Acclaim for

DAVID MALOUF'S

THE COMPLETE STORIES

"Remarkable.... Impressive.... Brings rich and finely honed language to bear." —*San Francisco Chronicle*

"An unrivaled delight." —*Milwaukee Journal Sentinel*

"Reading these rich, beautifully wrought stories, you can almost smell the ti trees and hear the screeching as the cockatoos take flight." —*The New York Times Book Review*

"Intensely vivid." —*O, The Oprah Magazine*

"Malouf is a master storyteller whose imagination inhabits shocking violence, quick humor, appealing warmth and harsh cruelty with equal intensity.... Readers won't want to skim a single page." —*The Journal Gazette* (Fort Wayne)

"There's enormous narrative power here.... [Malouf] is a very great short story writer of the F. Scott Fitzgerald, Leonard Michaels, Joyce Carol Oates sort." —*The Buffalo News*

"Wonderful.... These stories are compulsively readable, and while many of the locales are exotic, their inhabitants are as familiar as your own friends and family." —*Penthouse*

"A richly described and fascinating world." —*Deseret Morning News*

DAVID MALOUF

THE COMPLETE STORIES

David Malouf is the author of ten novels and six volumes of poetry. His novel *The Great World* was awarded both the Commonwealth Prize and the Prix Femina Étranger, and *Remembering Babylon* was shortlisted for the Booker Prize. He has also received the IMPAC Dublin Literary Award and the *Los Angeles Times* Book Award. He lives in Australia.

INTERNATIONAL

ALSO BY DAVID MALOUF

FICTION

Dream Stuff
The Conversations at Curlow Creek
Remembering Babylon
The Great World
Antipodes
Harland's Half Acre
Child's Play
Fly Away Peter
An Imaginary Life
Johnno

AUTOBIOGRAPHY

12 Edmondstone Street

POETRY

Selected Poems
Wild Lemons
First Things Last
The Year of Foxes and Other Poems
Neighbours in a Thicket
Bicycle and Other Poems

LIBRETTI

Jane Eyre
Baa Baa Black Sheep

THE COMPLETE STORIES

THE COMPLETE STORIES

DAVID MALOUF

VINTAGE INTERNATIONAL
Vintage Books
A Division of Random House, Inc.
New York

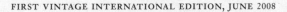

The Library of Congress has cataloged the Pantheon edition as follows:
Malouf, David.
[Short stories]
The complete stories / David Malouf.
p. cm.
Short stories.
I. Title.
PR9619.3.M265A6 2007
823'.914—dc22 2006037694

Vintage ISBN: 978-0-307-38603-8

Book design by Robert C. Olsson

www.vintagebooks.com

Printed in the United States of America
10 9 8 7 6 5 4 3 2 1

When I consider the brevity of my life, swallowed up as it is in the eternity that precedes and will follow it, the tiny space I occupy and what is visible to me, cast as I am into a vast infinity of spaces that I know nothing of and which know nothing of me, I take fright, I am stunned to find myself here rather than elsewhere, for there is no reason why it should be here rather than there, and now rather than then. Who set me here? By whose order and under what guiding destiny was this time, this place assigned to me?

—Pascal, *Pensées*

CONTENTS

EVERY MOVE YOU MAKE

The Valley of Lagoons

WHEN I was in the third grade at primary school it was the magic of the name itself that drew me.

Just five hours south off a good dirt highway, it is where all the river systems in our quarter of the state have their rising: the big, rain-swollen streams that begin in a thousand threadlike runnels and fall in the rainforests of the Great Divide, then plunge and gather and flow wide-banked and muddy-watered to the coast; the leisurely watercourses that make their way inland across plains stacked with anthills, and run north-west and north to the Channel Country, where they break up and lose themselves in the mudflats and mangrove swamps of the Gulf.

I knew it was there and had been hearing stories about it for as long as I could remember. Three or four hunting parties, some of them large, went out each year at the start of August, and since August was the school holidays, a good many among them were my classmates. By the time he was sixteen, my best friend, Braden, who was just my age, had been going with his father and his two older brothers, Stuart and Glen, for the past five years. But it was not marked on the wall-map in our third-grade schoolroom, and I could not find it in any atlas; which gave it the status of a secret place, accessible only in the winter when the big rains eased off and the tracks that led into it were dry enough for a ute loaded down with tarpaulins, cookpots, carbide lamps, emergency cans of petrol, and bags of flour, potatoes, onions, and other provisions to get in without sinking to the axle: a thousand square miles of virgin country known only to the few dozen families of our little township and the surrounding cane and dairy farms that made up the shire.

It was there, but only in our heads. It had a history, but only in the telling: in stories I heard from fellows in the playground at school, or from their older brothers at the barbershop or at the edge of an oval or on the bleachers at the town pool.

These stories were all of record "bags" or of the comic mishaps and organised buffoonery of camp life—plus, of course, the occasional shocking accident—but had something more behind them, I thought, than mere facts.

Fellows who went out there were changed—that's what I saw. Kids who had been swaggering and loud were quiet when they spoke of it, as if they knew more now than they were ready to let on, or had words for, or were permitted to tell. This impressed me, since it chimed with my own expectations of what I might discover, or be let into, when I too got there.

I stood in the shadows at the edge of what was being told, tuning my ear to the clamour, off in the scrub, of a wild pig being cornered while a kid no older than I was stood with an old Lee Enfield .303 jammed into the soft of his shoulder, holding his breath.

An occasion that was sacred in its way, though no one, least of all the kid who was now retelling it, would ever speak of it that way.

All that side of things you had to catch at a glance as you looked away. From the slight, almost imperceptible warping upwards of a deliberately flattened voice.

IN THE FIRST freshening days of June, and increasingly as July came on, all the talk around town, in schoolyards and changing sheds, across the counter at Kendrick's Seed and Hardware, along the veranda rails and in the dark public bars of the town's three hotels, where jurymen were put up when the district court was in session, and commercial travellers and bonded schoolteachers and bank clerks roomed, was about who, this year, would be going, and in which party and when.

In the old days, which were still within living memory, they had gone out on horseback, a four-day ride, the last of it through buffalo grass that came right to the horses' ears, so that all you had to go on was bush sense, and the smell in the horses' nostrils of an expanse of water up ahead.

Nowadays there were last year's wheel-marks. A man with a keen eye, crouched on the running-board of a ute or hanging halfway out the offside cabin window, could indicate to the driver which way to turn in the whisper of high grassheads, till the swishing abruptly fell away and you were out in the shimmering, insect-swarming midst of it: sheet after sheet of brimming water, all lit with sky and alive, like a page of Genesis, with spur-winged plover, masked plover, eastern swamphen, marshy moorhen, white-headed sheldrake, plumed tree duck, gargery teal, and clattering skyward as, like young bulls loose in pasture, the utes swerved and roared among them, flocks of fruit pigeon, squatters, topknots, forest bronzewings . . .

MY FATHER was not a hunting man. The town's only solicitor, his business was with wills and inheritance, with land contracts, boundary lines between neighbours, and the quarrels, sometimes fierce, that gave rise to marriage break-ups, divorce, custody battles, and, every two or three years, the odd case of criminal assault or murder that will arise even in the quietest community. He knew more of the history of the shire, including its secret history, its unrecorded and unspoken connections and disconnections, than any other man, and more than his clients themselves did of how this or that parcel of their eighty- or hundred-acre holdings had been taken up out of what, less than a hundred years ago, had been uncharted wilderness, and how, in covert deals with the bank or in deathbed codicils, out of spite or through long years of plotting, this or that paddock, or canebrake, or spinney, had passed from one neighbour or one first or second cousin to another.

When he and my mother first came here in the late Thirties, he'd been invited out, when August came round, on one of the parties—it was a courtesy, an act of neighbourliness, that any one of a dozen locals would have extended to an acceptable new-comer, if only to see how he might fit in.

"Thanks, Gerry," I imagine him saying in his easy way—or Jake, or Wes. "Not this time, I reckon. Ask me again next year, eh?" And had said that again the following year, and the year after, until they stopped asking.

He wasn't being stand-offish or condescending. It was simply that hunting, and the grand rigmarole, as he saw it, of gun talk and game talk and dog talk, was not his style. He had been a soldier in New Guinea and had seen enough perhaps, for one lifetime, of killing. It was an oddness in him that was accepted like any other, humourously, and was perhaps not entirely unexpected in a man who had more books in his house than could be found in the shire library. He was a respected figure in the town. He was even liked. But he wore a collar and tie even on weekdays, and men who were used to consulting him in a friendly way about a dispute with a neighbour, or the adding of a clause to their will, developed a sud-den interest in their boots when they ran into him away from his desk.

My mother too was an outsider. Despite heavy hints, she had not joined the fancy-workers and jam- and chutney-makers at the CWA, and in defiance of local custom sent all three of us to school in shoes. This was understandable in the case of my sisters. They were older and would grow up one day to be ladies. It was regarded as unnecessary and even, perhaps, damaging in a boy.

After more than twenty years in the district my father had never been to the Lagoons, and till I was sixteen I had not been there either, except in the dreamtime of my own imaginings and in what I had overheard from others.

I might have gone. Each year, in the first week of August, Braden's father, Wes McGowan, got up a party. I was always invited. My father, after a good deal of humming and ha-ing and using my mother as an excuse, would tell me I was too young and decline to let me go. But I knew he was uneasy about it, and all through the last weeks of July, as talk in the town grew, I waited in the hope he might relent. When the day came at last, I would get up early, pull on a sweater against the cold and, in the misty half-light just before dawn, jog down the deserted main street, past the last service station at the edge of town, to the river park where the McGowans' Bedford ute would be waiting for the rest of the party to appear, its tray piled high with tarpaulins, bedrolls, cook-pots, a gauze meat safe, and my friend Braden settled among them with the McGowan dogs at his feet, two Labrador retrievers.

Old Wes McGowan and his crony, Henry Denkler, who was also the town mayor, would be out stretching their legs, stamping their boots on the frosty ground or bending to inspect the tyres or the canvas water bag that hung from the front bumper-bar. The older McGowan boys, Stuart and Glen, would be squatting on their heels over a smoke. I would stand at the gate of the ute chatting to Braden for a bit and petting the dogs.

When the second vehicle drew up, with Matt Riley, the "professional," and his nephew Jem, Matt too would get down and a second inspection would be made—of the tyres, of the load—while Jem, with not much more than a nod, joined the McGowan boys. Then, with all the rituals of meeting done, Henry Denkler and Wes McGowan would climb back into the cabin, Glen into the driver's seat beside them, Stuart into the back with Braden and the dogs, and I would be left standing to wave them off; and then, freezing even in my sweater, jog slowly back home.

The break came in the year after I turned sixteen. When I went for the third or fourth year running to tell my father that the McGowans had offered to take me out to the Lagoons and to ask if I could go, he surprised me by looking up over the top of his glasses and saying, "That's up to you, son. You're old enough, I reckon, to make your own decisions." It was to be Braden's last trip before he went south to university. Most of the shooting would be birds, but to mark the occasion as special Braden would also get a go at a pig.

"So," my father said quietly, though he already knew the answer, "what's it to be?"

"I'd really like to go," I told him.

"Good," he said, not sounding regretful. "I want you to look out and be careful, that's all. Braden's a sensible enough young fellow. But your mother will worry her soul case out till you're home again."

What he meant was, *he* would.

BRADEN MCGOWAN had been my best friend since I was five years old. We started school on the same day, sharing a desk and keeping pace with one another through pot-hooks and the alphabet, times tables, cursive, and those scrolled and curlicued capitals demanded by our Queensland State School copybooks. We dawdled to and from school on our own circuitous route. Past the Vulcan Can Company, where long shiny cut-offs of raw tin were to be had, which we carted off in bundles to be turned into weapons and aids of our own devising, past the crushing-mill where we got sticks of sugar cane to chew. Narrow gauge lines ran to the mill from the many outlying farms, and you heard at all hours in the crushing season the noise of trundling, and the shrill whistle of the engine as a line of carts approached a crossing, and rumbled through or clanked to a halt.

In the afternoons after school and in the holidays, we played together in the paddocks and canebrakes of the McGowans' farm, being, as the mood took us, explorers, pirates, commandos, bushrangers, scouts on the track of outlaws or of renegade Navaho braves.

Usually we had a troop of the McGowan dogs with us, who followed out of doggy curiosity and sometimes, in the belief that they had got the scent of what the game was, moiled around us or leapt adventurously ahead. But for the most part they simply lay and watched from the shade, till we stretched out beside them and let the game take its freer form of untrammelled thinking-aloud that was also, with its range of wild and rambling surmise, the revelation—even to ourselves, though we were too young as yet to know it—of bright, conjectural futures we would have admitted to no one else.

"You two are weird," Braden's brother Stuart told us with a disgusted look, having caught on his way to the bails some extravagant passage of our talk. "*God,* you're weird. You're *weird!*"

Stuart was four years older. He and the eldest of the three brothers, Glen, had farm work to do in the afternoons after school. Braden in those days was still little and free to play.

They were rough kids, the McGowans, and Stuart was not just rowdy, I thought, but unpredictably vicious. He scared me.

I had come late into a family of girls, two sisters who, from the beginning, had made a pet of me. Going over to the McGowans' was an escape to another world. Different laws were in operation there from the ones I was used to. Old Mr. McGowan had a different notion of authority from the one my father followed. Quiet but firmer. His sons, who were so noisy and undisciplined outside, were subdued in his presence. Mrs. McGowan, unlike my mother, had no interests beyond the piles of food she brought to the table and the washing—her men's overalls and shirts and singlets, and the loads of sheets and pillowcases I saw her hoist out of the copper boiler when I came to collect Braden on Monday mornings.

She too had a softening influence on the boys. They might complain when she called them in from kicking a football round the yard, or working on a bike, to fetch in an armful of wood for the stove or to carry a basket of wet sheets to the line, and they squirmed when she tried to settle an upturned collar or hug them. But they did do what she asked in the end, and even submitted, with a good show of masculine reluctance, to hugging.

I liked the roughness and ease I found at the McGowans', but even more the formality, which was of a kind my parents would have wondered at and found odd, old-fashioned.

My sisters, Katie and Meg, were exuberantly opinionated. Our mealtimes were loud with argument in which we all talked over one another, our parents included, and the food itself was forgotten.

There was no arguing at the McGowans'. Glen and Stuart, rough and barefooted as they were, showed their hands before they were allowed to table, sat up straight, kept their elbows in, and lowered their heads for grace—the McGowans said grace!

They passed things without speaking. Barely spoke at all unless their father asked a question, or in response to a story he told, or to tell their mother how good the stew was in hope of a second helping.

I loved all this. When Braden began to have his own jobs to do after school, I stayed to help. I learned to milk, to clean out the bails, to handle a gun and shoot sparrows in the yard, and rabbits in the brush, then stayed for the McGowans' early tea. I wanted to be one of them, or at least to be like them. Like Glen. Like Stuart even. I wasn't of course, but then neither was Braden.

When we were very young it did not occur to me that Braden might be odd. He was often in trouble at home for being "dreamy," but then so was I. "What's the matter with you," Stuart would demand of him, genuinely exasperated, "are you dumb or something?"

He wasn't, but he found a problem at times where the rest of us did not, and to a point of inertia that infuriated Stuart (who suspected him, I think, of doing it deliberately) was puzzled by circumstances, quite ordinary ones, that the rest of us took for granted. Other kids found him slow. Some of them called him a dill.

I understood Braden's puzzlement because I shared it at times, and since we were always together, I took it that we were puzzled in the same way. I had for so long been paired with Braden, we had shared so many discoveries and first thoughts, that I had assumed we were in every way alike; that in all the hours we had spent spinning fantasies and creating other lives for ourselves, we had been moving through the same landscape and weather, and were one. When Stuart told us, "You two are weird. You're weird," I was pleased to see in his savage contempt the confirmation that in Stuart's eyes at least we were indistinguishable.

I did not want to know what I had already begun in some part of me to suspect. That Braden's oddness might be quite different from anything I could lay claim to.

For as long as I could remember, we had known, each one, what the other was thinking. The same things amused or excited or scared us. Now, almost overnight, it seemed, Braden knew stuff I had never dreamed of. His mind was engaged by questions that had never occurred to me, and the answers he came up with I could not follow. It was a habit of mind, I thought, that must have been there from the start, but moving underground in him and hidden from me; a music, behind the rambling stories he told, that I had all along been deaf to.

At the same time, in the six months before he turned fifteen, he put on height, six inches, and bulked up to twelve and a half stone. He was suddenly a big fellow. Bigger than either of his brothers. Not heavy, but big.

Then one day he showed me, in a copy of *Scientific American,* what it was that he was into. Cybernetics. I had never heard the word, and when he tried to explain it to me in his usual style, all jumps and sideways leaps into a silence I had believed I could interpret, I was lost.

I understood the science well enough. Even the figures. What I could not grasp was the excited vision of what he saw in it: a realm of action he saw himself moving through as if it had come into existence precisely for him. And this was the opening of a gap between us. Not of affection—no question of that—but of where our lives might take us. Braden, who had always been so vague and out of it, was suddenly the most focused person I knew. Utterly single-minded and sure of what he wanted and what he was for.

For the first time in my life I felt lonely. But not so lonely, I think, so finally set apart as *he* felt. From his family. His brothers. Who were still puzzled by him but in a new way.

Here he was, a big boy who had outgrown them and his own strength, and ought, in springing up and filling out, to have become a fellow they could deal with at last on equal terms. Instead he seemed odder than ever. More difficult to get through to. Content to be away there in his own incommunicable universe.

Glen, who had always had a soft spot for the boy, was confused, but also I think impressed. He still teased him, but in a soft-handed affectionate way. As if Braden's difference, which had always intrigued him, had turned out to be something he might respect.

Glen, because he was so much older, had for the most part left us alone. We had always been a source of mild amusement to him, but except for the odd burst of impatience he had, in a condescending, big-brotherly way, ignored us. Stuart could not.

In the early days the mere sight of us drove him to fury. All jeers and knuckles, he was always twisting our arms and jerking them up under our shoulder blades to see how much we could take before we turned into crybabies and sissies.

He felt easier with me, I think, because I fought back. Braden disarmed him by taking whatever he could dish out with scornful defiance, never once, after our baby years, yielding to tears.

All this, I knew, belonged to a side of their life together that I had no part in, to hostilities and accommodations, spaces shared or passionately disputed, in rooms, at the table, in their mother's affection or their father's regard or interest.

But the fullness of the change in Braden, when it finally revealed itself, dismayed Stuart. He simply did not know what to do with it.

I think it scared him to have someone who was close, and who ought therefore to have been knowable, turn out to be so far from anything he could get a hold on. It suggested that the world itself might be beyond his comprehension, but also beyond his control. The only way he could deal with Braden was by avoiding him. Which made it all the more odd, I thought, that he began at the same time to latch on to me.

He had left school by now, was working in a garage and ran with a set of older fellows, all of whom were wild, as he was, and had "reputations." But suddenly we were always in one another's path.

He would appear out of nowhere, it seemed, on my way back from the pool, and offer me dinks on his bike. And when he exchanged his Malvern Star for a Tiger Cub he would stop, talk a bit, and offer to take me pillion.

I was wary. I had too often been on the wrong side of Stuart's roughness to be easy with him. It was flattering to be treated, in my own right, as a grown-up, but I did not trust him. He was trying to win me over. Why? Because he had seen the little gap that had opened up between Braden and me and wanted to widen it? To bring home to me that if Braden was odder than any of us had thought, then I had proved to be, like Stuart himself, more ordinary?

I resented his attention on both counts, and suspected that his unlikely interest in me was a form of mockery. It took me a while to see that mockery was not Stuart's style, and that by seeking me out, a younger boy and the brother of a girl he was sweet on (I learned this amazing fact from a bit of conversation overheard while I was sunbaking on the bleachers at the pool), he was putting himself helplessly in my power; making himself vulnerable to the worst mockery of all. That he trusted me not to take advantage of it meant that I never would of course, but I hated the familiarity with which he now greeted me as "Angus, old son," or "Angus, old horse," as if there was already some special relationship between us, or as if getting close to me brought him closer somehow to her. My own belief was that Stuart McGowan was just the sort of rough, loud fellow she wouldn't even look at. Then suddenly he and Katie were going out together, and he was at our house every night of the week.

Taking a break from my homework or the book I was absorbed in, and going through to the kitchen to get a glass of water or cold milk from the fridge, I would hear them whispering together on the couch in our darkened front room, and would turn the tap on hard to warn them I was about.

Or if it was late enough, and Stuart was leaving, I would run into them in the hall: Stuart looking smug but also, somehow, crestfallen, Katie hot and angry, ready I thought to snap my head off if I said more in reply to his " 'lo, Angus, how's it going?" than a "Hi, Stuart," and ducked back into my room.

The truth was, I had no wish to know what was going on between them. I did not like the look of shy complicity that Stuart cast me, as if I had caught him out in something, but in something that as another male I must naturally approve.

Two or three nights each week he ate with us. I have no idea what he thought of the noisy arguments that marked our mealtimes.

Perhaps it attracted him, as I was attracted by the old-fashioned formality I found at the McGowans'.

Occasionally, to kill time while Katie was helping in the kitchen, he would drift to the sleepout on the side veranda where I would be sprawled on my bed deep in a book. I would look up, thinking, God, not again, and there he would be, hanging awkwardly in the open doorway, waiting for me to acknowledge him and taking my grunt of recognition as an invitation to come in.

Oddly restrained and self-conscious, he would settle at the foot of the bed, take a book from the pile on the floor, and say, with what I thought of as a leer, "So what's this one about?" The way he handled the book, his half-embarrassed, half-suggestive tone, the painful attempt to meet me, as I saw it, on unfamiliar ground, made me uncomfortable. "You don't have to pretend you're interested," I wanted to tell him, "just because you're going out with my sister." On the whole, I preferred the old Stuart. I thought I knew better what he was about. It did not occur to me that what I was reading, and what I found there, might be a genuine mystery to him; which disturbed his sense of himself, and had to do with how, in this strange new household he had blundered into, with its unfamiliar views and distinctions, he might learn to fit in.

He would run his eyes over a few pages of the book he had in hand and shake his head. Thinking, I see now, of her, of Katie, and waiting for me to provide some clue—to me, I mean, to *us*—that would help him find common ground with her.

I would make a rambling attempt to explain who Raskolnikov was, and Sonia, and about the horse that had fallen down in the street. He would look puzzled, then stricken, then, trying to make the best of it, say, "Interesting, eh?" Waiting for some sign perhaps that I recognised the effort he was making to enter my world, and what this might reveal about *him:* about some other Stuart than the one I thought I knew, and knew only as a "bad influence." After about ten minutes of this, I would swing my legs off the bed and say, "Tea must be about ready, we'd better go out," and to the relief of both of us, or so I thought, it would be over.

I had begun to dread these occasions of false intimacy between us that were intended, I thought, to be rehearsals for a time when we would be youthful brothers-in-law, close, bluff, easily affectionate. If he could get me to accept him in this role, then maybe she would.

Once, as he moved towards the door, I caught him, out of the corner of my eye, making a quick appraisal of himself in the wardrobe mirror. Starched white shirt with the sleeves rolled high to show off his biceps. Hair slicked down with Potter and Moore jelly. In the hollow of his underlip the squared-off, dandified growth of hair he had begun to affect in recent weeks, a tuft, two or three degrees darker than his hair colour but with flecks of gingery gold, that I had overlooked at first—I thought he had simply neglected to shave there. When I realised it was deliberate I was confused. It seemed so out of character.

Now, watching him take in at a casual glance the effect he made in my wardrobe mirror, I thought again. What a bundle of contradictions he is, I told myself.

He gave me a sheepish grin, and stopped, pretending to examine his chin for a shaving nick. But what his look said was, Well, that's how it is, you can see that, eh, old son? That's what they do to us.

When Katie first began to go out with him I'd felt I should warn her. That he was wild. That he had a "reputation." Only I did not know how to begin. We had always been close, and had grown more so since my older sister Meg got married, but for all that, and the boldness in our household with which we were willing to air issues and deliver an opinion, there were subjects, back then, that we kept clear of, areas of experience we could not admit knowledge of.

And it seemed to me that Katie must know as well as I did, or better, what Stuart was like. She was the one who spent all those hours of fierce whispering with him in the dark of our front room.

For weeks at a time they would move together in what seemed like a single glow. Then I would feel an anger in her that needed only a word on my part, or a look, to make her blaze out, though the real object of her fury, I thought, was herself. Stuart, for a time, would no longer be there, on the back veranda or in the lounge after tea. Things were off between them. When I ran into him at the baths, or when he stopped and offered me a lift on the Triumph, he would look hangdog and miserable. "How are you, Angus, old son?" he'd ask, hoping I would return the question.

I didn't. The last thing I wanted was to be his confidant; to listen to his complaints about Katie or have him ask what she was saying about him, what I thought she wanted. These periods would last for days, for a whole week sometimes. Then he would be back, all scrubbed and spruced up and smelling like a sweet shop. Narrow-eyed and watchful. Like a cat, I thought. But also, in a way he could not help and could not help showing, happily full of himself and of his power over her. Couldn't he see, I thought, how mad it made her, and that it was this in the long run that would bring him down?

THE CRISIS CAME a year or so after they first began.

Nothing was said—my parents were the very spirit of tact in such matters—but I guessed Katie had given him his marching orders. Again. *Again.* Because for two nights running he did not appear. Then, late on the second night, I looked out and the little Anglia he sometimes ran around in was parked under the street light opposite.

It was there at nine and was still there at half past ten. What was he doing? Just sitting there, I guessed, hunched and unhappy, chewing on his bitten-down nails.

To see if she had some other fellow calling?

More likely, I thought, just to be close to her. Or if not her, the house itself. To reassure himself that since we were all in and going about our customary routine, no serious breach had occurred. Then, remembering the old Stuart, I thought, No, it's his way of intimidating her. It's a kind of bullying. Didn't he know the first thing about her? Had he learned nothing in all those hours in the dark of the lounge room or the back veranda? Did he think that because she had sent him packing on previous occasions, all he had to do now was apply pressure and wait?

I could have told him something about those other occasions. That she was the sort of girl who did not forgive such demonstrations of her own weakness or those who caused them. There was only a limited number of times she would allow herself to be so shamefully humiliated. I stood hidden behind the slats of my sleepout and watched him there. Was she watching too?

I was surprised. That he should just drive up like that and park under the street light where everyone could see him. Was he more inventive than I'd guessed?

It seemed out of character too. Melodramatic. The sort of thing people did in the movies. Was that where he had got it?

Next morning at breakfast I glanced across at Katie to see if she too had seen him, and got a defiant glare. Then that night, late, when I went out to the kitchen to get a drink, she confronted me.

"So what do *you* think?" she demanded.

It was a clammy night. Airless. Without a breath. She was barefoot, her hair stuck to her brow with sweat. We stood side by side for a moment at the kitchen window.

"He's been there now for three nights running," she said. "It's ridiculous!"

I passed behind her and opened the fridge.

"Maybe you should go down," she said, "and sit with him."

"What? What would I want to do that for?"

"Well, you're mates, aren't you?"

I had turned with the cold-water bottle. She took it from me and rolled it, with its fog of moisture, across her damp forehead, then her throat and chest.

"Is that what Stuart says?"

"Not what he *says*. Stuart never says anything, you know that."

"What then? What do you mean?"

"Oh, nothing," she said wearily. She handed the bottle back. "Let's drop it."

"Braden's my friend," I told her. "If Stuart wasn't here every night I wouldn't even see him from one week's end to the next."

"Okay," she said, "let's drop it. Maybe I don't understand these things."

"What things?"

"Oh, boys. Men. You're all so—*tight* with one another."

"No we're not. Stuart and I aren't—tight."

"I thought you were."

"Well, we're not." I finished my glass of water, rinsed it at the sink, and went to pass her.

Suddenly, from behind, her arms came round me. I felt the damp of her forearms on my chest, her face nuzzling the back of my neck.

"Your hair smells nice," she said. "Like when you were little."

I squirmed and pretended to wriggle free, but only pretended. "Stop," I said, "you're tickling," as she held me tighter and laughed.

"There," she said, glancing away to the window, "he's gone."

Neither of us had heard the car move off. She continued to hold me. "Stay a minute, Angus," she said. "Stay and talk."

"What about?"

"Oh, not him." She let go of me. "That wouldn't get us far."

I sat at the kitchen table, awkward but expectant, and she sat opposite.

In the old days we had been close. When I came out of my room at night to get a glass of water or milk from the fridge, she would join me and we would sit for a bit, joking, exchanging stories, larking about. Stuart's arrival had ended that. He was always there, and when he wasn't she avoided me. Either way, I missed her and blamed Stuart for coming between us. We liked each other. She made me happy, and I made her happy too.

"I know you're on his side," she said now. "But there are things you don't know about."

"I'm not on his side," I told her. "Are there sides?"

She laughed. "No, Angus, there are no sides. There never will be for you. That's what I love about you."

I was defensive. "What's that supposed to mean?"

"It means you're nicer than I am. Maybe than any of us. And I love you. Listen," she said, leaning closer, "I'm going away."

"Where to?"

"I don't know yet. Maybe I'll go and stay with Meg and Jack for a bit. Or I'll take the plunge and just go to Brisbane."

"What would you do down there?"

"Get an office job, work in a shop—what do other girls do? I'm doing nothing here. Reading a lot of silly novels—what's the use of that? You know what this place is like. You won't stay here either."

"Won't I?"

It pleased me at that time when people told me things about myself. Sometimes they surprised me, sometimes they didn't. Even when they confirmed what I already knew I was filled with interest.

"I've *got* to get out," she told me passionately, "I've *got* to. Nothing will ever happen if I stay here. I'd end up marrying Stuart, or someone just like him, and it'd kill me. It doesn't matter that he wants me, or thinks he does, or what I think of *him*. Even if he was kind—which he wouldn't be in fact. He'd be a rotten husband. What he really loves is himself. Maybe I won't get married at all. I don't know why everyone goes on all the time about marriage, as if it was the only thing there is."

I was bewildered. She was telling me more than I could take in.

"So when?" I asked. "When will you go?"

"I don't know," she said miserably. "I've got no money."

"I have. I've got forty pounds."

She leaned across the table and took my hand. "I love you, Angus. More than anyone. Did you know that?" Then, after a pause, "But you should hang on to your money, you'll need it yourself if you're ever going to get out of this dump. I'll get it some other way. Now go to bed or you won't be able to get up in the morning. It's after eleven."

I got up obediently, and was at the door when she said, "I suppose you'll be inseparable now."

"Why?" I asked her. "Why should we be?"

"Because that's the way he is. Once he realises this is the end, really this time, he'll want you to see what a bitch I am and how miserable he is."

"That's all right," I said. "I won't listen."

"Yes you will. But don't worry—"

"Katie—"

"No, no," she said. "Go to bed now."

She came and kissed me very lightly on the cheek.

"We'll talk about it some other time. I told you, I love you. And thanks, eh? For the offer of the money. You sleep well now."

THAT WAS in mid-April. The weeks passed. There was no reconciliation. Stuart stopped driving up to keep a watch on the house. Katie did not go away.

But she was right about one thing. Despite my reluctance, Stuart and I did become mates of a sort. Hangdog and subdued, he was in no mood to go out on the town with his mates, the daredevil rowdies he normally ran with, who did shift work at the cane mill, or were plumber's mates, apprentice builders, counter-jumpers in drapery shops or hardware stores, or helped out in their father's accounting business. Fellows whose wildness, which involved a lot of haring around late at night, scaring old ladies and Chinamen or the occasional black, was winked at as a relatively harmless way of letting off steam; the sort of larrikin high jinks that on another occasion might take the form of dashing into a burning house to rescue a kiddie from the flames or dragging a cat from a flooded creek or, if there was another war, performing feats of quicksilver courage that would get their names on the town memorial.

What Stuart needed me for, I decided, was to be a witness to his sorrows. Which he thought I might best be able to confirm because so much of what he gave himself up to came out of books. He was literary in the odd way of a fellow who did not read and who trusted my capacity to appreciate what he was feeling because I did. Perhaps he believed that if I took him seriously, then she would; though with a fineness of feeling I had not expected, he never once, in all our times together, mentioned her. Which made me more uneasy than if he had, since at every moment she was there as an unasked question between us, and as the only reason, really, why I was there at all.

He would pick me up in the Anglia at the bottom of our street, usually around nine when I had finished my homework, and we would drive out to some hilltop and just sit there in the cool night air, with the windows down, the sweet smell of cane flowers coming in heady wafts and the night crickets shrilling.

Stuart's self-pitying tone, and his self-conscious half-jokey way of addressing me as "Angus, old boot," or "Angus, old son," suggested more than ever, I thought, a character out of some movie, or a book he had been impressed by, and had more to do with the way he wanted me to see him, or the way he wanted to see himself, than with anything he really was.

Then it was July at last. The McGowans asked me to go out to the Lagoons. And I was going.

JUST BEFORE SUN-UP the McGowans' heavy-duty Bedford ute swung uphill to where I was waiting with my duffel bag and bedroll on our front veranda. Behind me, the lights were on in our front room and my mother was there in her dressing gown, with a mug of tea to warm her hands, just inside the screen door. I was glad the others could not see her, and hoped she would not come out at the last moment to kiss me or to tuck my scarf into my windcheater. But in fact, "Look after Braden" was all she said as I waved to the ute, shouted "See you" over my shoulder, and took three leaps down to the front gate.

Glen was driving, with his father and Henry Denkler in the cabin beside him. Braden, Stuart, and the dogs were in the back. Stuart leapt down, took my bedroll, and swung it up into the tray where Braden, on his feet now, was barely managing the dogs. "Hi, Angus," Stuart said, "all set for the boat race?" He laid his hand on my shoulder, but his glance, I saw, went to the house, in case *she* was there.

If she was, she did not make herself visible.

I climbed over the gate of the truck and Stuart followed. We staggered, the dogs around our legs, and Braden, to make room for us, settled on the pile of bedrolls at the back.

"Get down, you stupid buggers," Stuart told the dogs, and grabbing the head of one of them under his right arm, plumped down heavily next to Braden.

I sat opposite, drawing the other dog, Tilly, between my knees. Braden banged the flat of his hand on the cabin roof and we were off.

He had said nothing as yet. Now he looked at me, grinned, and pulled his hat down firmly over his ears.

"Hi," I said.

"Cold, eh?" was all he said in return.

Stuart laughed. "He's always cold, aren't you, Brade? The warm blood in this family ran out with me."

Stuart was wearing an old plaid shirt frayed at the collar and with the sleeves rolled loosely at the elbow. No jacket, no woolly.

Braden, hunched into his thick turtle-necked sweater, made a face, and looked away. A draught of cold air streamed over us as we rolled down to the town bridge with its drift of bluish mist and up to where the other ute, with Matt Riley and his nephew Jem and their dogs, was parked at the petrol station before the entrance to the highway. Matt Riley, the white breath streaming from his mouth, was out of the ute, checking one of the offside tyres. Jem was driving.

I had known Matt Riley for as long as I could remember, though we had never had a proper conversation. His wife, Eileen, was our ironing lady. Every Monday morning he dropped her off in his ute, and he was there when I got home, silent, drinking tea at our kitchen table, waiting to take her back again. She ignored his presence, laying aside the shirt she was working on to make me a malted milk.

I was fond of Eileen. She was full of stories, told in a language, all jumps and starts, that I had got so used to at last that it seemed the only language for what she had to tell. I had never asked myself what might be peculiar about it, or where it came from. As I never asked myself why Matt Riley was so subdued and retiring in our kitchen and yet so quietly sure of himself, and so readily deferred to, when he was inspecting tyres or setting right an unbalanced load.

As for Jem, he had been one of the big boys when I started school. In the same class as Glen McGowan. A dark, sulky fellow, I thought. Although he was a big boy he could neither read properly nor write. At fourteen he had gone off to become a roo-shooter like his uncle.

He was no longer sulky. Just big and silent, almost invisible. His uncle Matt's shadow.

AN HOUR LATER we had left the bitumen and were bouncing due west on a clay highway cut clean through the scrub. The sun was up and had burned off the early-morning chill. The dogs were alert but quiet. Braden, his knees drawn up, one of the dog leads round his wrist, was dozing, his head toppled forward under his hat. Stuart, after a bit, leaned across, unwound the lead and passed it to me. The big dog, Jigger, turned its head in my direction but did not stir. "Good dog, Jigger," I told him, roughening the gingery ears, "good old boy." He lowered his head and settled.

I was beginning to feel good. We were riding high up on the camber of the yellow-clay road, which had been washed by the rains so that it was all exposed pebbles with eroded channels on either side, then tough grass, then forest.

Stuart shook a cigarette out of the packet in the breast pocket of his shirt, dipped his head to take it between his lips. He offered me one. I shook my head. Smoke blew towards me. Sharp and sweet.

"Big day, eh, Angus?"

It was. He knew how long I had wanted this. To come out here, be one with the others, part at last of whatever it was. The sky above us was high and cloudless, as it is up here in winter. Stuart followed my gaze as if there was something up there that I had caught a glimpse of, a hawk maybe; but there was nothing. Just the huge expanse of blue that made the air so clean as it tumbled over us; as if all this—sky, forest, the warmth of the big dog between

my knees—was part of the one thing, a consciousness—not simply my own—that belonged not only to the body I was in, back
hard against the metal side of the truck, muscles flexed in my
calves and thighs, belly empty, but also to something out there
that I had melted into as one melts into sleep, and was infinite.

I did sleep, and was woken by Stuart punching me lightly in the
shoulder. "Wake up, Australia!"

We climbed down. The other ute was already parked.

We were at the little junction station where the Chillagoe line
branches west into anthill country: a water tank and pump, a general store, and the two-roomed cottage-cum-stationmaster's hut.
It was the established custom for parties going out to the Lagoons
to stop here for breakfast, before going down to the general store
to fill the emergency petrol cans.

"I'm famished," Braden announced. It was after eight.

I agreed.

"Don't worry, son, you'll get a good feed here," Matt Riley told
me. "Trust Miss Appin, eh, Jem?"

Like most of the older members of the party, Matt Riley had
been stopping here for nearly forty years.

Suddenly in a storm of dust a dozen or so guineafowl darted
out from under the house, which stood on three-foot stumps, and
got between our legs and began to peck around the tyres of the
trucks. There was a clatter of hooves, and a young nanny goat skit-
tered down the stairs from Miss Appin's dining room, with three
more guineafowl at her heels, and behind them Miss Appin herself flourishing a tea towel in her fist.

"Morning, Millie," Henry Denkler called across to her, and
took the hat from his stack of white hair and made a decent sweep
with it. "Mornin', Millie," Wes McGowan echoed.

"Drat the thing," Miss Appin shouted after the goat, which had
propped in the yard ten paces off and with its wide-set, sad-looking
eyes stood its ground looking offended.

"Garn," Jem told it, and at something in his unfamiliar growl it
started and fled.

"Good on you, lad," Miss Appin told him. Then, reverting to

her role as hostess, "It's all ready, gentlemen. Eight of you—is that right?"

I knew about Miss Appin. She had been described to me a dozen times by kids at school who had been out here and known what to expect, but had still, when they came face to face with her, been startled.

Forty years before she had been a beauty. Her family ran the biggest spread in this part of the state. She was one of those girls that a young Wes McGowan or Henry Denkler might dream of but could not aspire to. The best horsewoman in the district, she had been to school in Europe, spoke French, and had been "presented" at Government House in Brisbane.

But at twenty, in a single moment, fate had exploded out of a trusted corner and turned her whole world upside down. A horse had kicked in all one side of her face, flattening the bony ridge above her right eye, shattering her cheekbone and jaw. Over the years, the damaged side of her face had aged differently it seemed from the other, so that they appeared to belong to different women, or to women who had lived very different lives. Only one of these faces smiled, but you saw then why a girl who had been so lively and pleased with herself might have chosen to live in a place where she saw no more than a few dozen people each week, and most of them the same people, over and over.

Miss Appin was responsible for changing the points on the line, and had turned her front room into the station buffet, where twice a week, while the two-carriage train waited and took on water, she served freshly baked scones and tea out of thick white railway crockery, and in winter, breakfast to shooting parties like ours that called up beforehand and put in their order.

Two tables with chequered cloths had been laid for us. Otherwise, the small neat room was a front room like any other. There was an upright piano with brass candelabra and the walls were covered from floor to picture rail with photographs of Miss Appin's nephews and nieces, all of them known, it seemed, to Henry Denkler and Wes McGowan and even, though he was shy to admit it, to Matt Riley: family parties on lawns, the ladies with their skirts spread; young men with axes at wood-chopping shows or looking solemn in studio poses in the uniforms of the two wars; other boys (or the same ones when younger) in eights on a sunlit river or standing at ease beside their oars; five-year-olds in communion suits with bow ties, or like baby brides in a cloud of tulle. Three or four guineafowl crept back, and flitted about under the tables. There was a smell of bacon.

"Come on now, Braden," Miss Appin jollied, "and you too—what's-your-name—Angus, was it?—I need a couple of willing hands."

She ushered us into the little blackened scullery and we fetched back plates of eggs, a great platter of sizzling rashers, bread, butter, scones. We were ravenous, all of us. But when we were seated even Jem Riley, who was a rough fellow, ate in a restrained, almost dainty way, swallowing quietly, blushing at every mouthful in an effort to keep up to the standard set by Henry Denkler and Wes McGowan, which was clearly what they thought was due to Miss Appin's "background." As soon as he had gulped the last of his tea, Jem excused himself and bolted. He would drive their ute down to the store and fill the emergency cans.

Glen, in a high state of amusement at Jem's confusion, got to his feet, thanked Miss Appin with an old-world formality that delighted his father and which the McGowan boys could turn on quite effortlessly when occasion demanded, and went after Jem to help.

"So then, Millie," Wes McGowan began, pushing back from the remains of his breakfast while Braden and I tucked into seconds, "what have you got to tell us about this *pig*?"

A SEVEN-MILE DRIVE south of Miss Appin's, the old Jeffries place where the boar had been sighted was no more now than an isolated chimney stack in a pile of rubble and a steel windmill whose spindly tower and blades could be seen in the long grass off the north–south highway.

We drove in slowly—there was no longer a track—and parked

in a clump of water gums. I was directed to take charge of the McGowan dogs, Jigger and Tilly, but also of Matt Riley's dog, Archer, an Irish setter as new to all this as I was and very nervous, though Jem assured me, as the dog rubbed against him and licked his hand, that he was sweet-natured enough if you handled him right. And it was true. When I leaned down and hugged him a little, he immediately shoved his nose into my groin. I settled in the shade of the water gums, but the three dogs, excited by the sense that something was about to begin, remained standing, heads raised, lean flanks trembling, pulling hard at the leash. It was just after ten. The sun was fierce, the long grass a wave of cicada-voices rising and skirling, then lapsing, then rising again.

Matt, with Jem as usual at his side, went off to do some scouting and it was confirmed. There was a pig, a good-sized one.

Wes McGowan, whose party this was, had ceded authority for the moment to the professional. He was seated now, sweating under his hat, in the shade of the Bedford, having a quiet smoke.

Matt Riley, meanwhile, had taken Braden aside and was giving him instructions, pointing across the open grassland to where the boar was holed up and sleeping in the sun, somewhere between the windmill and the darker treeline that marked the course of a creek.

The other old-timer of the party, Henry Denkler, had set up a folding stool, and with his hat drawn down and his .303 across his arm, was dozing, for all the world as if he was having a quiet snooze in his own backyard in town.

The others, Glen, Stuart, Jem, were squatting on their heels in the shadows behind me. Not speaking. All their attention, like mine, was on the group Matt Riley and Braden made, Braden the taller by a head, which was all Matt-talk, low-voiced and slow, no more, as I strained my ears to catch it, than a few broken sibilants at moments when the cicadas cut out.

Braden was nodding. Allowing himself to be sweet-talked into a kind of high-pitched ease. Yet another area in which Matt was a professional.

I glanced back quickly at the others.

They too had been gathered in. A moment ago, Glen and Stuart had been as tense almost as the dogs, out of concern perhaps for Braden—more family business. They were subdued now. Almost dreamy. As if Matt had worked his spell on them also, as he had done three or four years back, when they had been where Braden stood now.

I too had a place made for me, but it was up to me what I made of it. I held fast to the dogs, watching their shoulders quiver in expectation. Something of their animal sense that we were set down now in a single world of muscle and nerve, mind both present and dreamlike afloat, communicated itself to me, entered my fists, where they held fast to the twined leashes and took the strain of the dogs' forelegs and rump, ran back down my forearms to my chest and belly, set my heart steadily beating.

Matt had his hand now on Braden's shoulder and was singing to him—that's how I heard it. Slowing him down. Creating in him a steady state of being inside himself. In the eye that would sight along the barrel of the rifle. In the index finger that would gently squeeze the trigger. In the softness of his shoulder that would take the impact of the shot down through his spine, his buttocks, the muscles at the back of his calves to the balls of his feet where they were spread just wide enough to balance the six feet two of him squarely on the earth.

I wished that Matt was singing, in that low voice whose words I missed but whose tune I was straining to catch, to me, or to something *in* me. That he was discovering for me that state of detachment but deep immersion, beyond mere attention or nerve, that, once I had hit upon it, I might go back and back to—the sureness of something centred that I lacked.

I watched Braden and thought I saw it entering him. When Matt nodded and released his shoulder at last he would be fully equipped. They would go forward and the others would get up and follow, even Henry Denkler, waking abruptly from his doze as if even in sleep he too had been quietly listening. Twenty minutes from now, Braden would have it for ever. Even if he never returned to any of this, it would be his.

It was this, rather than the business of simply putting a shot into the brain of a maddened beast, that he had come out here to get hold of so that these witnesses to it—his father, his brothers, the professional, Matt Riley, Henry Denkler—would know he had it, that they had passed it on.

On some signal from Matt Riley that I failed, for all my tenseness, to register, Wes McGowan got to his feet, came to where I was sitting, and leaned down. His big hand covered Tilly's skull, tickling her with his finger behind the ears. "Angus," he told me, "I want you to stay back here with the dogs."

I swallowed hard, nodded glumly. I'd known this was coming, and Mr. McGowan, not to embarrass me by witnessing my youthful disappointment, turned away. I knew what he was doing. He was keeping me out of harm's way. But there was something else as well. If anything went wrong out there my inexperience might be dangerous, and not only to myself.

"Come on, boys," I told the dogs, and I put my arms around Tilly, who turned and licked my face.

Glen and the others were on their feet now. Braden cast me a quick look and I nodded. I too got to my feet. The little party formed in three lines, Matt Riley and Jem in front to do the tracking, Braden, Glen and Stuart behind. They set off through the waist-high grass. Once again I would be on the sidelines watching, as I had been so often before when it was a matter only of the telling. I urged the dogs up into the tray of the Bedford and, scrambling up behind them, stood straining my eyes for a better view.

The shoulders and hats, which were all I could see above the sunlit grasstops, moved slowly forward. Twenty, thirty yards further and Matt Riley sheered off to the left. The rest of the party came to a stop. Waited. I could hear the silence like a hotter space at the centre of the late-morning heat. Big grasshoppers were blundering about. Flies simmered and swarmed. The dogs, on tensed hind legs, leaned into the still air, tautening the leash. "Easy, Jigger," I whispered to the younger dog, though he paid no attention. His mind was away up ahead, low down in the grass roots, close to the earth. "Tilly," I told the other, "quiet, eh? Be quiet now." My own mind too was out there somewhere. Beside Braden. Who would be sweating hard now, every muscle tense, preparing for the moment when he would move on out of himself. I saw Matt Riley, without looking behind, raise his arm.

"Quiet now, Tilly."

I laid my hand on the old dog's quivering flank. The sky hung above like a giant breath suspended over the shifting light and shadow of the grass and I watched the hats, and below them the upper bodies, part the still grassheads as they waded towards the treeline. They were moving in dreamlike slow motion, Matt Riley still in front. "What can you see now, Tilly?" I whispered.

They had stopped again. I saw Matt, still without turning, beckon to Braden.

He moved forward and Matt passed to his right. Braden was half a head taller than anyone else among them except Henry Denkler, who towered above the rest.

Matt raised an open hand, and I saw Braden lift the .303 very slowly to his shoulder.

The cicadas stopped dead in the heat. There was a sound, more like a happening in the sky I thought than a shot, and dozens of birds that had been invisible in the grass were suddenly in the air, wildly flapping.

There was a swift movement among the hats, then another shot, and the dogs were barking and straining so hard at the leash that I was almost pulled out of the truck, too busy shouting at them to shut up, and cursing and jerking at the leash, to see what was happening off in the distance, till there was another shot and I risked it, and saw the knot around what I knew must be the kill.

At that moment, a quarter of a mile to my left and well out of the vision of the others, I saw the two ancient carriages of the Chillagoe train come puffing across the horizon, pouring out smuts. It would have made its mid-morning stop at Miss Appin's, taken on water, and was now heading west into anthill country.

I could see Wattie McCorkindale, the driver, in the cabin, a tough nut of a man with tight grey curls like a woolly cap. I passed him each morning on my way to school, always in the same faded, washed-out overalls and carrying his black lunch tin. Beside him in the cabin was his mate, Bill Yates.

For a moment, as it swung close, I heard the hammering of the wheels on the track, then it swung back again, and it was the little gated platform at the rear that was facing me, and a woman was there, shading her eyes as she peered into the sunlight. She must have heard the shots. I was tempted to wave. I wondered what she must be making of all this. The shots, then a lone boy standing in the tray of a ute, in a grassfield in the middle of nowhere, holding hard to a mob of crazy hounds. Meanwhile, the party of pig-shooters, in a tight bunch now, was coming back.

Braden was flushed and looked innocently pleased with himself. Stuart and Glen were on either side of him. They had never seemed such a close and affectionate group.

I let the dogs loose. They leapt down from the ute and went running in excited circles around him. He dropped to one knee; happy, I thought, to be in a group where he could be the focus of another sort and exhibit an easier and more exuberant affection. He hugged Tilly, then Jigger, who was jostling to be gathered in, and they licked at his face and hands. Perhaps they could smell the pig on him, or some other smell he carried that was whatever had passed between him and the three hundred pounds of malevolent fury, in beast form, that had come hurtling towards him in the blood-knowledge and small-eyed, large-brained premonition of its imminent death.

He looked up, with his arms round Tilly, who for the past eight years had shared so many of our games and excursions, and in her own way, with doggy intuition, so many of our secrets. I saw then what a relief it was to him that all this was done with at last, and done well.

He had wanted it to go well for his father's sake as much as his own; out of a wish, just this once and for this time only, to be all that his father wanted him to be. All that Glen wanted him to be as well, and Stuart, because this was the last time they would be together in this way. When he left at the beginning of the new year it would be for a life he would never come back from; even if he did, physically, come back.

Except for Braden himself, I was the only one among us, I thought, who knew this. And because I knew it, I felt, as he must have, the sadness that was in Wes McGowan's pride in him, and in what he had shown of himself in front of Henry Denkler and Matt Riley, whose good opinion the old man set such store on. Had it crossed his mind, I wondered, that Braden, even in this moment of being most immediately one with them, was already lost to him?

I glanced at Stuart. He knew Braden just well enough to see what was at stake for the boy in that other world he was about to give himself to, though not perhaps how commanding it might be, or how clearly Braden understood that there was no other way he could go.

Glen saw nothing at all. It was inconceivable to him that a fellow of Braden's sort, his brother, who had grown up in the same household with him, could imagine anything finer or more real than what had just been revealed to him: the deep connection between himself and these men he was with; his even deeper connection with that force out there, animal, ancient, darkly close and mysterious, which, when he had stood against it and taken upon himself the solemn distinction of cancelling it out, he had also taken in, as a new and profounder being.

What surprised me, and must have surprised Braden too, was the glow all this gave him. It was real, in a way I think that even he had not expected: the abundant energy surging through him that lit his smile when he glanced up at me, then gave himself, all overflowing warmth and affection, to the dogs.

AN HOUR LATER, with Matt Riley's battered ute in front and Matt himself hanging out the cabin window to guide us, we bumped and lurched into the Valley. Which wasn't a valley in fact but a waterland of drowned savannah forest, reedy lagoons stained brownish in the shallows, sunlit beyond, or swampy places, half-earth, half-ooze, above which ti-trees stood stripping their bark or rotting slowly from the roots up. We parked beside an expanse of water wide enough to suggest a lake and with a good deal of leg-stretching, and expressions of satisfaction at the number of game birds in evidence, made camp, Matt directing.

Matt's precedence out here, I saw, had nothing to do with Braden's business with the pig or his "professionalism." It was something else. Very lightly ceded, the authority that Wes McGowan might have claimed as the getter-up of our party, or old Henry Denkler as its senior member and as mayor, had passed naturally, and with no need for explanation, to the younger man. And though no one had spelled it out I knew immediately what it was. I looked at Matt—at Jem too—with new eyes.

The land out here was Matt's grandmother's country, and the moment he entered it he had a different status: that was the accepted but unspoken ground of his authority. That and the knowledge of the place and all its workings that came with the land itself.

I had heard of this business of "grandmothers." The grandfathers were something else. Overdressed men with beards and side-whiskers—farmers, saddlers, blacksmiths, proprietors of drapery shops and general stores—they had given their names to streets, towns, shires all over the North. You saw their photographs, looking sternly soulful and patriarchal, round the walls of shire halls and in mouldy council chambers; men who, in defiance of conditions so hard that to survive at all a man had to be equally hard in return (in defiance too of the niceties of law as it might be established fifteen hundred miles away, in Brisbane), had carved out of the rainforest a world we took for granted now, since it had all the familiar amenities and might have been here for ever.

In fact, they had made it with their bare hands, and with axes and bullock-wagons. Doing whatever had to be done to make it theirs in spirit as well as in fact. Brooking no question, and suffering, one guesses, no regrets, since such work was an arm of progress and of God's good muscular plan for the world. All that so short a time ago that Wes McGowan might well have been one of the children in long clothes you saw seated on the knee of one of those bearded ancients, or in the arms of one of the pallid women in ruched and ribboned silk who sat stolidly beside him flanked by her brood.

No one would ever have spoken of Matt Riley's "grandfather." That would have given something away that in those days was still buried where family history meant it to stay, in the realm of the unspoken. "His grandmother's country" was a phrase that referred, without raising too precisely the question of blood, to the relationship a man might stand in to a particular tract of land, that went deeper and further back than legal possession. When used in town it had "implications," easy to pick up but not to be articulated. A nod to the knowing.

Out here, in the country itself, though what it referred to was still discreetly unspecified, it was actual. From the moment we climbed down out of the trucks and let the light of its broken waters enter us, and breathed in its sweetish water-smelling air, and took its dampness on our skins—from that moment something was added to Matt Riley, or given back; and he took it, with no sign of change in the quietness with which he went about things, or in his understated way of offering his own opinion or disagreeing with another's. He had re-entered a part of himself that was continuous with the place, and with a history the rest of us had forgotten or never known.

It was a place he both knew and was a stranger to; so deep in him that only rarely perhaps, save in sleep or half-sleep, did he catch a whisper of it out of some old story he had heard from one side of his family—the other would have a different story altogether—and which, the moment he stepped into it, became a language he understood in his bones and through the soles of his feet, though he had no other tongue in his head, or his memory, than the one we all spoke.

At home I had been shy of Matt—mostly, I think, because he was so shy of me. Out here things were different. All those afternoons in our kitchen when, with Eileen at the ironing board, I had sat at the table and drunk the milkshake she had stopped to make for me, and ate my biscuit or slice of cake, though we had barely addressed a word to one another, constituted a kind of intimacy, out here, that could be drawn on and made to bloom. "Com' on, son," he'd tell me, "I got somethin' you oughta take a look at."

Alone, or with Braden, and always with Jem in tow, he would uncover for me some small fact about the world we were in—a sight or ordinary but hidden wonder that I might otherwise have missed. Brushing the earth away with a grimy hand, or delicately lifting aside a bit of crumbling damp, he would open a view into some other life there, at the grub or chrysalis stage, that in moving through several forms in the one existence was in progress towards miraculous transformation, and whose unfolding history and habits, as he evoked them in his grunting monosyllabic style, moved almost imperceptibly from visible fact into half-humourous, half-sinister fable.

He showed us how to track, to read marks in the softly disturbed earth that told of the passage of some creature whose size and weight you could calculate—sometimes from observation, sometimes from a kind of visionary guesswork—by getting down close to the earth and attending, listening. The place was for him all coded messages; hints, clues, shining particulars that once scanned, and inwardly brooded on, opened the way to another order of understanding and usefulness.

WE ATE EARLY, before it was dark, Matt choosing what should go into the pot and Jem doing the chopping and seasoning.

Afterwards, bellies full of the cook-up and of the damper Jem had made to soak up the last of the gravy, we sat on as the ghostly late light on the tree trunks faded, and the trees themselves stepped back into impenetrable dark. Slowly the world around us re-created itself as sound. The occasional flapping, off in the distance, of a night bird on the prowl, an owl or nightjar. Low calls. Bush mice crept in, and tumbled with a chittering sound in the undergrowth beyond the fire, lured perhaps by our voices, or by our smell, or the smell of the stew and Jem's damper, the promise of scraps. There was the splash, from close by in the lagoon, of waterfowl, the clicketing of tree frogs or night crickets, a flustering of scrub-turkey or some other shy bush creature that had been drawn to the light, here in the great expanse of surrounding darkness, of our fire.

We sat. Not much was said. Talk out here, at this hour, was not so much an exchange of the usual observations and asides as a momentary reassurance, subdued, unassertive, of presence, of company and speech. The few words, an occasional low laugh, mingled as they were with the hush and tinkle of bush sounds, lulled something in me as I lay stretched on one side on top of my sleeping bag, face to the flames, and led me lazily, happily towards sleep.

The one jarring note was Stuart.

He too said little. But often, when I glanced up, I would find his eyes on me, dark, hostile I thought, in the glow of the fire. His beard had grown. He looked a little mad. Sometimes, when I dropped some word into the conversation, I would hear him grunt, and when I looked up there would be a line of half-humourous disdain to his mouth that in the old days would have been a prelude to one of his outbursts of baffled fury. Braden saw it too. But out here, Stuart kept whatever he was thinking to himself.

I stayed clear of him. Not consciously. But with Braden here it was easy to fall into the old pattern in which Braden and I were a pair and Stuart was on the outer. Perhaps he thought I had told Braden something—I hadn't. That I'd betrayed him in some way, and that we were ganging up on him. Then there was Matt Riley and the things he had to show. It simply happened that for the first two or three days we barely spoke.

IT WAS MY JOB, first thing each morning, to take a couple of billies down to the edge of the lagoon and draw water for our breakfast tea. Usually Braden went with me, but that morning, when I rolled out of the blanket and pulled on my jeans, he was still sleeping. I sat to tie my bootlaces, waiting for him to stir. When he didn't I took the billies from beside the fire and set out. The grass was white with frost. Pale sunlight touched the mist that drifted in thin low banks above the lagoons. Cobwebs rainbowed with light were stretched between the trees, their taut threads beaded with diamond points that flashed and burned gold, then fiery red.

Later, in the heat of the day, the bush smell would be prickly, peppery with sunlight. Now it had the freshness in it of a sky still moist with dew.

I climbed down the weedy bank and trawled the first of the billies through the brownish water, careful not to go too deep. I heard someone behind me, and thought it was Braden, but when I looked up it was Stuart who was swinging his long legs over a fallen branch and glowering down at me.

"Hi, Angus," he said, "how's it goin'?" His tone had an edge to it. "You havin' a good time out here?" He reached down and I passed the first of the two billies up to him, then set myself to filling the second.

"Great," I said. "Great!"

"That's nice," he said. He rested the billy on the log beside him. It sat there, balanced and brimming. "I been hopin' to catch you an' have a bit of a talk," he said at last. "You been avoidin' me?"

I found it easier to ignore this than deny it.

"Aren't you goin' to ask me what about?"

"I suppose it's about Katie," I said. I was wondering why, after so many weeks, he had broached the subject at last, and so directly. Did being out here make things different, relax the rules? Or was it that he had somehow come to the end of his tether? I emptied the second billy and for a second time drew it slowly across the surface of the lagoon. I had caught the little smile he had given me. Good shot, Angus. You got it in one. Satirical, I thought.

He waited for me to stop fooling with the second billy, then reached down and I handed it up to him.

"So," he said, holding on to the handle but not yet taking its weight so that I was caught looking up at him, "what do you know about all this, eh, Angus? What's happening? One minute everything was fine—you saw that. An' the next she's gone cold on me."

"Honestly, Stuart, I don't *know* what's happened. She wouldn't say anything to me."

He looked doubtful.

"I'm beat," he said suddenly, taking the billy at last and hoisting it over to sit beside the other one on the log. I thought there were tears in his eyes. I was shocked.

"I just don't know what she wants out of me."

"Stuart—"

"Yair, I know," he said. "I'm sorry, Angus." He sniffled and brushed his nose with his knuckled fist. "If you knew what it was like . . ."

I thought I did, though not from experience.

"The thing is," he said, sitting on the low branch, his face squared up now, the cheeks under the narrowed eyes wooden, the eyes gazing away into himself, "if this goes wrong it'll be the finish of me. For me it's all or nothing. If she would just have me—let *me* have *her*—it'd be all right—my life, I mean—hers too. If she won't I'm finished. She knows that, she must. I told her often enough. So why's she doing it?"

I found I couldn't look at him. We remained poised like that, the question hanging, the open expanse of water like glass in the early light. He got up, took one of the billies, then the other, and set off back to camp.

I sat on at the bank for a moment. Then I crouched down and splashed cold lagoon water over my face, then again, and again.

Stuart's misery scared me. My own adolescent glooms I had learned to enjoy. I liked the sense they gave me of being fully present. Even more the bracing quality I felt in possession of when I told myself sharply to stop play-acting, and strongly, stoically dealt with them. Did I despise Stuart because he was so self-indulgent? Was he too play-acting, but not alert enough to his own nature to know it? I preferred that view of him than the scarier one in which his desperation was real. I didn't want to be responsible for his feelings, and it worried me that out here there was no escape from him.

He tackled me again later in the day.

"You know, Angus," he said mildly as if he had given the matter some thought and got the better of it, "you could put in a good word for me. If there was the opportunity."

We were standing together on a shoot, just far enough from the others not to be heard, even in the late-afternoon stillness.

Braden was with his father and Henry Denkler, a little away to the left. The air was still, the ground, with its coarse short grass, moist underfoot. Steely light glared off the nearby lagoon. The dogs, in their element now, had discovered in themselves, in a way that impressed me, their true nature as bird-dogs, a fine tense quality that made them almost physically different from the rather slow creatures they were at home. They were leaner, more sinewy.

"You could do that much," he persisted, "for a mate. We are mates, aren't we?"

I turned, almost angry, and found myself disarmed by the flinching look he gave me, the tightness of the flesh around his eyes, the line of his mouth.

I was saved from replying by a clatter of wings, as a flock of ducks rose out of the glare that lay over the surface of the big lagoon and stood out clear against the cloudless blue. But it was too late. I had missed my chance at a shot and so had Stuart. The others let off a volley of gunfire and the dogs went crashing through the broken water to where the big birds were tumbling over in the air and splashing into the shattered stillness of the lake, or dropping noiselessly into the reeds on the other bank.

"Damn," I shouted. "Damn. Damn!"

"What happened?" Braden asked, when we stood waiting in a group for the dogs to bring in the last of the birds. "Why didn't you fire?"

I shook my head, and Braden, taking in Stuart's look, must have seen enough, in his quick way, not to insist. The dogs were still coming in with big plump birds. There were many more of them than would go into the pot.

"Good girl, Tilly," he called, and the dog, diverted for a moment, gave herself a good shake and ran to his knee. He leaned down, roughly pulled her head to his thigh and ruffled her ears. The strong smell of her wet fur came to me.

I spent the rest of the day stewing over my lost chance, exaggerating my angry disappointment and the number of birds I might have bagged, as a way of being so mad with Stuart that I did not have to ask myself what else I should feel. Braden and I spent the whole of the next morning with Matt Riley and Jem, but in the afternoon I came upon Stuart sitting on a big log a little way off from the camp, with a scrub-turkey at his feet. I stopped at a distance and spent a moment watching him. I thought he had not seen me.

"Hi," he said. I stepped out into the clearing. "What are you up to?"

"Nothing much," I told him.

I settled on the log a little way away from him.

"Listen, Stuart," I began, after a bit.

"Yair, I know," he told me. "I'm sorry."

"No," I said, "it's not about yesterday. You've got to stop all this, that's all. She won't change her mind. I know she won't. Not this time."

"Did she tell you that?"

"No. Not in so many words. But she won't, I know she won't. Look, Stuart, you should leave me out of it, that's what I wanted to say. I don't know anything so I can't help you. You've got to stop."

"I see," he said. "That's pretty plain. Thanks, Angus. No, I mean it," he said, "you're right, I've been foolin' myself. I can see that now."

"Look, Stuart—"

"No, you're right, it was hopeless from the start. That's what you're telling me, isn't it? That I might as well just bloody cut my throat!"

I leapt to my feet. "Shut up," I told him fiercely. "Just stop all this. Bloody shut up!"

He was so shocked that he laughed outright.

"Well," he said after a moment, with bitter satisfaction. "Finally."

What did *that* mean? He gave me a look that made me see, briefly, something of the means he might have brought to bear on *her*. But she was harder than I was. I knew the contempt she would have for a kind of appeal that she herself would never stoop to.

I stood looking at him for a moment. I did not know what more I could say. I turned and walked away.

"I thought you were on *my* side," he called after me.

I had heard this before, or an echo of it. I looked back briefly but did not stop.

"I thought we were mates," he called again. "Angus?"

I kept walking.

I did know what he was feeling, but he confused me. I wanted to be free of him, of his turmoil. The nakedness with which he paraded his feelings dismayed me. It removed all the grounds, I thought, on which I could react and offer him real sympathy. It violated the only code, as I saw it then, that offered us protection: tight-lipped understatement, endurance. What else could we rely on? What else could *I* rely on?

I walked.

The ground with its rough tussocks was swampy, unsteady underfoot, the foliage on the stunted trees sparse and darkly colourless, their trunks blotched with lichen. I had no idea where I was headed or how far I needed to go to escape my own unsettlement. Little lizards tumbled away from my boots or dropped from branches, dragonflies hung stopped on the air, then switched and darted, blazing out like struck matches where the sun caught their glassy wings.

I walked. And as I moved deeper into the solitude of the land, its expansive stillness—which was not stillness in fact but an interweaving of close but distant voices so dense that they became one, and then mere background, then scarcely there at all—I began to forget my own disruptive presence, receding as naturally into what hummed and shimmered all round me as into a dimension of my own being that it had taken my coming out here, alone, in the slumbrous hour after midday, to uncover. I felt drawn, drawn on.

I had enough bush sense, a good enough eye for recording, unconsciously as I passed, the little oddnesses in the terrain—the elbow of a fallen bough, a particular assembly of glossy-leaved bushes that would serve as signposts on my way back—to feel confident I wouldn't get lost. I let Stuart, seated gloomily back there on his log, hugging his rifle, hugging even closer his dumb grief, fade from my thoughts, and moved deeper into the becalmed early-afternoon light, over spatterings of ancient debris, crumblings of dried-out timber. Slowly, all round and under me, an untidy grey-green world was continuously, visibly in motion. Ti-tree trunks unfurled tattered streamers; around their roots a seepage like long-brewed tea.

I walked, and the great continent of sound I was moving into recorded my presence, the arrival, in its close-woven fabric of light, sound, stilled or moving shadow, of a medium-sized foreign body, displacing the air a moment as it advanced, and confusing, with the smell of its sweat and the shifting of its breath, the tiny signals that were being picked up and translated out there by a myriad of forms of alien intelligence. I was central to it but I was also nothing, or close to nothing.

In the compacted heat and drowsy afternoon sunlight, I could have kept walking for ever, all the way to the Gulf. It was time, not space, I was moving into. Years it might be. And there was more of it—not just ahead but on all sides—than I could conceive of or measure.

There was no specific point I was heading for. I could stop now, turn back, and it would all still be here. It was myself I was moving into.

One day, far off down the years, I would come stumbling back in my body's last moments of consciousness and here it would be: crumbling into itself and dispersing its particles and voices, reassembling itself cell by cell in a new form that was also the old one remade. I had no need to go on and actually see it, the place where I would lie down in the springy marsh-grass, among the litter and mould, letting the grass take the impression of my weight, the shape of my body's presence, and keep it long after I was gone.

Away back, when I first heard about the Valley and let it form itself in my mind, I had thought that everything I found unsatisfactory in myself, in my life but also in my nature, would come right out here, because that is what I had seen, or thought I had, in others. Kids who had been out here, and whom I had thought of till then as wild and scattered, had come back settled in their own aggregation of muscle, bone, and flesh, and in some new accommodation with the world.

Nothing like that had come to me. I was no more settled, no less confused. I would bring nothing back that would be visible to others—to my father, for instance. I had lost something; that was more like it. But happily. As I walked on into this bit of grey-green nondescript wilderness I was happily at home in myself. But in my old self, not a new one.

I don't know how far I had gone before I paused, looked around, and realised I was lost. For the last ten minutes I had been walking in my sleep. The landscape of small shrubs and ti-trees I had been moving through was now scrub.

I consulted the sun and turned back the way I had come. Minutes later I looked again and changed tack. It was hot. I had begun to sweat. I took my shirt off, draped it round my neck, and set off again.

Five minutes more and I stopped, told myself sternly not to panic and, standing with my eyes closed and the whole landscape shrilling in my head, took half a dozen slow breaths.

THE SHOT CAME from closer than I would have expected, and from a direction—to my left—that surprised me. How had I gone so wrong? It was only when I had got over a small rush of relief that it struck me that after the first shot there had been no other. I quickened my pace, then began to run, my boots sinking and at times slipping on the swampy ground. When I arrived back at the clearing Stuart lay awkwardly sprawled, white-lipped and holding his shirt, which was already soaked, to his bloodied thigh.

"Hi, Angus," he said, his tone somewhere between his old, false jauntiness and a dreamy bemusement at what had occurred and at my being the one who had arrived to find him.

"Better get someone. Quick, eh?"

He glanced down to where blood, a lot of it, I thought, was flooding through the flimsy shirt.

I fell to my knees, gaping.

"No," he said calmly. "Just run off as quick as you can, mate, and fetch someone. But be quick, eh? I'll be right for a bit."

I wasn't sure of that. I felt there was something I should be doing immediately, something I should be saying that would make him feel better and restore things, maybe even cancel them out, and I was still nursing this childish thought as I sprinted towards the camp. Something I would regret for ever if he bled to death before I got back. *Was* he bleeding to death? Could a thing like that just happen, without warning, out of the blue?

In just minutes I had shouted my breathless announcement and we were back.

He was still sitting, awkwardly upright, his back against the log. I took in the rifle this time. It lay on the ground to his right. There was also the heap of dull black feathers that was a scrub-turkey. He was no longer holding the soaked rag to his outflung leg. A pool was spreading under him. He was streaming with sweat. Great drops of it stood on his brow and were making runnels down his chest.

"It's all right, Dad," he said weakly when the old man and Matt and the others reached him. "Bugger missed."

It took me a moment to grasp that it was the bullet he was referring to.

They got his boot off and Matt slashed the leg of the scorched and bloodied jeans all the way to the crotch and worked quickly to apply a tourniquet. "You'll be right," he told Stuart. "Bugger missed the main artery, you're a lucky feller. Bone too." Blood was seeping out between his hands. There was a smell that made me squeamish. Seared meat. Stuart, bluish-white around the mouth, was raised up on his elbows and staring, fascinated by the throbbing out of the warm life in him. Like a child who has borne a bad fall manfully, but bursts into tears at the first expression of sympathy, he seemed close to breaking.

I was dealing with my own emotions.

I had seen Stuart stripped any number of times, in the changing room at the pool, in the noise and general roughhouse of the showers afterwards. A naked body among other naked bodies, with clear water streaming over it and a smell of clean soap in the air, is bracing, functional, presents an image too common to be remarkable or to draw attention to itself. But a single ravaged limb thrust out in the dirt, the soaked denim of the jeans that covered it violently ripped and peeled away, black hairs curling on the hollow of the thigh and growing furlike close to the groin, has a brute particularity that brought me closer to something exposed and shockingly intimate in him, to the bare forked animal, than anything I had seen when he stood fully naked under the shower. I was shaken. His jockeys, where they showed, sagged, and were worn thin and greyish. A trail of blood, still glistening wet, made its way down the long ridge of the shank bone.

Not much more than half an hour ago I had walked out on him. Exasperated. Worn down by the demands he put on me. At the end of my patience with his turmoil, the poses he struck, his callow pretensions to martyrdom. Now I was faced with a shocking reality. It was Stuart McGowan's blood I was staring at. What impressed me, in the brute light of day, was its wetness, how much there was of it, the alarming blatancy of its red.

He caught the look on my face, and something in what he saw there encouraged him back into a bravado he had very nearly lost the trick of.

"Angus," he said. He might just have noticed me there in the tense crowd around him and recalled that I was the one who had found him. "Waddya think then?" He managed a crooked smile, and his voice, though strained, had the same half-jokey, half-defensive tone as when on those early visits to my sleepout he had picked up one of my books and asked, "So what's this one about?"

As if on this occasion too he were faced with a puzzle on which

I might somehow enlighten him, and in the same expectation, I thought, of being given credit for the seriousness of his interest.

A smile touched the corner of his lips.

He was pleased with himself!

At being the undoubted centre of so much drama and concern. At having done something at last that shocked me into really looking at him, into taking him seriously. The wound was worth it, that's what he thought. All it demanded of him was that he should grit his teeth and bear a little pain, physical pain, be a man; he had all the resources in the world for that. And what he gained was what he saw in *me*. Which, when I got back, I would pass on to her, to Katie. When she was presented with the facts—that hole in his naked thigh with its raw and blackened lips, the near miss that had come close to draining him of the eight pints of rude animal life that was in him—she would have to think again and accept what she had denied: the tribute of his extravagant suffering, the real and visible workings of his pure, bull-like heart. He had done this for *her*!

"Okay," Matt Riley was saying. "That's the best we can do for now."

He got to his feet, rubbed his hands on the cloth of his thighs, and told Jem: "You—Jem—we'll need some sort of stretcher to get 'im to the truck. See what you can knock up." Then, quietly, to Wes McGowan: "The quicker we get 'im back to town now the better. It's not as bad as it looks. Bullet went clean through. Bugger'll need watchin', but."

It took me a moment to grasp that what was being referred to this time was the wound.

In all the panic and excitement around Stuart, I had lost sight of Braden. He was hunched on the ground a little way off, his back to Stuart and the rest, his head bowed. I thought he was crying. He wasn't, but he was shaking. I squatted beside him.

"You okay?" I asked. I thought he hadn't heard me. "It's just a flesh wound," I told him. "Nothing serious. He's lost a bit of blood, but."

He gave a snort. Then a brief contemptuous laugh.

Was that what it was? Contempt?

He thought Stuart had done it deliberately! I was astonished. But wasn't that just what I had assumed a moment back, when I told myself "He's done this for her"?

I touched Braden lightly on the shoulder, then got up and turned again to where Stuart, wrapped in a blanket now and with his eyes closed, but still white-lipped and sweating, lay waiting for the pallet to be brought.

I told myself that it had never occurred to me that he would go so far. It was too excessive, too wide of what was acceptable to the code we lived by. A hysterical girl might do such a thing but not a man, not Stuart McGowan's sort of man. But at the edge of that I was shaken. Maybe what I thought I knew about people—about Stuart, about myself—was unreliable. I looked at Stuart and saw, up ahead, something that had not come to me yet but must come some day. Not a physical shattering but what belongs to the heart and its confusions, the mess of need, desire, hurt pride, and all the sliding versions of himself as lover triumphant, then as lover rejected and achingly bereft, that had led him to force things—had he?—to such lurid and desperate conclusions.

I considered again the nest of coppery hair he sported in the scoop of his underlip.

When it first appeared I had taken it, in a worrying way, as a dandified affectation, out of character with the Stuart I knew. I was less ready now with my glib assumptions. What did I know of Stuart McGowan's "character" as I called it? Of what might or might not belong to it?

After a moment he opened his eyes, caught me watching, and in an appeal perhaps to some old complicity between us that for a good time now had been under threat, but which the shock of his near miss had re-established, he winked. Only when I failed to respond did it strike him that he might have miscalculated.

He struggled to one elbow, his head tilted, his brow in a furrow, and grinned, but sheepishly, as if I had caught him out in something furtive, unmanly. "So how's tricks, Angus? How's it goin'?" he enquired. "You okay?"

This time I did not turn my back on him, but I did walk away, even while I stood watching. Jem and Glen had come up with their makeshift stretcher, and Matt Riley and his father, with Henry Denkler directing, rolled him onto it, all of them quieting his sharp intakes of breath with ritual assurances, most of them wordless. For some reason, what I remember most clearly is the three-day grime on the back of Glen McGowan's neck as he bent to settle Stuart. And through it all, deep in myself, I was walking away fast into a freshening distance in which my own grime was being miraculously washed away.

Walking lightly. The long grass swishing round my boots as the sparse brush drew me on. Into the vastness of small sounds that was a continent. To lose myself among its flutings and flutterings, the glow of its moist air and sun-charged chemical green, its traffic of unnumbered slow ingenious agencies.

An hour later we had loaded up and were on our way home: Stuart well wrapped in an old quilt, laid out in the tray of the McGowans' ute with his father to tend him, Glen driving, and Henry Denkler, who seemed troubled and out of sorts, in the cabin beside him. Braden and I, seated high up on a pile of bedrolls and packs, rode in the back of Matt Riley's beaten-up ute with the guns, a mess of dogs, and all our gear.

I sat, my back to the side of the truck, with Tilly between my knees, leaning forward occasionally to hug her to me, and receiving in return a soulful, brown-eyed look of pure affection. How straightforward animals are, I thought. As compared to people, with their left-handed unhappy agendas, their sore places hidden even from themselves.

I thought uneasily of Stuart, bumping about now in the other ute as it wallowed through waist-high grass down the unmarked track; still believing, perhaps, that Katie would be impressed by the badge of a near fatality he would be wearing when we got back.

Would she be? I didn't think so, but I could no longer be sure. She kept eluding my grasp. As Stuart had. And Braden.

I glanced across at him. He had pushed his hat off, though the

cord was still tight under his chin, and his eyes were narrowed, his
cheeks taut as he grasped the side of the ute with one hand to
steady himself against its rolling and stared into space. After a
moment, aware of my scrutiny, he turned, and for the first time in
a while he smiled his old wry smile, which meant he had returned,
more or less, to being relaxed again. Inside his own head. But not
in a way that excluded my being in tune with him. I sat back, giving myself up to the air that came streaming over the cabin top as
the ute emerged at last on to bitumen, turned north, and put on
speed.

We were less than thirty miles from home now. The land was
growing uneven. Soon there would be canefields on either side of
the steeply dipping road, dairy farms smelling of silage, and little
smooth-crowned hills that had once been wooded and dark with
aerial roots and vines, till the loggers and land-clearers moved in
and opened all this country to the sky, letting the light in; creating
a landscape lush and green, with only, in the gully breaks
between, a remnant of the old darkness and mystery, a cathedral
gloom where a smell of damp-rot lingered that was older than the
scent of cane flowers or the ammoniac stench of wet cow flop, and
where creatures still moved about the forest floor, or hung in rows
as in a wardrobe high up in the branches, or glided noiselessly
from bough to bough.

I must have nodded off. When I looked up, we were already
speeding through settlements I recognised and knew the names
of: wooden houses, some of them no more than shacks, set far back
and low among isolated forest trees, the open spaces on either side
of the bitumen strip narrowing so quickly that what there was of a
township—a service station, a Greek milk bar and café—was
gone again before you could catch the name on a signpost or register the slightly different smell on the air that signified settled life
and neighbourliness.

I loved all this. But Katie was right. I too would leave. As she
would, as Braden would.

He met my eye now and then, as the ute swung out to pass a
slower vehicle and we had to reach for the side and hang on to

steady ourselves, but I was less certain now that I could read his looks. He had already begun to move away.

The difference was, I thought, that he, like Katie, would not come back. But for me there could be no final leaving. This greenish light, full and luminous, always with a heaviness in it that was a reminder of the underlying dark—like the persistent memory, under even the most open of cleared land, of the dankness of rainforests—was for me the light by which all moments of expectation and high feeling would in my mind for ever be touched. This was the country I would go on dreaming in, wherever I lay my head.

We were bounding along now. Sixty miles an hour. From the cabin of the truck, Jem Riley's voice, raw and a little tuneless, came streaming past my ear. "Goodnight, Irene," was what he was singing, "I'll see you in my dreams."

Braden took it up and grinned at me. I followed. A doleful tune, almost a dirge, full of old hurt, that people were drawn to sing in chorus, as if it were the sad but consoling anthem of some loose republic of the heart, spontaneously established, sustained a moment, then easily let go. Before we were done with the last of it the quick-falling tropical night had come. A blueness that for the last quarter of an hour had been gathering imperceptibly round fence posts and in the depths of trees had swiftly overtaken us, with its ancient smell of the land and its unfolding silence that was never silence. "Goodnight," we sang at full pelt, foolishly grinning, "goodnight, goodnight, I'll see you in my dreams."

Every Move You Make

WHEN JO FIRST CAME to Sydney, the name she heard in
every house she went into was Mitchell Maze. "This is a
Mitchell Maze house," someone would announce, "can't you just
tell?" and everyone would laugh. After a while she knew what the
joke was and did not have to be told. "Don't tell me," she'd say, taking in the raw uprights and bare window frames, "Mitchell Maze,"
and her hostess would reply, "Oh, do you know Mitch? Isn't he the
limit?"

They were beach houses, even when they were tucked away in
a cul-de-sac behind the Paddington Post Office or into a gully
below an escarpment at Castlecrag. The group they appealed to,
looking back affectionately to the hidey-holes and treehouses of
their childhood, made up a kind of clan. Of artists mostly,
painters, session musicians, filmmakers, writers for the *National
Times* and the *Fin Review,* who paid provisional tax and had kids at
the International Grammar School, or they were lawyers at Free-
hills or Allen, Allen & Hemsley, or investment bankers with
smooth manners and bold ties who still played touch rugby at the
weekends or belonged to a surf club. Their partners—they were
sometimes married, mostly not—worked as arts administrators,
or were in local government. A Mitchell Maze house was a sign
that you had arrived but were not quite settled.

Airy improvisations, or—according to how you saw it—calculated and beautiful wrecks, a lot of their timber was driftwood
blanched and polished by the tide, or had been scrounged from
building sites or picked up cheap at demolitions. It had knotholes,
the size sometimes of a twenty-cent piece, and was so carelessly

stripped that layers of old paint were visible in the grain that you could pick out with a fingernail, in half-forgotten colours from another era: apple green, ox-blood, baby blue. A Mitchell Maze house was a reference back to a more relaxed and open-ended decade, an assurance (a reassurance in some cases) that your involvement with the Boom, and all that went with it, was opportunistic, uncommitted, tongue-in-cheek. You had maintained the rage, still had a Che or Hendrix poster tacked to a wall of the garage, and kept a fridge full of tinnies, though you *had* moved on from the flagon red. As for Mitch himself, he came with the house. "Only not often enough," as one of his clients quipped.

He might turn up one morning just at breakfast time with a claw hammer and rule at the back of his shorts and a load of timber on his shoulder. One of the kids would already have sighted his ute.

"Oh great," the woman at the kitchen bench would say, keeping her voice low-keyed but not entirely free of irony. "Does this mean we're going to get that wall? Hey, kids, here's Mitch. Here's our wall."

"Hi," the kids yelled, crowding round him. "Hi, Mitch. Is it true? Is that why you're here? Are you goin' t' give us a *wall*?"

They liked Mitch, they loved him. So did their mother. But she also liked the idea of a wall.

He would accept a mug of coffee, but when invited to sit and have breakfast with them would demur. "No, no thanks," he'd tell them. "Gotta get started. I'll just drink this while I work."

He would be around then for a day or two, hammering away till it was dusk and the rosellas were tearing at the trees beyond the deck and dinner was ready; staying on for a plate of pasta and some good late-night talk then bedding down after midnight in a bunk in the kids' room, "to get an early start," or, if they were easy about such things, crawling in with a few murmured apologies beside his hosts. Then in the morning he would be gone again, and no amount of calling, no number of messages left at this place or that, would get him back.

Visitors observing an open wall would say humourously, "Ah, Mitch went off to get a packet of nails, I see."

Sensitive fellows, quick to catch the sharpening of their partner's voice as it approached the subject of a stack of timber on the living-room floor, or a bathroom window that after eleven months was still without glass, would spring to the alert.

As often as not, the first indication that some provisional but to this point enduring arrangement was about to be renegotiated would be a flanking attack on the house.

"Right, *mate*," was the message, "let's get serious here. What about that wall?"

Those who were present to hear it, living as they did in structures no less flimsy than the one that was beginning to break up all around them, would feel a chill wind at their ear.

All this Jo had observed, with amusement and a growing curiosity, for several months before she found herself face to face with the master builder himself.

Jo was thirty-four and from the country, though no one would have called her a country girl. Before that she was from Hungary. Very animated and passionately involved in everything she did, very intolerant of those who did not, as she saw it, demand enough of life, she was a publisher's editor, ambitious or pushy according to how you took these things, and successful enough to have detractors. She herself wanted it all—everything. And more.

"You want too much," her friends told her. "You can't have it, you just can't. Nobody can."

"You just watch me," Jo told them in reply.

She had had two serious affairs since coming to Sydney, both briefer than she would have wished. She was too intense, that's what her friends told her. The average bloke, the average *Australian* bloke—oh, here it comes, *that* again, she thought—was uncomfortable with dramatics. Intimidated. Put off.

"I don't want someone who's average," she insisted. "Even an average Australian."

She wanted a love that would be overwhelming, that would

make a wind-blown leaf of her, a runaway wheel. She was quite prepared to suffer, if that was to be part of it. She would walk barefoot through the streets and howl if that's what love brought her to.

Her friends wrinkled their brows at these stagy extravagances. "Honestly! Jo!" Behind her back they patronised and pitied her.

In fact they too, some of them, had felt like this at one time or another. At the beginning. But had learned to hide their disappointment behind a show of hard-boiled mateyness. They knew the rules. Jo had not been around long enough for that. She had no sense of proportion. Did she even *know* that there were rules?

THEY MET AT LAST. At a party at Palm Beach, the usual informal Sunday-afternoon affair. She knew as soon as he walked in who it must be.

He was wearing khaki shorts, work boots, nothing fancy. An open-necked unironed shirt.

Drifting easily from group to group, noisily greeted with cries and little affectionate pecks on the cheek by the women, and with equally affectionate gestures from the men—a clasp of the shoulder, a hand laid for a moment on his arm—he unsettled the room, that's what she thought, re-focused its energies, though she accepted later that the unsettlement may only have been in herself. Through it all he struck her as being remote, untouchable, self-enclosed, though not at all self-regarding. Was it simply that he was shy? When he found her at last she had the advantage of knowing more about him, from the tales she had been regaled with, the houses she had been in, than he could have guessed.

What she was not prepared for was his extraordinary charm. Not his talk—there was hardly any of that. His charm was physical. It had to do with the sun-bleached, salt-bleached mess of his hair and the way he kept ploughing a rough hand through it; the grin that left deep lines in his cheeks; the intense presence, of which he himself seemed dismissive or unaware. He smelled of physical work, but also, she thought, of wood shavings—blond transparent curlings off the edge of a plane. Except that the special feature of his appeal was the rough rather than the smooth.

They went home together. To his place, to what he called "The Shack," a house on stilts, floating high above a jungle of tree ferns, morning glory, and red-clawed coral trees in a cove at Balmoral. Stepping into it she felt she had been there already. Here at last was the original of all those open-ended unfinished structures she had been in and out of for the past eight months. When she opened the door to the loo, she laughed. There was no glass in the window. Only a warmish square of night filled with ecstatic insect cries.

SHE WAS PREPARED for the raw, splintery side of him. The sun-cracked lips, the blonded hair that covered his forearms and the darker hair that came almost to his Adam's apple, the sandpapery hands with their scabs and festering nicks. What she could not have guessed at was the whiteness and almost feminine silkiness of his hidden parts. Or the old-fashioned delicacy with which he turned away every attempt on her part to pay tribute to them. It was so at odds with the libertarian mode she had got used to down here.

He took what he needed in a frank, uncomplicated way; was forceful but considerate—all this in appreciation of her own attractions. She was flattered, moved, and in the end felt a small glow of triumph at having so much pleased him. For a moment he entirely yielded, and she felt, in his sudden cry, and in the completeness afterwards with which he sank into her arms, that she had been allowed into a place that in every other circumstance he kept guarded, closed off.

She herself was dazzled. By a quality in him—*beauty* is what she said to herself—that took her breath away, a radiance that burned her lips, her fingertips, every point where their bodies made contact. But when she tried to express this—to touch him as he had touched her and reveal to him this vision she had of him—he resisted. What she felt in his almost angry shyness was a kind of distaste. She retreated, hurt, but was resentful too. It was unfair of him to exert so powerful an appeal and then turn maidenly when he got a response.

She should have seen then what cross-purposes they would be at, and not only in this matter of intimacy. But he recognised her hurt, and in a way, she would discover, that was typical of him, tried out of embarrassment to make amends.

He was sitting up with his back against the bedhead enjoying a smoke. Their eyes met, he grinned; a kind of ease was re-established between them. She was moved by how knocked about he was, the hard use to which he had put his body, the scraps and scrapes he had been through. Her fingertips went to a scar, a deep nick in his cheekbone under the left eye. She did not ask. Her touch was itself a question.

"Fight with an arc lamp," he told her. His voice had a humorous edge. "I lost. Souvenir of my brief career as a movie star."

She looked at him. The grin he wore was light, self-deprecatory. He was offering her one of the few facts about himself—from his childhood, his youth—that she would ever hear. She would learn only later how useless it was to question him on such matters. You got nowhere by asking. If he did let something drop it was to distract you, while some larger situation that he did not want to develop slipped quietly away. But that was not the case on this occasion. They barely knew one another. He wanted, in all innocence, to offer her something of himself.

When he was thirteen—this is what he told her—he had been taken by his mother to an audition. More than a thousand kids had turned up. He didn't want the part, he thought it was silly, but he had got it anyway and for a minute back there, because of that one appearance, had been a household name, a star.

She had removed her hand and was staring.

"What?" he said, the grin fading. He gave her an uncomfortable look and leaned across to the night table to stub out his cigarette.

"I can't believe it," she was saying. "I can't believe this. I know who you are. You're Skip Daley!"

"No I'm not," he said, and laughed. "Don't be silly."

He was alarmed at the way she had taken it. He had offered it as a kind of joke. One of the *least* important things he could have told her.

"But I saw that film! I saw it five times!"

"Don't," he said. "It was nothing. I shouldn't have let on."

But he could have no idea what it had meant to her. What *he* had meant to her.

Newly arrived in the country, a gangly ten-year-old, and hating everything about this place she had never wanted to come to— the parched backyards, the gravel playground under the pepper trees at her bare public school, the sing-song voices that mocked her accent and deliberately, comically got her name wrong—she had gone one Saturday afternoon to the local pictures and found herself tearfully defeated. In love. Not just with the hard-heeled freckle-faced boy up on the screen, with his round-headed, blond, pudding-bowl haircut and cheeky smile, his fierce sense of honour, the odd mixture in him of roughness and shy, broad-vowelled charm, but with the whole barefoot world he moved in, his dog Blue, his hardbitten parents who were in danger of losing their land, the one-storeyed sun-struck weatherboard they lived in, which was, in fact, just like her own.

More than a place, it was a world of feeling she had broken through to, and it could be hers now because *he* lived in it. She had given up her resistance.

On that hot Saturday afternoon, in that darkened picture theatre in Albury, her heart had melted. Australia had claimed and conquered her. She was shocked and the shock was physical. She had had no idea till then what beauty could do to you, the deep tears it could draw up; how it could take hold of you in the middle of the path and turn you round, fatefully, and set you in a new direction. That was what he could know nothing of.

All that time ago, he had changed her life. And here he was more than twenty years later, in the flesh, looking sideways at her in this unmade lump of a bed.

"Hey," he was saying, and he put his hand out to lift aside a strand of her hair.

"I just can't get over it," she said.

"Hey," he said again. "Don't be silly! It was nothing. Something my mother got me into. It was all made up. That stupid kid wasn't me. I was a randy little bugger if you want to know. All I could think about was my dick—" and he laughed. "They didn't show any of that. Truth is, I didn't like myself much in those days. I was too unhappy."

But he was only getting himself in deeper. Unhappy? He caught the look in her eyes, and to save the situation leaned forward and covered her mouth with his own.

FROM THE START he famished her. It was not in her nature to pause at thresholds but there were bounds she could not cross and he was gently, firmly insistent. He did give himself, but when she too aggressively took the initiative, or crossed the line of what he thought of as a proper modesty, he would quietly turn away. What he was abashed by, she saw, was just what most consumed her, his beauty. He had done everything he could to abolish it. All those nicks and scars. The broken tooth he took no trouble to have fixed. The exposure to whatever would burn or coarsen.

A series of "spills" had left him, at one time or another, with a fractured collarbone, three bouts of concussion, a broken leg. These punishing assaults on himself were attempts to wipe out an affliction. But all they had done was refine it: bring out the metallic blue of his eyes, show up under the skin, with its network of cracks, the poignancy—that is how she saw it—of his bones.

Leaving him sprawled, that first morning, she had stepped out into the open living room.

Very aware that she was as yet only a casual visitor to his world, and careful of intruding, she picked her way between plates piled with old food and set on tabletops or pushed halfway under chairs, coffee mugs, beer cans, gym socks, ashtrays piled with butts, magazines, newspapers, unopened letters, shirts dropped just anywhere or tossed carelessly over the backs of chairs. A dead light bulb on a glass coffee-table rolled in the breeze.

She sat a moment on the edge of a lounge and thought she could hear the tinkling that came from the closed globe, a distant sound, magical and small, but magnified, like everything this morning. The room was itself all glass and light. It hung in mid-air. Neither inside nor out, it opened straight into the branches of a coral tree, all scarlet claws.

She went to the kitchen bench at the window. The sink was piled with coffee mugs and more dishes. She felt free to deal with those, and was still at the sink, watching a pair of rainbow lorikeets on the deck beyond, all his dinner plates gleaming in the rack, when he stepped up behind her in a pair of sagging jockey-shorts, still half asleep, rubbing his skull. He kissed her in a light, familiar way. Barely noticing the cleared sink—that was a *good* sign—he ran a glass of water and drank it off, his Adam's apple bobbing. Then kissed her again, grinned, and went out on to the deck.

The lorikeets flew off, but belonged here, and soon ventured back.

OVER THE WEEKS, as she came to spend more time there, she began to impose her own sort of order on the place. He did not object. He sat about reading the papers while she worked around him.

The drawers of the desk where he sometimes sat in the evening, wearing reading glasses while he did the accounts, were stuffed with papers—letters, cuttings, prospectuses. There were more papers pushed into cardboard boxes, in cupboards, stacked in corners, piled under beds.

"Do you want to keep any of this?" she would enquire from time to time, holding up a fistful of mail.

He barely looked. "No. Whatever it is. Just chuck it."

"You sure?"

"Why? What is it?"

"Letters."

"Sure. Chuck 'em out."

"What about these?"

"What are they?"

"Invoices. 1984."

"No. Just pile 'em up, I'll make a bonfire. Tomorrow maybe."

SHE HAD a strong need for fantasy, she liked to make things interesting. In their early days together, she took to leaving little love notes for him. Once under the tea caddy, where he would come across it when he went out in the morning, just after six, to make their tea. On other occasions, beside his shaving gear in the bathroom, in one of the pockets of his windcheater, in his work shorts. If he read them he did not mention the fact. It was ages before he told her, in a quarrel, how much these love notes embarrassed him. She flushed scarlet, did not make that mistake again.

He had no sense of fantasy himself. He wasn't insensitive—she was often touched by his thoughtfulness and by the small things he noticed—but he was very straight-up-and-down, no frills. Once, when his film was showing, she asked if they could go and see it. "What for?" he asked, genuinely surprised. "It's crap. Anyway, I'd rather forget all that. It wasn't a good time, that. Not for me it wasn't."

"Because you were unhappy?" she said. "You told me that, remember?"

But he shut off then, and the matter dropped.

HE TOLD HER nothing about his past. Nothing significant. And if she asked, he shied away.

"I don't want to talk about it," was all he'd say. "I try to forget about what's gone and done with. That's where we're different. You go on and on about it."

No I don't, she wanted to argue. You're the one who's hung up on the past. That's why you won't talk about it. What I'm interested in is the present. But all of it. All the little incidental happenings that got you here, that got *us* here, made us the way we are. Seeing that she was still not satisfied, he drew her to him, almost violently—offering her that, his hard presence—and sighed, she did not know for what.

HE HAD no decent clothes that she could discover. Shirts, shorts, jeans—workclothes, not much else. A single tie that he struggled into when he had an engagement that was "official." She tried to rectify this. But when he saw the pile of new things on the bed he looked uncomfortable. He took up a blue poplin shirt, fingered it, frowned, put it down.

"I wish you wouldn't," he said. "Buy me things. Shirts and that." He was trying not to seem ungracious, she saw, but was not happy. "I don't need shirts."

"But you do," she protested. "Look at the one you've got on."

He glanced down. "What's wrong with it?"

"It's in rags."

"Does me," he said, looking put out.

"So. Will you wear these things or what?"

"I'll wear them," he said. "They're bought now. But I don't want you to do it, that's all. I don't *need* things."

He refused to meet her eye. Something more was being said, she thought. I don't deserve them—was that what he meant? In a sudden rush of feeling for something in him that touched her but which she could not quite catch, she clasped him to her. He relaxed, responded.

"No more shirts, then," she promised.

"I just don't want you to waste your money," he said childishly. "I've got loads of stuff already."

"I know," she said. "You should send the lot of it to the Salvos. Then you'd have nothing at all. You'd be naked, and wouldn't be able to go out, and I'd have you all to myself." She had, by now, moved in.

"Is that what you want?" he asked, picking up on her lightness, allowing her, without resistance for once, to undo the buttons on the offending shirt.

"You know I do," she told him.

"Well then," he said.

"Well then what?"

"Well, you've *got* me," he said, "haven't you?"

HE HAD a ukulele. Occasionally he took it down from the top shelf of the wardrobe and, sitting with a bare foot laid over his thigh, played—not happily she thought—the same plain little tune.

She got to recognise the mood in which he would need to seek out this instrument that seemed so absurdly small in his hands and for which he had no talent, and kept her distance. The darkness in him frightened her. It seemed so far from anything she knew of his other nature.

SOME THINGS she discovered only by accident.

"Who's Bobby Kohler?" she asked once, having several times now come across the name on letters.

"Oh, that's me," he said. "*Was* me."

"What do you mean?"

"It's my name. My real name. Mitchell Maze is just the name I work under."

"You mean you changed it?"

"Not really. Some people still call me Bobby."

"Who does?"

"My mother. A few others."

"Is it German?"

"Was once, I suppose. Away back. Grandparents."

She was astonished, wanted to ask more, but could see that the subject was now done with. She might ask but he would not answer.

THERE WERE TIMES when he did tell her things. Casually, almost dismissively, off the top of his head. He told her how badly, at sixteen, he had wanted to be a long-distance runner, and shine. How for a whole year he had got up in the dark, before his paper run, and gone out in the growing light to train on the oval at their local showground at Castle Hill. He laughed, inviting her to smile at some picture he could see of his younger self, lean, intense, driven, straining painfully day after day towards a goal he would never reach. She was touched by this. But he was not looking for pity. It was the folly of the thing he was intent on. It appealed to a spirit of savage irony in him that she could not share.

There were no evocative details. Just the bare, bitter facts. He could see the rest too clearly in his mind's eye to reproduce it for hers. She had to do that out of her own experience: Albury. The early-morning frost on the grass. Magpies carolling around a couple of milk cans in the long grass by the road. But she needed more, to fix in a clarifying image the tenderness she felt for him, the sixteen-year-old Bobby Kohler, barefooted, in sweater and shorts, already five inches taller than the Skip Daley she had known, driving himself hard through those solitary circuits of the oval as the sunlight came and the world turned golden around him.

One day she drove out in her lunch hour to see the place. Sat in her car in the heat and dazzle. Walked to the oval fence and took in the smell of dryness. There was less, in fact, than she imagined.

But a week later she went back. His mother lived there. She found the address, and after driving round the suburb for a bit, sat in her car under a paperbark on the other side of the street. Seeing no one in the little front yard, she got out, crossed, climbed the two front steps to the veranda, and knocked.

There was no reply.

She walked to the end of the veranda, which was unpainted, its timber rotting, and peered round the side. No sign of anyone.

Round the back, there was a water tank, painted the usual red, and some cages that might once have held rabbits. She peeped in through the window on a clean little kitchen with a religious calendar—was he a Catholic? he'd never told her that—and into two bedrooms on either side of a hall, one of which, at one time, must have been his.

He lived here, she told herself. For nearly twenty years. Something must be left of him.

She went down into the yard and turned the bronze key of the tap, lifting to her mouth a cupped handful of the cooling water. She felt like a ghost returning to a world that was not her own, nostalgic for what she had never known; for what might strike her senses strongly enough—the taste of tank water, the peppery smell of geraniums—to bring back some immediate physical memory of the flesh. But that was crazy. What was she doing? She had *him,* didn't she?

That night, touching the slight furriness, in the dark, of his earlobe, smelling the raw presence of him, she gave a sob and he paused in his slow lovemaking.

"What is it?" he said. "What's the matter?"

She shook her head, felt a kind of shame—what could she tell him? That she'd been nosing round a backyard in Castle Hill looking for some ghost of him? He'd think she was mad.

"Tell me," he said.

His face was in her hair. There was a kind of desperation in him. But this time she was the one who would not tell.

HE WAS EASY to get on with and he was not. They did most things together; people thought of them as a couple, they were happy. He came and went without explanation, and she learned quickly enough that she either accepted him on these terms or she could not have him at all. Without quite trying to, he attracted people, and when "situations" developed was too lazy, or too easy-going, to extract himself. She learned not to ask where he had been or what he was up to. That wasn't what made things difficult between them.

She liked to have things out. He wouldn't allow it. When she raged he looked embarrassed. He told her she was overdramatic, though the truth was that he liked her best when she was in a passion; it was the very quality in her that had first attracted him. What he didn't like was scenes. If she tried to make a scene, as he called it, he walked out.

"It's no use us shouting at one another," he'd tell her, though in fact he never shouted. "We'll talk about it later." Which meant they wouldn't talk at all.

"But I *need* to shout," she shouted after him.

Later, coming back, he would give a quick sideways glance to see if she had "calmed down."

She hadn't usually. She'd have made up her mind, after a bout of tears, to end things.

"What about a cuppa?" he'd suggest.

"What you won't accept—" she'd begin.

"Don't," he'd tell her. "I've forgotten all about it." As if the hurt had been his. Then, "I'm sorry. I don't want you to be unhappy."

"I'm not," she'd say. "Just—exasperated."

"Oh, well," he'd say. "That's all right then."

What tormented her was the certainty she felt of his nursing some secret—a lost love perhaps, an old grief—that he could not share. Which was there in the distance he moved into; there in the room, in the bed beside her; and might, she thought, have the shape on occasion of that ukulele tune, and which she came to feel as a second presence between them.

It was this distance in him that others were drawn to. She saw that clearly now. A horizon in him that you believed you alone could reach. You couldn't. Maybe no one could. After a time it put most people off; they cut their losses and let him go. But that was not her way. If she let him go, it would destroy her. She knew that because she knew herself.

There was a gleam in him that on occasion shone right through his skin, the white skin of his breast below the burn-line his singlet left. She could not bear it. She battered at him.

"Hey, *hey*," he'd say, holding her off.

He had no idea what people were after. What she was after. What she saw in him.

FOR ALL the dire predictions among the clan, the doubts and amused speculations, they lasted; two people who, to the puzzlement of others, remained passionately absorbed in one another. Then one day she got a call at work. He had had a fall and was concussed again. Then in a coma, on a life-support system, and for four days and nights she was constantly at his side.

For part of that time she sat in a low chair and tuned her ear to a distant tinkling, as a breeze reached her, from far off over the edge of the world, and rolled a spent light bulb this way and that on a glass tabletop. She watched, fascinated. Hour after hour, in shaded sunlight and then in the blue of a hospital night lamp, the fragile sphere rolled, and she heard, in the depths of his skull, a clink of icebergs, and found herself sitting, half frozen, in a numbed landscape with not even a memory now of smell or taste or of any sense at all; only what she caught of that small sound, of something broken in a hermetic globe. To reach it, she told herself, I will have to smash the glass. And what then? Will the sound swell and fill me or will it stop altogether?

Meanwhile she listened. It demanded all her attention. It was a matter of life and death. When she could no longer hear it—

At other times she walked. Taking deep breaths of the hot air that swirled around her, she walked, howling, through the streets. Barefoot. And the breaths she took were to feed her howling. Each outpouring of sound emptied her lungs so completely that she feared she might simply rise up and float. But the weight of her bones, of the flesh that covered them, of the waste in her bowels, and her tears, kept her anchored—as did the invisible threads that tied her body to his, immobile under the crisp white sheet, its head swathed in bandages, and the wires connecting him to his other watcher, the dial-faced machine. It was his name she was howling. Mitch, she called. Sometimes Skip. At other times, since he did not respond to either of these, that other, earlier name he had gone by. Bobby, Bobby Kohler. She saw him, from where she was standing under the drooping leaves of a eucalypt at the edge of a track, running round the far side of an oval, but he was too deeply intent on his body, on his breathing, on the swing of his arms, the pumping of his thighs, to hear her.

Bobby, she called. Skip, she called. Mitch. He did not respond. And she wondered if there was another name he might respond to that she had never heard. She tried to guess what it might be, certain now that if she found it, and called, he would wake. She found herself once leaning over him with her hands on his shoulders, prepared—was she mad?—to *shake* it out of him.

And once, in a moment of full wakefulness, she began to sing, very softly, in a high far voice, the tune he played on the ukulele. She had no words for it. Watching him, she thought he stirred. The slightest movement of his fingers. A creasing of the brow. Had she imagined it?

On another occasion, on the third or fourth day, she woke to find she had finally emerged from herself, and wondered—in the other order of time she now moved in—how many years had passed. She was older, heavier, her hair was grey, and this older, greyer self was seated across from her wearing the same intent, puzzled look that she too must be wearing. Then the figure smiled.

No, she thought, if that is me, I've become another woman altogether. Is that what time does to us?

It was the night they came and turned off the machine. His next of kin, his mother, had given permission.

TWO DAYS LATER, red-eyed from sleeplessness and bouts of uncontrollable weeping, she drove to Castle Hill for the funeral.

His mother had rung. She reminded Jo in a kindly voice that they had spoken before. Yes, Jo thought, like this. On the phone, briefly. When she had called once or twice at an odd hour and asked him to come urgently, she needed him, and at holiday times when he went dutifully and visited, and on his birthday. "Yes," Jo said. "In June." No, his mother told her, at the hospital. Jo was surprised. She had no memory of this. But when they met she recognised the woman. They *had* spoken. Across his hospital bed, though she still had no memory of what had passed between them. She felt ashamed. Grief, she felt, had made her wild; she still looked wild. Fearful now of appearing to lay claim to the occasion, she drew back and tried to stay calm.

The woman, Mitch's mother, was very calm, as if she had behind her a lifetime's practise of preserving herself against an excess of grief. But she was not ungiving.

"I know how fond Bobby was of you," she told Jo softly. "You must come and see me. Not today. Ring me later in the week. I can't have anyone at the house today. You'll understand why."

Jo thought she understood but must have looked puzzled.

"Josh," she said. "I've got Josh home." And Jo realised that the man standing so oddly close, but turned slightly away from them, was actually with the woman.

"I can't have him for more than a day or so at a time," the woman was saying. "He doesn't mean to be a trouble, and he'd never do me any harm, but he's so strong—I can't handle him. He's like a five-year-old. But a forty-year-old man has a lot of strength in his lungs." She said this almost with humour. She reached out and squeezed the man's hand. He turned, and then Jo saw.

Large-framed and heavy-looking—hulking was the word that came to her—everything that in Mitch had been well-knit and easy was in him merely loose. His hands hung without occupation at the end of his arms, the features in the long large face seemed unfocused, unintegrated. Only with Mitch in mind could you catch, in the full mouth, the heavy jaw and brow, a possibility that had somehow failed to emerge, or been maimed or blunted. The sense she had of sliding likeness and unlikeness was alarming. She gave a cry.

"Oh," the woman said. "I thought you knew. I thought he'd told you."

Jo recovered, shook her head, and just at that moment the clergyman came forward, nodded to Mitch's mother, and they moved away to the open grave.

They were a small crowd. Most of them she knew. They were the members of the clan. The others, she guessed from their more formal clothes, must be relatives or family friends.

The service was grim. She steeled herself to stay calm. She had no wish to attract notice, to be singled out because she and Mitch had been—had been what? What had they been? She wanted to stand and be shrouded in her grief. To remain hidden. To have her grief, and him, all to herself as she had had him all to herself at least sometimes, many times, when he was alive.

But she was haunted now by the large presence of this other, this brother who stood at the edge of the grave beside his mother, quiet enough, she saw, but oddly unaware of what was going on about him.

He had moments of attention, a kind of vacant attention, then fell into longer periods of giant arrest. Then his eye would be engaged.

By the black fringe on the shawl of the small woman to his left, which he reached out for and fingered, frowning, then lifted to his face and sniffed.

By a wattlebird that was animating the branches of a low-growing grevillea so that it seemed suddenly to have developed a life of its own and began twitching and shaking out its blooms. Then by the cuff of his shirt, which he regarded quizzically, his mouth pouting, then drawn to one side, as if by something there that disappointed or displeased him.

All these small diversions that took his attention took hers as well. At such a moment! She was shocked.

Then, quite suddenly, he raised his head. Some new thing had struck him. What? Nothing surely that had been said or was being done here. Some thought of his own. A snatch of music it might be, a tune that opened a view in him that was like sunlight flooding a familiar landscape. His face was irradiated by a foolish but utterly beatific smile, and she saw how easy it might be—she thought of his mother, even more poignantly of Mitch—to love this large unlovely child.

The little ukulele tune came into her head, and with it a vision of Mitch, lost to her in his own world of impenetrable grief. Sitting in his underpants on the floor, one big foot propped on his thigh. Hunched over the strings and plucking from them, over and over, the same spare notes, the same bare little tune. And she understood with a pang how the existence of this spoiled other must have seemed like a living reproach to his own too easy attractiveness. It was that—the injustice of it, so cruel, so close— that all those nicks and scars and broken bones and concussions, and all that reckless exposure to a world of accident, had been meant to annul. She felt the ground shifting under her feet. How little she had grasped or known. What a different story she would have to tease out now and tell herself of their time together.

The service was approaching its end. The coffin, suspended on ropes, tilted over the hole with its raw edges and siftings of loose soil. It began, lopsidedly, to descend. Her eyes flooded. She closed them tight. Felt herself choke.

At that moment there was a cry, an incommensurate roar that made all heads turn and stopped the clergyman in full spate.

Some animal understanding—caught from the general emotion around him and become brute fact—had brought home to Josh what it was they were doing here. He began to howl, and the sound was so terrible, so piteous, that all Jo could think of was an animal at the most uncomprehending extreme of physical agony. People looked naked, stricken. There was a scrambling over broken lumps of earth round the edge of the grave. The big man, even in the arms of his mother, was uncontrollable. He struck out, face congested, the mouth and nose streaming, like an ox, Jo thought, like an ox under the hammer. And this, she thought, is the real face of grief, the one we do not show. Her heart was thick in her breast. This is what sorrow is that knows no explanation or answer. That looks down into the abyss and sees only the unanswering depths.

SHE RECALLED NOTHING of the drive back, through raw unfinished suburbs, past traffic lights where she must dutifully have swung into the proper lane and stopped, her mind in abeyance, the motor idling. When she got home, to the house afloat on its stilts among the sparse leaves of the coral trees, above the cove with its littered beach, she was drained of resistance. She sat in the high open space the house made, feeling it breathe like a living thing, surrendering herself to the regular long expansions of its breath.

Against the grain of her own need for what was enclosed and safe, she had learned to live with it. What now? Could she bear, alone, now that something final had occurred, to live day after day with what was provisional, which she had put up with till now because, with a little effort of adjustment, she too, she found, could live in the open present—so long as it *was* open.

Abruptly she rose, stood looking down for a moment at some bits of snipped wire, where he had been tinkering with something electrical, that for a whole week had lain scattered on the coffee-table, then went out to the sink, and as on that first morning washed up what was there to be washed. The solitary cup and saucer from her early-morning tea.

For a moment afterwards she stood contemplating the perfec-tion of clean plates drying in the rack, cups turned downwards to drain, their saucers laid obliquely atop. She was at the beginning again. Or so she felt. Now what?

There was a sock on the floor. Out of habit she retrieved it, then stood, surveying the room, the house, as you could because it was so open and exposed.

Light and air came pouring in from all directions. She felt again, as on that first occasion, the urge to move in and begin set-ting things to rights, and again for the moment held back, restrained herself.

She looked down, observed the sock in her hand, and had a vision, suddenly, of the place as it might be a month from now when her sense of making things right would already, day after day, imperceptibly, have been at work on getting rid of the maga-zines and newspapers, shifting this or that piece of furniture into a more desirable arrangement, making the small adjustments that would erase all sign of him, of Mitch, from what had been so much of his making—from her life. Abruptly she threw the sock from her and stood there, shivering, hugging herself, in the middle of the room. Then, abruptly, sat where she had been sitting before. In the midst of it.

So what did she mean to do? Change nothing? Leave every-thing just as it was? The out-of-date magazines, that dead match beside the leg of the coffee-table, the bits of wire, the sock? To gather fluff over the weeks and months, a dusty tribute that she would sit in the midst of for the next twenty years?

She sat a little longer, the room darkening around her, filling slowly with the darkness out there that lay over the waters of the cove, rose up from the floaty leaves of the coral trees and the shadowy places at their roots, from around the hairy stems of tree ferns and out of the unopened buds of morning glory. Then, with a deliberate effort, she got down on her knees and reached in to pick up the match from beside the leg of the coffee-table. Shocked that it weighed so little. So little that she might not recall, later, the effort it had cost her, this first move towards taking up again, bit by bit, the weight of her life.

Then, with the flat of her hand, she brushed the strands of wire into a heap, gathered them up, and went, forcing herself, to retrieve the sock, then found the other. Rolled them into a ball and raised it to her lips. Squeezing her eyes shut, filling her nostrils with their smell.

Then there were his shirts, his shorts, his jeans—they would go to the Salvos—and the new things she had bought, which lay untouched in the drawers of his lowboy, the shirts in their plastic wrappers, the underpants, the socks still sewn or clipped together. Maybe Josh. She had a vision of herself arriving with these things on his mother's doorstep. An opening. The big man's pleasure as he stroked the front of his new poplin shirt, the sheen of its pure celestial blue.

She sat again, the small horde of the rolled socks in her lap, the spent match and the strands of wire in a tidy heap. A beginning. And let the warm summer dark flow in around her.

War Baby

C HARLIE DOWD spent the last weeks before he was inducted and went to Vietnam riding round town on a CZ two-stroke, showing himself off to people and saying goodbye.

It was August and cold: high dry skies, the westerlies blowing. He wore a navy blue air force greatcoat of his father's, who had been a Spitfire pilot in the war. It was belted and double-breasted with wide lapels, and when you turned the collar up your ears were covered. The skirts were so long that what Charlie saw in the long wardrobe mirror in his room (he'd been reading *War and Peace*) was a French cavalry officer in the Napoleonic Wars in flight from Cossacks. Anticipating his first day in camp he had been down to Sam Harker and had his hair cut short on top and shaved at the sides. When he stood and contemplated himself in the mirror, he really looked the part.

He had a routine. He got up late, ate the breakfast his aunt made for him, which doubled as lunch, then sat for a couple of hours in warm winter sunlight in the window of the pub. Always in the same place, looking out across the veranda rails to the median strip of the town's one main street, with a schooner of beer at his elbow on the chocolate-brown sill, and beside it, as a way of making himself at home, his pen, his wallet, the paperback he was reading, and the makings of the roll-your-owns he liked to smoke—papers, Drum tobacco in a plastic wrap, and an oblong tin not much bigger than a matchbox that contained the simple mechanism for turning them out. He took trouble over this, giving the roller a practised spin between forefinger and thumb, and when he ran his tongue along the edge of the paper, putting just enough spit into it for the spill to be dry but perfectly, almost professionally, sealed. He smoked a little, read a little, wrote in his notebook.

He was keeping notes. Not a diary exactly, just random thoughts. As they came to him in the drowsy sunlight in the slow early session after midday, and as they took off, the moment he began to set them down, and led him into all sorts of unpredictable and shadowy places where he was pleased to roam. Bemused speculations.

If he tired of writing, and had no book at hand, he would read the contents of his wallet: his library card and driver's licence, several torn-off corners of a notepad or newspaper with names and phone numbers on them that he could barely decipher, ads from magazines that he must have thought, when he folded them small and tucked them away in one of his wallet's many pockets, might one day come in useful. With a cigarette at his lips, the sun on his hands, a crease between his brows, he would give these exhibits his solemn attention, as if this time he might catch, in the evidence they offered of unfulfilled needs and momentary promises, some reflection of himself that till now had subtly eluded him.

Occasionally when he looked up he would find upon him the pink-rimmed, rheumy eyes of one of the old-timers, pensioners and retired tradesmen or storekeepers, who were the regulars of this hour: thin-faced, silent fellows with elongated ears and noses who had been turned out of the house by their daughters or daughters-in-law, and towards two or two thirty in the afternoon dropped in, very formally attired in coat and hat, for a beer and whatever talk might be going. In the early days one or two of them had enquired from a distance what he was writing. They seemed ready to start a conversation. Charlie put his pen down and let them go on.

It wasn't really a conversation. What they wanted was to tell him their story—well, not him exactly, anyone would have done.

He listened. That they had a story, and took it for granted they did, confirmed him in the assumption that he too had one. But he was glad when they drifted off at last and went back to their beer, and after a time they ceased to be curious about him. He had become one of them.

They were becalmed at the end of their lives, that's what he saw, and he was becalmed in the middle of his, but nearer the beginning. Waiting out these last days as if they were an enforced holiday, which was why his aunt let him sleep till past midday and did not complain, as she would have done earlier, when the breakfast she made him was also his lunch.

Afternoons had always been a trouble to him, going right back to when he was little and had to take a nap each day beside his mother on a high double bed in their cool spare room. He would play afterwards on the lino and watch his mother laugh on the phone or do her nails on the back veranda, or with her skirt hoicked up and her bare feet propped on the rail, sit tanning herself while the radio played, "Music, music, music," and willy-wagtails switched about on the grass.

Time passed slowly after midday, before tea. That's what he had found. The air grew thicker. There was a weight that dragged. It had something to do with the clouds, loaded at times with thunder, that at that hour gathered and rolled in over the Range. Summer or winter, it made no difference: trees, houses, grass, sky—the whole world seemed to be waiting only for the coming on of dark.

Lately, that quality he had felt of a whole world hanging on what was to come, nightfall, had become the keynote of his own existence. He had waited. First for his birthday to come around, then for his name to come up. He was waiting now for the last days to pass before his induction. All that time had been a mixture in him of restless impatience for each day to dawn and pass, and a kind of inertia which, if he had not deliberately taken a hand, would have made a sleepwalker of him, just when he needed to be most fully awake.

The truth was that Vietnam, and his going, was the certainty he had needed to give his life direction; to close off an open and indeterminate future where he might have gone on stumbling about in a maze that had no end. He was going. He would see action—the phrase brought a prickle of excitement to his skin that scared and at the same time gravely enlivened him. Meanwhile, though others need not see it in this light, he had organised a small carnival for himself.

Around four in the afternoon, with the sun gone from the sill where his empty beer glass sat—he never had more than two—he set out on his rounds.

HIS ARRIVAL on their doorstep puzzled some people. They had not seen him in a while; in some cases, a long while. They did not immediately recognise the crop-headed boy in uniform greatcoat who loomed in the door frame as if he had come to deliver something official, and stood smiling and stamping on the doormat in the assurance of being invited in. They had difficulty remembering who he was.

They did remember at last—and would have known the name anyway, because of his grandfather—but could not guess why on earth he had called, and why, when he settled, his long legs extended, the skirts of the greatcoat open like dark wings, he looked from one to another of them with so much wide-eyed alertness—in expectation of what, they wondered.

More than puzzled, some of them were embarrassed. But Charlie wasn't. He knew very well what he was after. He wanted to know, before he went away, what impression his having lived here for a whole twenty years had made on people. Not much, he guessed. But that was just the point. They would remember his going. They would remember that he had come to say goodbye.

One or two of them were old friends of the family who had known him when he was little and whom his aunt had mentioned. They were surprised to see him after so long but soon made him feel at home.

In other cases they were fellows a little older than himself who, two or three years back, had been on the school swimming team with him but could not, when he turned up now, come up with his name.

"Who did you say he was?" he heard a girl whisper out in the kitchen while he sat alone in the front room with a round-eyed baby and the TV. "Have I met him? Was he at the wedding?"

In households where he had, for a time, been the schoolfriend of a son or daughter now lost to the city, it was recalled that he had always been odd—old-fashioned they had called it then; a consequence of his having no one to bring him up but his grandfather and an old-maid aunt.

Well, he was even odder now. The way he had of just sitting and looking. With his ears sticking out above the lapels of his greatcoat. And the greatcoat itself. What was that? What was that about?

For all his affability, some older men looked him over and were put off. They had been to a war themselves. They hadn't gone around making a song and dance of it, parading about in what looked like fancy dress. He was young of course, but no younger than they had been. Young people these days made too much of themselves. That came from the sort of pop music they listened to, and from the TV. Life for them was all play-acting, dressing up. Sideburns, old double-breasted suits and striped collarless shirts they'd raked up from a deceased uncle's lowboy or picked up cheap at the St. Vincent de Paul's. Fleecy-lined bomber jackets, and if the leather was cracked and worn so much the better. Camouflage battledress and other fads. Sergeant Pepper Band uniforms!

In a way that would never have occurred to them at that age, this feller was making a show of himself, and enjoying it too. What gave him the right to prance around drawing attention to himself?

All this would have surprised Charlie.

He *was* enjoying himself, and it was true, he did want to be noticed. But play-acting? He was on his way to Vietnam. Wasn't that real enough? There had been a ballot, a lottery. The world had cast him one of its backhanded prizes, and since he had no notion himself of what his life was to be, he had accepted it. Not passively, but without complaint. He'd let a roll of the barrel decide things. Given himself over to hazard, to chance. In a spirit, as he thought, of existential stoicism.

The war itself, when he got to it, would present hazards of a different sort. He had seen something of that. Body bags, statistics, fellows who brought back, in one way or another, a good deal less of themselves than they had taken away. He had no illusions. But chance in that case was tempered with something else. Something you yourself brought to the bar.

Guts. A feeling for where to put your foot down and where not. The good-luck charm of life itself—the one you were intended for. He believed, though none of this, of course, had yet been tested, that he was the possessor of all three.

Beyond that you could present yourself as you wanted to be seen and then try to live up to it. With a rough outline in your head of a story, you could do everything in your power to act it out; to incorporate the accidents that hit you into its form, as he had incorporated the lottery and his conscription. Later parts of it, in his case, included Paris, which he definitely saw himself visiting one day, a language or two he meant to pick up, a wife of course—he had a whole list of things he'd barely started on. He had already read *War and Peace*, but he had not, as yet, fired a gun or been up in a plane. He had never tasted Tokay, or champagne or oysters, or slept with a girl or been further from home—this small town tucked into a hollow behind the Range—than Brisbane once on a rugby trip while he was at school: he had been sick, both ways, on the coach. But he was young, and believed, even with Vietnam up ahead, that he had time.

He had discovered in the eyes of others, beginning with his grandfather, an affectionate wish that all things should go well with him. It was partly out of a desire to extend to as many people as possible the privilege of exercising their large goodwill towards him that he appeared on so many doorsteps of what was still, for the time being, his own little world.

ONE OF THE PLACES he liked to go was a household where he *was* known; the family of his best friend Brian Whelan, who at the end of the previous year had decided on university and was away now in Brisbane.

The Whelans had known him since he was ten years old. The difference, when he went there now, was that Brian was gone and his sister Josie, who was three years older and had been away, was back. It was Josie who had opened the door to him when, after a six-month absence, he turned up one weekday around five in the afternoon, a little light-headed from the two beers he had drunk and with his hair, and the hairlike filaments of the greatcoat, touched with tiny droplets of moisture, silvery and weblike from the drizzling rain he had driven through.

"Well, look what the cat dragged in," Josie announced to the lighted room behind her as he stood stamping on the threshold.

It was three years or more since he had last seen her. She had changed. She was thinner with longer hair. But her voice had not changed. It still had its edge of dismissive irony.

She had never really liked him, that's what he felt. His closeness to Brian had shut her out. He had never intended that and was sorry for it. He wished now that he had known her better and that she was more pleased to see him.

"Come in, love," Mrs. Whelan called.

In a little while there were mugs of tea and his favourite Tim Tams. The greatcoat was draped over the back of a chair.

"I'm going to Vietnam," he announced.

"Oh," Mrs. Whelan said, and Josie, who was standing with her back against the sink, made a huffing sound.

"Brian's older than you," Mrs. Whelan said after a bit. "Isn't your birthday in March, love?"

"May," he told her.

"Yes," she said, "Brian's is February the ninth."

What she meant was that Brian's birth date had put him in a previous ballot; he was safe. She held out the plate of Tim Tams, as if offering him a small consolation, and when Charlie saw it he wanted to laugh. He had, he felt, grasped so clearly what was in her mind.

Lately he had found himself looking at the world—at people—as if he had developed another sense, beyond the usual five, for what was happening around him, for what was being said. Listening, really listening, was a kind of looking. For the way a glance passed from one person to another, or a soft mouth was compressed into a hard line, as Josie's was now, or cheeks were momentarily sucked in. As often as not that was where the real conversation was being conducted.

The younger boys of the family, Luke and Jack, came crashing into the room. They were eleven and fifteen. Barefooted, in out-at-elbow woollies, they had been tempted in by his arrival—and the promise of Tim Tams—from practising hoops at the basketball ring where he and Brian had spent long afternoons just a year ago.

"I've seen you riding," Luke told him. His eyes went to the greatcoat.

Jack, the older boy, laughed, as if this intended more than it said.

"CZ," Luke said admiringly.

The greatcoat and the bike, that's what they saw.

What Josie saw was a warmonger.

"I suppose you're proud of yourself," she accused, "going off to blow a lot of women and children to pieces who've never done you any harm."

He was surprised by her vehemence, but when he looked he saw that her eyes were bright with something different.

"Leave Charlie alone now," her mother told her. "Have another Tim Tam, love."

"Can I?" Luke asked.

"He's had two already," the older boy protested.

"Don't be a tittle-tat," his mother told him.

"Well, he has!"

"She's a real Tartar, eh?"

This, proudly, came from the father, who had just stepped in from work and overheard the scene. "Good to see you, son."

He shook Charlie's hand, and they stood a moment in what might have been manly solidarity while Josie scowled.

"He's going to Vietnam," Luke told his father.

"Hmmm," Mr. Whelan said.

He gave Charlie another look and accepted the mug Josie was passing him.

"Well," he said gravely, "I suppose someone's got to go. Good on you, son."

"No they don't," Josie insisted.

"Josie's been on demos"—this was Luke again—"in Sydney."

"That's enough, Luke," his mother told the boy.

But Josie was not so easily silenced. She gave them her opinion of various politicians, local and overseas, and in no uncertain terms stated her convictions about wars in general, men, and this war in particular.

"I told you she was a Tartar," her father said with a laugh, and Charlie wondered what side he was on. "Hope you've got your crash helmet handy."

Charlie was amused. He enjoyed being so immediately the centre of attention here, and the little sensual kick he got from her high colour and excitement. He'd never looked at Josie in this light. She had always been simply "Brian's sister." But there was something as well that confused him. All this talk of politics, all these fierce convictions.

He had no convictions himself and did not consider what he was about to do as involving him in "politics." There was nothing in the notebook about that. His going or not going concerned only himself. It had to do with where he stood with the world and what it had put in his way, the claims *that* made on him. With how he saw himself and wanted others to see him. With what he could live with. Maybe—though he believed this would not be demanded of him—with what sort of death he might make.

Josie's insistence that what really mattered was some larger question of right or wrong made nothing of all that. And made nothing too—this is what affronted him—of his presence here, a little heated as he was by all the sensations of the moment and the turmoil of these last weeks. As if his life, *his* life, the one he felt so strongly pulsing through him, was of no account.

"You've got no imagination," Josie accused.

"And you have, I suppose," he shot back. Surprising himself.

"That's it, son," Mr. Whelan laughed. "You speak up for yourself."

"Enough of a one," Josie told him mildly.

Charlie tried not to show how angry he felt. The implication was that his rude good health, his youth, his high spirits, put some things that she saw with blinding clarity beyond his comprehension. That something boyish and crudely warlike in him, male bravado, the rush of hormonal mayhem, made him insensitive to the price that others would have to pay—women and the old, and little helpless terrified kids—so that his brand of swagger and mindlessness could have its way. He felt acutely, under her gaze, the bunched muscles of his shoulders in the old school sweater and eased them a little.

But the fact was, he did see these things, and no less clearly perhaps than she did. He *knew* about blood. His own, just at the moment, was very much present to him, in his forearms and wrists, in the veins of his neck. He meant to keep it there. But also, if he could, to preserve his honour as well. That was *his* argument.

It involved words it would have embarrassed him to use. Things that could be thought, and warmly felt, but not stated. There was no way he could lay claim—or not openly—to so much for himself. But he was sorry just the same that she had not seen it.

There were ways in which she too was insensitive—and she didn't see that either.

Still, all this intrigued him. He kept coming back.

"A glutton for punishment, eh, son?" was how Mr. Whelan put it.

AT HOME in his grandfather's house they never argued about politics. They never argued about anything. If his grandfather and his aunt had convictions he had never heard them. His aunt's view was that some things, most things as it turned out, were better left unsaid, and Charlie had learned to see the point of this, having learned early that a good deal that went unsaid was too cruel, or too painful, for speech. The unspoken, in his grandfather's house, had mostly to do with his father.

Charlie had few memories of his father, and none of them substantial. The earliest was a character called Charlie that his mother and aunt spoke of in passionate whispers, and ceased to discuss the moment he appeared. He had assumed at first that they were speaking of him (he must have been three years old) and wondered what he had done that they should be so disturbed; his aunt so angry, his mother so weakly tearful. Only over time did it come to him that *this* Charlie, whose shadow fell so darkly over the house, was his father. Who had, it seemed, once more *failed* them—but mostly himself—and whom his aunt sometimes defended, and sometimes his mother, but never both at the same time and never in front of his grandfather.

Sometimes, when his grandfather laid a hand on his shoulder and asked sadly: "So how's it going, Charlie? How are they treating you?" he understood that it was not really him that his grandfather was speaking to but that other, who once, before he failed them all, had also been young, and had not yet discovered, or not yet revealed, that failure was what he was inevitably heading for. His father seemed frighteningly present then in his own name and skin.

There was a photograph on the piano in the front room of a young man in RAAF uniform and cap, much the same age as Charlie was now and bearing a resemblance to him that Charlie found unsettling. He looked out of the frame with such a guileless sense of his own presence and future that Charlie, on those occasions when he was led to take a good hard look, felt—along with curiosity and a shy affection for this stranger who was so uniquely close to him—a pang of doubt about his own too easy optimism.

No hint of failure there, or of failings either. What clung to the image was the romance of a period when his father had been a hero fired with a belief in his own physical survival into a time to come. It was in this spirit, it seemed, that he had got hold of Charlie's mother; the suggestion being that she had been deceived.

But perhaps, Charlie thought, she had wanted to be. And wasn't his father also deceived? By a belief that the high spirits that had swept him up, and the high action he had been involved in, were an aspect of his own nature rather than of the times; were in *him* rather than in the air, and could be confidently extended. And that the old weakness in him had been burned away. By a boyish delight in immediate danger and the nerve with which, in mission after mission, he had met it and come through.

Charlie was inclined to identify with this youthful warrior, and had developed, from what he knew of his own doubts and confusions—his own anxiety about getting what he was, or might be, out into a world that was so undependable and chancy—an understanding, a sympathy even, for what might have gone wrong in the man, though he did not mean to repeat it.

Perhaps the dramatic excitements of that brief year of scrambles and dogfights and ditchings had exhausted what was in him. He had made demands on his spirit that he could meet only once, and could not match under other, more ordinary circumstances.

But then he had never seen, as his mother had—his aunt, too, perhaps—what weakness was *like* close up; the sly deceits and fierce self-justifications that were the daily accompaniment of it.

The clearest sense he had of his father's actual presence was of standing—he must have been six—at his father's grave.

Men in dark suits, their hats clasped to their chest, hair plastered to their skulls and sweating, stood on the far side of the grave and all around it, looking hard at him and frowning. The ladies at their side wore gloves and were also looking, but their eyes were hidden under wide-brimmed hats that they were allowed to keep on.

It was hot. The midsummer sky was a blanched yellow-white, and the gum trees at the edge of the cemetery shimmered as if they were not real trees at all, only their reflection in water.

He stood very still, trying not to shift his feet, but could not tell if he was standing the right way, and thought he must be doing it wrong, which was what made people over there look at him so hard, and frown.

He had frequently been encouraged by his aunt to be a good little soldier in the matter of grazed elbows and bloodied knees, and plasters that had to be ripped off, but no one had told him how it would be at his father's funeral and how he should stand.

His grandfather was close behind him. His hand, blotched, with lumpy veins, rested on his shoulder, and occasionally drew him in to the soft belly and the hot smell of his woollen suit.

His mother and his aunt were on the other side of him, his aunt crying. He had never thought of his aunt as a woman who cried.

His mother cried very often, and noisily. She was what his aunt called theatrical. When his father met her, in London, she had been on the stage. Being theatrical was something, later, when his mother was gone, that he would be severely warned against; as he was against being, like his father, weak—it was the double inheritance he must constantly fight against.

But at his father's funeral his mother did not cry, she simply stood, and he thought of her later as having already left, as he understood by then she must already have decided to do. So that what he recalled of that day was his aunt's tears, the weight of his grandfather's hand on his shoulder, and the dry, peppery smell of the bush, along with a ladies' smell of talcum powder and sweat.

The white gravestones all around pulsed with light and might have been preparing to rise straight up like rockets. Which was just what was required, he thought, to free him from the scrutiny of the strangers over there and the need to hold himself so strictly to attention. Then suddenly the trees on the skyline exploded. Dozens of snow-white, sulphur-crested cockatoos flocked skyward, the noise of their shrieking so fierce, so like the sound of souls in torment, that all the people turned their heads.

That was his father's funeral. His father had always been absent in one way. Now he was absent in another. And beginning then, at the edge of the open grave, so was his mother. She went home to her family in England. From where she rang regularly twice each year, on his birthday and at Christmas, long distance, tearfully. And sent presents in elaborate wrappings that his aunt resented and referred to, though never to him, as "extravagant."

He had heard often enough from his grandfather that every man had his justifications, though one did not have to believe that they were always good; and since every man clearly meant every woman too, he wondered what his mother's might be. For having left him—temporarily at first, then permanently—in the charge of his grandfather and aunt.

Had she already given him over so completely to them and what they had to offer that she felt her own claim was weak, and that by taking him with her she would deprive him of more than she could give—even in the matter of love? Was he unlovable? Did he remind her too much of his father? Was she simply—he felt the implication of this in his aunt's silence on the matter— *weak?*

The word hung in the air so often, though unspoken like so much else, because his grandfather, and even more his aunt, were so fond of the word "strong."

He felt the house was full of watchers. Not just his grandfather and aunt, but those presences, invisible but by no means to be underestimated, who were watching *them*—which was as far as his grandfather went in the matter of religion.

But all this meant was that the forces under whose watchful gaze they were living—who missed nothing, he came to feel, and were pitilessly demanding—had no names, no faces, and were difficult therefore to get a hold on, to approach and reason with. No doubt they too had their justifications, impossible to challenge.

He wondered sometimes, since his grandfather did not actually refer to them, how he had got so clearly into his head, and so early, that they were there. As palpably there as the furniture—big old-fashioned dining chairs with high backs, ample seats, solid legs, bedroom suites with mirrored wardrobes and dressing tables— that his grandfather had had made in Brisbane, and which, as newly-weds, his grandparents had brought up here after the First World War.

He reminded himself that his father too had grown up among these heavy presences. Perhaps it was the furniture, and the shadow it cast, that had alarmed his mother and driven her from the house.

These were the perplexities and childish conclusions of a lively seven-year-old. But a dozen years later he had got no further with them.

SOMETIMES, in the early afternoon, he rode out to the edge of town and spent an hour or two with Cliff Hodges, who had sold him the CZ and was prepared to take it back again when he left.

Cliff was twenty-four. An easy-going fellow and a big drinker on Friday and Saturday nights, he was popular with the girls. Married women mostly, if his own stories were to be believed. Charlie was never sure he did believe them, but it didn't matter. Cliff glowed so convincingly in the aura of them.

He was a mechanic. He worked out of a corrugated-iron shed on a lot where two giant pepper trees grew out of broken concrete. A dozen oil drums and some old car parts, now gone to rust, were piled against a fence that seemed to be held up only by the woody rose bush, all outbursts of yellow buds and creamy, extravagant blooms, that climbed in and out of its grainy slabs.

Charlie looked forward to the afternoons he spent out here; his back to the corrugated-iron wall of the shed, his long legs thrust out before him, while Cliff, sprawled out of sight, flat on his back under the car he was working on, put easy questions to which he gave his own wry answers, or launched into a live-wire account, all crude but colourful riffs and clownish avowals of contrition, of his latest night out with the boys. The desultory nature of these exchanges, the easy pace, which included a good many silences, none of them heavy as elsewhere with the unsaid, was tonic. Charlie laughed. He let go.

Very little that passed between them was personal. What they shared were the formal rituals of taking an engine apart and putting it together again, which Charlie, under Cliff's instruction, had quickly grasped and become expert in. The dexterity it involved, the easiness about getting your hands mucky, the masculine talk punctuated with *shit, fuck, come on you bitch, give,* which was the almost musical accompaniment to this, led naturally, while the fingers worked delicately with wires and screws, to discussion of that other area of male expertise where the parts were anatomical. Charlie was less expert here but once again looked to Cliff's instruction as a likely way ahead.

Later in the afternoon it was the Beach Boys or Cream or Hendrix that filled the air between them, when Cliff, at a point of exasperation with some bit of machinery that would not yield to him, took time out, and they sat side by side with a mug of hot coffee to warm their hands, and floated—mostly on drags of the good grass Cliff had access to.

What Charlie found so appealing in these afternoon hours was that they led nowhere and could have no consequence. Two years from now, when he got back, Cliff would be just the same, or he would be married with a kid and would be the same anyway. And *he* would have Vietnam behind him. Because he had chosen that, and all that it involved and would bring. To mark him; mark him off. To set the seal on a certain way of living that a man could choose, and which Cliff had *not* chosen and might never know. It was a difference between them that was already in operation, because in spirit he was already gone. It gave him, despite his being so much younger, and quite without experience in some matters, an advantage here that Cliff recognised and did not resent.

"Rather you than me, boy," Cliff had said after a pause when Charlie first made his announcement.

The respect, a matter of taking him seriously, Charlie thought, had come about later. A kind of concern for him too, which in Cliff's case took a particular form.

"We better set you up with a girl, eh? Before you go and get your collateral blown off." This was a reference, witty to an extent that surprised Charlie, to a Dylan song they were fond of.

So far it had gone no further than that, the offer. In the meantime they sat with their backs to the wall and took in the music along with the grass.

The nice thing, around Cliff, was that there was no need to hurry.

. . .

So he came to the last days. He had a strong sense, as he made his rounds, of other people stopping, in the ordinary flow of their lives, to make room for him. He had made that much at least of an impression. Perhaps it was simply that they knew it would soon end: that he would in a few days now be gone. They could afford to grant him room.

He had no illusions. The moment he was no longer here their lives would flow on again without him; not because they did not care but because that's the way it is, the way we are.

He felt he existed in a space which, the moment he stepped out of it, would close behind him, and he began practising; in mind stepping out, then looking back at the space he had filled for a little with his warmth and watching it cool and give up all sign of his presence.

This sort of thinking was new to him. That there might be in you a ghostly quality of your own absence even when you were most warmly there; when you were most conscious of your long, blunt-ended fingers flattened against a mug of scalding tea, your breath visibly blowing across the earthenware rim, your smile and your last words hanging in the silence. And their eyes on you, also smiling, and telling you how substantially present you were.

He would glance briefly towards the greatcoat tossed over the back of a chair, its thick serge bunched and shapeless. His father's greatcoat. Which he had commandeered for a bit. And where was his father?

He shrugged, and the cough he gave was half a chuckle.

It was an uncomfortable feeling only for a moment. The mug was warm against the soft flesh of his palm. The coffee or tea, when he lowered his head to hide his confusion, and sipped, was hot in his mouth.

There was a design of painted flowers on the tiles behind the sink in the Whelans' kitchen: detached yellow petals round a dob of red, with a green stem and two symmetrical green leaves—the kind of flower he remembered painting when he was first at school, the flower a five- or six-year-old paints. Not a real flower, one you've seen—they're too difficult, too complicated and raggedy. The stripped-down *idea* of a flower. The one from which all other flowers might have evolved.

The rightness of these flowers, each one planted in the centre of its tile and repeated all over the bit of wall, pleased him in a way he could not have explained, and centred him for a moment, but only for a moment, in a space of his own.

One afternoon, when he was leaving the Whelans', Josie followed him out to where his bike was parked under the overhanging canopy of a camphor laurel.

She dawdled, and he wondered, as he sat astride the CZ, at a hesitancy in her that was unusual and which, for all the little crease between her brows, softened her features and brought her close, in a way that created a soft feeling in him as well.

It was a time of day when everything was in suspense. The light high up in the sky just yielding to the first smokiness of dark. A hint of night-time coldness in the air. Birds restless in the grass and beginning to flock low now over the neighbouring roofs. He waited.

Josie too had an offer to make. What she had access to, if he wanted, was a line of safe houses. In Sydney. He could, even at this point, refuse to go, declare himself an objector—and people down there, good people, would pass him on from one house to another till the war was over.

He listened quietly. To the agitation of birds. To some boys off in the distance, shouting as they kicked a ball about.

"How would I get there?" he asked. Not because he might actually do it but out of curiosity, to catch himself briefly in the light of an unexpected possibility. "To Sydney, I mean."

"I could arrange it," Josie told him. He was impressed by her intensity. "There's an organisation."

He nodded but remained sceptical. She made it sound like the underground during the war. It had the air of a game.

What was no game was where *he* was going.

"I'll think it over," he told her, turning his head to where the voices of the footballers were raised in a triumphant shout. She touched the sleeve of the greatcoat. "No, I will," he assured her, "I'll think about it. I really will."

But he wondered that she should have seen so little of what was in him. When his last visit came and he gave her his answer, feeling clumsy though he tried not to be—they were once again in the half-dark under the camphor laurel tree—she was silent and did not try to persuade him, though she accepted none of his "reasons." What he could not tell her was that since the ballot was announced his life had had a shape. He could see himself. He had begun to see, in the events he had organised for himself, the outline of what he was to be.

She kissed him lightly to one side of his mouth and turned back into the house.

He sat a moment—he was not reconsidering—he had never in fact considered—before he kicked the bike into sputtering life and went roaring off.

The other proposition that had been put to him, Cliff's offer to set him up with a girl, he did accept. He was shy, he found, about such matters, even with Cliff, and feared afterwards that he had not hit the right note between throwaway ease and the sort of eagerness that might have been expected of red-blooded youth when he told Cliff, "What you said that time—you know, about a girl—I've been thinking, and I'd really appreciate it." Cliff seemed to have forgotten his offer. They agreed, however, to meet up at the pub on his last night.

HE ARRIVED ON TIME but missed Cliff, who had already been there and left. He bought a beer, talked to one or two people, but after half an hour pushed his way out again and took a slow ride around town.

It was Saturday night. Everyone was out. He felt an odd affection for the place now that he was about to leave it, though it had nothing to recommend it really and he was eager to go.

The usual Saturday-night crowd of fellows and their girls was milling round the entrance to the pictures, which was all lit up;

the girls with hair buffed and lacquered, a little top-heavy in their miniskirts and skintight sweaters, the boys trying not to look dressed up, but dressed up just the same in camouflage battledress or motorcycle jacket and cord flares. Some with long hair, one or two with the beginnings of a beard. A good many of those who were still at school, or worked in banks or stores, had short hair with just the sideburns left to thicken.

Charlie felt distanced from them. He rode slowly, scanning the crowd, then did a circuit of the local War Memorial.

Groups of lone youths sat on the backs of benches in the low-walled park there, and smoked or skylarked; others stood leaning against the cars parked along the kerb, making remarks to the passers-by that flared up on occasion into shouting matches. But on the whole a fairground atmosphere prevailed.

He stopped and shouted across to a group of fellows he recognised from school.

"I'm looking for Cliff Hodges," he called. "Anyone seen Cliff Hodges?"

"You seen him?" one of them asked another.

The boy pursed his lips.

"We haven't seen him," the first boy called. "Try the pub."

Charlie drove off, did another slow circuit of the park. He felt let down, decided to look in again at the pub, just in case.

An hour later he was still there. He hadn't found Cliff but had got into conversation with a fellow he'd known at primary school when they were eleven.

Still reddish-blond and freckled, Eddie McPhee was not much bigger than he had been then. Charlie towered over him. He was an apprentice jockey at a local stables. For a good two hours before Charlie met up with him he had been drinking vodka and orange and Charlie decided now to join him. He was very noisy and argumentative, but so slight and pallidly childlike that none of the fellows he picked on thought it honourable to hit him. The worst they did was tell him to get lost and walk away, which made him all the madder. After his second vodka Charlie found this extraordinarily amusing.

He remembered Eddie as a kid who couldn't spell and was always getting whacked across the palm with a ruler. He had grown up cocky and sure of himself. This surprised Charlie but impressed him too. He began to feel happily light-headed, then elated, then affectionately grateful to Eddie for having at this point reappeared out of his primary-school years to take him on a long loop backwards that he might otherwise have missed.

"Remember that bastard Hoyland?" Eddie shouted. This was the wielder of the ruler. "Remember Frances Jakes?" She was a girl who, at twelve, had had the most enormous tits. I'm really enjoying myself, Charlie thought. Too bad about Cliff.

When the pub closed, he redeemed his overcoat from a bar stool where he had abandoned it and offered Eddie a lift back to the stables on the other side of town.

It was after midnight, and cold. What he was aware of, as they rode between the houses down deserted street after street, was the closeness of the stars overhead and the distance between his hands on the handlebars of the bike and his head, where it just managed to stay put at the top of his body. This made the business of keeping the bike upright—and steering it through space with the cold night air pouring over them, and the bitumen, with its starry sheen, ribboning out before and behind—a skill that for all its familiarity approached the miraculous. If anyone was looking down from up there, he thought, how amazing all this must look. And us too. How amazing *we* must look!

"I'm fucken freezing," Eddie shouted in his ear, crouched behind the wall of his back.

"Yahwee!" Charlie shouted in return and, aiming at the stars, he jerked the bike upwards so that for a moment they sailed along on one wheel.

HE WOKE, feeling stiff and sorry for himself, as the first light was coming. His head was heavy, still thick with sleep, his mouth dry. He couldn't think for a moment where he might be, swaddled in the bulkiness of the greatcoat, its collar round his ears.

There was a sharp ammoniac smell. Ah! Eddie! The stables.

He saw the wooden walls of the stall then. Sat up in straw. Heard the snuffling close by of horses.

Eddie, in thick socks and greyish longjohns that sagged at the knees, was already upright, pulling a sweater over his head. "I gotta go," he explained.

"I'll go with you," Charlie told him and got to his feet.

Eddie sat to pull on his boots. Charlie discovered he was still wearing his.

They staggered out into the pearly light, unbuttoned, and standing side by side took a good long piss, watching it stream and puddle between the pebbles in the yard. Eddie hitched up his pants and went back inside. Charlie walked up and down, hands deep in the pockets of his greatcoat, which was still unbuttoned, his head and shoulders drawn inside the collar, hunched in on the warmth of himself. "Jesus," he hissed.

He couldn't believe how cold it was out here. There was a bluish frost on the paddock; on the fence post, where it had split and hardened, a glint of ice.

"Here," Eddie said when he reappeared, "give us a hand with these."

He was weighed down with a load of gear. Charlie allowed him to heft a pouched bag over his shoulder that weighed a ton. He released a hand from his pocket to steady it. They went out of the yard, where the CZ rested against the fence, and down a gravel drive beside a slip-rail fence towards the highway. Other figures loomed up in the misty light.

"Is it always as cold as this?" Charlie asked.

Eddie had almost disappeared under the load he was carrying. "Yair. You never fucken get used to it!"

They came to a T-junction. There was no traffic. Horses were being brought up in a long line; silvery shadows in the misty half-light, their hooves making a hollow sound on the bitumen. They might have been packhorses setting out across a continent. Charlie was reminded of a troop of soldiers—or was it Indians?—out of some black-and-white movie. Something unfamiliar anyway, not part of his world. Yet here it was, and routine to Eddie, who was grumping along at his side. Just another Sunday morning.

If I hadn't missed Cliff last night, and the girls, Charlie thought, I wouldn't know all this was here. How much else was there, he wondered, that he wouldn't have time now to discover?

He felt a little cloud of doubt, of depression, puff up in him. But just then the sun broke through, touching the grass on either side of the road, and with its sudden warmth came a strong earth smell, comfortingly dark, along with the rankness of the horses.

He dumped the bag. "I should get going," he said.

Eddie, standing beside him at the fence, was absorbed now with what was happening out in the paddock.

"Yair, good," he said in an absent voice. "See you round."

He continued to stare out into the distance.

Charlie, standing for a moment, felt the pull of Eddie's absorption. In a world. In work. There was so much liveliness in the way the horses pranced about, proud and full of themselves and their power, the air blowing white from their nostrils, light rippling on their coats. When he turned and walked back briskly to where the CZ was parked, he felt in himself some of the energy they moved with, the touch of coming warmth in the air, the beginning excitement of realising that this was it, it had arrived. The day.

AT HOME he showered, got his few things together.

He was very much aware, in a sentimental way, that these would be his last moments, for a while at least, in this room.

It had been his for the whole of his life. Its view, into the branches of an old liquidambar, was one of the first he could recall, the luminous green of star-shaped leaves in the early-morning light that went gold then rusted at the end of May, then crisped and yielded to a faint line of hills; bluish, but sometimes with the red of the sun behind them, and a flash as it was sucked down and disappeared behind their blackness.

He stood now looking out over the sill. There was just an instant when it struck him—repeating an episode from a conventional

Boy's Own story—that he could still climb over the sill, grab one of those branches, swing to the ground ten feet below and be away. But where to? To Josie and the limbo, the dangling interim, of a series of safe houses?

He turned back into the room. He had slept here virtually every night of his life for almost twenty years. Seven full years that would make in all, of being laid out here in a state of suspension, colouring its darkness with his dreams. Its walls bore the record, meagre as it might be, of the dedications and brief enthusiasms of his passage—it too seemed brief—from childhood to wherever he had arrived at now of imperfect manhood. When he closed the door on it, it would remain here, complete to a point, while four thousand miles away the same body that had trusted itself each night to unconsciousness, and done its daily push-ups here on the polished floor, and sat at the desk sweating over the binomial theorem and making its way through *Sons and Lovers* and the *Iliad* and *War and Peace,* would be putting itself through a new set of experiences, as yet unimaginable, which it might or might not at last get back from.

He hung the greatcoat in the wardrobe—the period of that particular uniform was over—and closed the door, then stood and examined himself, hair still wet from the shower, in the mirror.

He had expected these last weeks to resolve in some way the puzzle of what he was—they had not. To provide something, caught from others, that he could take away and hang on to, refer back to, measure himself against.

He opened the door of the wardrobe and looked again at the greatcoat on its hanger, bulky and familiar. He buried his nose in it. The odour of mothballs had faded over the weeks. There was another smell now, not quite familiar. Was *that* him?

Once more he closed the wardrobe door and, avoiding his image, sat for a moment, hands placed lightly on his knees, very quiet and still, on the edge of his bed, the way the characters do in a Russian novel before a journey. Then went out to where his aunt, in her dressing gown, was just coming from the bathroom.

She kissed him, laying her hand very gently to his cheek. It was so unusual, the touch of her fingers added to the regular, rather formal kiss, that it came to him with a little start of reality, which those last moments in his room had not quite produced, that he was actually going.

They were quiet at breakfast, though no more than usual. His grandfather complained, which *was* unusual, of a neighbour's dog, which had kept him awake half the night, he insisted, with its barking—growing, as he went on, more and more aggrieved, then angry.

What Charlie saw, his aunt too, was that he really *was* angry, though not with the neighbour. And not with me either, Charlie said to himself, but with the fact that I am going. Maybe even with the war. But nothing of this—the war, his going or not going—had ever been discussed between them, and he wondered why. He had simply taken it for granted that if his number came up he would go, and that his grandfather and aunt, however they might fear for his safety and miss him, would expect him to, because it was the *strong* thing to do. Wasn't that what they had always been looking for in him? A sign that the moral weakness, or whatever it was that had made his father run, and had then brought him back again destroyed by his own hand, had passed him over. Now, when they shook hands on the veranda step and he felt himself briefly hugged and pushed away, his grandfather's anger, or sorrow, suggested something shocking: that in his own unaccustomed weakness, the old man might be willing to accept even a lack of strength in this last of his line if he could be kept home and safe from harm.

"Look after yourself, boy," was what he said.

His aunt kissed him. Again her fingertips. Soft on his cheek.

And that, on a quiet Sunday morning in August 1968, was how Charlie Dowd went to a war.

THREE YEARS LATER he was back, almost unscathed and nearly two stone heavier, an ex-sergeant, released to take up civilian life where he had left off—after a period of adjustment, of course.

The house he had left was much changed. His grandfather had died the previous year and the first thing his aunt did was suggest that he move into his grandfather's room, which had been cleared and cleaned and was the best room in the house.

He declined. Though his own room now felt small, he preferred, by keeping it, to make the point that his stay was to be temporary. Till he got on his feet, worked out what he wanted to do with himself.

His aunt did not press him. Her enquiries into his plans were tactful and oblique. So were her attempts, which amused him—he thought of Cliff—to set him up with girls. *Nice* ones.

In fact, he had no need of help in this direction but for the moment was taking things, in this area as in all others, slowly.

The world he had come back to struck him as being very different from the one he had known. More relaxed in some ways, more strenuous in others, and his aunt's life was a measure of it.

It wasn't simply that she no longer had her father to care for, his exacting standards to meet. She no longer had *him*—and only now did he understand how much of her life had been devoted to fulfilling what his mother, by leaving, had passed to her in the way of duty, and of affection too. He was shocked now at what it might have cost her, and abashed at how little of this he had appreciated or shown gratitude for, perhaps because she made so little of it herself. He had scarcely considered her then in separation either from his grandfather or himself. He saw, now that things were more equal between them, that she was a woman with her own interests, and was in her own way interesting. She had a sharp eye when it came to the affairs of the town and her various friends; a sharp tongue too, now that her father was not here to monitor it. They got on well together. She still worried about him but did not fuss.

She had had the kitchen, which had been an old-fashioned place of leadlight cupboards and scrubbed-wood draining boards, fitted out with a good deal of Laminex and stainless steel. A skylight filled the whole space with the kind of light that would once have been considered dangerous, in the way of fading curtains or exposing the lurking places of ineradicable grime.

There were no curtains now, and little fear of grime. The archway into the dining room had been removed and the new space furnished with pieces of a spare "modern" design—bold fabrics, pale wood. Hard, he thought, for the old presences to find harbour in a world that was so shadowless and bright.

He wondered where his aunt had found in herself such a capacity for lightness. Had it always been there, waiting to establish itself the moment the old man was gone? A refutation, long unspoken, of his world of solid truths?

Charlie was surprised, but he enjoyed surprise. It was one of the small surprises his own nature had yielded him in recent years.

She was made wary, he saw, by his experiences. Since he offered no account of them and gave no outward sign of how they had touched him, she had had to make them up out of horrors she had read about in the papers or seen on TV. That he did not need to talk about what he had seen, and did not bring to breakfast with him the smell of napalm or of the night sweats that must accompany his dreams, was not in itself a reassurance. Neither was his lack of visible wounds. His father too had come home without wounds.

What worried her was what might be there in his head. Deep-hidden, unspoken. In the meantime they took refuge, both, since he proved to be such an obedient pupil of her rules, in good-humoured banter and routine.

But neither of them any longer believed in rules. That's what he saw. The new rule was to pretend they did, while knowing perfectly well, on each side, that the other did not.

But perhaps, he thought, she never had. Maybe that was another of the ways in which, over the years, he had misread her.

HE DEVELOPED his own routine: got up late, did odd jobs around the yard that he found oddly satisfying—putting new palings into the back fence, climbing up on to the roof to replace a length of guttering. He read, sat with his hands in his lap idling an hour away on the new couch in front of the TV. Took long walks along the roads that led out of town.

Walking, he found, set just the right pace for the sort of think-ing he had to do; and watching people at their ordinary occupa-tions, in a world where the commonest source of disruption was the weather, comforted him—he didn't mind the tedium of it.

People talked about the weather in a way he had never noticed till now. As if they looked to the sky for *relief*. For a mild irruption into their lives of chance or change that might at one time have come from the gods, but in the clear assurance now that the worst it could produce was a fistful of hail.

"Looks like it might rain," men who stood behind a fence with a pair of shears would call across to him—entire strangers.

It was a way of invoking a link between them within a dispensa-tion so easily admissible on both sides, and so large and all-embracing, that no answer was required.

It was in such moments that he felt closest to being home.

Sometimes, on one of his walks, he dropped in at the pub and, feeling like an old-timer himself these days, settled in his old place by the window with a beer.

He recognised one or two of the old fellows sitting alone in the sunlight, but had changed too much for them to see in him the thin-shouldered youth in the air force greatcoat who had once sat scribbling in his notebook at the sill.

He no longer wore the greatcoat or had a notebook with him, and in a general doing-over in which the whole place had been subjected to progress, the sill was no longer chocolate-coloured but a spanking white.

But when he looked across, the boy was still there, his wallet and the little machine for producing roll-your-owns, which he had long since abandoned, on the sill before him. Urgently, solemnly setting down his thoughts. Looking up. Biting the end of his pen. Writing again. Thoughts. Endless lists. Impossible now to get back into that boy's head.

Tenderly curious, he had gone in search of the notebook, but had hidden it so well from others who might stumble across it in his absence that he could not find it himself.

Occasionally a phrase came back to him, or an item from one of the lists, and he blushed, then found himself feeling oddly, indulgently protective of his former self. He had been so full of the easy belief that his thoughts, and the careful formulation of them, mattered. Perhaps it was better that the notebook was lost.

But the boy continued to haunt him. There in silhouette against the light of the window, or as a slighter sharer of his own more solid flesh. Which he shared now with other presences as well. Ghosts he carried in him who saw things in their own way.

What they felt, what they had seen, formed a glow around his own feelings that on occasion confused him and was the chief reason why he kept clear of old friends. He did not know how to present himself to them or what he had to present. In the other lives that now haunted him he had lived a different history, lighter or darker than the one he had brought home and could show.

As for the boy at the sill, the tenderness he felt for him was of a brotherly kind; blood-closeness, but with an element, as well, of distance.

It wasn't a question of innocence, or the loss of innocence—he found these days he could no longer talk in such terms, and people who did made him angry.

There were fellows he had come across "up there" who were, in a childlike way, unknowing; others who, again like children, seemed unmarked by the evil they had come up against. The first was just that—childishness. The second, maybe, a form of grace. We lose whatever innocence we might have laid claim to the moment we are drawn into that tangle of action and interaction, of gesture and consequence, where the least motion on our part, even the drawing of a breath, may so change things that another, close by or far off, will be nudged just far enough out of the clear line of his life as to be permanently impaired.

That, so Charlie would have written now, if he still had his notebook and thought it worth the effort of setting down, was the price of living. To that extent, no man is innocent. As for the loss of innocence, how could you lose what you'd never had? He had never claimed to be innocent. Only alive.

Ah, thoughts. Thoughts.

He saw himself as a man who, whole as he might look, in that he had no wound to show, had come back just the same with a limb missing, a phantom limb that continued to putrify.

Or with fragments of shrapnel in his flesh that sent metal detectors into electronic fits, whether others had ears for it or not.

Or bearing on his breath spores from the soil of a disorderly and darkly divided country where for two whole years he had taken the infected air into his lungs, so that that too—along with the dulled habit of boredom, the unnatural excitements and dreams he had been dragged through, the brutal descents into degradation and a blundering despair without hope of renovation—had come home with him, in selves who had their own other and haunting lives to live.

It scared him at times that one of these ghostly selves who now sheltered in him might speak up and send a conversation skidding in some new and terrible direction. He would have to deal then with a look on the face of whatever companion he had found of startled incomprehension, as if with no warning a mask had slipped.

So he watched himself. Watched *them*. These others who had set up in him, who insisted at times on drawing attention to themselves and had motives that were not his own.

The need to be heard was theirs, not his. He had no wish to discuss what he had been witness to, and there was no way of doing it anyway. So he did not mention that he had been to the war.

Some people knew it already. They did not mention it either. Embarrassed for him, and for themselves, in case it led to argument. There was a lot of argument on the subject, but only, up here, on the TV, which had smuggled itself now into every household all up and down the country, where it dominated the front room like a child overexcited by the power to say at last the once unsayable.

Up here an older decorum prevailed. People had as little appetite as ever for open dispute.

He thought of Josie and wondered how deep she was now in her hostility to the war, and her disappointment with fellows, like him, who had been duped into going. But he wasn't sure of that—of having been duped. He had had no illusions. The experience had offered itself, that's all, and he had accepted. He did not disagree with the arguments he heard against the war, and his aunt, he suspected, was fiercely opposed to it, though she did not say so. He picked this up from the line of her profile as they sat watching the news together. Her sharp little glances to see how he was taking it. She was afraid of offering some insult to what he had "been through."

He recognised this and was touched. Her fierceness, he knew, was on his behalf. She meant to protect him. But it was too late for that.

What affronted him was not the opinions he heard but the gap between their glib abstractions and what he himself had come across in the way of fact: the heaviness of a soaked pack and mudcaked army boots; grime, dank sweat, the death smell of bloated corpses; the incessant tense preoccupation with keeping all the parts of a body that was suddenly too large, and could not effectively be hidden, clear of the random brute agents of destruction that kept hurtling in from every direction; death-dealing but indifferent. For whom you, warm and intelligently alive as you might be, were no more than another object in their path, though the roar with which they came at you was specific and the collision, when it came, so wet and personal.

On the few occasions when people did argue he turned his back. He had only his experience—combustive actualities—to offer, and they weren't an argument. He screwed his mouth shut and sat sullen over his beer.

The wall of silence he felt between himself and others, which he refused to breach, was noise of a kind they could not even begin to conceive: so dense with the scream of metal and the lower but distinguishable screams of men, with the splash of heavy objects through oil-slicked swamp, and night calls out there in the stilled other world of nature that might be birds but might also be the location signals of a waiting enemy, and with heartbeats and the thump-thump of rotor blades, that not even the music he liked to listen to, and which his aunt thought unnecessarily loud, could block it out.

WEEKS PASSED. He drifted.

In the month before he left things had been like this. He had felt the same way. Detached. Floating. But those days had not been entirely aimless. They had a fixed termination; he had known then what he was moving towards. Now he did not.

And he himself had been different, not simply younger. With a different sense of where he might look for enlightenment. Intrigued still by the spectacle of his own existence, and open to every clue he might pick up—a look here, a passing comment there—of what he might be. Still making himself up out of what others saw in him. Or wanting to. Because it was easier than looking too clearly into himself.

He had tried that too, but it was confusing. What he had found there was contradictory, or the evidence was in a code he could not crack.

Was he wiser now?

Not much, he thought.

What he had learned in the heat of action was useful only in moments of extremity, of violent confrontation. The pressures now were soft, the dangers more insidious because not deadly. Or not immediately so.

His aunt went easy on him, was not demanding. She had become sociable and went out a good deal, leaving his meals on a plate in the fridge with a note telling him how they should be heated. The notes were jaunty, an easier and more playful form of communication than talk, and became more so as the weeks rolled on.

He ate alone in the kitchen with the radio playing, for the comfort of some other voice in his head than his own, which wearied him, or in the new lounge in front of the news.

He ate slowly, trying not to let the images that flashed from the TV connect with his own low-level anger; which was more like a taste in his mouth that no other could quite displace than an emotion, a subtle disturbance of his vision that bled the world of vividness and gave everything he looked at a yellow tinge.

He watched a group of young men in battledress run hunched and stumbling towards a medevac chopper that swayed and tilted. Its blades churned the fetid air, whipped up a tornado of smashed grass stalks and twigs. He felt a damp heat on his skin. Found he was sweating.

He watched a bunch of young men, much the same age as in the previous clip, but in T-shirts and jeans and with young women among them—and some older women too, not unlike his aunt, grey-haired, in glasses—push hard against a line of uniformed police. Banners hung askew above their heads, like thought bubbles in a cartoon. All capitals, all pointing in the same direction. The young men, animal spirits fiercely mobilised in a violent forward movement, were engaged in their own version of war. And the enemy?

He ate. Chewing slowly. Swallowing it down.

"You know," his aunt remarked one morning at breakfast, "there's some money. You haven't asked, but it's yours, you know, whenever you want it."

"I don't need it yet," he told her.

"Well," she said, not pressing, "it's there. Just ask when you do."

On another occasion: "Have you thought of getting in touch with your mother?"

This surprised him. He looked up, but could not tell from her eyes—she glanced quickly away—what she was thinking. Did she want him to or not?

"No," he said. "I can barely remember what she looks like."

This wasn't quite true.

"She thinks you're angry with her."

"I'm not," he said. "Not anymore. There are too many other things. Anyway, I try not to be angry at all. It does no good."

"You're right," she said, but seemed unconvinced.

"Do you keep in touch then?"

"Not regularly. But there *is* a tie. Your father—"

She foundered, unwilling to go further, and he was glad—he did not want her to. He wanted, just for a moment, to think of himself as a free agent, no ties—or at least to tell himself he had none. The ties, such as they were, he could pick up later. When he was ready. When.

"She's moved to Aberdeen," his aunt told him.

"Aberdeen!"

The word fell into the room out of nowhere. He knew where Aberdeen was, he could see it on the map, but had never expected to have any connection to it. Hadn't thought of his connections as being so worldwide. He gave a little laugh, more a snigger perhaps, and his aunt looked alarmed.

"I can't imagine her," he said, "in Aberdeen," and laughed again.

It denied, of course, what he had already claimed. That he had no clear picture of her at all. And what did he know of Aberdeen?

HE WALKED. From one end of town to the other. Walking was another form of thinking—or maybe *un*thinking—in which the body took over, went its own way and the mind went with it; the ground he covered, there and back, measurable only by the level of quietude he had arrived at, and the change, when he came out of himself, in the atmosphere and light.

One of the places he liked to go when the weather was fine was to a river park at the far end of town. Willow-fringed along the brown, rather sluggish stream, it was featureless save for an elaborate rotunda of timber and decorative wrought iron that was unusual in that it offered more in the way of fantasy than you got in other parts of town, and a children's playground where, in the afternoon, mothers brought their kids to climb, swing, and roll about in a sandpit. He liked to sit high up in the bandstand, where he had a good view over the expanse of park and an oval beyond, and lose himself in a book.

Towards the end of January it rained for three days. He stopped his walks and stuck to the pub.

Finally the rain gave up, though the air remained saturated.

There were still heavy clouds about and the ground was soggy underfoot. He took his usual walk out towards the river. And the park when he came to it was a place transformed. Great sheets of water broke the green of its surface, and hundreds of seagulls had flocked in, bringing with them the light of ocean beaches and of the ocean itself. They were crowding the shores of the newly formed ponds: huge white creatures that had made their way a hundred miles from the coast to translate what had been one kind of landscape into something entirely other. The children had deserted the swings and ladders of the playground and were chasing about among the big birds, delighted by the novelty they presented, the news they had brought—not just of another world, but of a world inside the one at their feet that they had scarcely dreamed of.

He too felt the miracle of it. It was as if a breath of fantasy, that had existed as no more than an unlikely possibility in the lightness and whiteness of the bandstand, had re-created itself as fact in these hundreds of actual bodies, independent organisms and lives, that were shifting about over the green or making brief flights across the expanse of silvery, sky-lit water.

What he felt in himself was an equal lightness, that reflected, he thought, the persistence out there in the world, of the unexpected—an assurance that nothing was final, or beyond surprise or change. The dry little park had transformed itself into a new shore, but the force he felt in touch with was in himself. It was as if he had looked up from a book he was lost in and found that what his eyes had conceived of on the page was shining all round him.

Half a dozen children were chasing along the banks, delighted that by rushing at them they could drive the big birds skyward, half expecting perhaps to find in themselves the power to join them and go heavily circling and gliding. One small boy, unready to challenge the birds as the others were doing, stood stranded on the sidelines. He was maybe five years old. Skinny with pale reddish hair. Doubtful but tempted.

Charlie stood looking at him, and the boy, aware of it, turned to meet Charlie's gaze, drawing his underlip in, which only made his moist eyes rounder.

"Magic," Charlie told the boy with a laugh, and made a sweep with his arm that sent a dozen birds streaming aloft.

The boy's mouth fell open, and Charlie saw in the look of sudden enlightenment in his eyes that the child had taken the word literally, as a claim on Charlie's part to be the presiding genius here who had turned a bit of the local and familiar into something extraordinary, and for a moment Charlie actually felt a breath of what the child's belief had accorded him.

A girl of ten or eleven appeared, also skinny but more vigorously red-headed than the boy. She took him sternly by the hand.

"Kelvin," she scolded in a whisper, "you know you're not allowed!" Fiercely protective, she cast a baleful look in the direction of the stranger who had been *speaking* to him. But the boy, suddenly defiant, broke away, and with arms outspread launched headlong into a flock of gulls, which lifted with excited shrieks and went flapping past his head. Glancing back a moment to make sure that he was the one who had been the actual cause of this commotion, he tilted his arms like outstretched wings and made another rush among the birds.

Charlie turned away, lightly amused. But he would think of this inconsequential moment afterwards as being for him the end of one thing and the beginning of another, though which element in it, if any, had been decisive he would never know: the translation of the park to another shore; the boy Kelvin's mistaken belief that, like a conjuror at a children's party, he had produced all this shifting light, all these plump white bodies, out of his sleeve; the sister's defiance of him as a dangerous stranger. Perhaps it was all these in odd collusion with one another, or in collusion with something in himself that had been waiting for just this concatenation of small events to touch it awake and open a way to the future. Or something else again that he had no possibility of bringing to consciousness. Some chemical change in him even more miraculous at one level, though ordinary and explicable at another, than the appearance overnight, out of nowhere as it were, of a thousand sea creatures so far from the sea.

Walking home he had no sense that anything momentous had

occurred. He was aware only of his immediate mood; an amusement that continued to work on him, quiet but quickening, and a glimpse—for the moment it was no more than that—of how small the pressures might be that determine the sum of what is and what we feel, the fugitive deflections and instinctive blind gestures that might be the motor of change.

He did not know as yet that there *was* a change. Only that it was possible, and that the agents of it could be small. But that, for the moment, was enough.

Towards Midnight

WHAT CAME to her ear was the hovering close by of mechanical wings, that had come, she thought, to carry her off. In her dream-state she felt only the relief it would be to pass the weight of her body, light as it now was, to some other agency.

The wings beat closer. She started awake, and the familiar objects of her upstairs sitting room, as if a second earlier she might have surprised them in a temporary absence, settled back into place.

The TV screen was dancing, white with static. It was after midnight. For a good hour and a half, it seemed, she herself had been absent. She reached for the remote. But the sound out of her dream persisted. It was the clatter of the filter boxes in the pool two levels below. A breeze must have sprung up. She stirred herself, gathered up her things.

But against the blue Tuscan night the cypress tops in the window were as still as if they were painted.

She stepped out on to her terrace and, half hidden in shadow, peered down through the darkness of pomegranate and bay. Someone was down there, swimming. All she could make out were the streamers of light at his shoulders, and when he came, too quickly, to the end of a length, the heap of silvery bubbles he left as he tucked over into the turn. Up and down he went, in a dozen powerful strokes, and the pool, which for so many weeks had lain heavy and still in the heat, under a mantle of olive florets, drowned midges, beetles paddling in clumsy circles, expanded and contracted like a living thing.

If Gianfranco was here, or one of her sons, Tommy or Jake, what a ruckus there'd be! They'd feel bound to go down and shout at the fellow. Chuck him out.

Well, she wasn't going to try that. She was alone in the house, a kilometre from the village. No neighbours in calling distance. But she felt no particular alarm. Only surprise, and a kind of delight at the unexpectedness of it, exhilaration in the presence of so much effort. As if she had got herself hooked up to some new chemical—neat starlight—that glowed in her veins and quickened her awareness of her own body, but as a thing alive and part again of the living scene.

With her elbows propped on the parapet of her terrace, she watched—hard to say for how long—and was taken out of herself, till at the end of a length like any other he did not tumble into a turn, but with his head streaming moonlight came to his feet, and in the same agile movement sprang on to his splayed hands, heaved himself up, and was out.

No one she recognised.

A sturdy peasant type, in a bathing-slip that might have been red.

She stepped back in case he glanced up and caught her there.

But he was too absorbed for that. Standing with his arms forced back hard behind him, fingers linked, he did half a dozen stretching exercises, dipping his head swiftly like a bird; then straightened and moved out of sight under the pergola.

The pool, meanwhile, had settled to clear moonlight again.

She felt let down, as if he had taken with him part of the night and what was vital to it. Was it over? Was that it?

She stood peering into the darkness of the pergola. He must have gone already, through one of the gaps in the fence. The fence had gaps, but there were so many brambles along its length, and the bank was so steep, that they hadn't bothered to have it mended. Was he really gone?

A gust of fragrance came on the air, then thinned and came again. So strong! Her lime tree.

Out of sight on the other side of the house, and taller now than

the house itself, its scent was so overpowering on these warm May
nights that in her mind she could actually see the great dark mass
of it looming against the stars.

How good it is to be here, she thought, at just this moment.
With the moon resting like that on the tip of a cypress, the air
freighted with the scent of *tiglio*, the clear bright notes of the
nightingale dropping so precisely into place, off in the dark. It was
a moment, she thought, when all things were just as they should
be. Not a degree lighter or heavier or louder or more intense.

Ah, her swimmer!

Wearing rough workman's trousers but still bare-chested, he
moved to the edge of the pool and stood there towelling his hair
with his T-shirt; then, rather dreamily, began to dry his chest.

He might have looked up then and seen her. She drew back. But
something else had caught his attention.

He was gazing out over the wall of bay to the hills with their
swathes of blue-black *macchia*. Looking, perhaps, for where the
nightingale was dinning from its post in the olive grove, establish-
ing, note on note, its claim to territory.

There, she could have told him. Further to the left. Down there.

He turned his head as if he had heard, but in the wrong direction. Then kneeling, laced his sneakers and, with the soaked T-
shirt across his shoulders, ducked down beside the fence and was
gone.

She continued to stand. Looking at the place where he had vanished, but with no sense of being left. Rather of remaining, of
being here and in possession of all this. The place. The hour. Most
of all, of herself.

The moon, which just a moment ago had been straw-coloured,
when she looked at it now was paling, as if it had been subjected to
immersion in some fast-working chemical. Again the scent of lime
came to her, and with it the quickening sense of a whole world
astir and on the move. Small nocturnal creatures, destructive in
fact—but so what—were nosing in around the fleshy roots of her
iris. A cat was on the prowl—or was it a fox? Other lives, intent on
their interests. Invisibly close and companionable.

She felt settled, wonderfully so. And by a situation that on another occasion or in a different mood might have alarmed her. Why hadn't it? She did not know and did not need for the moment to ask. What she needed now was to tumble into her bed and sleep.

SHE WAS ALONE because she chose to be. Later it might not be possible, she knew that, but for the time being she could manage, and it was what she preferred. She had worked through her period of rage and hard words, but wasn't sure she could trust herself, just yet, with others.

Each night at seven she boiled herself an egg or heated a pan of soup, and at half past, right on the dot, Gianfranco rang. She was comfortably settled in her routine.

No, she told him, everything was fine, just fine. Marisa came to clean each morning. Corrado looked after the *orto* and the pool.

Gianfranco, she knew, was nodding, but what she could hear in his silence, even at this distance, was the terrible humming of anxiety in him, the fear that there was something—there was always *something*—that she was holding back. She raged up and down beside her kitchen cupboards, the receiver tight in her fist. But her voice when she spoke was soothing (or so she hoped).

"No, no," she cooed. "Gianfranco! Darling! I'm perfectly okay, I promise I am. Stop fussing."

She gave a little laugh that was meant to assure him that this, like all the other things he fretted over—the boys, his office, money, the house—was nothing, he was being silly.

He said goodnight, made her promise to ring if there was the slightest problem, the least change.

Then waited, as he always did, for her to reconsider and tell him the bad news. She refrained. And in fact there *was* none.

At last, on his third goodnight, he rang off.

She gave a subdued scream of a theatrical kind—seeing herself in a jokey, self-dramatising way helped to keep up her spirits— and sat down hard on a stool.

But it was over. She was alone again. Free. The whole night before her.

She thought sometimes that she would like it if Tommy was here; Jake, her second son, was mid-Atlantic somewhere on someone's yacht. There were afternoons when she found herself gazing out of her window and wishing she could just call down to the terrace, where, his mobile on the glass-topped table within easy reach, Tommy would be lazing on a daybed. She would get him to come up then and put on one of the Roy Orbison albums she liked to listen to only when he was here. Or wishing that she would look up, having caught a scent, and find him there in the doorway of her room, filling its space with his hungry presence.

What she meant was, she would like it for about *five minutes*. Any longer and she would discover all over again the things about this favourite child that exasperated and enraged her.

The way he stalked about, clutching his mobile like a small instrument of torture. Waiting pathetically for someone to call.

And when he gave in at last, and himself did the calling, the way he pursed his lips at the thing, as if it was a mouth; arguing with his ex-wife and sounding so mild and reasonable, or sweet-talking some girl he'd picked up on the train. Then, the moment he hung up, going glowery and dark again, casting about, like the bewildered four-year-old she saw so clearly at times in the big unhappy man, for some mischief he could get up to that would make someone pay.

Somebody, it didn't matter who.

She had been paying for more than thirty years.

Well, she could do without that just for the moment. What she needed, just for the moment, was solitude, and blessèd, blessèd routine.

THREE DAYS each week she went up to Siena for her chemo. They taped a plastic bubble like a third breast to the soft flesh below her shoulder and it fed mineral light into her at a slow run. The nausea it left her with was like space sickness. As if they were minerals from another planet, changing her slowly into a space creature who would be free at last of the ills of earth.

Well, she knew what *that* was code for!

Between visits she wore a holster packed with a flattish canister that for twenty-four hours a day played with the weather of her body—its moods, her dreams; filling her mouth with the taste of metals straight off the periodic table, getting her ready for the thing itself—the taste of earth.

For Siena she had a driver from the village and a big old Audi. Soft-leathered, air-conditioned. She sat in magisterial coolness, closed off from the straw-coloured, treeless hills, the vine rows where the grapes, as yet, were like hard little peas, but swelling, swelling towards October.

At intervals along the highway, black girls in six-inch heels toting fake Gucci handbags paced up and down in the dust. Some of them in skintight leather miniskirts, others in gold Lurex pants tight at the ankle. In the middle of nowhere! With nothing in sight but oakwoods or a distant viaduct, they paced elegantly up and down beside the hurtling traffic, in a tide of ice-cream sticks, paper cups, dried acacia blossom. She watched them from the closed-off sanctuary of the car, and sometimes, to pass the time, kept count. On long car journeys in her Queensland childhood, she and her brother had watched for white horses. The appearance in the timeless Tuscan landscape of opulent, overdressed black girls seemed no less marvellous.

They came from as far away as Cape Verde and Sierra Leone, these girls, and drove out here in taxis to wait for the long-distance lorry drivers. Their managers (or so she had heard) were women: big African mammas who were also witches and used old-country spells to keep them in fear of their lives, or their children's lives, but to be doubly sure held their passports—a modern touch. In bodies that seemed entirely their own, and giving no hint of being fearful or enslaved, they walked up and down as if the dirt under their heels were the paving stones of some fashionable piazza in Florence or Milan.

She watched them. Hard not to envy, whatever the facts, the grace and assurance they brought to this new version of pastoral.

Till one of the lorries, with a whine of its air brakes, came powerfully to a halt, and the driver—the god—stepped down.

Her own body was *not* her own. In some moment of ordinary distraction, while she was on her knees in the rose bed pulling up weeds, or waiting idly for the kettle to boil, her mind God knows where, her body had taken a wrong turning, gone haywire, and now did exactly as it pleased. It was like being in the hands of a loony housebreaker who did not have your interest at heart. Who had moods and notions of his own. Was savagely perverse, and curious to see how far he could push you. And was there at every moment, making his obscene, humiliating demands. To get away from him she read, or rather, reread. Chasing up old friends in the pages of her favourite books to see how she or they had changed over the years, or to rediscover, with a little shock of affection, the earlier self who at sixteen or thirty had first been touched by them.

Effi Briest, who was in favour of living, poor girl, but had no principles. Mrs. Copperfield, one of the two Serious Ladies, who had always wanted to go to pieces. Gratefully she went back to them. And found herself, towards midnight, with her book in her lap and her glasses at the end of her nose, listening impatiently for the familiar clap-clap of the filter boxes and the arrival of her intruder.

SHE KNEW NOW who he must be.

There were woods on the far side of the village. The men who worked there these days, cutting and stacking logs, came from Eastern Europe. Poles or Yugoslavs. They had rooms in the village and sat around playing cards outside the bar. She had seen them riding through the square on top of a truck piled with firewood, their muddy boots dangling. He would be one of those. She didn't need to know which one or to see him close. She liked the idea of his being a stranger in the further sense of his having other words in his head, when she looked down and saw him gazing out over the hills, for *owl, fence, distance*. Of there being nothing between them but his body, either in vigorous action down there in the pool or in dreamy repose; which he did not know was being watched, and in the long hour before he made his appearance, impatiently waited for.

He came every night, not always at the same hour. Sometimes earlier—a surprise!—mostly later. There would come the clatter of the filter boxes as he brought the pool to life, and with it the quickening of her heart, which laughed quietly as she took her book up again and pretended for a moment to go back to her reading. Then she would rise, draw her robe about her, and step out on to the terrace.

Sipping her coffee each morning she caught glimpses of the pool as it shimmered and flashed between the leaves, an electric, unnatural blue. Housemartins, in their furious hunger, would be swooping for insects that danced in swarms on its surface, taking the pool's reflected light in flushes on their under-bodies. The air, down there, as it heated, would be sharp with the scent of bay.

She might have gone down to lie for a little on one of the sunbeds. It was still cool at this hour and she would get down easily enough. But where would she find the strength to climb back again?

As they moved deeper into June, the afternoons grew fiery, she could not sleep. Elbows on the parapet of her terrace, sipping cold tea, her thoughts went to a young man, Justin Ferrier, who, fifteen years before, had come out from England to be her summer help in the garden.

The son of a business contact of Gianfranco's, he was the same age as Jake and just down from Eton. Hard-working, sociable, the perfect guest.

Unused to their southern habits, he had spent long afternoons, under the low bronze sky, at work on an old 350cc motorbike he had acquired from a mechanic in the next village and set up like an idol on the terrace below her window.

Sometimes, when it was too hot to sleep, she would lean over the parapet and chat to him while he squatted like a child in his open sandals and worked, or she simply rested there on her elbows and watched. Drawing back at times in dazzled embarrassment at the intensity with which, under his flop of sun-bleached hair, he devoted all his shining attention to the mucky business of laying out on sheets of yesterday's *Repubblica* all the dismantled parts of the god he worshipped: chain, gears, grease-slicked carburettor, screws.

He'd put his stamp on the summer—even Jake and Tommy felt that. Whenever they talked of it later it was always "the year Justin was here."

Because it would have seemed shameful to shout or call one another names in front of him, they had, for a whole two months, been on their best behaviour, playing just the sort of nice *per bene* family he believed them to be.

Her friend Jack Chippenham, Chipper, was with them and had immediately been smitten. He had made a big play for the boy—but in a jokey way, as if it was accepted, a part of that summer's special mood, that they should all be a little in love with him.

She and Chipper had grown up together. They had met at a birthday party in Toowoomba when they were still at school. Chipper, at sixteen, was already in possession of things—style, a humourous take on the world, and himself and others—that she had only begun to be aware of. "You saved my life," she told him on that first occasion. Meaning that without him the party would have been a write-off. He had been doing it, in different ways, ever since.

Justin, like everyone Chipper set his sights on, was charmed, and was charming in return. He let Chipper drive him across to Monteriggione and Sinalunga to expensive meals, and to the summer discos all up and down the coast. There was nothing in it, of course, she knew that. But when Chipper's attentions began to be so obvious that even Gianfranco noticed, she took him aside and gave him a good talking to. After all, she was *in loco parentis* here. She actually said that: *in loco parentis.*

Chipper's response was to pretend astonishment. That she should turn out, in her old age, to be so moralistic. And humourless. It was the second charge that hurt.

And he was right. The boy enjoyed being made a fuss of, and why not? He knew just how to handle such things. There was no harm in it. But the next day, while they were having drinks before lunch, she suggested to Justin that he might like to bring his girlfriend Charlotte out, and for the rest of the summer Charlotte too worked in the garden, and they had a tent in the olive grove.

"Uh-huh," Chipper had said. "Nice." He might have been referring to the sip he had taken from the Bloody Mary she had just passed to him.

Maintaining *his* sense of humour right to the end.

One morning, to amuse the young people, as she thought of them, she raked out a dress she had kept from their Rome days twenty years before, a sleeveless low-waisted Yves Saint Laurent that came just to the knee, and which, when she tried it on, still miraculously fitted. After consulting the mirror in her room she had gone down to where they were sunbathing beside the pool— Justin, Chipper, the girl—and was flattered that the young people, when they glanced up, did not at first recognise her.

Justin had had to take his sunglasses off, and she could tell that he was seeing her as if for the first time.

"Oh my, my," Chipper had said, and Yes, she was saying to herself as she stood there transformed, here I am at last, this is the *real* me.

The dress, which was of dark green silk, fitted like a secret skin. The fashion of that particular year had been made for her. It had been her moment, her season. Which she had stepped back into as if it had never passed.

Well, it had of course. It was Chipper who got gallantly to his feet, took her hand and led her, while the others applauded, through her one celebratory twirl.

Poor Chipper! It was, after all, Chipper that this memory had been moving towards. He was dead. Six years ago in San Francisco.

"I'm not sorry," he had written, just before the end, "to have wasted my time on such an agreeable planet."

THE LAST DAYS of June came on. One night of intense moonlight, when the whole landscape, fields, vineyards, river meadows, the densely wooded surrounding hills, had the glow of midday in some other part of the universe, she realised that for several evenings now she had not heard what she thought of as the embodiment of so much silvery stillness, the bright little hammer-strokes and exuberant volleys of the nightingale. He had said "Enough" and was gone.

Standing behind her parapet, in the hard shadow of the terrace, she was even more aware of her swimmer, who had not. A small blessing, but one, she knew, that must also have its term. One night soon he would come to his feet at the end of a length and that would be that. All unknowing, she would wait the next night and he would not appear. And the next. Till she was used once again to getting through the midnight hours without him. But for the moment—maybe for the last time—he was here. The disturbance he made as he rocked the water, which was all tilted planes of moonlight and dark, set the filter boxes dancing and beating the air just as she had first heard it. Like the arrival of wings.

Back and forth he hurled himself. Effortless, the body its own affair. Weightless. As if there was no limit to the energy that powered it. As if the breath it drew on might have no end.

Elsewhere

W HEN DEBBIE LARCOMBE died she had not been home to her family for nearly three years. Her father decided at once that he would go down to Sydney for the funeral, which was already arranged. There was no suggestion of her being brought back to Lithgow. Her sister Helen couldn't go. She had the children. So Harry's son-in-law, Andy Mayo, would go with him. The two men worked together down the mine and were mates.

Andy was a steady fellow of thirty-three. He'd been to Sydney once, with a rugby team, when he was nineteen. The prospect of driving down and seeing something of the Big Smoke excited him, but he felt he should disguise the fact. After all it was a funeral. "Are you sure?" he asked Helen, who was kneeling at the bathtub bathing their youngest.

"It's only for the day," she told him. "And Dad would like it. I'd be worried about him going down all on his own."

She paused at her work and said for the third or fourth time, "It's so sudden! I can hardly believe it."

Andy, stirred by a rush of tenderness, but also of tender sensuality, brought his fingertips to a strand of hair, damp with steam, that had stuck to the soft white of her neck. Responding, she leaned back for a moment into the firmness, against her nape, of his extended forefinger and thumb, which lightly stroked.

He'd barely known Debbie; in fact he'd met her only twice. She had already left home when he arrived on the scene. After training college at Bathurst she had taught in country towns all up and down the state and had ended up at Balmain, in Sydney. She was four years older than Helen.

The one occasion they'd spent any time together—he had sat up late with her on the night of her mother Dorothy's funeral— Andy had been impressed but had also felt uneasy. She was nothing like Helen, except a little in looks—same nose, same big hands. Keen that she should see him as more than the usual run of small-town fatheads and mug lairs she had known before she left, but unpractised, he was soon out of his depth. They'd gotten drunk together—she was quite a drinker—and he was the one, being unused to spirits, who had ended up fuzzy-headed.

She sat with her legs crossed and smoked non-stop. Her legs were rather plump, but the shoes she wore, which had thin straps across the instep, were very fashionable-looking. Expensive, Andy thought. Though in no way glamourous, she was a woman who took trouble with herself.

The impression he'd got was that she moved in a pretty fast crowd down there, and some of what he caught on to of what Balmain was, and the people she knew—poets and that—and the fact that she lived now with one poet, and had been the girlfriend earlier of another, excited him. He had had very little of that sort of excitement in his own life.

He'd been a football player, good but not good enough. At sixteen he'd gone down the mine. Married at twenty. That there was another life somewhere he had picked up from the magazines he saw and the talk, some of it rough, of fellows who got down to the city pretty regularly and had much to tell. In Debbie, he had, for an hour or so, felt the breath of something he had missed out on. Something extra, something more. Now she was dead.

At thirty-six, some woman's problem. An abortion he guessed, though Helen had done no more than raise a suspicion and the old man of course knew nothing at all. So far as Harry knew, all Debbie had been was a high-school science teacher.

It hadn't struck Andy till now, but everything he'd heard of Debbie's doings had come from Helen and he wondered how much more she knew than she let on. Out of loyalty to Debbie no doubt—but also, he thought, to protect him from a side of herself that might be less surprised by Debbie's way of life, and less disapproving of it, than she pretended.

He felt, vaguely, that here too he had missed out. There was something more he hungered for, and occasionally pushed towards, that Helen would not admit. Because for all the twelve years they had passed in the closest intimacy, she did not want him to see in her the sort of woman who might recognise or allow it.

THE DRIVE DOWN was uneventful. Harry was silent, but that wasn't unusual. They were often silent together.

All this, Andy thought, must be hard on him. He'd never asked himself how Harry felt about Debbie's being away. Proud of her, certainly, as the only one of them who had got enough of an education to make a new life for herself. Sad to see so little of her. Worried on occasion. Now this.

Andy followed these thoughts on Harry's behalf—he was fond of Harry—then followed his own.

Which sprang from the lightness he felt at having a day off like this in the middle of the week. The sunlight. The high white clouds set above open country. The freedom of being behind the wheel. The freedom too—he felt guilty to be thinking this way—of being off the hook, away from home and its constrictions. And along with all that, the exhilaration, the allure, of a faster and more crowded world "down there" that he would finally get to see and feel the proximity of.

He was surprised at himself. Here he was, a grown man, twelve years married, two kids, seated side by side with his father-in-law, both of them in suits on the way to a funeral, and he might have been seventeen, a kid again, he was so full of expectation at what the day might offer. In some secret place where the life in him was most immediately physical, he still clung to a vision of himself that for a time back there had seemed golden and inextinguishable. He thought he had dealt with it, outgrown it, let it go, and without too much disappointment replaced its bouts of extravagant yearning with the reality of small prospects, work, the life he and Helen had made together. And now this.

He was surprised, ashamed even. What would Harry think? But not enough, it seemed, to subdue the flutter he had felt in his belly the moment the idea of the trip came up, or the heat his body was giving off inside the suit.

THEY ARRIVED EARLY. To kill the time they drove out to Bondi and sat in the car eating egg hamburgers in greasy paper and watching the surf.

Boardriders miraculously rose up and for long moments kept their balance on running sunlight, then went down in a flurry of foam.

Mothers, their skirts round their thighs, tempted little kiddies too far past the waterline for them to run back when the sea, in a rush, came sparkling round their feet. Surprised beyond tears, they considered a moment, then squealed with delight.

Andy thought of his girls. He should bring them down here, show them the ocean. They hadn't seen it yet. He had only seen it one other time himself.

On their rugby trip they had come down here in the dark, half a dozen of them, seriously pissed, and had chased about naked on the soft sand after midnight, skylarking, taking flying tackles at each other, wrestling, kicking up light in gritty showers, then stood awestruck down at the edge, watching a huge surf rise up like a wall, and roar and crash against the stars.

He glanced sideways now to see what Harry was making of it, this immense wonder that at every moment surrounded them.

"That's South America out there," Harry informed him. "Peru."

As if, by narrowing your eyes and getting the focus right, you might actually see it.

Andy narrowed his eyes. What his quickened senses caught out there was the outstretched figure of a long-bodied woman under a sheet, thin as a veil, slowly turning in her sleep.

. . .

THE FUNERAL was a quiet affair, with everyone more respectable-looking than Andy had expected, though the fellow who gave the service, which wasn't really a service—no prayers or hymns—was jollier than is normal on such occasions. He talked of Debbie's life and how full it had been. How full of life *she* had been, and how they all liked her and what a good time they'd had together.

He did not refer to the fact that she was actually here, screwed down now inside the coffin they'd carried in.

Andy himself was acutely aware of that. It made him uncomfortably hot. He pushed a finger into his collar and eased it a bit, but felt the blood swelling in the veins of his neck.

It was the bulk of his own body he felt crammed into a coffin. How close the lid would be over his head. And how dark it must be in there when the chapel all around was so full of sunlight and the pleasantness of women in short-sleeved frocks, and a humming from the garden walks outside, of bees. The big-boned woman he'd spent a night drinking vodka with seemed very close: the heaviness of her crossed legs in the expensive-looking shoes, and her determination, which he had missed at the time but saw clearly now, to outdrink him. He wondered what shoes she was wearing in there. Then wondered, again, what Harry was thinking.

Harry looked very dignified in his suit and tie. Andy had last seen him in it at Dorothy's funeral, a very different affair from this. It was hard to tell from the straightness of him, and the line of his jaw, what he might be feeling. Andy looked more than once and could not tell.

It's his daughter, he thought. He's the father. Someone ought to have mentioned that.

But there was no talk of Debbie's family at all. Didn't they have families, these people? Or was it that they thought of *themselves* as a family? He couldn't work it out, their ties to one another—wives and husbands, mothers and fathers.

Still, it went well. People listened quietly. One or two of the women cried. People laughed, a bit too heartily he thought, at the speaker's jokes. They were private jokes that Andy did not catch, and he wondered what Harry thought of *that*. A couple of poems were read, by an older fellow with a ponytail who seemed to be drunk and swallowed all his words. When the curtains parted and the coffin tilted and began to slide away, there was music.

At least that part was like a funeral. Except that the music was another fellow singing to a guitar: Dylan's "Sad-eyed Lady of the Lowlands." Andy cast a glance at Harry and laid his hand for a moment on the soft pad of his father-in-law's shoulder, but Harry gave no sign.

THEY DROVE for nearly half an hour to the wake, through heavy traffic, the city dim with smoke but the various bits of water they crossed or saw in the distance—the Harbour—brightly glinting. They stopped at a phone box and he called Helen, who was full of questions he found it hard to answer. He had really called—the idea occurred to him towards the end of the service—so that Harry could speak to her.

When Harry took the phone he walked away from the box and stood on the pavement in the sun, and only once looked back to see how things were going.

It was hot in the sun. Too hot for a suit. He was sweating under the arms and in the small of his back. Most of the passers-by wore jeans and T-shirts. It was a run-down neighbourhood of old factory buildings, with a view of wharves stacked with containers, and on the dirty waters of the bay a busy movement of ships.

He took his jacket off, hooking his finger into the collar and letting it trail over his shoulder.

He felt easier back in his own loose body, though he continued to sweat. He rolled his shirtsleeves, but only halfway.

At last Harry appeared. He pursed his lips and nodded, which Andy took as an indication that the talk with Helen had gone well. Well, that was something. When they got back into the car he remained silent, but his silence, Andy thought, was of a different kind. More relaxed. Something had broken.

When they got to the house and found a parking place, Harry, who had not removed his jacket, stood waiting for Andy to resume his. Which he did, out of respect. For Harry. For the fact that Harry thought it was the right thing to do.

The front door of the house was open and a crush of people, all with drinks in hand, spilled out on to the narrow veranda of the one-storeyed house and down on to the footpath. They pushed through, conspicuous, Andy thought, in their suits. People looked and raised an eyebrow. Maybe they think we're cops, Andy thought. It made him smile.

The hallway, which ran right through to the back door, was crowded. It was noisy in the small rooms with their tongue-and-groove walls, so noisy you could barely hear yourself speak. Music. Voices.

"Debbie's brother-in-law," he shouted to a fellow who gave him a beer, and offered the man his hand. The man took it but looked surprised.

"Debbie's father," he explained when, with just a glance, the fellow looked to where Harry was standing, towering in fact, in his pinstriped double-breasted suit, against the wall.

The fellow was fifty or so, in a black skivvy, and bearded, with a chain and a big clanking medal round his neck.

"Well, cheers," he said, looking uncertain.

"Cheers," Andy replied, raising the can.

He took a good long swig of the beer, which was very cold and immediately did something to restore him—his confidence, his interest. He looked around, still feeling that he stuck out here like a sore thumb; so did Harry. But that was to be expected.

This was *it*. Elsewhere. He was in the middle of it.

But he wished Harry would relax a bit. Trouble was, he didn't know what to do or say that would help. He had to tell himself again that Harry was a man standing in the hallway of a house full of people shouting at one another over a continuous din of party music, at his daughter's wake. He felt protective of Harry, most of all of Harry's feelings, but he also wanted to range out. All this represented a set of possibilities that might not come his way again. His own impatience, the itch he felt to move away, be on his own, see for himself what was going on here, seemed like a betrayal.

"Listen," he said to a woman who was pushing past with two cans of beer in her hand and a fag hanging from the corner of her mouth. "Where can I get a drink for my mate?" He jerked his head in Harry's direction. "He's Debbie's father," he told her, lowering his voice.

The woman looked. "Agh!" she said. "Here, take one a' these." Then, with lowered voice and a stricken glance in Harry's direction, "I didn't know that was Debbie's father."

"It is," he told her. "I'm her brother-in-law."

He took the beer, thanked her, then carried it over to Harry. They stood together, side by side in the hallway, and drank.

"Thanks, mate," Harry told him.

ANDY STOOD, taking in the changing scene. People pushing past to the front door and the veranda. Pausing to greet others. Joking, laughing. More guests kept arriving, some with crates of beer. He still hadn't said more than a word or two to anyone else, but felt a rising excitement. He would move out and get into it in a minute. He was very willing to be sociable. It was just a matter, among these people, of how to make a start.

He was curious, considering the mixture, about who they were, how they were related to Debbie and came to be here, and increasingly confident, looking around, of what he himself might have to offer. He caught that from the eye of some of the girls— the women—who went by. Things were developing.

He had another beer, then another, lost track of Harry, got involved with one group, then a second—but only at the edge. Just listening.

He drifted out to the kitchen, where people were seated around a scrubbed-pine table stacked with empties and strewn with scraps. Others leaned against the fridge and the old-fashioned porcelain sink. He leaned too.

No one paid any attention to him, though they weren't hostile. They just went on arguing.

Politics. Though it wasn't really an argument either, since they all agreed.

He stepped past them to a little back porch with three steps down to a sloping yard, grassy, the edges of it, near the fence, thick with sword fern in healthy clumps. It was getting dark.

There was a big camphor laurel tree, huge really, and a Hill's Hoist turning slowly in the breeze that he felt, just faintly, on his brow, and clothes pegged out to dry that no one had bothered to bring in. They were hung out just anyhow. Not the way a woman would do it.

He watched them for a while: the shirts white in the growing darkness, filling with air a moment, then collapsing; the tree, also stirring, filling with air and all its crowded gathering of leaves responding, shivering. He too felt something. Something familiar and near.

He thought of Helen. Of the girls. He did not want the feeling of sadness that came to him, which had been there all day, he felt, under the throb of expectation, and which declared itself now in the way these clothes had been hung out, the tea towels all crooked, the shirts pegged awkwardly at the shoulder so that the sleeves hung empty and slack.

Back in the hallway he got talking to a very young woman in a miniskirt, hot pink, with a tight-fitting hot-pink top and a glossy bag over her shoulder, and glossy cork-heeled sandals, her toenails painted the same hot pink as her lips and clothes. He hadn't seen her at the funeral. She had just arrived. He introduced himself. "I'm Debbie's brother-in-law," he told her, but without making it sound, he hoped, like a claim.

The girl took a sip from her glass and looked up at him, all eyelashes. "Who's Debbie?" she asked, genuinely stumped.

He opened his mouth but felt it would be foolish to explain. Still, he was shocked.

A little later he found himself engaged with another woman, older and very drunk, who in just minutes began pushing herself against him. He was a bit drunk himself at this stage. Not very drunk, but enough to go where his senses took him. He stood with his back against a wall of the crowded hallway and the woman pushed her knee between his thighs in the thick woollen suit and her tongue into his mouth. Her fingers were in his hair. He was sweating.

She undid a button on his shirt, put her nose in. "Ummm," she murmured, "*au naturel,* I like it. Where have they been keeping *you?*" When they broke briefly to catch their breath he glanced around in case Harry was close by.

All this now was what he had expected or hoped for, but he was surprised how little of the initiative was his. Somewhere in the back of his head, as the woman urged her tongue into it and her hand went exploring below, he was repeating to himself: "I'm Debbie's brother-in-law. She's dead, this is her wake." Since he had arrived in this house he was the only one, so far as he knew, who'd volunteered her name.

Things were going fast down in his pants, the woman luxuriously leading. He liked it that for once someone else was making the moves. A small noise struggled in his throat. No one around seemed to care, or even to have noticed. He wondered how far all this was to go, and saw that he could simply go with it. He was pleased, in a quiet, self-congratulatory way, that this was how he was taking it.

The woman drew her head back, looked at him quizzically, and smiled. "Umm," she said, "nice. I'll be back." Then, fixing her hair with a deft hand, she disengaged; gently, as he thought of it, set him down. He was left red-faced and bothered, fiercely sweating.

He dealt with his own hair, a few flat-handed slaps, discreetly adjusted things below. He felt like a kid. What was he supposed to do now? Wait for her to come back? Follow? He leaned against the wall and stared at the plaster ceiling. His head was reeling. He decided to stumble after her, but she was gone in the crowd and instead he found Harry, squatting on a low three-legged stool that was too small for him, his thumb in a book.

"Harry?"

Harry glanced up over the big horn-rimmed glasses he used for reading. He looked like a professor, Andy thought with amusement, but could not fathom his expression. Harry handed him the book.

It was a poetry book. There were more, exactly like the one he was holding, on the shelf at Harry's elbow, with the gap between them where he had pulled this one out. Andy shifted his shoulders, rubbed the end of his nose, consulted Harry. Who nodded.

Andy rubbed his nose again and opened the book, turning one page, then the next. *To Debbie,* he read on a page all to itself. All through, he could see, her name was scattered. Debbie. Sometimes Deb.

He was puzzled. Impressed. The book looked substantial but he had no way of judging how important or serious such a thing might be, or whether Harry, in showing it to him, had meant him to see in it a justification or an affront. It was about things that were private, that's what he saw. But here they were in a book that just anyone could pick up.

He turned more pages, mostly so as not to face Harry. Odd words jumped out at him. "Witchery" was one—he hoped Harry hadn't seen that one. In another place, "cunt." Right there on the page. So unexpected it made his stomach jump. In a book of poetry! He didn't understand that. Or any of this. He snapped the book shut, and moved to restore it to the shelf, but Harry reached out and took it from him.

Andy frowned, uncertain where Harry's mind was moving.

Using both hands, Harry eased himself upright, slipped his glasses into one pocket of his jacket, forced the book into another, and turned down the hallway towards the front door.

Andy followed.

So it was over, they were leaving. It struck Andy that he had never discovered whose house this was.

"You need to say goodbye to anyone?" he asked Harry.

"Never bloody met anyone," Harry told him.

Outside it was night-time, blue and cool. Some people on the steps got up to let them through. One of them said, "Oh, you're leaving," and another, "Goodbye"—strangers, incurious about who they might be but with that much in them of politeness or affability.

They found the car, and Andy took his jacket off and tossed it into the back seat. Harry retained his.

They drove across bridges, through night traffic now. Past water riddled with red and green neon, and high tower blocks where all the fluorescent panels in the ceilings of empty offices were brightly pulsing.

After a bit, Harry asked out of nowhere, "What's a muse? Do you know what it means? A muse?"

"Amuse?" Andy asked in turn. "Like when you're amused?" He didn't get it.

"No. A — muse. M-U-S-E."

Andy shook his head.

"Don't worry," Harry told him. "I'll ask Macca. He'll know."

Andy felt slighted, but Harry was right, Macca would know. Macca was a workmate of theirs, a reader. If anyone knew, Macca would. But the book in Harry's pocket was a worry to Andy. He hoped Macca wouldn't uncover *too* much of what was in it. He'd seen enough, himself, to be disturbed by how much that was personal, and which you might want to keep that way, was set down bold as brass for any Tom, Dick, or Harry—ah, Harry—to butt in on. He didn't understand that, and doubted Harry would either.

Suddenly Harry spoke again.

"She was such a bright little thing," he said. "You wouldn't credit."

Andy swallowed. This was *it*. A single bald statement breaking surface out of the stream of thought Harry was adrift in—which was all, Andy thought, he might ever hear. He kept his eyes dead ahead.

What Harry was thinking of, he knew, was how far that bright little thing he had been so fond of, all that time ago, had moved away from him, how far he had lost track of her.

He had his own bright little girl, Janine. She was ten. He felt sweetly bound to her—painfully bound, he felt now, in the prospect of inevitable loss. She too would go off, go elsewhere.

At the time Harry was recalling, Andy thought, he would have been a young man, the same age I am now. He had never thought of Harry as young. There was a lot he had not thought of.

He glanced at Harry. Nothing more would be said. Those last few words had risen up out of a swell of feeling, unbearable perhaps, that Harry was still caught up in, but when Andy looked again—the look could only be brief—he got no clue.

A wave of sadness struck him. Not only for Harry's isolation but for his own. He was fond of Harry, but they might as well have been on different planets.

"Have a bit of a nap if you like," he told Harry gently. "You must be buggered. I'll be right." What he meant, though Harry would not take it that way, was that he wanted to be alone.

In just minutes Harry had sunk down in the seat, letting the seat belt take his weight, and had followed his thoughts deeper, then deeper again, into sleep. Andy focused on the road ahead, his hands resting lightly on the wheel. Free now to follow his own thoughts. Not thinking exactly. Letting the thoughts rise up and flow into him. Flow through him.

Something had come to him back there and changed things. When? he wondered. In the noisy hallway? Where in a world that was so far outside his experience, and among people whose lives were so different from his own, he'd given himself over to what might come? No, he'd been fooling himself, and he blushed now, though no one but himself would ever know about it. Earlier than that.

His body, which knew better than his slow mind, set him back in the bluish dusk of that back porch.

For a moment there he had been out of things, looking down from high up into a quiet backyard. A camphor laurel tree, its swarming leaves lifted by a quickening of the air. The same breeze touching shirts pegged awkwardly on a line, filling them with breath. Then like fingers in his hair. It was something in those particular objects that had struck him. Something he felt, almost grasped, that was near and familiar.

Or it was a way of looking at things that was in himself. That *was* himself. A lonely thought, this—the beginning, perhaps, of another kind of loss, though his own healthy resilience told him it need not be.

He drove. The road was straight now, a double highway running fast through blue night scrub. Under banks of smoky cloud a rounded moon bounced along treetops. He put on speed and felt released. Not from his body—he was more aware than ever of that, of its blockiness and persistence—but from the earth's pull upon it. As if, seated here in this metal capsule, knees flexed, spine propped against tilted leather, it was the far high universe they were sailing through, and those lights off to the side of the ribboning highway—small townships settled down to the night's TV, roadside service stations all lit up in the dark, with their aisles of chocolate biscuits and potato crisps—were far-flung constellations, and Harry, afloat now in the vast realm of sleep, and he, in a lapse of consciousness of a different kind, had taken off, and weightless as in space or in flying dreams, were flying.

Mrs. Porter and the Rock

THE ROCK is Ayers Rock, Uluru. Mrs. Porter's son, Donald, has brought her out to look at it. They are at breakfast, on the second day of a three-day tour, in the Desert Rose Room of the Yullara Sheraton. Mrs. Porter, sucking voluptuously, is on her third cigarette, while Donald, a born letter writer who will happily spend half an hour shaping and reshaping a description in his head, or putting a dazzling sheen on an ironical observation, is engaged on one of the airy rockets, all fizz and sparkle and recondite allusions, that he can barely wait, once he is out of town, to launch in the direction of his more discerning friends. In a large, loose, schoolboyish hand, on the Sheraton's rich notepaper, he writes:

To complete the scene, only the sacred river is missing, for this resort is surely inspired by the great tent city of Kubla Khan. Nestling among spinifex dunes, it rises, like a late vision of the impossible East, out of the rust-red sands, a postmodern Bedouin encampment, all pink and apricot turrets and slender aluminium poles that hum and twang as they prick the skyline. Over the walkways and public spaces hover huge, shadow-making sails that are meant to evoke, in those of us for whom deserts create a sense of spiritual unease, the ocean we left two thousand miles back.

So there you have it. The pitched tents of the modern nomads. That tribe of the internationally restless who have come on here from the Holy Land, or from Taos or Porto Cervo or Nepal, to stare for a bit on an imaginable wonder—when, that is, they can lift their eyes from the spa pool, or in pauses between the Tasmanian Salmon and the Crème Brûlée...

Mrs. Porter is here on sufferance, accepting, with minimal grace, what Donald had intended as a treat. Frankly she'd rather be at Jupiter's playing the pokies. She takes a good drag on her cigarette, looks up from the plate—as yet untouched—of scrambled egg, baked beans, and golden croquettes, and is astonished to find herself confronting, high up on the translucent canopy of the dining-room ceiling, a pair of colossal feet. The fat soles are sloshing about up there in ripples of light. Unnaturally magnified, and with the glare beyond them, diffuse, almost blinding, of the Central Australian sun. She gives a small cry and ducks. And Donald, who keeps a keen eye on her and is responsive to all her jerks and twitches, observing the movement but not for the moment its cause, demands, "What? What's the matter? What is it?"

Mrs. Porter shakes her head. He frowns, subjects her to worried scrutiny—one of his what's-she-up-to-now looks. She keeps her head down. After a moment, with another wary glance in her direction, he goes back to his letter.

Mrs. Porter throws a swift glance upwards.

Mmm, the feet are still there. Beyond them, distorted by fans of watery light, is the outline of a body, almost transparent—shoulders, a gigantic trunk. Black. This one is black. An enormous *black* man is up there wielding a length of hose, and the water is red. The big feet are bleeding. Well, that's a new one.

Mrs. Porter nibbles at her toast. She needs to think about this. Between bites she takes long, sweet drags on her cigarette. If she ignores this latest apparition, she thinks, maybe it will go away.

Lately—well, for quite a while now—she's been getting these visitations—apparitions is how she thinks of them, though they appear at such odd times, and in such unexpected guises, that she wonders if they aren't in fact *re*visitations that she herself has called up out of bits and pieces of her past, her now scattered and inconsiderate memory.

In the beginning she thought they might be messengers—well, to put it more plainly, angels. But their only message seemed to be one she already knew: that the world she found herself in these days was a stranger place than she'd bargained for, and getting stranger.

She had wondered as well—but this was only at the start—if they might be tormentors, visitors from places she'd never been, like Antarctica, bringing with them a breath of icebergs. But that, she'd decided pretty smartly, was foolish. Dulcie, she told herself, you're being a fool! She wasn't the sort of person that anyone out there would want to torment. All *her* apparitions did was make themselves visible, hang around for a bit, disturbing the afternoon or whatever with a sudden chill, and drift off.

Ghosts might have been a more common word for them—she believes in ghosts. But if that's what they are, they're the ghosts of people she's never met. And surely, if they were ghosts, her husband, Leonard, would be one of them.

Unless he has decided for some reason to give her a miss.

She finds this possibility distressing. She doesn't particularly want to see Leonard, but the thought that he could appear to her if he wanted and has chosen not to puts a clamp on her heart, makes her go damp and miserable.

All this is a puzzle and she would like to ask someone about it, get a few answers, but is afraid of what she might hear. In the meantime she turns her attention to Donald. Let the feet go their own way. Let them just go!

Donald looks sweet when he is writing. He sits with one shoulder dipped and his arm circling the page, for ever worried, like a child, that someone might be looking over his shoulder and trying to copy. His tongue is at the corner of his mouth. Like a sweet-natured forty-three-year-old, very earnest and absorbed, practising pot-hooks.

Poor Donald, she thinks. He has spent his whole life waiting for her to become a mother of another sort. The sort who'll take an interest. Well, she *is* interested. She's interested, right now, in those feet! But what Donald means is interested in what interests him, and she can't for the life of her see what all this stuff *is* that he gets so excited about, and Donald, for all his cleverness, can't tell her. When she asks, he gets angry. The questions she comes up with are just the ones, it seems, that Donald cannot answer. They're too simple. He loses his cool—that's what people say these days—but all that does is make him feel bad, and the next moment he is coming after her with hugs, and little offerings out of the *Herald* that she could perfectly well read for herself, or out of books! Because she's made him feel guilty.

This capacity she appears to possess for making grown men feel guilty—she had the same effect on Donald's father—surprises her. Guilt is not one of the things she herself suffers from.

Duty. Responsibility. Guilt. Leonard was very strong on all three. So is Donald. He is very like his father in all sorts of ways, though not physically—Leonard was a very *thin* man.

Leonard too would have liked her to take an interest. Only Leonard was kinder, more understanding—she had almost said forgiving. It wasn't her fault that she'd left school at thirteen— loads of girls did in those days, and clever men married them just the same. Leonard was careful always not to let her see that in this way she had failed him; that in the part of his nature that looked out into the world and was baffled, or which brought him moments of almost boyish elation, she could not join him, he was alone.

She was sorry for that, but she didn't feel guilty. People are what they are. Leonard knew that as well as she did.

Donald's generation, she has decided, are less willing to make allowances. Less indulgent. Or maybe that is just Donald. Even as a tiny tot he was always imposing what he felt on others. His need to "share," as he calls it, does have its nice side, she knows that. But it is very consuming. "Look at this, Mum," he would shout, his whole tiny body in a fury. "You're not *looking*! *Look!*"

In those days it would be a caterpillar, some nasty black thing. An armoured black dragon that she thought of as Japanese-looking and found particularly repulsive. Or a picture of an air battle, all dotted lines that were supposed to be machine-gun bullets, and jagged flame. Later it was books—Proust. She'd had a whole year of that one, that *Proust.* Now it was this Rock.

High maintenance, that's what they called it these days. She got that from her neighbour, Tess Hyland. Donald was high maintenance.

"What's up?" he asks now, seeing her dip her shoulder again and flinch. "What's the matter?"

"Nothing's the matter," she snaps back. "What's the matter yourself?"

She has discovered that the best way of dealing with Donald's questions is to return them. Backhand. As a girl she was quite a decent tennis player.

She continues to crouch. There is plenty of space up there under the cantilevered ceiling, no shortage of space; but the fact that twenty feet over your head the splayed toes of some giant black acrobat are sloshing about in blood is not an easy thing to ignore, especially at breakfast. She is reminded of the roofs of some of the cathedrals they'd seen—with Leonard it was cathedrals. They visited seven of them once, seven in a row. But over there the angels existed mostly from the waist up. You were supposed to ignore what existed below. They hung out over the damp aisles blowing trumpets or shaking tambourines. Here, it seems, you did get the lower parts and they were armed with hosepipes. Well, that was logical enough. They were in the southern hemisphere.

Donald is eyeing her again, though he is pretending not to. They are all at it these days—Donald, Douglas, Shirley. She has become an object of interest. She knows why. They're on the lookout for some sign that she is losing her marbles.

"Why aren't you eating your breakfast?" Donald demands.

"I am," she tells him.

As if in retaliation for all those years when she forced one thing or another into their reluctant mouths—gooey eggs, strips of limp bread and butter, mashed banana, cod-liver oil—they have begun, this last year, to torment her with her unwillingness to do more than pick about at her food. When Donald says, "Come on now, just one more mouthful," he is reproducing, whether he knows it or not, exactly the coax and whine of her own voice from forty years ago, and so accurately that, with a sickening rush, as if she had missed a step and fallen through four decades, she finds herself back in the dingy, cockroach-infested maisonette at West End that was all Leonard was able to find for them in the shortage after the war. The linoleum! Except in the corners and under the immoveable sideboard, roses worn to a dishwater brown. A gas heater in the bathroom that when she shut her eyes and put a match to it went off like a bunger and threatened to blast her eyebrows off. Donald in his high chair chucking crusts all over the floor, and Douglas hauling himself up to the open piano, preparing to thump. To get away from that vision she's willing even to face the feet.

She glances upwards—ah, they're gone!—then away to where an oversized ranger in a khaki uniform and wide-brimmed Akubra is examining the leaves of a rainforest shrub that goes all the way to the ceiling. For all the world as if he was out in the open somewhere and had just climbed out of a ute or off a horse.

"You shouldn't have taken all that," Donald is saying—she knows this one too—"if all you're going to do is let it sit on your plate."

Dear me, she thinks, is he going to go through the whole routine? The poor little children in England? What a pain I must have been!

In fact, she doesn't intend to eat any of this stuff. Breakfast is just an excuse, so far as she is concerned, for a cigarette.

But the buffet table here is a feature. Donald leads her to it each morning as if it was an altar. Leonard too had a weakness for altars.

This one is garishly and unseasonably festive.

A big blue Japanese pumpkin is surrounded by several smaller ones, bright orange, with shells like fine bone china and pimpled.

There are wheatsheaves, loaves of rye and five-grain bread, spilled walnuts, almonds, a couple of hibiscus flowers. It's hard to know what is for decoration and what is to eat.

And the effect, whatever was intended, has been ruined because some joker has, without ceremony, *unceremoniously,* plonked his saddle down right in the middle of it. Its straps all scuffed at the edges, and with worn and frayed stitching, its seat discoloured with sweat, this saddle has simply been plonked down and left among the cereal jars, the plates of cheese, sliced ham and smoked salmon, the bowls of stewed prunes, tinned apricots, orange quarters, crystallised pears . . .

But food is of no interest to her. She has helped herself so generously to the hot buffet not because she is hungry and intends to eat any of this stuff but so she'll have something to look at. Something other than *it*.

It is everywhere. The whole place has been designed so that whichever way you turn, it's there, displaying itself on the horizon. Sitting out there like a great slab of purple-brown liver going off in the sun. No, not liver, something else, she can't think quite what.

And then she can. Suddenly she can. That's why she has been so unwilling to look at it!

She is seven, maybe eight years old. Along with her friends of that time, Isobel and Betty Olds, she is squatting on her heels on the beach at Etty Bay in front of their discovery, a humpbacked sea creature bigger than any fish they have ever seen, which has been washed up on this familiar bit of beach and is lying stranded on the silvery wet sand. Its one visible eye, as yet unclouded, which is blue like a far-off moon, is open to the sky. It is alive and breathing. You can see the opening and closing of its gills.

The sea often tosses up flotsam of one kind or another. Big green-glass balls netted with rope. Toadfish that when you roll them with a big toe puff up and puff up till you think they'd burst. But nothing as big and sad-looking as this. You can imagine putting your arms around it like a person. Like a person that has maybe been *turned* into a fish by a witch's curse and is unable to tell you that once, not so long ago, it was a princess. It breathes and is silent. Cut off in a silence that makes you aware suddenly of your own breathing, while the gulls rise shrieking overhead.

They have the beach to themselves. They sit there watching while the tide goes out. No longer swirling and trying to catch your feet, it goes far out, leaving the sand polished like a mirror to a silvery gleam in which the light comes and goes in flashes and the colours of the late-afternoon sky are gaudily reflected.

And slowly, as they watch, the creature begins to change—the blue-black back, the golden belly. The big fish begins to throw off colours in electric flashes. Mauve, pink, a yellowish pale green, they have never seen anything like it. Slow fireworks. As if, out of its element, in a world where it had no other means of expression, the big fish was trying to reveal to them some vision of what it was and where it had come from, a lost secret they were meant to remember and pass on. Well, maybe the others had grasped it. All she had done was gape and feel the slow wonder spread through her.

So they had squatted there, all three, and watched the big fish slowly die.

It was a dolphinfish, a dorado, and it had been dying. That's what she knew now. The show had been its last. That's why she didn't want to look at this Rock. Just as she wouldn't want to look at the dolphinfish either if it was lying out there now. No matter what sort of performance it put on.

She finds herself fidgeting. She stubs out the last of her cigarette, takes up a fork.

"My mother," Donald writes to his friend Sherman, offering yet another glimpse of a character who never fails to amuse, *"has for some reason taken against the scenery. Can you imagine? In fact it's what she's been doing all her life. If she can't accommodate a thing, it isn't there. Grand as it is, not even Ayers Rock stands a chance against her magnificent indifference. She simply chain-smokes and looks the other way. I begin to get an idea, after all these years, of how poor old Leonard must have felt.*

"The hotel, on the other hand, has her completely absorbed. She devotes whole mealtimes to the perusal of the menu.

"Not that she deigns to taste more than a bite or two. But she does like to know what is there for the choosing."

He pauses and looks up, feeling a twinge at having yet again offered her up as a figure of fun, this woman who has never ceased to puzzle and thwart him but who still commands the largest part of his heart. He knows this is odd. He covers himself by making her appear to his friends as a burden he has taken on that cannot, in all honour, be thrown off; an endless source, in the meantime, of amusing stories and flat-footed comments and attitudes.

"What would Dulcie think of it?" his friends Sherman and Jack Anderson say, and try, amid shouts of laughter, to reproduce one of her dead ordinary ways of looking at things, without ever quite catching her tone.

She eludes them—"One for you, Dulcie," Donald tells himself—as she has for so long eluded him.

He watches her now, fork in hand, pushing baked beans about, piling them into modest heaps, then rearranging them in steep hills and ridges, then using the prongs of the fork to redistribute them in lines and circles, and finds himself thinking of the view from the plane window as they flew in from Alice: a panorama of scorched, reddish rock that must have been created, he thinks, in a spirit of wilfulness very like his mother's as she goes now at the beans.

He smiles. The idea amuses him. His mother as demiurge.

He continues to watch, allowing the image to undergo in his head the quiet miracle of transformation, then once more begins to write.

MRS. PORTER sits in the tourist bus and smokes. Smoking isn't allowed of course, but there is nobody about. She has the bus to herself. She has no qualms about the breaking of rules.

The bus is parked in the shade but is not cool. Heated air pours in at the open window, bearing flies. She is using the smoke to keep them off. Outside, the earth bakes.

To her left, country that is flat. Orange-red with clumps of grey-green spiky bushes. *It,* the Rock, is a little way off to her right. She does not look.

People, among them Donald, are hauling themselves up it in relays; dark lines of them against the Rock's glowing red. Occasionally there is a flash as the sun bounces off a watch or a belt buckle, or a camera round someone's neck. Madness, she thinks. Why would anyone want to do it? But she knows the answer to that one. Because it's *there.*

Except that for most of the time, it hadn't been—not in her

book. And what's more, she hadn't missed it, so there! When they drew maps at school they hadn't even bothered to put it in! She had got through life—dawdling her way past picket fences, barefoot, in a faded frock, pulling cosmos or daisies through the gaps to make bouquets, parsing sentences, getting her teeth drilled, going back and forth to the dairy on Saturday mornings for jugs of cream—with no awareness whatsoever that this great lump of a thing was sitting out here in the middle of nowhere and was considered sacred.

She resents the suggestion, transmitted to her via Donald, that she had been missing out on something, some other—dimension. How many dimensions are there? And how many could a body actually cope with and still get the washing on the line and tea on the table?

That's the trouble with young people. They think everything outside their own lives is lacking in something. Some dimension. How would they know, unless they were mind-readers or you told them (and then you'd have to find the words, and they'd have to *listen*), what it felt like—that little honey-sack at the end of a plumbago when it suddenly burst on your tongue, or the roughness of Dezzy McGee's big toe when he rubbed it once on her belly while she was sunbaking at the Townsville Baths. "Waddabout a root, Dulce?" That's what he had whispered.

She laughs, then looks about to see if anyone has heard, then laughs again. Eleven she was, and Dezzy must have been twelve. Blond and buck-toothed, the baker's boy.

All that seems closer now than this Rock ever was. Closer than last week.

Plus a butcher-bird her uncle Clary owned that was called Tom Leach after a mate he'd lost in France. Which was where—a good deal later of course—she lost Leonard. It could whistle like a champ. And a little stage set, no bigger than a cigar box, that belonged to Beverley Buss's mother, that consisted of a single room with walls that were all mirrors, and little gold tables and chairs, and a boy in silk breeches presenting to a girl in a hooped skirt a perfect silver rose. It played a tune, but the mechanism was broken so she never got to hear it. She had pushed her face so close once, to the tiny open door, that her hot breath fogged up all the mirrors, and Beverley Buss had said, "Look, Dulce, you've made a different weather."

Cancer. Beverley Buss, she'd heard, had died of cancer. Beverley McGowan by then.

She had loved that little theatre, and would, if she could, have willed herself small enough to squeeze right in through the narrow doorway and join that boy and girl in their charmed life that was so different from her own barefooted one—she bet *that* girl didn't have warts on her thumb or get ringworm or nits—but had managed it only once, in a dream, and was so shocked to be confronted with herself over and over again in the seven mirrors, which were only too clear on that occasion, that she burst into tears and had to pinch herself awake not to die of shame in front of such a perfect pair.

So what did this Rock have to do with any of that?

Nothing. How could it? It wasn't on the map. It wasn't even on the *list*—there was a list, and you had to find out where the names belonged and mark them in. Capes, bays, the river systems, even the ones that ran only for a month or two each year. You marked them in with a dotted line. But this Rock that everyone makes such a fuss of now wasn't on the list, let alone the map. So there!

It certainly wasn't on *her* map. Her map, in those days, was five or six cross-streets between their weatherboard, her school, the open-air pictures where coloured people sat on the other side of a latticed partition, and the Townsville Baths. Later, in Brisbane after the war, it was the streets around West End as she dragged Douglas and pushed Donald, up to the shops and then back again in the boiling sun, her route determined by the places where you could get a stroller over the kerb.

Big grasshoppers would be chugging past, and at nesting time you had to watch out for magpies. Nothing to see on the way. A stray dog sniffing then lifting its leg in the weeds round a lamp-post. Roadmen at work round a fenced-off hole. A steamroller laying a carpet of hot tar, and that smell, burning pitch or hellfire, and the fellers in army boots and shorts at work beside it, most of them leaning on shovels or sitting on one heel with a fag hanging from their lip, waiting for the billy to boil over a pile of sticks. The tar smell thinning at last to the peppery scent that came through a paling fence. Dry stalks in a spare allotment.

Sometimes she stopped off to have morning tea with her only friend at that time, a Chinese lady called Mrs. Wau Hing.

Mrs. Wau Hing had a cabinet in her front room made of carved cherrywood, with shelves and brackets and appliquéd ivory flowers, chrysanthemums and little fine-winged hummingbirds. It was beautiful. Though you wouldn't really know what to do with it. Mrs. Wau Hing called it decorative.

Mrs. Wau Hing called *her* Blossom (which was silly really, but she liked it) and gave her chicken in garlicky black sauce to take home, which Leonard said was "different." Too different for her, but never mind, it was the thought.

What pleased her was the fine blue-whiteness of the bowl her friend sent it home in, with its design of pinpricks filled with transparent glaze.

When she went out barefoot in her nightie to get a glass of water at the kitchen sink, there it was, rinsed and shining in the wooden rack along with her own familiar crockery.

So what did the Rock have to do with any of that? Or with the stones she had in her kidneys in 1973?

These days, mind you, it's everywhere. Including on TV. Turns up dripping with tomato sauce as a hamburger, or as a long red-clay mould that starts to heave, then cracks open, and when all the bits fall away there's a flash-looking car inside, a Ford Fairlane—stuff like that. Its red shadow turned into a dingo one night and took that baby.

Suddenly it has plonked itself down in the middle of people's lives like something that has just landed from outer space, or pushed up out of the centre of the earth, and occupies the gap that was filled once by—by what? She can't think. Movie stars? Jesus? The Royal Family? It has opened people's minds—this is Donald again—in the direction of the *incommensurable*. What a mouthful! It is exerting an *influence*. Well, not on her it isn't! She gives it a quick dismissive glance and takes another deep drag on her Winfield.

Cathedrals. With Leonard it was cathedrals. As soon as the war was over and the big liners were on the go again he started planning their trip. They made it at last in 1976.

Cathedrals. Great sooty piles at the end of crooked little streets, more often than not with something missing, like the veterans they made a space for, *mutilés,* on every bus.

Or on islands. Or high up on cliffs. Leonard's eyes went all watery just at the sight of one of them and she felt him move quietly away.

He wasn't religious in a praying way. When Leonard got down on his knees each morning it was to polish his boots—Nugget boot polish was what he believed in. The smell of it hung about in the hallway long after he had taken his briefcase and hat and run off to the tram. But with cathedrals, she'd decided, it was the gloom that got him. Which had been brewing there for centuries, and connected with some part of his nature she recognised, and felt soft towards, but had never felt free to enter. She associated it with the bald patch on top of his head, which you saw, or *she* did, only when he got down on his knees in the hallway on a sheet of newspaper, and held one boot, then the other, very lovingly to his heart, and stroked it till it shone.

She felt such a surge of tenderness for him then. For his reliability, his decency. And for that bald spot, which was the one thing she could see in him that he couldn't, a hidden weakness. That's the sort of thing that got her. But cathedrals, no thanks!

When she did manage to feel something, other than a chill in her bones that was like creeping death, was if the organ happened to be playing, or the sun, which was rare enough, was dropping colours from a stained-glass window on to the stony floor, in a play of pink and gold.

As for the proportions, as Leonard called them, well, she didn't go in for height, she decided; all *that* gave you was a crick in the neck. What she liked was distance. A good long view towards the sunset, or at a certain soft hour at home, towards an empty intersection, and if you got a glimpse of something more it would be the way the hills blurred off into blueness beyond the last of the flashing roofs. You would feel small then, in a way she found comforting.

What really put her off was when Leonard, half lying in one of the pews, with the guide laid open in his lap and his arms extended along the wooden back, rolled his eyes up, like suffering Jesus or one of their Catholic saints. Where, she wondered, had he got *that* from? As far as she knew he was a Methodist.

As they moved on from Cologne to those others—the French ones—she'd taken against the cathedrals, started to really resent them. The way you can resent a teacher (that Miss Bishop in third grade for instance) who has got a set against you and decided you're a dill, or some little miss at the bank.

She had never had to worry, as some do, about other women, but she'd felt then that Leonard was being stolen from her. The moment they pushed through the doors and the cold hit her heart, she felt the change in him. Lying awake at his side in poky rooms, she would stare up at the ceiling and have to prevent herself from reaching out to see if he was still there.

She began to feel a kind of dread. The sight of yet another of those Gothic monsters looming up out of a side street and opening its stone arms to him was more than she could face.

But when it happened it wasn't in a cathedral but in one of the hotels, and for two days afterwards she sat waiting in the room beside their ports, eating nothing, till at last Donald arrived to reclaim her and take his father home.

"It's something you should *see*," Donald had told her, speaking of this Rock.

"Why?"

"Because you should, that's all."

"You mean before I die," she said, and gave a rough laugh.

It's what Leonard had said. "I want to see Cologne Cathedral before I die." But after Cologne he had got in another six.

"Are there any more of these things?" she asked of the Rock. "Or is there just the one?"

Donald gave her a hard look. He wondered sometimes if she wasn't sharper than she let on.

She had come out here to please him. He was easily pleased and she knew that if she didn't he would sulk. It was a break as well from the unit, and from having to show up at Tess Hyland's every afternoon at five thirty—the Happy Hour—and listen to her complaints about the other owners and what the dogs were doing to her philodendrons.

Tess Hyland had been a convent mouse from Rockhampton when, in all the excitement after the war, she was recruited by UNRWA and went to work in the DP camps in Europe, then spent twenty-five years as a secretary at the UN in New York, where she had picked up a style that included daiquiris at five thirty in the afternoon and little bits of this and that on "crackers."

Five thirty, the Happy Hour. Personally it was a time she had always hated, when a good many people might think seriously of cutting their throat.

She would also miss out, just this once, on babysitting her three grandchildren, Les, Brett and Candy, on a Saturday night, and her drive in the back seat of Douglas's Toyota on Sunday afternoon.

They had given her a room out here with an en suite, and the menu, even at breakfast, was "extensive." It was only three nights.

THE FIRST THING she'd done when Donald left her alone in the room was to have a good go-through of the cupboards. She didn't know what she was looking for, but people, she knew, were inclined to leave things, and if there was a dirty sock somewhere, or a suspender belt or a used tissue, she wouldn't feel the place was her own.

The drawers for a start. There were two deep ones under the table where they had put her port, and two more at the end of the long cupboard. When you opened the cupboard a light came on. There was a good six feet of hanging space in there, with a dozen or so good hangers. Real ones, not fixed to the rail so you couldn't walk off with them like the ones in France.

But all that hanging space! All those shelves and drawers! Who had they been expecting? Madame Melba? How many frocks and matinee coats and smart little suits and jackets would you have to have, how many hankies and pairs of stockings and undies, to do justice to the facilities they had provided? She had brought too little. And even that, when she opened her port and looked at it, seemed more than she would need. And why were there two beds? Both *double*.

In the fridge, when she looked, and in the bar recess above, was all you would need to put on a good-sized party: cans of VB, bottles of Carlsberg, Cascade, champagne, wicker baskets packed like a Christmas hamper with Cheezels, crisps, Picnic and Snickers bars and tins of macadamia nuts and cashews.

So what am I in for? she wondered. Who should I be expecting? And what about those double beds?

Casting another panicky glance in the direction of so many tantalising but unwelcome possibilities, she fled to the en suite and snicked the lock on the door.

The whole place gleamed, you couldn't fault them on that. Every steel bar and granite surface gave off a blinding reflection. There was a band of satiny paper across the lid of the lav. You had to break it to use the thing. Like cutting the ribbon on a bridge.

You could crack your skull in here. That's what she thought. Easily. It was so shiny and full of edges. Or fall and break a hip.

She settled on the rim of the bath and considered her predicament. Just stepping into a place like this was a *big risk*.

Suddenly she saw something.

On the floor between the gleaming white lav and the wall was a cockroach, lying on its back with its curled-up legs in the air. It could hardly be the victim of a broken hip, so must have died of something the room had been sprayed with, that was safe for humans—well, it had better be!—but fatal to cockies and such. She got down on her knees and took a good look at it.

Cockroaches, she had heard, were the oldest living creatures on earth. Survivors. Unkillable. Well, obviously you could kill individuals like this one, but not the species. They would outlast anything. Even a nuclear explosion. She sat back on her heels and considered this.

The cockie statistics were impressive, but when it came to survival you couldn't beat people, that was her view. People were amazing. They just went on and on. No matter how poor they were, how pinched and cramped their lives, how much pain they had, or bad luck, or how unjust the world was, or how many times they had been struck down. Look at Mrs. Ormond with her one breast and that husband of hers who was always after the little boys. Look at those fellers in Changi and on the railway—Dezzy McGee had been one of those. Look at that cripple you saw down at the Quay, in a wheelchair with his head lolling and the snot running down into his mouth. Living there—sleeping and all—in a wheelchair, with no other shelter, and young fellers running in off the ferries in relays to wheel him into the Gents and put him on the lavvie and clean him up afterwards at one of the basins. Look at the derros with their yellow beards and bare, blackened feet, shifting about among the suits in Martin Place. They were all up and moving—well, not that one in the wheelchair—pushing on to the next day and the next and the one after, unkillable, in spite of the bombs and the gas chambers, needing only a mouthful of pap to live on, like those Africans on the TV, and the least bit of hope. Hanging on to it. To life and one another.

She took the cockroach very gingerly by one of its brittle legs, used the side of the bathtub to heave herself upright, went through to the bedroom, and tossed it out into a garden bed. Something out there, ants or that, would get a meal off it. Good luck to them!

But when she turned back to the room and saw the wide-open empty cupboard with its blaze of light she regretted it. She could have thrown the cockroach in there. A dead cockroach was all right. It wouldn't have disturbed her sleep. Not like a dirty sock.

She closed the cupboard door and squinnied through a crack to see that the light was off, then sat very quietly on one of the beds. Then, after a moment, shifted to the other.

She was saved by a light knocking at the door. Donald. Afternoon tea. But when she came back the problem was still there. All that cupboard space, the second bed.

She did what she could by distributing her belongings in as many places as possible—one shoe in one drawer, one in another, the same with her undies, her four hankies, and the things from her handbag: lipstick, a little hand mirror, an emery board, half a roll of Quick-Eze, a photograph of Donald and friends from the Arts Ball in Shanghai, another of Les, Brett, and Candy in school uniform. But it looked so inadequate after a moment or two, so hopeless, that she gathered everything up again, put it back into her handbag, then repacked her port and left it to sit there, all locked and buckled, on the rack, as if only her unclaimed luggage had arrived in the room, and she as yet had acquired no responsibilities. Then she stretched out fully clothed on one of the beds and slept.

"What now?"

Donald had lowered the novel he was reading and was watching her, over the top of his glasses, slide down, just an inch at a time, between the arms of the yielding silk-covered lounge chair. They were in one of the hotel's grand reception rooms after dinner.

"What now what?" she demanded.

"What are you doing?"

"Nothing," she told him. "Getting comfortable."

Dim lighting, the lampshades glowing gold. Outside the beginnings of night, blue-luminous. The long room suspended out there in reflection so that the lounge chairs and gold-legged glass-topped tables floated above a carpet of lawn, among shrubs that might simply have sprouted through the floorboards, and they too, she and Donald and some people who were standing in a group behind them, also floating and transparent, in double exposure like ghosts.

Meanwhile, shoes off, stockinged feet extended, slumped sideways in the welcoming softness, she was getting her right hand down between the arm of the chair and the cushion, almost to the elbow now, right down in the crease there, feeling for coins, or a biro or lost earring. You could find all sorts of things in such places if you got deep enough, as she knew from cleaning at home. Not just dustballs.

Once, in a big hotel at Eaglehawk Neck in Tasmania, where she had gone to play in a bridge tournament, Tess Hyland had found a used condom. Really! They must have been doing it right there in the lounge, whoever it was, late at night, in the dark. She hoped her fingers, as they felt about now, didn't come across anything like that! But she was ready—you had to be. For *whatever*.

The tips of her fingers encountered metal. She slipped lower in the chair, settling in a lopsided position, very nearly horizontal, like a drunk, and closed her fist on one, two, three coins, more— and a pen, but only plastic.

"For heaven's sake," Donald exploded.

Maybe she looked as if she was having an attack. She abandoned the pen. With some difficulty she wiggled her fist free and, pushing upright, smoothed her skirt and sat up, very straight now and defiant. Donald, with a puzzled look, went back to his novel but continued to throw her glances.

She snapped her handbag open, met his gaze, and, very adroitly she thought, slipped the coins in. Two one-dollar pieces, a twenty cents, and some fives. Not bad. She estimated there were about thirty such armchairs in the lounge, plus another half-dozen three-seaters. Up to a hundred dollars that would make, lurking about as buried treasure in the near vicinity. Quite a haul if you got in before the staff.

She wondered if she could risk moving to the third of the armchairs round their table, but decided she'd better not. Donald was already on the watch.

What pleased her, amid all these ghostly reflections, was that the coins down there in their hidden places, like the ones she had just slipped into her purse, maybe because they had slipped deep down and smuggled themselves out of sight, had retained their lovely solidity and weight. That was a good trick.

What she had to do was work out how *she* might manage it.

· · ·

MID-MORNING. They were out under the sails beside the pool. Donald was writing again. She wondered sometimes what on earth he found to say. She had been with him all the time they were here. Nothing had *happened*.

On the wide lawn bodies were sunbaking, laid out on folding chairs, white plastic, that could also become beds, their oiled limbs sleek in the sun.

Three Japanese boys who looked like twelve-year-olds, and not at all the sort who would rape nuns, were larking about at the deep end, throwing one another over and over again into the pool. They were doctors, down here, Donald had discovered, to celebrate their graduation.

Four women in bikinis that showed their belly buttons and yellow-tanned bellies—women as old as herself she thought—were at a table together, sipping coloured drinks. They wore sunglasses and a lot of heavy gold, though all one of them had to show was a stack of red, white, and green plastic bangles up her arm. She recognised her as a person she had spoken to once before, maybe yesterday. She was from a place called Spokane. Or was she the one from Tucson, Arizona? Either way, she had found their encounter disturbing.

Spokane! She'd never heard of it. Never even knew it existed. A big place too, over four hundred thousand. All learning to talk and walk and read and getting the papers delivered and feeling one another up in the backs of cars. This woman had lived her whole life there.

What you don't know can't hurt you, her mother used to say. Well, lately she'd begun to have her doubts. There was so much. This Rock, for instance, those people in the *camps*. All the time she had been spooning Farax into Douglas, then Donald, these people in Spokane or Tucson, Arizona, had been going to bed and the others into gas ovens. You couldn't keep up.

"Where is it?" she had asked the woman from Tucson, Arizona, who was perched on the edge of one plastic chair with her foot up on another, painting her toenails an iridescent pink.

The woman paused in her painting. "Well, do you know Phoenix?"

"What?"

"Phoenix," the woman repeated. "Tucson is a two-hour drive from Phoenix. South."

"Oh," she'd said.

So now there was this other place as well. She'd never heard of either one. But then, she thought, these people have probably never heard of Hurstville!

Still, it disturbed her, all these unknown places. Like that second *bed*.

There were six old men in the spa, all in a circle as if they were playing ring-a-ring-a-rosie, their arms extended along the tiled edge, the bluish water hopping about under their chins.

They were baldies most of them, but one had a peak of snow-white hair like a cockatoo and surprisingly black eyebrows, in a face that was long and tanned.

Occasionally one of them would sink, and as he went down his toes would surface. So there was more to them than just the head and shoulders.

These old fellers had not lost their vim. You could see it in their eyes and in the champagne that bubbled up between their legs. The spa was *buzzing*. Most of it was these old guys' voices. It was like a ceremony, that's what she thought.

She shifted her chair to hear them better.

"Tallahassee," she heard. That was a new one! "Jerusalem."

She pretended to be looking for something under her chair, and trying not to let Donald see, jerked it closer to the spa. These old fellers were up to something.

Gnomes, is what she thought of. The gnomes of Zurich. Shoulders, some of them with tufts of white hair, long faces above the boiling surface. Hiding the real source of things, the plumbing. Which was lower down.

She had never fathomed what men were really up to, what they wanted. What it was they were asking for, but never openly, and when they didn't get it, brooded and fretted over and clenched their jaws and inwardly went dark, or clenched their fists and beat one another senseless, or their wives and kiddies, or rolled their eyes up and yearned for in a silence that filled their mouths like tongues.

The pool was whispering again.

"Odessa," she heard. "Schenectady." Then, after a whole lot more she couldn't catch, very clearly, in a voice she recognised over the buzzing of the water, "unceremonious," a word she wouldn't have picked up if she hadn't heard it on a previous occasion.

Unceremonious.

MRS. PORTER stood in the middle of her room and did not know which way to turn. Each time she came back to it, it was like a place she was stepping into for the first time. She recognised nothing.

When something like that happens over and over again it shakes you. As if you'd left no mark.

It wasn't simply that the moment she went out they slipped in and removed all trace of her. It was the room itself. It was so perfect it didn't need you. It certainly didn't need *her*.

She thought of breaking something. But what? A mirror would be bad luck.

She picked up a heavy glass ashtray, considered a moment, then flipped it out the window. Like that cockroach. It disappeared with a clunk into a flower bed.

Well, that was a start. She looked about for something else she could chuck out.

The one thing she couldn't get rid of was that Rock. It sat dead centre there in the window. Just dumped there throbbing in the late sunlight, and so red it hurt her eyes.

To save herself from having to look at it she shut herself in the bathroom. At least you could make an impression on that. You could use the lav or turn the shower on and make the place so steamy all the mirrors fogged up and the walls lost some of their terrible brightness.

The place had its dangers of course, but was safe enough if all you did was lower the toilet lid and sit. Only how long could a body just sit?

Unceremonious.

He had saved that up till the last moment, when he thought she was no longer listening, and had hissed it out, but so softly that if she hadn't had her head down trying to catch his last breath she mightn't have heard it at all.

What a thing to say. What a word to come up with!

She thought she might have got it wrong, but it wasn't a word *she* could have produced, she hardly knew what it meant. So what was it, an accusation? Even now, after so long, it made her furious.

To have *that* thrown at you! In a dingy little room in a place where the words were strange enough anyway, not to speak of the food, and the dim light bulbs, and the wobbly ironwork lift that shook the bones half out of you, and the smell of the bedding.

One of her bitterest memories of that dank little room was of Leonard kneeling on that last morning in front of the grate and putting what must have been the last of his strength into removing the dust of France from the cracks in his boots. His breath rasping with each pass of the cloth. His body leaning into the work as if his blessèd soul depended on the quality of the shine.

And then, just minutes later, that word between them. "Unceremonious."

For heaven's sake, what did they expect? How many meals did you have to dish up? How many sheets did you have to wash and peg out and fold and put away or smooth over and tuck under? How many times did you have to lick your thumb and test the iron? How many times did you have to go fishing with a safety pin in their pyjama bottoms to find a lost cord?

Angrily she ripped a page off the little notepad they provided on the table between the beds and scribbled the word. Let someone else deal with it, spelled out there in her round, state-school hand.

She opened a drawer and dropped it in. *Unceremonious.* Posted it to the dead.

Then quickly, one after another, scribbled more words, till she had a pile of ripped-out pages.

Dimension, she wrote.

Bon Ami.

Flat 2, 19 Hampstead Road, West End, she wrote.

Root, she wrote, and many more words, till she had emptied herself, like a woman who has done all her housework, swept the house, made the beds, got the washing on the line, and, with nothing to do now but wait for the kiddies to come home from school and her husband from work, can afford to have a bit of a lie-down. She posted each page in a different drawer until all the drawers were occupied, then stretched out on one of the beds, the one on the left, and slept. Badly.

Back home in her unit, dust would be gathering, settling grain by grain on all her things: on the top of the television, between the knots of her crocheted doilies, in the hearts of the blood-red artificial roses that filled the glass vase on her bedside table.

On one petal of each rose was a raindrop, as if a few spots of rain had fallen. But when you touched the drop it was hard, like one of those lumps of red-gold resin they used to chew when they were kids, that had bled out of the rough trunk of a gum.

If it was rain that had fallen, even a few spots, her things would be wet and the heart of the rose would have been washed clean. But what she found herself sitting in, in her dream, was a slow fall of dust. Everything, everything, was being covered and choked with it.

Well, it's what they'd always said: dust to dust—only she hadn't believed it. The last word. *Dust.*

It worried her now that when she'd made her list she had left it out, and now it had got into her head she'd never be rid of it. She'd just go on sitting there for ever watching it gather around her. Watching it fall grain by grain over her things, over *her,* like a grainy twilight that was the start of another sort of night, but one that would go on and on and never pass.

The Hoover, she shouted in her sleep. Get the Hoover.

She woke then. On this double bed in a room from which every bit of dust, so far as she could see, had been expunged.

And now, at last, the others arrived.

One of them lay down beside her. She refused to turn and look, and the bed was wide enough for her to ignore him, though at one point he began to whisper. More *words*.

The others, a couple, lay down on the second bed and began to make love, and so as not to see who it was who had come to her own bed, and most of all not to have to listen to his words, she turned towards them and watched. They were shadowy. Maybe black.

She didn't mind them using the bed, they didn't disturb her. Probably had nowhere to go, poor things. And they weren't noisy.

She must have gone back to sleep then, because when she woke again the room seemed lighter, less thick with breath. She was alone.

There was a humming in the room. Low. It made the veins in her forehead throb.

She got up and went, in her stockinged feet, to the window.

It was as if something out there at the end of the night was sending out gonglike vibrations that made the whole room hum and glow. The Rock, darkly veined and shimmering, was sitting like a cloud a hundred feet above the earth. Had simply risen up, ignoring the millions of tons it must weigh, and was stalled there on the horizon like an immense spacecraft, and the light it gave off was a sound with a voice at the centre of it, saying, *Look at this. So, what do you reckon now?*

Mrs. Porter looked at it askance, but she did look. And what she felt was an immediate and unaccountable happiness, as if the Rock's new-found lightness was catching. And she remembered something: a time when Donald had just begun to stand unsteadily on his own plump little legs and had discovered the joy of running away from her towards a flower he had glimpsed in a garden bed, or a puppy dog or his brother's red tricycle. When she called he would give a quick glance over his shoulder and run further. Suddenly unburdened, she had had to hang on to things— the sink, Leonard's Stelzner upright—so as not to go floating clean off the linoleum, as if, after so many months of carrying them, inside her body or on her hip, first the one, then the other, she had forgotten the trick of letting gravity alone hold her down.

Now, looking at the Rock, she felt as if she had let go of something and was free to join it. To go floating. Like a balloon some small child—Donald perhaps—had let go of and which was free to go now wherever the world might take it. She glanced down. She was hovering a foot above the carpet.

So it had happened. She was off.

Immediately she began to worry about Donald. She needed to get word to him.

That did it. She came down with a bump. And with her heart beating fast in the fear that it might already be too late, she made for the door. She needed to reassure him, if he didn't already know, that she hadn't really minded all those times when he'd hung on to her skirt and dragged her off to look at this and that. So full of need and bullying insistence, she saw now, because if she didn't look, and confirm that yes it was amazing, it really was, he couldn't be sure that either he or it was there.

She had gone grudgingly, and looked and pretended. Because she had never given up the hard little knot of selfishness that her mother had warned would one day do her in. Well, her mother was wrong. It had saved her. Without it she would have been no more than a space for others to curl up in for a time then walk away from. All this, in her newfound lightness, she understood at last and wanted to explain to the one person who was left who might understand it and forgive. Still wearing the frock she had lain down in, she flung the door open and, barely hearing the click as it closed behind her, stepped out into the hotel corridor. Only then did she realise that she did not know the number of Donald's room.

"You fool, Dulcie," she told herself. The voice was Leonard's. In these latter years, Leonard's had become the voice she used for speaking to herself. It made her see things more clearly. Though Leonard would never have said to her the sort of things she said to herself. "Stupid *woman*. Bloody old fool."

She walked up and down a little. All the doors looked the same. She put her ear to one, then to another, to see if she could hear

Donald's snoring, but behind their identical doors all the rooms preserved an identical breathless silence.

A little further along, beside the door to a linen closet where she had sometimes seen a trolley stacked with towels and the little coloured bottles and soap packs that went into the various bathrooms, there was a chair. In a state now of angry alarm, she seized occupation of it and sat, commanding the empty corridor. She'd been too quick off the mark. She needed to sit now and have a think.

But the corridor, with its rows of ceiling lights and doors all blindly closed on their separate dreams, gave her the creeps. She felt breathless.

She made for a small flight of stairs at the far end that went down to a door, and when she opened it, and it too clicked shut behind her, found herself outside the building altogether, standing in her stockinged feet on stone flags that were still warm. The warmth came right up through her, and all about were night-flowering shrubs, and bigger trees with boughs that drooped. She took a good breath. The air was heavy with scent—with different scents. Night insects were twittering. All was clear moonlight, as still as still.

She began to walk—how simple things could be!—enjoying her own lightness and wondering if she wasn't still asleep and dreaming. Only in dreams did your body dispose of itself so easily. She walked on springy lawn. But they must have been watering it, because almost immediately her stockings were soaked. She sat down on a low wall and peeled them off, and when she looked back gave a little laugh at the look of them there on the shadowy grass. Like two snakeskins, a couple. That'll make 'em guess!

Soon she was in a car park, empty but flooded with moonlight, then out again into soft sand. Red sand, still with the warmth of the sun in it, but cooler when you worked your naked toes in. Luxurious. She waded to the top of a dune and let herself go, half sliding, half rolling, till she came to a stop and was on level ground again. She righted herself and, seated in warm sand, checked for broken bones. All around her the bushes, which were spiky and had seemed dull by day, were giving off light like slow-burning fireworks. Big clouds rolled across the moon, thin as smoke, then darker. There was a twittering, though she could see no birds. Everywhere, things were happening—that's what she felt. Small things that for a long time now she had failed to notice. To see them you had to get down to where she was now, close to the ground. At kiddie level. Otherwise there were so many other things to demand your attention that you got distracted, you lost the habit of looking, of listening, unless some kiddie down there dragged at your skirt and demanded, "Look, Mum, look."

That twittering for instance. She knew what it was now. Not birds but the Station Master's office at Babinda. It was years, don-key's years, since that particular sound had come to her, yet here it was. Must have been going on all around her for ages, and she was too busy listening to other things to notice.

Babinda.

For a whole year after she was married, with Leonard away in New Guinea, she had been with the Railways, an emergency worker while the boys were at the war. Those were the days! She was off the shelf, so that was settled, and she had no domestic responsibilities. She had never in her life felt so free. She loved the noise and bustle of the Station Master's office when things were on the go; the buzzing and tinkling when the First Division was held up by floods below the Burdekin or when, outside the regular timetable, a Special came through, a troop-transport with all the boys hanging out the windows wolf-whistling and calling across the tracks to where she was walking up and down with a lantern, to ask her name. Then the long sleepy periods when nothing was happening at all and you could get your head into *Photoplay*.

The Station Master, Mr. O'Leary, was a gardener, his platform a tame jungle of staghorns, elkhorns, hoyas, maidenhair ferns in hanging baskets, tree orchids cut straight from the trunk. He was out there in all weathers in his shirtsleeves whispering to his favourites. "Hullo, ducky," he'd be singing, "here's a nice drop of water for you. That's a girl! You'll enjoy this."

She'd pause at her knitting to listen to him. He used the same tone when he was talking to her. It made her feel quite tender towards him. But he was always respectful—she was, after all, a married woman.

Sometimes, in the late afternoon, when everything was at a low point and even the bush sounds had dropped to nothing, he would talk of his son Reggie, the footballer, who had been in her class at primary school and was now a POW in Malaya. Reggie had played the mouth organ, that's what she remembered. A chunk of honeycomb at his lips and his breath swarming in the golden cells, that's what she remembered. *The Flight of the Bumble Bee.*

"It's a blessing his mother's already gone," Mr. O'Leary would tell her softly while the light slanted and turned pink. "At least she's spared the waiting. Once you've got kiddies, Dulce, you're never free, not ever. I spend half my time asking myself what he's getting to eat, he's such a big feller. If he's got a mate an' that. I'm only half here sometimes."

She listened and was sympathetic but did not understand, not really. Douglas and Donald were still way off in the future, waiting there in the shadows beyond the track; they had not yet found her. But she liked listening to Mr. O'Leary. No one had ever thought her worth confiding in, not till this. She felt quite grown up. An independent woman. She was all of twenty-three.

Under the influence of the many unscheduled trains that were running up and down the line, all those lives the war had forced out of their expected course, she was led to wonder what direction she herself might be headed in. Odd, she thought now, that she had never considered her marriage a direction, let alone a terminus. But that was the times, the war. Everything normal was suspended for the duration. Afterwards, anything might be possible.

"You won't find me stickin' round once the war is over."

This was Jim Haddy, the Station Master's Assistant. "No fear! I'll be off like a shot. You watch my dust!"

At sixteen, Jim Haddy was the most amazing boy she'd ever come across. He was so full of things, so dedicated. He thought the Queensland Railways were God and got quite upset if you threw off at them or said things like "You know the theme song of the

Queensland Railways, don't you? 'I Walk Beside You.'" He thought Mr. O'Leary was "slack" because when they went out with their flags and lamps and things to wave a train through, he left the tabs on his waistcoat unfastened. Jim was a stickler. He did not roll his sleeves up on even the muggiest days. Always wore his soft felt railway hat. And his waistcoat, even if it was unbuttoned in front, was always properly buckled at the sides.

He was a soft-faced kid who got overexcited and had, as Mr. O'Leary put it, to be watched. He knew all there was to know about the Royal Houses of Europe, and talked about the Teck Mecklenburgs and the Bourbon Parmas as if they owned cane farms down the road, and Queen Marie of Romania and King Zog as if they were his auntie and uncle. He spent a lot of the Railway's time settling them like starlings in their family trees on sheets of austerity butcher's paper.

"What a funny boy you are," she would tell him dreamily as she leaned over his shoulder to watch.

The summer rain would be sheeting down, a wall of impenetrable light, and when it stopped, the view would be back, so green it hurt your eyes, and the earth in Mr. O'Leary's flower beds would steam and give off smells. The little room where they sat at the end of the platform would be all misty with heat. She'd be thinking: When I get home I'll have to take Leonard's shoes out of the lowboy and brush the mould off. "Where *is* Montenegro?" she'd ask, and Jim was only too happy to tell, though she was none the wiser.

That boy needs watching.

But she had lost sight of him. Like so much else from that time. And from other times. She was surprised now that he had come back, and so clearly that as she leaned over his shoulder she caught the vinegary smell of his neck under the raw haircut.

"What happened to you, Jim Haddy?" she found herself asking in her own voice, her feet in the powdery red soil. "Where are you, I wonder? And where are Queen Marie and King Zog?" She hadn't heard much of them lately either.

"I'm here," she announced, in case Jim was somewhere in the vicinity and listening.

She looked about and saw that she was in the midst of a lot of small grey-green bushes, with daylight coming and no landmarks she could recognise.

"My God," she said to herself, "where? *Where* am I? This isn't my life."

Off in the distance a train was rumbling in over the tracks: a great whooshing sound that grew and grew, and before she knew it passed so close to where she was standing that she was blown clear off her feet in a blaze of dust. It cleared, and she realised that high up in a window of one of the carriages as it went thundering past she had seen her own face, dreaming behind the glass and smiling. Going south. She picked herself up and got going again.

The Rock was there. Looming. Dark against the skyline. She made for that.

The sun was coming up, hot out of the oven, and almost immediately now the earth grew too hot to walk on. The bushes around her went suddenly dry; her mouth parched, she sat down dump. There was no shade. She must have dozed off.

When she looked up again a small boy was squatting in front of her. Not Donald. And not Douglas either. He was about five years old and black. He squatted on his heels. When her eyes clicked open he stared at her for a moment, then took off shouting.

When she opened her eyes again there were others, six or seven of them. Shy but curious, with big eyes. They squatted and stared. When she raised a hand they drew back. Dared one another to come close. Poked. Then giggled and sprang away.

At last one little girl, older than the rest, trotted off and came back with some scraps of bread and a cup full of water. The others looked on while the little girl pushed dry crusts into the open mouth, as if feeding a sick bird, and tipped the cup. The cup was old and crumpled, the child's fingers rather dirty. Oh well, she thought, it's a bit late to be worrying over my peck of dirt.

She swallowed, and the children watched as her old throat dealt with the warmish water, got it down.

She saw that it was a test. To see what she was. Old woman or spirit.

No need to look so puzzled, she told them, though not in so many words. It's just me, Dulcie MacIntyre. It's no use expecting anything more. This is it.

But they continued to watch as if they were not convinced.

She lay like a package while they sat waiting. As if, when the package finally unwrapped itself, it might contain something interesting. Oh well, she thought, they'll find out. If they're disappointed, that's their lookout.

After a while she must have seemed as permanent and familiar to them as any other lump of earth because they got bored, some of them—the littlies—and went back to whatever game they'd been playing when that first one interrupted them, shouting, "Hey, look what I found! Over here!"

But two or three of them stayed. Watching the old lizard turn its head on the wrinkled, outstretched neck. Slowly lifting its gaze. Shifting it north. Then east. The dry mouth open.

They fed her dribbles of water. Went off in relays and brought back armfuls of dry scrub and built a screen to keep the sun off, which was fierce, and moved it as the sun moved so that she was always in shade. She had never in all her life felt so closely attended to, cared for. They continued to sit close beside her and watch. They were waiting for something else now. But what?

"I told you," she said weakly, "it's no good expecting anything more." They had been watching so long, poor things. It was a shame they had to be disappointed.

They must have waited all day, because at last she felt the sun's heat fall from her shoulders, though its light was still full in the face of her watchers. Then a shadow moved over them. The shadow of the Rock. She knew this because they kept lifting their eyes towards it, from her to it then back again. The Rock was changing colour now as the sun sank behind it.

The shadow continued to move, like a giant red scarf that was being drawn over them. The Rock, which had been hoarding the sun's heat all day, was giving it off now in a kindlier form as it turned from orange-red to purple. If she could swing her body around now to face it, to look at it, she might understand something. Might. But then again she might not. Better to take what she could, this gentle heat, and leave the show to these others.

I'm sorry, she chuckled, I can't compete.

She was beginning to rise up now, feeling even what was lightest in her, her thoughts, drop gently away. And the children, poor things, had their eyes fixed in the wrong place. No, she wanted to shout to them. Here I am. Up here.

One of the little ones, sitting there with a look of such intense puzzlement on his face, and baffled expectation, was Donald. I'm sorry, Donald, she said softly. But he too was looking in the wrong place.

THE BIG DOLPHINFISH lay stranded. The smaller waves no longer reached it. There were sandgrits in its eyes, the mouth was open, a pulse throbbed under its gills. It was changing colour like a sunset: electric pink and mauve flashes, blushings of yellow-green.

"What is it?" Betty Olds asked. "What's happening to it?"

"Shush," Isobel told her.

So they sat, all three, and watched. The waves continued to whisper at the edge of the beach. The colours continued to play over the humped back and belly, flushing, changing, until slowly they became less vivid. The pulsing under the gills fluttered, then ceased, and the flesh, slowly as they watched, grew silvery-grey, then leaden.

"What happened?" Betty asked again. "Is it dead now?"

"I think so," Isobel told her. Then, seeing Betty's lip begin to quiver, put her arm around her sister's shoulder and drew her close. "It's all right, Bets," she whispered. "It was old."

Dulcie said nothing. She too was breathless. This was a moment, she knew, that she would never forget. Never. As long as she lived. She also knew, with certainty, that she would live for ever.

The Domestic Cantata

S TARTING BACK before he stumbled, the man groaned, then raised his voice in protest.

"Maggie," he shouted. "Maaggieee!"

The ten-geared blue-and-gold Galaxy had been propped against the panelled wall of the staircase and was sprawled now on its side in the hallway outside his room, like a giant insect that had blundered in and expired there, or a stunned, iridescent angel— one more example of the chaos they lived in, the clutter and carelessness. Nobody in this house, so far as Sam could see, ever rinsed a coffee mug or returned a book to its shelf, or threw out a newspaper, or picked a wet towel up off the sopping bathroom floor. He knew the savagery he was assailed with had nothing to do, specifically, with the bike, but he kicked it just the same, and saw even as he did so what a spectacle he was making of himself. A grown man in the hallway of his own home, putting his boot into a defenceless machine!

Maggie had appeared at the kitchen door.

"Maggie," he moaned, "*look* at this!" His voice had the arch and droop of classic lament. "That boy wants a good hiding. Look at it!" A good hiding was a phrase that Sam McCall was excessively fond of. It belonged to the world of his boyhood—maybe even of his father's boyhood, though the truth was that neither he nor any one of his children had ever had a hand laid on them.

Maggie looked, but not at the bike. Hot blood suffused his brow. There were veins in his neck.

"I'm sorry, love," she said mildly, and came out into the hallway drying her hands on her skirt. "I tell them and they don't listen."

She reached down, hoisted the bike upright, and stood for a moment, bare-armed, poised on her solid legs as if, tempted by its promise of velocity, she might be about to leap into the saddle, sprint down the hallway, over the threshold and away. Instead, she turned the beast into its stall under the stairs.

"There," she said. All was restored, made good again.

Sam watched. Quiet but unappeased.

"Would you like a cup of coffee, pet?"

He shook his head.

She waited. He might be amenable to some other distraction.

"Well," he said in a tone of aggrievement, "I'll get back to it. I came out to make a phone call."

What he meant was that the moment of tender sociability that had drawn him away from his work had been spoiled now and was irretrievable. He turned, went back to his workplace, and a moment later she heard, tentative, in one chord, then another, the notes of the piano.

Redeeming a football boot he'd failed to notice, she set it on the bottom step—she'd carry it up later—and went back to the kitchen, a little song rising in her throat, set off perhaps by a suggestion in one of the chords. She sang three or four bars of it, then returned in silence to the sink, where, in a high, soft head voice, she launched into the rest while she topped and tailed celery sticks and scored a dozen radishes that, when they were plunged into cold water, would open and transform themselves into peppery, pink-and-white roses.

TWELVE YEARS AGO, when they first moved in, this house had seemed perfect.

It was a big Federation house on three levels, with pierced work above the solid doors and in the archway between the ground-floor rooms, leadlight windows that in the early morning threw dancing colours on the walls, and balconies that broke out in unexpected places on a view of palm crowns and glinting water. The children had been more manageable then, and fewer.

These days, everything above the ground floor, which Maggie tried to keep clear, had been abandoned to general mayhem and din. She tolerated this, and only intermittently dealt with it, so long as there was no clattering on the stairs, no shouting in the hallway, and, above all, no argument with the law that "down here," and the garden outside their father's window, was the sacred realm of Silence. Silence, in this house, was a positive not a negative commodity, a breathing space and pause that was essential not only to the production of their father's work but to the work itself, as they knew very well from counting out the fixed measures of it, either in their head or with the muted tapping of a foot, when they played or sang.

But silence, outside music, was hardly absolute.

"What about the birds?" Miranda had demanded once, meaning the bad-tempered Indian mynahs that carried on an incessant warfare around the bottlebrush and pomegranates below their father's window, screaming and driving off the natives.

She kept her voice civil, draining it of any suggestion—she was twelve then—of rebelliousness or irony. Her father already suspected her of the first. He did not consider her old enough, as yet, for the second.

"Nature," he told her, "is different."

Miranda held her tongue but made a face at the twins, who each raised an eyebrow and looked away.

It was Cassie, too young for the codes that were in operation here, who in all innocence had demanded, "But what about us? Aren't *we* nature?"

"Of course you are, darling," Maggie told her. "What Daddy means is, he knows what distracts him. Little people stomping. Shouting in the hallway or on the stairs. You know that."

They all did, and accepted it for the most part without question. However they might whisper among themselves, and complain against their father's moods, his grouchiness, his angry descents and tyrannies, they acknowledged that he was himself a force of nature, a lightning rod for energies, for phenomena that people were impressed by and wrote about in the newspaper in terms that Miranda tended to mock—but only the terms, not the fact. She would read these pieces aloud at the breakfast table, while Sam, his face screwed up with distaste and embarrassment, shook his head—disguising, he hoped, a certain measure of delight—and Maggie said flatly, "Well, I didn't understand a word of that. But what would I know? I only sang the thing."

"Impeccably," Miranda quoted.

Now it was her mother's turn to make a face.

Their father's alternation of moods constituted the weather of their lives, which, like the weather itself, it was useless to quarrel with or resist.

In his phases of exuberant good humour he could be wilder and noisier than any of them. Then there were what their mother called his "dumps," whole days it might be when he was like a ghost at the table and even Cassie could not get a good word out of him, and all you heard at mealtimes, since no one else dared speak either, was the clink of knives and spoons against crockery and the grinding of jaws.

He lived in two worlds, their father—with, so far as they could see, no traffic between them.

When it suited him he was like a boy who had never grown up, full of stories made up on the spot about stones that yodelled and perambulating washing machines that went on trips to Vienna or London and gave performances as Brünnhilde at the Met.

He would settle into a beanbag and watch cartoons with them, utterly absorbed, producing great hoots of laughter at things even they thought silly. Then in the middle of one of his rambling tales, full of grunts, whistles, clicks, and hums, the mood of boisterous hilarity in him would lapse and go underground; he would ease off his lap whichever of the littlies had climbed there and, without a word of explanation, go off. They would wait a moment to see if it was just a call of nature, in which case he would be back. But mostly it wasn't. He had been *struck*. Just like that—*kazoom*, as Tom put it.

You got used to it, of course, but it was disconcerting. Annoying too. *They* couldn't have got away with it.

So however much they stood in awe of whatever force it was that he had given himself up to, they resented it, and took their own form of revenge.

Asked what it was that their father did, Miranda would say blandly, "Oh, he works for the council. He's a sewage inspector." Or as Tom once put it, "He's a burglar."

Intimidated by his father and puzzled by a side of him that did not keep to the rules, Tom had conceived a picture of Sam as an anarchic schoolboy, pretending to be hard at work behind closed doors but in reality reading a comic, or picking his nose, or no longer there at all but off robbing a bank.

It was a boyish vision, to be explained not only by Tom's easy tendency to attribute to others what he would most wish for himself but by the resentment he felt at being the odd man out. Not only because he was the only boy in the family but also because, through some quirk of nature, he alone among them had no ear. He suffered this affliction without complaint, and even allowed himself to be teased about it with clownish good humour, but in a household where singing was as natural as speech he felt disabled, and since his first inclination was to conform, it unnaturally set him apart. He also felt, painfully, that Sam, whom he longed to please, was disappointed in him.

Lately, out of defiance, not of his father but of fate, he had taken to sneering at every form of "artiness" as "female business."

It would have surprised Tom to know that his father understood his perplexity and was undismayed. Composing, for Sam, was work—it was the only thing he had ever been good at—and music a condition that could manifest itself in other ways than as notes on a page or in flights of calibrated sound. He was waiting for Tom to stop feeling sorry for himself and discover his own form of the thing.

They must have had some inkling, Sam felt, of what nature was up to in Tom's case, when they named the girls Miranda, Rosalind, Cressida and—in a moment of recklessness—Cassandra, but for the boy had immediately settled on Tom. Not even Thomas, but Tom. Tom-tom. There was, from the beginning, something wonderfully bull-like in him that would not be rarefied—even, Sam suspected, by time. He had grown up around his own literalness, and to Sam was all the more precious for it.

As for Maggie, though she believed without question in the energy Sam poured into his work—always had, from the first note he struck in her presence—the deeper music of the household flowed, for her, from what each of her children, with all their different natures and needs (even the twins, Ros and Cressie, were of contrary colour and temperament), brought to the routine and daily muddle of their lives: hurt feelings, tantrums, head colds, the shooting pain of a new tooth pushing into the house, complaints of misunderstanding and unfairness, squeals of protest at a shampooing against head lice or as a strip of Elastoplast was ripped off. For all the time and fret this cost her she would not have had it otherwise. Not one little difficult nature, or demand, or crotchet. Not one. Though she was glad she did not have to find a system of notation for it, and even more that she did not have to sing it.

S A M, looking sleek and youthful, his locks wet-combed from the shower, wandered into the kitchen, on the prowl now that he was done with work for the day, for something he could pick at—a stick of celery, a sliver of carrot, something one of the children had been up to.

"Where is he, anyway?" he demanded, meaning Tom. He was still fretting over that business with the bike. "They'll be here any minute now. Can't we eat as a family for once?"

"He's taken his surfboard to Manly," Maggie told him, busying around behind him. "He did ask. I said it was okay. He's to be back by five."

"And the girls?"

"They're at the pool."

There was an open-air saltwater pool just ten minutes away, on a walk along the Harbour.

"Miranda should have stayed," he grumbled. "You shouldn't have to do all this." Including the guests, there would be more than a dozen of them. He picked a round of cucumber out of the tuna salad, ruining one of her attempts at symmetry, and leaned with his back to the refrigerator.

"What can *I* do?"

"Open the wine and get me something to drink."

Instead, he came up from behind, put his arms around her, and buried his face in her hair. Maggie laughed.

"That was lovely," she told him, "but what about my drink?"

He opened three bottles of red, set them on the bench with the corks laid across their mouths, then drew her a glass of flagon white with soda.

For a few minutes they moved easily together in the space between table and cupboards, her stacks of empty egg boxes, the spilled waste from the bin; not touching, but in an easy association of bodies that was a kind of dance before the open-mouthed wine bottles.

The upper part of the house, its rooms all disorder and stopped noise, hung above them like a summer cloud, dense but still, alive with events that were for the moment suspended. The door to his workroom was closed for the day, its flow of sound also suspended, but on a chord that continued to reverberate in his head and teasingly unfold. It was there, humming away, and could wait. He would find his way back to it later.

Maggie turned and looked at him. Seeing herself reflected in his gaze, she brought the back of her hand to her forehead where a strand of hair had come loose.

It was difficult to say at such moments, she thought, whether this was before or after; whether the children were about to come bursting back into their lives from the pool, from the surf, all wet towels and hair, complaints and appetites, riddles, the smell of suntan oil and Bacon Crispies—or whether they were still waiting in youthful expectancy in that one year when there had been just the two of them, in the long nights, the short days. Not so long ago really.

They stood for a moment outside time, outside their thickened bodies, in renewed youthfulness. He nibbled. She sipped. The chord moved out through the house, discovering new possibilities in what might have passed for silence.

The doorbell rang.

"Damn," she said. "That'll be Stell. They're always early."

At the same moment, from the back porch, came the voices of the girls, little Cassie's breathless with grievance.

"Mummy, they tried to run away from me."

"We did not."

"They were chasing boys."

"We were *not*."

The bell sounded again.

"You get it," Maggie told Sam, and turned to face the onslaught.

"Now, Cassie," she told the child, who was clinging to her hip, "stop whinging. We've got visitors. Lars and Jens are here. Cressie—Ros—you should be ashamed of yourselves."

Miranda, hair dyed pink and green in the punk style she now affected, stood in the frame of the doorway, frowning, unwilling to be drawn in.

"And so should you, miss," Maggie told her. "I let them go with you because you're sixteen and supposed to be responsible. Sometimes I wonder."

But the rebuke, as Miranda knew, was ritual. There was no conviction in it.

"Now go and get yourselves decent, all of you. Before the real guests appear."

THE REAL GUESTS were an American visitor, Diane Novak, and her friend Scott McIvor, a much younger man than they had expected who turned out to be a local sailmaker. The others were family: Maggie's sister Stella and her two boys, Lars and Jens, and Stella and Maggie's old singing teacher, Miss Stinson. Then— invited unannounced by Miranda, it seemed, but more likely uninvited and hastily vouched for—Miranda's "best friends" of the moment, an odd pair called Julie and Don, also known as "The Act."

Sam was appalled. "How did *they* get here?" he demanded fiercely, the minute he got Maggie alone.

"I don't know," Maggie told him. "Any more than you do. I suppose Miranda asked them. They'll be all right. I've put all the kids out in the sunroom. You just look after the drinks. And, Sam, love," she pleaded, "try not to make a fuss."

Julie was an intense, waiflike creature. Tossed out of home (or so she claimed) by her stepfather, she had taken herself out of school and was living now in a squat—a plywood cubicle in an empty warehouse at Marrickville. Like Miranda she was sixteen. She got herself up, Sam thought, like an anorexic teenaged widow, entirely in black, and painted her lips black and her fingernails as well—in mourning, Sam had once suggested, for her own life.

Her partner Don, the other half of The Act, was a slight, sweet-faced boy, girlish but not it seemed gay, whose pale hair had been trained to fall perpetually over one eye and who affected little pink silk ballet slippers that Julie had embroidered with vivid scarlet and emerald-green thread. Julie was a designer. She created fashion garments from scraps picked up at the Salvation Army and St. Vincent de Paul op shops. Miranda today was wearing one of Julie's "creations," a recent present. It was a flared skirt made entirely of men's ties, in heavy satins and silks, a little grimy some of them but all vivid in colour and glossily shimmering.

She was always giving Miranda presents. Trashy jewellery she bought with her outsized allowance, miniature artworks of her own devising and of a crazy intricacy: cages in search of an inmate, efficient tiny guillotines involving razor blades and springs—bad-luck charms all, which Sam did not want smuggled in among them. Offerings, he had once observed, to some god of ultimate unhappiness.

"Honestly," Miranda told him. "I can't believe you'd say a thing like that! You're so ungenerous! And you think Julie's the crazy one."

Miranda liked to scare them with lurid accounts of what Julie, poor thing, had "been through." How at seven she was abused by a favourite uncle. How three months ago she'd been raped in her plywood cubicle by half a dozen ethnic youths but had declined to press charges.

Was any of this true? Or was it, as Maggie assured him, just another of Miranda's stories? Designed to shock them into admitting how out of touch they were, how little they knew of what was really going on.

"Young people these days see all sorts of things," Maggie told him, trying for an unconcern she did not quite feel. "Things we had no notion of. They survive, most of them—if they're sensible. Miranda is *very* sensible, you know that. All this is just showing off. She wants you to be impressed."

"Impressed!" Sam exploded.

"In your case, love," she told him with a twisted smile, "that means scared."

"Well, I am," he admitted. "I'm bloody petrified. I don't know how you can be so cool about things."

But that was just the point, the point of difference between them. And it was the mystery of this, more than anything Maggie actually said or did, that had its effect on him, a belief that Maggie did know something he did not, and that he could rely on this to get him through all doubts and difficulties. It was what she offered him. He had no idea what it might be that he offered her in return. Now, ignoring the irruption of Julie and her pallid companion into what was meant to be a private celebration, he followed Maggie's instructions and set himself to dealing with the drinks, but was not happy. It was a mistake—that's what he now decided—to have made his first meeting with Diane Novak a family affair.

For one thing, it had become clear that she hadn't made this trip "down here" only to see him. However eager she appeared to be, and full of interest in his workplace, the house, the bottlebrush with its sprays of pink-and-gold blossom that drooped over the front porch—"Callistemon, I think," she pronounced accurately—all the flow of energy in her, and it was considerable, was towards the young sailmaker, Scott, one of those easy-going, utterly likeable, ponytailed young fellows from good North Shore families and the best private schools who, instead of following their fathers into accountancy or the law, went back, led by nothing more radical than their own freewheeling interest, to trades their grandfathers or great-grandfathers had practised, and became carpenters and did up houses, or built boats, or made surfboards or sails.

Diane Novak was from Madison, Wisconsin. Three years ago Sam had come across one of her poems in an anthology and was led to set it to music. Later he sought out others and had ended up with a loose cycle. He wrote to her. Diane Novak wrote back. A correspondence developed.

Correspondence.

He had never given much consideration to the word till then, but "correspondence" and all it implied seemed entirely rich and right for what had since then flowed so easily between them: the current of curiosity and interest, of shy revelations on his part, flights of extravagant fancy on hers; jokes, wordplay, essays in boldness that took them, he had sometimes felt, to the edge of flirtation; small hints at the erotic. A hint too of darker things. Disappointment. Pain. Which his music had found in the poems, and which corresponded, he felt—there! that word again—to something in himself that had remained to this point wordless, though not entirely unspoken.

There was nothing dangerous in it. No suggestion of an affair, even a long-distance one. He passed all Diane's letters on to Maggie, though he suspected she did not read them, and could, without fear, have shown her his own. The deeper connection was impersonal. It lay in the inwardness with which he had taken her words, felt out the emotion there that had given them just their own shape, weight, texture, and found music for it. Released, she might have said, the music that was already in them and in her. She recognised that. Had felt it strongly as something secret, though not quite hidden, that he had subtly but again secretly made plain, for which she was grateful to the point of an agreeable affection that constituted a correspondence of an even more intimate kind. Inexpressible, or rather not needing expression, because he had already expressed it for them in the thing itself—the music.

So there was no need for them to meet, she told him. They had already done that, in their own chaste but public consummation, *there.*

In the meantime, they could joke about passing one another as intimate strangers on the moving walkway in some airport, Hawaii or Atlanta, or pressing fingertips on either side of a glass partition in Anchorage.

When she wrote out of the blue announcing a visit, he had assumed, foolishly, and with some trepidation, that she was coming because of him. But then, from her hotel, she had called and admitted to another interest "down here," this Scott the sailmaker, whom she had met at a poetry reading in Seattle. And now they were seated, Diane Novak, this Scott, who at twenty-seven or so was a good twenty years younger than his companion, at the big pinewood table in their front room, together with Maggie's sister, Stella, and Miss Stinson. Maggie and Diane, Sam thought, seemed entirely relaxed and easy with one another, like old friends united in understanding.

Of what? he wondered. Him?

Only now did it strike him that Maggie might have her own correspondence with Diane Novak. Through the words he had found music for. To which Maggie, in performance, had brought an exploratory sense, which she was now testing, of the other's shifting emotions, but also her own presence and breath. Is that why he felt so uncomfortably displaced, the only one here who seemed out of tune with the occasion?

The truth was, he was confused.

Very blonde and tanned, very carefully presented, but in a stringy way that was a mite too "American," Diane Novak was not what he had pictured. There were angularities to her that he had not foreseen. Something in the way she came at things—too directly, he thought—set him ill at ease. He wondered now if there had not been in her letters a suggestion of—what? Artfulness and high self-mockery that she had expected him to share but that he had mistaken or missed.

In her letters, not in the poems. She was rounder, softer there.

Or was that because he had translated the poems so fully into Maggie's sphere?

Either way, while remaining excited, fascinated even, he had begun to doubt his clear sense of Diane Novak, and was disconcerted by the speed with which she and Maggie, for all the differences between them, had caught one another's tone.

DIANE NOVAK was also disconcerted. She had brought presents, of course: jewellery of various kinds for the girls, a Ferragamo scarf for Maggie. For Sam a pair of Indian moccasins. He had received them, she thought, as if they were an exchange, not quite adequate, for something she had deprived him of, rather than as a gift, and was suddenly aware of all those little signs of unease she had felt between the lines of his letters and put out of mind, but which in the man himself were too close to the surface to be ignored. Goodness, she thought, what have we got here? She was disturbed a little, amused a little, but also touched.

Because the music he had found for her was so inward, so intuitive and acute, she had assumed a degree of knowingness in him that had led her into a kind of playful exaggeration that she saw now might have been a mistake. He wasn't at all knowing. He was, for all his sleekness, altogether boyish and at the mercy of his own wild starts and emotions.

Proprietorial too, she saw. Of herself, of Maggie. Of everything. She would have to be careful of wounding him. She would have to rely on Maggie to get them through.

Thank goodness, she thought, for Maggie.

She shot Sam a glance that was meant to be reassuring, collusive even, but all he did was look alarmed, and she was reminded yet again of how much of what life cannot deal with may be taken up, taken care of and reconciled, in the work.

She was well aware of what this meant for her own work, and had assumed that he too must know it—which is why she had responded so completely to him. She saw now that he might not.

And saw too, almost too clearly, how much of "life" his work might have to make up for.

Scott, meanwhile, had transferred his attention to Miss Stinson, who, seventy-five if she was a day, was glowing in the full light of his interest.

He was amazing, Scott. He had a fund of attention, of youthful excitement over this, that—everything in fact—that seemed inexhaustible and which he bestowed, in an unself-conscious way, on everything in his vicinity. Which was a bit of a problem really. She knew from her own case how easy it was to be misled. But not, in her own case, dangerously; she was pretty skilled, at this point, at protecting herself from ultimate disappointment.

Miss Stinson was telling them how she had discovered Maggie and Stella, while Stella, the subject of the story, sat placid and indulgent, but frowning. It bored her to have these ancient wonders trotted out again—as she would have said, for the forty-second time. Any glory they involved was more important, these days, to Miss Stinson than to Stella herself, who had long since put well behind her the tattered, if once glowing, clouds they trailed.

"Such funny little things, they were," Miss Stinson told. "With no shoes, and scars on their knees, real harum-scarums. Tomboys." They were her next-door neighbours, their father a removal man. They were always hanging over the fence to hear the scales that rose and fell behind the blinds of the little house she shared with her sister, and the big practise pieces their students performed. Longing to join in. Well, she had taken them on at last, in exchange for a couple of hours of ironing each week, because their mother had wanted something more for them—but without much enthusiasm. And lo and behold, miracle of miracles, by one of those quirks of fate that make you wonder at things—life was such a lottery, so unexpected, so unpredictable— little Stella Glynn had turned out to be just what her name suggested—a star. The one undisputed triumph of Miss Stinson's career. She won the Sun Aria. Went to study in Paris, then London. Sang at Covent Garden and the Met and was for ten years an

international "singer of renown," and was still described that way
when her records turned up on local radio. But the gift she had
been endowed with had never meant as much to Stella as it did to
others. As soon as she could manage it she gave up the irregular
life of glitter and savage discipline, married her Swede, and came
home. These days she co-managed a successful travel agency. It
suited her to a T.

Scott, dazzled to find himself in the presence of a real star, even
one who seemed little interested in her own faded glow, was leaning intensely towards Miss Stinson, who was telling her story now,
in an oddly flirtatious way, entirely for him.

"Go on," he said, when Miss Stinson paused and seemed for a
moment to be following some vivid memory of her own. "What
happened then?"

"Isn't this amazing," he said aside to Diane, with no hint of
irony.

Diane was quietly amused. Clearly, whatever else she might be
to Scott McIvor, she was not a star.

Sam too was listening, also moved in his way by the familiar
tale.

Long ago when they were all young, it was Stella he had been
drawn to. She had obsessed and tormented him.

He was studying piano then with Miss Stinson's sister, Miss
Minnie. Without Stella, he thought, his real life—the one he had
imagined and must at all costs have—would be for ever closed to
him.

He had been wrong; had almost made a fatal error, and not only
of the heart. When he listened these days to the two pieces Stella
had inspired in him, and which he had written for her extraordinary voice, he got a cold feeling at the base of his spine that was
only partly for what came back to him, unbidden, of that old
attraction, and the young man's bitter hurt with which it was still
sometimes infused.

What scared him more was the echo he caught, the *pre*-echo, of
the works he might have gone on to produce; the way his nature,
his own gift might have gone if Stella, grand as she was, had con-

tinued to be his goal and inspiration. But she had been wiser than he was. Crueller. More honest. Less vain. She had understood, long before he saw it, that the true voice of what he might have in him was Maggie's. When he saw it too he was dismayed and humbled, then swept away by how obvious it was.

Miss Stinson was right. How unexpected, how simple life could be. Though not, perhaps, just at the moment.

He turned his attention to the sunroom where the children were gathered. Frowned. Got to his feet. Maggie, seeing his frown and reading the question in it, waited a beat then followed.

Sprawled on the floor out there the twins were engaged in a game of Monopoly with their cousin Jens. Cassie, who distrusted Jens and often complained about him, but succumbed immediately to the smallest attention he showed her, had been permitted to mind his cash. Jens, of course, was winning. Lars, Stella's older boy, was plugged into a Walkman. Miranda and the two interlopers, as Sam thought of them, were in a huddle of green, pink, and ash-blond heads half hidden behind the door.

Sam surveyed the scene and settled on Jens and Lars as the source of what he felt in the air as a threat of imminent disorder. They had only to step across the threshold, these two, for the twins to be transformed from awkward, leggy little girls stuck on Michael Jackson to beings who gave off a seductive glow that terrified him, it was so naked—though innocent of course. They didn't know what it meant.

Lars was sixteen. He played in a pop group and was reputed to have got a schoolgirl pregnant—they had actually heard this from the twins! He was keeping his distance today, big feet in Nike joggers thrust out into the centre of the room, head bobbing, eyes closed under bluish lids. A great six-foot *lump* attached to a Walkman, exerting some sort of diversionary influence on the Monopoly board by disabling the twins, who could never quite ignore him.

But Jens was the one. It was Jens with his berserker's blue eyes and con man's smile who was the killer.

"I hope you'll tell that Jens he's not allowed upstairs. I don't want him going through my things."

This, earlier in the day, from Cassie, who was possessive of her "treasures."

"The last time he was here he walked off with a scent bottle I was keeping. He's a thief!"

And here she was, three hours later, entirely under his spell.

Once, when he was five, they had surprised Jens with his thing out, attempting to put it into one of the twins.

Stella, who ought, Sam thought, to have been as appalled as he was, had laughed when he faced her with it.

"Oh for heaven's sake, Sam, he's five years old!" she told him. "It'd be like marshmallow in a moneybox."

She and Maggie had collapsed at that, and Sam, enraged, had felt once again what a gap there was between the way he saw things and the world these sisters came out of, and so easily reverted to the moment they were together. Two minutes in one another's company and they were barefooted kids again, back in that disastrous household that had once, he admitted, when he was young, seemed so liberating. The easy-going carelessness and good humour. The very amenable terms these sturdy, down-to-earth sisters had appeared to be on with their own very different styles of beauty and with the world—with Life, as he would have put it then.

Well, he was less indulgent these days of that sort of carelessness. He knew now what it led to. On a daily basis.

Eighteen years he and Maggie had been together, but there were times when he was astonished all over again by how differently they took the world and what it threw at them.

As for Jens, five years old or not, he could have killed the little shit. And he could have killed him all over again right now.

Maggie, who had come up quietly behind him, laid her hand very lightly on his back.

"What is it, love? What's the matter?" she enquired. But almost immediately one of the twins, Rosalind, complained: "Mummy, Jens is cheating."

"He *is* not," Cassie told her.

"He is too."

"Play quietly, girls," Maggie said, barely paying attention. She was concerned now with getting Sam back to the table. She barely noticed the buzzing behind the half-open door where Miranda was closeted with her friends.

"What about Tom?" Sam now demanded, as if this all along was what had really been troubling him. "You said five. It's gone half past."

As if she knew any more than he did. The boy was fifteen.

"Oh, you know what he's like," Maggie told him. "He gets carried away. He'll be back."

Stella's eye was on them from the table next door. Maggie caught it and winked.

"What are you two doing out there?" Stella called. "Come here, Sam, and explain to Diane about fire-farming. You know what a dud I am, and Scott's no help." She was sacrificing the sailmaker, who was too pleased to have been named by her in such a familiar way to take offence.

Maggie relaxed a little. If there was anyone who could break Sam's mood it was good old Stell.

It was nearly six now and beginning to be dusk. The conversation at table was muted. The bottles of wine Sam had opened earlier, and one Stella had brought, stood empty before them among half-filled glasses and plates piled with peelings and scraps.

Diane Novak consulted her watch.

She was uncertain of the conventions here. People seemed settled in and gave no sign of moving, but she thought they should get going, that it was time to whip her sailmaker away. Suddenly there was a commotion from the sunroom—actual screams.

Miss Stinson, who was in full flight again, looked alarmed as the heads turned—she was deaf—and first Maggie, then Sam, then Stella, leapt to their feet.

"What is it?" she cried. "What's happened?"

It was at moments like this that her "condition," which for the most part she contrived very successfully to hide, came home to her—the prospect of not hearing the car that was bearing down to lift you bodily off your feet.

The scene in the sunroom when Maggie arrived was confused. It was Sam, immediately behind her, who took it all in and saw at once how things stood: Jens rushing past them to his mother in the hallway, Lars, still plugged in to his Walkman, upright now in the middle of the room, around him and under his feet small houses scattered as by a tornado among the dice and cards of the Monopoly game, the twins and Cassie, big-eyed all three, clinging together in the bay window. Still half out of sight behind the door, Miranda, Don, and the girl Julie were scrabbling in a heap on the floor. It was Julie who was screaming. But she was also flailing her arms and kicking her legs while Don and Miranda tried to hold her still and shouted her name. It was only a moment before Sam, uncomfortably sprawled with the writhing body half under him, had her controlled, but in that moment, he thought, the room was like an animal pit, as the others must have seen, coming up behind Stella—the sounds that were coming out of the child's body so little resembled anything that belonged to human speech. Sam looked back over his shoulder to where Maggie had pulled Cassie and the twins, who were staring white-faced but silent, close against her. Jens had his head hidden in his mother's shirt.

A moment. Then it was past. They were back in their ordered lives again.

"It's okay, pet," Maggie was telling Cassie, "everything's fine now."

She moved to relieve Sam, who was stricken, now that the girl was quiet, to find her sobbing against his chest. He let go and Maggie took over.

Picking Cassie up in his arms, Sam carried her past the others, the twins following, to the dining room, but turned back when Miss Stinson said, to no one in particular, "I expect she's taken something, poor girl. They should find out what it is."

That "taken something" reminded him. Years back—twenty, twenty-five—Miss Stinson's sister, Miss Minnie, had "taken something."

In her late forties, Miss Minnie had fallen passionately in love with a bus-driver, and when, after a series of approaches and ambiguous responses, he had, deeply embarrassed, made it plain that she had mistaken his interest, the poor woman had swallowed a whole bottle of aspirin. She survived, but it was a shaming business, and Miss Stinson had been devastated to find herself brought so close to a passion whose destructive consequences she too had to bear.

What surprised Sam was how entirely he had submerged and forgotten what to Miss Stinson must, for so long, have been a source of immediate and almost daily sorrow. He kissed Cassie briefly on the ear and told her: "Here, sausage, why don't you go to Miss Stinson for a moment." They were old friends, Cassie and Miss Stinson. "I'll just go and see how Mummy is doing. And you girls," this to the twins, "why don't you make us all a good cup of coffee. A big pot. Real grains."

But when Sam got to the sunroom, Maggie and the others were gone. Only the boy Don, with his floppy hair and lolly-pink slippers, was there, hovering on the threshold. Like everyone else, Sam had forgotten him.

It was Diane Novak's young man Scott who stepped in. "Are you okay, mate?" he asked, at Sam's side. The boy looked tearful. "Come on here." He came obediently, and Scott, without self-consciousness, put his arm around the boy and held him close; and at just that moment, the women reappeared at the top of the stairs—Stella, Miranda, Diane. Maggie had shushed them off and remained with Julie.

"She'll be fine," Stella told them, "she's a bit overwrought, that's all." She made a face at Sam, indicating that for Miranda's sake he should ask no questions.

Overwrought, they both knew, was an understatement, but for the moment must suffice.

Sam nodded. With a revulsion he could not hide, at least from himself, he turned away, but felt again in his back muscles and in the tendons of his hands the unnatural strength with which her body, slight as it was, had thrashed and jerked against his hold. Her hot breath in his ear. And the sounds that issued from her, wildered howlings at such a pitch of animal fury and uncomprehending anguish that he had almost been overcome.

By her terrible closeness. By the birdlike fragility against his ribcage of her bones and the alien power they were endowed with as he used all his weight to keep her still.

Her presence had always unnerved him. The funereal black of the miniskirts and shawls she got herself up in, her black eye make-up and the black fingernails and lips. The toxic disaster stuff she carried. Which he was afraid might brush off on Miranda, or on Cassie or the twins.

Now Maggie too reappeared at the top of the stairs. "She's sleeping," she told them.

She came on down, touching Sam's hand briefly as she passed. The twins were at the kitchen door, with a pot of coffee and a tray of mugs. "Good girls," she said. They all made their way to the dining room and went back to being a party, but a single one now, sipping, passing things. Even Lars appeared, tempted by chocolate biscuits.

"Miss Stinson," Maggie suggested, "why don't you play us something." In the early days of their marriage they had often had musical evenings. Miss Stinson had always played.

Too old and too much the professional to be coy, Miss Stinson got her ancient bones together and moved to the piano.

The Schubert she chose was safe, its fountain of notes under her fingers brightly lit and secure. The regretful middle section when it appeared, with its shifts, on the same note sequence, from trancelike sureness to throbbing hesitation, its wistfulness and quiet stoicism, spoke of a world of recoveries that could still rouse itself and sing. Even the repeats, which might have been too many, as she reached for them were new-found and welcome.

Sam, under the influence of the music, and the hour and the light, which seemed one, met Diane Novak's eye across the table. She smiled and nodded.

Nothing had been said. They had barely spoken. But he felt

easy again. Their meeting had not, after all, been the central event of the occasion, but had not been a mistake.

The last notes died away. Miss Stinson sat a moment, as if she were alone out there, somewhere in the dark, and they, like shy animals, had been drawn in out of the distance to listen; drawn in, each one, out of their own distance and surprised, when they looked about, that music had made a company of them, sharers of a stilled enchantment. It was only when Miss Stinson, still absent and absorbed, lifted her hands at last from the keys that Tom, who had been waiting, respectful but impatient in the doorway behind them, bursting with his news, spoke up at last, red-faced and over-wrought.

"I had an accident," he hooted.

He was triumphant, despite the bump on his forehead and his discoloured eye. "I got hit by a board. I had to have stitches!"

Still pumped, still caught up in the world of mishap and risk he had come from, but torn now between the wish to astonish them and at the same time not to alarm, he came forward to show his mother the wound.

"It's not serious," he told her. "I had to go in an ambulance. Is that okay? Do we belong?"

It was true, it was nothing, nothing much. A gash that would heal, leaving a scar over his left eye that would be interesting. But it must have been close just the same, and because it was so physical, and came so soon after their earlier commotion, Maggie shocked the boy by suddenly clasping him to her and bursting into tears. He faced the others—his father, Miranda—over her shoulder and did not know what he had done.

"Honestly," he told them, "it's nothing. I hardly felt it."

Sam, recalling how angry he had been with the boy, was suddenly heartsick. Tom saw it.

"Hey, Dad," he said, "I'm sorry. I didn't mean to upset you."

"That's all right, son," Sam told him, playing calm. "We've had a bit of an afternoon, that's all. Come and get something to eat." It surprised him that his tone was so much one that Maggie might have used. She too caught it, gave him a swift look, and laughed.

"Well," she said, releasing Tom, then drawing him back to give him a light kiss on the corner of his mouth, "welcome back from the wars."

THE GUESTS WERE GONE, the children settled. Upstairs was quiet, all the lights out except in Tom's room; the rooms left and right down the hallway filled with quiet breathing, their windows half open to the summer night of clicking insects and the barely audible slow flapping past of flying foxes, the stirring of possums among leaves. Downstairs the washing-up was stacked in racks above the sink.

Sam and Maggie, having shut the kitchen door behind them, were in Sam's sleepout workroom, Maggie, with closed eyes, in an upright chair by the door, Sam at the piano. Idly his fingers struck a chord, the same one that earlier in the day, out in the kitchen, had led her to an old song that was there somewhere in the four ordinary notes. But what moved out into the silence now was full of other, stranger possibilities that brought the room into a different focus: the air, rather thick and heated; the bright ellipse of the lamp under its hood, where it lit the keys and the reddish wood of the piano; Sam's profile, lips slightly apart in anticipation; the glare of the louvres, parted to let in a scent of leaves and distant water.

"Do you want me to try it?" Maggie asked.

"You're not too tired?"

She made the effort, sprang upright. Sam briefly laughed. She took the sheet from the piano, and Sam handed her two more that she ran her eye over in preparation as his fingers found one chord, then, in a way that made her draw herself together and attend, another. And now the focus was in *her*. In her shoulders, her legs where she settled the column of her body on the worn carpet, and reaching in the spaces of her head for the first note let out her breath.

Ah! Sam turned his head. He felt the whole surface of his skin thrill at the wonder of it, the purity of this voice she harboured so mysteriously in a body he had lived with now for nearly twenty years and which never failed to astonish him. Fleetingly their eyes met and Maggie smiled, as sounds he had with so much difficulty drawn out of himself now poured forth, without effort it seemed, on her breath, and on the same breath climbed and spread. So much part of her, of her actual being, yet entirely independent. As they had been of him too, even before she took them over, took them into herself, gave them life.

With the turn of his head Sam showed a different profile, and Maggie recorded it while all her attention remained fixed on the page and on what, with all her body's susceptibilities and claims in perfect collusion, she was miraculously translating into this other self he had discovered for her, and which her breath, pushed almost to its limit, was once again amply reaching for.

UPSTAIRS, with the blanket drawn up high under his chin, Tom contemplated his sister Miranda, who sat on the edge of the low bed and regarded him with a look he preferred not to meet. She was preparing, he thought, to rebuke him. He felt warm and comfortably indulged. He did not want to be told, yet again, how hopeless he was. There had been a moment down there in the sitting room when he had been the centre of all their attention and concern—not just his mother's, his father's, and Miss Stinson's, but everyone's, and had felt, beyond his usual awkward self-consciousness, a kind of glow, an assurance of how loved he might be. He did not want that spoiled.

But Miranda did not mean to spoil it. She wanted to tell him how fond she was of him, how often she thought of a time, before the twins appeared, when there had been just the two of them and he had been her dumb, soft, wet-mouthed little brother who needed her to watch out for him and trailed after her and did everything she did.

There were moments when she still saw him that way.

Recently, when she began to colour her hair and explore the decorative resources of the safety pin, her mother had told her angrily:
"This is very silly, Miranda, your father is disappointed. Is that why
you're doing it? To get at him? And it's such a bad example!"

"Who to, for heaven's sake?"

Her mother had had to stop and think.

"To Tom," she decided. "You know how he copies everything
you do."

Miranda had laughed outright. "Honestly," she said. "Tom!"

But it was true. He did follow, in his odd, half-hearted way.
Careful always not to stray too far from his own stolid centre. He
had acquired a pair of black parachute pants, put colour in his hair
that would wash out for school, wore a stud in his ear.

"What *is* that?" their father had taunted. "That *thing* in your ear.
A hearing aid?"

She too wished he would stop trying so hard and just be his own
lovable self.

What he really wanted, she thought, was that they should be
twins; whereas what she wanted, in her contradictory way, was to
be an only child. What she said now was: "I could sleep here, if
you like. On the floor."

Tom was surprised. Wary.

"Julie's in my bed anyway. It'd be better if she just stayed there."

"Well, if you want to," he said. "But I don't need it."

"I know you don't," she said. "I do."

He snuggled down into the blankets.

"I'm pretty tired now," he told her. "I might just go to sleep."

"That's all right. I'll be tired myself in a bit."

She took his hand.

His eyes were closed but he was smiling. Already sinking downwards into sleep.

Far off in the depths of the house their mother's voice rose in a
long sweet arc of sound, pure and unwavering.

Tom heard it, a shining thread he was following in the dark that
step by step was leading him down into his own private underworld.

Julie too heard it. Still stiffly awake in the next room, she was puzzled for a moment. She lay breathless, listening, salt tears in her throat—not for the music, though the throbbing of it seemed one with her own silent weeping. As if it had appeared just at this moment to reassure her that what she felt, her unassuageable misery, was part of something larger that was known, shared, and could take this lighter form, a high pure sound out of elsewhere. Something more than this hot welling in her throat, this salty wetness in her nostrils and on her lips.

Maggie was on the last page now, and aware, as she moved with ease along the line of notes, of the silence she was approaching, which began just a little way up ahead, where he had laid down his pen.

As she came closer to it Sam's head turned further in her direction and his eye caught hers. She was coming to what had stopped him.

He was looking right at her now, as she reached the small difficulty he had set himself there. Had set *her*. She closed her eyes, to free herself from his look of anxious expectancy, so that without anxiety she could allow what was purely physical in her to take over and get her through. She heard his breath go out. Then silence.

But not quite silence. A slight hissing of night through the parted slats of the louvres. Nature. Then again their breathing.

"That's it for the moment," he said—unnecessarily, but to return them, she understood, to the ordinariness of speech.

She nodded. Laid the last sheet beside the others on the stand.

Her body was still attuned to what she had just been so caught up in. She felt the vibrations still. No longer emanating from her, they went on where the music continued to flow and spread. Beyond the page. In his head. In the silence which was not quite silence. On the lines of score-paper as yet still empty.

Which would sit where she had just set down the last uncompleted page, in the dark of this room, after he had put the lamp out and closed the door behind them, and they had gone upstairs, undressed, lain down side by side in the dark; for a few moments simply going over the day's events, Diane Novak, whatever it was that had afflicted the child—not one of their own—who now lay sleeping across the hall, Tom's accident, Miss Stinson. Till once again he turned to her and whispered her name.

And this, waiting below.

To be resumed. To be continued.

DREAM STUFF

At Schindler's

1

A T SCHINDLER'S Jack woke early. The sound of the sea would find its way into his sleep. The little waves of the bay, washing in and receding, dragging the shell-grit after them, would hush his body to their rhythm and carry him back to shallows where he was rolled in salt. It was his own sweat springing warm where the sun struck the glass of his sleepout, which was so much hotter than the rest of the house that he might, in sleep, have drifted twenty degrees north into the tropics where the war was: to Borneo, Malaya, Thailand. He would throw off even the top sheet then to bake in it, till it was too hot, too hot altogether, and he would get up, go down barefoot to pee in a damp place under one of the banana trees and take a bit of a walk round the garden. Until Dolfie, the youngest of the Schindlers, came out bad-tempered and sleepy-eyed to chop wood, he had the garden's long half-acre to himself.

There was a pool at Schindler's. In the old days Jack and his father had swum there each morning. Jack would cling to the edge and kick, while his father, high up on the matted board, would leap, jackknife in the air, hang a moment as if he had miraculously discovered the gift of flight, then plummet and disappear. Then, just when Jack thought he was gone altogether, there would be a splash and he would reappear, head streaming, a performance that gave Jack, after the long wait in which his own breath too was held, a shock of delighted surprise that never lost its appeal.

Schindler's was a boarding-house down the "Bay" at Scarborough. They went there every holiday.

The pool these days was empty, closed, like so much else, for the "duration." But Jack, who this year would have been old enough to use the board, liked each morning to walk out to the end and test its spring. Toes curled, arms raised, beautifully balanced between the two blues, the cloudless blue of the early-morning sky and the painted one that was its ideal reflection, he would reach for what he remembered of his father's stance up there, grip the edge, strain skyward with his fingertips, push his ribcage out till the skin felt paper-thin, and hang there, poised.

He had got this part of it perfect. For the rest he would have to be patient and wait.

HIS FATHER was missing—that was the official definition. Or, more hopefully, he was a prisoner of war. More hopefully because wars have a foreseeable end, their prisoners come home: to be missing is to have stepped into a cloud. Jack's mother, who was aware of this, never let a mealtime pass without in some way evoking him.

"I suppose," she would say, "your daddy will be having a bite to eat about now."

They knew quite well he wouldn't be sitting down, as they were, to chops and boiled pudding, but it kept him, even if all he was doing was pushing a few spoonfuls of sticky rice into his mouth, alive and in the same moment with them.

When St. Patrick's Day came round she would say: "Sweet peas. They're your father's favourites. You should remember that, Jack. Maybe by the time they're ready he will be home."

One year, struck by one of the models in a Paton and Baldwin pattern book, she knitted a cable-stitch sweater for him. Jack held the wool when it was wound, watching the yards and yards it would take pass over his hands. Twenty skeins! When all the parts were finished and had been assembled into the shape of a sweater, his mother held it up to her shoulders. "Look, Jack."

He was astonished by the bulkiness of it. He hadn't remembered his father's being so big. In a moment when his mother was out of the room he held its roughness to his cheek, but all he could smell was new wool.

Collapsed now between layers of tissue, it lay in a drawer of his father's lowboy acquiring an odour of naphthalene.

But as the months slipped by and they still had no news of him, no postcard or message on the radio, Jack saw that his mother's assurance had begun to fail. She still spoke as if his father were just out of the room for a bit, at a football match or having a drink down at the boat club, but she was pretending. For his sake—that is what he felt—and it worried him that she might realise that he knew. They would have to admit something then, and it was imperative, he thought, that they should not. If she no longer had faith, then he must. If his father was to survive and get home, if he was to hang on to whatever light thread was keeping him in the world, then *he* was the one who must keep believing. It was up to him.

"NOW, MILLY! You can't just sit around mooning. Stan wouldn't want that. You're young, you need a break. You need to get out and have a bit of fun."

This was his aunt Susan speaking, his father's sister. Jack wondered how she could do it.

"Look," she said, holding his mother's hair up, "like this. You've got such lovely bones."

They looked into the mirror, his aunt lifting the thick hair in her hands like a live animal, their two bodies leaning close.

His mother regarded herself. "Do you really think so?" she said dreamily. "That I could get away with it?"

Jack frowned. Don't, Mum, he said silently.

The two figures in the mirror, his mother smiling now, her head turned to one side, disturbed him; there was a kind of complicity between them. When they looked at one another and leaned closer, their eyes full of daring and barely suppressed hilarity, he felt they had moved away into a place where he was not invited to follow. Other rules applied there than the ones he knew and wanted her to keep.

"Well, I don't know," his mother was saying. But she looked pleased, and his aunt Susan giggled. "Maybe," she said. "What do you think, Jack?"

He looked away and did not answer. She must know as well as he did that his father hated anything of that sort—rouge, painted toenails, permed hair. What was wrong with her?

For the past few weeks she had been working one night a week at a canteen. Now, under his aunt Susan's influence, she changed her hairstyle to a glossy pompadour, put on wedgies, and, drawing Jack into it as well, began to teach herself the newest dances. They tried them out with old gramophone records, on the back verandah; Jack rather awkward in bare feet and very aware that he came only to her shoulder. I'm only doing it to make her happy, he told himself. He felt none of the pride and excitement of the previous year, when he had gone along each Saturday night in a white shirt and bow tie to be her beau at the Scarborough dances.

Americans began to appear at their door. Escorts, they were called. It had a military ring, more formal, less personal than partner. They brought his mother orchids in a square cellophane box and, for him, "candy," which only Americans could get. He accepted, it was only polite, but made it clear that he had not been bought.

His mother asked him what he thought of these escorts and they laughed together over their various failings. She was more critical than Jack himself might have been and this pleased him. She also consulted him about what she should wear, and would change if he disapproved. He was not deceived by any of this, but did not let her see it.

And in fact no harm was done. New dances replaced the old ones every month or so, and in the same way the Rudis, the Dukes, the Vergils, the Kents, were around for a bit and sat tugging at their collars under the tasselled lamps while his mother, out in the kitchen, fixed her corsage and they made half-hearted attempts to interest or impress him, then one after another they got their marching orders. Within a week or two of making themselves too easily at home, putting their boots up on the coffee-table, swigging beer from the bottle, they were gone. The war took them. They moved on.

MILT, Milton J. Schuster the Third, was an air force navigator from Hartford, Connecticut, a lanky, fair-headed fellow, younger than the others, with an Adam's apple that jumped about when he was excited and glasses of a kind Jack had never seen before, just lenses without frames. Jack took to him immediately.

He wasn't a loud-mouth like so many of the others, he did not skite. And for all that he was so young, he had done a lot, and was full of odd bits of information and facts that were new to Jack and endlessly interesting. But most of all, it was Milt who was new. He was put together with so much lazy energy, had so many skills, so much experience that he was ready, in his good-humoured way, to share.

"Jack," his mother protested, "give us a break, will you? That's the fifty-seventh question you've asked since tea."

But where Milt was concerned Jack could never get to the end of his whats and whys and how comes and who said sos, or of Milt's teasing and sometimes crazy answers.

Milt was a fixer. Humming to himself a tuneless tune that you could never quite catch, comfortable in a sweat-stained singlet with the dog-tags hanging, he would, without looking up from the screwdriver he was spinning in his long fingers or the fuse-wire he was unravelling, say "Hi, kiddo," the same for Jack and his mother both, and just go on being absorbed. It wasn't an invitation to stay, but it wasn't a hint either (Jack was sensitive to these) that you should push off. He accepted your presence and went on being alone. Yet somehow you were not left out.

In fact the jobs Milt did were things Jack's mother could do quite well herself, but she was happy now to have Milt do them. When he made a lamp come on that had, for goodness knows how long, failed to work, he wore such a look of beaming satisfaction that he might have supplied the power for it out of his own abundant nature, out of the same energy that fired his long stride and lit his smile.

So what was his secret? That's what Jack wanted to know. That was where all his questions tended. And what was the tune he hummed? It seemed to Jack that if he could only get close enough to hear it, he would understand at last Milt's peculiar magic. Because it was magic of a sort. It put a spell on you. Only Milt didn't seem to know that he possessed it, and it was this not-knowing, Jack thought, that made it so mysterious, but also made it work.

Milt was twenty-two. In the strict code of those times it was inconceivable that a woman should be interested in a man who was younger. Jack could imagine his mother breaking some of the rules, smoking in the street for instance, or whistling, but not this one. So he had come to think of Milt as *his* friend.

When Christmas came they took him to Schindler's.

2

THEY HAD been going to Schindler's for as long as Jack could remember. His mother and father had spent their honeymoon there. Unlike the other guests, who ate in the little sunlit dining room at midday and half past six, they took their meals at the big table in Mrs. Schindler's kitchen, and Jack had permission to go in at any hour and ask for milk from the fridge, or an ice-block, or one of Mrs. Schindler's homemade biscuits. On days when they went fishing at Deception, Mary, the Schindlers' girl, packed them a lunch-tin with things only the family ate: salami, sweet-and-sour gherkins, strudel.

The soil at Scarborough was red. So were the eroded cliffs, which you could slide down and whose granular, packed earth could be trickled through a fist to colour sand-gardens. So were the rocks that formed a Point at each end of the beach, and the escarpments of the reef that at low tide emerged from the dazzle about sixty yards out, where fishermen, standing on the streaming shelf, cast lines for rock-cod or bream.

When the tide was in, the Points were covered, the beach was isolated. But at low tide, walking on what had just an hour before been the bottom of the sea, you could go round by the beach way to Redcliffe in one direction or Deception in the other.

No need to consult the *Courier Mail* for high- and low-water times at the Pile Light. When the tide was coming in your sandfly bites grew swollen and itched. When it went out, they stopped.

The beach at Scarborough was a family camping-ground. Bounded on one side by a grassy cliff-top—where at Christmas there was a fairground with hoopla stalls and an Octopus and a woozy merry-go-round—and on the other by a storm-water drain, it was a city of tents; or if not a city, at least a good-sized township, where the same groups, established in the same pozzies each year, made up a community as fixed in its way as any on the map.

It was a lively and relaxed world. When the tent flaps were up people's whole lives were visible, the folding table where they ate, the galvanized or enamel tub where they washed their clothes and did the dishes, the primus stove, camp-stretchers and carbide or petrol lamps. Jack spent his whole day moving from tent to tent asking if his friends could come out, or being gathered into the loose arrangements that were other people's lives. There were a dozen families where he could simply step in under the flap, which would be golden where the sun beat through, and be offered a slice of bread with condensed milk or, in the afternoon, a chunk of cold watermelon.

At home in Brisbane, people's lives were out of sight behind lattice and venetians. Here, it was as if, in some holiday version of themselves, they had nothing to hide. All you had to do to be one of them was to make yourself visible; and if, in tribute to settled convention, you did say "knock, knock," it was a kind of joke, the merest shadowy acknowledgement of the existence elsewhere of doors and of a privacy that had already been surrendered or was dissolved here like the walls.

"Come on in, pet." That is what Mrs. Chester or Mrs. Williams would call, the comfortable mothers of his holiday friends. And if strangers were there, other women like themselves, barefoot, in

beltless frocks, they might add: "This is Jack. He's one of the family, aren't you, love?"

It was a manner of speaking, a temporary truth like all their
arrangements down here. Rivalries, gangs, friendships existed
with a passionate intensity for the six weeks of Christmas and two
more at Easter, and for the rest of the year, like some of the rivers
they drew in Geography, went underground, became dotted lines.

Jack loved these broken continuities. They were reassuring.
You let things drop out of sight, then you picked them up again
further on. Nothing was lost. Even a single day could have that
pattern. For a whole morning, while you played Fish or Ludo, you
were one of the Chesters. Then in the afternoon you became a
loose adjunct of the Ludlow family or returned to your own.

It was his own family that was the puzzle.

The way Jack saw it was this. He and his mother were two
points of a triangle, of which the third point was over the horizon
somewhere in a place he could conceive of but never reach,
though there were times when his whole body ached towards it,
and so intensely that he would wake at night with the torment of
it. Growing pains, his mother called it. And it was true, he was
growing; he had shot up suddenly into a beanpole. But that wasn't
the whole of it.

Down here at Scarborough, where he was most keenly aware of
his body as the immediate image of himself, the sun's heat, day
after day, and especially in the early morning when it struck the
glass of his hot-house sleepout, would draw him in a half-waking
dream to some tropic place where everything grew faster. His
limbs would be stretched then across three thousand miles of real
space till every joint was racked, and he would experience at last
the thing he most hungered for: a smell of roll-your-owns as sharp
as if his father were actually there in the room with him, or a light-
headed feeling of being hefted all along the verandah-boards on
his father's boot, the two of them laughing, Jack a little out of fear,
and his father shouting: "Hang on, Jack, that's the boy. Hang on!"

It was the voice he found hardest to keep hold of. He strained to
hear it, vigorously lifted, under the beating of the shower, "All

together for the Floral Dance," but got nowhere. When he did sometimes discern the peculiar line of it on a stranger's lips it was in one of the phrases his father liked to use: "fair crack o' the whip" or "you wouldn' credit it." He would try for the tune of it then under his breath.

So HERE they were at Schindler's; Jack, his mother, and Milt. Jack was in his element.

Even Mrs. Schindler, who had treated Milt at first with a kind of coldness, was won over by the drawling stories he told, a way he had of kidding people that was rough but inviting. By the end of their first meal together she adored him and from then on insisted on making all his favourite dishes, waiting breathlessly, like a girl, for him to taste and approve. Once it had been Jack who was consulted on whether the precious dessert-spoons should be used for ice-cream or for pudding. Now it was Milt. And Jack didn't mind at all. How could he be resentful of someone he himself was so eager to see pleased?

Milt kidded Mrs. Schindler the way he kidded Jack's mother, with a mixture of courtliness and plain tomfoolery. He hung around the kitchen benches, beating eggs and dipping his finger into bowls. He set up a little speaker so that Mrs. Schindler could listen in to the news from the lounge-room wireless while she helped Mary wash up. He danced her all round the kitchen, on the black-and-white tiles, whistling "Wiener Blut."

Jack still spent the day with his friends down at the beach, but in the evenings he and Milt played Chinese Checkers or Fiddlesticks, or the three of them played Euchre, or Milt worked with him on the crystal set he was making while his mother read. They went fishing at Deception, roller-skating at Redcliffe, and some afternoons he and Milt went off alone to the Redcliffe Pictures. Milt was crazy about cartoons. He sat with his long legs drawn up, cracking peanuts, and afterwards acted it all out again for Jack's mother—Bugs Bunny, Tom and Jerry, Goofy, Pluto—running about all over the room being a rabbit, a tom-cat, a mouse, and reducing her to helpless laughter as she never would have been by the real thing. Once, walking home the beach way, he told Jack about the fossils he wanted to study: palaeontology—bones. He got excited, threw his own bones about, arms and legs, and Jack had to run backwards on his heels over the wet sand not to miss any of it, since so much of what Milt was telling was in the dance of his Adam's apple, the electric spikes of his crew-cut hair.

"How do you do it?" Jack shouted, excited himself now and breathless with trying to run backwards fast enough to stay in front. "How do you work it out? What they were like? If they've been extinct for millions of years? If all you've got is a few bones?"

"Logic," Milt told him, looking wild. "There are laws. We don't get this way by accident, you know. We aren't just thrown together." Though the way his limbs were flying about, as if they were about to dislocate and break loose of his frame, might have denied it. "The body's got laws, and the bones follow 'em, just like everything else. It's a kind of—grammar—syntax. You know, everything fits and agrees. So if you've got one bit you can work out the rest, you can—resurrect it. By logic. But also by guessing right. There's a lot of guesswork involved, hunches. You've got to think yourself inside the thing, into the bones."

It had all gone too fast for Jack. Running backwards wasn't the ideal way to hear something so important and take it in. But he felt, just the same, that in this shouted exchange he had got hold at last of an important clue, one that convinced him because, in some obscure part of himself, he already knew it. When they fell into step again, saying nothing now, just letting the fall of the waves fill the silence between them, they were together, and in a way that utterly settled him in his own skin.

It was a happy time for Jack's mother too.

A lively girl with ideas of her own, she had been brought up to despise a view of women in which dependency and a sweet incapacity for everything practical were the chief attributes of the eternally feminine.

"For heaven's sake," she was fond of saying, "what's the advantage, I'd like to know, of sitting around in the dark until some *man* comes along who can fix a fuse."

She knew how to fix a fuse, and use a soldering iron, and how to bowl overarm and putt a ball. She had done these things when Jack's father was there, and when he was gone had taught Jack to do them, but with some concern that in having only her to learn from he might be missing something, some male thing, beyond the mere acquiring of a competence, that would ground him in the world of men. So she was glad to have Milt around. Glad too that Jack had taken to him. He had a new sense of himself that she found attractive—she had found it attractive in his father, whom he more and more resembled—and she was grateful that Milt, out of a natural generosity, should have reserved for Jack something that was special. It was part of Milt's instinct for things that he knew how to draw back and leave room for something special between Jack and herself as well.

"No good asking you to play," she would tease when they set up for cricket. And her mocking tone, which Milt only pretended not to recognise, kept him lightly in view, even as it lightly excluded him.

It was a tone Jack had never heard her use till now. And once he was alerted to it, he noticed something else as well. A little shift in her way of speaking—it was only on certain words—that was an imitation, a mockery perhaps, of Milt's. It occurred to him, but so fleetingly that he was barely conscious of it, that if he could determine which words, he would have a clue to what they talked about, Milt and his mother, when he was not there.

Meanwhile Milt's replies, all Yankee ceremony, had an edge of their own.

"No use at all, ma'am. None at all." And as he said it he would lie back, extend his long legs and, with his arms folded under his head, prepare to take a nap.

He was grinning, so was Jack's mother, and Jack had the feeling that their game of two-man cricket was not the only game in play. When his mother got hold of the bat she hit out with a flair, a keenness and accuracy, that had him running all over the yard.

In time he came to feel uncomfortable with all this. There was something in his mother's heightened glow on these occasions, when Milt lay sprawling in the grass, a loose spectator, not playing but none the less exerting a quiet attraction, that was more disturbing to Jack's fixed idea of her than other and more obvious changes—the ribbon she wore in her hair when they went skating, her acceptance now and then of a stick of gum.

He had a good think about it.

Milt, he decided, lying off to the side there, broke the clear line of force between batsman and bowler. His mother was too aware of him. Even more, he unsettled the map Jack carried in his head, in which the third point of their triangle, however far out of sight it might be, was already occupied.

They would be out on the pier at Deception, all three, their handlines trailing, stunned to a heap by the sun and with the glare off the water so strong that when you looked out across it everything dazzled and disappeared. Above the lapping, against the piles, of waves set off by a distant rowboat, Jack would catch a voice he could no longer characterize naming the peaks of the Glasshouse Mountains on the opposite shore: Coochin, Beerwah, Beerburrum, Ngungun, Coonowrin, Tibrogargan, Tiberoowuccum. Smokily invisible today in their dance over the plain, but nameable, even in a tongue in which they were no more than evocative syllables.

"Hey, kid! Jack! Don't jerk the line like that. Take it easy, eh?"

That was Milt. And his voice, with its unmistakable cadence, was sufficiently unlike the one Jack had been listening for that it was a comfort. It so plainly did not fit.

3

AMONG JACK'S special friends this year were two brothers, Gerald and Jamie Garrett, who were new down here. Tough State School kids, they swore, told dirty jokes, and could produce prodigious gobs of spit that they shot like bullets from between their teeth. But what gave them a special glamour in Jack's eyes was their father's

occupation. Back home in Brisbane, Mr. Garrett was the projection-
ist at the Lyric Pictures where Jack went on Saturday afternoons,
and was responsible as well for putting up the posters that appeared
in three places on Jack's way to school and which on Monday mornings he read, right down to the smallest print, with an excitement
that cast a glow over the whole week ahead.

What they proclaimed, these posters, was the existence of
another world, of such modernity, such intensified energy and
speed, of danger too, that their local one of weatherboard houses
and bakers' carts, unweeded pavements, and trams that filled the
night sky with electric sparks, seemed by comparison flimsy and
becalmed. America, that world was called. It moved on numbered
highways at a hundred miles an hour. It was twenty storeys high,
all steel and glass. It belonged to a century that for them was still
to come. Jack hungered for it, and for the dramas that it would
unfold, as for his own manhood.

He had looked for some reflection of all this in his mother's
escorts. But once you had got to the end of whatever magic could
be extracted from "Santa Fe" or "Wisconsin" or "Arkansas," they
had turned out to be ordinary fellows off farms, or small-town car
salesmen or pharmacists' assistants. As for Milt, he was just Milt.
But in Mr. Garrett the power of that projected world was primary,
and he found it undiminished in Gerald and Jamie as well, who
would have been astonished to know that in Jack's eyes they were
touched with all the menacing distinction of the gun-slinger or
baby-faced killer.

There was a third brother. Arnold he was called. A year older
than Jack, he was spending the first three weeks of the holidays at
their grandfather's, out west. Gerald and Jamie, as if they needed
his being there to know quite how they stood with one another
and the world, were for ever evoking his opinion or using his
approval or disapproval to justify their own. Before long the tantalising absence of this middle brother had become a vital aspect of
the Garretts as Jack saw them, and he too found himself looking
forward to Arnold's arrival. "Arnold'll be here next week, eh?"
Then it was "Saturday." Then "this arvo."

But Arnold, when he got off the green bus and was there at last, was not at all what Jack had expected. The quality he found in the others, of menace and tough allure, far from being intensified in this third member of the family, appeared to have missed him altogether. Blond where the others were dark, and tanned and freckled, he seemed dreamy, distant. When they told him stories of what had been, for them, the high points of these last weeks, he listened, but in the way, Jack thought, that adults listen to kids. Not disdainfully, he was too easy-going to be disdainful, but as if he could no longer quite recall what it was like to be involved in adventures or crazes. When he left school next year he would be out west permanently. On the land.

His most prized possessions were a pair of scuffed riding boots that sat side by side under his camp-bed and a belt of plaited kangaroo hide that cinched in the waist of his shorts with a good seven or eight inches to spare. He had ridden buckjumpers. He could skin a rabbit.

He did not boast of these things. He was not the sort to draw attention to himself or be loud. But the assurance they gave him, the adult skills they represented, set in a different light the excitements that had marked their weeks down here; even the abandoned fuel tank that had drifted in one afternoon and which they had believed, for a long, breathtaking moment while it bobbed about just out of reach, might be a midget sub.

"Anyway," Arnold assured them, "them Japs wouldn' get far, even if they did land. Not out there." And he evoked such horizons when he lifted his eyes in the following silence that the walk to Redcliffe or Deception, even the bush way, seemed like nothing.

Arnold Garrett had the slowest, drawliest voice Jack had ever heard. Secretly, high up on the diving-board or in the privacy of his room, he would reach for the growling flatness of it, "Aout theere," in the belief that if he could get the tone right he might catch a glimpse, through the other boy's eyes, of what it was.

There were times, listening to Arnold and narrowing his eyes in the same heat-struck gaze, when Jack felt turned about. Away from the Bay and its red rocks, away from their gangs, their games, this particular school holidays and everything to do with being eleven, or twelve even, towards—

But there he came to a barrier that Arnold Garrett, he felt, had already crossed.

THEY WERE sitting around after a late-afternoon swim. Jack was in the middle of a story, one of those flights of fancy with which he could sometimes hold them, all attention, in a tight group, when Arnold said lightly: "Hey, are you a Yank or something? You talk like a Yank," and he repeated a phrase Jack had used, with such dead accuracy, such perfect mimicry of Jack's pitch and tone and the decidedly un-local accent he had given to the otherwise inno-cent word "water," that the whole group, Gerald, Jamie, the Williams boys, laughed outright. Jack was dumbstruck. It wasn't simply that it was, of all people, Arnold who had caught him out in this small defection from the local, but the thing itself. He flushed with shame.

"It's his mum," Jamie explained. "She goes out with one." He said this in a matter-of-fact way. There was a touch of scorn but no malice in it.

"She does not," Jack shouted, and even as he flung the insinua-tion back at them he saw that it was true.

"Doesn't she?" Jamie said. "It's what Dolfie Schindler said. What about—"

But Jack, his face burning, had already leapt to his feet. Filled with the crazy conviction that if he denied it with his whole body it would cease to be true, he struck out, though not at Jamie. Hon-our would not allow him to strike a younger boy.

"Hey," Arnold yelled, throwing him off. "Hey! Are you crazy or something? Lay off!" Then, seeing that Jack could not be stopped, he weighed in with his fists and they fought, all knuckles, elbows, and knees, tumbling over one another on the coarse seagrass and pigface in a flurry of sand. When it was over they were both blood-ied, but neither had won. "You're crazy," Jamie shouted after him as he strode away.

He was still shaking. Not only with the passion of the fight and the hard blows he had taken, but with the shock of what he had discovered, which the furious involvement of blood and limbs and sweat and breath had failed to mitigate or change. He went and sat under the pump where the campers came to fetch water, tugging on the bit of looped wire that worked the handle and letting gush after gush of chill water pummel his skull. He sat with his arms around his drawn-up knees, uncontrollably shaking, and the tears he shed were hidden by the rush of water, and the din it made replaced for a moment the turbulence of his thoughts.

"Looks like you picked the wrong guy," Milt remarked when he came in. One cheek was raw and he had the beginnings of a black eye.

"Jack!" his mother exclaimed. "This isn't like you."

He couldn't look at either of them and shrugged his shoulders when they asked if he was all right.

They treated him gently after that. Warily. Trying not to make too much of it. As if, he thought, they preferred not to know why he had been fighting, or not to have it said. It was Mrs. Schindler who tended his cheek. But when she tried to cuddle him, he slipped out of her grip, and when Dolfie, at the end of their meal, waited as usual for him to help carry scraps out to the chooks, he turned his back on him. "You can drop dead," he hissed. His only comfort was his wounds.

AT EITHER END of the beach at Scarborough was a twelve-foot-high slippery-slide, a tower of raw saplings with a ladder on one side, its rungs so widely spaced that you had to be nine or ten years old to climb them, and on the other a polished chute. On the platform between, four or five kids could huddle, waiting their turn and threatening to shove one another off, or sit with their legs dangling while sunlight crusted the salt on their backs.

For a long time Jack had been too young for the slippery-slide. Then, last Christmas, when he was ready, he had been shocked to discover that he had no head for heights. The climb was all right;

so was the slide. The bad bit was having to wait on the platform. In his dream he found himself alone up there with a king tide running.

He was in deep trouble. Dark water rushed and foamed out of sight below, the flimsy structure shuddered and creaked. Worse still, the saplings that supported the platform had done their own growing in his sleep, so that when he shuffled forward on his knees to look over the edge, his head reeled. How had he found the courage to climb so high, to make his arms reach across the space between the rungs? No wonder his whole body ached. In the end there was nothing for it but to jump himself awake. It was the only way down.

He was sweating. Silvery flashes lashed the louvres of the sleep-out. They rattled in their frames. The tin roof drummed. They got these storms along the coast down here, in January when the king tides were running.

He rolled out of bed.

Barefoot, in just his pyjama bottoms and still shaken by his dream, he stepped outside and, like a child younger than his present self, a six-year-old still scared of the dark, started off down the verandah to where his parents slept.

Rain was beating in under the rails, forming pools of lightning round every post. Rivulets followed the cracks in the floorboards. Careful not to get his feet wet, he stepped over them—he was awake enough for that—and turned the corner towards his mother's room, which was halfway down the long side of the house, facing the front.

When he came to the french doors, they were open. The rain on the roof was deafening.

His first thought was that he had found his way back to a time, three years ago, when his father was still here. There were two figures on the bed.

Or—his mind worked slowly—or his mother had hit upon a way of summoning his father to her in the night. Some spell. His heart leapt. Daddy! Dad! The words were already on his lips.

The two figures were fiercely engaged. He knew what it was,

what they were doing. He had heard the facts of it. But nothing he had been told or imagined was a preparation for the extent to which, in their utter absorption in one another, they had freed themselves of all restraint. They were at a point of concentrated savagery that for all its intensity of thrusting and clutching was not violent, not at all, and not scary either, though it did set his heart beating.

His mother's head was thrown back and flinging from side to side. Her mouth was open, moaning. And Milt's breadth of shoulders and long back—for it was Milt, he could see that now—was rising and falling to the tune she sang, or it was Milt's tune they moved to, and she had discovered it, the one he hummed under his breath. What Jack was reminded of was moments when, in a kind of freedom that only his body had access to, he ceased for a time to be a boy and became a porpoise, rolling over and under the skin of sunlight all down the length of the Bay. Under the waves, then over. Entering, emerging. From air to water, then back again.

There was a lightning flash. The whole room for a moment was blindingly illuminated, the high ceiling, the walls, the rippled sheet and the figures beneath it. And there, on the other side of the bed, glimpsed only for the merest second before it fell back into the half-dark, was another figure, also watching.

It was his father. Bare-ribbed, long-necked, in a pair of old pyjama bottoms that hung below the hollow of his belly, he stood watching, in an exclusion that made him ghostlike, as if the world he belonged to was the otherworld of the dead. Jack strained to make him out there, to hold on to the sight of him. And realised, with a little shock, what the apparition really was. Not a ghost, but himself, fantastically elongated in the glass of the old-fashioned wardrobe.

Something snapped then. He heard it. A sound louder than the crack of thunder or the rising climax of their cries, or his own smaller one, which they were too far off now in the far place to which their bodies had carried them to hear.

. . .

HE STOOD, barefoot and still in pyjamas, at the very edge of the diving-board above the empty pool, using his weight to test the springs. He did not raise his arms or practise his pose.

The garden had been badly hit. There were smashed branches all over, and the pool had leaves in it and puddles where tiny frogs squatted and leapt. There was a strangeness. Some of it was in the light. But some of it, he knew, was in him. Keeping as close as possible to his normal routine, he went in, changed into a pair of shorts, and went out through the gate, across the road and down the red-soil track to the beach.

It was early, just before six, but men were already out tightening guy-ropes, digging new trenches round their camps. There was a high tide running. It was grey, its dull waves crested with weed as if a gigantic shark out there were showing first its back, then its belly, leaden, dangerous. Little kids, standing on isolated hillocks in the dunes, were gesturing towards it, marvelling at the absence of beach, dancing about on a ledge of soft sand that fell abruptly to foam.

He went on to the north end where the storm-water channel ran all the way to the water's edge, in a tangle of yellow-flowering native hibiscus so dense and anciently intertwined that without once setting your foot to the ground you could move on through it all the way to the beach. He swung up on to a low branch and made his way along it, gripping with his toes and using his arms for balance, then hauled himself on to a new branch higher up.

It was another world up here, a place so hidden and old, so deeply mythologized by the games they played in the twists and turns of its branches, their invented world of tribes and wars and castles, that the moment you hauled yourself up into its big-leafed light and shade you shook loose of the actual, were freed of ground rules and the habits of a life lived on floorboards and in rooms.

Hauling himself up from branch to branch, higher than he had ever been before, he found a place where he was invisible from below but had the whole bay before him.

It was an established custom that they came to the Trees only in the afternoon. He had the place to himself. Feeling the damp air begin to heat, he settled and let himself sink into an easy state where it was his blood that did the thinking for him, or his thumbs, or the small of his back where it was set hard against rough bark. From high up among leaves he watched the tide turn and begin, imperceptibly at first, then with swiftness, to go out.

His father would not be coming back. That was the first fact he had to face. And the second was that his mother already knew and had accepted it. Somewhere too deep for thought, he too had known it. The pain and bafflement of his first reaction had been at some failure of his own: he had let his father go; his will had not been strong enough to prevent him from slipping away. But he saw now that that was foolish. There were things that were out of your control. And if this was scary, it was also a relief. There were happenings out there in the world that you were not responsible for.

He must have slept then, because when he looked out again the morning had moved on. The sun was out. Mothers were pegging clothes to improvised lines, along with towels and old rags that had been used to sop up the rain. Others were dragging out furniture as well, stretcher-beds and mattresses, suitcases, the wooden, gauze-sided cupboards where groceries were kept. Fathers were going from tent to tent inspecting damage, tendering advice. He could see it all from up here. Weak rays were lighting the tent flaps and the tarpaulins laid out on the grass, but would soon be stronger.

Inside, card games would be starting up, Fish or Grab for the littlies, Euchre for the older kids, or Pontoon or Poker. He did not have to look in to see any of this.

Fran Williams would be laid across a stretcher with *The Count of Monte Cristo* open on the grass below. The Ludlow girls would have set up their grocery shop, its cardboard shelves stacked with tiny packets of tea, rice, sugar, sago, and little stamped coins in piles to shop with. Along the shoreline, processions of treasure hunters were poking about among the rubble of seaweed and cuttlefish shells and Have-a-Heart sticks.

Eventually, not long from now, he would go down and join them, and later again, not too late, not too early either, but at his usual hour, he would make his way back to Schindler's.

He sat a little longer, enjoying the sense that there was no rush. In a state of easy well-being. Refreshed, restored. Then, as slowly as he had come, he began to make his way back down through the open tangle; at one moment poised upright, at another crouched and reaching out till he could find a further branch to swing on, then hanging, then swinging out again in the slowest sort of flying twenty feet above the ground.

If he had bothered to think about it he would have said that he was happy. But as he came to the last of the trees and dropped lightly to the sand, he was thinking only that he was hungry and could do with a bit of breakfast and how hot the sun felt on his shoulders and how good it would be to put his hand out, have Arnold Garrett take it, and know that all was well again.

Not entirely well. There was a shadow on his heart that would be there for many years to come, a feeling of loss from which he would only slowly be released. But he was too young to conceive of more years than he had known, and the sun was getting hotter by the minute, and a little kid he had seen often enough but had never spoken to was hailing him from the top of a dune. "Hey," he called, "is your name Jack? There's some boys been lookin' for you, all over. I know where they are if you like. Hey," he said, "what about that? They been lookin' all over and I'm the one that found you."

No you didn't, he might have told him, I wasn't lost. But the boy was so pleased with himself that Jack did not want to disappoint him. "Come on," he said, and they set off together down the ravaged beach.

Closer

THERE WAS A TIME, not so long ago, when we saw my uncle
Charles twice each year, at Easter and Christmas. He lives in
Sydney but would come like the rest of us to eat at the big table at
my grandmother's, after church. We're Pentecostals. We believe
that all that is written in the Book is clear truth without error. Just
as it is written, so it is. Some of us speak in tongues and others
have the gift of laying on hands. This is a grace we are granted
because we live as the Lord wishes, in truth and charity.

My name is Amy, but in the family I am called Ay, and my
brothers, Mark and Ben, call me Rabbit. Next year, when I am ten,
and can think for myself and resist the influences, I will go to
school like the boys. In the meantime my grandmother teaches
me. I am past long division.

Uncle Charles is the eldest son, the firstborn. When you see
him in family photographs with my mother and Uncle James and
Uncle Matt, he is the blondest; his eyes have the most sparkle to
them. My mother says he was always the rebel. She says his
trouble is he never grew up. He lives in Sydney, which Grandpa
Morpeth says is Sodom. This is the literal truth, as Aaron's rod,
which he threw at Pharaoh's feet, did literally become a serpent
and Jesus turned water into wine. The Lord destroyed Sodom and
he is destroying Sydney, but with fire this time that is slow and
invisible. It is burning people up but you don't see it because they
burn from within. That's at the beginning. Later, they burn visibly,
and the sight of the flames blistering and scorching and blacken-
ing and wasting to the bone is horrible.

Because Uncle Charles lives in Sodom we do not let him visit.

If we did, we might be touched. He is one of the fools in Israel—
that is what Grandpa Morpeth calls him. He has practised abomi-
nations. Three years ago he confessed this to my Grandpa and
Grandma and my uncles James and Matt, expecting them to welcome his frankness. Since then he is banished, he is as water
spilled on the ground that cannot be gathered up again. So that we
will not be infected by the plague he carries, Grandpa has forbidden him to come on to the land. In fact, he is forbidden to come at
all, though he does come, at Easter and Christmas, when we see
him across the home-paddock fence. He stands far back on the
other side and my grandfather and grandmother and the rest of us
stand on ours, on the grass slope below the house.

We live in separate houses but on the same farm, which is
where my mother and Uncle James and Uncle Matt, and Uncle
Charles when he was young, grew up, and where my uncles James
and Matt still work.

They are big men with hands swollen and scabbed from the
farm work they do, and burnt necks and faces, and feet with toenails grey from sloshing about in rubber boots in the bails. They
barge about the kitchen at five o'clock in their undershorts, still
half asleep, then sit waiting for Grandma to butter their toast and
pour their tea. Then they go out and milk the herd, hose out the
bails, drive the cows to pasture and cut and stack lucerne for winter feed—sometimes my brothers and I go with them. They are
blond like Uncle Charles, but not so blond, and the hair that
climbs out above their singlets, under the Adam's apple, is dark.
They are jokers, they like to fool about. They are always teasing.
They have a wild streak but have learned to keep it in. My mother
says they should marry and have wives.

Working a dairy farm is a healthy life. The work is hard but
good. But when I grow up I mean to be an astronaut.

Ours is a very pleasant part of the country. We are blessèd. The
cattle are fat, the pasture's good. The older farmhouses, like my
grandfather's, are large, with many rooms and wide verandahs,
surrounded by camphor laurels, and bunyas and hoop-pines and
Scotch firs. Sodom is far off, but one of the stations on the line is at

the bottom of our hill and many trains go back and forth. My uncle Charles, however, comes by car.

His car is silver. It is a BMW and cost an arm and a leg. It has sheepskin seat covers and a hands-free phone. When Uncle Charles is on the way he likes to call and announce his progress.

The telephone rings in the hallway. You answer. There are pips, then Uncle Charles says in a jokey kind of voice: "This is GAY 437 calling. I am approaching Bulahdelah." The air roaring through the car makes his voice sound weird, like a spaceman's. Far off. It is like a spaceship homing in.

Later he calls again. "This is GAY 437," the voice announces. "I am approaching Wauchope."

"Don't any one of you pick up that phone," my grandfather orders.

"But, Grandpa," my brother Ben says, "it might be Mrs. McTaggart." Mrs. McTaggart is a widow and our neighbour.

"It won't be," Grandpa says. "It will be him."

He is a stranger to us, as if he had never been born. This is what Grandpa says. My grandmother says nothing. She was in labour for thirty-two hours with Uncle Charles, he was her first. For her, it can never be as if he had never been born, even if she too has cast him out. I heard my mother say this. My father told her to shush.

You can see his car coming from far off. You can see it *approaching*. It is very like a spaceship, silver and fast; it flashes. You can see its windscreen catching the sun as it rounds the curves between the big Norfolk Island pines of the golf course and the hospital, then its flash flash between the trees along the river. When it pulls up on the road outside our gate there is a humming like something from another world, then all four windows go up of their own accord, all together, with no one winding, and Uncle Charles swings the driver's door open and steps out.

He is taller than Uncle James or Uncle Matt, taller even than Grandpa, and has what the Book calls beautiful locks. They are blond. "Bleached," my grandfather tells us. "Peroxide!" He is tanned and has the whitest teeth I have ever seen.

The corruption is invisible. The fire is under his clothes and inside him, hidden beneath the tan.

The dogs arrive, yelping. All bunched together, they go bounding over the grass to the fence, leaping up on one another's backs with their tails wagging to lick his hands as he reaches in to fondle them.

"Don't come any closer," my grandfather shouts. "We can see you from there."

His voice is gruff, as if he had suddenly caught cold, which in fact he never does, or as if a stranger was speaking for him. Uncle Charles has broken his heart. Grandpa has cast him out, as you cut off a limb so that the body can go on living. But he likes to see that he is still okay. That it has not yet begun.

And in fact he looks wonderful—as far as you can see. No marks.

Once when he got out of the car he had his shirt off. His chest had scoops of shadow and his shoulders were golden and so smooth they gave off a glow. His whole body had a sheen to it.

Uncle James and Uncle Matt are hairy men like Esau, they are shaggy. But his chest and throat and arms were like an angel's, smooth and polished as wood.

You see the whiteness of his teeth, and when he takes off his sunglasses the sparkle of his eyes, and his smoothness and the blondness of his hair, but you do not see the marks. This is because he does not come close.

My grandmother stands with her hands clasped, and breathes but does not speak. Neither does my mother, though I have heard her say to my father, in an argument: "Charlie's just a big kid. He never grew up. He was always such fun to be with."

"Helen!" my father said.

I know my grandmother would like Uncle Charles to come closer so that she could really see how he looks. She would like him to come in and eat. There is always enough, we are blessèd. There is an ivory ring with his initial on it, C, in the dresser drawer with the napkins, and when we count the places at table she pretends to make a mistake, out of habit, and sets one extra.

But not the ring. The place stays empty all through our meal. No one mentions it.

I know it is Grandpa Morpeth's heart that is broken, because he has said so, but it is Grandma Morpeth who feels it most. She likes to touch. She is always lifting you up and hugging. She does not talk much.

When we go in to eat and take up our napkins and say grace and begin passing things, he does not leave; he stays there beside his car in the burning sunlight. Sometimes he walks up and down outside the fence and shouts. It is hot. You can feel the burning sweat on him. Then, after a time, he stops shouting and there is silence. Then the door of his car slams and he roars off.

I would get up if I was allowed and watch the flash flash of metal as he takes the curves round the river, past the hospital, then the golf course. But by the time everyone is finished and we are allowed to get down, he is gone. There is just the wide green pasture, open and empty, with clouds making giant shadows and the trees by the river in a silvery shimmer, all their leaves humming a little and twinkling as they turn over in a breeze that otherwise you might not have felt.

Evil is in the world because of men and their tendency to sin. Men fell into error so there is sin, and because of sin there is death. Once the error has got in, there is no fixing it. Not in this world. But it is sad, that, it is hard. Grandpa says it has to be; that we must do what is hard to show that we love what is good and hate what is sinful, and the harder the thing, the more love we show Him.

But I don't understand about love any more than I do about death. It seems harder than anyone can bear to stand on one side of the fence and have Uncle Charles stand there on the other. As if he was already dead, and death was stronger than love, which surely cannot be.

When we sit down to our meal, with his chair an empty space, the food we eat has no savour. I watch Grandpa Morpeth cut pieces of meat with his big hands and push them between his teeth, and chew and swallow, and what he is eating, I know, is ashes. His heart is closed on its grief. And that is what love is. That is what death is. Us inside at the table, passing things and eating, and him outside, as if he had never been born; dead to us, but shouting. The silver car with its dusky windows that roll up of their own accord and the phone in there in its cradle is the chariot of death, and the voice announcing, "I am on the way, I am approaching Gloucester, I am approaching Taree"—what can that be but the angel of death?

The phone rings in the house. It rings and rings. We pause at the sink, in the middle of washing up, my grandmother and my mother and me, but do not look at one another. My grandfather says: "Don't touch it. Let it ring." So it keeps ringing for a while, then stops. Like the shouting.

This Easter for the first time he did not come. We waited for the telephone to ring and I went out, just before we sat down to our meal, to look for the flash of his car along the river. Nothing. Just the wide green landscape lying still under the heat, with not a sign of movement in it.

That night I had a dream, and in the dream he did come. We stood below the verandah and watched his car pull up outside the fence. The smoky windows went up, as usual. But when the door swung open and he got out, it was not just his shirt he had taken off, but all his clothes, even his shoes and socks. Everything except his sunglasses. You could see his bare feet in the grass, large and bony, and he glowed, he was smooth all over, like an angel.

He began to walk up to the fence. When he came to it he stood still a moment, frowning. Then he put his hand out and walked on, walked right through it to our side, where we were waiting. What I thought, in the dream, was that the lumpy coarse-stemmed grass was the same on both sides, so why not? If one thick blade didn't know any more than another that the fence was there, why should his feet?

When he saw what he had done he stopped, looked back at the fence, and laughed. All around his feet, little daisies and gaudy, bright pink clover flowers began to appear, and the petals glowed like metal, molten in the sun but cool, and spread uphill to where we were standing, and were soon all around us and under our shoes. Insects, tiny grasshoppers, sprang up and went leaping, and glassy snails no bigger than your little fingernail hung on the grass stems, quietly feeding. He took off his sunglasses, looked down at them, and laughed. Then looked across to where we were, waiting. I had such a feeling of lightness and happiness it was as if my bones had been changed into clouds, just as the tough grass had been changed into flowers.

I knew it was a dream. But dreams can be messages. The feeling that comes with them is real, and if you hold on to it you can make the rest real. So I thought: if he can't come to us, I must go to him.

So this is what I do. I picture him. There on the other side of the fence, naked, his feet pressing the springy grass. *Stretch out your hand*, I tell him. *Like this.* I stretch my hand out. *If you have faith, the fence will open for you, as the sea did before Moses when he reached out his hand.* He looks puzzled. *No*, I tell him, *don't think about it. Just let it happen.*

It has not happened yet. But it will. Then, when he is close at last, when he has passed through the fence and is on our side, I will stretch out my hand and touch him, just under the left breast, and he will be whole. He will feel it happening to him and laugh. His laughter will be the proof. I want this more than anything. It is my heart's desire.

Each night now I lie quiet in the dark and go over it. The winding up of the smoky windows of the chariot of death. The swinging open of the door. Him stepping out and looking towards me behind his sunglasses. Me telling him what I tell myself:

Open your heart now. Let it happen. Come closer, closer. See? Now reach out your hand.

Dream Stuff

1

COLIN'S EARLIEST MEMORY was of the day his mother's Doberman Maxie died, of heartworm, they said; he had dragged himself up under the house near the front steps and would not come out.

Late in the morning Colin slipped away and, crawling on his hands and knees in the dirt, though the place had always scared him—it was all dustballs and spiders, some of them just shells but others alive and skittering—he had gone up after Maxie and crouched there holding the big floppy creature in his arms.

The slats that closed in their under-the-house made the place dim, even in daylight. But up where Maxie lay, still drawing breath, there was the fleshy green light of the gladioli stems that rose stiffly on either side of their front steps.

Colin stayed up there the whole day, hugging Maxie and listening to footsteps in the rooms overhead: Mrs. Hull going from room to room as she swept and made beds, then coming heavy-footed down the hallway to the postman, then going out the back again for the ice.

About lunchtime they began calling to him. Casually at first, then with increasing anxiety. Mrs. Hull, then his mother, then, joining them, the first of the ladies who had arrived for Bridge. Finally—it was afternoon by now—his father, who had been called home from work.

"Colin," his father said severely from far off where their washtubs stood, "come on out of there."

But he turned his face away and would not be persuaded.

His father, handing his jacket to Mr. Hull, started up through the forest of stumps, crouched at first, then crawling, then wriggling on his belly. His tie was loose, his cufflinks jingled. Colin could hear them and the heavy breathing as his father emerged from the middle darkness and came up to where there was light.

"Colin," he said, "what are you doing? Come on out, son. It's time to come out."

"No," he said. "Not unless Maxie does."

"Colin, Maxie is very sick, we can't help him. Now, be a good fellow and come out." The voice was exasperated but calm, holding on hard against shortness of breath rather than shortness of temper.

Colin had no memory of what happened next. The story as they told it simply trailed off, or led, in that anthology of anecdote and legend that is family history, to another story altogether. The occasion remained suspended at a point where he was still crammed into the close space under the floorboards, with the big dog warm in his arms and the whole weight of the house on his shoulders, while his father, dark-faced and wheezy with hayfever, stretched a hand towards him, all the fingers tense to grasp or be grasped, and his brow greasy with sweat; as if he were the one who was trapped up there dying—the worm at his heart taking all his breath.

This image was overlaid with another from perhaps a year later.

They were staying at his grandfather's house at Woody Point. His father was teaching him to swim. One afternoon, after several attempts to make him let go and strike out for himself, his father carried him out of his depth in the still, salty water and, breaking contact, stepped away. "Now, Colin," he commanded, "swim."

His father's face, just feet away, was grim and unyielding. He floundered, flinging his arms about wildly, gasping, his throat tight with the saltiness that was both the ocean and his own tears. He dared not open his mouth to cry out. He choked, while his father, his features those of a stony god, continued to urge him and back away.

As Colin saw himself, he wore, as he gasped and thrashed at the surface, the same look of desperation that he had seen in his father when, with his chin thrust up and the muscles of his neck horribly distended as his whole body fought for breath, he lay stretched on his belly in the dust.

So it was from somewhere far up under their house at Red Hill, or choking in the waters off Woody Point, that he woke now to his hotel bedroom and a climate established somewhere in an unearthly season between autumn and early spring, in a place that might have been anywhere but was in fact, for the first time in nearly thirty years, home—that is, the city he had grown up in, though when he went to the window there was little that recalled that exotic and far-off place save a lingering warmth out of his dream and a tightening of anxiety in his throat.

All that belonged to the interior view. Down below, in the real one, the big country town of his childhood, with its wharves and bond-stores and two-storeyed verandahed pubs, had been levelled to make way for flyovers, multi-level car parks, tower blocks that flashed like tinfoil and warped what they reflected—which was steel girders, other towers like themselves and cranes that swung like giant insects from cloud to cloud. Brisbane, as his cousin Coralie put it, had "gone ahead." It was a phrase people used here with a mixture of uneasy pride and barbed, protective humour, expecting him, out of affection for the slatternly, poor-white city of his youth, to deplore this new addiction to metal and glass.

Well, he did and he did not. It wasn't nostalgia for a world that had long since disappeared under fathoms of poured concrete that had led him, in half a dozen fictions, to raise it again in the density of tropical vegetation, timber soft to the thumb, the drumming of rain on corrugated-iron roofs. What drew him back was something altogether more personal, which belonged to the body and its hot affinities, to a history where, in the pain and longing of adolescence, he was still standing at the corner of Queen and Albert Streets waiting for someone he knew now would never appear.

He had long understood that one of his selves, the earliest and most vulnerable, had never left this place, and that his original and clearest view of things could be recovered only through what had first come to him in the glow of its ordinary light and weather. In a fig tree taller than a building and alive with voices not its own, or a line of palings with a gap you could crawl through into a wilderness of nut-grass and cosmos and saw-legged grasshoppers as big as wrens.

It was the light they appeared in that was the point, and that at least had not changed. It fell on the new city with the same promise of an ordinary grace as on the old. He greeted it with the delight of recovery, not only of the vision but of himself.

HE HAD LEFT the place when he was not yet twenty. That was the year his mother went back to Sydney.

Twenty-three years earlier, his father, on a weekend rowing trip, had discovered her there and brought her north. She had never really settled. When she put the old house up for auction and went home, Colin had seized the chance to make his own escape. He went to London. Till now he had not come back.

In the twenty years that they lived together he had found his mother a puzzle, and where his need for affection was concerned, a frustration.

A lean ghost of a woman, intense, but not in his way, she had prowled the house with an ashtray in her hand, distractedly chain-smoking, argued with friends on the phone, mostly men-friends, gone to committee meetings and charity drives, and was always interested, out of a sense of duty, in his doings but reticent about her own. Dissatisfied, he thought, maybe desperate—he could not tell, and he knew she would not have wanted him to ask. She made no enquiry about *his* feelings. They got through his childhood and adolescence without ever being close.

Then something unexpected occurred. Freed by distance, they found a way of being intimate at last. Perhaps it was the writing itself that did it. Anyway, the letters she sent him, warm, inventive, humourously critical of everything she came across (he recognised, he thought, and with curiosity now, the tone of her telephone conversations), were those of a woman he more and more wanted to know. So much of what he was haunted by, all that underworld of his early memories and their crooked history, was in her keeping. If he was ever to get to the heart of it he would need her as his guide.

He no longer tormented himself with the wish that things had been different. They had made him what he was. But he did want to know why the world he had grown up in had been so harsh and uncompromising, and had made so little room for love.

Then there was the question of his father. His father had disappeared in the waters off Crete in May 1942. Swimming out on a night of no moon to be rescued along with other remnants of a defeated army by the British submarine *Torbay*, he had tired and gone under.

Colin, who was just six, had believed for a time that he was actually there and had seen it happen, but understood at last that he had been imposing on that moonless night on the far side of the world the only clear memories he had of his father and their time together; though even then there was part of him in which his presence out there, in those dark unknown waters, remained more vivid than either.

Each year as Christmas drew near he would suggest to his mother that he should come and visit. They would see one another at last and talk.

How wonderful, she wrote. How she would look forward to it. But she managed, each time, to find excuses, and he guessed that she was unwilling to put to the test this long-distance intimacy that had grown up between them. Her dying suddenly, with no suggestion of a previous illness, made him wonder how much more she had been keeping from him.

Arriving before the last of his letters, he put it into the coffin along with the many other questions to which he must accept now that there would be no answer, and since he was here, and unlikely to come back a second time, accepted an invitation to fly up to Brisbane and give a reading.

It was a strange homecoming. He knew no one in Brisbane but his cousin Corrie. He was forty-eight years old and nobody's child.

ONE OF THE FEW mementoes his father had left was a little green-bound pocket diary in which, for a few days in Athens, in the year of his death, he had recorded in his Queenslander's big copybook hand what he had seen of a city whose every monument he had already wandered through in dreams, but which had to be excavated, by the time he got there, from towers of rubble.

What moved Colin when he first turned its pages was the passion he found even in the driest details, and the glimpse he got, which was clear but fleeting, of a young man he felt close to but had barely known, and who had himself to be resurrected now from scribbled notes and statistics, tiny painstaking sketches of capitals and the motifs off daggers in a dusty museum, and from half a dozen hastily scrawled street maps.

He stuffed the diary into the bottom of his rucksack and when, at the end of his first year in Europe, he went to Athens, spent a whole day trying to match the sketches to a modern map of the city.

What he had hoped to recover was some defining image of his father, some more intimate view of the amateur classicist and champion athlete who had played so large and yet so ghostly a part in his existence. He stood at corner after corner turning the sketch-map this way and that until, admitting at last that he was bushed, he took himself off to a café on Venizelou.

He was settled there in front of a cold beer, still sweating, when he was approached by a dandified stranger, a fellow not much older, he guessed, than himself, but with a gold wedding-band on his finger, who seemed to have mistaken him for someone else. Anyway, they got talking, and when his new friend, out of pure pride in the place, offered to show him around a little—the sights, the real sights—he accepted.

His guide was so knowledgeable, he talked so well and in such impeccable English, that Colin, who had been wary at first, was soon at his ease. And it was astonishing how often it happened that

Giorgios in his excitable way said: "Look, Colin, now look at this," and there it was, just what the diary had described as being wonderful but hard to come upon and which on his own he had been unable to find.

They moved deeper and deeper into a maze. After the classical sights, the Byzantine—though "after" in fact was not quite accurate, because everything here was a patchwork in which bits of one period were used to hold up or decorate another, a half-column here, a slab there with two peacocks and a laurel wreath, so that styles and centuries tended to collapse into one another. As the afternoon wore on, the sights closed in. They were in a tangle of narrow streets where men with baskets were selling twists of salt-crusted bread and sticky honey-cakes; a crowded place, noisy, garish, where his new friend seemed to know everyone they met, and introduced him to men who showed him brasswork and filigree silver and other antique relics, but gave out, in an obscure way, that they had other wares to dispose of, though he could not guess what they might be and his new friend did not elucidate.

They stepped into one dark little taverna to drink ouzo, and into another to smoke, and afterwards he had the sensation that time, as he had already discovered among the monuments, was more a continual looping here than a straight line. He half expected, as a narrow street turned back upon itself, to see his father appear in the shadowy crowd, though there was no indication in the diary that he had been in this place. Then quite suddenly, in a poky alleyway with stalls full of brazen pots and icons, his friend was gone.

It was the oddest thing imaginable. One minute he was there, as affable and eager as ever, and the next he had slipped away.

There was no misunderstanding. Or if there was, Colin had failed to observe it. Perhaps his guide had lost patience with him, with his failure—was that it?—to catch at suggestions. Or he had seen friends close by and, not wishing to desert him openly—anyway, the occasion was broken off, that is what Colin felt. Things had been moving towards some event or revelation that at the last moment, for whatever reason, had been withheld.

He was disappointed for a time, but came at last to feel that it might have been the best thing after all. He heard tales later of tourists, too trusting like himself, who had been led on and then robbed or assaulted. Perhaps the fellow had thought better of it and let him off. But the teasing suggestion of something more to come, which was unseen but strongly felt, and had to be puzzled over and guessed at, appealed to him. To a side of him that preferred not to come to conclusions. That lived most richly in mystery and suspended expectation. The afternoon had a shape that he came to feel was exemplary, and his readers might have been surprised to know how often the fictions he created derived their vagrant form, but even more their mixture of openness and hidden, half-sought-for menace, from an occasion he had never got to the bottom of, for all that he had gone back time after time and let his imagination play with its many possibilities.

So NOW, shaved, showered and with a pot of strong coffee at his elbow, he got down to it, the usual routine.

He wrote quickly, his blood brightening the moment he took up where he had left off the day before. His people drew breath again, turned their mute, expectant faces towards him.

He had moved the desk so that it faced the wall. The sun was already high and the city in a swelter, but the room he was writing in seemed within reach of invisible snow peaks. He wrote in coolness, while down there in weatherboard houses under weeping figs, behind mango and banana trees and spindly rust-coloured palms, his people sweated it out; till just on four in the afternoon, as a longish paragraph found its way towards that hour, the sky cracked, struck, and a storm broke, turning closed rooms into gigantic side-drums crazily beaten and shutting off, for a time, all chance of speech.

He put his pen down. It was almost ten. Quite soon his hosts would appear. That cloudburst had cleared the air. He could leave his people suspended in it, waiting to hear how they should go on.

It had cleared his own head as well, giving things, when he went to the window, an intense glow as if lit from within. The big trees in the Gardens opposite, that in their darkness of packed leaves might have been sinister, seemed filled with a powerful energy: gigantic angels momentarily stilled.

Greenness, that was the thing. Irresistible growth. Though it wasn't always an image of health or of fullness.

He thought of the mangroves with their roots in mud, and under their misshapen arches the stick-eyes of crabs and their ponderous claws. They had been banished for a time under concrete freeways, but would soon be pushing up fleshy roots, their leathery leaves, black rather than green, agleam with salt.

Vegetation spread quickly here. Everything spread quickly— germs, butter, rumours. There was talk of plantations outside the city, in pockets deep in the foothills of the Range, where cannabis was being grown in dense plantations. Each night late, trucks would move into the city, on the lookout for teenagers who had nowhere to sleep or were simply loose in the streets, available for whatever might bring a little action into their lives. They would be approached, hired, loaded on to trucks, and driven blindfolded to the marijuana fields, where in long rows, until first light, they would go about the business of harvesting the green stuff, the dream stuff. Then, towards four thirty, when the sun began to show, after being paid and blindfolded again, they would be driven back and dropped off in the Valley or at Stones Corner, or along the various bus routes into the city.

True? It did not have to be. It was convincing at some deeper level than fact. It expressed something that was continuous with the underground history of the place, with triangles and flayed ribs, the leper colony on its island in the Bay, the men with scabbed and bloody hands sleeping on sacks behind the Markets, an emanation in heavy light and in green, subaqueous air, of an aboriginal misery that no tower block or flyover could entirely obliterate.

He moved one of his characters into place somewhere along

Petrie Terrace where he could be approached. Loose, open, waiting for the truck that had just set out from a covered shed and was wobbling, low down on a rutted track, under moonlit leaves.

It was ten. Precisely. Any moment now his cousin Corrie would ring.

2

HE AND CORALIE had grown up together. In the war years, with his father gone and his mother taken up with a social round that had a new definition as war work, he had spent the long weeks of the Christmas holidays at his Grandfather Lattimer's house at Woody Point, in a muddle of uncles and aunts and their children of whom Coralie James, who was just his age, had always been closest to him. In the obsessive way of only children they had done everything in tandem, having discovered in one another feelings they had thought too private, too much their own and only theirs, to be shared. They exchanged whispered secrets, scared one another with ghost stories, had their own coded language full of private jokes and references, which they would recognise only later as another version of the Lattimer exclusivity, and had, at eight or nine years old, to the amusement of the grown-ups, committed themselves to marriage. They had even picked out the house they meant to live in. A two-storeyed cottage with dormer windows, it was sufficiently unlike the houses they and their friends lived in to suggest possibilities of behaviour, of feeling too, quite different from the ones they found unsatisfactory at home.

Well, it had come to nothing, of course. A childish dream. Only once after those early years had he and Coralie spent any time together.

At twenty-five she had turned up in Swinging London, at a time, just after the birth of their second daughter, when he and Jane were still dealing happily with broken nights, babies' bottles, and wet nappies drying on a ceiling rack in the damp little kitchen. Coralie, while she made up her mind between a teaching job in Portugal and a return to the arms of a boy in Brisbane who was prepared to wait, though not perhaps for ever, had spent six weeks on the floor of their basement living room.

It was the time, as well, of his first novel, which he wrote each night at the kitchen table, in the early hours while his family slept in the room next door; getting up every half-hour or so and stepping away from the warm sunlight of his Brisbane childhood to feed the coke-fire or make himself a mug of tea, and when the baby woke to walk her up and down a little while a bottle heated. His head would be so brimming with sunlight, and images and whole sentences that he needed to set down before they were gone, that he would write on sometimes with the baby over his shoulder, feeding off her warmth, in a state of wholeness and ease with his life and work that he was never to know so completely again.

In the conspiratorial way of lovers, he and Jane had made alliance against their wanted, unwanted guest. When he crept to bed at last, Jane would tease him about his other woman out there—and he could never be sure how serious she was and whether it was Coralie she meant or his book.

And in fact there was a sense in which they could scarcely be separated, that's what he saw after a time, since it was Coralie's presence he was drawing on when so many vivid pictures came back to him. Of blue sand-crabs spilled from a gunnysack and setting out over the red-earth floor of a hut, till they could be grabbed by the back legs and dropped squealing into the pot. Of tiger-moths at a wire-screen door and the peculiar light of a ribbed sandbank when the tide rippled out and a whole battalion of soldier crabs wheeled and flashed, then darkened.

"She's still in love with you," Jane whispered. "She thinks I'm a mistake. She thinks I'm the interloper."

"Don't be silly," he protested.

"She thinks you two were made for each other. And you love it—you really love it. Being the rooster with two hens."

"Do I?" he asked, genuinely surprised but not entirely displeased with this new and more dashing version of himself.

"Yes, you do—bastard!" Her voice, in playful accusation, had a throatiness, a sensuality that stirred him. "At heart you're a philanderer."

"No I'm not," he told her. "What do you mean? I'm not," and he clasped her more warmly in the rumpled bed.

It became a joke between them, one of her ways of playing up to his ego and exciting him. It had taken him another seven years to see that it was also true.

But she had been wrong about Coralie. Their moment was past. He found her presence at the edge of his enclosed and sufficient family an irritation. Too keen-eyed, too deeply imbued with their Lattimer scepticism, she was an infidel. He resented her humourous disbelief in his being so easily settled. Being settled was important to him—too important, perhaps, that is what she had seen, and if he had been less concerned to defend his own small victory over aimlessness and the fear that without the constraints of a conventional family life he would sink back into the perplexities and self-destructiveness of adolescence, he too might have seen it.

How little he had known himself! What a mess he had made of things. And now, after half a lifetime, this late reunion.

It did not help that Coralie and Jane had remained friends, and that she knew, from Jane's side, all the sorry details, the whole sad story. And would have heard as well that of his two daughters, Eleanor would see him only to make their meetings, each time, the occasion of bitter recriminations and punishment, and Annabel, who had been his favourite, would not see him at all.

THEY HAD BEEN to the North Coast—a patchy occasion, despite the perfect weather. Now, sun-dazed, they were having drinks on the Pedersens' verandah above the river. Coralie, shoes discarded, her bare legs tucked away under her, had retreated into silence. It was Eric who did the talking.

All day, intimidated perhaps by the years they had known one another, his wife and this almost famous cousin, and the times they had shared, or by a kind of play between them which was too

light, too full of allusions he could not catch, and which represented a side of Corrie he did not feel comfortable with, Eric had
been sulky, watchful, determined, Colin thought, not to be drawn
in or impressed. Now, suddenly, he had sprung to life. He
expanded, he was voluble. It was as if he and Coralie shared a
single source of energy, and when one of them drew on it the
other wilted. Or perhaps it was simply that he was on home
ground at last.

He had just made a surprising discovery. That Colin, who in all
other respects seemed a well-informed sort of chap, was entirely
ignorant on the subject of futures.

"I can't believe it," he kept saying. "Corrie, can you believe it?"
Futures, it seemed, were what everyone was into.

Eric, in a way that was almost winning, he was so shyly passionate about the thing, began a lecture on futures and how they
worked, keeping the tone light—he did not want to appear ponderous—but making certain that Colin should not miss the fact
that here too a certain imagination and flair might be demanded.
The thing had its own sort of drama, and considering the dreams
that were dependent on it, and the suspense and disappointments,
might have the makings of a plot.

Colin nodded, but it was like listening to something that, however coherent it might be, made no sense; like a poem in another
tongue. Did Coralie follow it? Was she even listening? He could
make nothing of the little smile she wore. Anyway, she must have
tired of whatever amusement it gave her to see him so easily dis-
comfited. After a moment or two she got up and said: "Well, I'd
better see what I can rustle up to eat." She was abandoning—no,
relinquishing—him. When she called them in, twenty minutes
later, Eric had his arm across Colin's shoulder and had become
cheerily sentimental. They might have been old friends who had
just recaptured, in a series of boyish reminiscences, a moment
forty years back when as spirited ten-year-olds they had slit their
wrists Indian style and shared blood and spit. Colin did not trust
himself to look in Coralie's direction.

"Big things are happening here," Eric was telling him. "We're

going on by leaps and bounds. No holding us. You ought to come
back and be part of it, Colin. We need him, don't we, Corrie?"

"Mango," Coralie told Colin, who was separating something
from the green of his salad, "and shredded ginger," and their eyes
did meet for a moment. But any alliance between them could only
be fleeting. And Eric was too deep in his pleasure in the occasion
to see how lightly they let him off. Was she always so indulgent,
Colin wondered.

Forgive me, she was saying.

No, he said. No need. I'm the one.

The fact was, he was a disappointment to her. She had read too
many of his books. Eric's advantage was that he had read none of
them. Then there was Jane, and London, and all those years when
they had been so close that he could barely separate, when he
looked back, what had been his experience and what hers. He had
stolen a good deal of it—she of all people must know how
much—and made it his own. But the fact that he had used it in his
work did not mean that he had used it up, or got to the end of its
mysteries. It was still precious to him, all of it, and she was so
much part of the way it played on his mind and on his senses,
especially here among so many familiar sounds and objects, that
his feeling for her was as fresh and real in him as it had ever been.
This is what he had wanted, all day, to say to her. But they had
spent the time in small talk. He had said nothing. And in the end it
was Eric who had stepped in and claimed him, and would establish the tone of their last hours together.

There was a kind of comedy in that, and they might have to
settle for the recognition of it in a shared glance as the nearest
they would get, this time round, to their old closeness or the
promise of a new one.

"Goodnight, Colin," she said softly when the taxi arrived and
they went out into the gathered nightsounds of the verandah. The
touch of her hand very softly on his cheek was an assurance.

"Goodnight, mate—keep in touch," Eric told him, leaning into
the window of the taxi. And he called again from the foot of the

steps where Coralie fitted into the hollow of his arm: "And remember, we need you. Come back soon."

3

THE EVENTS of the following hours he would have rejected outright if they had presented themselves to him as the components of a plot. They were too extravagant for the web of quiet incident and subtle shifts of power that were the usual stuff of his fiction. But they occurred and he was not granted the right of refusal. From the moment the Pedersens saw him into the cab (the front seat beside the driver) he was aware that some agency had taken over whose imagination was wilder than his own and which he could neither anticipate nor control.

The driver himself was part of it. Young, bearded, in boxer shorts and sneakers, he was one of the sociable ones, an Armenian or Yugoslav with the broad vowels of the local accent drawlingly prolonged and the consonants of another tongue altogether.

When a few direct questions established that Colin was a visitor, he began evoking possibilities for the remainder of the night: a gambling club, a massage parlour, other darker, more dangerous amenities that were not to be named. When Colin, with a wave of his hand, rejected them, he shrugged and removed himself to a sulky distance, one hairy arm on the steering wheel, the other angled out of the window and drumming lightly on the roof. After five minutes or so of this Colin said abruptly: "Look, just let me out at the next corner, will you? I need a breath of air. I'll walk."

The driver pulled in. "Please yerself," he said. "You're the driver."

He sniggered at his own joke, consulted a card, made calculations, very slowly as if the figures wouldn't add up, and named a price. Safely outside, Colin passed him a note and relinquished the change.

The driver grinned. It wasn't a pleasant grin, and Colin wondered, as he set off beside a row of dingy shops that appeared sinister but were merely unlit, if the fellow hadn't after all delivered him over to one of those obscure and perhaps hazardous occasions that had not been named.

THE CITY AT THIS HOUR was deserted. The street (and he could see down a dip a good half-mile of it) was clear. He thought of flagging down another cab. But that was silly. He knew this place, he had grown up in it, his hotel was five minutes away, and he had the odd conviction that if he did hail a cab it would turn out to be the one he had just got out of making a circle around the block.

He had gone no more than forty yards—past a gunsmith's, its barred windows stacked with rifles and binoculars, a jeweller's, the frosted windows of a bank—when he was aware of a car, a battered Kingswood, that had slowed to walking pace and was travelling close to the pavement beside him. The driver's head was thrust out, in an effort, he realised, to see him more clearly in the diminished light.

He tried to conceal his anxiety, but began to walk faster. When the Kingswood put on speed at last and swung round the next corner, he crossed briskly against the lights, and was just beginning to regain his composure and admonish himself for being a fool when he heard behind him the footfalls of someone running, and a moment later was being pushed back hard against a wall.

It was a matter of seconds. His attacker, too close for him to get any impression except of damp flesh, had him pinioned and was breathing heat into his neck.

"You din' expect that, didja," the man hissed. "Didja? Didja?" With each question he pushed his face closer and jerked Colin's arm. "You cunt!"

He whispered this almost lovingly into Colin's ear.

"I seen you get outa that cab. I knew I'd catch up with you sooner or later. Cunt!"

Colin's panic, now that the situation had declared itself, had given way to raging anger. He was surprised at the intensity of it and at how clear-headed he felt.

"Get off," he shouted, and raised his elbow and pushed.

"Oh no you don't," the fellow warned, and he held him even closer, half smiling, very pleased with himself. A lean-faced fellow of maybe thirty, red-headed, unshaven, wearing a singlet. Colin could smell the excitement that came off him, a yeasty sourness. When he was satisfied his grip was firm, he leaned back a little and said easily: "So here we are, eh? Just the two 'v us." He gave a short laugh, but seemed now to lose concentration, as if he did not know what should come next. Perhaps his arm was tiring and it had occurred to him that he could not go on holding Colin for ever. "I seen you get outa that cab," he said again. Then he found what it was he really wanted to say. "You din' think I'd face up to yer, didja? Well, you made a bad mistake, feller. I'm fed up t' th' gizzard. I'd rather fucken finish off the both of us." He said this with passion, his voice rising to a sobbing note, but did not move.

"Look," Colin said, "this is crazy. I don't even know who you are."

"Don't you? Don't you? Well, that's what you would say."

Once again the energy had gone out of him. He swung his head from side to side as if looking out for something. "Only I'm not that much of a mug. I know you've been with 'er. I wanta hear you say it. Say it, cunt! Bloody say it!"

These were not so much orders as desperate appeals. When Colin did not respond, the fellow looked about again, and with a forceful motion broke his grip, then stood slumped, his arms hanging. His face was distorted with a pain so naked and hopeless that Colin, who was free now and might have run, was mesmerized. The man raised his voice in a dismal howl. "Say it," he sobbed. But hopelessly now, as if the words were a spell that had failed to work, or whose purpose he could no longer recall.

I should get away now, Colin told himself. This is the dangerous bit. That other stuff was nothing. Just bluster. This is it. And almost on the thought a knife appeared in the man's hand. He

stepped back, the knife flashed, and with a series of anguished
cries he began slashing at the freckled, dead-white flesh of his own
neck and shoulder and at the dirty singlet, which was immediately
drenched with blood.

"For God's sake!" Colin shouted.

But the man was now triumphant. He stood at the edge of the
pavement with his head thrown back in the light of a streetlamp
and wielded the knife in slow motion while Colin, helplessly,
watched. "There!" he sobbed, "There! There!"—as if what he had
wanted all along was not Colin's life but his attention, and the sobs
came as regular as the gushes of his blood.

Colin, without thinking, made a grab for the knife and felt himself cut.

There was blood everywhere now, some of it on the man's body,
some of it on him. The knife slid away into the gutter and they
were locked fiercely together on the pavement, grunting and
shouting wordlessly between breaths until, with a mechanical
whooping and a pulsing of blue light, a car came screaming to a
halt beside them and Colin felt himself hauled skyward by a hefty
cop. "Okay, feller," he was being advised, "you just calm down,
eh?" The incident was at an end.

He was covered with blood. The other man, savagely wounded,
was weeping and on his knees.

It wasn't till he was in the squad car, and his heart had slackened
a little, that he caught up with the enormity of the thing. The
blood that covered his shirt and jacket in a sticky mess was the
stranger's. He was barely scratched.

"BUT IT DOESN'T make sense, now does it, Colin?" the larger of
the two detectives told him. He was speaking gently, with toler-
ance for a naïvety that might, after all, be genuine; as one talks to a
bemused and stubborn child.

The room seemed too small for the three of them. There was
too much light.

"Now, tell us again, Colin. You get out of the cab. Why? What was it that upset you? In what way did this Armenian, or Yugoslav, seem threatening?"

The more often he told it the less probable it became. He saw that. A taxi-driver he had been eager to get away from, at midnight, half a mile from his hotel. A perfect stranger who first attacked and abused him and then turned the knife on himself. The only fact he could produce was his identity.

These sceptical fellows, who had never heard of him of course, were not impressed. "What sort of books, Colin?" the blond one, who was larger, enquired with a sneer. He was called Lindenmeyer, the other Creager.

After a time they allowed him to ring the Pedersens, and Coralie verified that, yes, he had been with them. They had seen him off in the taxi. The driver was dark. Greek maybe, Lebanese. "Listen, Colin," she whispered, when they passed the phone to him, "don't tell them anything till we get hold of a lawyer. Eric will be there to bail you out. Don't say a word. And most of all, don't provoke them. You don't know what they're like."

Looking sheepishly at the two detectives, he thanked her. They were grinning. Perfectly aware of what Coralie was telling him, they seemed amused by their own reputation—which did not mean that it was undeserved.

But Coralie was wrong, he did know these men. They were boys he had grown up with, and Lindenmeyer might even have been familiar. It was a name he knew from school.

He was very blond and bony, and must, in early adolescence, have been girlishly pretty. There was, behind his rather high voice and beefy grin, a hint of fineness savagely repressed. Only with women, Colin thought, might he feel free to reveal it. But of the two, it was Lindenmeyer he was wary of. His brutality, like his coarseness, was assumed. Having no necessary cause, it would also have no limit. Creager, more obviously the bully, had no need to make a show. Red Irish and with freckles that in places had turned to open sores, he was all bluster, but too lazy to do more than put a blow in now and then to keep up his name for toughness. It was Lindenmeyer who asked the questions.

So he claimed to be local. Didn't sound it.

And had stepped out of nowhere into a situation with which he had absolutely no connection. Well, he was in the clear then.

Given the state of his clothes and the amount of blood he was covered with, very little of which was his own, and the crusting of it in the cracks of his knuckles and under his nails, there was some justification, he saw, for Lindenmeyer's irony. Blood needs explaining. He recalled, with astonishment now, the sense of elation in which, just before he was hauled off the man, he had been aiming blow after blow at his face.

"Will he be all right?" he found himself asking, and was uncertain whether the question put him in a better light or a worse.

It was recorded, but neither Lindenmeyer nor Creager gave him an answer. The role of questioner, here, was theirs.

"All right, Colin," Lindenmeyer said for the third or fourth time, "let's go over it again. This taxi-driver, this Armenian or Lebanese—"

LATER, lying stripped on the cot of a clean cell, he considered his position.

When he was brought down here he had not been thrown into the communal cell at the end of the corridor, which was crowded and stank and from which, as they passed, came catcalls and curses against the constable who was accompanying him, followed by gobs of spit, but he was alarmed just the same. It was a low throb in him, sign of some larger unrest that he had become part of.

He wished desperately that they had allowed him to wash. More than his assailant's blood, it was the man's smell, which once it got into his head might be ineradicable, that he felt all over him; the rancidness and close animal stink of self-loathing. He began to tremble with delayed shock. Not for the danger he had been in but for how close he had stood to an anguish so intense that the only escape from it was into self-extinction. When he did fall at last into a fevered sleep he was in a place where there were no walls; his sleep was open to the communal cell opposite, he was surrounded by broken mutterings and cries whose foul breath he took into his lungs and breathed out as protests that found no sound except as echoes in his skull.

At some point he woke, or half-woke. Three or four black youths were being dragged to the door of his cell, shouting obscenities; but the constable must have thought better of it and pushed them on. There was a scuffle. Hard blows against something soft or hollow. Then a violent eruption as the cell opposite burst into a howling, and again he had in his nostrils the odour of his assailant's sweat. It was overpowering. He started up, shouting, and his cry was immediately taken up in a renewed frenzy of cat-calls and yells.

He did not sleep again. He lay stiff and still, aware of the exchange of heavy night-heat for the clearer heat of day. Light came, and with it the shrill clattering among palm fronds and fig trees of thousands of starlings.

"Right, mate," the new duty-officer told him, "you c'n have a bit 'v a wash. Inspector'll see yer."

He stood in the open doorway, severely official, and let Colin pass.

The working day had begun. The cells were being unlocked. Bleary-eyed but subdued, the night's pick-ups had begun shuffling out: drunks, derelicts, young toughs, barefoot and with tattoos on their calves, who had been hauled out of fist fights just on closing time or from round the doors of discos, thin young Aborigines, one or two with dreadlocks—the agents, or victims or both, of a violence that was random but everywhere on the loose. You had only to step into the path of it to be picked up and whirled about and shattered. It was something he had always known about the place but had allowed himself to take for metaphor. He was being reminded again that it was fact.

He washed, when his turn came, at the dirty basin, and drew wet fingers through his hair.

In the metal mirror above the tap he barely recognised himself. The metal distorted, but there was also the puffed eye and thickened lip. He looked, he thought, like a dead ringer of himself who

for thirty years had lived a different and coarser life—maybe even
that of the man he had been mistaken for.

THE INTERROGATION ROOM appeared different in daylight.
Larger. But the real difference was that Lindenmeyer and Creager
had been pushed to the edges of it, one lounging in a chair by the
typewriter, the other hunched into the window frame. The
younger man who occupied the centre immediately offered Colin
his hand. His name was McKinley.

"I'm sorry, Mr. Lattimer," he said, all affability, "we've finally
got things sorted out. You'll be free in just a minute."

Without being obvious he made it clear that he knew quite well
who he was dealing with, and might even, if pressed, have been
able to produce a title.

Lindenmeyer and Creager watched closely, wearing faces that
expressed different styles of contempt—whether for him or for
their superior he could not guess.

Creager might have spent the remainder of the night in the
derros' cell. His tiny blue eyes had disappeared into the beef of his
cheeks. He kept hitching his belt over the roll of his belly. Lindenmeyer, too intelligent not to feel that this writer bloke and the
inspector made an oaf of him, boiled with resentment. Whatever
residue of violence the room contained came from him.

"The man's out of danger," McKinley was telling Colin.
"Superficial wounds is what the report says. It wasn't a serious
attempt." He cleared his throat. "Mind you, he's still pretty convinced that he's got some grudge against you."

The hint of a question in his voice made Colin say very firmly,
for perhaps the twentieth time in the last eight hours, "I never saw
the man in my life before."

McKinley nodded.

"Well, don't concern yourself. On the evidence," he said, as if
evidence might not be the only thing to go by, "we accept that. The
man doesn't, that's all. We're waiting for the psychiatrist's report."

Lindenmeyer and Creager were grinning. McKinley paused,

regarding him, Colin thought, with anticipation, as if, now that he was officially cleared, he might offer some private explanation of an affair that was still worryingly obscure. McKinley's interest at this point could be thought of as personal, literary—that was the suggestion—and Colin's obligation to explain, that of an author to a loyal but puzzled reader.

But Colin himself was in the dark. It might have helped, he thought, if he had had a name for the man he had struggled with, held close, beaten, and whose blood and sweat, mingled with his own, had discoloured the water in the dirty handbasin and gone swirling to join the rest of the city's scourings, the accumulated debris and filth of nearly a million souls.

What he had not been able to wash off was the claim that had been laid upon him. In some ward, in a hospital somewhere in the city, a man lay sedated, physically restrained perhaps, who still inwardly pursued him, consumed with resentment for the harm done to him by a shadowy third party to whom, Colin thought, he too was connected, but in ways so dark and undeclared that they might never be known.

But if McKinley did have a name, he did not offer it, and Colin knew that he could not ask.

"I'll just call your friend in," he said, closing what had been for a moment an open silence.

Eric was outside and immediately turned to face them, substantial looking in a suit and tie, and already preparing, Colin saw, to take charge. His face was a mixture of concern for an old friend—"Are you okay, Colin?"—and prickly disdain for the ways of local officialdom.

McKinley too saw it, but stood back, too polite to let his irritation show. His attention was not on Eric but on a woman on the bench opposite, who looked up, and as she did so, met Colin's eye.

He knew immediately who she must be, and was aware too of the inspector's awakened interest. He was on the watch. Not out of professional interest now, but with that curiosity about human behaviour and its shifts and by-ways that made him both a policeman and a reader.

She was blonde, and coarse but sexy. He took in the soiled tank-top, the feet, which were dirty, in their high-heeled, patent-leather sandals, and felt a little shameful kick of desire.

A smile, half-scornful, drew down the corner of her mouth. She had caught the spark of attraction in him that might have confirmed, to a practised onlooker like the inspector, that his assailant's suspicions had to this extent at least been entirely plausible. For a moment they made a triangle, a second one, this woman, the inspector and himself. The tension of the moment was felt by all three.

It was Eric who broke it. "Come on, Colin," he said. "Let's get you out of here."

So it was over—or almost. In moving too quickly away under the double gaze of the inspector and the woman, Colin stumbled, very nearly fell, and found himself caught and supported by an arm that shot out from nowhere and belonged, when he looked up, to a young man in a crash-helmet who had been waiting at the counter to report a theft.

"Hey, steady on."

"Sorry," Colin said as he righted himself. Then, "Thanks."

"She's right, mate." The young man produced a grin that was all friendliness and good humour and a frankness that knew no guile.

"Come on," Eric said, in a tone that suggested a growing apprehension at how accident-prone his new friend might be. "I'll get you back to the hotel, we can ring Coralie from there."

SAFELY BACK in his room at the hotel, he splashed cold water over his face, and as soon as he had recovered a little, rang London. Emma's voice was thick with sleep.

"I'm sorry," he said. "I just wanted to hear your voice."

He closed his eyes, and her breathing in his ear was so close that she might have been lying half-curled against his body in the dark.

"What is it?" she asked. "What time is it?"

"Nothing. It's nothing to worry about. Go on back to sleep."

The closeness, the familiarity of her, collapsed the hemispheres, the vast spaces across which her voice was being projected towards him. With his eyes close-shut he could believe that the slight hissing he could hear in the gaps of her breathing came from the high-ceilinged room where she lay, their flat high up above Redcliffe Square, and felt himself settle in the stillness and order, even in its customary disorder, of their shared life: dishes left overnight in the sink, books on shelves, LPs, newspapers.

"Go back to sleep," he said again. "I'm fine. I just wanted to hear your voice."

"No, it's nothing," she was calling now, her head turned away from the mouthpiece. "It's Colin. From Australia."

That would be Marcus. He saw the boy standing in striped flannel pyjamas and his Manchester United jersey at the door to their room.

He was sixteen and diabetic, so used to his disease and its regimen that you were barely aware of it except for the chocolate biscuits he carried in the pockets of his coat. He liked to go to discos. He was so easy and serious and assured that Colin, who, in the three years that he and Emma had been together, had grown fond of the boy, was sometimes intimidated. He expected the young to be confused, as he had been.

"That was Marcus," Emma told him unnecessarily. "Are you sure you're all right?"

"Yes, I'm fine, I'll be there on Friday. Go on back to sleep. I'll ring in the morning."

He listened for a moment after she hung up to the different quality of silence—which was no longer that of their bedroom and the warmer, reassuring spaces of the flat, but the white noise, the rubbing together in a soft, functional hissing, of a myriad random particles colliding and parting in the high wastes of air.

AT SEVEN that evening, uneasily assured and with a puffiness about the lip that gave him a disreputable look, which must have been a puzzle to those readers of newspaper and magazine articles

for whom he was always "distinguished," he read to a modest gathering at a popular bookshop, then fielded the usual questions,
some effusively respectful but others aggrieved. What did he
think of the place? Why had it taken him so long to come back?
How had his work suffered by his having abandoned, as they said,
his roots? Still feeling battered, he moved to one of the vast plate-
glass windows and looked out.

The city he knew, and in one part of himself still moved in, was
out there somewhere, but out of sight, underground. Unkillably,
uncontrollably green. Swarming with insects and rotting with a
death that would soon once again be life, its salt light, by day,
blinding to the eye and deadening of all thought, its river now,
under fathoms of moonlight, bursting with bubbles, festering, fer-
menting.

Inescapable. Far from having put it too far behind him, he felt
entangled, caught.

He thought of the flying foxes hanging in furry rows under the
boughs of the Moreton Bay figs, the metho-drinkers on the Victo-
ria golf-links, the teenage blacks and dropouts on their cots at the
watchhouse or in gutters in the lanes off Mary and Margaret
Streets. The frowsy blonde in the back room of a massage parlour,
the taxi-driver with one hairy arm out the window, drumming
impatiently on the roof. And in a darkened room somewhere, a
man, restrained or sedated, who long after the scars had healed on
his neck and chest would go on stalking down midnight pavements the one who had wronged him.

LATER, in the cool of a room nine storeys above the street, he fell
into a reviving sleep and was for a time nowhere—or nowhere
that can be found on any map.

He was standing at a street corner, lounging against a wall in
the neon dark and watching the headlamps of a truck rise slowly
between lightpoles over the crown of a hill. He did not move.
Even when the truck drew level, stopped, and he was called to.
Till, being called a second time, he pushed away from the wall,

ambled to the kerb, and setting his hand on the high cabin window, listened, shrugged his shoulders, looked to where others, already blindfolded, were packed together in the open truck, and shrugged again. Then, blindfolded himself, he was hauled up to join them, and they began a long ride out through the sleeping suburbs towards wherever it was out there in the foothills that the green stuff, the dream stuff, was.

The truck came to a halt, high among insect voices. He shuffled to the edge of the tray, a little breathless. How long a drop was it? He put his hand out, feeling air. Then there was a hand. He had only to take it and launch off.

And now, in a stretch of time where before and after had no meaning, in which none of the things had yet occurred that had so shaken his world and none of the people who most mattered to him had yet left his life or come into it, or they had and he was not yet aware of it—in that neither before nor after, he was high up under the floorboards of the house, and though the light was almost gone, he knew that the pale stems in which he could see the endless pushing upwards of a liquid green were the stems of gladioli, and that the great weight of darkness in his arms, which was still warm, was Maxie. The heart he could feel beating had a worm in it but had not yet stopped. It still made a regular, reassuring thump against his ribs.

He heard them call. They were calling to him.

"Come on out now. Come out," and a hand was stretched towards him.

But he would not for a while yet, for a good while yet, respond to the voices, or reach out and put his own into the outstretched hand.

Night Training

THE DAY GREG NEWSOME turned seventeen he joined the University Air Squadron. It was 1951. The memory of one war, which had been in progress all through his childhood, was still strong in him, gathering to it all the appealing mementoes and moods of those years, and the Cold War had recently thrown up another conflict, a smaller one, in Korea. War seemed to him, and to others like him, a natural thing. It galvanized people's energies and drew them to a pitch. It clarified meanings. It held you in the line of history. It also cleansed the spirit by offering occasions where mere animal energy and the noblest aspirations could meet at a point of vivid exultation, and mind and body, which at a certain age seem like divergent states of being, were instantly reconciled.

When Greg went to be medically examined he had to wait for more than an hour in a poky enclosure with walls of three-ply. There were a dozen other fellows there, on benches; he didn't know a single one of them. He plunged into his book, a Loeb Classic. When he was called at last he had to strip and sit on a chair to one side of the examiner's desk.

The man was a civilian but with one of those handlebar moustaches that in those days still evoked the image of a fighter pilot in the war. He looked at Greg's birth date, then at Greg, and was silent. Greg blushed. It was odd to be sitting stark naked on a chair beside a desk with his flesh sticking to varnish. He hung on mentally to his Plato.

"So," the doctor said, "we've got around to you lot." His face expressed a profound weariness.

. . . .

ON THEIR FIRST CAMP three months later he was assigned to the Intelligence Unit and shared a hut with the other baby of the squadron, a country boy from Harrisville, Cam Brierly. They were so much the youngest that they took it in turns on official mess nights, when all the officers of the station were assembled, to be Mister Vice: that is, to reply to toasts and initiate the passing of the port. It was a role in which you appeared to be the centre of the occasion, but only in the clownish sense of being a king of fools.

They stuck together, he and Cam. Not because they had anything in common but to conceal from others their appalling innocence.

Their task by day was to catalogue and reshelve the station library, under the eye of the Chief Education Officer, Dave Kitchener, a cynical fellow who did nothing himself but lounge behind his desk and was by turns a bully and a tease. He resented having them fobbed off on him.

At night, after dinner, while other fellows got drunk, played darts or snooker, or sang round the piano in true wartime style, they tried, one after another, a series of exotic liqueurs of lurid colour and with enticing names: Curaçao, Crème de Menthe, Parfait d'Amour. They were sickly, every one.

The mess late at night got rowdy, then out of hand. Understanding, though they never admitted it, that if they hung around too long they would very likely become butts, for their youth was in itself ridiculous, they slipped away before eleven and were soon asleep.

ONE OF THE WILDEST FIGURES at these nightly gatherings was Dave Kitchener, the officer who gave them such a hard time by day. A bit of an outsider with his fellow officers, he was always looking for trouble. When he got a few drinks under his belt he turned sarcastic, then aggressive, and went on the prowl; they had, more than once, caught him glaring in their direction. If he once got up, they thought, and came across, it would be to lash them with his tongue. They knew him by now. He couldn't be trusted to keep to the rules. He might pass muster in the office, and on official parade, but in the mess at night his uniform was loosened at the neck, and his hair, which was longer than permitted, fell uncombed over his brow. He had a sodden look.

Six or seven years back—Greg had the story from a fellow who had known him at Charters Towers when he was a geography master at All Souls—he had been caught climbing into the room of a woman from the sister school, Blackheath, and after a scandal that was quickly hushed up, they were both dismissed. One night when there were women in the mess, air force nurses, Dave Kitchener went up to one of them and threw a glass of beer in her face.

They had been in camp for two weeks when he appeared for the first time in their hut.

IT MUST HAVE BEEN between one and two in the morning. Greg stirred, aware of a presence in the room that registered itself first as a slight pressure on his consciousness, then on the mattress beside him. He woke and there he was, sitting on the edge of the bed. Just sitting. Quietly absorbed, as if he had come in, tired, to his own room and was too sleepy to undress.

He's made a mistake, Greg thought.

His cap was off, his tie loose, and there was a bottle in his hand.

Greg lay quiet. Nothing like this had ever happened to him before. He didn't know what to do. When the man realised at last that he was being watched, he turned, fixed his eyes on Greg, made a contemptuous sound deep in his throat, and laughed. He lifted the bottle in ironic salute. Then, reaching for his cap, which he had tossed carelessly on to the bed, he set it on his head, got to his feet, and took a stance.

"All right, cadet," he said. "Get out of there."

Greg was astonished.

"Didn't you hear? That was an order." His nails flicked the stripes on his sleeve. "Get your mate up. I said, get up!"

Greg rolled out of bed. He was out before he properly realised it. This must be a dream, he thought, till the cold air struck him. Skirting the officer, who stood in a patch of moonlight in the centre of the room, he crossed to Cam's bed and hung there in a kind of limbo, looking down at his friend. He still couldn't believe this was happening.

"Go on," the man told him.

Cam was sound asleep, and Greg, still touched by a state that seems commonplace till you are unnaturally hauled out of it, was struck by something he had never felt till now: the mystery, a light but awesome barrier, that surrounds a sleeping man. Which is meant to be his protection, and which another, for reasons too deep to be experienced as more than a slight tingling at the hair roots, is unwilling to violate.

Cam's head rested on the upper part of his arm, which was thrust out over the edge of the mattress. Under the covers his legs were moving, as if he were slowly running from something, or burrowing deeper into the dark.

Greg glanced across his shoulder at the officer, hoping, before this new breach was made, that he would reconsider and go away. But the man only nodded and made an impatient sound. Greg put his hand out. Gingerly, with just the tips of his fingers, he touched Cam's shoulder, then clasped it and shook.

But Cam was difficult. He put up a floppy arm and pushed Greg off. Even when Greg had got him at last into a sitting position he wasn't fully awake. Sleep was like a membrane he was wrapped in that would not break. It made everything about him hazy yet bright: his cheeks, his eyes when they jerked open. Greg began to be impatient. "Come on, Cam, get up," he whispered. "Stop mucking about."

The man, standing with the cap at a rakish angle, laughed and took a swig from his bottle.

"Wasser matter?" Cam muttered. The words were bubbly. " 'S middle o' the night."

Greg hauled him up, cursing, and propped him there: he kept giggling like a child and going loose. "Cut it out," Greg hissed, staggering a little in the attempt to hold him. He hadn't realised before what a spindly, overgrown fellow he was. But at least he was on his feet, if not yet fully present. Greg turned to the officer.

Dave Kitchener had been watching his struggles with a mixture of amusement and contempt. He seated himself, as before, on the edge of Greg's bunk, his legs apart, the cap pushed now to the back of his head, his feet firmly planted. He was enjoying himself.

"Right," he said. "Now. Get stripped."

Greg was outraged. After all his exertions with Cam, it still wasn't finished. This is wrong, he told himself as he started on the buttons of his pyjama jacket. He shouldn't be wearing his cap that way. He shouldn't be sitting on my bed. He wrenched at the buttons in a hopeless rage, the rage a child feels at being unjustly punished, feeling it prickle in his throat. Tears, that meant. If he wasn't careful he would burst into tears. His concern now was to save himself from that last indignity. He lifted his singlet over his head, undid the cord of his pants. They were in winter flannels. In the mornings here, when you skipped out barefoot to take a piss, the ground was crunchy with frost.

Cam was still dazed. He stood but was reeling. Greg looked towards the officer; then, with deliberate roughness, began to undo the buttons on Cam's jacket.

"We've got to take them off," he explained as to a three-year-old. When they were naked Dave Kitchener had them drill, using a couple of ink-stained rulers. He kept them at it for nearly an hour.

HE DID NOT COME every night. Three or four might pass and they would be left undisturbed, then Greg would be aware again of that change of pressure in the room.

After the first occasion there was no need for commands. As soon as Greg was awake, Dave Kitchener would rise, stand aside for him to pass, and Greg would go obediently to Cam's bed and begin the difficult exercise of getting him to his feet. It was always the same. Cam had to be dragged to the occasion. He resisted, he pushed Greg off. Laughing in his sleep in a silly manner and muttering sentences or syllables from a dialogue of which only the one side could be heard, he reeled and clung on.

Dave Kitchener showed no interest in these proceedings. They were Greg's affair. He left him to it. And because the officer no longer made himself responsible, Greg found all this intimate business of getting Cam out of bed and awake and stripped more repugnant than ever. Damn him! he thought—meaning Cam. He had come to see this peculiarity in the other boy, his reluctance to come awake, as a form of stubborn innocence. It set his own easy wakefulness in a shameful light. He resented it, and his resentment carried over into their dealings in the library as well. They began to avoid one another.

Meanwhile the waking and drilling went on. And afterwards, while they stood naked and shivering but at ease, the lectures.

EACH MORNING the squadron was broken up into specialist units, but in the afternoons after mess, they came together for a series of pep talks that were intended to develop a spirit of solidarity in them as well as providing an introduction to the realities of war. Some of these talks were given by men, bluff self-conscious fellows not much older than themselves, who were just back from the fighting in Korea. They made everything, even the rough stuff, sound like Red Rover or some other game, where getting a bloody knee, or your shirt torn, was the risk you took for being in it. One fellow told them that his liaison officers up there had been called Cum Suk and Bum Suk, then went on to describe the effects of something called napalm.

In the break between lectures they stood about smoking, or formed circles and tossed a medicine-ball.

DAVE KITCHENER'S LECTURES were of a different sort, and they came, after a time, to signify for Greg the real point of these midnight sessions, for which the rest, the dreamlike ritual of ordering and presenting arms, of turning left, right, about face, coming to attention, standing at ease and easy, was a mere preliminary, a means of breaking them down so that they would not resist. They drilled. Then they stood at ease, they stood easy, and Dave Kitchener, walking in slow circles around them, began.

After the formal hectoring of the bullring, the roars of official rage and insult that were a regular thing out there, Dave Kitchener's voice, which seldom rose above a whisper in the room, was unnerving. They felt his breath at moments on the back of their necks. Then, too, there was their nakedness. They were like plucked chooks—that's how Greg felt. Goose-pimpled with cold and half-asleep on their feet, they stood, while the voice wove round and round them.

"What I'm trying to do is wake you up to things. You're so wet behind the ears, both of you, you're pitiful! Have you got any idea how pitiful you look? Because your mothers love you and you've been to nice little private schools, you think you've got it made. That nothing can touch you. That you're covered by the rules. Well, let me tell you, lad, there *are* no rules. There's a war on out there, you're heading right for it, and there are no rules. Oh, I know that's not what they tell you in those jolly pep talks they give you. What I'm talking about is something different. The real war. The one that's going on all the time. Right here, now, in this room." He laughed. Greg heard the spittle bubble on his tongue. "The one where they've already got you by the balls." He stood back, looked them over, turned away in disgust. "You poor little bastards. You don't even know what I'm talking about, do you? You should see yourselves. You're pitiful. You're fucking pitiful. I'm wasting my time on you."

He would go on like that for the best part of an hour, a mixture of taunts, threats, insults, concern, and blistering anger at the quality in them that most offended him, their naïve confidence in things; which he was determined to relieve them of, and which they were unable to give up—it belonged too deeply to the power they felt in themselves, the buoyancy and resistance of youth. Greg discovered after a time how to handle it. You did just what you were ordered to do down to the last detail, with scrupulous precision, as you never did out there on the bullring. Not in mockery of the thing itself—that would have been to enter into collusion with him, for whom this was already a mockery—but to mock his authority with its limits. Your body obeyed to the letter. The rest of you stayed away.

THEIR LAST DAY in camp was a passing-out parade. Several of the older fellows were to get commissions, which would entitle them to wear their caps without the virginal white band. Three of them were getting wings.

The bullring dazzled in the sun; they sweated in their heavy uniforms. A band played. The voices of the drill sergeants leapt out and they responded. "Stand at ease, stand easy." Dave Kitchener was there, his cap straight, his collar fastened. He saluted when the others did.

Watching from his company in the ranks, Greg was puzzled by a kind of emptiness in himself, a lack of connection with all this. Something in him had moved away, and might have been lounging off there in the shade of one of the huts, with its spine against a wall and the curl of a smile on its lips, bored now with the whole show: these movements that were so fixed and refined that the discipline they embodied seemed like another nature, the swing of their arms that brought the rifles down, the clunking of boots, their bodies aligned and responding as one to snapped commands. His own body was too constant for him not to remember that he had performed these movements smartly elsewhere. He had an impulse to make some deliberate error and break the line. He closed his lids and swallowed. "Eyes right!" The image that fixed itself in his head was of the bullring empty, lit only by the moon, with the bluish shadow of the flag-mast, also empty, falling far across it.

HE SAW CAM BRIERLY only once in the following year. They were no longer the youngest, and since that had been the only thing in common between them, they were free to keep apart. They never spoke of Dave Kitchener or made any mention of the night training. In time, those shameful episodes took on a quality of unreality that belonged to the hour, somewhere between one and three in the morning, when they had taken place: the hours of regulated dark when they, like all those others laid out in officers' huts and barracks, should have been safe under the blankets pursuing innocuous dreams. It was almost, in the end, as if they had been. Greg's anger faded in him. So did the sense of injury he felt. When sometimes, in the following years, he thought of Dave Kitchener he understood, from the midst now of that other war he had spoken of, what it was that had fired and frustrated the man. He felt a kind of pity for him.

It was about this time that he had a dream. He was standing once again beside Cam Brierly's bed, looking down at the sleeping figure from a height, a distance of years, and with a mixture of tenderness and awe that arrested every possibility of movement in him. He could no more have leaned down and broken the other's sleep at that moment than woken himself. Some powerful interdiction was on him. He looked back over his shoulder and said firmly: "No!"

But the one who had been there in his dream was not there to hear it. He found himself staring into darkness, fully awake.

Sally's Story

S ALLY PRENTISS was one of those girls who in the last days of the Vietnam War were known as "the widows."

For a week or ten days as required they would set up in a one-bedroom apartment—thoughtfully supplied with candles in a kitchen drawer for intimate evenings and a box of geraniums on the sill—with an American GI or marine (sometimes an officer) who, for months amid the welter and din of war, had been hoarding some other dream than the ones that were generally on offer at the Cross: an illusion of domestic felicity in the form of a soft-mouthed girl and the sort of walk-up city-style living that is represented by an intercom and a prohibition against the playing of loud music after eleven o'clock.

To lie in until midday while the sun shone in on the bedcovers, then go off to the beach or an afternoon movie, then come back and fuck—but in a leisurely way, with no need to hurry, and with the luxury sometimes, which is another sort of pleasure, of not having to fuck at all—was the ordinary bliss they had set their sights on, a rehearsal for the settled life to come, when, their term of duty over, they would have no other obligation than to get pleasurably and without effort from one day to the next.

Sally Prentiss was an actress. That is, she was preparing to audition for NIDA. She had taken up this work because it paid better than anything else she had been offered. At just nineteen she was very aware that she had no real experience of life and she thought this might supply it. She was a down-to-earth person who knew how to stick up for herself; she did not think it would be damaging. She would only be doing it for a few months, and the men who wanted this sort of arrangement—or so she thought—would be nicer than the average, and since they would be pretending while they played house that everything was normal, would make fewer demands. They *were* nice for the most part, but she was wrong about the damage, and she was wrong about the demands as well.

They came in every variety, these boys, these men.

Some of them were barely house-trained. They licked the flat of their knives when they were eating—she pretended not to notice; they did not know how to wash properly or when they should change their socks. "Oh Delilah," she said to herself in a voice of commiseration, "not another one!" She had a whole cast of voices that she used for bucking herself up or giving herself a good talking-to, or for commenting, in a half-mocking way, on the irony of things and the rebounds and reversals that made up her world.

As for the demands—of course, all some of them wanted, or thought they wanted, was sex, laid on and guaranteed at any hour of the day or night. A wife out of the porno magazines. But even these boys wanted sometimes to just hang in the doorway and, in a proprietorial way, watch her do something as simple as make her face up in the bedroom mirror or wriggle into her jeans.

They would come up behind her while she was washing dishes at the sink, shoes off, hair damp with sweat, and, slipping their arms around her waist, rock her gently against them to an unheard tune—a moment, sweetly evocative, out of an old movie they had seen on TV. Or, with an ease that suggested an intimacy so long established that it no longer vibrated with even a hint of the provocative, walk in while she was in the bath, lower the toilet seat, and have a good old-fashioned talk.

What many of them wanted was to have reinforced the illusion of mastery. To a point sometimes just short of brutality. But there were times when even these fellows wanted to be relieved of all that and just lie back and be petted.

Then there were the ones—she got to recognise them after a bit—who just sat around all day in their undershorts and never left the flat. They were uncomfortable with air and sunlight, or had seen too much of it. One big foot up on the edge of the coffee-table, eyes glued to the TV, downing can after can of beer, they ignored her; but at every moment, whatever she was doing, kept her in view. However far off she might move, she was never quite out of reach. Idly, almost abstractedly, without taking their eyes off the game they were watching, they would put a hand out, and with the same easy affection for the body's demands with which they might shift themselves more comfortably in their under-shorts or scratch their heel, take possession of her neck and push her down.

They were almost completely cut off from speech, these fellows. Their denial of words, like their body smell, was something they imposed, on the room, on her, with a satisfaction they were barely aware of since it had to do entirely with themselves.

She put up with it but was filled with rage. This pleased some of them, though they might also use it later as an excuse for complaint, then violence. The blows were real enough, but the words they found to spit out at her, the routine obscenities, were half-hearted, a formula for keeping them excited, for reminding themselves that she was there.

God, she thought, what a nightmare! Imagining years of marriage on such terms.

Then there were the ones who felt an obligation to teach her things. Very solemn and little-mannish, their freshly scrubbed faces intent on the task of relieving her of some aspect, suddenly revealed, of female ignorance, they would deliver long, sometimes incomprehensible lectures on politics or the Market or the workings of some bit of equipment they had fallen in love with, while she, barely attending, sipped at a Coke or did her nails.

Usually this sort of boy did not care to be interrupted. All she had to do was keep nodding. But one or two of them wanted her to repeat what she had learned, and there were others who liked her to argue, but when she did would get mad and shout at her. This aroused some of them. To the point where they would all of a sudden forget that they were engaged in the business of instruction and want to fuck—right there on the living-room rug.

There was no way of guessing beforehand the quite ordinary things that would turn them on.

One moment they would be as still as a pond, everything would be relaxed and easy between them. The next they would have dived into themselves and be staring. Some gesture she had made, something she had said or done, had made her suddenly alive to their senses, provoked in them a rush of blood. What alarmed her was that for her there was no connection; she had felt nothing herself and almost never knew what it was.

There were times, faced with this impersonal power she possessed, when she wanted, quite simply, to run. But mostly what she felt was a kind of pity. They were so utterly at the mercy, these boys, of their needs; and they hated it, some of them, and could convince themselves, even while they were fiercely pushing into her, that *she* was the source of this fever they were afflicted with, this animal dependency without which they might have been hard and pure and self-sufficient.

They were just boys, she knew that, but they made her mad. She often quarrelled with them and said things that were mocking and cruel, but only in her head. Laying the responsibility for their failings on her, making her responsible for their weakness, was unfair. They did not play fair.

But the quality in them that she found hardest to live with was their restlessness. They were always looking at their watches and could not settle. Something was always missing. And this was just what they had feared. That having survived and come so far, the thing they had come for might still be out of reach, or be happening elsewhere, and at every moment time was passing. "Peter, Paul, and Mary," she whispered, "save our souls!"

But she saw at last that this was only part of a larger fear, and she learned after a time never to look, never to really look, into their eyes. What she saw there when she did was scary and might be catching. She wanted to keep clear. But there was no way of touching them and keeping clear.

She had thought, since they had been through so much and were *boys*, were *men*, that they would by now have learned to deal with it; or that being here in the quietness of the city, with a glint of sunlit water at the end of the street, they might forget. But they did not. It wasn't a mental thing. So long as their body was there, big and pulsing with heat, so was the fear. They brought it to bed with them, in dreams from which they woke shouting, and the only thing then that might drive it off was sex. Terrifyingly possessed, they thrashed and sweated in the effort to push their body through to the other side, gasping at the limit of their breath, crying out into her mouth. And when they subsided and lapsed immediately into unconsciousness, it was a dead man's weight that was on her, a dead man's sweat she was drenched with.

All this, she came to understand, was why so few girls were willing to do this work and why those who did the same work, but on a one-time or one-night basis, held them in contempt. They gave too much of themselves: it was indecent. And as "widows," they carried with them the taint of death.

She had thought this was ridiculous when she first heard it. Mere superstition. She thought she could outface it. But more and more now she had her doubts, especially in the last days of an engagement, when she had to deal with the ways—different in each case—in which these boys came to accept that their time was at an end. The war wasn't over. All they had done was step for a while out of the immediate line of it.

They paid the price then for their escape into make-believe, and she for having let herself, as she did at times, get too close. But how could she help it?

In a moment when her guard was down, when one of them was tickling her ear with some breathy story of the small town he came from, she would get a glimpse—that's all it took—into the odd, individual life of him; at the small naked creature in there, beyond the boastfulness and swagger, that was helpless and soft as a worm.

Often enough it was something physical that did it, the mother-of-pearl whiteness of an appendix scar, or some blemish she had not seen before, and which close up filled the whole of her view. Suddenly a body she had managed till now to touch without touching was *there*, heavy with its own meaty poundage, and hot, and real. It made their last moments together, if she did not deal sternly with herself, very nearly unbearable. As if, in allowing his body to lay itself bare to her, in her touching of it, there, and there, it was death itself that he had made himself open to, and what she was feeling out in him was the entry-place of a future wound.

As for the partings themselves, they too could take any form, and though they were final enough, were not always the end.

In some cases, the boy had already begun to leave a day or more beforehand, moving away in his head. All she had to do then was stay quiet and small while he got on with it. Others avoided the actual moment. Leaving her curled up in bed, they would pretend to be slipping out as usual to get the paper or a packet of cigarettes. She would lie there waiting to hear him lift his bags, which had been sitting all night in the hallway, then hold her breath for the last clicking of the latch.

But some wanted to believe that this was only the beginning. They would write, they would be back. She smiled and nodded, stirring her coffee with too much vigour. She hated to lie, but let herself cry a little, and her tears after a moment were real.

Then there were the ones who put on a turn. Like spoiled kids, toddlers. Big-shouldered in their freshly laundered shirts, they would sit beside their bags looking so plaintive, so stricken, that she had to pull the sheet over her head to save herself from the awfulness of it. You saw so nakedly what was being snatched away from them.

With the sheet pulled close over her head she would hear him deep-breathing out there, pumping himself up. Huh huh huh, on ten now!

She began to feel haunted. By so much that remained unfinished, unresolved in her relations with this or that one of them.

A phrase would come back to her, or a look, that was so sunny, so touched with ease and well-being, that she thought it must belong to some boy she had known back home. Then she would remember. It was one of them. Jake, or was it Walt, or Kent, or Jimmy? So this is what it means, she thought, to be a widow. She felt as if she had already, in just a few months, discovered things that made her older than the oldest woman alive. She had used up too many of her lives, that is what it was, in these phantom marriages.

At school last year their English teacher, Miss Drury, had given them a poem to crit. "To speak of the woe that is in marriage" it was called. It was American. Modern.

She was good at English. It was her best subject. "Woe," she had argued, was old-fashioned and melodramatic, a poet's word. Now she saw that the feeling it carried, the weight in it of all that was human and hopeless, made it utterly right. She knew now what it meant. Pay a fine of one hundred dollars, she told herself, and return to Go! She considered writing to Miss Drury and telling her of this late enlightenment, though not the means by which she had come to it.

PERHAPS IT WAS a recollection of simpler days, of HSC English and Miss Drury, that made her decide to take time off and spend a week or two at home.

But by the second day she remembered again why she had left.

Her mother worked at a check-out counter in the one-storeyed main street of the little country town, where all the cars were angle-parked to the kerb and everyone knew one another and there was nothing to do.

Boys, as soon as they were old enough, congregated at the pub, spilling out barefoot in stubbies and football jerseys on to the pavement, which was lined with empty glasses. The girls, over-dressed and with too much make-up, walked up and down from one of the two coffee-shops to the other, much preoccupied with their hair, too brightly on the lookout for occasions they feared might never occur. At home, after work, her mother took photographs of little kids in their school uniforms with slicked-down wetted hair or all decked out in white for their first communion, then, at the weekend, of wedding groups. She had a studio and dark-room on the closed-in back verandah and rented a window in the main street, full of examples of her work: smiling couples, good-looking boys in uniform, cute tots.

Her younger brother, Brian, who was fourteen, spent all his time in the camouflage battledress of his school cadet corps, including a khaki net that he wore round his shoulders like a shawl.

Sometimes he wrapped his head in it and stalked the corridors of the house in his big boots, moving warily through an atmosphere of damp heat and dripping bamboo while the boards under the linoleum creaked. He even wore the uniform when he was practising shots out in the yard at their basketball ring, and once, looking into his room, she saw him, his face swathed in the net, sitting crouched under the desk-lamp, doing his maths homework. Did he sleep in it?

Only once did she see him when he wasn't in full rig. He had taken the jacket off to chop wood in the yard. She was shocked by his thinness and by the whiteness of his hairless arms and chest.

At breakfast she asked, "Don't you ever take it off?"

He grunted, his face in a bowl of cornflakes.

"Does he ever wash?" she asked her mother.

Her mother looked at him and frowned, as if she were seeing this warrior who had seated himself at her kitchen table for the first time.

"Brian," she said wearily, "a shower! Tomorrow, eh? Did you hear what I said?"

"Huh," he grunted.

Her sister, Jess, who was two years younger but the same height, worshipped him. She longed for a uniform and was sometimes allowed to wrap her head in the camouflage net while they practised shots at the ring. They never stopped sniping at one another and appealing to her mother to adjudicate.

ON THE SATURDAY she went off with her mother to a wedding. In the yard of the reception hall at the School of Arts they ran into Mrs. Preston, who was a guest at the wedding and the mother of her oldest friend, Jodie. She and Jodie had been at school together.

"Oh, didn't you hear?" Mrs. Preston told her. "Jodie's married. They're living out at Parkes. Clive—her husband—is in the railways."

"And Jodie?" Sally asked. She had been the wildest of their group. She was surprised to hear that Jodie was married.

Mrs. Preston looked beatific. "Jodie," she told them, "is getting on with her cake decoration."

Today's wedding, as usual up here, was a very grand affair: three bridesmaids attended by groomsmen in suits of the same pastel blue. All shoulders, and uncomfortable with their buttonholes and formal bow ties, they had played rugby with the groom. One of them, Sally noticed, fooled about a lot. He was a broad-faced, well-set-up fellow with a full mouth, but otherwise very square and manly. He had a thatch of blond hair that would not stay down, and kept beating at it with the flat of his hand. He got drunk on the cheap champagne and made bawdy remarks that people laughed at, and chatted up all the girls, and was at every moment in a state of high excitement, but in the photographs when they were developed looked dark, almost surly. This was surprising.

"Who's this?" she asked her mother.

"Oh, that's Brad Jenkins; don't you remember him?"

"No," she said. "I don't think so. Should I?"

"Works down at McKinnon's Hardware. Used to work for Jack Blade at the service station. Don't you remember him?"

"No," she said.

"Poor boy, his wife left him. Lives out Dugan way with two little kiddies. It can't be much fun."

"Why?" she asked, examining the photo. "Why did she leave?"

"Who knows? Just packed up one day and when he got home she was gone. People say she ran off with a fellow she was engaged to before Brad. You know, she got pregnant to Brad, and—" Her mother consulted the photograph. "Maybe he isn't as nice as he looks," she said. "Sometime these happy-go-lucky fellers—"

She didn't finish. She was thinking, Sally knew, of their father, who had been nice-looking and charming enough but grew sullen

when there were no more hearts to win, and more and more disappointed with himself, and angry with them, and beat their
mother, and at last, when they were still quite small, took off.

Sally, with her new understanding of these things, threw her
arms around her mother, who was too surprised by this burst of
affection to resist.

"Lordy, Lordy," Sally said to herself in the old black mammy's
voice she used for one set of exchanges with herself, "life is *saaad*."

IN THE AFTERNOONS she had taken to going for long walks over
the low, rather treeless hills. It pleased her, after so many months
in the city, to be in the open again, alone and with no one to consider but herself.

The air in these late-spring days had a particular softness. There
were birds about, there was the scent of blossom. She felt a lighten-
ing of her spirits that was more, she thought, than just a response to
the soft weather. She was beginning to recover some of her old
good humour in the face of what life presented, its sly indignities.
The errors she had made need not, after all, be fatal. "Things will
turn out all right, I'll survive. I'm young, I'm tougher than I look."

This was the way she argued with herself as she strode out
under the high clouds, with the rolling landscape before her of
low hills and willow-fringed creeks and their many bridges.

One day, when she was out later than usual and had turned
back because the sky far to the west had darkened and was growling, she was overtaken on the white-dust road by a Ford Falcon
that tooted its horn, went past, then came to a halt and stood waiting for her to catch up. A dirty-blond head appeared at the window. "Want a lift?"

"No thanks," she called, still twenty yards off. "I'm walking."

"You'll get drenched," the voice told her. "Gunna be a storm."

When she came level she saw who it was. She might not have
recognised him without the blue suit and groomsman's bow tie,
but it was him all right. Same unruly head of hair, same look of
broad-faced amusement.

"That's all right," she told him. "I'll risk it."

He looked at her, his eyes laughing. "Okay," he said, "suit yourself. We don't mind, do we, Lou?"

She saw then that there was a child in the back, a boy about four years old, and a baby strapped in beside him and slumped sideways, sleeping.

"No," the boy shouted, "we don't mind. We got ourselves, eh?" He laughed and repeated it. It was a formula.

"That's right," the man said.

"Hi," said Sally, ducking her head to be on a level with the boy.

"Hi," the boy said, suddenly shy.

They looked at one another for a moment, then he said, shouting: "Hey, why don't you ride with us? We're not goin' far."

"Where?" she asked, "where are you going?"

"Anywhere! We're ridin' the baby. She likes it, it stops 'er screamin'. We just ride 'er and she stops. Anywhere we like. All over. We like havin' people ride with us, don't we, Brad?"

"Sometimes," the man said. "It depends."

"We like girls," the boy shouted.

The first drops of rain began to fall. They bounced in big splashes off the roof of the car.

"All right," Sally said, "I'll ride with you for a bit," and she ran round the back of the car and got in.

"Well," he said to the boy, "we got lucky, eh?"

"We did," the boy crowed, "this time we got lucky."

"Brad Jenkins," the man told her, starting the car up. "And that's Lou and Mandy."

"I'm four," the boy announced, "an' Mandy's one. Nearly. Our mum ran off an' left us. He's our dad."

She looked at the man. Oh Delilah, that mouth! she thought. He lifted an eyebrow and gave a slow grin. "Reuters," he said, "all the news as soon as it happens. That's enough, eh, Lou? We don't want to give away *all* our secrets."

"What secrets?" the boy shouted. "What secrets, Daddy? Have we got secrets?"

"It's true," he told her, still grinning. "No secrets."

The boy looked puzzled. Something was going on here that he didn't get. "Hey," he said, "you didn't tell us your name."

"Sally," she told him. And added for the man's benefit, "Prentiss."

"I know," he said. "Jumbo's wedding."

Almost immediately the heavens opened up and water began pouring into her lap. Not just a few drops, but a torrent.

"Sorry," he said.

She shook her head. There was not much use complaining. The car swooped up and down the low hills.

"Hey, Brad," the boy shouted over the sound of the storm, "are we gunna take Sally to our house? Like the last one?"

"Steady on," the man told him. "She'll think we're kidnappers."

"We are. We're kidnappers."

"Don't worry," he told her seriously. But she wasn't worried. It amused her to think of him riding round the countryside letting Lou do the talking for him, using the kids as bait. She didn't expect to find herself tied up at the back of a barn.

"He goes on like that all the time. Non-stop."

"What?" The boy shouted. "Was that about me?"

"Yes it was," the man told him. "I said you talk too much."

"I do, don't I?" the boy said. He was very pleased with himself. "I'm a chatterbox."

"Okay, now, a bit of silence, eh? While we work out what we're doin'. You're soaked," he told Sally. "We could get you some dry clothes if you like. I could take you back after we've eaten. We'd be goin' out anyway t' get the baby to sleep—No, Lou," he told the boy, who was trying to interrupt, "I'll handle it. It's true, we *would* like it. I'm a pretty good cook."

She wasn't taken in by any of this and he didn't expect her to be. Part of his charm, she saw, was that he expected you to see through him and become complicit in what all this playfulness, with its hidden urgencies, might lead to. But nothing else had happened to her in the last week.

"Okay," she said. "But you're looking after me, eh, Lou?"

"Am I? Am I, Brad? What for?"

"It's all right, mate," he told him, "she's jokin'," and he gave her a bold, shy look that was meant to disguise with boyish diffidence his easy assurance that she was not.

W HEN THEY GOT THERE it proved to be a house on wheels, a portable barrack-block for workers on the line. Long and narrow, like a stranded railway carriage, it consisted of a dozen rooms all of the same size along a single corridor, with a kitchen unit at one end and a shower and a couple of toilets at the other. The rain had stopped as suddenly as it had begun, and the land, all washed and dripping, glowed under a golden sky.

"Well," he said, "this is it—nice, eh? We aren't cramped. Lots of room for expansion, if you'd like to move in. We can put up any number. We could open a hotel."

Only four of the rooms were in use. The others, when she looked in, were thick with dust, the little square windows grimed with months, maybe years, of muck. One or two of them had old pin-ups on the walls. Another was piled with dusty cartons and magazines, and there were tools, several shovels, and a pick or two in a pile in one corner.

"That's it," he told her; "have a poke around. I'll find something for you to put on in a minute while we dry your clothes."

It was true. She was soaked. Her hair was dripping.

He was kneeling while he got Lou's wet shoes off. The baby was gurgling in an armchair.

"Sorry," he said; "take a towel. In that basket there—it's clean— and dry your hair. Children can't wait."

After a minute, with the children settled: "You watch baby for a bit," he told Lou and, soft-footed in his socks, led Sally two doors down the corridor to a bedroom.

As soon as she stepped in, though he was careful to leave the door open, she felt the change in him; a heightening of his physical presence, a heat that glowed under his clothes, out of the open-necked shirt, and a wet-grass smell that was his excited sweat. She recalled what her mother had said: "Two kids—that can't be much fun," and was impressed by how easily her mother had found, in that word fun, just the light in which he should be looked at. What was essential in him, what you might need to take most seriously in him, was a capacity he had for being light-spirited, for making himself easy with the world.

"Well," he said, breaking the tension between them, "let's see what we've got."

He found a pair of jeans in one drawer—his, she guessed, but they were clean enough—and among a jumble of T-shirts and jumpers in another, a woollen shirt, also his. He put his face into it and smelled to see if it was clean.

"Okay? Will they do?" he asked. "I've got t' look after the baby now." He hovered a moment, hesitant, apologetic, appealing to her to understand that he was not entirely free.

She closed the door behind him, but it was unnecessary really, and as soon as she did so she knew it was not to preserve her own privacy but so that she could peek a little into his. She changed quickly, then opened the door of the wardrobe.

Dresses, all neatly on hangers, and at the bottom a pile of shoes. In a drawer, jeans, shirts, all ironed and folded. His wife's clothes. Why hadn't he offered her something from here?

But she could see why. All this was untouched.

And what had she expected? To find them torn from their hangers and ripped? She felt a sadness in these things. In their emptiness. In their remaining just as the woman had left them, untouched. No, not untouched—she could imagine him opening the wardrobe and letting his hand move among them. Undisturbed. His own things, as she had seen when he found the shirt for her, were a mess.

She opened the drawer again, took up one of his T-shirts, and held it to her face; saw the girlie magazine underneath, and the stiff, crumpled handkerchief.

"How's it going?" he called.

"Fine," she said, closing the drawer.

"We'll toss these in the drier," he said, when she emerged with her pile of wet clothes.

"I will! I will!" Lou shouted, and rushed to take them from her.

"It's okay," he said, "he knows how t' work it. I've got to bathe the baby. Do you mind? Then I'll get us some tea."

She watched while he sat the baby in a tub of warm water and washed her, supporting her very gently with one hand while he soaped and splashed with the other. He spoke to the baby, who crowed and gurgled, soft-talking her, and was absorbed. The habitual nature of what he was doing absorbed him and for moments at a time he seemed unaware of her presence. But at others he grew self-conscious, and the soft-talk, the way he handled the baby, she felt, was for her. Or perhaps it was simply that she was aware of *him*.

The jeans she wore, which were too big for her, were his. So was the shirt. Her own clothes were tumbling away in the drier.

Lou had come back. With the baby's fresh clothes in his lap, he was sitting very quietly watching them both. He too was subdued.

"Is she gunna stay?" he asked at last.

The man cast her one of his shy looks. "I don't know," he said. "Why don't you ask her."

"*Are* you?" the boy asked.

"We'll see," she said.

The man turned away, but was smiling, she knew, and, holding the baby high, smacked a kiss on its wet belly. The baby laughed.

"Okay, Lou," he said when the child was dried and set down, "you can take over."

"We're a team," he told her.

"Oh, I can see that," she said.

SHE DID STAY, and did not hold it against him that he was so obviously pleased with himself, and so eager to show how good he was—he was—and that it wasn't because of *that* that his wife had left.

What was it then? she wondered. Why did she? Would she too find out?

Lying awake beside him, this almost stranger with his warmth against her, listening to the depth of his breathing, she was aware of the watchers she would have to deal with: the ghostly versions of Hedda and Rosalind and Blanche Du Bois waiting silently in the dark for her breath to release them. Behind the flimsy pine door of the wardrobe, just feet away, the rows of empty frocks.

Then there was the hurt she had felt in him. She could heal that. It seemed to her, at this moment, that she wanted nothing more in the world than to be his healing. She did not see, or not immediately, that his presenting himself to her in this light, with so much tremulous need, and when he felt her response to it, so much commanding passion, might be her healing as well.

Sometime in the night she woke to find him gone, and when he came back again he had the baby.

"Sorry," he whispered, as he set it down in the bed between them. "Do you mind?" He lay down again holding the child close to his chest, cradling its head.

So there was that, too.

She began to laugh.

"What is it?" he asked; "what's so funny? She won't be in the way. You go on back t' sleep. I'm used to it." And reaching across the baby, he had another hand for her, his fingers gently stroking her cheek.

Lordy, Lordy, she said to herself, looking at the two of them, the rough thatch of his blond head, the baby nestling into the warmth of him, snuffing his scent, burrowing deep into the familiar bulk of him.

Life is so—

But she was not sure that she believed, quite yet, in such happy turnabouts, and feared it might be tempting fate if she were to find a word, a new one, to finish the phrase. Instead she too snuggled down and let herself float free on the unloaded breath.

Jacko's Reach

So it is settled. Jacko's Reach, our last pocket of scrub, has been won for progress. It is to be cleared and built on. Eighteen months from now, after the usual period of mud pies and mechanical shovels and cranes, we will have a new shopping mall, with a skateboard ramp for young daredevils, two floodlit courts for night tennis and, on the river side, a Heritage Walk laid out with native hybrids. Our sterner citizens and their wives will sleep safe at last in a world that no longer offers encouragement to the derelicts who gather there with a carton of cheap wine or a bottle of metho, the dumpers of illegal garbage, feral cats, and the few local Aborigines who claim an affinity with the place that may or may not be mystical.

Those four and a half acres were an eyesore—that's the council's line: openly in communication, through the coming and going of native animals and birds, or through seeds that can travel miles on a current of air, with the wilderness that by fits and starts, in patches here and great swathes of darkness there, still lies like a shadow over even the most settled land, a pocket of the dark unmanageable, that troubles the sleep of citizens by offering a point of re-entry to memories they have no more use for—unruly and unsettling dreams. Four and a half acres.

Boys riding past it on their way to school are caught by a sudden impulse, and with a quick look over their shoulder, turn in there and are gone for the day on who knows what adventures and escapades.

Driving slowly past it, you see a pair of boots sticking out from under a bush. At eight thirty in the morning! A drunk, or some

277

late-night rover who has been knocked on the head and robbed. A flash of scarlet proclaims the presence of firetails lighting the grass.

Jacko's Reach: once known, and so marked on older maps, as Jago's. How, and at what point, by what slip of the tongue or consonantal drift, did the name lurch backwards into an earlier, not-quite-forgotten history, so that the white man's name became a black one and the place reverted, if only in speech, to its original owner's? Jacko's.

For as long as anyone can remember the people who had a legal right to the Reach, and are responsible for its lying unkept and unimproved, are Sydneysiders, but there are no Jacks or Jagos among them. They themselves have fallen back to a single remnant, a Miss Hardie of Pymble, who claims to have been a pupil of Patti, speaks with a German accent, and sold Jacko's over the telephone, they say, for a song.

It is a place you have to have seen and been into if you are to have any grasp of it. Most of all, you have to have lived with it as the one area of disorder and difference in a town that prides itself on being typical: that is, just like everywhere else. Or you have to have been hearing, for as long as you can recall, the local stories about the place, not all of them fit to be told—which does not mean that they are not endlessly repeated. Or you have to have lost something there—oh, years back. A little Eiffel Tower off a charm bracelet, or your first cigarette lighter, which you have never given up hope of kicking up again, and go searching for in sleep. Or you have to have stumbled there on something no one had warned you of.

Back before the First World War, two bullockies (they must have been among the last of their kind) settled a quarrel there. No one knows what it was about, but one party was found, the next day, with his skull smashed. The other had disappeared. The bullocks, no longer yoked to the wagon, had been left to wander.

Then, two days later, the second bullocky turned up again, hanging by his belt from a bloodwood. An eight-year-old, Jimmy Dickens, out looking for a stray cow and with the salt taste of porridge in his mouth and that day's list of spellings in his head, looked up and saw, just at eye level, a pair of stockinged feet, and there he was, all six feet of him, pointing downwards in the early light. Old Jimmy was still telling the story, in a way that could make the back of your neck creep, fifty years later, in my youth.

The facts of the case had got scrambled by every sort of romantic speculation, but it was the awe of that dumbstruck eight-year-old as he continued to look out, in a ghostly way, through the eyes of the gaunt old-timer, that was the real story. That, and the fact that it was still there, the place, and had a name. You could go out yourself and take a look at it. That particular patch of Jacko's, that tree, had been changed for ever, and become, for all of us who knew the story, the site of something you could touch. A mystery as real as the rough bark of the tree itself, it could change the mood you were in, and whatever it was you had slipped in there to get away from or do.

Well, that's Jacko's for you.

When I was seven or eight years old we used to play Cops and Robbers there. It seemed enormous. Just crossing it from the main road to the river gave you some idea, at the back of your knees, of the three hundred million square miles and of Burke and Wills.

Later it became the place for less innocent games, then later again of games that were once again innocent, though some people did not think so. Jacko's became a code-word for something as secret as what you had in your pants: which was familiar and close, yet forbidden, and put you in touch with all the other mysteries.

The largest of those you would come to only later; in the meantime, Jacko's, just the word alone, fed your body's heated fantasies, and it made no odds somehow that the scene of those fantasies was a place you had known for so long that it was as ordinary as your own backyard. It was changed, it was charged. And why shouldn't it be? Hadn't your body worked the same trick on you? And what could be more familiar than that?

What Jacko's evoked now was not just the dusty tracks with

their dried leaves and prickles that your bare feet had travelled a thousand times and whose every turning led to a destination you knew and had a name for, but a place, enticing, unentered, for which the old name, to remain appropriate, had to be interpreted in a new way, as if it had belonged all the time to another and secret language. Girls especially could be made to blush just at the mention of it, if your voice took on a particular note. For them too it had a new interest, however much they pretended.

Those four and a half acres, dark under the moon on even the starriest nights, could expand in the heat of Christmas and the months towards Easter till they filled a disproportionate area of your head.

On sultry nights when you had all the sheets off, they suggested a wash of air that could only be fresher and cooler on the skin, a space you could move in with the sort of freedom you had known away back when you were a kid. You walked out there in your sleep and found it crowded. There were others. You met and touched. And those who were bold enough, or sufficiently careless of their reputation, or merely curious about the boundary of something too vague for the moment to be named, actually went there, in couples or foursomes. They weren't disappointed exactly, but they came out feeling that their mothers had exaggerated. There was no danger, except in what people might make of it through talk, and about that their mothers had not exaggerated, not at all.

Valmay Mitchell was thirteen. She got no warning from her mother because she did not have one. She lived with her father in an old railway hut out on the line.

Every fellow of my generation knows Valmay's name. If she were to come back here, to take a last look at Jacko's for instance before it goes under for ever, she would be astonished at her fame.

She was a plain, blonde little thing who left school in the sixth grade. She wore dresses that were too big for her, went barefoot, and her one quality that anyone recalls was her eagerness to please. She would do anything—that was the news. Then one day, when we were all in the seventh grade, she disappeared. She was nowhere to be found.

People immediately thought the worst. Valmay Mitchell was the sort of girl that acts of violence, which haunt the streets like ghosts on the lookout for a body they can fill, are deeply drawn to. She had last been seen going into Jacko's with a boy on a bike. Which boy? He was found—it was the bike that gave him away— but never publicly identified, though we all knew his name. He admitted he and Valmay had been in there. They had both come out. But Valmay stayed missing. They combed Jacko's inch by inch and found no trace of her, though some of the searchers found things they, or others, had lost there and had spent years looking for. It was a real treasure-trove that came out of the hunt for Valmay. You could have weighed her against the heap of it and the heap would have weighed more.

They dug in places where the ground was disturbed, they dragged the river. Nothing.

Rumours flew about. She had been seen getting into a car—a Holden, or a Ford ute, or a Customline—poor little thing! It was her innocence now, suddenly restored, that people were drawn to. Then the news came back that she was in Sydney, in a Salvation Army Home, having a baby. One boy got a postcard from her. Several others spent anxious days in the weeks afterwards running out to waylay the postman in the fear that she might drop them a line as well. They are middle-aged now, my generation. One is our local baker, another a real-estate agent, another a circuit judge. Our lives these days barely cross. One of them does odd jobs out at the golf course and we exchange a few words now and then. Not about Valmay. Others I see driving their daughters to dances or calling for them afterwards, just as in the old days, or at football matches where their grandsons are playing.

Still, it's an older fellowship we share than the ones we belong to now, Rotary, or the Lions, or the BMA; and in a ghostly, dreamy area of ourselves, some of us are still willing to acknowledge it. The gangs we ran with back there, whose passionate loyalties did not last—the scratch teams for rounders, with captains choosing in turn. You can look about, if you have an eye for these things, at a public meeting where people are vociferously taking sides, or round the spectators at a concert, or in the thin gathering at an Anzac Day service, and re-form, in a ghostly way, those older groups, and see something that is oddly moving: darker loyalties, deeper affinities, submerged now under the more acceptable ones. The last luminous grains of a freer and more democratic spirit, that the husbands and wives of my generation still turn to in dreams. It's like having the power to see into someone's pocket, where among the small change and dustballs he is still turning over a favourite taw.

It is this, all this, that will go under the bars of neon lights and the crowded shelves and trolleys of the supermarket, the wheels of skateboards, the bitumen walks and solid, poured-concrete ramps.

Jacko's, as we knew it, will enter at last into what a century and more has already prepared it for, the dimension of the symbolic. Which is of course what it has always been, though the grit of it between your bare toes and the density of its undergrowth, the untidy mass of it against the evening sky, for a long time obscured the fact. After all, you don't lose something as palpable as a solid silver cigarette lighter, not to speak of your innocence, in a place that is purely symbolic. Or gash your foot there so that you carry for ever after the consequent scar. Or stand, day after day, waiting to be called as the possible ninth, the tenth man of a team, in an agony of humiliation you feel may never end.

So it will be gone and it won't be. Like everything else.

Under.

Where its darkness will never quite be dispelled, however many mushroom-lights they install in the parking lot.

Where it will go on pushing up under the concrete, reaching for the wilderness further out that its four and a half acres have always belonged to and which no documents of survey or deeds of ownership or council ordinances have ever had the power to cancel. The possibility of building over it was forestalled the moment it got inside us. As a code-word for something so intimate it can never be revealed, an area of experience, even if it is deeply forgotten, where we still move in groups together, and touch, and glow, and spring apart laughing at the electric spark. There has to be some place where that is possible.

If there is only one wild acre somewhere we will make that the place. If they take it away we will preserve it in our head. If there is no such place we will invent it. That's the way we are.

Lone Pine

Driving at speed along the narrow dirt highway, Harry Picton could have given no good reason for stopping where he did. There was a pine. Perhaps it was that—its deeper green and conical form among the scrub a reminder out here of the shapeliness and order of gardens, though this particular pine was of the native variety.

May was sleeping. For the past hour, held upright by her seat-belt, she had been nodding off and waking, then nodding off again like a comfortable baby. Harry was used to having her doze beside him. He liked to read at night, May did not. It made the car, which was heavy to handle because of the swaying behind of the caravan, as familiar almost as their double bed.

Driving up here was dreamlike. As the miles of empty country fell away with nothing to catch the eye, no other vehicle or sign of habitation, your head lightened and cleared itself of thoughts, of images, of every wish or need. Clouds filled the windscreen. You floated.

The clouds up here were unreal. They swirled up so densely and towered to such an infinite and unmoving height that driving, even at a hundred Ks an hour, was like crawling along at the bottom of a tank.

A flash of grey and pink flared up out of a dip in the road. Harry jerked the wheel. Galahs! They might have escaped from a dozen backyard cages, but were common up here. They were after water. There must have been real water back there that he had taken for the usual mirage. Like reflections of the sky, which was pearly at this hour and flushed with coral, they clattered upwards and went streaming away behind.

"May," he called. But before she was properly awake they were gone.

"Sorry, love," she muttered. "Was it something good?"

Still half-asleep, she reached into the glovebox for a packet of lollies, unwrapped one, passed it to him, then unwrapped another and popped it into her mouth. Almost immediately she was dozing again with the lolly in her jaw, its cherry colour seeping through into her dreams.

THEY WERE on a trip, the first real trip they had ever taken, the trip of their lives.

Back in Hawthorn they had a paper run. Seven days a week and twice on weekdays, Harry tossed the news over people's fences on to the clipped front lawns: gun battles in distant suburbs, raids on marijuana plantations, bank holdups, traffic accidents, baby bashings, the love lives of the stars.

He knew the neighbourhood—he had to: how to get around it by the quickest possible route. He had got that down to a fine art. Conquest of Space, it was called, just as covering it all twelve times a week in an hour and a quarter flat was the Fight against Time. He had reckoned it up once. In twenty-seven years bar a few months he had made his round on ten thousand seven hundred occasions in twelve thousand man-hours, and done a distance of a hundred thousand miles. That is, ten times round Australia. Those were the figures.

But doing it that way, piecemeal, twice a day, gave you no idea of what the country really was: the distances, the darkness, the changes as you slipped across unmarked borders.

Birds that were exotic down south, like those galahs, were everywhere up here, starting up out of every tree. The highways were a way of life with their own population: hitch-hikers, truckies, itinerant fruit-pickers and other seasonal workers of no fixed address, bikies loaded up behind and wearing space helmets, families with all their belongings packed into a station wagon and a little girl in the back waving or sticking out her tongue, or a boy putting up two fingers in the shape of a gun and mouthing Bang, Bang, You're Dead, kids in panel-vans with a couple of surfboards on the rack chasing the ultimate wave. Whole tribes that for one reason or another had never settled. Citizens of a city the size of Hobart or Newcastle that was always on the move. For three months (that was the plan), he and May had come out to join them.

Back in Hawthorn a young fellow and his wife were giving the paper run a go. For five weeks now, their home in Ballard Crescent had been locked up, empty, ghosting their presence with a lighting system installed by the best security firm in the state that turned the lights on in the kitchen, just as May did, regular as clockwork, at half past five; then, an hour later, lit the lamp in their living room and flicked on the TV; then turned the downstairs lights off again at nine and a minute later lit the reading lamp (just the one) on Harry's side of the bed in the front bedroom upstairs.

Harry had spent a good while working out this pattern and had been surprised at how predictable their life was, what narrow limits they moved in. It hadn't seemed narrow. Now, recalling the smooth quilt of their bed and the reading lamp being turned on, then off again, by ghostly hands, he chuckled. It'd be more difficult to keep track of their movements up here.

There was no fixed programme—they took things as they came. They were explorers, each day pushing on into unknown country. No place existed till they reached it and decided to stop.

"Here we are, mother," Harry would say, "home sweet home. How does it look?"—and since it was seldom a place that was named on the map they invented their own names according to whatever little event or accident occurred that made it memorable—Out-of-Nescaf Creek, Lost Tin-opener, One Blanket—and before they drove off again Harry would mark the place on their road map with a cross.

This particular spot, as it rose out of the dusk, had already named itself. Lone Pine it would be, unless something unexpected occurred.

"Wake up, mother," he said as the engine cut. "We're there."

. . .

TWO HOURS LATER they were sitting over the remains of their meal. The petrol lamp hissed, casting its light into the surrounding dark. A few moths barged and dithered. An animal, attracted by the light or the unaccustomed scent, had crept up to the edge of a difference they made in the immemorial tick and throb of things, and could be heard just yards off in the grass. No need to worry. There were no predators out here.

Harry was looking forward to his book. To transporting himself, for the umpteenth time, to Todgers, in the company of Cherry and Merry and Mr. Pecksniff, and the abominable Jonas—he had educated himself out of Dickens. May, busily scrubbing their plates in a minimum of water, was as usual telling something. He did not listen.

He had learned over the years to finish the Quick Crossword while half tuned in to her running talk, or to do his orders without making a single blue. It was like having the wireless on, a comfortable noise that brought you bits and pieces of news. In May's case, mostly of women's complaints. She knew an inordinate number of women who had found lumps in their breasts and gone under the knife, or lost kiddies, or had their husbands go off with younger women. For some reason she felt impelled to lay at his feet these victims of life's grim injustice, or of men's unpredictable cruelty, as if, for all his mildness, he too were one of the guilty. As, in her new vision of things, he was. They all were.

Three years ago she had discovered, or rediscovered, the church—not her old one, but a church of a newer and more personal sort—and had been trying ever since to bring Harry in.

She gave him her own version of confessions she had heard people make of the most amazing sins and of miraculous conversions and cures. She grieved over the prospect of their having, on the last day, to go different ways, the sheep's path or the goat's. She evoked in terms that distressed him a Lord Jesus who seemed to stand on pretty much the same terms in her life as their cats, Peach and Snowy, or her friends from the Temple, Eadie and

Mrs. McVie, except that she saw Him, Harry felt, as a secret child now grown to difficult manhood that she had never told him about and who sat between them, invisible but demanding, at every meal.

Harry, who would have defended her garrulous piety against all comers, regarded it himself as a blessèd shame. She was a good woman spoiled.

Now, when she started up again, he vanished into himself, and while she chattered on in the background, slipped quietly away. Down the back steps to his veggies, to be on his own for a bit. To feel in his hands the special crumbliness and moisture of the soil down there and watch, as at a show, the antics of the lighting system in their empty house, ghosting their lives to fool burglars who might not be fooled.

HARRY WOKE. His years on the paper run had made him a light sleeper. But with no traffic sounds to give the clue, no night-trains passing, you lost track. When he looked at his watch it was just eleven.

He got up, meaning to slip outside and take a leak. But when he set his hand to the doorknob, with the uncanniness of a dream-happening, it turned of its own accord.

The young fellow who stood on the step was as startled as Harry was.

In all that emptiness, with not a house for a hundred miles in any direction and in the dead of night, they had come at the same moment to opposite sides of the caravan door: Harry from sleep, this youth in the open shirt from—but Harry couldn't imagine where he had sprung from. They faced one another like sleepers whose dreams had crossed, and the youth, to cover his amazement, said "Hi" and gave a nervous giggle.

He was blond, with the beginnings of a beard. Below him in the dark was a woman with a baby. She was rocking it in a way that struck Harry as odd. She looked impatient. At her side was a boy of ten or so, sucking his thumb.

"What is it?" Harry asked, keeping his voice low so as not to wake May. "Are you lost?"

He had barely formulated the question, which was meant to fit this midnight occasion to a world that was normal, a late call by neighbours who were in trouble, when the young man showed his hand. It held a gun.

Still not convinced of the absolute reality of what was happening, Harry stepped back into the narrow space between their stove and the dwarf refrigerator, and in a moment they were all in there with him—the youth, the woman with the baby, the boy, whose loud-mouthed breathing was the only sound among them. Harry's chief concern still was that they should not wake May.

The gunman was a good-looking young fellow of maybe twenty. He wore boardshorts and a shirt with pineapples on a background that had once been red but showed threads now of a paler colour from too much washing. He was barefoot, but so scrubbed and clean that you could smell the soap on him under the fresh sweat. He was sweating.

The woman was older. She too was barefoot, but what you thought in her case was that she lacked shoes.

As for the ten-year-old, with his heavy lids and open-mouthed, asthmatic breathing, they must simply have found him somewhere along the way. He resembled neither one of them and looked as if he had fallen straight off the moon. He clung to the woman's skirt, and was, Harry decided, either dog-tired or some sort of dill. He had his thumb in his mouth and his eyelids fluttered as if he was about to fall asleep on his feet.

"Hey," the youth said, suddenly alert.

Down at the sleeping end, all pink and nylon-soft in her ruffles, May had sat bolt upright.

"Harry," she said accusingly, "what are you doing? Who are those people?"

"It's all right, love," he told her.

"Harry," she said again, only louder.

The youth gave his nervous giggle. "All right," he said, "you can get outa there."

Not yet clear about the situation, May looked at Harry.

"Do as he says," Harry told her mildly.

Still tender from sleep, she began to grope for her glasses, and he felt a wave of odd affection for her. She had been preparing to give this young fellow a serve.

"You can leave those," the youth told her. "I said *leave 'em!* Are you deaf or what?"

She saw the gun then, and foggily, behind this brutal boy in the red shirt, the others, the woman with the baby.

"Harry," she said breathlessly, "who *are* these people?"

He took a step towards her. It was, he knew, her inability to see properly that most unnerved her. Looking past the man, which was a way also of denying the presence of the gun, she addressed the shadowy woman, but her voice had an edge to it. "What is it?" she asked. "Is your baby sick?"

The woman ignored her. Rocking the baby a little, she turned away and told the youth fiercely: "Get it over with, will ya? Get 'em outa here."

May, who had spoken as woman to woman, was deeply offended. But the woman's speaking up at last gave life to the boy.

"I'm hungry," he whined into her skirt. "Mummy? I'm hun- greee!" His eye had caught the bowl of fruit on their fold-up table. "I wanna banana!"

"Shuddup, Dale," the woman told him, and put her elbow into his head.

"You can have a banana, dear," May told him.

She turned to the one with the gun.

"Can he have a banana?"

The child looked up quickly, then grabbed.

"Say ta to the nice lady, Dale," said the youth, in a voice rich with mockery.

But the boy, who really was simple-minded, lowered the banana, gaped a moment, and said sweetly: "Thank you very much."

The youth laughed outright.

"Now," he said, and there was no more humour, "get over here." He made way for them and they passed him while the woman and the boy, who was occupied with the peeling of his banana, passed behind. So now it was May and Harry who were squeezed in at the entrance end.

"Right," the youth said. "Now—" He was working up the energy in himself. He seemed afraid it might lapse. "The car keys. Where are they?"

Harry felt a rush of hot anger.

Look, feller, he wanted to protest, I paid thirty-three thousand bucks for that car. You just fuck off. But May's hand touched his elbow, and instead he made a gesture towards the fruit bowl where the keys sat—now, why do we keep them there?—among the apples and oranges.

"Get 'em, Lou."

The woman hitched the baby over her shoulder so that it stirred and burbled, and was just about to reach for the keys when she saw what the boy was up to and let out a cry. "Hey you, Dale, leave that, you little bugger. I said leave it!"

She made a swipe at him, but the boy, who was more agile than he looked, ducked away under the youth's arm, crowing and waving a magazine.

"Fuck you, Dale," the woman shouted after him.

In her plunge to cut him off she had woken the baby, which now began to squall, filling the constricted space of the caravan with screams.

"Shut it up, willya?" the youth told her. "And you, Dale, belt up, or I'll clip y' one. Gimme that." He made a grab for the magazine, but the boy held on. "I said, give it to me!"

"No, Kenny, no, it's mine. I found it."

They struggled, the man cursing, and at last he wrenched it away. The boy yowled, saying over and over with a deep sense of grievance: "It's not fair, it's not fair, Kenny. I'm the one that found it. It's mine."

Harry was flooded with shame. The youth, using the gun, was turning the pages of the thing.

"Someone left it in a café," Harry explained weakly. "Under a seat."

The youth was incensed. He blazed with indignation. "See this, Lou? See what the kid found?"

But the woman gave him only the briefest glance. She was pre-occupied with the baby. Moving back and forth in the space between the bunks, she was rocking the child and sweet-talking it in the wordless, universal dialect, somewhere between syllabic spell-weaving and an archaic drone, that women fall into on such occasions and which sets them impressively apart. The others were hushed. May, lowering her voice to a whisper, said: "Look here, if you're in some sort of trouble—I mean—" She indicated the gun. "There's no need of that."

But the youth had a second weapon now. "You shut up," he told her fiercely. "Just you shut up. You're the ones who've got trouble. What about this, then?" and he shook the magazine at her.

She looked briefly, then away. She understood the youth's out-rage because she shared it. When he held the thing out to her she shook her head, but he was implacable.

"I said, look!" he hissed.

Because of the woman's trouble with the baby he had lowered his voice again, but the savagery of it was terrible. He brandished the thing in her face and Harry groaned.

"Is this the sort of thing you people are into?"

But the ten-year-old, excited now beyond all fear of chastise-ment, could no longer contain himself.

"I seen it," he crowed.

"Shuddup, Dale."

"I seen it . . ."

"I'll knock the bloody daylights out of you if you don't belt up!"

"A cunt, it's a cunt. Cunt, cunt, cunt!"

When the youth hit him he fell sideways, howling, and clutched his ear.

"There," the youth said in a fury, swinging back to them, "you see what you made me do? Come here, Dale, and stop whinging. Come on. Come on here." But the boy had fled to his mother's skirts and was racked with sobs. The baby shrieked worse than ever. "Jesus," the youth shouted, "you make me sick! Dale," he said, "come here, mate, I didn't mean it, eh? Come here."

The boy met his eye and after a moment moved towards him, still sniffling. The youth put his hand on the back of the child's neck and drew him in. "There," he said. "Now, you're not hurt, are you?" The boy, his thumb back in his mouth, leaned into him. The youth sighed.

"Look here," May began. But before she could form another word the youth's arm shot out, an edge of metal struck her, and "Oh God," she said as she went down.

"That's enough out of you," the youth was yelling. "That's the last *you* get to say."

She thought Harry was about to move, and she put out her hand to stop him. "No, no," she shouted, "don't. It's all right—I'm all right." The youth, in a kind of panic now, was pushing the gun into the soft of Harry's belly. May, on her knees, tasted salt, put her fingers to her mouth and felt blood.

"All right, now," the youth was saying. He was calming himself, he calmed. But she could smell his sweat. "You can get up now. We're going outside."

She looked up then and saw that it made no difference that he was calm. That there was a baby here and that the mother was concerned to get it to sleep. Or that he was so clean-looking, and strict.

She got to her feet without help and went past him on her own legs, though wobbling a little, down the one step into the dark.

THE TROPICAL NIGHT they had stepped into had a softness that struck Harry like a moment out of his boyhood.

There were stars. They were huge, and so close and heavy-looking that you wondered how they could hold themselves up.

It seemed so personal, this sky. He thought of stepping out as a kid to take a piss from the back verandah and as he sent his jet this way and that looking idly for Venus, or Aldebaran, or the Cross. I could do with a piss right now, he thought, I really need it. It's what I got up for.

They were like little mirrors up there. That's what he had sometimes thought as he came out in the winter dark to load up for his round. If you looked hard enough, every event that was being enacted over all this side of the earth, even the smallest, would be reflected there. Even this one, he thought.

He took May's hand and she clutched it hard. He felt her weight go soft against him.

The youth was urging them on over rough terrain towards a patch of darker scrub further in from the road. Sometimes behind them, but most often half-turned and waiting ahead, he could barely contain his impatience at their clumsiness as, heavy and tender-footed, they moved at a jolting pace over the stony ground. When May caught her nightie on a thorn and Harry tried to detach it, the youth made a hissing sound and came back and ripped it clear.

No words passed between them. Harry felt a terrible longing to have the youth speak again, say something. Words you could measure. You knew where they were tending. With silence you were in the open with no limits. But when the fellow stopped at last and turned and stood waiting for them to catch up, it wasn't a particular point in the silence that they had come to. A place thirty yards back might have done equally well, or thirty or a hundred yards further on. Harry saw with clarity that the distance the youth had been measuring had to do with his reluctance to get to the point, and was in himself.

The gun hung at the end of his arm. He seemed drained now of all energy.

"All right," he said hoarsely, "this'll do. Over here."

It was May he was looking at.

"Yes," he told her. "You."

Harry felt her let go of his hand then, as the youth had directed, but knew she had already parted from him minutes back, when she had begun, with her lips moving in silence, to pray. She took three steps to where the youth was standing, his face turned away now, and Harry stretched his hand out towards her.

"May," he said, but only in his head.

It was the beginning of a sentence that if he embarked on it, and were to say all he wanted her to know and understand in justification of himself and of what he felt, would have no end. The long tale of his inadequacies. Of resolutions unkept, words unspoken, demands whose crudeness, he knew, had never been acceptable to her but which for him were one form of his love—the most urgent, the most difficult. Little phrases and formulae that were not entirely without meaning just because they were common and had been so often repeated.

She was kneeling now, her nightie rucked round her thighs. The youth leaned towards her. Very attentive, utterly concentrated. Her fingers touched the edge of his pineapple shirt.

Harry watched immobilised, and the wide-eyed, faraway look she cast back at him recalled something he had seen on television, a baby seal about to be clubbed. An agonized cry broke from his throat.

But she was already too far off. She shook her head, as if this were the separation she had all this time been warning him of. Then went back to *him*.

He leaned closer and for a moment they made a single figure. He whispered something to her that Harry, whose whole being strained towards it, could not catch.

The report was sharp, close, not loud.

"Mayyeee," Harry cried again, out of a dumb, inconsolable grief that would last now for the rest of his life, and an infinite regret, not only for her but for all those women feeling for the lump in their breast, and the ones who had lost kiddies, and those who had never had them and for that boy sending his piss out in an exuberant stream into the dark, his eyes on Aldebaran, and for the last scene at Todgers, that unruly Eden, which he would never get back to now, and for his garden choked with weeds. He meant to hurl himself at the youth. But before he could do so was lifted clean off his feet by a force greater than anything he could ever have imagined, and rolled sideways among stones that after a moment cut hard into his cheek. They were a surprise, those stones. Usually he was careful about them. Bad for the mower.

He would have flung his arms out then to feel for her comfortable softness in the bed, but the distances were enormous and no fence in any direction.

Her name was still in his mouth. Warm, dark, filling it, flowing out.

THE YOUTH STOOD. He was a swarming column. His feet had taken root in the earth.

Darkness was trembling away from the metal, which was hot and hung down from the end of his arm. The force it contained had flung these two bodies down at angles before him and was pulsing away in circles to the edges of the earth.

He tilted his head up. There were stars. Their living but dead light beat down and fell weakly upon him.

He looked towards the highway. The car. Behind it the caravan. Lou and the kids in a close group, waiting.

He felt too heavy to move. There was such a swarming in him. Every drop of blood in him was pressing against the surface of his skin—in his hands, his forearms with their gorged veins, his belly, the calves of his legs, his feet on the stony ground. Every drop of it holding him by force of gravity to where he stood, and might go on standing till dawn if he couldn't pull himself away. Yet he had no wish to step on past this moment, to move away from it into whatever was to come.

But the moment too was intolerable. If he allowed it to go on any longer he would be crushed.

He launched himself at the air and broke through into the next minute that was waiting to carry him on. Then turned to make sure that he wasn't still standing there on the spot.

He made quickly now for the car and the group his family made, dark and close, beside the taller darkness of the pine.

Blacksoil Country

THIS IS BLACKSOIL COUNTRY. Open, empty, crowded with ghosts, figures hidden away in the folds of it who are there, who are here, even if they are not visible and no one knows it but a few who look up suddenly into a blaze of sunlight and feel the hair crawl on their neck and know they are not the only ones. That they are being watched or tracked. They'll go on then with a sense for a moment that their body, as it goes, leaves no dent in the air.

Jordan my name is. Jordan McGivern. I am twelve years old. I can show you this country. I been in it long enough.

When we first come up here, Pa and Ma and Jamie and me, we were the first ones on this bit of land, other than the hut-keepers and young inexperienced stockmen that had stayed up here for a couple of seasons to establish a claim, squatting in a hut, running a few cattle, showing the blacks they'd come and intended to stay and had best not be interfered with.

When we come it was to settle. To manage and work a run of a thousand acres, unfenced and not marked out save on a map that wouldn't have covered more than a square handkerchief of it and could show nothing of what it was. How black the soil, how coarse and green the grass and stunted the scrub and how easy a mob can get lost in it. Or how the heat lies over it like a throbbing cloud all summer, and how the blacks are hidden away in it, ghosts that in those days were still visible and could stop you in your tracks.

Mr. McIvor, who owned the run, had no thought of coming up here himself. He was too comfortable out at Double Bay, him and his wife and two boys in boots and collars that I saw when I went out with Pa to get our instructions. I talked to them a bit, and the

older one asked me if I could fight, but only asked; he didn't want
to try it. This was in a garden down a set of wooden steps to the
water, with a green lawn and a hammock, and lilies on green stalks
as long as gun barrels, red.

Mr. McIvor meant to stay put till the land up here was secured
and settled and made safe. He might come up then and build a
homestead. Meantime, my pa was to be superintendent, with a
wage of not much more than a roof over our heads and a box of
provisions that come up every six months by bullock dray, eleven
days from the coast. To hold on to the place and run the mob he
had stocked it with.

Our nearest neighbours were twelve miles off, southwest, and
had blacks to work for them out of a mob that had settled on
the creek below their hut. We only heard of this, not seen it. We
had just ourselves. Pa believed it was better that way, we relied
on nobody but ourselves. It was the way he liked it. Ourselves and
no other. He wouldn't have slept easy with blacks in a mob close
by, in a camp and settled. Maybe wandering in and out of the
yards, or the hut even, and sleeping close by at night. Or not
sleeping.

"You trust nobody, boy, there's nobody'll look out for you better'n yourself. I learned that the hard way. I'm learnin' it to you
the easy way, if you'll listen. We're on our own out here. That's the
best way to be. No one watchin', or complainin' about this or that
you done wrong, or askin' you to do it their ways. Just us. We're on
to a good thing this time. We'll make it work. Damn me if we
won't!"

There had been other places, a good many of them, where it
didn't work. He had no luck, Pa. After a time there was always
some trouble. There was something in the work he was asked to
do, or the way the feller asked it, got his goat, and irked or
offended him. He'd begin to walk round with that set, ill-used
look to him that you knew after a time to avoid, and I would hear
him, low and sulky, complaining to Ma after they had gone to bed.
You could hear the aggrievement in his voice and the stubborn-
ness and pride in his justifications.

I don't know when I first begun to see he wasn't always in the right. I might have picked it up in the first instance from Ma, from her silence, or from the way she'd start packing up her bits and pieces, things she had had from way back before I was born—a tea caddy made of tin with little pigtailed Chinamen on it, a good-sized greenish stone from the Isle of Skye, which is where she was from—them and whatever else she had an affection for and had saved out of our many wrecks. She had already begun to pack them up in her head before he even come out with it, that we were on the move again.

"I won't be treated like a bloody nigger," he'd be telling her. "A man's got a right to a bit of respect." I don't know how many times I heard him say that, and saw the fierce look he wore, and felt the air hiss out of him and saw the scared look in her eye.

It was his pride. His impatience, too. Something in him that made doing things another man's way impossible to him.

I never once heard him put it down to anything he had done himself, to the trouble he had knuckling under or settling. It was always someone else was to blame. Or some power of bad luck or malice against him that all his life had dogged and downgraded him, going right back, and which he saw in the many forms it took to bring him low. In a look on one feller's face that said: "This work is not done the way I want it. It is not to my liking. Do it again. An' if you can't do it my way, then we'd better part company." Or in a finger moving slowly up a column of figures, and a frown that said: "Hello, what's this?" Then that cloud of old hurt and misjustice on his face for being once again doubted and disrespected, and while he raged and justified, the bundling up, all in a rush, of our few bits of things.

Always the same end to every venture, no matter how hopeful he started out: anger and disappointment. But what I saw on those occasions was more than disappointment. It was shame. In front of Ma, and of me too I think, once he begun to consider me. At having so little power to hold us in one place and safe. At being always at the mercy of another man's discontents.

He wasn't always right. But Ma did not once, that I ever heard, cross him or argue back. We stuck together. We were loyal. If I learned that, it was not so much from what he told me of the necessity of it, which he did often enough, but from watching her.

Whatever strung the different places together was in what she made. In the first meal we ate there, the plates set out the same way as at the last meal we'd sat down to, and a bit later the line of clothes she'd have drying, with the wind of the new place lifting and puffing them full of sunlight. In the smile she'd allow herself when he told her, with all his old false confidence: "This is a good place, Ef—an' he's a good man, I reckon. This'll do us for a bit— what d'you say?"

But I'd noticed something else by then. That people somehow, where he was concerned, were not well-disposed, they were not kindly. He lacked whatever it is that makes people respond.

Maybe he was just too much himself. Too ungiving. Or maybe it was the opposite—he wasn't ready enough to receive. Anyway, he could never get it right, never manage to ask for a thing in a way that won men over. He'd ask and they'd frown and hum and shift their feet in the dirt, and he'd already have took offence or lost his temper before they'd even come up with an answer. They'd feel then that they'd been right to hold back, and him that he'd been a fool ever to ask.

He also discovered after a while, and long before I even knew what it was, that I did have it—the power, whatever it is, to soften people, win them over. He'd get me to ask for things he knew no amount of asking on his part could get him, and laugh up his sleeve at the way they'd been hooked. And even if it was a gift he despised and wouldn't have wanted for himself, he was happy enough for me to make use of it. He'd just stand there and listen while I soft-soaped them, and I could tell from the way he looked and smiled to himself, but it was a sour smile, that he scorned me. He was pleased I could do it, but it was something in me that he scorned and might come to hate in the long run—that's what I thought. He didn't know how I'd got hold of it, where it had come from. Not from him, not from his blood. So I needed all the more to stick close and show him, whatever he thought, that there was a connection. That I was loyal, blood-loyal, and always would be, come whatever. Whatever.

IT WAS BLACKSOIL COUNTRY, and when the rains come, all mud. The land flowed then like a river as wide as the horizon in all directions. In the dry it was baked hard, and cracked. The low scrub got so green that the light of it hurt your eyes, and when the grass sprung up it was a lawn for two or three days, like Mr. Mclvor's lawn out at Double Bay, then it was swaying round your knees and next thing you knew the cattle were lost in it. He cursed it and had a complaint about every aspect of it. Most of all about the blacks, as if all the faults of the country were their doing. As if they'd made it the way it was.

"They'd better keep clear a' this place, that's all I got to say," he'd tell people. Our neighbours the Jolleys, for instance, the one or two times we met.

"Oh, the blacks are all right if you treat 'em right," Mick Jolley would say.

"Yair," he'd say, "well, my idea of treatin' 'em right is to keep 'em where they bloody belong. Which is not on my property. Not while I'm in charge of it." And he spat, and wiped the sweat off his face with a red handkerchief he wore, and screwed his eyes up against the glare of green.

Fact is, I loved this place we'd come to. Better than any other we'd been in.

He didn't. Not really. Nor Ma neither. For her it was a kind of horror, I knew that, though she would never have admitted it.

It was further out than we'd been before, and for her it was too far. All the things that tied her to the world—a store where she could turn things over at a counter, even if she couldn't afford to buy, a bit of material or that to pass through her fingers, a bit of talk, the sight of other women and what they were wearing—a new style of bonnet or the cut of a pair of shoes. All that, and the comfort of neighbours, of being linked that way, was gone. She went out only to hang the wash on the line, and even then I don't believe she ever raised her eyes to the country. She just acted as if it wasn't there.

But I loved it.

This is my sort of country, I thought, the minute I first laid eyes on it. And the more I explored out into it the more I felt it was made for me and just set there, waiting.

It was more than it looked. You had to give it a chance to show itself. There were things in it you had to get up close to, if you were to see what they really were—down on your knees, then sprawled out flat with your chest and your kneecaps touching it, feeling its grit. Then you could see it, and smell the richness of it too, that only come to your nostrils otherwise after a good fall of rain, when the smells were in the steam that rose up for just seconds and were gone.

Most of all I liked the voices of it. The day voices, magpies and crows and the rattle of cicadas, and the night voices, spotted nightjars calling caw-caw-caw gabble-gabble-gabble, and owls, and frogs I had never seen by day but heard after dark, so I knew they must be there, and found them at last, so small it was no wonder I'd missed them, and with the trick of taking on the colour, green or stripy-bark-like, of whatever they were clamped to, and only their eyes catching the light like tiny dewdrops, liquid and gleaming, till they blinked.

Nothing in it scared me. Not even the tiger snakes or diamond-heads you saw basking in the sun, then slithering off between hissing stems.

After a bit I would get up nights, let myself out, and lie in some place out there under the stars. Letting the sounds rise up all around me in the heat, and letting a breeze touch me, if there was one, so I felt the touch of it on my bare skin like hands.

KEEPING THE BLACKS off the land was a difficult proposition. Little groups of them—women and children dawdling along and chatting as they dug with sticks, bands of fellers on a hunting party— were for ever straying across what we knew were our rightful boundaries.

Pa would put up with it for a bit, then go out with a gun and shout at them. There would be scowls and mutterings, and a shaking of spears on their side if it was the men, and on our side Pa, standing square and hard-mouthed, showing no fear, whatever he might have felt, with his shotgun across his arm.

He didn't have to point it. It was enough that he had it across his arm. They knew by now what it could do.

They were noisy and fierce-looking, them fellers, but it was show; and so on Pa's side was the shotgun. Only our show was more convincing, I reckon. Our noise, if it come to that, would be a single blast. Louder than anything they could produce, and they knew it. Louder, and from a darker place than a mere mouth.

I think Pa liked what it felt like to just stand there and watch them fellers dance and shout, singing out loud enough, but powerless. It made him all the quieter, just standing and watching how the puff went out of them after a bit. One or two of the fiercer ones among them would make a run, but only two or three steps, and he'd stand his ground, smiling to himself, no need to react.

It was a feeble token. They'd already decided to back off. And when they did, slinking off one by one and throwing dark looks over their shoulder, and muttering, he'd keep standing. I think it was the best he ever got to feel maybe in his life, being left like that facing the empty bush, the last one in the field.

If it was a bunch of just women and little kids he didn't even bother to confront them. He'd just fire the shotgun once in the air, and laugh at the way they squealed and run about rounding up their kids, then scattered.

Most of the time I was there beside him, since most of the work to be done round the place we did together. I was his off-sider, his chief helper. We had no others.

I was too half-grown and scrawny to offer him much physical support, but me being not yet a grown man, even by their lights, was a constraint on them, and in that I gave him an advantage he didn't maybe appreciate. I know this because when I didn't have any jobs to do for Ma, and wasn't out working with him, I'd wander off alone and pass right close to them and all they'd do, whatever they were engaged in, was look. They never offered any word of threat. They'd just look. Like I was some curious creature that had come into view, that was of no use to them because I couldn't be hunted, and was just there—but in a way maybe that changed things and made them curious.

They didn't give me any acknowledgement, either one way or the other, except just with their long looks.

And no trouble, neither. But I'd feel the skin creep on my skull, and I'd walk on as if I was walking on eggshells or air, and I'd just whisper to Jamie, if he was with me, "Just keep on walkin', Jamie, and don't give 'em no notice," and felt there was a kind of magic around us, that come from their looking and protected us from harm. Though all it might be was us being so young.

And that day?

It seemed no different from any of the other occasions. We were in the home paddock grubbing out the last of a patch of low mulga scrub, him all strained and sweating with a rope around his middle, me with a crowbar under the dug-out roots. Suddenly he looked over my head and said quietly: "Get me gun, Jordie. Leave that now."

I looked to where he was looking and didn't move quick enough for him. He had slipped clear of the rope. He jerked his elbow at me and I jumped and run. When I come back he was standing with an odd little smile on his face. I don't think I'd ever seen him so good-humoured, so playful-looking.

Before he took the gun from me he rubbed his palms on the side of his pants; they were grimed with dirt and sweat from the rope. Then, still smiling a little, he ran his fingers through his hair.

He had curls that sometimes flopped into his eyes. Now, with his fingers, he smoothed them back and his bronze-coloured hair was dark wet.

I handed him the gun and he kept watching while he loaded it.

He had never taken his eyes off them. But what I remember, even more than what was happening, was the mood that was on him. That was what was unusual. The rest was like any other occasion. He shot me a lively look that said, "Watch this now, Jordie," as if what was coming was to be the purest fun. I loved him at that moment. He was so easy. So happy-looking.

The blacks, all near naked, were striding along through the scrubby dust and in the heat-haze seemed to bounce on their heels and rise up a little. To float.

There were three of them. The leading one carried something slung across his shoulders; they weren't near enough yet for us to see what it was. And there was a small mob at their back, not many. A dozen, no more. About thirty yards back, in the scrub.

There was no way we could have known what it was. We'd had no notice they were coming.

Pa put his hand up to stop them. They kept coming at the same slow pace, their bodies swaying a little, or so it looked, as if they were walking on air. "Stop there," he shouted. They were closer than they had ever got before.

"That's far enough," he called. They were still coming.

I looked across to him then. He was all fired up, but not panicky. Not angry neither, but he had a brightness to him I had never seen before. It was like I could hear the blood beating in him, or maybe it was mine. I think it was the moment in his life, so long as I had ever known him, when he felt lightest, most sure of himself, most free. Five minutes back he'd been straining his guts out over that stump, every muscle of him strained—the sweat running out of him in streams. He was still sweating now, but it was a glow.

He raised the gun and I thought: "He'll just fire over their heads and scare them." He fired, and I saw the black, the leading one, take off into the air a little and what he was carrying on his shoulders fly up. And as he stumbled in mid-air and rolled towards us, the meat, the side of lamb, went rolling in front of him. Meantime, the other two were scurrying back, and the mob gave a cry, and the women begun wailing. It was done. It had happened.

Out of that slow-fired mood he was in. Which did not ebb away. So that even when he saw what he had done, and lowered the gun, he was still lightly smiling.

I was astonished. That he could stand there with the sound of the shot still in the air and all that yelling and be so cool. Inside the heat there had been a cold, clear place, and he had acted from there, lightly and without thought. It was like he had just hit on a new way of being inside his own skin, and from now on that was the way he would live, and I was the first, the very first, to get a glimpse of it. But he wasn't thinking of me. He just turned his back on the whole thing, and swaggering a little, walked away, leaving the blacks, who were quiet now, to creep forward and drag off the man who had been killed or wounded, while the side of meat just lay where it was, rolled in the dirt.

Later on I saw that it must have seemed like a good idea on Mick Jolley's part to send the blacks across like that. To show him, Pa, that they could be trusted. That he could just send them off like that with a gift and it would be delivered. Sort of a soft lesson to him. But how was he to know that that was what it was? All in a moment and with no warning. A mob of blacks just walking up where he had always resisted.

He was wrong, I know that. He was wrong every way. But I want to speak up for him too.

Even when Mick Jolley come across and yelled at him and tried to get him to pay the blacks what he called compensation, I was on his side; not just by standing there beside him, but in my heart.

He did not know that black was a messenger. Who had the right to pass through all territories without harm. How could he know that? And even if he had, he mightn't have cared anyway that it was a consideration in their world. It wasn't one in ours. That they should even have considerations—that there might be rules and laws hidden away in what was just makeshift savagery, hand-to-mouth getting from one day to the next and one place to another a little further on over the horizon—that would have seemed ridiculous to him. Given they had no place of settlement nor roof over their heads to keep the sun off, nor walls to keep out the wind and the black dust that made another duller blackness where they were already blacker than the most starless night. No clothes neither, to keep them decent, and had never raised even the skinniest runt of a bean or turnip, nor turned a single clod to grow what went into their mouths, only scavenged what was there for anyone to crawl about and pick up. "Consideration," he would have said. "Consideration, thunder!"

Yet it was true. There were messengers. Given a part to play like any sergeant or magistrate, and recognised as such even by strangers.

Though not by us.

Which made us, in some ways, the most strangers of all.

I don't believe he knew what he had done—the full extent of it. And with all that light in his blood that made him so glowing and reckless, I don't think he would have cared.

I didn't know neither, but I felt it. A change. That change in him had changed me as well and all of us. He had removed us from protection. He had put us outside the rules, which all along, though he didn't see it that way, had been their rules. The magic I'd felt when they just stood and looked, as if I was some creature like a unicorn maybe, had come from them. Now it was lifted.

These last months I had taken to going about the place with Jamie. I was just beginning to show him things, things I had discovered and knew about our bit of land that no one else did except maybe the blacks, and places no one else had ever been into, except maybe them, when it was theirs. I don't reckon those hut-keepers and shepherds had ever been there. They were places you could only reach by letting yourself slide down a bank into a gully or pushing in under the low underbrush along a creek, so low you had to go on your knees, then on your belly. Jamie would have followed me anywhere, I knew that, but I was careful always to show him marks and signs along the way. Even when he was too little to talk, he was quick to see, and knew the signs again on the way back. He had known no other place than this. There were times, little as he was, when I felt he was showing it to me. Only now I kept a good eye open when we were out together. The whole country had a new light over it. I had to look at it in a new way. What I saw in it now was hiding-places. Places where they were hidden in it, the blacks. Places too where ghosts might be, also hidden.

THE STORY I have been telling up till now is my story. But at this point it becomes his. Pa's.

It is the story of a twelve-year-old boy treacherously struck down in the bush by unknown hands, his body hidden away in the heart of the country and for days not found, though many search parties go looking.

The mother is distraught. She has only one woman to comfort her. All the rest of those who gather at the hut, take a hasty breakfast, and set out in small groups to scour the countryside, are men, embarrassed to a profound silence by the depth of her grief. Only when they have stepped into the sunlight again, to where their horses stand restless in the sun, do they let their breath out and express what they feel in head-shaking, then anxious whispers.

They feel a kind of shyness in the presence of the father as well, but there are forms for what they can say to him. They clap him roughly on the shoulder, and impressed by the rage he is filled with, which they see as the proper form for his grief, they reach for words that will equal his in their stern commitment, their vehemence.

He is a man who has been touched by fate, endowed with the dignity of outrage and a cause. It draws together, in a tight knot, qualities that they felt till now were scattered in him and not reliable. When the body comes to light at last, the skull caved in, the chest and thighs bearing the wound-marks of spears, and he rides half-maddened about the country urging them to ride with him and kill every black they come across, he inspires in them such a mixture of horror and pity that they feel they too have been lifted out of the ordinary business of clearing scrub and rounding up cattle and are called to be heroic.

He is a figure now. That is why it is his story. The whole country is his, to rage up and down in with the appeal of his grief. His brow like thunder, his blue eyes bleared with weeping, he speaks low (he has no need to shout) of blood, of the dark pull of it, of its voice calling from the ground and from all the hidden places of the country, for the land to be cleared at last of the shadow of blood. He is a new man. He has discovered one of the ways at last to win other men to him and he blazes with the power it brings him. He is monstrous. And because he believes so completely in what he must do, is so filled with the righteous ferocity of it, others too are convinced. They are drawn to him as to a leader.

One clear cool act, the shedding of a little blood, and all that old history of slights and humiliations, of being ignored and knocked back, of having to knuckle under and be subservient—all that is cancelled out in the light he sees at last in other men's eyes, in their being so visibly in awe of the distinction that has descended upon him.

But that little blood was my blood, not just that black feller's. Pa's blood too. So he did come to see at last that I was connected.

For a season my name was on everyone's lips, most of all on his, and in the newspapers at Maitland and Moreton Bay and beyond. Jordan McGivern. A name to whip up fear and justified rage and the unbridled savagery of slaughter. For a season.

The blacks in every direction are hunted and go to ground. They too have lost their protection—what little they had of it. And me all that while lying quiet in the heart of the country, slowly sinking into the ancientness of it, making it mine, grain by grain blending my white grains with its many black ones. And Ma, now, at the line, with the blood beating in her throat, and his shirts, where she has just pegged them out, beginning to swell with the breeze, resting her chin on a wet sheet and raising her eyes to the land and gazing off into the brimming heart of it.

Great Day

1

U P AT THE HOUSE, Angie told herself, they would be turning in their bunks and pushing off sheets in the growing heat, still dozing but already with their sights on breakfast. Bacon and eggs and Madge's burnt toast. "Burnt?" Madge would bluster; "I don't call that burnt, I can do better than that. Besides, burnt toast never did your father any harm. It didn't kill him off, he thrived on it, so did your uncles. Now, who's for honey and who wants Vegemite? That's the choice." The children would yowl and make faces but bite into the burnt toast just the same. It was a ritual that would begin precisely at seven with the banging of Madge's spoon.

Meanwhile, down here on the headland, in an expanding stillness in which clocks, voices, and every form of consciousness had still to come into existence and the day as yet, like the sea, had no mark upon it, it was before breakfast, before waking, before everything but the new tide washing in over rows of black, shark-toothed rocks that leaned all the way inland, as they had done since that moment, unimaginable ages ago, when the earth at this point whelmed, gulped, and for the time being settled. Angie drew her knees up and locked them in with her arms.

On the reef to her left, out of sight behind the headland, her father-in-law, Audley, was fishing.

Dressed in the black suit and tie he wore on all occasions, even before breakfast, even for fishing, and standing far out on the rocky ledge with its urchin pools and ropes of amber worry-beads, he would, she thought, if you were sailing away and happened to glance back, be the last you would see of the place, a sombre column—if you were coming from the other direction, the first of the natives, providing, with his fishing rod and jacket formally buttoned, an odd welcoming party.

She raised her eyes to the sea and let herself drift for a moment in its dazzling stillness, then, dawdling a little, got to her feet and started up the path towards the house.

A FOUR-SQUARE STRUCTURE of sandstone blocks, very massive and permanent-looking, it stood immediately above the sea. Its first builder was Audley's grandfather. Successive owners had simply added on in the style of the times: two bedrooms on the south in Federation shingles; later, for the children, the product of wartime austerity, a fibro sleepout. More recently Audley had added a deck of the best kauri pine where in winter they could eat out, protected at last from the prevailing southerlies, and where, when the whole clan was gathered, the overflow, as Madge called it, could bed down in sleeping bags. The grass below the deck was scythed—no mower could have dealt with it—and roses, mixed with native shrubs, threw out long sprays forming an enclosure that was alive at this time of day with wrens and long-beaked honey eaters. Angie, lifting aside a thorny shoot, came round past the water tank. She paddled one foot, then the other, in the bucket of salt water Madge had set below the verandah and came round to the kitchen door.

"Hey, here's Angie."

Her son, Ned, leapt up among the scattered crusts.

"Angie," he shouted as if she were still fifty yards off, "did you know Fran was coming?"

"Yes," she said, "Clem's bringing her."

Ned was disappointed. He loved to be the bearer of news.

Always ill at ease in Madge's kitchen, fearful she might register visible disapproval of the mess or throw out some bit of rubbish that her mother-in-law was specially keeping, Angie perched on

the end of a form as in a class she was late for and accepted a mug
of scalding tea.

"But I thought they were divorced," Ned protested. His voice
cracked with the vehemence of it. "Aren't they?"

Madge huffed. "Drink your tea," she told him.

"But aren't they?"

"Yes, you know they are," Angie said quietly, "but they're still
friends. I saw Audley," she added, to change the subject.

Jenny looked up briefly—"Has he caught anything?"—then
back to the album where she was pasting action shots of her
favourite footballers. She was a wiry child of nine, her hair cut in
raw, page-boy fashion. Angie cut it for her.

"The usual, I should think," said Madge. "A cold."

"I thought when people got divorced," Ned persisted, "it was
because they hated one another. Why did they get divorced if
they're still friends? I don't understand."

Jenny, who was two years younger, drew her mouth down,
looked at her mother, and rolled her eyes.

"Ned," Angie said, "why don't you go and see if Ralph's up?"

"He is, I've already seen him," Jenny informed her. Ralph was
their father. "He's writing. He told me to stay away."

"People never tell me anything," Ned exploded. "How am I
ever going to know how to act or anything if I can't find out the
simplest thing? How will I—"

"You'll find out," Madge said. "Now—I want a whole lot of wild
spinach to make soup. I'm paying fifty cents a load. Any takers? A
load is two bucketfuls."

"Oh, all right," Ned agreed, "I'll do it, but fifty cents is what you
paid last time. Haven't you heard of inflation?"

"Ned," Madge told him firmly, "it's too early in the morning for
an economics lecture. Besides, you know what a dumb-cluck I am.
Leave me in blessèd ignorance, that's my plea." She made a clown's
face and both children laughed. "Small hope in this family!"

When she had armed the children with short knives and buckets she flopped into a chair and said: "Do you think we'll get
through today? I'm a dishrag already and it isn't even eight."

. . .

THE TYLERS were what people called a clan. Not just a family with the usual loose affinities, but a close-knit tribe that for all its insistence on the sociabilities was hedged against intruders. Girls brought home by one or another of the four boys would despair of ever getting a hold on the jokes, the quick-footed allusions to books, old saws, obscure facts, and references back to previous mealtimes that made up a good deal of their table-talk, or of adapting to Madge's bluntness or Audley's sombre, half-joking pronouncements, the latter delivered, in the silence that fell the moment he began to speak, in a voice so subdued that you thought you must have been temporarily deafened by the previous din.

Even when they had been gathered in as daughters-in-law, they felt so out of it at times that they would huddle in subversive pockets, finding relief in hilarity or in whispered resentment of the way their husbands, the moment they crossed the family threshold, became boys again, reverting to forms of behaviour that Madge, in her careless way, had allowed and which Audley, for all his fastidiousness, had been unable to check: shouting one another down, banging with their great fists, grabbing at the food or scattering it to left and right in a barbarous way that in minutes left any table they came to a baronial wreck.

Audley claimed descent from two colonial worthies, a magistrate and a flogging parson, both well recorded. His roots were as deep in the place as they could reasonably go. Madge, on the other hand, had no family at all.

Adopted and brought up by farm people, she had been, when Audley first knew her, in the days when they came down here only for holidays, the Groundley girl, who helped her old man deliver milk.

"Goodness knows where you kids spring from," she used to tell the boys when they were little. "Only don't go thinking you might be princes. Just as well Audley knows what little sprigs of colonial piety and perfect breeding you are because there's nothing I can tell you. Gypsies, maybe. Tinkers. Malays. Clem could be a Malay, couldn't you, my pet? Take your pick."

"I was fascinated, you see," Audley would put it, taking people aside as if offering a deep confidence. "I'd been hearing all my life about my lot—the Tylers and the Woolseys and the Clayton Joneses—made me feel like something in a dog show. Then Madge came along with those blue eyes and big hands that belonged to no one but herself—old Groundley was a little nut of a fellow. In our family everything could be traced back. Long noses, weak chests, a taste for awful Victorian hymns—it could all be shot home to some uncle or aunt, or to a cousin's cousin that only the aunt had heard of. My God, I thought, is there no way out of this? Whereas I can look at one of the boys and say, Now I wonder where he got that from? Can't be my side, must be her lot. The berserkers. The Goths-and-Vandals. It's made life very interesting."

People who were not used to this sort of thing were embarrassed. But it was true, the boys all took after their mother, except for Clem, who took after no one. They were big-boned, fair-headed, with no physical grace but an abundance of energy and rough good humour. Not a trace of Audley's angular refinement, though they were free as well of his glooms.

As little lads Madge had let them run wild, go unwashed, barely fed—in the upper echelons of the public service where Audley moved it was a kind of scandal—but had been ready at any time to down tools and read them a story or show them how to spin pyjama cord on a cotton-reel or turn milkbottle-tops into bells. She wrote children's books, tall tales for nine-year-olds. Twice a year, regardless of household moves or daily chaos or childhood fevers or spills, she had produced a new title—she was proud of that—using as models first her children, then her grandchildren, all thinly disguised under such names as Bam or Duff or Fizzer for the boys and for the tomboyish girls, McGregor or Moo. "It's lucky," she told Ned and Jenny once, "that Audley had all those family names to draw on. I'd have let my fancy rove. If it'd been up to me I'd have called the boys all sorts of things."

"What would you have called Ralph?" Ned asked, interested in catching his father for a moment in a new light.

"I'd have called him—let me see now—Biffer!"

The children went into volleys of giggles. "That's a great name!" Ned yelled. "It really fits him. You should have called him that."

"I did," Madge said, "in one of my books, I forget which."

"I know," Jenny shouted, "*The Really-Truly Bush,* I've read it. The boy in that was Biffer."

"Well, hark at the child, she got it in one." Madge gave a snort of laughter.

But Ned was affronted. "That's not Ralph," he insisted; "that's nothing like him. That's not Ralph."

"No," Madge agreed, "but that's because a whole lot of different things happened to that boy. If they'd happened to Ralph he'd be just like it."

"Would he really?" This from Jenny.

Ned, whose idea of the world was very different, was unconvinced.

Madge laughed again. "Really and truly."

She got letters from her readers, which she answered in the same distracted style as the books and had been looked up to by three generations of children as the mother they most wished for, a cross between a mad aunt and a benign but careless witch.

The boys too had had no complaint, though they had from the beginning to give up all hope of shirts with all the buttons on or matching pyjama tops or even a decently cooked potato. It was Audley who had attended to them, wiping their noses, picking up their toys, dishing up Welsh Rarebit, which he had learned to make at cadet camp when he was a schoolboy and which had remained his only culinary skill. They had had to fend for themselves, shouting one another down in the war for attention and growing up loud and confident. They admired their mother without qualification and were fond of Audley as well—too much so, some would have said. "The true sign of a great soul," they would have replied, citing Goethe, "is that it takes joy in the greatness of others." They were quoting their father, of course.

Today was to be a meeting of the clan. All the Tylers would be there with their wives and children, a few cousins, and neighbours from as far as fifty kilometres off if they cared to drive over.

It was the Tylers' annual party, an occasion they celebrated as a purely family affair since it was Audley's birthday. That it coincided with a larger occasion was of only minor significance—though Audley, when he was a boy, had thought it might not be, and had built his dreams on the auspicious conjunction. Later, when some of those dreams became reality, he mocked his youthful presumption as tommy-rot, but by then it had already served its purpose.

"No, no, Audley's seventy-second," Madge was shouting into the phone. "Just come along as usual if you've got nothing better on, it won't be special. Oh no, Audley's birthday, like we always do. The other thing's too big. I couldn't cater."

WHEN AUDLEY came up the path he did have something: two blackfish, each the size of an Indian club.

"Oh la," Madge said, "now what am I going to do with those?" She stood with her hefty arms folded, looking down at where he had laid them side by side on the bench, the eyes in their heads alive but stilled, a pulse still beating under the gills. "The freezer's full of things for the party. Isn't he the last word?"

Audley, meanwhile, in his jacket and tie and with his long legs crossed, was perched on a form, hoeing into tea and burnt toast.

Angie watched him. He chewed on the blackened wafer as if he were doing penance. He appeared to enjoy it. He wants people to think he's humble, she thought.

She could never quite believe, despite the evidence, that in Audley she had come so close to power. He had none of the qualities you read about in books, but for thirty-seven years this odd, hunched figure, who was devoting himself at the moment to ingesting the last of a blackened crust, had been in charge, one after the other, of four government departments. Wasn't that power? His signature had appeared on the nation's banknotes. He had, as he put it, "had tea with the sharks," survived a dozen blood-lettings, dealt with thugs of every political persuasion. Six prime ministers at one time or another had slipped into his office, sometimes with a bottle of whisky, to steel their nerves before a vote or share a moment's triumph or grief, and still turned up, those of them who were among the living, to check a detail in their memoirs or clear up with him a matter of protocol or just talk over what was happening in the world—meaning Canberra.

He had disciples too. The oldest among them now ran departments of their own or were professors or the editors of journals. The youngest were alert, ambitious fellows who saw in him the proof that you could get to the top, and stay there too, yet maintain a kind of decency. He bit into the blackened crust, masticating slowly, while Madge, arms folded, regarded the fish.

"Well," she said at last, "this won't buy the baby a new blanket. Birthday or no birthday, I've got my words to do."

She hefted the two fish into the sink, scratched about on the windowsill among the biros, testing one or two of them to see if they were still active, then, using her forearms to push back a pile of plates, made space for herself at the table among the unwashed tea mugs. She opened a child's plastic-covered exercise book and began to write.

Angie wandered off. She ought by now to be used to Madge's off-hand discourtesies and Audley's tendency to withdraw, but the truth was that she always felt, down here, like a child who had been dumped on them for a wet weekend and could find nothing to do.

She went down the steps and stood shading her eyes, looking to where the children would be hunting the slopes above the sea for spinach. Suddenly, as if from nowhere, an arm came round her waist, so awkwardly that they nearly went over, both of them, into a blackberry bush.

"Hullo," Ralph said, "it's me. Are you up to a bit of no good?"

He kissed her roughly on the side of the neck. "Hope no one's looking." He kissed her again.

He was a big fair fellow who had never grown out of the school-boy stage of being all arms and legs, a bluff, shy man who liked to fool about, but then, without warning, would go quiet, as if his intelligence had just caught up with some other, less developed side of him that was all antics, leaving him suddenly abashed.

He pulled her down in the grass.

"Mmm," he mumbled into her mouth, "this is better than Mum's toast." He sat up. "Did Dad catch anything?"

She told him about the blackfish and he nodded his head, suddenly sober again.

"Oh, he'll be pleased with that, that's good," he said. "What a terrific day it's going to be."

2

AN HOUR LATER Jenny was shouting from the verandah rails. "Hey Ned, Mum, Fran's here." She ran down to the gravel turning-place to greet her.

"Where's Clem?" she demanded when she saw that Fran was alone. "Angie said you were coming with Clem."

Fran stuck her head out of the window to look behind and backed into a shady place under the trees.

"We came in separate cars," she explained. "He's closing the gates."

Almost immediately they heard his engine on the slope.

Fran swung out of the car carrying the little deerskin slippers she liked to wear when she was driving, coral pink, and a soft leather shoulder bag. She was very slight and straight, and with her cropped hair looked childlike, girlish or boyish it was hard to say.

"So," she demanded, glancing about, "what have you kids been up to?"

"When?"

"Since I last saw you, dope!" She gave Ned's head an affectionate shove, then threw her arm around him. She was barely the taller.

He grinned and hunched into himself but did not pull away.

"Our football team won the premiership," Jenny announced. "I got best and fairest."

"Gee," said Fran, "did you?"

Clem slammed the door of his car and came up beside her. Smiling, he took her hand. "Do we look like newly-weds?" he asked.

Jenny was suddenly suspicious. "Why?" she asked. "Why should you?"

"I don't know. Do we?"

The two children glanced away.

Since his accident Clem *said things*, just whatever came into his head. They felt some impropriety now and cast quick glances at Fran to see what she thought of it, but she didn't appear to have heard. "I'm going to look for Angie," she said jauntily. "I could do with a cuppa." She started off towards the house with her bouncy, flat-heeled stride. With the long scar across his brow, Clem was smiling.

At the step to the verandah Fran had turned and was waiting for him.

One night three years back, on a straight stretch between a patch of forest and the Waruna causeway, a child had leapt out suddenly on to the moonlit gravel. It was late, after ten. Clem was tired after a long drive. The boy, who was nine or ten years old, was playing chicken. He stood in the glare of the headlights, poised, ready to run, while his companions—who were all from the Camp, half a dozen skinny seven- or eight-year-olds—danced about on the sidelines yelling encouragement, and the little girls among them shrieked and covered their eyes.

Clem swung the wheel, narrowly avoiding the boy, and the whole continent—the whole three million square miles of rock, tree trunks, sand, fences, cities—came bursting through the windscreen into his skull. The remaining hours of the night had lasted for fourteen months. It had taken another year to locate the bit of him that retained the habit of speech.

Always the odd man out among them, the stocky dark one, he was a good-natured fellow, cheerful unless taunted, but slow, tongue-tied, aimless. Even at thirty he had been unable to see what sort of life he was to lead. It was as if something in him had understood that no decision was really required of him. The accident up ahead would settle that side of things.

When Fran first came to the house it was with one of the others. She had been Jonathon's girl. But in time the very qualities that had impressed her in Jonathon, the assurance he had of being so much cleverer than others, his sense of his own power and charm, appeared gross. They got on her nerves in a house where everyone was clever, and shouted and pushed for room.

An outsider herself, never quite sure that Madge approved of her and whether to Audley she was anything more than an angry mouse, she had seen Clem as a fellow sufferer among them and decided it was her role to save him. From Them. She would take him away, where he could shine with his own light. "There, you see," she wanted to tell them, "you have been harbouring a prince among you."

"You're making a grave mistake," Madge warned her once while they were in the kitchen washing up.

"Oh?" she had replied, furiously drying. "Am I?"

The marriage lasted two years.

After being at passionate cross-purposes for a year, they lived a cat and dog life for another, each struggling for supremacy, then separated. But when Fran got back from her year in Greece they had begun to see one another again, locked in an odd dependency. She was adventurous, what she wanted was experience, "affairs." Clem was the element in her life that was stable. And after his accident, she became the one person with whom he felt entirely whole.

"So," she demanded now, "what do they say about me turning up like this?" "They" meant Madge and Audley.

She had her bare feet up on a chair, a straw hat over her eyes. She looked, Angie thought, wonderfully stylish and free.

"Nothing. They wouldn't say anything to me."

"Huh!"

Fran pushed the hat back, screwed her nose up, and squinted against the glare off the sea.

They were friends. When Fran first appeared all those years ago—Angie was already a young wife, Fran then just another of the hangers-on—they had been wary of one another; they were so unalike.

She thinks I'm bossy, like them, Fran had told herself. A know-all. A skite.

She thinks, Angie had thought, that I'm a dope.

But then they became sisters-in-law and found common cause. Angie, with Fran to lead her, discovered how much stronger her resentments were now that she had someone to share them. She admired Fran's fierce sense of humour, was bemused by her assumption that being honest gave her the right to be cruel. Fran, when she wearied, as she often did, of her own intensity, was drawn to Angie's stillness, her capacity to just sit among all that Tyler ebullience and remain self-contained.

When they were alone together Fran made a game of her rage, doing imitations of Audley's voice and manner and little turns of phrase that kept them in a state of exhausted hilarity. But Angie could never quite free herself of a feeling of discomfort, of something like impiety, when Fran took her flair for mockery too far.

The fact was that for all his peculiarities, Audley was without doubt the most remarkable person she had ever known. On this point she agreed with Ralph. Then, too, there was something in him, a side of his odd, contradictory nature, that Fran had no feeling for and for which she had coined the nickname "Doctor Creeps." But it was just this quality in him that Angie felt most connected to, since she recognised in it something of herself. When Fran mocked it she felt the opening between them of a dispiriting gap, a failure of sympathy on Fran's part that must include herself as well.

Angie's darkness was inherited. The Depression was already a decade past when she was born, but she had grown up with it just the same. In her parents' house it had never ended; they were still waiting for the axe to fall. She had married to break free of that cramped and fearful world and had been surprised, when her father-in-law engaged her with a sorrowful look that said, Ah, *we* know, don't we, that even among the Tylers there was this pocket of the darkly familiar.

Audley had ways of disguising his moodiness with bitter jokes and a form of politeness that at times had an edge of the murderous. "Your glass is empty," he would say to some unsuspecting guest, leaning close and whispering, full of hospitable concern, and Angie would shudder and turn away.

"So," Fran said, "what's the cast list at this wake? As if I didn't know! Jonathon, Rupe and Di, the Rainbow Serpent—"

Angie laughed.

"God, why did I come? Am I really such a masochist? Well, you'd better not answer that."

Clem, meanwhile, was with his mother at the pinewood bench in the house, sipping tea from a chipped mug while she chopped and prepared spinach. Madge looked up briefly, then away. The scar across his brow was so marked that all other signs of age seemed smoothed away in him.

"Tell me when I was six, Mum," he was saying, and he gave a cheery laugh as at an old joke between them. Madge paused, then chopped.

It was a thing he used to say when he was a little lad of nine or so: "Tell me when I was six," he would say, "when I was four, when I was just born." It was an obsession with him. But no detail you gave was ever enough to convince him that he really belonged among them.

Madge had had no time for the game then. Too many other questions to answer. And the house, and their homework, and Audley's many visitors. Now she made time. Clem's questions were the same ones he had been asking for nearly thirty years, but these days they had a different edge. Ashamed to reveal how much of his life was a blank, he had become skilful at trapping others into providing the facts he was after. Starting up a conversation or argument with Audley and his brothers, he would turn his head eagerly from one to another of them like a child catching at clues that the grown-ups would give away only by default; or he would begin stories that the others, with their passion for exactitude, would immediately leap to correct.

"You should ask Audley," Madge told him now, turning her eyes from his glowing face. "He's the archive."

"But I want *you* to tell me."

She paused, looked at the worn handle of her knife. "You were a strange little lad," she began after a moment.

He laughed. "How was I strange?"

"You had this knitted beanie you liked to wear."

"What colour?"

"Red. It was a snow cap, in fact, though we never went near the snow. It looked like a tea-cosy. It was too big for you, but you wouldn't go anywhere without it. It made you look like a sort of mad elf. If I said no, you'd rage at me."

"What would I say?"

"I can't remember what you'd say. Just the look of you."

"Was this when I was six?"

"Five, six, something like that."

"Go on."

"Ralph used to refuse to go out with you. My God, what a pair you were! People will look, he'd tell me, they'll think he's a dill."

"Was I?"

"No, of course you weren't. You were just a funny little boy." She paused and looked at him. "Don't you remember any of this, Clem?"

"No," he said happily. "It's all news to me."

He wasn't a dill. He had, in fact, been an intense, old-fashioned little fellow, but with a form of intelligence that wasn't quick like the others—a sign, perhaps, an early one, of a relationship to the world that was to be obscure and difficult and a life that was not to shoot forward in a straight line but would move by missteps and indirections through all those crazes taken up and dropped again that had filled a cupboard with abandoned roller-skates, a saxophone, a microscope and slides, all the gear for scuba diving. He looked down now, embarrassed by what he had to ask, but hitched his shoulders and plunged in.

"Did you and Dad love me?"

His voice was painfully urgent, but what struck her, as she clutched the knife to her breast, was his odd, dislocated cheerfulness. She closed her eyes.

There were times, years back, when they were all shouting and clutching at her skirt, when she would, for just a second, close her eyes like this and pretend they were not there, that they had succumbed to lockjaw or whooping-cough, or had never found the way through her to their voices and demanding little fists. It was restful. She could rest in the emptiness of herself, but only for a second. Immediately struck with guilt, she would catch up the littlest of them and smother him with kisses, till he felt the excessiveness of it and fought her off.

"What's it like," some silly young woman had once asked her, one of the hangers-on, "to live in a house full of boys?"

She had given one of her straight answers: "The lavatory seat is always up."

Now, opening her eyes again, she looked at Clem, at the darkness of his brow, and said, "Of course we did. Do. How could we help it?" He stared at her with his blue eyes, so clear that they could see right through you. "You were Audley's favourite—always. You know that. If he was hard on you sometimes it was because he was afraid of his own feelings, you know how he is. Of being swept away."

"I thought I was a disappointment to him."

"Maybe. Maybe that too. Things get mixed up. Nothing's just one thing. You know that."

He nodded, fixing his eyes on her, very intent, an alert seven-year-old, as if there was something more to what she was saying than the words themselves expressed, some secret about Life, the way the world is, that he would some day catch and make use of.

"Ah, here's your father," she said, relieved at the promise of rescue. Audley was coming up the track between the banksias.

Clem immediately leapt to his feet. Hurling himself through the wire-screen door and down the steps, he flung his arms around his father, clasping him so tight that Audley, with his head thrown back and his arms immobilised, had the look of a black-suited peg-doll. "Clem," he said, clutching at his glasses, but allowing himself to be danced about as Clem hung on and shouted: "It's me, Dad, I'm so glad to see you!"

3

MOSEYING ABOUT on the slope beyond the house in swimming trunks, sneakers, and a green tennis-shade, Ned glimpsed through the trees a party of interlopers. Stopped on the stony track, among blackboys and leopard gums that had been blackened the summer before by a bushfire, they were gathered in a half-circle round a charred stump.

Slipping from tree to tree like a native, Ned began to stalk them. There were six adults and some children.

The men, who were young, wore jeans and T-shirts, except for one with hair longer than the others and tied with a sweatband, who wore a singlet and had tattoos. They carried sleeping bags, an esky, and the man with the tattoos had a ghetto-blaster. Two of the women carried babies.

Ned manoeuvred himself into a better position to see what it was that had stopped them.

An echidna, startled by their footfalls on the track, had turned in towards the foot of the stump and, with its spines raised, was burrowing into the ashes and soft earth, showing a challenge, but pretending, since it could not see them, that it was invisible.

"What is it?" one of the women was asking.

"Porcupine," one of the men told her, and the man with the tattoos corrected him: "Echidna."

"Gary, come away," the other woman said, and she hauled out a boy of five or six who was dressed as a space invader and carried a plastic ray-gun.

Ned, very quietly, squatted, took a handful of ashes, and smeared them over his cheeks, forehead, and neck, then took another and smeared his chest.

If I was really a native, he thought, and had a spear, I could drive them off. They don't even know I'm here.

It pleased him that while they had their eyes on the echidna, which was only pretending to be invisible, he had his eye on them and really was invisible, camouflaged with earth and ashes and moving from one to another of the grey and grey-black trunks like a spirit of the place. He was filled with the superior sense of belonging here, of knowing every rock and stump on this hillside as if they were parts of his own body. These others were tourists.

They were on their way to the beach. You could not legally stop them—the land along the shore was public, it belonged to everyone—but this headland and the next as well belonged to Audley and would one day be Ralph's, then his. He felt proprietorial, but responsible too. As soon as the party had moved on, he went and checked on the echidna, which was still burrowing. When he stepped out on to the track again he was surprised to find the space invader there, a sturdy, dark-headed kid with freckles.

"Hi," the boy said cheerfully. "We're gunna have a bonfire, you can come if you like. My name's Gary, I'm six."

Ned was furious. It hurt his pride that he had been crept up on and surprised. He was disarmed for a moment by the boy's friendliness and lack of guile, but affronted by his presumption. It wasn't his place to offer invitations here.

The boy meanwhile was regarding him with a frown. "You know what?" he said at last, "you've got stuff all over your face."

"I know," Ned told him sharply, "I don't need you to tell me," and he began to walk away. The space invader followed.

"Don't go," he shouted, as Ned, arms stiffly at his side, his body pitched forward at an odd, old-mannish angle, began to stride away downhill. "We got sausages. D'you like sausages? We got plenty."

Ned walked faster.

"We got watermelon, we got cherry cheesecake. Hey, boy," he shouted, "don't go away. My name's Gary, I already told you. What's yours?"

He was trotting after Ned on his plump little legs. "Hey," he panted, when he finally caught up, "why are we walking so fast?"

Ned swivelled. "You piss off," he said from a height.

The boy looked at him as if he might be about to burst into tears, and when Ned turned and started off again, did not follow.

"Ralph!" Ned shouted as soon as he was in sight of the house, "there's a whole heap of people up there going to make a bonfire. Can they?"

Ralph, hearing the note of hysteria in his voice, was tempted to laugh, but Ned was quick to take offence and Ralph was touched, as he often was, by the boy's intense concern about things. He was always in a blaze about something—the Americans in Nicaragua, what the Libs were up to in the Senate. Keeping his own voice even, he said: "Well, it's a free country, Ned. They can have a bonfire if they want. So long as they're careful."

Ned huffed. He had hoped his father might be more passionate. "Well, I'm going to tell Audley," he announced. He stalked off.

Audley was on the phone in the sitting room. All morning he had been receiving congratulatory messages, most of them from people who would later be at the party. He stood hunched and with his head bowed, murmuring politenesses into the mouthpiece while, with his eyes screwed up in acute distress, he did a little stamping dance on the carpet and tugged with his free hand at a button on his vest.

Ned waited impatiently; then, when the call went on longer than he had expected, sprawled in an armchair and took up a magazine. At last Audley replaced the receiver. He stood a moment, looking gravely down. Ned, who was still all eagerness and anger, held back.

He was impressed by this grandfather of his, and not only by his reputation; also by the sense he gave, with his deep reserve, of being worthy of it.

Audley was on all occasions formal. Ned liked that. He had a hunger for order that the circumstances of his life frustrated. He wished that Angie and Ralph, whom he otherwise approved of in every way, would insist a little more on the rules. He would have liked to call Ralph "sir," as kids did on TV. But everything around them was very free and easy—maybe because Ralph, when he was younger, had been a hippie.

"How are you, Ned?" Audley said at last, but went on standing, deep in thought. He might have been out in a paddock some-where, having got there, Ned thought, without even noticing, on one of his walks.

"Audley," he began, very quietly, but Audley was startled just the same.

"Ah," he said, "Ned!"

Ned went on bravely: "Do you know there are people on the headland? They want to make a bonfire."

He watched for Audley's reaction, which did not come, and was surprised how the urgency had gone out of the question, not just out of his voice, which he lowered out of consideration for Aud-ley, but out of what he felt. He had taken on, without being aware of it, some of Audley's subdued gravity.

Audley seemed not to have heard the question. Putting his hand on Ned's head in a gentle, affectionate way, he stood looking down at the boy. "So what do you think of today, eh, Ned?"

Ned was confused. He knew what Audley thought because it was what Ralph thought as well. They were to be non-participants in the national celebrations. "Not wet-blankets," Ralph had insisted. "If these fellers want an excuse for a good do, I'm not the one to deny them, but it's just another day like any other really, when we've got to get along with one another and keep an eye on the shop."

It was a view that did not appeal to Ned. It was unheroic. He would, if it could be done with honour, have gone out and waved a flag. He wanted time to have precise turning-points that could be marked and remembered.

"Well," Audley said now, and turned aside. Ned slumped in his chair. Dissatisfied on that question as on the one he himself had put.

This is how it always is, he raged to himself. They like things left up in the air. They never want anything settled.

. . .

LATER THAT MORNING, and again in the afternoon, he went back to the headland to see what those people were up to.

The first time, the four men, stripped to their bathers, were playing football on the wet beach, making long rugby passes and shouting, tackling, scuffing up sand.

Three of them were hefty fellows with thickened shoulders and thighs. The fourth, the long-haired one who had previously worn a singlet, was slimmer and fast. They were all very white as if they never saw the sun, except that the slim one with the tattoos had a work-tan on his neck and arms that made him look as if he was still wearing the singlet, only now it was cleaner.

The boy was down at the shoreline dragging a wet stick. The two women, lying head to toe opposite one another in the shade, were waving off flies from the babies, who were asleep. They were talking, and every now and then one of them gave a throaty laugh. Ned sat for a long time watching.

When he went back the second time the men were dressed and their hair was wet. They had been surfing and were busy now constructing a bonfire, shouting to one another across great stretches of air and energetically competing to see who could drag out the longest branch and heave it crosswise on to the pile. They laughed a lot and every second word was "fuck."

The two women, each with a child on her hip, were walking along the edge of the tide, almost in silhouette at this hour against the wet sand, which was lit with rays of sunlight that shot out from under the clouds. Oyster-catchers were running away fast from their feet.

Once again he sat for a long time and watched. He wondered how high the bonfire would go before the men tired of hauling dead trees and brush out of the sandhills, and how far, once it was alight, it would be visible out at sea. He admitted now that what he really regretted was that the bonfire was not theirs. It ought to be theirs. The idea of a bonfire on every beach and the whole map of Australia outlined with fire was powerfully exciting to him. The image of it blazed in his head.

He got up and began to walk away, and almost immediately stumbled on the boy, who had been squatting on the slope behind him.

"Hi," Ned said briskly, and walked on—a kind of reconcilement. It was too late for anything more.

4

UNDER THE INFLUENCE of his birthday mood, which was sober but good-humoured, and in honour as well of the larger occasion, Audley decided on a walk to town.

He often took such a walk in the afternoon. It helped him think. He could, while strolling along, turn over in his mind the headings of a report he had to write, or prepare one of the speeches that since his retirement were his chief contribution to public life, polishing and repolishing as he walked phrases that would appear on the late-night news bulletins, to be mulled over the morning after by politicians, economists, friends, rivals, and his successors in the various public-service departments he had once had at his command. It was an old trick, this recovery of the harmony between walking pace, our natural andante as he liked to call it, and the rhythms of the mind. "I think best with my kneecaps," he would tell young reporters, who looked puzzled but scribbled it down just the same. "I recommend it."

If he didn't feel like walking back he could get a boy from the garage to drive him, or there was always some local, a farmer with his wife and kids or a tradesman with a ute full of barbed wire or paint tins, who would offer him a lift. He was a familiar figure in these parts, traipsing along with his head down, his boots scuffing the dust.

His object was not, as gossip sometimes suggested, the Waruna pub, though he did sometimes drop in there for an hour or so to hear what the locals had to say, but the museum just beyond, the Waruna Folk and History Museum as it was rather grandly called, which was housed in a four-roomed workman's cottage next to the defunct bank.

It had been founded by his grandfather in the early Thirties, with furniture and other knick-knacks from the house and a rare collection of moths and beetles.

Other families over the years had added their own cast-offs and unfashionable bric-a-brac: superannuated washboards and mangles, butter-churns, a hip-bath, tools, toys, photographs. Holiday-makers on their way to the beach resorts further south would stop off to stretch their legs among its familiar but surprising exhibits. It was educational. They would point to a pair of curling-tongs or a shaving-dish that looked as if someone had taken a good-sized bite out of it, a ginger-beer bottle with a glass stopper, a furball as big as a fist that had been found in the stomach of a cat.

But the main body of the collection had come from the Tylers, so that stepping into the dark little rooms where everything was so cramped and crowded was for Audley like re-entering one of the abandoned spaces of his childhood, which had miraculously survived or been resurrected, but with different dimensions now and with all its furnishings rearranged.

The cedar table and twelve dining chairs, for example, that filled the front room, had once stood in the larger dining room at the house, whose windows looked down to the sea, and when Audley seated himself—as he liked to do, though a notice expressly forbade it—in one of the stiff-backed carvers by the wall, and gazed out across the glazed table top, he was disconcerted, startled even, when that view failed to materialize. He could not imagine mealtimes at this table in any other light.

He recalled such occasions vividly. The big people seated round the extended cedar table, he and the other children—his brother, various cousins—at side-tables by the wall.

The table, minus its extensions, was set now with dinner plates from some other household and just the sort of engraved glasses that his grandmother, who was a snob, would have relegated to the back of a cupboard. He could imagine the well-dressed ghosts coming in through the door (and one or two of them, uncles, through the windows) and seating themselves in their accustomed places, a bit surprised by some of the details, as if one of the long string of maids his grandmother found and then let go had made an error, but happy just the same to find themselves back, and taking up immediately the never-ending arguments his grandmother wished they would refrain from—"Not at the table, Gerry, please!"—and which as a boy he had longed to join.

Above the table hung a lamp. It was of an old-fashioned kind that was all the rage again, in coloured glass. He remembered climbing on to his father's shoulders to light it, and from that height seeing the room, as the flame took, spring into a new shape. It had looked foreshortened from up there, as if he had been seeing it as it was now, nearly seventy years later.

What he had failed to notice, on that occasion, was the old fellow in the suit seated on a chair against the wall.

His father's contribution to the museum was a collection of rock specimens and rare fossils, set out now in display-cases in the hallway, each piece labelled in neat copperplate, his father's hand, and the ink so faded it could barely be read. The shell fossils were of exquisite engineering, little spiral staircases in perfect section, the ferns indelible prints.

He had loved these objects as a child. As a young fellow of sixteen or seventeen he had often come here with his father to examine them and been led so deep by his awed contemplation of their age, and all his father had to tell, that he had thought that his fate, his duty, was to become a geologist and solve the mysteries of their land.

They still moved him, these dusty objects, but that particular fate had never been taken up, though it still hovered in his excited imagination, as if the dedication of his life to stones and minerals were still an option of his secretly enduring youth. Would the distinguished geologist he might have become—he had no doubt of the distinction—have been all that different? He doubted it.

Other people saw him, he knew, as if what he was now had been fixed and inevitable, a matter of character. He wished sometimes that he could introduce them to some of his favourites among those other lives he had been drawn to and had abandoned or let go. Like the jazz pianist who, for two or three summers, along with a saxophonist and drummer, had rattled round the countryside in an old Ford, using his left hand to vamp while he reached with the other for a glass—already on the way to an established drunkenness and sore-headed despair that he actually felt on occasion. As if that other self had never quite been dismissed. The museum was full of such loose threads that if he touched them would jerk and lead him back.

On a wall of the little ex-bedroom out the back were three photographs. One of them was of a class from the one-teacher school where he and old Tommy Molloy, the head-man out at the Camp, had started school together more than sixty years ago, singing the alphabet and their times-tables together at the same desk. If he poked his head out the window he could see the little verandahed schoolhouse under a pepper tree, in the grounds now of Waruna High.

The photograph had been taken two years before he and Tommy arrived there, in his brother Ralph's year.

He studied the faces. Sitting cross-legged in the front row, holding a slate on which Miss Curry, whose first name was Esme, had chalked Waruna One Teacher School, 1922, was Tommy's sister Lorraine.

She had been the best fisherman among them: that is what Audley recalled. Once, when the trevally were running, she had caught forty-three at a single go. The sea had been so thick with them that you could have walked on their backs from one side of the cove to the other, and he believed sometimes that they had done just that. It was one of the great occasions of his life.

Lorraine had gone off a year later to be a domestic somewhere. Her eyes in the photograph looked right through you. So alive and black you might think they were beyond defeat. Well, time had known better.

He set his fingertip to the glass—also forbidden, of course. The print it left was a mist of infinitesimal ghostly drops that in a moment faded without trace.

But it was something other than this old photograph, however moving he found it, that drew him to this room. In a display of children's toys—a jigsaw puzzle that some local handyman had cut with a fine jigsaw, a pipe for blowing bubbles, some articulated animals from a Noah's Ark—was a set of knucklebones. He had won them more than sixty years ago from a boy called Arden Robinson who, the year he was nine, had come to stay with neighbours for the Christmas holidays and for whom he had formed an affection that for five whole weeks had kept him in eager and painful expectation.

He had not meant to win. He had meant to give the knucklebones up as a token of the softness he felt, the lapse in him of the belief that he was the only one in the world who mattered. As a hostage to what he had already begun to think of as The Future. A sacrifice flung down to nameless but powerful gods.

But he had won after all. The holidays came to an end, he had never seen Arden Robinson again. He had kept the knucklebones by him as a reminder, then five years ago had given them over, his bones as he called them, into public custody, which was in some ways the most hidden, the most private place of all. It would be nice, he sometimes thought, if he could give himself as well.

Occasionally, sitting in a chair in one of the rooms, he would doze off, and had woken once to find a little girl preparing to poke a finger into him as if, propped up there in his old-fashioned collar and tie, he was a particularly convincing model of ancient, outmoded man. When he jerked awake and blinked at her she had screamed.

"I'd quite enjoy it, I think," he told them at home, "if instead of shoving me into a hole somewhere you had me stuffed and sat there. No need for a card. No need for anyone to *know* it was me."

5

AT HALF PAST SEVEN the first of the guests arrived. Jenny was the lookout. Hanging from one of the verandah posts, she could see headlamps swinging through the dusk and stopping at the first of their gates. Two cars. There would be two more gates to open and close before they reached the gravel slope.

She leapt down and darted into the house.

"Madge, Angie," she called, "they're on the way. Somebody's here."

Madge, in shoes now and a frock that emphasized the width of her hips, was standing at the sink, contemplating the two fish she had earlier found a place for at the bottom of the fridge but had now taken out again to make room for her dips.

Her whole life, she felt, had been a matter of finding room. For unhappy children, stray cats, pieces of furniture passed on by distant aunts, unexpected arrivals at mealtimes, visitors who stayed too long talking to Audley and had to have beds made up for them on the lounge-room sofa, gifts she did not want and could find no use for but did not have the courage to throw out. Now these fish.

"They're almost here," Jenny was shrieking.

Fortunately it was only her son Jonathon with one of his girls, though he did warn her that Lily Barnes was in the car behind.

"Oh Lord," she said. "Jenny, love, go and tell Audley Lily Barnes is here. Oh, and Jonathon." Only then did she embrace her son.

She took the flowers he had brought and dumped them absentmindedly into the sink. Then, not to appear rude, she turned and kissed his girl, in case she had been here before. All Jonathon's girls were of striking appearance—more appearance than reality, she had once quipped—but she could never tell one of them from the next.

"How is he?" Jonathon asked, taking a handful of nuts from one of the bowls she had laid out and tossing them, one by one, into his mouth. "What's been going on? What have I missed?"

"Nothing," she told him, moving the bowl out of his reach. "You haven't missed a thing. Now, if you're hungry, Jonathon, I'll give you some soup. I thought you'd have eaten on the way."

"We did. We had this terrific meal, didn't we, Susie? At Moreton." He reached behind her and took another handful of nuts. But immediately there was the sound of Lily's voice and Audley's greeting her.

"Well," said Madge, "that's the end of that."

She strode out to the stone verandah.

"Is she always like that?" the girl whispered to Jonathon.

He looked at her with his mouth full. "Oh," he said, "I thought you'd been here before."

"No," she said, coldly, "I have not."

Lily Barnes was an old flame of Audley's—that was Madge's claim, though he always denied it.

"Lily Barnes," he would say, "is a remarkable woman, but she's more than I could have handled."

"La, hark at the man!" Madge would tell the boys, who, when they were young, had been all ears for these interesting revelations. "That means he thinks he can handle me."

"Can you, Dad?" one of them would pipe up. "Can you?"

When Lily Barnes and Audley were at university they had been rivals for various medals and scholarships, which she had mostly won. But after they left, Audley had gone on to high public office; Lily had been, over the years, private secretary to a string of ministers, admired, feared, warily consulted, but a shadowy presence, unknown outside a narrow circle. Then when she retired three years ago she had published a book that upstaged them all, Audley included, and had become a celebrity. At seventy she was very plain and petite, twisted now with arthritis but always very formally and finely dressed.

Madge, years ago, had dubbed her the Rainbow Serpent, partly because of her sharp tongue but also because of a passion she had for coloured silks. She had meant it unkindly then, but in the years since the name had come to have a benign, overarching significance. It was an affectionate tribute.

She entered now wearing a russet-coloured skirt and a café-au-lait blouse, leaning as always on a stick, but making an impression, for all her crooked stance and diminutive size, of elegance and charm. She had with her a young fellow, the son of some people she knew, called Barney Shannon, who had been in trouble with drugs and was now employed to drive her about. Since he wanted to bring his surfboard and was also shifting house, they had come in his ute, the back of which was piled high with his futon, several bits of old iron from which he hoped to make lampstands, a Fifties cocktail cabinet, and his library of paperbacks, all in cartons and covered with a loose tarpaulin.

"Sorry, Madge," she called, "are we the first? It's Barney. He drives like a bat out of Hades. I think that ute of his may have cured my back by redistributing the vertebrae." She looked about and gave one of her winning smiles. "But how lovely to be here."

AN HOUR LATER the room was full. Little noisy groups had formed, mostly of men, all vigorously arguing. Lily, moving from one group to another and leaning on her stick, would linger just long enough to shift the discussion sideways with a single interjection, then move on. She did not join the other women, young and old, who sat on the sidelines.

Fran had been hovering at the edge of these groups. She too moved from one to another of them, growing more and more irritated by what she heard and angrier with herself for having come.

She knew these people. They were the same relations and old friends and nervous hangers-on that she had been seeing for the past fifteen years, people for whom disagreement was the spice of any gathering. She felt out of place. Not because her opinions were all that different from theirs, but from temperament, and because, as everyone knew, she was a backslider. She had married one of them, been taken to the heart of the clan, then bolted. Well, that was their version. Drink in hand, looking sad-eyed and defenceless, but also spikily vigilant, she kept on the move.

Clem watched her from cover. He had mastered the art of pretending that his attention was elsewhere while all his movements about the room, along the verandah, past the open windows, had as their single object her appearance in a mirror or between the shifting heads.

He watched. Not to monitor or restrict her freedom but to centre himself. Otherwise the occasion might have become chaotic. All that din of voices. All those faces, however familiar. The fear that someone without warning might open their mouth and expect an answer from him.

Once, briefly, she had come up beside him. Her head came only to his shoulder.

"Are you okay?"

"Yes," he told her, "I'm doing fine. What about you?"

She cast a fierce glance about the room. "I'll survive."

He loved this house. He had grown up on holidays here. It was where he could let go and be free. All its routines, from the dinning of Madge's early-morning spoon to the pieces Audley liked to play on the piano last thing at night, were fixed, known. Objects too.

He liked to run his fingertips along the edge of the coffee-table and feel the sand under its varnish. His brother Rupe had made that table at Woodwork when he was fifteen. Clem loved it. It was one of the objects he had clung to when he was floating out there in the absolute dark, finding his way back by clinging to anything, however unlikely, that came to hand. Rupe's table had played no special part in his life till then, but he had clung to it, it had shored him up, and squatted now, an ugly, four-legged angel, right there in the centre of the room, very solid and low to the floor, bearing glasses and a lumpy dish full of cashews. He would have knelt down and stroked it, except that he had learned to be wary of these sudden impulses of affection in himself, towards people as well as objects, that were not always welcome or understood.

He had moments of panic still when he looked up and had no idea where he had got to. It was important then that something should come floating by that he recognised and could fling his arms around. The house was full of such things. Rupe's table, Audley's upright, the jamb of the verandah door where a dozen notches showed how inch by inch he and his brothers had grown up and out into the world—Ralph always the tallest. He had never caught up with Ralph.

And the books! Old leather-bound classics that their grandfather had collected, Fenimore Cooper and Stevenson and Kipling, and magazines no one would ever look at again, except maybe him; tomes on economics and the lives of the great, Beethoven and Metternich, and the children's books he had loved when he was little. *The Tale of the Tail of the Little Red Fox* one of them was called. It contained a question that had deeply puzzled him then, and still did: how many beans make five? It sounded simple but there was a trick in it, that's what he had always thought, which was intended to catch quick-thinkers and save slow ones. But from what?

He could move among these familiar things and feel easy. But when Fran was here the course he followed, the line he clung to, was determined by her. He liked the way she led him without knowing it, the form she gave to his turning this way and that, and how she held him while herself moving free.

SHE CAME to the edge of a group where Jonathon, his new girl leaning on his shoulder and pushing segments of sliced apple between her perfect teeth, was listening to a story Audley's cousin, Jack Wild, was telling. Jack Wild was a judge.

Most of the group had heard the story before and were waiting, carefully preparing their faces, for the punchline. Catching her eye, Jonathon gave her one of his bachelor winks.

They had a compact, she and Jonathon. They steered clear of each other on these family occasions, but meeting as they sometimes did on neutral ground, at openings or at one of the places in town where they liked to eat, could be sociable, even affectionate, for twenty minutes or so, teasing, reliving the times before Clem, before the wars, when they had been like brother and sister, best mates. He wasn't hostile to her or sternly unforgiving, like Rupe and Di.

She winked back, and saw with satisfaction that the girl had seen it. A little crease appeared between her perfect brows.

A moment later she had moved to another group and was half listening, half inattentively looking about, when she caught the eye of someone she had never seen before, a boy—man—who was lounging against the wall and observing her over the rim of his glass.

She looked down, then away, and almost immediately he came up to her.

He was called Cedric Pohl and rather pedantically, a bit too sure of himself she thought, spelled it out for her: P-O-H-L. He already knew who she was. Oh yes, she thought, I'll bet you do! He was an admirer of Audley's, but his time with the clan had been in one of her periods away. He had been away himself. He was just back from the States.

She listened, looking into her glass, wondering why he had picked her out and searching for something she could hold against him, and settled at last on his expensive haircut. Her mouth made a line of silent mockery.

Because, his gathered attention said, the powerful energy he was directing at her—because you looked so lost standing like that. Alone and with your eyes going everywhere.

He was attracted, she saw, by her desperation. It attracted people. Men, that is. They felt the need to relieve her of it. To bring her home, as only they could, to the land of deep content. She had been through all this before.

She lifted her chin in sceptical defiance, but had already caught the note of vibrancy, of quickening engagement in his voice that stirred something in her. Expectancy. Of the new, the possible. Hope, hope. And why not? Again, the excitement and mystery of a new man.

Moments later, she was outside, taking breaths of the clear night air. On the grass below the new deck, some young people, children mostly, were dancing. A single high-powered bulb cast its brightness upwards into the night, but so short a distance that it only made you aware how much further there was to go. The stars were so close in the clear night that she felt the coolness of them on her skin.

She had moved out here to get away from the feeling, suddenly, that too much might be happening too fast. Glass in hand, she looked down at the dancers.

Ned was there. So was Jen, along with three or four of their cousins, one of them a little lad of no more than five or six, Rupe and Di's youngest. They were moving barefoot to the ghetto-blaster's tatty disco, looking so comically serious as they rotated their hips and rolled their shoulders in a sexiness that was all imitation—of sinuosity in the girls, of swagger in even the tiniest boys—that she wanted to laugh.

Jen glanced up and waved. Fran raised her hand to wave back and was suddenly a little girl again at the lonely fence-rails, waving at a passing train.

She had always been an outsider here; in the clan, among these people who believed so deeply in their own rightness and goodwill. They had meant to pass those excellent qualities on to her, having them, they believed, in their gift. But for some reason she was resistant and had remained, even after her marriage, one of the hangers-on, one of those girls in lumpish skirts and T-shirts (though in fact she had never worn clothes like that, even at nineteen) who'd got hooked on the Tylers, not just on whichever one of the boys had first brought them in but on Audley's soft attentions, Madge's soups, the privilege of being allowed to do the drying-up after a meal, the illusion of belonging, however briefly, to the world of rare affinities and stern, unfettered views they represented. Girls, but young men too, odd, lonely, clever young people in search of their real family, were caught and spent years, their whole lives sometimes, waiting to be recognised at last as one of them.

She had told herself from the beginning that she could resist them, that she would not, in either sense, be taken in.

In the early days, on visits like this, she had spent half her time behind locked doors, sitting on the lowered lavatory seat or cross-legged on her bed, filling page after page of a Spirex notebook with evidence against them: the terrible food they ate, their tribal arrogance and exclusivity, the jokes, everything they stood for—all the things she had railed against in grim-jawed silence when she was forced to sit among them and which, as soon as she was alone, she let out in her flowing, copybook hand in reports so wild in their comedy that she had to stuff her fist into her mouth so that they would not hear, gathered in solemn session out there, her outrageous laughter, and come bursting in to expose her as God's spy among them. At last, in an attempt to rid herself of all memory of her humiliations and secret triumphs, she had torn up every page of those notebooks and flushed them down the loo in a hotel in Singapore, on her way to Italy and a new life.

Remembering it now, she was tempted to laugh and free herself a second time, and was startled by Audley's appearance, out of nowhere it might have been, right beside her.

"Let me get you something," he said very softly, relieving her of her glass. Setting his sorrowful eyes upon her he gave her one of those looks that said: We know, don't we? You and I.

Do we? she asked herself, and felt, once again, the old wish to succumb, then the old repulsion and the rising in her of a still unextinguished anger.

These cryptic utterances were a habit with him, part of his armoury of teasing enticements and withdrawals. They were intended, she had decided long ago, in their suggestion of a special intimacy, to puzzle, but also to intimidate.

"You don't understand him," Clem would tell her; "you're being unfair." But the truth was, there was something phony in these tremendous statements. A challenge perhaps for you to call his bluff and unmask him. Crooked jokes.

He paused now and, after a silence that was calculated, she thought, to the last heartbeat, went off bearing her glass.

Once again she felt the need to escape. I'll find Angie, she thought. She'll get me out of this. The last thing she wanted now was to get caught in an exchange of soul-talk with Audley.

She saw Angie standing alone in a corner, in a dream as usual, wearing that dark, faraway look that kept people off. How beautiful she is, Fran thought.

She was in black—an old-fashioned dress that might have belonged to her mother, with long sleeves and a high neck that emphasized her tallness. Fran was about to push between shoulders towards her when she felt a hand at her skirt. It was Tommy Molloy's wife, Ellie.

"Hi, Fran," she said. "You lookin' good."

"Hi, El," Fran said, and, settling on the form beside her, stretched out her legs and sat a moment looking at her shoes.

"Wasser matter?" the older woman asked, but humourously, not to presume. She was Tommy's second wife, a shy, flat-voiced woman. "You in the dumps too?"

"No," Fran said. "Not really."

In fact, she added to herself, not at all. I'm holding myself still, that's all, so that it won't happen too quickly. So that I won't go spinning too fast into whatever it is that may be—just may be, beginning.

She let these thoughts sweep over her to the point where, suddenly ashamed of her self-absorption, she drew back. "What about you, El?" she asked. "Why are you in the dumps?"

"Oh, I dunno. Things. You know. It gets yer down."

Fran looked at her, smiled weakly, and really did want to know, but Ellie of course would not tell. Not just out of pride, but because she did not believe that Fran, even if her interest was genuine and not just the usual politeness, would understand.

I would, Fran wanted to say. Honestly, I would. Try me! But Ellie only smiled back and looked away.

Fran knew Ellie from the days before Audley's retirement, when, from the Camp, which was less than a mile away, she had kept an eye on the house and a key for visitors. Sitting beside her now, Fran felt a weight of darkness descend that for once had nothing to do with herself.

Occasionally, driving out to collect the keys, she had had a cup of tea in Ellie's kitchen, had sat at the rickety table telling herself, in a self-conscious way: I'm having a cup of tea in the house of a black person.

What she felt now, with a kind of queasiness, was how slight and self-dramatising her own turmoils were, how she exaggerated all her feelings, took offence, got angry, wept too easily, and all about what?

"See you, El," she said, very lightly touching the woman's hand. She pushed through to where Angie stood.

"Listen," she said, "can we get out of here? I'm being pursued."

Angie looked interested. "Who by?"

"You know who," she said. "He's got that look. He keeps—hovering." She frowned. This was only half the truth.

Angie laughed. "Come on," she said. "Let's go down to the beach."

WHEN AUDLEY returned to the deck, a moment later, Fran was nowhere to be found. He was disappointed. There were things he wanted to ask—things he wanted to say to her.

He set the glass of wine on the rails, an offering, and sat on a chair beside it.

He would have liked to consult her about one or two things. About Clem. About his own life. About Death: would she know anything about that? About love as well, carnal love. Which he thought sometimes he had failed to experience or understand.

Absent-mindedly, he took the glass he had brought for her— forbidden, of course—and sipped, then sipped again. Just as well, he thought, that Madge wasn't around!

6

FROM THE HEADLAND ABOVE, the sea was flat moonlight all the way to the horizon, but down in the cove among the rocks, almost below sea-level, it rose up white out of the close dark, heaped itself in the narrow opening, then came at them with a rush. Fran leapt back at first, up the shelving sand. "I don't want to get wet!" She had to yell against the sea as well as get out of the way of it. But when she saw how Angie just let the light wash in around her ankles, then higher, darkening all the lower part of her skirt, she laughed and gave in, but did tuck her dress up. It was grey silk and came to her calves. She did not want it spoiled.

They walked together, Angie half a head taller, along the wet beach, their heels leaving phosphorescent prints, and laughed, talked, regaled one another with stories.

It was a secret place down here. With the sea on one side and the cliffs on the other, you were walled in, but the clouds were so high tonight and the air so good in your lungs that you didn't feel its narrowness, only a deep privacy.

"Do you know this Cedric What's-his-name?" Fran asked after a time. "Pohl—Cedric Pohl. Isn't that a hoot?"

She disguised the spurt of excitement, of danger she felt at saying the name twice over. "He's a good-looking boy, isn't he?"

"He isn't a boy," Angie said. "He's thirty-three."

"He asked if he could drive back with me."

"I thought you were staying."

"No. That was a mistake. I can't stay."

They walked on in silence.

"Actually," Angie said at last, "he's a bit of a shit."

"Who is?"

"Your Cedric Pohl."

"He isn't mine," Fran said, but it exhilarated her to be speaking of him in these terms.

"So," she said when a decent interval had elapsed, "what do you know about him? He's married, I suppose."

"Was."

"Well, that's nothing against him."

"She left him and took the kids. He was two-timing her."

Fran gave a little laugh, then thought better of it. "Well," she said, "I haven't committed myself. He can go back with the Bergs."

They came round the edge of the knoll and once again the sea was before them.

A slope, low dunes held together by pigface and spiky grass, led down to the beach. On any other occasion they would have hauled up their skirts at this point and sprinted, but the beach was already occupied. There was a party down there round a leaping fire. They made a face at one another, lifted their skirts like little girls preparing to pee in the open (was that what gave the moment an air of the deliciously forbidden and set them giggling?) and sat plump down in the cool sand to spy.

The fire had been built in the most prodigal way, a great unsteady pyramid of flames. A man with a sleeping bag round his shoulders was tending it, occasionally tossing on a branch but otherwise simply contemplating it, watching the sparks fly up and the nest of heat at its centre breathe and glow. Something in his

actions suggested a trancelike meditation, as if the pyre had drawn
his mind out of him and he were living now as the fire did, subdued to its being but also feeding his and the fire's needs. Watching him you too felt subdued yet invigorated, taken out of yourself
into its overwhelming presence.

They sat with their arms round their knees, unspeaking, and
the silence between them deepened. Drawn in by the slow gestures of the man as he tossed branch after branch on to the pyre—
and, like him, by the pulse of the fire itself, which was responding
in waves to the breeze that came in from the sea, and which they
felt on the hairs of their arms—they might have stepped out of
time entirely.

The others—there were three little groups of them—lay away
from the fire but still in the light of its glow.

One couple was curled spoon-fashion on the sand. In the
curve of the woman's body, a child, its plump limbs rosy with fire-
light.

A little distance away another woman sat on a pile of blankets
with a baby at her breast and a boy of six or seven beside her. He
had his thumb in his mouth.

Further off, where the darkness began, two men sat cross-
legged and facing one another so that their brows almost touched.

One, his long hair over his eyes, his head bent, was playing a
mouth-organ, some Country and Western tune, very sad and
whining, to which the second man beat a rhythm on his thigh.

All around them, scattered without thought in the sand, were
bottles, paper plates, cartons, the remains of their meal.

The group of the man, woman, and baby shifted a little. The
man's arm had gone numb. He eased it, and the woman's body
moved with his into a new position. She drew the baby in.

The man with the sleeping bag threw another branch on to the
fire.

I could sit here for ever, Fran thought. If the fire went on burning and the man fed it and the others slept like that, and those two
men kept on playing that same bit of a tune, I could sit here till I

understood at last what it all means: why the sea, why the stars, why this lump in my throat.

Still seated in the sand with her skirt tucked between her knees and her spine straight, she saw herself get up and walk slowly to where the man with the sleeping bag stood. He turned, and without surprise, watched her come in out of the dark. She stood before him for a moment, then, as if granted permission, went and lay down on the sand among the others, between the group of the man, woman, and baby and the woman with the small boy, feeling the fire's warmth on one side and the breath of the sea on the other. The tune went on. She slept. And in her dream saw a thin, tight-lipped woman with big eyes like a bush-baby's, sitting far off in the dark of the dunes. Gently she beckoned to her, and the woman got up and came into the circle of light.

Long minutes had passed. They had grown cold. Angie wrapped her arms around herself and shivered. She got to her feet and began to walk on. Fran took up her shoes and followed.

The track led to the crest of the hill. From there a second track would take them down to the horse-paddocks, then the long way round to the house. But as they climbed there was a brighter glow in the sky.

"What is it?" Fran asked. "More bonfires?"

Then they came to the top and saw it. Great shoots of flame over the town.

7

FROM THE HOUSE a fleet of cars had already set off, their progress slowed by the many gates that had to be opened. They were barely out of sight when the telephone rang.

"Poor Audley," Madge said when Milly Gates from the Post Office gave her the news. She sat down in her black frock, closed her eyes and, worn out with all the preparations and the talk and because it was the only way she had of dealing with things, immediately fell asleep, her head back, snoring.

The half-dozen guests who had stayed behind with her were embarrassed, but felt free now to step out on to the deck and watch from a distance the play of flames across the inlet and the reflected glow in the sky.

In the cars they were still in doubt, as they came along the edge of the Lake, what it was that was making such a show.

"Looks like the police station," Rupe ventured.

"No," Ralph told him gloomily, having a good idea what it must be, "it's not the cop shop."

Tommy Molloy, sitting in the back seat between them, said nothing. He knew what it was. So did Audley. A vision of it had appeared spontaneously in Audley's head, the four rooms and all their objects in glowing outline, in a red essence of themselves, a final intensity of their being in the world before they collapsed into ash.

He sat very still in the front seat beside Jonathon, wearing a look, behind the startled eyes, of practised stoicism.

The first one away had been Barney Shannon in his ute, with Lily in the cabin beside him. When they came to the gates it was Barney who leapt out and ran forward in the headlamps' beam to open them.

In procession they crossed the causeway into town.

The street was jammed with cars. On the roofs of some of them young fellows in boardshorts were standing as if at a football match, with beer cans in their fists. Girls were being hauled up beside them, slipping and shrieking. Further on was the inner circle of those who had pushed in as close as the heat would allow.

Abandoning the cars, they began to ease their way through the crowd, Ralph staying as close as he could to his father's side. People turned to protest, but, when they saw who it was, made way, and Audley, finding himself the object of so much attention, felt his heart flutter.

A young fireman came hurrying up. He was in uniform but without his helmet.

"Sorry about this, Mr. Tyler," he shouted, "she's pretty far gone. Old stuff. That's what done it. Went up like a haystack."

He was a fresh-faced fellow of twenty-two or -three, recently married. The firebell must have got him out of bed. His hair was wild, his face aglow. There was something hectic and unreliable in his looks. He shouted as if afraid his rather high voice might not carry across the distance he felt between himself and a world that was entirely occupied now by the blaze; all the time casting quick little glances over his shoulder, anxious that if he took his eyes off it for even a second, this conflagration, this star-blaze whose heat he felt between his shoulder blades, and which sent runnels of sweat down his sides under the heavy uniform, might die on him before he had time to savour the excitement it had set off in him. Suddenly, unable to resist any longer the attraction of the thing, he swung round and took the full blast of it on his cheeks. He had, Audley saw, a proprietorial look.

Beautiful! His look said. She's a real beauty! It was his first big do.

If I were a policeman, thought Audley, I'd arrest that boy on the spot.

Surprised by his own excitement, which he had caught from the young fireman and which he felt too in the silent concentration and glow of the crowd, he approached the flames.

Don Wheelwright, the local policeman, materialized. "Don't worry, Mr. Tyler," he shouted, "we'll get 'em soon enough, the bastards that done it."

Audley did not respond. He knew who the fellow was referring to. And Don Wheelwright, feeling snubbed, put another mark in his book of grievances. He had had go-ins with Audley before. His promise of action was a challenge. Well, what about it, Mr. Tyler? Now it's something of yours the bastards have touched. As if, Audley thought, in Clem, he had not been touched already.

All these unofficial reports were an embarrassment to him, he did not want them. He had no doubt Don Wheelwright and his people would come up with a culprit—several, perhaps. There might even be among them the one who had struck the match. But standing here in the crowd was like being in the fire itself, there was such an affinity between the two, such a surge of intensity. It

stilled the mind, sucked up attention and subdued the individual
spirit in such a general heightening of crowd-spirit, of primitive
joy in the play of wind and flame, that he found himself saying,
with grim humour, out of the centre of it: "So we got our bonfire
after all—want it or not."

He felt, against all sense or reason, exhilarated, released. He
could have shaken his palms in the air and danced.

Looking about quickly to see if anyone, Lily for instance, had
noticed, he was struck again by the intensity of the faces. They
were like sleepwalkers who had come out, some of them still in
their nightwear, to gaze on something deeply dreamed.

What we dare not do ourselves, he found himself thinking, they
do for us, the housebreakers, the muggers, the smashers, the grab
merchants. When we punish them it is to hide our secret guilt.
There is ancient and irreconcilable argument in us between
settlement and the spirit of the nomad, between the makers of
order and our need to give ourselves over at moments to the imps
and demons, to the dervish dance of what is in the last resort dust.
We are in love with what we most fear and hide from, death. And
there came into his head some lines of a poem he had read, composed of course by one of the unsettled:

> And yet, there is only
> one great thing,
> the only thing:
> to live to see, in huts and on journeys,
> the great day that dawns,
> the light that fills the world.

As for the objects in there, brilliantly alive for a moment in the
last of what had been their structure and about to fall into themselves as ash—the dining table with its set and empty places, each
occupied now by an eddy of flame, the writhings on the double
bed, the glass cases exploding and tossing their rocks back into the
furnace of time—what was that but a final sacrifice, like his bones,

to the future and its angels, whose vivid faces are turned towards us but with sealed lips?

He glanced sideways, feeling an eye upon him.

It was Lily. Tilted at a precarious angle on her stick, her silks all flame, her twist of a smile saying: Don't think I can't see right through you, Audley Tyler, you sorrowful old hypocrite.

He too must have been smiling. She pitched a little and, using her stick to right herself, dipped her shoulder in acknowledgement and turned away.

There is no hope, he told himself, that's what the old know, that's our secret. It is also our hope, our salvation.

It was then that he remembered Tommy. Searching among the nearby crowd, he found him standing a little way off to the left, his face gleaming with sweat. He was watching along with the rest, and as always seeing the thing, the fire in this case, out of another history.

Audley, touched, went across and laid a hand on his old friend's shoulder. They had been through so much together, he and this old man, over the years. Battles won and lost; the night, which might so easily have divided them, of Clem's accident. They looked at one another, but only briefly, then stood side by side without speaking and went on gazing into the fire.

8

"LISTEN," Clem said, "listen, everybody. I want to say something."

They were a small group now, seated on the coarse-bladed lawn with just the lights from the house falling on them through the open windows, only one or two among them, Audley, Lily, in deck chairs; Barney Shannon lay full-length with his hands folded on his chest, but not sleeping. Subdued, each one, by the recent event, which no one referred to, but also by the overwhelming presence, at this hour, now that the music had packed up and they had run out of talk, of the moon, running full-tilt against a bank of fast-moving clouds, and by the bush, so dense and alive with sound, and down in the cove, the sea breaking. Clem could not have said which of these things moved him most. They were all connected.

The day was over, past, if what you meant by that was time strictly measured—it was past midnight. But what he meant by it was the occasion, though that too might end if one of them now made the move, got up and said: "Well, I'm off," or "Let's call it a day," or "Me for the blanket show." The group would break up then, and these last ones, the survivors, would go to join those who were already curled up in bunks and sleeping bags on their way to the next thing. Tomorrow. He wanted to forestall that. Something more was needed. Something had to be said. And if no one else was ready to say it, then it was up to him. He felt their eyes upon him, and saw Audley's look of disquiet and shook his head, meaning to reassure him: Don't worry, Dad, I know what I'm doing. It's all right.

He felt confident. The words were there, he still had hold of them. And these were friends, people he loved, who would understand if what he said went astray and did not come out the way he meant. Their faces, which just a moment ago had seemed weary and at an end, were expectant. A light of alertness and curiosity was in them, a rekindling.

"Listen," he said, "this is what I want to say.

"Out there—out there in space, I mean—there's a kind of receiver. Very precise it is, very subtle—refined. What it picks up, it's made that way, is heartbeats, just that. Every heartbeat on the planet, it doesn't miss a single one, not one is missed. Even the faintest, it picks it up. Even some old person left behind on the track, too weak to go on, just at their last breath. Even a baby in its humidicrib." He took a breath, growing excited now. He had to control the spit in his mouth as well as the sentences. But he had their attention, it did not matter that one or two of them were frowning and might wonder if he was all there.

"Once upon a time, all this bit of the planet, all this—land mass, this continent—was silent, there was no sound at all, you wouldn't have known it was here. Silence. Then suddenly a blip, a few little signs of life. Not many. Insects, maybe, then frogs, but it was registering their presence. The receiver was turned towards it and tuned in and picked them up. Just those few heartbeats. What a weak little sound it must have been, compared with India for instance or China, or Belgium even—that's the most crowded spot. How could anyone know how big it was with so few heartbeats scattered across it? But slowly others started to arrive, just a few at first, rough ones, rough—hearts—then a rush, till now there are millions. Us, I mean, the ones who are here tonight. Now. There's a great wave of sound moving out towards it, a single hum, and the receiver can pick up each one, each individual beat in it, this one, that one—that's how it's been constructed, that's what it's fixed to do. Only it takes such a long time for the sound to travel across all that space that the receiver doesn't even know as yet that we've arrived—us whites, I mean. Our heartbeats haven't even got there yet. But that doesn't matter—" he laughed, it was going well "—because we *are* here, aren't we? Others were here, now they're gone. But their heartbeats are still travelling out. Even though they stopped ages ago, they're still travelling. It doesn't matter one way or the other, which people, the living or the dead, it's all the same. Or whether they're gone now or still here like us. The birds too. You can feel the way their hearts beat when you pick one up, even when it's still in the shell. And rabbits. What I think is—" he prepared now for his conclusion "—is this. If we imagined ourselves out there and concentrated hard enough, really concentrated, we could hear it too, all of it, the whole sound coming towards us, all of it. It's possible. Anything is possible. Nothing is lost. Nothing ever gets *lost*."

He looked about, their attention was on him. And suddenly there was nothing more to say.

"That's all," he said abruptly, "that's all I wanted to say. Because of what day it is. You know, because of that. Because no one had said anything. So I did."

He smiled nervously but felt pleased with himself. He felt good about things. He grinned, gave a little laugh, then sat on the grass and saw that they were all smiling, except for Audley, who always had a few tears on these occasions. But that was all right. It was good. Only he wished that Fran had still been here. She had left half an hour ago and that put a damper on his heart, but not so much of a one. That was all right too. They could go to bed now. He could. They all could. The day was over.

But not yet, not quite yet. They would sit for a bit, letting the moon, the dark surrounding bush with its medley of nightsounds, hold them in its single mood, which his speech had not broken.

Fran had left in a group of a dozen or so, including Cedric Pohl, who did go with the Bergs. The cars made a procession down the rutted slope and through the three gates to the main road.

In the flurry of farewells, in the leaping torchlight as people stumbled over clods and picked their way among bushes to find their cars, she had had no chance to explain to Clem, simply to say what he already understood, that she felt out of things and would rather drive back tonight than in the heat of the day. He nodded, smiling. She kissed him quickly and climbed into her car.

The procession got under way and she closed her mind to everything but the drive ahead: her mind, not her body. The excitement she felt at the prospect of something new, a romance even, had settled now to a slow but regular ticking in her. Like a bomb, she thought, that was timed to explode somewhere up ahead. Well, she'd deal with that when she came to it.

As they swung down past the horse-paddocks and began to climb the moonslope, two figures appeared in the light of the headlamps and had to move away to the side of the road.

It was Ralph and Angie out walking—bailed up now by the line of cars. She would have stopped and spoken, but there were two more cars behind her and before she could wave even, they had been left standing, looking blanched and ghostlike, stunned by the blaze of lights. Still, the image of them together, isolated in the dark, Ralph in his white shirt, Angie in black, pleased her.

Ralph and Angie walked, as they often did at the end of the day, even at home in the city. Sharing a half-hour together after so many in which they had gone their separate ways.

Down here in the open they walked in whatever light there was from the moon, since they knew this place like the back of their hands. At home it was under humming streetlights, past fences behind which dogs leapt or growled and walls scribbled with graffiti—Yuppies Fuck Off or Eve Was Framed—stepping over rubbish spilled out of doorways, old-fashioned hearts drawn in chalk on the pavement and roughly initialled, through streets where the inhabitants were already sleeping; pausing sometimes before a lighted window to catch a couple of moments from a late-night movie. Ralph, who knew every movie ever made, would identify it for her. "That's Jack Palance, the rat! In *Panic in the Streets*." Or, "That's Marilyn in *Bus Stop*."

They seldom talked, or if they did it was to pass on bits and pieces of the day's news, none of it important. It was the walking together that held them close. Now, as they came up the hill in the dark, they could hear Audley at the piano. He liked to play quietly to himself when the rest of the household had gone to bed: simple things that he had learned when he was a boy. Tonight it was "Jesu, Joy of Man's Desiring." The flowing accompaniment brought them right up to the kitchen steps and they stood a moment in the dark to let him finish.

The piano was an old Bechstein upright, its black enamel finish chipped in places, worn in others. He played without music but with his eyes fixed ahead, as if the pages stood open on their rest; very straight on the stool, still hearing in his head that first voice telling him: Keep your shoulders back, Aud, sit up straight, and don't drop your wrists. Being stern with himself, as he was in everything.

When he came to a conclusion he sat with his hands on his knees, till Ralph called: "That was great, Dad. We just dropped in to say goodnight."

Angie had gone to the tap over the sink to get a glass of water. Nothing had been cleared. In the sink, still in its wrapping, was a big bunch of flowers—tuberoses, the air was drenched with their scent—and under them, Audley's blackfish.

"You go on," she told Ralph quietly. "I'll just clear up a bit."

Ralph kissed her on the back of the neck while she stood and sipped her glass of water, then went to say goodnight to his father. She unwrapped the flowers, found a pail to put them in, and ran cold water over the fish to freshen them up, then made room for them in the bottom of the fridge. When she looked up Ralph was gone and Audley was standing in the doorway behind her.

She turned and ran the tap to rinse her hands.

"Would you like me to make some tea?" she asked.

They were the night owls of the household. They often found themselves alone like this, last thing.

He did not like to go to bed, she knew that. He was scared, she suspected, that if he took his clothes off and lay down to sleep he would slip so far into the dark, into the night that becomes greater night, that he might never get back. He had never said any of this, he was too proud, but she had seen the same thing, the year before he died, in her father. Without waiting for an answer now she filled the electric jug and he sat down like a patient child on one of the forms.

The throbbing of the jug filled the silence. When it stopped she was aware, as she had not been before, of the odd little sounds that came from the house itself, its joists and uprights creaking as they shifted and settled like sleepers—or it was the sleepers themselves in their several rooms and out on the deck where the young were sleeping. She thought she could hear Ned, who was inclined to mutter in his sleep.

Taking her cup, she stepped to the window and looked down on half a dozen forms all huddled in their sleeping bags, and made out Ned's fair head, then Jenny's darker one. All safe as houses.

She came back and sat by Audley at the bench.

"What I've always admired about you, Angie," he said after a moment, "is the gift you have for attending—for attention. People never mention it among the virtues, but it might be the greatest of them all. It's the beginning of everything. Malebranche, you know, called it the natural prayer of the soul. I think it's what Clem's speech meant to say. You didn't hear it, did you?"

She shook her head, took a sip from her cup.

"I wish you had. It would have meant something to you. I was deeply moved. By the boy's intense—happiness. He spoke from a full heart—I think he was trying to say something to *me*. You know, about the fire—as well as all the rest. What a day we've had!" He sipped his tea. "Thank you," he said in his formal way.

They sat a little longer, saying nothing now.

Outside, a breeze had sprung up; it stirred the faded chintz at the windows, touched with freshness the stale air of the room. On the edge of town, the charred ashes of the museum glowed a moment so that here and there a flame appeared and wetly hissed.

Down in the cove, the bonfire, which had collapsed on itself, a shimmering mass, revived, threw up flames that cast a flickering redness over the sand, and one of the men, conscious perhaps of the renewed heat, sat up for a moment out of sleep and regarded it, then burrowed back into the dark. Till here, as on other beaches, in coves all round the continent, round the vast outline of it, the heat struck of a new day coming, the light that fills the world.

ANTIPODES

Southern Skies

Fʀᴏᴍ ᴛʜᴇ ʙᴇɢɪɴɴɪɴɢ he was a stumbling-block, the Professor. I had always thought of him as an old man, as one thinks of one's parents as old, but he can't in those days have been more than fifty. Squat, powerful, with a good deal of black hair on his wrists, he was what was called a "ladies' man"—though that must have been far in the past and in another country. What he practised now was a formal courtliness, a clicking of heels and kissing of plump fingers that was the extreme form of a set of manners that our parents clung to because it belonged, along with much else, to the Old Country, and which we young people, for the same reason, found it imperative to reject. The Professor had a "position"—he taught mathematics to apprentices on day-release. He was proof that a breakthrough into the New World was not only possible, it was a fact. Our parents, having come to a place where their qualifications in medicine or law were unacceptable, had been forced to take work as labourers or factory-hands or to keep dingy shops; but we, their clever sons and daughters, would find our way back to the safe professional classes. For our parents there was deep sorrow in all this, and the Professor offered hope. We were invited to see in him both the embodiment of a noble past and a glimpse of what, with hard work and a little luck or grace, we might claim from the future.

He was always the special guest.

"Here, pass the Professor this slice of torte," my mother would say, choosing the largest piece and piling it with cream, or "Here, take the Professor a nice cold Pils, and see you hand it to him proper now and don't spill none on the way": this on one of those community outings we used to go to in the early years, when half a dozen families would gather at Suttons Beach with a crate of beer bottles in straw jackets and a spread of homemade sausage and cabbage rolls. Aged six or seven, in my knitted bathing-briefs, and watching out in my bare feet for bindy-eye, I would set out over the grass to where the great man and my father, easy now in shirtsleeves and braces, would be pursuing one of their interminable arguments. My father had been a lawyer in the Old Country but worked now at the Vulcan Can Factory. He was passionately interested in philosophy, and the Professor was his only companion on those breathless flights that were, along with the music of Beethoven and Mahler, his sole consolation on the raw and desolate shore where he was marooned. Seeing me come wobbling towards them with the Pils—which I had slopped a little—held breast-high before me, all golden in the sun, he would look startled, as if I were a spirit of the place he had failed to allow for. It was the Professor who recognised the nature of my errand. "Ah, how kind," he would say. "Thank you, my dear. And thank the good mama too. Anton, you are a lucky man." And my father, reconciled to the earth again, would smile and lay his hand very gently on the nape of my neck while I blushed and squirmed.

The Professor had no family—or not in Australia. He lived alone in a house he had built to his own design. It was of pinewood, as in the Old Country, and in defiance of local custom was surrounded by trees—natives. There was also a swimming pool where he exercised twice a day. I went there occasionally with my father, to collect him for an outing, and had sometimes peered at it through a glass door; but we were never formally invited. The bachelor did not entertain. He was always the guest, and what his visits meant to me, as to the children of a dozen other families, was that I must be especially careful of my manners, see that my shoes were properly polished, my nails clean, my hair combed, my tie straight, my socks pulled up, and that when questioned about school or about the games I played I should give my answers clearly, precisely, and without making faces.

So there he was all through my childhood, an intimidating

presence, and a heavy reminder of that previous world; where his family owned a castle, and where he had been, my mother insisted, a real scholar.

Time passed and as the few close-knit families of our community moved to distant suburbs and lost contact with one another, we children were released from restriction. It was easy for our parents to give in to new ways now that others were not watching. Younger brothers failed to inherit our confirmation suits with their stiff white collars and cuffs. We no longer went to examinations weighed down with holy medals, or silently invoked, before putting pen to paper, the good offices of the Infant of Prague— whose influence, I decided, did not extend to Brisbane, Queensland. Only the Professor remained as a last link.

"I wish, when the Professor comes," my mother would complain, "that you try to speak better. The vowels! For my sake, darling, but also for your father, because we want to be proud of you," and she would try to detain me as, barefoot, in khaki shorts and an old T-shirt, already thirteen, I wriggled from her embrace. "And put shoes on, or sandals at least, and a nice clean shirt. I don't want that the Professor think we got an Arab for a son. And your Scout belt! And comb your hair a little, my darling—please!"

She kissed me before I could pull away. She was shocked, now that she saw me through the Professor's eyes, at how far I had grown from the little gentleman I might have been, all neatly suited and shod and brushed and polished, if they had never left the Old Country, or if she and my father had been stricter with me in this new one.

The fact is, I had succeeded, almost beyond my own expectations, in making myself indistinguishable from the roughest of my mates at school. My mother must have wondered at times if I could ever be smoothed out and civilized again, with my broad accent, my slang, my feet toughened and splayed from going barefoot. I was spoiled and wilful and ashamed of my parents. My mother knew it, and now, in front of the Professor, it was her turn to be ashamed. To assert my independence, or to show them that I did not care, I was never so loutish, I never slouched or mumbled or scowled so darkly as when the Professor appeared. Even my father, who was too dreamily involved with his own thoughts to notice me on most occasions, was aware of it and shocked. He complained to my mother, who shook her head and cried. I felt magnificently justified, and the next time the Professor made his appearance I swaggered even more outrageously and gave every indication of being an incorrigible tough.

The result was not at all what I had had in mind. Far from being repelled by my roughness the Professor seemed charmed. The more I showed off and embarrassed my parents, the more he encouraged me. My excesses delighted him. He was entranced.

He really was, as we younger people had always thought, a caricature of a man. You could barely look at him without laughing, and we had all become expert, even the girls, at imitating his hunched stance, his accent (which was at once terribly foreign and terribly English) and the way he held his stubby fingers when, at the end of a meal, he dipped sweet biscuits into wine and popped them whole into his mouth. My own imitations were designed to torment my mother.

"Oh you shouldn't!" she would whine, suppressing another explosion of giggles. "You mustn't! Oh stop it now, your father will see—he would be offended. The Professor is a fine man. May you have such a head on your shoulders one day, and such a position."

"Such a head on my shoulders," I mimicked, hunching my back like a stork so that I had no neck, and she would try to cuff me, and miss as I ducked away.

I was fifteen and beginning to spring up out of pudgy childhood into clean-limbed, tumultuous adolescence. By staring for long hours into mirrors behind locked doors, by taking stock of myself in shop windows, and from the looks of some of the girls at school, I had discovered that I wasn't at all bad-looking, might even be good-looking, and was already tall and well-made. I had chestnut hair like my mother and my skin didn't freckle in the sun but turned heavy gold. There was a whole year between fifteen and sixteen when I was fascinated by the image of myself I could get back from people simply by playing up to them—it scarcely mattered whom: teachers, girls, visitors to the house like the Professor, passers-by in the street. I was obsessed with myself, and lost no opportunity of putting my powers to the test.

Once or twice in earlier days, when I was playing football on Saturday afternoons, my father and the Professor had appeared on the sidelines, looking in after a walk. Now, as if by accident, the Professor came alone. When I came trotting in to collect my bike, dishevelled, still spattered and streaked from the game, he would be waiting. He just happened, yet again, to be passing, and had a book for me to take home, or a message: he would be calling for my father at eight and could I please remind him, or yes, he would be coming next night to play Solo. He was very formal on these occasions, but I felt his interest; and sometimes, without thinking of anything more than the warm sense of myself it gave me to command his attention, I would walk part of the way home with him, wheeling my bike and chatting about nothing very important: the game, or what I had done with my holiday, or since he was a dedicated star-gazer, the new comet that had appeared. As these meetings increased I got to be more familiar with him. Sometimes, when two or three of the others were there (they had come to recognise him and teased me a little, making faces and jerking their heads as he made his way, hunched and short-sighted, to where we were towelling ourselves at the tap) I would for their benefit show off a little, without at first realising, in my reckless passion to be admired, that I was exceeding all bounds and that they now included me as well as the Professor in their humourous contempt. I was mortified. To ease myself back into their good opinion I passed him off as a family nuisance, whose attentions I knew were comic but whom I was leading on for my own amusement. This was acceptable enough and I was soon restored to popularity, but felt doubly treacherous. He was, after all, my father's closest friend, and there was as well that larger question of the Old Country. I burned with shame, but was too cowardly to do more than brazen things out.

For all my crudeness and arrogance I had a great desire to act nobly, and in this business of the Professor I had miserably failed.

I decided to cut my losses. As soon as he appeared now, and had announced his message, I would mount my bike, sling my football boots over my shoulder and pedal away. My one fear was that he might enquire what the trouble was, but of course he did not. Instead he broke off his visits altogether or passed the field without stopping, and I found myself regretting something I had come to depend on—his familiar figure hunched like a bird on the sidelines, our talks, some fuller sense of my own presence to add at the end of the game to the immediacy of my limbs after violent exercise.

Looking back on those days I see myself as a kind of centaur, half-boy, half-bike, for ever wheeling down suburban streets under the poincianas, on my way to football practise or the library or to a meeting of the little group of us, boys and girls, that came together on someone's verandah in the evenings after tea.

I might come across the Professor then on his after-dinner stroll; and as often as not he would be accompanied by my father, who would stop me and demand (partly, I thought, to impress the Professor) where I was off to or where I had been; insisting, with more than his usual force, that I come home right away, with no argument.

On other occasions, pedalling past his house among the trees, I would catch a glimpse of him with his telescope on the roof. He might raise a hand and wave if he recognised me; and sprinting away, crouched low over the handlebars, I would feel, or imagine I felt, that the telescope had been lowered and was following me to the end of the street, losing me for a time, then picking me up again two streets further on as I flashed away under the bunchy leaves.

I spent long hours cycling back and forth between our house and my girlfriend Helen's or to Ross McDowell or Jimmy Larwood's, my friends from school, and the Professor's house was always on the route.

I think of those days now as being all alike, and the nights also: the days warmish, still, endlessly without event, and the nights quivering with expectancy but also uneventful, heavy with the scent of jasmine and honeysuckle and lighted by enormous stars. But what I am describing, of course, is neither a time nor a place but the mood of my own bored, expectant, uneventful adolescence. I was always abroad and waiting for something significant to occur, for life somehow to declare itself and catch me up. I rode my bike in slow circles or figures-of-eight, took it for sprints across the gravel of the park, or simply hung motionless in the saddle, balanced and waiting.

Nothing ever happened. In the dark of front verandahs we lounged and swapped stories, heard gossip, told jokes, or played show-poker and smoked. One night each week I went to Helen's and we sat a little scared of one another in her garden-swing, touching in the dark. Helen liked me better, I thought, than I liked her—I had that power over her—and it was this more than anything else that attracted me, though I found it scary as well. For fear of losing me she might have gone to any one of the numbers that in those days marked the stages of sexual progress and could be boasted about, in a way that seemed shameful afterwards, in locker-rooms or round the edge of the pool. I could have taken us both to 6, 8, 10, but what then? The numbers were not infinite.

I rode around watching my shadow flare off gravel; sprinted, hung motionless, took the rush of warm air into my shirt; afraid that when the declaration came, it too, like the numbers, might be less than infinite. I didn't want to discover the limits of the world. Restlessly impelled towards some future that would at last offer me my real self, I nevertheless drew back, happy for the moment, even in my unhappiness, to be half-boy, half-bike, half aimless energy and half a machine that could hurtle off at a moment's notice in any one of a hundred directions. Away from things—but away, most of all, from my self. My own presence had begun to be a source of deep dissatisfaction to me, my vanity, my charm, my falseness, my preoccupation with sex. I was sick of myself and longed for the world to free me by making its own rigorous demands and declaring at last what I must be.

. . .

ONE NIGHT, in our warm late winter, I was riding home past the Professor's house when I saw him hunched as usual beside his telescope, but too absorbed on this occasion to be aware of me.

I paused at the end of the drive, wondering what it was that he saw on clear nights like this that was invisible to me when I leaned my head back and filled my gaze with the sky.

The stars seemed palpably close. In the high September blueness it was as if the odour of jasmine blossoms had gathered there in a single shower of white. You might have been able to catch the essence of it floating down, as sailors, they say, can smell new land whole days before they first catch sight of it.

What I was catching, in fact, was the first breath of change—a change of season. From the heights I fell suddenly into deep depression, one of those sweet-sad glooms of adolescence that are like a bodiless drifting out of yourself into the immensity of things, when you are aware as never again—or never so poignantly—that time is moving swiftly on, that a school year is very nearly over and childhood finished, that you will have to move up a grade at football into a tougher class—shifts that against the vastness of space are minute, insignificant, but at that age solemnly felt.

I was standing astride the bike, staring upwards, when I became aware that my name was being called, and for the second or third time. I turned my bike into the drive with its border of big-leafed saxifrage and came to where the Professor, his hand on the telescope, was leaning out over the roof.

"I have some books for your father," he called. "Just come to the gate and I will get them for you."

The gate was wooden, and the fence, which made me think of a stockade, was of raw slabs eight feet high, stained reddish-brown. He leaned over the low parapet and dropped a set of keys.

"It's the thin one," he told me. "You can leave your bike in the yard." He meant the paved courtyard inside, where I rested it easily against the wall. Beyond, and to the left of the pine-framed house, which was stained the same colour as the fence, was a garden taken up almost entirely by the pool. It was overgrown with dark tropical plants, monstera, hibiscus, banana-palms with their big purplish flowers, glossily pendulous on stalks, and fixed to the paling-fence like trophies in wads of bark, elkhorn, tree-orchids, showers of delicate maidenhair. It was too cold for swimming, but the pool was filled and covered with a shifting scum of jacaranda leaves that had blown in from the street, where the big trees were stripping to bloom.

I went round the edge of the pool and a light came on, reddish, in one of the inner rooms. A moment later the Professor himself appeared, tapping for attention at a glass door.

"I have the books right here," he said briskly; but when I stood hesitating in the dark beyond the threshold, he shifted his feet and added: "But maybe you would like to come in a moment and have a drink. Coffee. I could make some. Or beer. Or a Coke if you prefer it. I have Coke."

I had never been here alone, and never, even with my father, to this side of the house. When we came to collect the Professor for an outing we had always waited in the tiled hallway while he rushed about with one arm in the sleeve of his overcoat laying out saucers for cats, and it was to the front door, in later years, that I had delivered bowls of gingerbread fish that my mother had made specially because she knew he liked it, or cabbage rolls or herring. I had never been much interested in what lay beyond the hallway, with its fierce New Guinea masks, all tufted hair and boar's tusks, and the Old Country chest that was just like our own. Now, with the books already in my hands, I hesitated and looked past him into the room.

"All right. If it's no trouble."

"No no, no trouble at all!" He grinned, showing his teeth with their extravagant caps. "I am delighted. Really! Just leave the books there. You see they are tied with string, quite easy for you I'm sure, even on the bike. Sit where you like. Anywhere. I'll get the drink."

"Beer then," I said boldly, and my voice cracked, destroying what I had hoped might be the setting of our relationship on a clear, man-to-man basis that would wipe out the follies of the previous year. I coughed, cleared my throat, and said again, "Beer, thanks," and sat abruptly on a sofa that was too low and left me prone and sprawling.

He stopped a moment and considered, as if I had surprised him by crossing a second threshold.

"Well then, if it's to be beer, I shall join you. Maybe you are also hungry. I could make a sandwich."

"No, no thank you, they're expecting me. Just the beer."

He went out, his slippers shushing over the tiles, and I shifted immediately to a straight-backed chair opposite and took the opportunity to look around.

There were rugs on the floor, old threadbare Persians, and low down, all round the walls, stacks of the heavy seventy-eights I carried home when my father borrowed them: sonatas by Beethoven, symphonies by Sibelius and Mahler. Made easy by the Professor's absence, I got up and wandered round. On every open surface, the glass table-top, the sideboard, the long mantel of the fireplace, were odd bits and pieces that he must have collected in his travels: lumps of coloured quartz, a desert rose, slabs of clay with fern or fish fossils in them, glass paperweights, snuff-boxes, meerschaum pipes of fantastic shape—one a Saracen's head, another the torso of a woman like a ship's figurehead with full breasts and golden nipples—bits of Baltic amber, decorated sherds of pottery, black on terra-cotta, and one unbroken object, a little earthenware lamp that when I examined it more closely turned out to be a phallic grotesque. I had just discovered what it actually was when the Professor stepped into the room. Turning swiftly to a framed photograph on the wall above, I found myself peering into a stretch of the Old Country, a foggy, sepia world that I recognised immediately from similar photographs at home.

"Ah," he said, setting the tray down on an empty chair, "you have discovered my weakness." He switched on another lamp. "I have tried, but I am too sentimental. I cannot part with them."

The photograph, I now observed, was one of three. They were

all discoloured with foxing on the passe-partout mounts, and the glass of one was shattered, but so neatly that not a single splinter had shifted in the frame.

The one I was staring at was of half a dozen young men in military uniform. It might have been from the last century, but there was a date in copperplate: 1921. Splendidly booted and sashed and frogged, and hieratically stiff, with casque helmets under their arms, swords tilted at the thigh, white gloves tucked into braided epaulettes, they were a chorus line from a Ruritanian operetta. They were also, as I knew, the heroes of a lost but unforgotten war.

"You recognise me?" the Professor asked.

I looked again. It was difficult. All the young men strained upright with the same martial hauteur, wore the same little clipped moustaches, had the same flat hair parted in the middle and combed in wings over their ears. Figures from the past can be as foreign, as difficult to identify individually, as the members of another race. I took the plunge, set my forefinger against the frame, and turned to the Professor for confirmation. He came to my side and peered.

"No," he said sorrowfully. "But the mistake is entirely understandable. He was my great friend, almost a brother. I am here. This is me. On the left."

He considered himself, the slim assured figure, chin slightly tilted, eyes fixed ahead, looking squarely out of a class whose privileges—inherent in every point of the stance, the uniform, the polished accoutrements—were not to be questioned, and from the ranks of an army that was invincible. The proud caste no longer existed. Neither did the army nor the country it was meant to defend, except in the memory of people like the Professor and my parents and, in a ghostly way, half a century off in another hemisphere, my own.

He shook his head and made a clucking sound. "Well," he said firmly, "it's a long time ago. It is foolish of me to keep such things. We should live for the present. Or like you younger people," bringing the conversation back to me, "for the future."

I found it easier to pass to the other photographs.

In one, the unsmiling officer appeared as an even younger man, caught in an informal, carefully posed moment with a group of ladies. He was clean-shaven and lounging on the grass in a striped blazer; beside him a discarded boater—very English. The ladies, more decorously disposed, wore long dresses with hats and ribbons. Neat little slippers peeped out under their skirts.

"Yes, yes," he muttered, almost impatient now, "that too. Summer holidays—who can remember where? And the other a walking trip."

I looked deep into a high meadow, with broken cloud-drift in the dip below. Three young men in shorts, maybe schoolboys, were climbing on the far side of the wars. There were flowers in the foreground, glowingly out of focus, and it was this picture whose glass was shattered; it was like looking through a brilliant spider's web into a picturebook landscape that was utterly familiar, though I could never have been there. *That is the place,* I thought. *That is the land my parents mean when they say "the Old Country": the country of childhood and first love that they go back to in their sleep and which I have no memory of, though I was born there. Those flowers are the ones, precisely those, that blossom in the songs they sing.* And immediately I was back in my mood of just a few minutes ago, when I had stood out there gazing up at the stars. *What is it,* I asked myself, *that I will remember and want to preserve, when in years to come I think of the Past? What will be important enough?* For what the photographs had led me back to, once again, was myself. It was always the same. No matter how hard I tried to think my way out into other people's lives, into the world beyond me, the feelings I discovered were my own.

"Come. Sit," the Professor said, "and drink your beer. And do eat one of these sandwiches. It's very good rye bread, from the only shop. I go all the way to South Brisbane for it. And Gürken. I seem to remember you like them."

"What do you do up on the roof?" I asked, my mouth full of bread and beer, feeling uneasy again now that we were sitting with nothing to fix on.

"I make observations, you know. The sky, which looks so still, is always in motion, full of drama if you understand how to read it. Like looking into a pond. Hundreds of events happening right under your eyes, except that most of what we see is already finished by the time we see it—ages ago—but important just the same. Such large events. Huge! Bigger even than we can imagine. And beautiful, since they unfold, you know, to a kind of music, to numbers of infinite dimension like the ones you deal with in equations at school, but more complex, and entirely visible."

He was moved as he spoke by an emotion that I could not identify, touched by occasions a million light-years off and still unfolding towards him, in no way personal. The room for a moment lost its tension. I no longer felt myself to be the focus of his interest, or even of my own. I felt liberated, and for the first time the Professor was interesting in his own right, quite apart from the attention he paid me or the importance my parents attached to him.

"Maybe I could come again," I found myself saying. "I'd like to see."

"But of course," he said, "any time. Tonight is not good—there is a little haze, but tomorrow if you like. Or any time."

I nodded. But the moment of easiness had passed. My suggestion, which might have seemed like another move in a game, had brought me back into focus for him and his look was quizzical, defensive. I felt it and was embarrassed, and at the same time saddened. Some truer vision of myself had been in the room for a moment. I had almost grasped it. Now I felt it slipping away as I moved back into my purely physical self.

I put the glass down, not quite empty.

"No thanks, really," I told him when he indicated the half finished bottle on the tray. "I should have been home nearly an hour ago. My mother, you know."

"Ah yes, of course. Well, just call whenever you wish, no need to be formal. Most nights I am observing. It is a very interesting time. Here—let me open the door for you. The books, I see, are a little awkward, but you are so expert on the bicycle I am sure it will be okay."

I followed him round the side of the pool into the courtyard and there was my bike at its easy angle to the wall, my other familiar and streamlined self. I wheeled it out while he held the gate.

AMONG MY PARENTS' oldest friends were a couple who had recently moved to a new house on the other side of the park, and at the end of winter, in the year I turned seventeen, I sometimes rode over on Sundays to help John clear the big overgrown garden. All afternoon we grubbed out citrus trees that had gone wild, hacked down morning-glory that had grown all over the lower part of the yard, and cut the knee-high grass with a sickle to prepare it for mowing. I enjoyed the work. Stripped down to shorts in the strong sunlight, I slashed and tore at the weeds till my hands blistered, and in a trancelike preoccupation with tough green things that clung to the earth with a fierce tenacity, forgot for a time my own turmoil and lack of roots. It was something to *do*.

John, who worked up ahead, was a dentist. He paid me ten shillings a day for the work, and this, along with my pocket money, would take Helen and me to the pictures on Saturday night, or to a flash meal at one of the city hotels. We worked all afternoon, while the children, who were four and seven, watched and got in the way. Then about five thirty Mary would call us for tea.

Mary had been at school with my mother and was the same age, though I could never quite believe it; she had children a whole ten years younger than I was, and I had always called her Mary. She wore bright bangles on her arm, liked to dance at parties, never gave me presents like handkerchiefs or socks, and had always treated me, I thought, as a grown-up. When she called us for tea I went to the garden tap, washed my feet, splashed water over my back that was streaked with soil and sweat and stuck all over with little grass clippings, and was about to buckle on my loose sandals when she said from the doorway where she had been watching: "Don't bother to get dressed. John hasn't." She stood there smiling, and I turned away, aware suddenly of how little I had on; and had to use my V-necked sweater to cover an excitement that might otherwise have been immediately apparent in the khaki shorts I was wearing—without underpants because of the heat.

As I came up the steps towards her she stood back to let me pass, and her hand, very lightly, brushed the skin between my shoulder blades.

"You're still wet," she said.

It seemed odd somehow to be sitting at the table in their elegant dining room without a shirt; though John was doing it, and was already engaged like the children in demolishing a pile of neat little sandwiches.

I sat at the head of the table with the children noisily grabbing at my left and John on my right drinking tea and slurping it a little, while Mary plied me with raisin-bread and Old Country cookies. I felt red, swollen, confused every time she turned to me, and for some reason it was the children's presence rather than John's that embarrassed me, especially the boy's.

Almost immediately we were finished John got up.

"I'll just go," he said, "and do another twenty minutes before it's dark." It was dark already, but light enough perhaps to go on raking the grass we had cut and were carting to the incinerator. I made to follow. "It's all right," he told me. "I'll finish off. You've earned your money for today."

"Come and see our animals!" the children yelled, dragging me down the hall to their bedroom, and for ten minutes or so I sat on the floor with them, setting out farm animals and making fences, till Mary, who had been clearing the table, appeared in the doorway.

"Come on now, that's enough, it's bathtime, you kids. Off you go!"

They ran off, already half-stripped, leaving her to pick up their clothes and fold them while I continued to sit cross-legged among the toys, and her white legs, in their green sandals, moved back and forth at eye-level. When she went out I too got up, and stood watching at the bathroom door.

She was sitting on the edge of the bath, soaping the little boy's back, as I remembered my mother doing, while the children splashed and shouted. Then she dried her hands on a towel, very carefully, and I followed her into the unlighted lounge. Beyond the glass wall, in the depths of the garden, John was stooping to gather armfuls of the grass we had cut, and staggering with it to the incinerator.

She sat and patted the place beside her. I followed as in a dream. The children's voices at the end of the hallway were complaining, quarrelling, shrilling. I was sure John could see us through the glass as he came back for another load.

Nothing was said. Her hand moved over my shoulder, down my spine, brushed very lightly, without lingering, over the place where my shorts tented; then rested easily on my thigh. When John came in he seemed unsurprised to find us sitting close in the dark. He went right past us to the drinks cabinet, which suddenly lighted up. I felt exposed and certain now that he must see where her hand was and say something.

All he said was: "Something to drink, darling?"

Without hurry she got up to help him and they passed back and forth in front of the blazing cabinet, with its mirrors and its rows of bottles and cut-crystal glasses. I was sweating worse than when I had worked in the garden, and began, self-consciously, to haul on the sweater.

I pedalled furiously away, glad to have the cooling air pour over me and to feel free again.

Back there I had been scared—but of what? Of a game in which I might, for once, be the victim—not passive, but with no power to control the moves. I slowed down and considered that, and was, without realising it, at the edge of something. I rode on in the softening dark. It was good to have the wheels of the bike roll away under me as I rose on the pedals, to feel on my cheeks the warm scent of jasmine that was invisible all round. It was a brilliant night verging on spring. I didn't want it to be over; I wanted to slow things down. I dismounted and walked a little, leading my bike along the grassy edge in the shadow of trees, and without precisely intending it, came on foot to the entrance to the Professor's drive, and paused, looking up beyond the treetops to where he might be installed with his telescope—observing what? What events up there in the infinite sky?

I leaned far back to see. A frozen waterfall it might have been, falling slowly towards me, sending out blown spray that would take centuries, light-years, to break in thunder over my head. Time. What did one moment, one night, a lifespan mean in relation to all that?

"Hullo there!"

It was the Professor. I could see him now, in the moonlight beside the telescope, which he leaned on and which pointed not upwards to the heavens but down to where I was standing. It occurred to me, as on previous occasions, that in the few moments of my standing there with my head flung back to the stars, what he might have been observing was *me*. I hesitated, made no decision. Then, out of a state of passive expectancy, willing nothing but waiting poised for my own life to occur; out of a state of being open to the spring night and to the emptiness of the hours between seven and ten when I was expected to be in, or thirteen (was it?) and whatever age I would be when manhood finally came to me; out of my simply being there with my hand on the saddle of the machine, bare-legged, loose-sandalled, going nowhere, I turned into the drive, led my bike up to the stockade gate, and waited for him to throw down the keys.

"You know which one it is," he said, letting them fall. "Just use the other to come in by the poolside."

I unlocked the gate, rested my bike against the wall of the courtyard, and went round along the edge of the pool. It was clean now but heavy with shadows. I turned the key in the glass door, found my way (though this part of the house was new to me) to the stairs, and climbed to where another door opened straight on to the roof.

"Ah," he said, smiling. "So at last! You are here."

The roof was unwalled but set so deep among trees that it was as if I had stepped out of the city altogether into some earlier, more darkly wooded era. Only lighted windows, hanging detached in the dark, showed where houses, where neighbours were.

He fixed the telescope for me and I moved into position.

"There," he said "what you can see now is Jupiter with its four moons—you see?—all in line, and with the bands across its face."

I saw. Later it was Saturn with its rings and the lower of the two pointers to the cross, Alpha Centauri, which was not one star but two. It was miraculous. From that moment below when I had looked up at a cascade of light that was still ages off, I might have been catapulted twenty thousand years into the nearer past, or into my own future. Solid spheres hovered above me, tiny balls of matter moving in concert like the atoms we drew in chemistry, held together by invisible lines of force; and I thought oddly that if I were to lower the telescope now to where I had been standing at the entrance to the drive I would see my own puzzled, upturned face, but as a self I had already outgrown and abandoned, not minutes but aeons back. He shifted the telescope and I caught my breath. One after another, constellations I had known since childhood as points of light to be joined up in the mind (like those picture-puzzles children make, pencilling in the scattered dots till Snow White and the Seven Dwarfs appear, or an old jalopy), came together now, not as an imaginary panhandle or bull's head or belt and sword, but at some depth of vision I hadn't known I possessed, as blossoming abstractions, equations luminously exploding out of their own depths, brilliantly solving themselves and playing the results in my head as a real and visible music. I felt a power in myself that might actually burst out at my ears, and at the same time saw myself, from *out there*, as just a figure with his eye to a lens. I had a clear sense of being one more hard little point in the immensity—but part of it, a source of light like all those others—and was aware for the first time of the grainy reality of my own life, and then, a fact of no large significance, of the certainty of my death; but in some dimension where those terms were too vague to be relevant. It was at the point where my self ended and the rest of it began that Time, or Space, showed its richness to me. I was overwhelmed.

Slowly, from so far out, I drew back, re-entered the present and was aware again of the close suburban dark—of its moving now in the shape of a hand. I must have known all along that it was there, working from the small of my back to my belly, up the inside of my thigh, but it was of no importance, I was too far off. Too many larger events were unfolding for me to break away and ask, as I might have, "What are you doing?"

I must have come immediately. But when the stars blurred in my eyes it was with tears, and it was the welling of this deeper salt, filling my eyes and rolling down my cheeks, that was the real over-flow of the occasion. I raised my hand to brush them away and it was only then that I was aware, once again, of the Professor. I looked at him as from a distance. He was getting to his feet, and his babble of concern, alarm, self-pity, sentimental recrimination, was incomprehensible to me. I couldn't see what he meant.

"No, no, it's nothing," I assured him, turning aside to button my shorts. "It was nothing. Honestly." I was unwilling to say more in case he misunderstood what I did not understand myself.

We stood on opposite sides of the occasion. Nothing of what he had done could make the slightest difference to me, I was untouched: youth is too physical to accord very much to that side of things. But what I had *seen*—what he had led me to see—my burst-ing into the life of things—I would look back on that as the real beginning of my existence, as the entry into a vocation, and nothing could diminish the gratitude I felt for it. I wanted, in the immense seriousness and humility of this moment, to tell him so, but I lacked the words, and silence was fraught with all the wrong ones.

"I have to go now," was what I said.

"Very well. Of course."

He looked hopeless. He might have been waiting for me to strike him a blow—not a physical one. He stood quietly at the gateway while I wheeled out the bike.

I turned then and faced him, and without speaking, offered him, very formally, my hand. He took it and we shook—as if, in the magnanimity of my youth, I had agreed to overlook his misde-meanour or forgive him. That misapprehension too was a weight I would have to bear.

Carrying it with me, a heavy counterpoise to the extraordinary lightness that was my whole life, I bounced unsteadily over the dark tufts of the driveway and out onto the road.

A Trip to the Grundelsee

T HEY WERE an ill-assorted party.
Gordon and Cassie, who had known one another almost since childhood, were still just friends, as they had been for so long now that Cassie despaired of their ever getting further. She had spent four years being in love with Gordon and felt a fool, but was still under his spell. His various forms of selfishness, all so frank and boyishly certain of their appeal, still worked on her, and she knew that if he made the least offer of himself she would say yes and spend the rest of her life typing his articles, keeping up with his interests and defending him from detractors. That's how she was, and that's how Gordon was as well.

She had simply rushed down here, for example, the moment she thought he was involved, but by the time she arrived he had already lost interest in the girl who had turned up so frequently in his letters of the previous month, and Cassie, who had disliked Anick at sight, soon made a friend of her, seeing quite clearly that this spoiled and rather unworldly French girl would be no more successful with Gordon than she had been. She had even at last grown fond of her—they had something in common; though Anick was elegant, almost beautiful, and Cassie had never been either.

Anick made up the third in their party, and the fourth was a soft American youth of not much more than twenty who earlier in the week had fallen in love with Anick and had since been following her about like a whipped puppy. Anick tended to laugh at him, but when he cried, as he often did, she let him sit with his head in her lap while she stroked his floppy hair, but at the same time made faces; and afterwards made the same faces when she described the scene to Cassie in her limited and brutal English.

Michael, the American boy, was really Austrian—that is, his parents were, but he spoke worse German than the rest of them (they were all doing a summer course at Graz) and was foolishly impressed by everything foreign and picturesque: by the Alpine cabins they passed with their carved wooden overhangs, by votive crosses high up in the mist of passes, the leather shorts and dirndls of villagers, a little steepled church in a cleft among firs, and the pumpy band-music that was being played in one place in the light of a thunderous waterfall. Gordon and Cassie were Australians, but they had never been so wide-eyed and impressionable as Michael, to whom all this might, after all, have been as familiar as home.

Michael had hired a car and they were driving down to the Grundelsee to visit two middle-aged women who had been friends of Michael's father before the war. It was, on Michael's part, a duty visit made on his father's behalf, but also to fulfil a promise he had given, when just a child, to the elder of the two women with whom he had had a schoolboy correspondence. Gordon and Cassie were along because Anick had invited them. She hadn't wanted to spend a whole day alone with Michael. Michael resented this and they felt uncomfortable, but had accepted for the sake of the trip, though Cassie, who took on new loyalties very easily, and stuck to them, included Anick in her reasons for going; she was offering female support. She rather despised Michael and found his mooning over Anick disgusting, whereas Gordon, intent on the landscape and excited by the prospect of adding yet another baroque abbey to his list—and such a remote one—was merely indifferent.

"Another Kaisersaal!" Gordon exulted. (Being impressed by a Kaisersaal rather than a cabin made him different from Michael. Superior.) "Another Kindertotentorte," Cassie thought, making up with this minor disloyalty for her slavish adoption of all Gordon's vagaries of taste.

An ill-assorted party.

"What are these ladies?" Anick demanded, preparing to find them dull.

"They were my father's closest friends in Vienna before the war," Michael told them solemnly. "In the days of Dollfuss, you know. Elsa Fischer and my father were going to be married, I guess. The other one, Sophie, is sort of my father's cousin. They were all in the same political group. My father was a Socialist—practically even a Communist—and they spent seven years—I mean Elsa and Sophie did—in camps. You know—concentration camps. They had a really terrible time. Boy! You should hear some of the things that happened to them. But they survived. And now they live together and have this little summer place on the lake."

Cassie was frowning. She had tried to keep up with it, to let it enter her imagination as well as her head, but Michael went too fast. His narrative made all events sound the same, and outside the sun was flashing.

"And your father?" she demanded, grabbing at a comprehensible fact.

"Oh, he escaped. He got away to America just before the Nazis came. It was a very close thing. He's told me all about it, it's a real adventure story. And of course he married my mother. But you know—he used to talk a lot about the old days, and after the war, when he and Elsa and Sophie made contact again, I used to write to Elsa—I was just a schoolkid—and well—now that I'm here it's the least I can do, to go and say hello."

The silence was filled with intensely dark fir trees, and above them the hard, unchanging whiteness of the Alps.

"They sound fascinating, these old women," said Anick.

Michael failed to catch her tone. "Well," he said, after a pause, "they're sort of special—you know what I mean?" He added a more specific recommendation: "They've *suffered* a lot."

It was a warm day. They had thrown their jackets aside, the two young men, and the girls were stockingless and in open sandals. They had already stopped once and eaten the most delicious cheesecake with cream on top, heaped Schlagobers that were absolutely continuous, Gordon assured them, with the confectionary clouds of local altars. The villages they passed were all very festive-looking, with boxes of bright red geraniums in the windows and in baskets on some of the wooden bridges, and the Alps were permanently, dazzlingly white along the skyline: so that Cassie wondered why she felt so depressed.

They were all four young and their whole lives were before them.

The big car waltzed and Michael took the mountain road at speed. They hoped to be at the Grundelsee before lunch.

THE LAKE WAS TINY—you could walk around it in under an hour—and glassily blue, with fir trees in dark clumps making wedge shapes and rhomboids on the slopes, and very green meadows. The summer places, scattered in groups, were all made of the same stained timber and had the same painted shutters, each with a heart cut out of it, and the same shingle roofs. A cow here and there made the scene look pastoral, productive, but bathers along the shore, and a yellow canoe out in the middle of the lake, pulling a long thread in its picture of blue mountain-peaks, certified that this was a pleasure park and that the slightly sinister atmosphere that hung over it was a matter of weather, the oppressive proximity of so much heaped sublimity.

Perfect Mahler, Gordon would have said.

What Cassie thought was: perfect Grimm.

The one piece of history the place boasted was the elopement, nearly a century before, of the postmaster's daughter and an archduke. A local inn commemorated the occurrence with a painted sign. There were portraits of the couple on all the fluttering racks on the news kiosks—she young and pretty, he an old buffer with side-whiskers—and within minutes of their arrival the two ladies had first asked if they knew the story and then recited, in tandem, its romantic facts, promising to show them later the exact spot where the lovers first met and the old post-house where the girl's parents had lived. Everything had been preserved, of course, and was properly kept up. People came from all over to visit, and apart from the beauty of the views it was the postmaster's daughter, Anna Plöhl, and the Archduke Johann who drew them. That gay fragment of not-too-recent history was what they came to savour and record.

The ladies were rather surprised by their ignorance but delighted that what they had come for was simply and entirely *them*. They hadn't been expected, of course—or not so many—but never mind, they were welcome anyway.

The more impressive of the two was definitely Elsa Fischer, a tall woman with a streak of steel-grey across her head. She was still handsome, and still preserved the assurance of what must once have been a remarkable beauty; but one felt she had long since dismissed that as a trivial gift and valued only the insights it had brought her. In learning to exploit her beauty she had learned how to deal with power; the one lasted after the other had become no more than good posture, good bones, and a little repertoire of gestures that still suggested availability—the promise of great sad occasions and moments of abandon. If she continued to play the game it was because men recognised in her a woman who knew the rules, and liked to experience, now that there was none, the sense of risk.

It was Cassie who saw all this. In her ugly-duckling way she valued beauty, had pondered the subject deeply, and was made aware of Elsa Fischer's great measure of that ambiguous gift in the effect it was having on Gordon. He had ceased to be plumply bored and was giving this sixty-year-old woman the sort of attention he reserved for churches, some paintings, and everything to do with himself.

Cassie was in anguish. She wanted her life, she wanted it at all costs. But she despised the means she had to use, and had been using, to get it—the humiliations, the pretence that she had no passion, no ambition of her own, no sense of honour. Most of all she was afraid that if it came to the point she might not be willing to suffer. She writhed in a dark and stolid silence.

The other woman, who was smaller in every way than Elsa Fischer, had red hair rather inexpertly coloured, red-rimmed eyes and a drooping nose, and seemed quite incapable of being still.

She had wept when Michael greeted her and clung to his neck: he was so much like his father.

"Isn't he just like Arnold?" she had said.

Elsa Fischer, who kissed him on the forehead and was not tearful, looked at him with her wide blue eyes.

"No," she said, "I do not see it. You already look American, Michael dear, and a good thing too. It's how you should look." She kissed him again. "I hoped you'd come."

"But of course," he began.

"No, there is no of course. But you are here, that is what matters." And immediately, since she was aware that she had given him all the attention so far, and since there were, after all, others, she had begun to ask questions, weigh answers, demand qualifications, put things together, and soon had them all clear; and since that is what plainly offered in Gordon's awakened interest, had settled her steady gaze on *him*. Cassie watched him respond, and grow alert and painfully attractive, and oh so youthfully promising as he took out all his little talents and made them shine.

She felt one of her black clouds, the one that had been riding just above her head all morning like a bleak halo, descend at last and smother her in gloom. She felt removed. She watched from a distance. And it occurred to her that if she ever stopped being under Gordon's spell she would hate him.

Was that the cloud?

The red-headed lady, in the meantime, had gone behind a partition, and Cassie, who might have been able to see through walls, saw her, at a little shelf, put slices of meat on pumpernickel and stand there in the half-dark pushing the stuff into one side of her face; vigorously working her jaws and gulping, so that her scalp, with its shock of coloured hair, moved up and down and her throat muscles formed stringy cords. She ate one slice, then another, then a third. Cassie was mesmerized. At last, after swallowing a difficult mouthful, she composed her features, swept her hair with a light hand, and came back into the room looking dignified. She sat, and when she caught Cassie looking at her, produced a smile that was all innocence.

Elsa Fischer, who looked untouchable and gave the impression of having always been so, had been speaking in a low concerned voice of Michael Pacher, his noble forms and glowing colours, while Gordon asked questions to which, Cassie reminded herself, he already knew the answers.

The questions blunt Cassie wanted to put were these. What about the suffering? How do you know if you can face it? Do you just go through it and come out the other side? Does time dull the pain and anger of it?

"Did you see?" Anick hissed, catching up with her on the lakeside path where they were walking to a restaurant. "She was *eating*. All by herself, behind the wall."

"Oh, well," said Cassie, as if there were extenuating circumstances. She hadn't Anick's clear notions of how people should and should not behave. People were extraordinary or plain odd, that was all.

"I was disgusted," Anick declared. "I found it insulting. Now she will come to the restaurant and say she is not 'ungree. I know such people. 'Orreeble!"

She was right. At the restaurant both ladies excused themselves and said they had already eaten, but Elsa Fischer drank a glass of wine and made recommendations and insisted they all try the local torte. It was uncomfortable, even Gordon looked uneasy. He didn't know how he should act, and felt that some situation he had been handling very well, very urbanely, just a while back had turned into something he couldn't handle at all. Only Michael seemed untroubled. He had done the right thing already, simply by coming. He smiled incessantly and looked softly angelic. He ate heartily, drank too much, and on the walk back tried to hold Anick's hand on the narrow path, and looked hurt when she shook him off.

Cassie's cloud refused to shift. Everything gave off a kind of blackness that added to it like smoke: the food they ate, the talk, the water, the damp meadows with the shadow of firs on them, the terrible peaks. It seemed to her that the lake might contain unbearable secrets—drowned babies, or the records, deep-sunk in leaden boxes, of an era—and that these made up the weather to which her cloud belonged, and enveloped her even in sunshine in deepest gloom. It might just be that she had stepped, back there, across a border into the rest of her life and it would go on like this for the next thirty, forty, fifty years—into another century.

AS THEY SPED back down the autobahn, through fields that threw off wave after wave of heat, she sat far back in the seat with her eyes closed and let the others, all of them, sink into the dark. Their faces faded, their voices. It seemed boundless, her depression, eternally deep; though in fact, ten years later, married to another quite different Australian, and with three exuberant daughters who liked to sing in the car as she drove them to and from school, she would not recall this particular gloom, or its cause, and had lost contact with all the members of their trip but Anick, who had started up a correspondence and then kept it going long after Gordon, the original reason, had departed from their lives.

"Who *is* Anick?" the little girls would chorus as they stared at an old album, finding it difficult to connect the slim girl under the peach tree with the lady in Paris who sent them expensive, rather inappropriate presents, or the bony figure in peasant skirt and T-shirt with their comfortable mother. Something more than time seemed to be involved here.

"Anick," Cassie would tell them, not quite sincerely, "is Mummy's best friend," and would add, out of loyalty to one or two neighbours, "in Europe."

Once a year, at Christmas, the presents arrived; and then on a trip to Paris, ten years after their first encounter, Cassie made her decision and looked Anick up. They had lunch together.

Anick was still unmarried. A hard, discontented girl of thirty, still strikingly good-looking, she had that mixture of slovenliness and chic that Cassie, to whom chic would be for ever foreign, thought of as uniquely French. She seemed much occupied with her digestion, eating little and accepting from the waiter, with only a nod of acknowledgement as she rattled on, the glass of mineral water she had not had to call for. It was for her medicine. Still talking, she took from her elegant bag a bottle of some thick white stuff, swallowed a spoonful, made a face that Cassie recalled from other occasions, and washed it down with a draught of Perrier and a wrathful "Ugh."

Thank God I don't have a digestion, Cassie thought. That'd be worse than the Black Cloud. She felt embarrassed by her bouncy good health. She was never ill—barring pregnancies of course, which didn't count.

"Cheers," Anick proclaimed dolefully, shaking the remains of her mineral water to make it fizz. And Cassie, who felt extraordinarily liberated, shouted in response, "Haro!," and might have done a little dance on the spot, in the manner of her youngest daughter when they were out on a hunting party being vengeful squaws. Anick looked astonished, and then delighted by what she recognised as a form of behaviour she couldn't have indulged in herself but which pleased her in others. Cassie had always, in her eyes, been marvellously free. "Haro!" Cassie shouted again, and gave one of her deep wheezy laughs, kicking up imaginary heels and draining her half of Burgundy.

Her smile was one of triumph. What she had caught sight of— the tail-end of a darker possibility, back there, that still haunted her at times—had gone to earth, startled perhaps by the exuberance of her war cry; it needn't again, for a moment, be disturbed. And Anick, who had never even caught sight of it or known they were on a hunting party at all, looked puzzled, but did her best to enter the spirit of things, though she didn't rise to a "Haro!"

They continued to face one another for a whole hour in the mutual perplexity of their national styles and from the vantage point of different lives, while Cassie tried to give some indication of the close web of her life as it involved three little girls, all extraordinarily different from one another and from herself, and a husband whose difficulty both challenged and pleased her. But the particulars of domesticity told nothing. They were flat, uninteresting. It was a holding warmth she needed to express, and she might have illustrated it best by simply leaning across the table and grasping Anick's neat little hand in her own larger, coarser one.

She did not. Instead she watched the details she provided in response to Anick's questions about colour of eyes and hair, the car—a station wagon!—the number of rooms in their house, slot in under the French girl's mascara and become a dead ordinary place—'orreebly provincial—where she had settled for a quiet, an ordinary fate.

But I am happy, she wanted to protest. I almost lost my life. And then, by the skin of my teeth, I saved it.

But there was no way of explaining this. They had no shared language, most of all when it came to the smaller words. She began to wonder, as her high spirits evaporated, what she and Anick had ever had in common.

Oh yes! She had almost forgotten. Gordon!

"No," she said matter-of-factly. It astonished her that it was Anick, after so long, who most clearly remembered. "I haven't seen him for years. Sydney's a big place. He's in town planning or something."

Anick nodded.

There was nothing more to be said. Or rather, there was what there had always been. Cassie continued to write long jaunty letters in her formal, seventeenth-century French, mostly because it pleased her to tell about her children, adding more and more to Anick's image of the 'orreeble place and describing in sinister detail trips to resorts Anick would never have wanted to visit and could never find on the map. Anick continued to send postcards and presents.

The time came when this was, for each of them, their oldest and most satisfying correspondence. The children no longer asked "Who is Anick?," not even to have the pleasure of hearing the known answer and of closing, with a rhythmic question and response, one of the gaps in their world. Instead they told their schoolfriends, rather grandly: "This is from Anick, our mummy's best friend—in Europe."

Europe was a place they would visit one day and see for themselves.

The Empty Lunch-tin

H E HAD BEEN THERE for a long time. She could not remember when she had last looked across the lawn and he was not standing in the wide, well-clipped expanse between the buddleia and the flowering quince, his shoulders sagging a little, his hands hanging limply at his side. He stood very still with his face lifted towards the house, as a tradesman waits who has rung the doorbell, received no answer, and hopes that someone will appear at last at an upper window. He did not seem in a hurry. Heavy bodies barged through the air, breaking the stillness with their angular cries. Currawongs. Others hopped about on the grass, their tails switching from side to side. Black metronomes. He seemed unaware of them. Originally the shadow of the house had been at his feet, but it had drawn back before him as the morning advanced, and he stood now in a wide sunlit space casting his own shadow. Behind him cars rushed over the warm bitumen, station wagons in which children were being ferried to school or kindergarten, coloured delivery vans, utilities—there were no fences here; the garden was open to the street. He stood. And the only object between him and the buddleia was an iron pipe that rose two feet out of the lawn like a periscope.

At first, catching sight of him as she passed the glass wall of the dining room, the slight figure with its foreshortened shadow, she had given a sharp little cry. Greg! And it might have been Greg standing there with only the street behind him. He would have been just that age. Doubting her own perceptions, she had gone right up to the glass and stared. But Greg had been dead for seven years; she knew that with the part of her mind that observed this stranger, though she had never accepted it in that other half where the boy was still going on into the fullness of his life, still growing, so that she knew just how he had looked at fifteen, seventeen, and how he would look now at twenty.

This young man was quite unlike him. Stoop-shouldered, intense, with clothes that didn't quite fit, he was shabby, and it was the shabbiness of poverty not fashion. In his loose flannel trousers with turnups, collarless shirt, and wide-brimmed felt hat, he might have been from the country or from another era. Country people dressed like that. He looked, she thought, the way young men had looked in her childhood, men who were out of work.

Thin, pale, with the sleeves half-rolled on his wiry forearms, he must have seen her come up to the glass and note his presence, but he wasn't at all intimidated.

Yes, that's what he reminded her of: the Depression years, and those men, one-armed or one-legged some of them, others dispiritingly whole, who had haunted the street corners of her childhood, wearing odd bits of uniform with their civilian cast-offs and offering bootlaces or pencils for sale. Sometimes when you answered the back doorbell, one of them would be standing there on the step. A job was what he was after: mowing or cleaning out drains, or scooping the leaves from a blocked downpipe, or mending shoes—anything to save him from mere charity. When there was, after all, no job to be done, they simply stood, those men, as this man stood, waiting for the offer to be made of a cup of tea with a slice of bread and jam, or the scrapings from a bowl of dripping, or if you could spare it, the odd sixpence—it didn't matter what or how much, since the offering was less important in itself than the unstinting recognition of their presence, and beyond that, a commonness between you. As a child she had stood behind lattice doors in the country town she came from and watched transactions between her mother and those men, and had thought to herself: *This is one of the rituals. There is a way of doing this so that a man's pride can be saved, but also your own.* But when she grew up the Depression was over. Instead, there was the war. She had never had to use any of that half-learned wisdom.

She walked out now onto the patio and looked at the young man, with just air rather than plate glass between them.

He still wasn't anyone she recognised, but he had moved slightly, and as she stood there silently observing—it must have been for a good while—she saw that he continued to move. He was turning his face to the sun. He was turning with the sun, as a plant does, and she thought that if he decided to stay and put down roots she might get used to him. After all, why a buddleia or a flowering quince and not a perfectly ordinary young man?

She went back into the house and decided to go on with her housework. The house didn't need doing, since there were just the two of them, but each day she did it just the same. She began with the furniture in the lounge, dusting and polishing, taking care not to touch the electronic chess-set that was her husband's favourite toy and which she was afraid of disturbing—no, she was actually afraid of *it*. Occupying a low table of its own, and surrounded by lamps, it was a piece of equipment that she had thought of at first as an intruder and regarded now as a difficult but permanent guest. It announced the moves it wanted made in a dry dead voice, like a man speaking with a peg on his nose or through a thin coffin-lid; and once, in the days when she still resented it, she had accidentally touched it off. She had already turned away to the sideboard when the voice came, flat and dull, dropping into the room one of its obscure directives: *Queen to King's Rook five;* as if something in the room, some object she had always thought of as tangible but without life, had suddenly decided to make contact with her and were announcing a cryptic need. Well, she had got over that.

She finished the lounge, and without going to the window again went right on to the bathroom, got down on her knees, and cleaned all round the bath, the shower recess, the basin, and lavatory; then walked straight through to the lounge room and looked.

He was still there and had turned a whole quarter-circle. She saw his slight figure with the slumped shoulders in profile. But what was happening? He cast no shadow. His shadow had disappeared. The iron tap cast a shadow and the young man didn't. It took her a good minute, in which she was genuinely alarmed, to see that what she had taken for the shadow of the tap was a dark patch of lawn where the water dripped. So that was all right. It was midday.

She did a strange thing then. Without having made any decision about it, she went into the kitchen, gathered the ingredients, and made up a batch of spiced biscuits with whole peanuts in them; working fast with the flour, the butter, the spice, and forgetting herself in the pleasure of getting the measurements right by the feel of the thing, the habit.

They were biscuits that had no special name. She had learned to make them when she was just a child, from a girl they had had in the country. The routine of mixing and spooning the mixture on to greaseproof paper let her back into a former self whose motions were lighter, springier, more sure of ends and means. She hadn't made these biscuits—hadn't been able to bring herself to make them—since Greg died. They were his favourites. Now, while they were cooking and filling the house with their spicy sweetness, she did another thing she hadn't intended to do. She went to Greg's bedroom at the end of the hall, across from where she and Jack slept, and began to take down from the wall the pennants he had won for swimming, the green one with gold lettering, the purple one, the blue, and his lifesaving certificates, and laid them carefully on the bed. She brought a carton from under the stairs and packed them in the bottom. Then she cleared the bookshelf and took down the model planes, and put them in the carton as well. Then she removed from a drawer of the desk a whole mess of things: propelling pencils and pencil-stubs, rubber-bands, tubes of glue, a pair of manacles, a pack of playing cards that if you were foolish enough to take one gave you an electric shock. She put all these things into the carton, along with a second drawerful of magazines and loose-leaf notebooks, and carried the carton out. Then she took clean sheets and made the bed.

By now the biscuits were ready to be taken from the oven. She counted them, there were twenty-three. Without looking up to where the young man was standing, she opened the kitchen window and set them, sweetly smelling of spice, on the window ledge. Then she went back and sat on Greg's bed while they cooled.

She looked round the blank walls, wondering, now that she had stripped them, what a young man of twenty-eight might have filled them with, and discovered with a pang that she could not guess.

It was then that another figure slipped into her head.

In her middle years at school there had been a boy who sat two desks in front of her called Stevie Caine. She had always felt sorry for him because he lived alone with an aunt and was poor. The father had worked for the railways but lost his job after a crossing accident and killed himself. It was Stevie Caine this young man reminded her of. His shoulders too had been narrow and stooped, his face unnaturally pallid, his wrists bony and raw. Stevie's hair was mouse-coloured and had stuck out in wisps behind the ears; his auntie cut it, they said, with a pudding-basin. He smelled of scrubbing-soap. Too poor to go to the pictures on Saturday afternoons, or to have a radio and hear the serials, he could take no part in the excited chatter and argument through which they were making a world for themselves. When they ate their lunch he sat by himself on the far side of the yard, and she alone had guessed the reason: it was because the metal lunch-tin that his father had carried to the railway had nothing in it, or at best a slice of bread and dripping. But poor as he was, Stevie had not been resentful— that was the thing that had most struck her. She felt he ought to have been. And his face sometimes, when he was excited and his Adam's apple worked up and down, was touched at the cheekbones with such a glow of youthfulness and joy that she had wanted to reach out and lay her fingers very gently to his skin and feel the warmth, but thought he might misread the tenderness that filled her (which certainly included him but was for much more beside) as girlish infatuation or, worse still, pity. So she did nothing.

Stevie Caine had left school when he was just fourteen and went like his father to work at the railway. She had seen him sometimes in a railway worker's uniform, black serge, wearing a black felt hat that made him look bonier than ever about the cheekbones and chin and carrying the same battered lunch-tin. Something in his youthful refusal to be bitter or subdued had continued to move her. Even now, years later, she could see the back of his thin neck, and might have leaned out, no longer caring if she was misunderstood, and laid her hand to the chapped flesh.

When he was eighteen he had immediately joined up and was immediately killed; she had seen it in the papers—just the name.

It was Stevie Caine this young man resembled, as she had last seen him in the soft hat and railway worker's serge waistcoat, with the sleeves rolled on his stringy arms. There had been nothing between them, but she had never forgotten. It had to do, as she saw it, with the two forms of injustice: the one that is cruel but can be changed, and the other kind—the tipping of a thirteen-year-old boy off the saddle of his bike into a bottomless pit—that cannot; with that and an empty lunch-tin that she would like to have filled with biscuits with whole peanuts in them that have no special name.

She went out quickly now (the young man was still there on the lawn beyond the window) and counted the biscuits, which were cool enough to be put into a barrel. There were twenty-three, just as before.

He stayed there all afternoon and was still there among the deepening shadows when Jack came in. She was pretty certain now of what he was but didn't want it confirmed—and how awful if you walked up to someone, put your hand out to see if it would go through him, and it didn't.

They had tea, and Jack, after a shy worried look in her direction, which she affected not to see, took one of the biscuits and slowly ate it. She watched. He was trying not to show how broken up he was. Poor Jack!

Twenty-two.

Later, while he sat over his chess set and the mechanical voice told him what moves he should make on its behalf, she ventured to the window and peered through. It was, very gently, raining, and the streetlights were blurred and softened. Slow cars passed, their tyres swishing in the wet. They pushed soft beams before them.

The young man stood there in the same spot. His shabby clothes were drenched and stuck to him. The felt hat was also drenched, and droplets of water had formed at the brim, on one side filled with light, a half-circle of brilliant dots.

"Mustn't it be awful," she said, "to be out there on a night like this and have nowhere to go? There must be so many of them. Just standing about in the rain, or sleeping in it."

Something in her tone, which was also flat, but filled with an emotion that deeply touched and disturbed him, made the man leave his game and come to her side. They stood together a moment facing the dark wall of glass, then she turned, looked him full in the face, and did something odd: she reached out towards him and her hand bumped against his ribs—that is how he thought of it: a bump. It was the oddest thing! Then impulsively, as if with sudden relief, she kissed him.

I have so much is what she thought to herself.

Next morning, alone again, she cleared away the breakfast things, washed and dried up, made a grocery list. Only then did she go to the window.

It was a fine clear day and there were two of them, alike but different; both pale and hopeless looking, thin-shouldered, unshaven, wearing shabby garments, but not at all similar in feature. They did not appear to be together. That is, they did not stand close, and there was nothing to suggest that they were in league or that the first had brought the other along or summoned him up. But there were two of them just the same, as if some *process* were involved. Tomorrow, she guessed, there would be four, and the next day sixteen; and at last—for there must be millions to be drawn on—so many that there would be no place on the lawn for them to stand, not even the smallest blade of grass. They would spill out into the street, and from there to the next street as well—there would be no room for cars to get through or park—and so it would go on till the suburb, and the city and a large part of the earth was covered. This was just the start.

She didn't feel at all threatened. There was nothing in either of these figures that suggested menace. They simply stood. But she thought she would refrain from telling Jack till he noticed it himself. Then they would do together what was required of them.

Sorrows and Secrets

"YOU'VE FALLEN on yer feet, son, you're in luck. This is the university 'v hard knocks you've dropped into but I've taken a fancy to yer. I'll see to it the knocks aren't too solid."

It was the foreman speaking, in a break on the boy's first day. The five of them had knocked off just at eleven and were sitting about on logs, or sprawled on the leaves of the clearing, having a smoke and drinking coppery tea.

The foreman himself had made the tea. Gerry had followed him about, watching carefully how he should trawl the billy through the scummy water so that what he drew was good and clear, how to make a fire, how the billy should hang, when to put in the tea and how much. The foreman was particular. From now on Gerry would make the tea. The foreman was confident he would make it well and that he would do all right at the rest of his work as well. The foreman was taking an interest.

He was a sandy, sad-eyed fellow of maybe forty, with a grey flannel vest instead of a shirt. Gerry felt immediately that he was a man to be trusted, though not an easy man to get along with, and guessed that it was his own newness that made him so ready on this occasion to talk. With the others he was reserved, even hostile. When they sat down to their tea he had set himself apart and then indicated, with a gesture of his tin mug, that Gerry should sit close by. Gerry observed, through the thin smoke of the fire, that the other fellows were narrowly watching, but with no more than tolerant amusement, as they licked their cigarette-papers and rolled them between thumb and finger. As if to say: "Ol' Claude's found an ear to bash."

They were quiet fellows in their thirties, rough-looking but clean-shaven, and one of them was a quarter-caste called Slinger. The others were Charlie and Kev. Gerry was to share a hut with them. The foreman Claude had his own sleeping quarters on the track to the thunderbox. He was permanent.

They were working for a Mister McPhearson, a shadowy figure known only to Claude; and even Claude had seen him less often than he let on. They were on McPhearson's land, using McPhearson's equipment, and it was his timber they were felling and to him, finally, that Claude was responsible. His name was frequently on the foreman's lips, especially when there was some question of authority beyond which there could be no appeal. "Don' ast me, ast McPhearson," he'd say. And then humourously: "If you can find 'im." Or: "Well now, there you'd be dealin' with McPhearson. That'd be his department," and there was something in Claude's smile as he said it that was sly. Inside, he was laughing outright.

Claude had a preference for mysteries. If McPhearson's name hadn't been stamped so clearly on all their equipment they might have decided he was one of Claude's humourous inventions.

Gerry had been sent here to learn, the hard way, about life. It was his father's intention that he should discover at first hand that his advantages (meaning Vine Brothers, which was one of the biggest machine-tool operations in the state) were accidental, had not been earned by him, and were in no way deserved; they did not constitute a proof of superiority. His mother spoiled him, as she did all of them. She had let him believe he was special. That's what his father said. He was out here to learn that he was not. The job had been arranged through a fellow his father knew at the Golf Club, who happened also to know McPhearson. Claude had started off by asking questions, as if he suspected a connection between Gerry and the Boss that had not yet been revealed, but there was none. Just that friend of his father's at the Club.

They worked hard and Gerry kept up with them. He didn't want it to show that what for them was hard necessity was for him a rich boy's choice. All day their saws buzzed, their sweat flew in the forest, and at night they were tired.

There wasn't much talk. Gerry, who usually fell asleep immediately they'd eaten, and had to be shaken to go to bed, got very little of the wisdom of the wider world out of what was said when they had swallowed their stew, drunk their tea, and were just sitting out in the smell of timber and burnt leaves under the stars.

"You should watch out f' loose women," one of the fellows said once. He seemed to be joking.

"I been watchin' out for 'em," Slinger said. "There ain't none around 'ere that I been able to discover." He looked off into the shifting, stirring dark.

"No," the third fellow said bitterly, "it ain't the loose women you need t' watch out for, it's the moral ones. A moral woman'll kill a man's spirit. The others—" But he bit off the rest of what he might have to tell. It went on silently behind his eyes, and the others, out of respect for something personal, fell into their own less heavy forms of silence.

It was Claude who provided most of the talk.

"One time," Claude told, "I was stoppin' at this boarding-house in Brisbane. I was workin' at the abatoors then, it was just after the war. Well, at the boarding-house there was this refugee-bloke, an' sometimes after tea, if I din' feel like playin' poker or listenin' t' Willy Fernell and Mo, this bloke an' me'd sit out on the front step in the cool. Not talkin' much—I wasn' much of a talker in them days. But I s'pose he reckoned I was sort of sympathetic, I din' rib 'im like the rest. He was a Dutchman, or a Finn—one of that lot. Maybe a Balt. Anyway a thin feller with very good manners, and exceptionally clean—exceptionally. On'y 'e was as mad as a meat axe. I mean, one day 'e'd be that quiet you couldn' get a word out of 'im, and the next 'e'd be on the booze and ravin'. 'E kept the booze under his bed. Vodka. Talked like a drain when 'e was pissed, an' all stuff you couldn' make sense of. He was hidin' from someone—some other lot, I never did find out who—you know what these New Australians are like. Look 'ere mate, I'd tell 'im, there's no politics here, this is Australia. But 'e'd just look at me as if I was soft or somethink. And in fact he was loaded—God knows what 'e didn' have stacked away, jewellery an' that—I saw some of

it—'e could of lived in any place he liked—at Lennon's even. 'E'd
be in his sixties now, that bloke—I often wonder what happened
to 'im . . . Anyway, we were sittin' out on the step one night, jus'
cool in our shirtsleeves, havin' a bit of a smoke, when the cicadas
start up. 'What's that?' 'e says, jumpin' to 'is feet. 'Cicadas,' I tell
'im. 'Chicago?' he says, all wild-eyed, 'the gangsters?' I had t'
laugh, but it was pathetic jus' the same. The poor bugger thought
'e'd got 'imself to America, thought it was machine-guns. Never
seemed t' know where 'e was half the time. You'd think a boarding-
house at Dutton Park 'd impress itself on *anyone*, but not him.
'Chicago,' 'e says, 'the gangsters!' God knows what sort of things 'e'd
been through—*over there*—I mean, you can't tell, can you? You
look at a bloke jus' sittin' there an' you can't tell. There's a lot of
misery about. You've only got t' go into some o' them boarding-
houses and see what blokes 'ave got in ports under their beds. Old
newspapers, bottles, stones. It'd surprise you. It'd surprise anyone."

Gerry listened to Claude's tales. They were interesting but he
could make nothing of them; they appeared to tell more than they
told. There was a quality in Claude's voice that asked for something more than interest, and it was just this that Gerry resisted.
He wanted Claude to be the foreman, only that, and preferred the
dour but dignified silence of the other men, who if they had stories to tell kept them entirely to themselves.

The hut where Claude lived was divided by a partition into
sleeping-quarters and storeroom. On one wall of the storeroom
there were tools, very neatly arranged on hooks. They might have
borne labels and been mistaken at first sight for a wall display in a
folk museum, or for the elaborate fan shapes and sunbursts that
native weapons assume when they have been stripped of their
power of violence and become flowerlike—till you examine the
points.

"I like t' see things in their place," Claude explained. "Order at
a glance." And he glanced up from where he was sitting at a desk
doing McPhearson's accounts.

He wore half-glasses and was peering over the straight tops of them. It made his eyes a weaker blue and gave him, for all his toughness, a scholarly look, like a failed monk. To his left were heavy ledgers, and immediately before him a pile of accounts waiting to be pushed down hard on a spike. Beyond, at the far end of the room, which was dark, Gerry could see the shelves of food-stuff—jars, tins, packets—from which Claude provided the ingredients for their meals, including a whole shelf of Claude's own homemade chutney.

Claude had surprised Gerry the first time he went there by what seemed like an act of disloyalty.

"Here," he had offered impetuously, "have a jar of peanut paste. On the house! McPhearson won't miss it. He's swimmin' in peanut paste that man. An' smoked salmon, they tell me." And when Gerry politely refused: "What about a packet a' Band-Aids?"

Claude shrugged his shoulders and looked disappointed, and Gerry was left with a puzzle. The foreman was strict but inconsistent.

As for the other side of the partition, where Claude slept, Gerry saw that only once, when Claude cut his leg, bled badly, and sent him off to get a fresh pair of shorts. There were cuttings from newspapers pinned to the bare boards—racehorses—and on the desk a box of old stereopticon plates that Claude had already told him about and promised to show: pictures from round the world. "You can stand right at the edge and see the waters of Niagara come thunderin' down—I tell yer, it's marvellous. I've stood there f' hours and even heard the noise of it. Imagined that, of course. The pyramids, the Taj Mahal, George the Fifth's Jubilee—you name it! A man can go round the world in 'is head with one a' these stereopticons, and it don't cost a brass razoo."

Gerry had looked round the narrow room, tried to make something of it—tried to make Claude of it—but saw nothing more than he already knew. He thought of his own room at home. He was untidy and his mother complained, but did his disorder reveal any more of what was going on in his head than Claude's fastidious habit of setting everything in its place? He had been able to tell Gerry, even through the pain of his wound, just where those clean shorts would be: in the second drawer to the left. Gerry had gone straight to them.

One day Claude came down to where he was working and asked him to go to town on a message. The town was twelve miles away. He was to go on Claude's two-stroke and deliver a letter. Claude drew a rough map of the town, showed him where the house was, and gave him very precise instructions about how he should open the gate, go up the four steps, and ring the doorbell—three long rings and then, after a pause, two short ones. "Like this," Claude explained, tapping it out on a metal cup. He was to leave the motorbike in the main street and go the rest of the way—it wasn't more than a hundred yards—on foot. Claude emphasized that he was putting great trust in the boy, and embarrassed perhaps by the air of mystery he had created, suggested that Gerry needn't hurry back; he could take time off if he wanted to have a milkshake at the Greek's. The message was in a plain white envelope with neither name nor address.

THE RIDE into town was a pleasant one. After three weeks of work Gerry was happy to have this time away, to feel released into his own body again and to be made free of the landscape and of the hot summer day.

The early part of the trip was rough. A narrow trail led upwards between thick-set pines. But he emerged at last on to a high rolling plateau where the clouds rode close overhead, struck a gravel road, then two miles before the town a stretch of bitumen. He opened his shirt and took the full thrust of the air. Crossing bridges over dry streams he heard the sound they made as he rattled across them, the *slog slog slog* of concrete balusters, a regular beating in his ear, and remembered the different rhythm—three longs, a pause and two shorts—that Claude had tapped out on the cup. Its meaning didn't concern him. It was Claude's business, or maybe it was McPhearson's. He was a messenger. He felt extraordinarily light-hearted. Perhaps because this was the first occasion in so long that he had been on his own, but also because, small as it might be, he was being entrusted with something. He had recently discovered, in the furthest reaches of himself, a capacity for what he thought of as noble action and was concerned now that it should find its proper form in the world; that when the occasion arose (as it surely must) that would demand the full stretch of his powers, he would recognise and meet it.

The problem of course was in the recognition. He was inexperienced but not romantic, and had perceived clearly enough that heroic occasions do not come ready-made, that they spring into existence only when they are grasped. You would need imagination as well as pluck. Two years ago he might have seen himself through drifts of gun-smoke bearing the colours, or as a dispatch-rider in one of the wars, vaulting shell holes on a BSA. But the next occasion wouldn't be like it, and any moment, even the most commonplace, might be either the call or the first step towards it. You had to be on the alert, and believe that when the opportunity came you would be ready for it.

All this was part of his most secret life. He let it out now that he was alone and flaring along a bitumen road—in the open air, under leaves, in sunlight; and all the more because for the last weeks he had held back, and tried among the others to seem acceptable, ordinary.

He came into the town over a bridge. Kids were swimming in the last of the season's water, among thick willows. He stopped the bike halfway across, and still easily astride it, leaned over the railings to watch. Slim bodies swung out on a knotted rope and went flying head-over-heels, their cries cut off in a splash. The sight pleased him. He was just out of that stage himself and might have allowed himself to regret it, but had set himself in the direction of manhood. He rode on into town, parked the bike, and was thirsty enough after his ride to consider going straight to the Greek's. But no, he told himself, Duty first. I'll deliver the message and have the milkshake afterwards.

The town was small and sleepy, but after his weeks up at the camp seemed to him to be bustling with life. Women clicked along the pavement in their high heels. A girl riding by on a bike

with her skirt up looked back over her shoulder, and he was taken
again by the variousness of the world and the number of paths
that were open in each moment of it. Later, that was for later. With
the envelope safe in his shirt pocket he turned out of the main
street with its row of two-storeyed buildings that went on for
another quarter of a mile, all pubs, banks, general stores, bakeries,
into the dusty streets behind. Crossed one, then another, till he
found the name he wanted, and was about to consult numbers
when he was hailed from a low verandah.

"Hey! Givvus a lift, wilya sonny?"

The man was holding one end of a genoa-velvet lounge as if he
had been standing there maybe all morning, waiting for someone
to come along, as Gerry had, and take the other.

Gerry hesitated—this was an interruption—but didn't see how
he could refuse. The man looked expectant. The lounge, with one
end on the ground and the other in the air, was ridiculous. After a
moment's hesitation he took it up as directed, walked backwards a
few paces, and helped the man push it on to the back of a lorry.

"The rest is a walkover," the man told him. He was a tall fellow
with teeth missing, wearing nothing but football shorts. "I'll bring
the armchair, you get the smokers' stands an' the side table."

He followed the man into the house and they cleared the front
room and loaded it, then carried out of a second room a dining
table, a sideboard, six chairs, and a framed oil painting of the Alps.
The lorry by now had about as much as it would carry. Gerry held
the other end of several ropes while the man strained, cursed,
knotted. Then, with a casual, "Thanks, son, I'll do the same f' you
some time," he climbed into the cabin and drove slowly away. He
had left the door of the house standing wide open.

Gerry wondered as he walked away if he mightn't have been
assisting at a burglary. But what else could he have done? He
noted the number of the house he had helped strip, in case there
were questions later, and saw now that the one he wanted was just
three doors off on the other side. He crossed, opened the gate
with as little sound as possible, went on up the steps, pushed the
bell three times as Claude had directed, waited, then rang twice

more. Almost immediately a curtain twitched aside in one of the front windows and a girl's face appeared. Then she was at the open door.

"For Christ sake!" she spat out. "What are you playin' at?" She gave an alarmed glance behind him and to both sides. "Who th' fuck are you?"

Barefoot, hastily wrapped in a gown with explosive red-and-gold flowers all over it, she smelled of soap and had the misty look of a woman who had come fresh from the bath.

The messenger for a moment failed to find his tongue, and she softened a little at his youth, at the way he flushed, and the movement of his eyes towards the mysterious darkness behind her.

She turned her head as if following his gaze, and said over her shoulder: "It's nothing. Just some kid." She gave him a look, half-knowing, half-ironical, but no longer alarmed. "Watcha want, son?"

"I've brought this," Gerry told her coldly, showing the envelope. "It's from Claude."

She took the envelope, tore it open, glanced quickly at both sides of the single sheet, and then burst out laughing. She began to close the door.

"Isn't there an answer?" Gerry asked foolishly.

"Are you kidding? How would you answer that?"

She showed him both sides of the page, and they stood at the half-open door with the blank sheet between them.

"Piss off," she said, not urgently: and the door was closed in his face.

HE RODE back fast, his face still burning. He hadn't after all stopped at the Greek's, and when he came bumping into the camp and parked the bike, and saw Claude coming down to meet him, would have turned away if he could and found work to do.

Claude came at him sideways. He screwed one eye up as if squinting at sunlight.

"Well," he said shyly, "how was the trip? Bike behave? Dja find the house alright?"

He answered Claude's questions, he rendered account; but would not, for all Claude's soft-talk, be sweetened.

Yes, he had rung the bell. Yes, it was a woman who had answered. She had been wearing a kimono. No, he hadn't seen into the house. Yes, he had delivered the envelope. What had she done? She'd laughed, that's what, and there was no answer.

Claude patted him on the shoulder, but when their eyes met he looked away, and Gerry, who had been glaring till that moment, was glad of it. There was something between them suddenly of which they were both, but for different reasons, ashamed.

"Thanks, Gerry," Claude said wearily. "Thanks, mate. You done well. If I ever had another message I'd—"

He broke off, as if he had heard Gerry's fierce, unspoken *Not me, you wouldn't! Not again!*

"Come 'n have tea," Claude was saying in his smallest voice, "I made puftaloons. They're yer favourite." He looked uncomfortably large in his grey flannel vest, but also beaten, and his tone was so wheedling and auntlike, so keen to make amends, that Gerry was torn between contempt and a kind of shameful pity. Without ceasing to be aggrieved he relented, and allowed himself to be drawn away.

"That's the style," the man said, as if it were Gerry who had to be got over a rough patch. "I make good puftaloons, even if I say so meself. Learned from a Chinese. Little feller with only one arm. It was out Charleville way . . ." And he was off on another of his tales.

THAT NIGHT they got drunk. Claude sat out in the moonlight on a stump, sucking a bottle of whisky, and the others, out of delicacy, kept away. Slinger the quarter-caste played his mouth organ.

"Wife-trouble," Kev whispered, and nodded his head seriously.

Gerry didn't admit that he knew something of that already; had been out earlier in the day, subjecting the woman to some mild terrorism.

Kev, staring off into the darkness, was lost in his own story.

Is life so sad then? Gerry asked himself. And was aware, with a sharpness he had not felt before, of the immensity of the darkness that surrounded them: all those leaves holding up individual fragments of it shaped exactly like themselves, the grassblades taking it down into their roots, the birds folding it away under their wings. Sorrows and secrets. All these men had stories, were dense with the details of their lives, but kept them in the dark. Only odd words broke surface and spoke for more than could be said.

"That's a nice tune, Slinger. I remember that one from the navy," Kev said. "Wartime."

"Wrong colour f' the navy," Slinger let out between chords, barely breaking the line of what he was playing.

Claude meanwhile had gone off, and when he appeared again it was from the door of his storeroom. He was carrying jars of the homemade chutney they had eaten at every meal Gerry had had here. "Mango chutney," Claude had explained, "off me own trees. I got two big 'uns in the backyard, with more mangoes than you could eat in a month a' Sundays. I make a big batch every year."

Now, armful after armful, he was carrying the labelled jars out of the storeroom and setting them down on the moonlit earth. The others fell silent and watched. He stacked them solemnly, neatly, so that they made a high but solid pyramid, and when the last one was out he closed and locked the storeroom door.

"Now we'll have some fun," he told them.

Standing bent-kneed and with his feet firmly apart, he balanced a jar on the palm of his hand, took it back over his shoulder, and hurled it against the storehouse wall. Moonlight splintered, and the dark golden stuff with its chunks of stringy fruit rolled slowly down.

"Here Slinger, Kev, Gerry—have a go!" He stooped and hurled another. "It's all right boys, this is on me, it's my bloody chutney. Nothin' t' do with McPhearson. I don't account t' him f' chutney."

But the others, suddenly sober, did not join in. At last one of them went up to him.

"Come on, mate, time t' turn in," he said. "We've got a heavy day."

It ended then. They went to bed. But were woken some time

later by what sounded like another jar of chutney being smashed
against the storeroom wall. They all started up at once and
trooped out in their underpants to see what it was. The clearing
was empty, still. It was Kev who knocked, with embarrassed
politeness, at the door to Claude's hut and pushed it open. They
heard him gasp.

"Aw, the poor bugger!"

It hadn't sounded like a shot.

There was a note, and beside it an envelope, exactly like the
one Gerry had carried earlier in the day. It was addressed to the
woman and the house in town. The note asked Gerry to deliver it,
and on this occasion to drive right up to the house on the bike. But
when the police came they took charge of the envelope along with
the body.

The remaining jars of chutney, all shot through with gold as the
sun struck them, were still stacked in a ruined pyramid in the
grass. The police found them difficult to fit into the picture, and
the others, faced with them and with the dried stains on the storehouse wall, which looked almost natural, as if the wood had experienced a new flow of thick golden sap, turned away in common
embarrassment. At last one of the policemen unlocked the storehouse door with Claude's keys, and Gerry and Charlie took the
jars back and set them neatly, darkly, on the shelf.

The sight of the storeroom, with everything fastidiously in
place and even the chutney now restored, unnerved Gerry. If he
were to go now into that space behind the partition, and note
every detail, and add to it the final disordering of all its objects by
the shot, nothing would be revealed, he thought, or added to what
he knew.

He watched the younger of the two policemen slip Claude's letter into his breast pocket. The policeman wore a uniform: boots,
cap, shirt with epaulettes and a flash—he was official. He would
ring the bell just once. And if the door wasn't answered immediately he would ring a second time, and again and again until it was.

That Antic Jezebel

CLIMBING TO HER SEAT in the organ gallery, up three flights of stairs, was such an arduous business, and she was so slow nowadays, that Clay had to begin early, even before the warning bells were sounded. She hated the thought of arriving breathless, of being locked out, or of looking, on the way up, like an old girl in need of aid. "He's cooked his goose—let him lie in it"; that was one of her sayings. Messy of course, but life is, you got used to it.

Clay McHugh had learned her survival tactics in Europe between the wars. She had studied there how to present an appearance that was never less than elegant and might be mistaken by snobs, and by the undiscerning and unworldly, for affluence. You lived in the best part of town, had one outfit of perfect cut that went to the cleaners each week, one piece of jewellery, and you never let anyone past the door.

Her present apartment was at Elizabeth Bay and she had spent all she had on it. Within its walls, among the last of her loot, she practised a frugality that would have surprised her neighbours and made social workers, and other Nosey Parkers, cry famine. Clay despised such terms. She ate a great deal of boiled rice, was careful with the lights, and on the pretext of keeping trim, she walked rather than took the bus. Her one outfit was black; her one piece of jewellery a chain of intimidating weight that chimed rather than tinkled but was too plain to suggest ostentation. Hung with mint-gold coins, seals, and medallions, it provoked questions and the answers told a story—in fact several stories, but never all. There was, each time, a little something-left-over.

This chain was her curriculum vitae. She shook it when she needed to remind herself that whatever hole she was now in, she had once been in a different one and this was her choice. The chain spoke of attachments: of men young and old, back there in Europe, who had wanted at one time or another to present her with their blue eyes, their lives, their titles, or with little flats in Paris or London or country houses near Antwerp or Rome—all of which, for good reason, she had declined. The men had slipped away, leaving only a family seal or rare coin or medal. The weight on her wrist was bearable and she thought of it as a tribute to her intention to keep free.

That was one way of putting it. Put another way, you might say that the men had escaped and that these coins were the price they'd been willing to pay. Clay looked at it different ways on different occasions, but mostly she thought of herself as having come out of all this—of *life*—as well as could be expected: that is, badly. But her freedom was important to her. All those dull dogs and bushy-tailed buffers, if they were still kicking, would be as old now as herself. She would, if she had accepted their offers, be no more than an expensive nursemaid to an old man's incontinence—though she was not without affection and she wouldn't have complained, even of that, after a lifetime of some other devotion, if it had been her fate; or if the right man—Karel for instance—had asked it of her. Things had turned out otherwise, that's all. She was lying with the goose.

Besides, she told herself in her scarier moments, I'll soon be in that state myself, except that I won't be. I won't hang around to get up at three in the morning like poor Grandma and make scones for people who've been dead for thirty years. I'll finish it first. I'll take the bun and the pills ...

(This grandmother had lived with them. As a grown girl of fifteen she had been sent out, burning with shame before the neighbours, but also before the old woman herself, to bring her in when she went aimlessly wandering. On several occasions that now seemed like one, they had stood shouting beside a fence in the overpowering smell of honeysuckle. The old woman whined, screeched, wheedled, tried to shake off the grip on her wrist; dogs barked, children stared, other old women shook their heads behind blinds—she could still feel the pain, the humiliation of it. But the centre of the occasion had shifted now from the unwilling and angry girl to the wilful old woman, who with her hair awry and her gown open stood barefoot under the streetlamp saying over and over, "Why are you doing this to me?" The old woman was herself.)

She shook her wrist and the chain clanked against the gallery rail, as leaning forward she allowed her eye, which was sharp, to sweep the crowded amphitheatre.

Eleanor had just come in, high up in the stalls. Tall, in an emerald cloak, she was waiting for the people in her row to get up and let her through.

How like her! There was stacks of room up there, not like these gallery boxes—stacks of it! But Eleanor continued to stand, and when at last the whole row had risen to its feet, the silly woman, holding her cloak about her, moved through, gracefully inclining her head and smiling and thanking people. Settled at last, with the cloak thrown back for later, when the air-conditioning would turn the place into an ice-box, she looked about; then cast her gaze upwards to the gallery and waved.

Clay immediately relented. Oh God, she told herself, I'm such a *bitch*. It was touching really, Eleanor's little wave—a real leap in the dark. Too vain to wear glasses, and half-blind by habit (as who wouldn't be after forty years with the dreaded doctor) she could barely see her face in the glass.

Clay produced in response one of her brisk salutes, a real one made by bringing two fingers of her right hand up to the temple and flicking them sharply away. It was her trade-mark; from the days when she had modelled little suits of a military cut for Molyneux in Paris and was considered a sport. It too was a leap in the dark since Eleanor couldn't see it. But she made the gesture just the same—as an acknowledgement to herself of the old, the unkillable Clay McHugh, since there was, God knows, so little left of her.

(She had taken to avoiding herself in mirrors and in ghostly shop windows; her eyes were too sharp; she hadn't, like Eleanor, developed the habit of not-seeing-clearly-anymore. But at some point back there she had let her attention wander, lost her grip on things, and the spirit of disintegration had got in. Well, she was fighting it—tooth and claw—she was holding on; she got tired, that's all. Your attention wandered. You got tired.)

She came quickly to the alert now. Eleanor was making a play in the air with her fingers that meant they should meet later and share a taxi home. They would—they always did—and Eleanor, who was generous and tactfully tactless, would see to it that they did not share the fare.

They were neighbours. Eleanor, Mrs. Adrian Murphy, lived in a unit-block three doors from her own, and once a week, on Fridays, they went down in the Daimler (Eleanor drove only in daylight now) and had coffee together: down among the heavy-eyed Viennese, all reading air-mail papers that were two weeks old, and those deeper exiles who had been born right here, in Burwood or Gulgong or Innisfail, North Queensland, but were dying of hunger for a few crumbs of Sacher Torte and of estrangement from a life they had never known. What a place! What a country!

Years ago, in Brisbane, where they had been at the same convent school, she and Eleanor Ure had hated one another. "That stuck up goody two-shoes" was the phrase she found herself repeating in her twelve-year-old's voice; though she couldn't recall how Eleanor, who had been mousey, could have deserved it—not then. It fitted her better twenty years later when the dreaded doctor appeared.

But that period too had passed; and now, with nearly sixty years between them and the girls they once were, she could accept Eleanor Murphy for what she was: a spoiled and frightened woman, too insistent on her own dignity, but generous, loyal, and very nearly these days a friend.

That first winter after they found themselves neighbours, Eleanor had slipped and broken her leg. Clay had gone across each afternoon to sit with her: not in the spirit of a little nursing-sister—she had none of that—but in a spirit of brisk cheerfulness, of keeping one's stoic end up, that revived the bossy schoolgirl in her. Eleanor was happy to be organised. They spent the afternoons playing cards (rummy) while the westering light touched with Queensland colours the baskets of maidenhair and the tree-orchids and staghorns of Eleanor's rainforest loggia, and Mrs. Thring, who came in to clean, and who served when Eleanor entertained, made them scones and tea.

Things had levelled between them. She was no longer "that Clay McHugh," unmarried and trailing clouds of dangerous appeal. And Eleanor, with the dreaded doctor gone, was no more the gilded and girlish dependent of a Household Word. They were alone, alive (widowed or not, what did it matter?) and had no one close but one another.

(Eleanor in fact had a son whom she doted on, worried over, and never mentioned; a forty-four-year-old hippie and no-hoper called Aidan, for God's sake!, who wore beads, wrote unpublishable poetry, had two broken marriages behind him, and lived in a rainforest—a real one—on sunflower-seeds, bananas, and old rope. Eleanor's bedroom was full of photographs of him when he was an angelic six-year-old. Clay knew all this, but was meant not to. There were days when all Eleanor had to say in the long silences between them was "Aidan, Aidan, Aidan, Aidan." It was hard then not to cry out, "For God's sake, Eleanor, I thought we were friends, why can't we talk about him?" "About who?" Eleanor would have said. "Who can you possibly mean?")

The Year of Eleanor's Leg had been followed by The Year of the Rapist. For five months their Point was at siege. The rapist specialized in high unit-blocks and only assaulted older women (they had shared, she and Eleanor, a phone code that made Eleanor at least feel safe) and had turned out to be a twenty-two-year-old cat-burglar, so round-chinned and mild-looking that nobody believed it was really him.

Clay did. Standing at the glass door to her balcony, with her old dragon-robe about her, she had come face to face with him. He was

spreadeagled against the wall, his cheek flat to the bricks. There
were only feet between them; he in the cold air, high up above the
fig tree and its voracious flying foxes, she safe behind glass. Below,
the whole Bay was lit. The police were on to him. Their searchlights crossed and re-crossed the fern-hung balconies.

Let me in, his eyes had pleaded. He was blond, with a two-day
growth that made a shadow above his lips. She shook her head.

He had smiled then and nodded; as if she were some silly old
girl who could be fooled by a soft look and didn't know he was a
tiger, a beast of prey, and these tower blocks were his jungle. Nervously his tongue appeared, just the tip, and slicked his lips. He
was perplexed, he was thinking with it.

If she hesitated a moment then it wasn't because she was fooled
but because she saw his animal mind at work. They were a pair.
She too had been "out there."

She didn't let him in. Another night she might have, it wasn't
final; but not that one. She stood and watched the searchlight play
across the balcony; go on, back-track, then stop, isolating him like
an acrobat, an angel, in its glare. He had his eyes closed. He was
pressing his body hard against the wall, pretending, like a child, to
be invisible.

Being more vulnerable than ever at that moment she had
turned quickly away . . .

So there was Eleanor, safely settled in the stalls. And there, in
their box, were the Scarmans, Robert and Jeanette, who always
appeared for the first half but seldom for the second. Cool ash-
blonds, very still and fastidious, they tried again and again but real
players never came up to what they were used to on Robert's
equipment. Robert had been Karel's favourite student (that was
how she knew them), but he was fonder now of Jeanette.

She caught their eye, and Jeanette made little window-cleaning
motions that meant See-you-later-in-the-usual-place. (That was
the Crush Bar on the harbour side.)

All this was ritual. She watched Jeanette wave to the Abrams,
and the Abrams a moment later caught her own eye, and Clay
gave them her salute. Then Doctor Havek, whom she had known

in Paris before the war, then in Cairo, and who was now her doctor at Edgecliff, shuffled to his seat in the third row—down in Middle Europe among the garlic and ashes; but before he was seated, he too waved to the Abrams and then leaned over and shook hands with the Scorczenys, whom she had also known in Paris but had nothing to do with here.

She began to tap her foot. Karel hadn't arrived. They had spoken on Thursday—no, Friday, and he had said yes, he definitely was well enough, he would be here.

It was just before eight. Downstairs the last bleeps would be sounding, like a nasty moment in a beleaguered submarine. But the seat between the blond woman and the couple who hummed, Karel insisted, through all of Mozart and Beethoven and most of Schubert (though they were pretty well stumped by Bartók) was empty, the only one in its row.

"Would you like to see the programme?" the young man on her right was enquiring. He was a sweet rather effeminate boy who had struck up a conversation at the start of the season and chattered on now whether she answered or not. She thanked him, turned the pages politely and handed it back.

"Martinů," the boy said with excitement. He had apple cheeks and a great deal of fluffy bronze hair.

Martinů too she had known for a time. She did not say so. She was too puzzled.

Down in the hall a character in a double-breasted suit had paused at the end of Karel's row, and after turning his head this way and that to examine the ticket, was pushing in towards the empty seat. It was a mistake—he had the wrong row; she leaned forward across the tense air to inform him.

Short, fair, balding, he pushed his way along the row, pausing frequently to excuse himself, and seemed unaware of his error. When he reached the seat at last he stood flicking it with a handkerchief, then settled. But uncomfortably, sitting too far forward, and went to work now, with the same handkerchief, on his brow. He mopped, consulted his watch, mopped again—all the time in the wrong seat; then sat with the handkerchief crumpled up in his right hand like an unhappy child, and sitting too far forward, as if his legs would not reach the ground.

It was this vision of him as an unlikely middle-aged child that gave her the clue. She saw a plump nine-year-old with sloping shoulders in front of a row of newly planted poplars. The poplars were meant to civilize a wilderness, and the child, who wore khaki shorts and sand-shoes, was bearing a spade. It was a snapshot. He squinted into the sun. Well, those poplars now must be sixty-, seventy-feet high, sending their roots to block someone's drains. And the child would be—Nicholas. Nicholas!

Her heart thumped and she half rose to her feet. But the hall was ringing with applause now and the chamber group was trooping on, the lights were fading. Too late! There was a scraping and plucking as they tuned up, and she joined them with a hiss of desperation at her own slowness. It was loud enough for the boy who was her neighbour to swing his head in alarm. She made violent motions—no, it's nothing, nothing—and subsided into noiseless gloom.

That Nicholas. He had sided against his father, turned clean against him all those years ago, and now here he was occupying his father's seat. "Traitor," she wanted to shout down at him, "you broke his heart!"

But on an abrupt and sickening change of key, old injustice and indignation gave way to alarm. Why wasn't Karel here, that was the real point. What had he said—on Friday was it?—no, Saturday. What had they talked about? What did they *ever* talk about, these days, these days! The music kept switching pace. She couldn't fit his voice to it. The violins were doing impossible things, leaping about off key, scraping below the bridge; no voice could be fitted to that! Oh my God, she thought, my God. The music was approaching a violent end. It ended. And the boy beside her held his hands clasped a moment, with his head thrown back and all his hair electrically tingling, before he joined the applause. "Wasn't that terrific?" he breathed. Then, when she clenched her jaw at him: "Are you all right?"

No, she was *not* all right! Where was Karel? Why hadn't he rung if he wasn't coming?

She got to her feet again, determined this time to rush down and call; but her head was filled with the sound of a phone ringing in an empty room, and she sat down again, plump, just like that, and covered her eyes. There was a hush. She steeled herself. Terrible Tchaikovsky bloomed all over the hall.

SHE MANAGED to push her way through the harbourside bar without encountering Robert and Jeanette, or Eleanor, or the Abrams, and after an eternity of searching (Where *was* the man? He couldn't spend the entire interval in the loo) she found him pacing up and down under the sloping panes that gave on the dark; nervously consulting his watch and looking so like the child of thirty years ago that she immediately felt thirty years younger herself.

"Nicholas!" she accused.

He looked startled. His hands jumped and opened. There was no need to introduce herself.

"Where is he?" she demanded.

The man frowned and lowered his gaze.

The worst, she thought, it's always the worst. Damn him!

He was looking desperately about for a place they could slip away to that wouldn't be loud with people, all standing too close and with glasses in their hands, shouting.

For God's sake, she thought, why doesn't he get it over with? I know already, it's only words. The stoop of his shoulders and his look of pained, concentrated concern was too irritating; she would have preferred him to be cruel. (It struck her then that all the bad news she had ever heard had come to her in public places: in railway stations, hotel foyers, bars, or over public address systems in crowded squares. It was a mark of the century.) Go on, damn you, she thought now, say it, shout it why don't you?

At last, in desperation, he did. He tipped his balding head towards her, and with one hand cupped to his mouth, bellowed softly: "My father died this morning. I tried to ring you. He collapsed while he was out shopping. I'm very sorry."

The vision of spilled parcels hit her harder than she expected; and Nicholas, made bold by the fear that she too might be about to fall down in a public place, took her, not quite firmly, by the elbow, and kept up a dismal muttering.

They had become a centre of concern. The crowd about them had drawn back. People were staring, she must have cried out. Nicholas, deeply embarrassed, was making little gestures towards them. He was explaining why he was clutching her, that it was not this that had provoked her cry. Meanwhile, to her, he was offering more complex explanations. "You see," he stammered, "I found the ticket—and I—well I just didn't want the seat to be empty."

His soft eyes appealed to her for understanding of his pious but perhaps foolish sentiment.

She did understand, and suddenly felt sorry for him—for his awkward emotion and the need to explain it, but also for his grief. But it hurt, that. They must have been closer than she had guessed, Karel and this grown-up Nicholas; who would be, of course—why had she never let herself think it?—the father of the grandchildren: of Elsa and Ross. She had known about the grandchildren—she even knew their birthdays, but had thought of them as having come to him without intermediaries. And now here he was, one of the *intermediaries*, thin, distressed, too formal, with the sweat breaking out on his bald crown—the bearer of a weight of filial piety that she did understand and which did after all do him credit, but which she felt like a knife in her bowels.

"Listen," she said harshly, "do you think you could find me a drink? Something good and strong. I'll be fine till you get back."

She swayed a little but recovered. How odd it was after all the turmoil they had created—the promises, threats, curses, the real and imaginary violence—to have reached in a public place in Sydney this moment of utter aloneness: Elizabeth gone, that devout vindictive woman, now Karel also gone, and nothing left but this numbness before the brute fact. Karel! Tipped out on the pavements of a town he had never meant to live in, let alone die in, and the hot sky pulsing overhead as the angel zoomed, found his easy mark—there under the ribs—and pushed. She too felt it, the knife; and the closeness of his breath.

She looked up sharply at a gentler touch. Nicholas, with a double cognac and nothing for himself.

She smiled, thanked him, and playing the tough old girl, threw her head back and tossed it off. Then stood with the balloon resting lightly on her palm.

She looked at it—it was so fine. Tough but delicate. If she closed her fist and pressed hard enough it would splinter.

He must have felt the thought pass through her; she was surprised. He took the glass in his own pudgy fist, but had nowhere to put it.

"I'll see you home," he was saying in that heavy, Middle-European way, all breathless gallantry, that she had found absurd even in his father and which thirty years in Australia, the rough example of contemporaries, and the half-mocking acquiescence of women like herself, had done nothing to change.

"No," she said. "The seat. You must stay."

He looked down again and was embarrassed. "The seat doesn't matter."

"Oh but it does!" she said firmly. "You've been kind enough already—Nicholas. I'll get a taxi."

He did not insist. "Then I'll find you one."

Still holding the glass in one hand, and with the fingers of the other just pinching her elbow, he led her down the shallow steps. When they came to the foyer he made a wide arc towards one of the bars, and reaching in between packed shoulders, fumbled and set the thing down, grinning a little for the awkwardness of it.

At last they were in the open air. Out here she had no need of support. The night was fresh, and the sky, beyond harbour-rails and fig-trees, an electric blue. He stood with his hands clasped behind him, rocking gently on his heels.

"It seems a shame," he began, "that we've never—that we had to wait so long. I'm sorry."

She shook her head. No good going into all that. Too late, too late.

But he was determined she saw, in his discreet, passionate, pedantic way, to deal with it, an image of her that must have been, like her own picture of him as a slope-shouldered child in shorts, a stereotype: the flashy homebreaker and Jezebel who had stolen his father and left him to be the little man of the house, the resentful mother's boy. Or perhaps what he was dealing with was his father's nakedness. Well, either way, either way, he was too late.

"If you don't mind," he was saying, "I'll call up tomorrow and see how you are. It's no trouble."

She shook her head and made deprecating motions with her lips. What was it—kindness?—was he *kind*? More of his filial piety?

Fortunately the taxi had arrived. The driver gave her a look—some old girl who'd had too much to drink, and while Nicholas was giving him the address, she heard, as often before, the sound of a note being passed.

"Thank you," she murmured, eager for nothing now except to be moving on in the dark.

"You all right, ol' lady?" the driver asked over his shoulder. There was mockery in his voice.

"Get stuffed," she told the fellow. That fixed him.

ELEANOR'S late-night telephone voice was full of concern. "No, no, I'm okay, no trouble—I was tired, that's all. How was the Schoenberg?" Then, because she was tired of making mysteries, and because sooner or later it would have to be said, she let a voice that was not quite her own announce flatly: "Karel died this morning—a heart attack. In the street . . ." Poor Eleanor! "No, no, I'm okay—I promise. Yes, I'll call you in the morning."

She replaced the receiver and stood for a moment looking down at the Bay. She must have been doing that for the last hour. There were no searchlights tonight; and no angel was clamped like an aerial frogman to the wall out there, with his animal eyes upon her and his angelic, unshaven cheek pressed close to the bricks. Only below, in the dark of the Moreton Bay figs—those exiles of her own northern shore—the flying foxes, gorging on fruit.

She turned the lights out and went into her bedroom. Brightness and squalor of a small star's dressing room—den of a sorceress whose spells were expert and false according to the times, and whose powers had been worked up always out of improvident energies. Well, that spring was dry. All that was left were the half-empty bottles of the witch's fakery: cut-glass in what the boys these days called Deco, plastic jars full of liquors, creams, milks, balms, emulsions—unmagic potions. Unzipping the good black dress, she hung it like an empty skin in the closet—one of the rules—then sat and rolled off her stockings, leaving them anyhow on the floor; underclothes the same—she had always been messy. "You're impossible," people told her, "you're such a perfectionist." "No," she had sometimes answered, bitter at being misunderstood, "I'm a slob." The nuns had known. "Clay McHugh," she heard an old nun, Sister Ignatia complain, "if your mind in any way resembles your closet you're in for a hard time. We shall say nothing of your soul." They had none of them said anything of her soul.

So she was naked.

She groaned aloud now, since there was no one to hear, and drew back the sheet. She laid her body out: the slack flesh of her arms and thighs, her wrinkled belly, her skull and her feet and her hands that were covered with blotches, patches of darkness that would spread.

I am lying with the goose, she told herself, that's how they'll find me. Only nobody dies of grief—grief doesn't kill us. We're too damned selfish and strong—and what we love in the end is the goose.

She unsnapped the chain. It was too heavy to sleep with. It dragged you down into dreams. With a solid clunk it hit the night table, all her stories, her insoluble mysteries: a dead sound, *clunk,* just like that—the last sound before silence.

The Only Speaker of His Tongue

HE HAS ALREADY BEEN pointed out to me: a flabby, thickset man of fifty-five or sixty, very black, working alongside the others and in no way different from them—or so it seems. When they work he swings his pick with the same rhythm. When they pause he squats and rolls a cigarette, running his tongue along the edge of the paper while his eyes, under the stained hat, observe the straight line of the horizon; then he sets it between his lips, cups flame, draws in, and blows out smoke like all the rest.

Wears moleskins looped low under his belly and a flannel vest. Sits at smoko on one heel and sips tea from an enamel mug. Spits, and his spit hisses on stone. Then rises, spits in his palm, takes up the crowbar. They are digging holes for fencing-posts at the edge of the plain. When called he answers immediately, "Here, boss," and then, when he has approached, "Yes, boss, you wanna see me?" I am presented and he seems amused, as if I were some queer northern bird he had heard about but never till now believed in, a sort of crane perhaps, with my grey frock coat and legs too spindly in their yellow trousers; an odd, angular fellow with yellow-grey side-whiskers, half spectacles, and a cold-sore on his lip. So we stand face to face.

He is, they tell me, the one surviving speaker of his tongue. Half a century back, when he was a boy, the last of his people were massacred. The language, one of hundreds (why make a fuss?) died with them. Only not quite. For all his lifetime this man has spoken it, if only to himself. The words, the great system of sound and silence (for all languages, even the simplest, are a great and complex system) are locked up now in his heavy skull, behind the folds of the black brow (hence my scholarly interest), in the mouth with its stained teeth and fat, rather pink tongue. It is alive still in the man's silence, a whole alternative universe, since the world as we know it is in the last resort the words through which we imagine and name it; and when he narrows his eyes, and grins and says, "Yes, boss, you wanna see me?," it is not breathed out.

I am (you may know my name) a lexicographer. I come to these shores from far off, out of curiosity, a mere tourist, but in my own land I too am the keeper of something: of the great book of words of my tongue. No, not mine, my people's, which they have made over centuries, up there in our part of the world, and in which, if you have an ear for these things and a nose for the particular fragrance of a landscape, you may glimpse forests, lakes, great snow peaks that hang over our land like the wings of birds. It is all there in our mouths. In the odd names of our villages, in the pet-names we give to pigs or cows, and to our children too when they are young, Little Bean, Pretty Cowslip; in the nonsense rhymes in which so much simple wisdom is contained (not by accident, the language itself discovers these truths), or in the way, when two consonants catch up a repeated sound, a new thought goes flashing from one side to another of your head.

All this is mystery. It is a mystery of the deep past, but also of now. We recapture on our tongue, when we first grasp the sound and make it, the same word in the mouths of our long dead fathers, whose blood we move in and whose blood still moves in us. Language *is* that blood. It is the sun taken up where it shares out heat and light to the surface of each thing and made whole, hot, round again. *Solen,* we say, and the sun stamps once on the plain and pushes up in its great hot body, trailing streams of breath.

O holiest of all holy things!—it is a stooped blond crane that tells you this, with yellow side-whiskers and the grey frock coat and trousers of his century—since we touch here on beginnings, go deep down under Now to the remotest dark, far back in each ordinary moment of our speaking, even in gossip and the rigma-role of love words and children's games, into the lives of our fathers, to share with them the single instant of all our seeing and making, all our long history of doing and being. When I think of my tongue being no longer alive in the mouths of men a chill goes over me that is deeper than my own death, since it is the gathered death of all my kind. It is black night descending once and for ever on all that world of forests, lakes, snow peaks, great birds' wings; on little fishing sloops, on foxes nosing their way into a coop, on the piles of logs that make bonfires, and the heels of the young girls leaping over them, on sewing-needles, milk pails, axes, on gingerbread moulds made out of good birchwood, on fiddles, school slates, spinning-tops—my breath catches, my heart jumps. O the holy dread of it! Of having under your tongue the first and last words of all those generations down there in your blood, down there in the earth, for whom these syllables were the magic once for calling the whole of creation to come striding, swaying, singing towards them. I look at this old fellow and my heart stops, I do not know what to say to him.

I am curious, of course—what else does it mean to be a scholar but to be curious and to have a passion for the preserving of things? I would like to have him speak a word or two in his own tongue. But the desire is frivolous, I am ashamed to ask. And in what language would I do it? This foreign one? Which I speak out of politeness because I am a visitor here, and speak well because I have learned it, and he because it is the only one he can share now with his contemporaries, with those who fill the days with him— the language (he appears to know only a handful of words) of those who feed, clothe, employ him, and whose great energy, and a certain gift for changing and doing things, has set all this land under another tongue. For the land too is in another language now. All its capes and valleys have new names; so do its creatures—even the insects that make their own skirling, racketing sound under stones. The first landscape here is dead. It dies in this man's eyes as his tongue licks the edge of the horizon, before it has quite dried up in his mouth. There is a new one now that others are making.

So. It is because I am a famous visitor, a scholarly freak from another continent, that we have been brought together. We have nothing to say to one another. I come to the fire where he sits with the rest of the men and accept a mug of their sweet scalding tea. I squat with difficulty in my yellow trousers. We nod to one another. He regards me with curiosity, with a kind of shy amusement, and sees what? Not fir forests, surely, for which he can have neither picture nor word, or lakes, snow peaks, a white bird's wing. The sun perhaps, our northern one, making a long path back into the dark, and the print of our feet, black tracks upon it.

Nothing is said. The men are constrained by the presence of a stranger, but also perhaps by the presence of the boss. They make only the most rudimentary attempts at talk: slow monosyllabic remarks, half-swallowed with the tea. The thread of community here is strung with a few shy words and expletives—grunts, caws, soft bursts of laughter that go back before syntax; the man no more talkative than the rest, but a presence just the same.

I feel his silence. He sits here, solid, black, sipping his tea and flicking away with his left hand at a fly that returns again and again to a spot beside his mouth; looks up so level, so much on the horizontal, under the brim of his hat.

Things centre themselves upon him—that is what I feel, it is eerie—as on the one and only repository of a name they will lose if he is no longer there to keep it in mind. He holds thus, on a loose thread, the whole circle of shabby-looking trees, the bushes with their hidden life, the infinitesimal coming and going among grass roots or on ant-trails between stones, the minds of small native creatures that come creeping to the edge of the scene and look in at us from their other lives. He gives no sign of being special. When their smoking time is up, he rises with the rest, stretches a little, spits in the palm of his hand, and goes silently to his work.

"Yes, boss, you wanna see me"—neither a statement nor a question, the only words I have heard him speak . . .

I must confess it. He has given me a fright. Perhaps it is only that I am cut off here from the use of my own tongue (though I have never felt such a thing on previous travels, in France,

Greece, Egypt), but I find it necessary, in the privacy of my little room with its marble-topped washbasin and commodious jug and basin, and the engraving of Naomi bidding farewell to Ruth—I find it necessary, as I pace up and down on the scrubbed boards in the heat of a long December night, to go over certain words as if it were only my voice naming them in the dark that kept the loved objects solid and touchable in the light up there, on the top side of the world. (Goodness knows what sort of spells my hostess thinks I am making, or the children, who see me already as a spook, a half-comic, half-sinister wizard of the north.)

So I say softly as I curl up with the sheet over my head, or walk up and down, or stand at the window a moment before this plain that burns even at midnight: *rogn, valnøtt, spiseskje, hakke, vinglass, lysestake, krabbe, kjegle* ...

Out of the Stream

T HE BOY STOOD in the doorway and was not yet visible.
The others were at breakfast. He stood leaning against the
refrigerator, which was taller than he was, a great white giant that
made ice, endlessly made ice, and whose shelves (the brightest
place in the house) were packed with bowls of asparagus tips,
beetroot, egg-custard, roll-mops, tubs of Neapolitan gelati,
cheesecake, pizzas, T-bone steaks. No one bothered to look up.

He would step out soon—but as what? A stranger from the
streets, filthy from sleeping on building-sites or at the end of alleys
among the rubbish-tins and piss; demanding that they take him in
and feed him, or find a place for him in their beds. As a courier of
the air, one of those agents of apocalypse that are for ever in course
about the planet, bearing news of earthquake, epidemic, famine,
and the coming now of the last invaders. As an exterminating angel
swinging a two-edged sword and bringing them back to the first
things of all, to blood and breath. As anything but the fourteen-
year-old he was, descending only from a night among the hot
sheets and a room whose Cat Stevens poster (which belonged to
the time when he was a Cat Stevens fan), and his dictionaries, cal-
culator, tape-recorder, and head-set—and the silhouettes of all the
ships of cruiser class in the Japanese navy of forty years ago—
might define the whole of his interests and what he was.

He stepped out of the lee of the white giant, in T-shirt and
jeans, his hair combed wet from the shower. The two-edged sword
went swinging.

"You're late," his mother complained, without even looking to
see who it was.

"It's all right," he said. "I don't want anything. Just tea."

His mother poured it with her back to him, where she was preparing salads for their picnic, and he came and took it from the bench.

His father was eating toast, snapping clean rounds out of it with his teeth and devouring the *Sun*. Michael was on the floor with the comics. Only Julie, all in white for tennis, her shoulders brown and bare, was sitting up straight and eating the way people were supposed to eat; and doing it beautifully as she did everything.

She was sixteen, two years older than Luke, and did not know how extraordinary she was. Her presence among them was a mystery. It had always amazed him that they were of the same family, especially in the days before Michael when there had been just the two of them. People were always proclaiming in that silly way, "What beautiful children!" But they had meant Julie. Any likeness between them was illusory, and when Michael appeared and was such an ugly duckling, Luke had felt easier, as if a balance was restored. He had a special fondness for Michael's batlike ears.

"Well, are you coming out or aren't you?" his father demanded.

"No. I promised to see Hughie."

His mother made a straight line with her mouth. Hughie was the son of the man who had made the sails for their boat. She didn't approve of that. It was all right when they were just kids at primary school, but now he was supposed to have other friends. He did not.

"But you said you would," Michael wailed. "You promised! I don't want to go either."

Michael was eight and still said exactly what he felt. It embarrassed Luke that Michael was so fond of him and did not dissemble or hide it. He felt Michael's affection as a weight that he might never throw off. He hated to hurt people, and was always doing it, whichever way he turned—Michael, Julie, his mother.

"I can't," he said again. "I promised Hughie."

Michael turned away and his mother gave him one of her looks of silent reproval: he was so selfish.

He had in fact made no promise to Hughie, but ten minutes

later he came round the harbour path with its morning glory vines and its wall of moss-covered, dripping rocks to where the Hutchins's house was built above the water, with a slatted ramp beside it. The walls of the house were of stained shingles, and at night you could hear water lapping below and the masts of pleasure-boats tapping and clicking.

Luke had known it always. It was a big open house full of light and air, but since Hughie's mother died, six months ago, had been let go. There were cartons in the hallway crammed with old newspapers and boating magazines that no one had bothered to move, already cobwebbed and thick with dust. In the kitchen, away to the right, flies buzzed among open jam-jars and unscraped plates where T-bones lay congealed in fat and streaks of hardened tomato sauce, a bottle of which, all black at the rim, stood open on the oilskin cloth. It was all mess—Luke didn't mind that; but beyond the mess of the two or three rooms where Hughie and his father camped, you were aware of rooms that were empty, where nobody ever went. They gave your voice in this house a kind of echo—that is what Luke thought—and made Hughie, these days, a bit weird. As if all those empty rooms were a part of him he could no longer control. "Is that you, Luke?" he called now, and his voice had the echo. "C'mon through."

He was the youngest of three brothers. The eldest, Ric, was a panel-beater. He lived in the Western suburbs with a girl who was just out of school. The other had got in with a drug crowd, and after a period of hanging round the city in a headband and waistcoat, had gone to Nimbin and was raising corn. Hughie was the baby. Spoiled and petted by his mother when she was alive, he had been drifting since. He spent his days in front of the TV or up at the Junction, barefooted in boardshorts, with the Space Invaders.

An excessively skinny kid, always tanned but still unhealthy-looking, he was sprawled now on the vinyl lounge in front of the TV, wearing the stained blue boardshorts that he never changed and with his fist in a packet of crisps. He took his hand from the packet and crammed a fistful into his mouth, then licked the salt from his fingers before it dropped. "Want some?" he asked through the crunching.

Luke shook his head. "Why do you eat that stuff?"

"Because I saw it on TV," Hughie answered straight off. "And because I'm dumb and don't know any better. Besides, it beats ice-cubes."

A few months back there was never anything to eat in this house except ice-cubes. They used to suck them in the heat while they watched the cricket. "There's a choice," Hughie would tell him, "ice-cubes boiled or fried or grilled. Take your pick." That was while Mrs. Hutchins was still dying in the next room. "I figure," Hughie told him now, "that if I eat all that stuff they eat on television—you know, potato crisps, Cherry Ripe, Coke, all that *junk,* I'll turn into a real Australian kid and have a top physique. Isn't that what's supposed to happen?"

"Maybe you'll turn into a real American kid and stay skinny."

"Y' reckon?" Hughie's hand was arrested in mid-lift.

"Maybe you'll just get spots."

"Nah! Nunna the kids on TV get spots. Look at 'em. They're all blond 'n have top physiques, and the girls are unreal."

"They've got spots. That's why they use Clearasil."

"I use Clearasil."

"Does it do any good?"

"No, but that's because I pull off so much."

"So do the kids on TV."

"Y' reckon?"

He leaned out, flicked to another channel, then another, then pushed the off-switch with his big toe.

"Maybe you'll just turn into yourself," Luke said, "only you'll be too full of junk to see what it is."

"But that's just what I *don't* want. You ever see anyone on TV looked like me? I wanna be a real Australian kid. You know—happy. Sliding down a water-chute with lots of other happy kids, including girls. Climbing all over a big ball and making things go better with Coke. That's why I'm into junk food. Junk food makes you tanned and gives you a terrific physique. It's pulling off gives you spots."

"No. It doesn't do anything."

"Yes it does. It turns you into a monster."

Hughie jumped up, made jerking movements with his fist, and turned into a pale skinny version of King Kong. He hopped about on flat feet with his knees bent, his arms loose, and his tongue pushed into his upper lip, grunting. Luke jumped up, made the same motions, and was Frankenstein. Laughing, they fell in a heap.

"No," Luke said, sitting upright, "it doesn't do any of that. They just tell you that because they can't sell it on TV."

Hughie went back to munching crisps.

"So what'll you do?" he said, returning to a conversation of several days back.

"I don't know. What about you?"

"My dad says I can leave school if I want to and go in with him. There's a lot of money in sailmaking. You know?" He said it without enthusiasm. "Everyone wants sails."

"I want to do Japanese," Luke said, moving to the window and looking across to the marina, where half a mile off, among a crowd of Sunday craft, he could see *Starlight* just beginning to make way. He was thinking of a time, a year back, when with his grandfather as guide he would go crawling about in the strange light of the sea off Midway, among the wrecks of the Japanese carriers *Soryu, Kaga, Hiru,* Admiral Nagumo's flagship the *Akagi,* the heavy cruiser *Mikuma,* and the *Yorktown.* "My grandad says we might have been better off," he said reflectively, "if we hadn't won the Battle of Midway after all and the Japs had come instead of the Americans. I don't know, maybe he's right. He says winning all those wars was the worst thing ever happened to us."

"Is this your grandfather who was in the Wehrmacht?" Hughie enquired.

Luke giggled. "No, you nut! They lost all *their* wars. My dad's father. The one who was in the AIF."

Hughie, still hugging the carton of crisps, got up and went to the other side of the room.

"Listen Luke," he said seriously, "I've been meaning to tell you. If you need any money I've got stacks of it."

"What?"

"Money. Com'n look."

He was standing over an open drawer.

"My dad's got this woman he goes to, and every time he goes off and leaves me alone I get ten dollars. I mean, he *gives* it to me. I'm making a fortune!" The two boys stood looking at the drawer full of bills. "He feels guilty, see? I ran into them once, up at the Junction, and they were both so embarrassed. She's a sort of barmaid. I had to stop myself from laughing. I feel like I'm living off her immoral earnings, ten dollars a time. If you want any of it, it's yours."

Luke looked at the drawer and shook his head. "No," he said, "I get pocket money, they give me pocket money. Anyway, all I need now is ninety-five cents for the train fare."

"I dunno," Hughie said before the open drawer. "Why does 'e do it? What's 'e scared of?" He looked sad standing there in the boardshorts, so buck-toothed and skinny, peering into the drawer full of bills. They had called him Casper at school. Casper the ghost.

"My parents," Luke said, "are scared of all sorts of things." And at first to take Hughie's mind off his problem, but soon out of a growing contempt and bitterness of his own, he began to list them. "They're scared one of us will go on drugs or join the Jesus freaks or the Hari Krishnas. Or grow up and marry a Catholic. My mother's scared of being poor, the way they were in Europe after the war. She's scared my father's dad'll get sick and have to come and live with us. She's scared of cancer. My dad's scared the tax people will catch up with him." He turned away to the window, and *Starlight* was just moving down towards the point opposite. He could see his father amidships, in his captain's cap, directing: "There's only one captain on this boat," he would be saying. "Most of all," Luke said, "he's scared of my mother. He thinks he's not good enough for her." At the prow was Michael, a lonely child, dangling his legs on either side of the bowsprit. Luke could see one dazzling white sneaker.

"Listen, I'll tell you what," he said, "why don't we go out and fly the kites? We haven't done that for ages."

"You really want to?"

"Yes, it's *just* what I want." He hadn't thought of it till this moment but it was true. "It's what I came for."

Last year when they had both seemed so much younger they had spent hours flying the kites, two big box-kites that Hughie's father had made with the same craftsman's skill he brought to his sailmaking. They were beautiful machines, and for a while Luke had liked nothing better than to be at the end of a string and to feel the gentle tugging of the birdlike creation that was three hundred feet up under the ceiling of cloud and gently afloat, or plunging in the breeze—feeling it as another freer self, almost angelic, and with a will of its own. No other activity he knew gave him such a clear sense of being both inside his own compact body and far outside it. You strained, you held on, the plunging was elsewhere.

Hughie was delighted to drag the kites out of the back room where they had been gathering dust for the past months and to check and re-wind the strings. He did it quickly but with great concentration. He tied the sleeves of a light sweater round his waist and they were off.

Twenty minutes later the kites with their gaudy tails were sailing high over the rocky little park on the Point and far out over the water. Luke too had removed his shirt and was running over the grass, feeling the kite tug him skyward: *tug, tug.* He could feel the sky currents up there, the pure air in motion, feel its energy run all the way back along the string into his gorged hands. It took him to the limits of his young strength.

"This is great," Hughie was shouting as if they had suddenly stepped back a year. "Feel that? Isn't it unreal?"

They let their animal selves loose and the great kites held and sustained them.

"What really shits me," Luke said later when they had drawn the machines in, wound the strings, and were lying stretched in the shade, "is that no one has the guts to be what they pretend to be. You know what I mean? My father pretends to be a big businessman. He makes deals and talks big but it scares the hell out of him, and at the weekend he pretends to be the skipper of a boat. He gets all dressed up in his whites and does a lot of shouting but all the time he's terrified a storm'll blow up or he'll ram someone or that Michael will fall in and get drowned. People are all the same. You can see it. Scared you'll call their bluff. It makes me puke."

Hughie looked puzzled. Luke worried him. Most of the time he was just like anyone, the way he was when they were flying the kites: then suddenly he'd speak out, and there was more anger in what he said than the words themselves could contain.

"So?" he said.

"So someone, sometime, has to go through with it."

"How do you mean?"

Luke set his mouth and did not elaborate, and Hughie, out of loyalty to an old understanding between them, did not push for an answer.

They had known one another since they were five or six years old. It was, in terms of their short lives, a long friendship, but Hughie had begun to perceive lately, and it hurt him, that they might already have grown apart. There was in Luke something dark, uncompromising, fanatical, that scared him because it was so alien to his own nature. He was incapable of such savagery himself, and might be the shallower for it. His mind struggled to grasp the thing and it hurt.

"Listen Luke," he began, then stopped and was defeated. There was no way of putting what he had seen into words. He swallowed, picked at his toe. Luke, hard-mouthed and with brows fiercely lowered, was staring dead ahead. "Hey, Luke," he called across the narrow space between them, and knocked the other boy's shoulder, very lightly, with the heel of his hand.

"What?"

"I don't know, you seemed—far away." He screwed his eyes up and looked out across the burnished water. The idea of distance saddened him.

"Thanks," Luke said softly after a moment, and Hughie was relieved.

"For what?" he answered, but it wasn't a question.

They grinned, and it was as if things between them were clear again. Luke got up. "I'd better get going," he said. "I'll give you a hand with the kites."

Two hours later he was getting down at the empty northern station with its cyclone-wire fence strung on weathered uprights. The view beyond was of the sea.

He made his way along a tussocky path that led away from the main settlement, and along the edge of the dunes to where his grandfather's shack, grey fibro, stood in a fenceless allotment above rocks. There were banksias all leaning one way, shaped by the wind and rattling their dry, grey-black cones. It was a desolate place, not yet tamed or suburban: the dunes held together by long silvery grass, changing their contours almost daily under the wind; the sea-light harsh, almost brutal, stinging your eyes, blasting the whole world white with salt. Inland, to the west, great platforms of sandstone held rainwater in rusty pools and the wild bush-plants, spiky green now but when they were in flower a brilliant white, thrust clean through rock.

His grandfather was a fisherman. It was his grandfather who had led Luke to the sea, and his grandfather's war (or rather the Occupation Forces of the years afterwards) that had led him, through yarns quietly told and a collection of objects too deeply revered to be souvenirs—touchstones rather—to his consuming interest of this last couple of years. He had touched every one of those objects, and they had yielded their mystery. He had listened to his grandfather, read everything he could lay his hands on, and had, he thought, understood. He felt now for the key, on a hook by the water tank, and let himself in.

A shack, not a house, but orderly and to Luke's eyes, beautiful. Washing-up was stacked on the primitive sink. There was a note on the kitchen table: "Luke—be back around five. Love, Pa." Luke studied it. He took a glass of water, but only wet his lips, and went through to the one large room that made up the rest of the place. It was very bare. Poor-looking, some would have thought. Everything was out and visible: straw mats of a pale corn colour, still with a smell; his grandfather's stretcher; the hammock where Luke himself slept when he stayed overnight. On the walls, the tabletop, and on the floor round the walls, were the objects that made this for Luke a kind of shrine: masks, pots, the two samurai swords, and daggers.

He went straight to the wall and took one of the daggers from its hook—it was his, and walking through to the open verandah, he stood holding it a moment, then drew the sharp blade from its sheath.

He ran his finger along the edge, not drawing blood, then, barely thinking, turned the point towards him and made a hard jab with his fist. It was arrested just at the white of his T-shirt.

He gave a kind of laugh. It would be so easy. You would let each thing happen, one thing after the next, in an order that once established would carry you right through and over into—

He stood very still, letting it begin.

At the moment of his first stepping in across the threshold out of the acute sunlight, he had entered a state—he couldn't have said what it was, but had felt the strangeness of it like a trance upon his blood, in which everything moved slowly, slowly. He was not dulled—not at all—but he felt out of himself, free of his own being, or aware of it in a different way. It came to him, this new being of his, as a clear fact like the dagger; like the light off the walls, which was reflected sea-light blasting the fibro with a million tumbling particles; like the individual dry strands of the matting.

You fell into such states, anyway he did, but not always so deeply. They began in strangeness and melancholy—you very nearly vanished—then when you came back, it was to a sense of the oneness of things. There was a kind of order in the world and it was in you as well. You attended. You caught a rhythm to which each gesture could be fitted. You let it lead you out of your body into—

It had begun. Slowly he removed his watch—it was twelve past four—and laid it on a ledge. Then he took off his gym-shoes, pushed his socks into them, and set them side by side on the floor. He pulled his T-shirt over his head and, folding his jeans, made a pile of them, jeans, T-shirt, shoes. They looked like the clothes, neatly arranged, of one who had gone into the sea or into the air—how could you be certain which?—or into the earth. The sea was glittering on his left and was immense. He did not look at it. Earth and air you took for granted. Wearing only the clean jockey-shorts now, he knelt on the verandah boards, carefully arranging his limbs: bringing his body into a perpendicular line with his foot soles, and thighs and trunk into alignment with the dagger, which lay immediately before him. He sat very straight, his body all verticals, horizontals, strictly composed; in a straight line with sea and earth, or at right angles to them. He began to breathe in and out, deeply, slowly, feeling the oxygen force its way into his cells so that they exerted a pressure all over the surface of him where his body met the air, in the beginning muscles of his forearms and biceps, in his throat, his lips, against the thinness of his closed lids. He clenched his teeth, the breath in his nostrils now a steady hiss, and took up the dagger. All there was now was the business of getting the body through and over into—

He paused. He set the point of the dagger to the skin of his belly above the white jockey-shorts (death was so close—as close as that) and all the muscles of his abdomen fluttered at the contact. He felt his sex begin to stiffen, all of itself.

A wave, not very big, had begun making for the shore and would reach it soon with a scuffling of pebbles, one of which, the one in his mouth, had a taste of salt. He sucked on it, and over a long period, after centuries, it began to be worn away, it melted, and his mouth, locked on the coming cry, was filled with the words of a new language, on his tongue, his tooth ridge, as a gurgling in his throat: the names of ordinary objects—tools, cookpots, baskets—odd phrases or conversations on which a life might depend, jokes (even crude ones), lyrics praising the moon or lilies or the rising of a woman's breast, savage epics—

"That you, Luke?"

The boy came back into himself, the wave passed on. He opened his eyes, picked up the sheath, pushed himself to his feet, and with dagger and sheath still in hand, walked barefoot, and naked save for his jockeys, to the door.

His grandfather was there. He had a heavy sack over his shoulder and a rod and reel.

"Hullo, Luke," he called. He swung the sack down hard on the concrete path. "I had a good day," he said. He gave a crack-lipped grin. "Take a look at this." He lifted the end of the sack, tumbling its contents in a cascade of shining bodies. Luke was dazzled. Some of them were still alive and flipping their tails on the rough concrete, throwing light.

The boy restored the dagger to its sheath, rested it on the edge of the sink, and stepped down among them. "Terrific," he said.

"Yairs," the man breathed, "pretty good, eh? You stoppin' the night?"

Luke nodded, moving quickly away to catch a fish that was flapping off into the coarse grass. It continued to flutter in his hands.

"Good," said the man. He went off to fetch buckets and knives. "We'll get started, eh?"

While his grandfather went through into the kitchen to get clean basins, Luke took one of the buckets round to the side of the house and filled it from the tank. He came back staggering.

"Good," his grandfather said. "Let's get into it."

They seated themselves side by side on the step and worked swiftly.

It was a job Luke was used to, had been skilled at since he was nine years old. The blade went in along the belly; the guts spilled, a lustrous silver-blue, and were tossed into the one bucket; in the other you plunged to the forearm and rinsed.

The work went on quickly, silently; they seldom talked much till after tea. Luke lost himself in the rhythm of it, a different rhythm from the one he had given himself to earlier. A kind of drowsiness came over him that had to do with the falling darkness, with the repeated flashing of the knife and his swinging to left and right between buckets, and with the closeness of so much raw flesh and blood. His arms and bare legs were covered with fishscales. His face, neck, chest were flecked with gobbets of the thin fish blood.

At last they were done. The fish, all scaled and gutted, were in the basins. One bucket was full of guts, the other with water that was mostly blood. The doorstep too was all shiny with scales (Luke would come out later and flush it clean).

"Good," his grandfather said. "We've done well." He carried in the basins of fish, then took the two heavy buckets and poured them into a dip in the sand where they could be covered. Luke sat, too drowsy to move; but stirred himself at last. He went round to the side of the house and let water run over his legs, and washed the scales from his neck and arms.

It was almost dark. You could hear the sea washing against the rocks below, a regular crashing; but further out it was still, and he stood a moment, clean again, drying off in the breeze, and watched it. He felt oddly happy—for no reason, there *was* no reason. Just happy, as earlier with the kites. It was like a change of weather, a sudden transformation, that might not last but for as long as it did would fill the whole sky and touch everything around with its steady light. He was back in the stream again— one of the streams.

He went in and began to dress: jeans (not caring that he was still half wet), T-shirt. His grandfather was frying fish for their tea. The fish smelled good and he was hungry.

"Set the table, Luke," his grandfather told him. "She'll be ready in a jiff."

So he set the two places at the kitchen table, then stood for a moment at the open door and looked out into the dark. It seemed larger, more comprehensible, because it lay over the sea and you saw it as an ocean whose name you knew and knew the other shore of, glittering full under the early stars; though the dark was bigger than any ocean, bigger even than the sky with its scattered lights.

"Right," the old man called. "We're all set, Luke. You hungry?"

The boy turned back to the lighted table. His grandfather, humming a little, was just setting down the pan.

The Sun in Winter

I T WAS DARK in the church, even at noon. Diagonals of chill sunlight were stacked between the piers, sifting down luminous dust, and so thick with it that they seemed more substantial almost than stone. He had a sense of two churches, one raised vertically on Gothic arches and a thousand years old, the other compounded of light and dust, at an angle to the first and newly created in the moment of his looking. At the end of the nave, set far back on a platform, like a miraculous vision that the arctic air had immediately snap-frozen, was a Virgin with a child at her knee. The Michael-angelo. So this church he was in must be the Onze Vrouw.

"Excuse me."

The voice came from a pew two rows away, behind him: a plain woman of maybe forty, with the stolid look and close-pored waxy skin of those wives of donors he had been looking at earlier in the side panels of local altars. She was buttoned to the neck in a square-shouldered raincoat and wore a scarf rather than a wimple, but behind her as she knelt might have been two or three miniatures of herself—infant daughters with their hands strictly clasped—and if he peeped under her shoes, he thought, there would be a monster of the deep, a sad-eyed amorphous creature with a hump to its back, gloomily committed to evil but sick with love for the world it glimpsed, all angels, beyond the hem of her skirt.

"You're not Flemish, are you," she was saying, half in question (that was her politeness) and half as fact.

"No," he admitted. "Australian."

They were whispering—this was after all a church—but her

"Ah, the *New* World" was no more than a breath. She made it sound so romantic, so much more of a venture than he had ever seen it, that he laughed outright, then checked himself; but not before his laughter came back to him, oddly transformed, from the hollow vault. No Australian in those days thought of himself as coming under so grand a term. Things are different now.

"You see," she told him in a delighted whisper, "I guessed! I knew you were not Flemish—that, if you don't mind, is obvious— so I thought, I'll speak to him in English, or maybe on this occasion I'll try Esperanto. Do you by any chance know Esperanto?" He shook his head. "Well, never mind," she said, "there's plenty of time." She did not say for what. "But you *are* Catholic."

Wrong again. Well, not exactly, but his "No" was emphatic, she was taken aback. She refrained from putting the further question and looked for a moment as if she did not know how to proceed. Then following the turn of his head she found the Madonna. "Ah," she said, "you are interested in art. You have come for the Madonna." Relieved at last to have comprehended him she regarded the figure with a proprietary air. Silently, and with a certain Old-World grandeur and largesse, she presented it to him.

He should, to be honest, have informed her then that he had been a Catholic once (he was just twenty) and still wasn't so far gone as to be lapsed—though too far to claim communion; and that for today he had rather exhausted his interest in art at the little hospital full of Memlings and over their splendid van Eycks. Which left no reason for his being here but the crude one: his need to find sanctuary for a time from their killing cold.

Out there, blades of ice slicing in off the North Sea had found no obstacle, it seemed, in more than twenty miles of flat lands crawling with fog, till they found *him,* the one vertical (given a belltower or two) on the whole ring of the horizon. He had been, for long minutes out there, the assembly-point for forty-seven demons. His bones scraped like glaciers. Huge ice-plates ground in his skull. He had been afraid his eyeballs might freeze, contract, drop out, and go rolling away over the ancient flags. It seemed foolish after all that to say simply, "I was cold."

"Well, in that case," she told him, "you must allow me to make an appointment. I am an official guide of this town. I am working all day in a government office, motor-vehicle licences, but precisely at four we can meet and I will show you our dear sad Bruges—that is, of course, if you are agreeable. No, no—please— it is for my own pleasure, no fee is involved. Because I see that you are interested, I glimpsed it right off." She turned up the collar of her coat and gave him an engaging smile. "It is okay?" She produced the Americanism with a cluck of clear self-satisfaction, as proof that she was, though a guide of this old and impressively dead city, very much of his own century and not at all hoity-toity about the usages of the New World. It was a brief kick of the heels that promised fun as well as instruction in the splendours and miseries of the place.

"Well then," she said when he made no protest, "it is decided— till four. You will see that our Bruges is very beautiful, very *triste*, you understand French? *Bruges la Morte*. And German too maybe, a little? *Die tote Stadt*." She pronounced this with a small shiver in her voice, a kind of silvery chill that made him think of the backs of mirrors. At the same time she gave him just the tips of her gloved fingers. "So—I must be off now. We meet at four."

Which is how, without especially wanting it, he came to know the whole history of the town. On a cold afternoon in the Fifties, with fog swirling thick white in the polled avenues and lying in ghostly drifts above the canals, and the red-brick façades of palaces, convents, museums laid bare under the claws of ivy, he tramped with his guide over little humpbacked bridges, across sodden lawns, to see a window the size of a hand mirror with a bloody history, a group of torture instruments (themselves twisted now and flaking rust), the site, almost too ordinary, of a minor miracle, a courtyard where five old ladies were making lace with fingers as knobbled and misshapen as twigs, and the statue of a man in a frock coat who had given birth to the decimal system.

The woman's story he caught in the gaps between centuries and he got the two histories, her own and the city's, rather mixed, so that he could not recall later whether it was his lady or the daughter of a local duke who had suffered a fall in the woods, and her young man or some earlier one who had been shut up and tortured in one of the many towers. The building she pointed to as being the former Gestapo headquarters looked much like all the rest, though it might of course have been a late imitation.

She made light of things, including her own life, which had not, he gathered, been happy; but she could be serious as well as ironic. To see what all this really was, she insisted—beyond the relics and the old-fashioned horrors and shows—you needed a passion for the everyday. That was how she put it. And for that, mere looking got you nowhere. "All you see then," she told him, "is what catches the eye, the odd thing, the unusual. But to see what is common, that is the difficult thing, don't you think? For that we need imagination, and there is never enough of it—never, never enough."

She had spoken with feeling, and now that it was over, her own small show, there was an awkwardness. It had grown dark. The night, a block of solid ice with herrings in it, deep blue, was being cranked down over the plain; you could hear it creaking. He stamped a little, puffing clouds of white, and shyly, sheepishly grinned. "Cold," he sang, shuffling his feet, and when she laughed at the little dance he was doing he continued it, waving his arms about as well. Then they came, rather too quickly, to the end of his small show. She pulled at her gloves and stood waiting.

Something more was expected of him, he knew that. But what? Was he to name it? Should he perhaps, in spite of her earlier disclaimer, offer a tip? Was that it? Surely not. But money was just one of the things, here in Europe, that he hadn't got the hang of, the weight, the place, the meaning; one of the many—along with tones, looks, little movements of the hands and eyebrows, unspoken demands and the easy meeting of them—that more than galleries or torture chambers made up what he had come here to see, and to absorb too if he could manage it. He felt hopelessly young and raw. He ought to have known—he had known—from that invisible kick of the heels, that she had more to show him than this crumblingly haunted and picturesque corner of the past, where sadness, a mood of silvery reflection, had been turned into the high worship of death—a glory perhaps, but one that was too full of shadows to bear the sun. He felt suddenly a great wish for the sun in its full power as at home, and it burned up in him. He *was* the sun. It belonged to the world he had come from and to his youth.

The woman had taken his hand. "My dear friend," she was saying, with that soft tremor in her voice, "—I *can* call you that, can't I? I feel that we *are* friends. In such a short time we have grown close. I would like to show you one thing more—very beautiful but not of the past. Something personal."

She led him along the edge of the canal and out into a street broader than the rest, its cobbles gleaming in the mist. Stone steps led up to classical porticoes, and in long, brightly lit windows there were Christmas decorations, holly with red ribbons, and bells powdered with frost. They came to a halt in front of one of the largest and brightest of these displays, and he wondered why. Still at the antipodes, deep in his dream of sunlight and youth, he did not see at first that they had arrived.

"There," the woman was saying. She put her nose to the glass and there was a ring of fog.

The window was full of funerary objects: ornamental wreaths in iridescent enamel, candles of all sizes like organ pipes in carved and coloured wax, angels large and small, some in glass, some in plaster, some in honey-coloured wood in which you saw all the decades of growth; one of them was playing a lute; others had viols, pan pipes, primitive sidedrums; others again pointed a slender index finger as at a naughty child and were smiling in an ambiguous, un-otherworldly way. It was all so lively and colourful that he might have missed its meaning altogether without the coffin, which held a central place in the foreground and was tilted so that you saw the richness of the buttoned interior. Very comfortable it looked too—luxuriously inviting. Though the scene did not suggest repose. The heavy lid had been pushed strongly aside, as if what lay there just a moment ago had got up, shaken itself after long sleep, and gone striding off down the quay. The whole thing puzzled him. He wondered for a moment if she hadn't led him to the site of another and more recent miracle. But no.

"Such a coffin," she was telling him softly, "I have ordered for myself. Oh, don't look surprised!—I am not planning to die so soon, not at all! I am paying it off. The same. Exactly."

He swallowed, nodded, smiled, but was dismayed; he couldn't have been more so, or felt more exposed and naked, if she had climbed up into the window, among the plump and knowing angels, and got into the thing—lain right down on the buttoned blue satin, and with her skirt rucked up to show stockings rolled tight over snowy thighs, had crooked a finger and beckoned him with a leer to join her. He blushed for the grossness of the vision, which was all his own.

But his moment of incomprehension passed. His shock, he saw, was for an impropriety she took quite for granted and for an event that belonged, as she calmly surveyed it, to a world of exuberant and even vulgar life. The window was the brightest thing she had shown him, the brightest thing he had seen all day, the most lively, least doleful.

So he survived the experience. They both did. And he was glad to recall years after, that when she smiled and touched his hand in token of their secret sympathy, a kind of grace had come over him and he did not start as he might have done; he was relieved of awkwardness, and was moved, for all his raw youth, by an emotion he could not have named, not then—for her, but also for himself—and which he would catch up with only later, when sufficient time had passed to make them of an age.

As they already were for a second, before she let him go, and in a burst of whitened breath said, "Now, my dear, dear friend, I will exact my fee. You may buy me a cup of chocolate at one of our excellent cafés. Okay?"

Bad Blood

O DD THE CONJUNCTIONS, some of them closer than any planet, that govern a life. I am an only child because of my father's brother, Uncle Jake. In an otherwise exemplary line of seven brothers and sisters he made so sharp a detour, and so alarmed my mother with the statistical possibilities, that she refused, once my father's desire for an heir had been satisfied, to take further risks. She was not, needless to say, a gambler—even one chance was one too many—and she spent a good deal of her time watching for signs of delinquency in me. As the years passed and familiar features began to emerge, a nose from one side of the family, a tendency to bronchitis from the other, she grew more and more apprehensive, and was only mildly relieved when I came to resemble the plainest of her sisters.

A nose is obvious enough, it declares itself. So does a tendency to wheeze when the skies grow damp. But bad blood is a different matter. It takes a thousand forms and loves to disguise itself in meek and insidious qualities that allay suspicion and then endlessly and teasingly provoke it. My mother could never be sure of me. I was too quiet—it was unnatural. And Uncle Jake did leave his mark.

Was he really so bad?

Bad is hard to define. I am speaking of a time, the middle Thirties, and a place, Brisbane, in which it took very little in the way of divergence from the moderately acceptable for heads to come together and for a young person to get a reputation—and all reputations, of course, were bad.

There are crimes that defy judgment because they defy understanding. A mild-mannered newsagent shuts his shop one evening, goes out to the woodpile where chooks are dealt with, takes an axe, sits for ten minutes or so listening to the sounds of the warm suburban night, then goes in and butchers his whole family, along with a child from next door who has come in for the serials. The law-courts do what they can, and so too, at a level where local history becomes folk-lore, do the newspapers; but horrors of this sort cannot be gathered back into the web of daily living, there is too much blood, too much darkness in them. We must assume the irruption among us of some other agency, a wild-haired fury that sets its hand on a man and shakes the day-lights out of him, or a god in whom the rival aspects of creation and chaos are of equal importance and who knows no rule. But bad is civil; it is small-scale, commonplace—something the good citizen, under other circumstances, might himself have done and is qualified to condemn.

"Shadily genteel" is how a famous visitor once described our city, and she was not referring, I think, to its quaint weatherboard houses with their verandahs of iron lace or to the hoop-pines and glossy native figs that make it so richly, even oppressively green.

Brisbane is a city of strict conventions and many churches, but subtropical, steamy. Shoes in a cupboard grow mould in the wet months, and on the quiet surface of things there are bubbles that explode in the heat and give off odours of corruption; everything softens and rots. There are billiard-saloons and pubs where illegal bets can be laid on all the local and southern races, and there were, not long ago, houses in Margaret and Albert Streets in the City, and at Nott Street South Brisbane, that were tolerated by the civil authorities and patronised by a good part of the male popula-tion but which remained for all ordinary purposes unmention-able—and given the corrugated-iron walls with which they were surrounded, very nearly invisible as well. Brisbane is full of shabby institutions that society turns its gaze from, and in a good many of them my Uncle Jake was known to have a hand. Always flush with money and nattily dressed, he rode to the races in a Black and White cab with his friend Hector Grierley, and could be seen on Saturday nights at the Grand Central, blowing his winnings in the company of ladies who smoked in public, painted their toenails, and wore silk. Uncle Jake wore his Akubra at an unserious angle and had a taste for two-toned shoes. Loud is what people called him, but I knew him only in his quieter moments.

He liked to come around while my mother was ironing, and would stand for long hours telling her stories, trying to impress her (she was never impressed) and seeking her womanly advice.

She gave him the advice and he did not take it. It always ran clear against his nature, or interfered, just at the moment, with some scheme he had in hand. My mother made a face that said "See, I knew it—why did you ask?"

She didn't dislike Uncle Jake. Quite the contrary. But she was afraid of his influence and she resented his idleness, his charm, his showy clothes, and the demands he made on my father. The youngest of my grandmother's children, he was also, for all the sorrow he had caused, her favourite, and it was the bad example, which even my father followed, of forgiving him every delinquency in the light of his plain good nature that my mother deplored. It seemed monstrous to her that on at least one occasion, when the police were involved, my steady, law-abiding father had had to go to a politician, and the politician to an inspector of police, to save Uncle Jake from his just deserts.

It hadn't always been so. As a very young man he had been an apprentice pastrycook. His paleness, the white cap and apron he wore, and the dusting of flour on his bare arms, had given him the look of a modest youth with a trade whose very domestic associations made him harmless or tame. He was cheeky, that's all; a good-natured fellow who liked a drink or two and was full of animal spirits, but in no way dangerous. He deceived several girls that way and some married women as well, and got the first of his reputations.

But people ignored it. He was so likeable, so full of fun, such a ready spender, and so ready as well to share his adventures in the stories he told, which were all old jokes remade and brought back into the realm of actuality. Then, at not much more than twenty, he fell in love. The girl was called Alice—she was two years older—and with rather a sheepish look before his mates (he was, after all, betraying the spirit of his own stories), he married her.

The girl's beauty made a great impression on everyone. She had the creamy blonde look that appealed to people in those days—big green eyes, a thinned-out arch of eyebrow, hair that hugged her head in a close cap then broke in tight little curls. Uncle Jake was crazy about her. He worked at the hot ovens all night and brought home from the bakery each morning a packet of fresh breakfast rolls that they ate in bed, and he made her cakes as well in the shape of frogs with open mouths, and piglets and hedgehogs. They were happy for a time, only they didn't know how to manage. The girl couldn't cook or sew and was reluctant to do housework, and Uncle Jake was ashamed to be found so often with his sleeves rolled up, washing dishes at the sink. He had always, himself, been such a clean fellow, such a neat and careful dresser. He couldn't bear dirt. They had house after house, moving on when the mess got too much for them.

They had a child as well, a little girl just like the mother, and Alice didn't know how to look after the baby either. She didn't change its nappies or keep it clean. It was always hungry, dirty, crawling about the unswept floor covered with flies. Uncle Jake was distracted. At last he stopped going to work—there were no more fresh little rolls, no more green iced frogs with open mouths. He stayed home to care for the child, while Alice, as lazy and beautiful as ever, just sat about reading *Photoplay* till he lost his temper and blacked her eye. Uncle Jake doted on the child but felt dismayed, un-manned. He fretted for his old life of careless independence.

Things went from bad to worse and when the little girl got whooping cough and died it was all over. Uncle Jake was so wild with grief that Alice had to be got out of the house, he might have killed her. She went to her mother's and never came back, and was, in my childhood, a big, blond woman, even-tempered and fattish, who drank too much.

As for Uncle Jake, he recovered his spirits at last, but he never went back to the bakery or to any settled life. He had had his taste of that. Nobody blamed Alice for what had happened to him. He had simply, people said, reverted to his original wildness, which the apprenticeship to flour and icing-sugar, and his diversion for a time into suburban marriage, had done nothing to change.

All this had happened long before I was born. By the time of my earliest childhood Uncle Jake was already a gambler. It was the period of his flash suits, his brushes with the law, and the little orange car.

This beautiful machine, quite the grandest present I ever received, was his gift for my fourth birthday. "There," he exulted when we all trooped out to the verandah to look, "it's for the kid." It sat on the front lawn in its cellophane wrappers like a miniature Trojan Horse.

My father was embarrassed: partly at being so ostentatiously outdone (my parents' present had been a cricket bat and ball), but also because he was fond of my uncle, knew how generous he could be, and was certain that my mother would disapprove.

She did. She regarded the machine, all gleaming and flame-coloured, as an instrument of the devil. Whenever I rode in it, furiously working the pedals and making a *hrummm hrumm hrummm* sound as I hurtled round the yard, she would look pained and beg me after a time to spare her head. The little orange car brought out a recklessness in me, a passion for noise and speed, that appalled her. I had always been such a quiet little boy. Was this it? Was this the beginning of it? Just working my legs so fast to get the wheels going introduced me to realms of sweaty excitement I couldn't have imagined till now—to scope, to risk! I had discovered at last the power that was coiled in my own small body, the depth of my lungs, the extraordinary joys of speed and dirt and accidents—of actually spilling and grazing a knee. Uncle Jake was beside himself. He had thought of me till then as a bit of a sissy, but look at this! "He's a real little tiger," he said admiringly. "Just look at him go!"

Uncle Jake was too attractive. My mother tried to keep him away but it wasn't possible. He was family. He was always there.

I remember catching my parents once in a rare but heated quarrel. There was a family wedding or funeral to attend and the question had arisen of who might look after me.

"No," my mother whispered, "he's irresponsible. I won't have the child traipsing around billiard-saloons or sitting in gutters outside hotels. Or riding in a cab with that Hector Grierley. He's an abortionist! Everyone knows it."

"He could spend the day at Ruby's."

I heard my mother gasp.

"Have you gone off your head?"

Ruby was one of Uncle Jake's girlfriends, a big china-doll of a woman who lived with her daughters at Stones Corner.

What my mother did not know was that I had been to Ruby's already. Uncle Jake and I had dropped in there for an hour or so after an outing, and I had been impressed by his insistence that I swear, scout's honour, not to let on. The act of swearing and the establishment of complicity between us had made me see the quite ordinary house, which was on high stumps with a single hallway from front to back, in a special light.

Ruby wore pink fur slippers and was sitting when we arrived on the front doorstep, painting soft, mustard-yellow wax on her legs, which she then drew off like sticking plaster, in strips. She had a walnut-veneer cocktail cabinet, and even at three in the afternoon it came brilliantly alight when you opened the doors. I was allowed, along with the two skinny daughters, to sip beer with lemonade in it; and later, while Uncle Jake and Ruby had a little lie down, I went off with the two girls, and a setter with a tail that swept the air like a scarlet feather, to see their under-the-house.

"Watch out for the dead marines, love," Ruby had called after us in her jolly voice, and one of the daughters, giggling at my puzzlement, indicated the stack of Fourex bottles on the back landing. "She means *them,* you dill!"

Among the objects that had taken my eye at Ruby's was a bowl of roses, perfect buds and open blooms in red, yellow, and pink, that looked supernaturally real but were not. I had never seen anything so teasingly beautiful, and when I left, one of the scarlet buds went with me. In crossing the hallway on my way to the toilet I had stopped, unhooked the most brilliant of them from its wire basket, and taking advantage of my time behind the bathroom door, had slipped it easily into my pants.

"Ruby's," my mother said firmly, "is out of the question. I'm surprised at you even suggesting it."

So with Ruby's hotly in mind, and exaggerated in retrospect as a carnival place of forbidden colour, I spent the day with a neighbour, Mrs. Chard, who took me on a tram-ride to the Dutton Park terminus, questioned me closely about Jesus, and informed me that she was descended from Irish kings, "though you mightn' think it." (I didn't, but at nearly seven was too polite to say so.) She had a place above her lip where she shaved—you could see the shadow picked out in sweat drops—and seemed quite unaware of how the afternoon in her company was transfigured by the pink glow of my imagination, and how her louvred weatherboard became for a moment, as we approached it, the site of lurid possibilities—not perhaps a cocktail cabinet, but some equally exotic object that would be continuous with the world of Ruby's where it had been decided I should *not* spend the day.

But there was nothing. Only the smell of bacon fat in the kitchen, that clogged the back of my throat the way it clogged the drains, and an upright with candleholders.

Mrs. Chard played something classical in which she crossed her plump, freckled wrists; then "Mother McCrea." After which she showed me photographs, all of children who were dead. Then, acting on some compulsion of her own, or responding perhaps to a mood that I myself had created, she disappeared into a room across the hallway and came back holding her hands behind her back and looking very coy and knowing.

I was fascinated. She hadn't seemed at all like a woman who could tempt.

Suddenly, with a little cry and a not-quite-pleasant giggle, she produced from behind her back a pair of glossy dancing-shoes such as little girls in those days wore to tap-dancing classes, and waggled them seductively before me. They were Kelly green, and were too small for her hands, which she was using to make them dance soundlessly on the air. Uncertain how to react, I smiled, and Mrs. Chard fell to her knees.

She set the Kelly green shoes on the linoleum, where they sat empty and flat; then shuffling forward, she lifted me up, set me on the piano stool, and while I watched in a trancelike state of pure astonishment, she removed my good brown shoes, took up the Kelly greens, and forced my left foot—was she mad?—into the right one and my right into the even tighter left. Then she rose up, breathy with emotion, and set me down. I stood for what seemed ages among the bone china and maidenhair in an agony of humiliation, but unable, despite every encouragement, to make the shoes take flight and release their magic syncopations.

I refused to cry. Boys do not. But Mrs. Chard did. She hugged and kissed me and called me her darling, while I quailed in terror at so much emotion that both did and did not involve me; then quietened at last to heaving sobs, she fell to her knees again, snatched the shoes off, and left me to resume my own.

After our fit of shared passion she seemed unwilling to face me. When she did she was as cool as a schoolmistress. She stood watching me sweat over the laces, fixing me with a look of such plain hostility that I thought she might at any moment reach for a strap. The tap-shoes had disappeared, and it was clear to me that if I were ever to mention them, here or elsewhere, she would call me a liar and deny they had ever been.

Of course all my mother's predictions, in Uncle Jake's case, came true. He did go to gaol, though only for a month, and as he got older his charm wore off and the flash suits lost their style. The days of Cagney and George Raft gave way to years of tight-lipped patriotism—to austerity, khaki. The Americans arrived and stole the more stunning girls. Uncle Jake was out of the race. Something had snapped in him. He had bluffed his way out of too many poker-hands, put his shirt on too many losers. He began to be a loser himself, and from being a bad example in one decade became inevitably a good one in the next—the model, pathetically threadbare and unshaven, in a soiled singlet and pants, of what not to be. I came to dread his attempts to engage my ear and explain himself. His rambling account of past triumphs and recent schemes that for one reason or another had gone bung ended always in the same way, a lapse into uneasy silence, then the lame formula: "If you foller me meanings." I was growing up. I resented his assumption of an understanding between us and the belief that I was fated somehow to be his interpreter and heir.

"Poor ol' Jake," my father would sigh, recalling the boy he had grown up with, who had so far outshone him in every sort of daring. He would every now and then slip him a couple of notes, and with his usual shyness of emotion say, "No mate—it's a loan, I'm keeping tag. You can pay me when your ship comes in."

My mother had softened by then. She could afford to. So far as she knew I had escaped contagion. "Poor ol' Jake," she agreed, and might have felt some regret at her own timidity before the Chances.

So it was Uncle Jake who came to spend his days in the third bedroom of our house, and as he grew more pathetic, as meek as the milk puddings she made because it was the only thing he could keep down, my mother grew fond of him. She nursed him like a baby at the end. It's odd how these things turn out.

A Change of Scene

1

HAVING COME like so many others for the ruins, they had
been surprised to discover, only three kilometres away, this
other survival from the past: a big old-fashioned hotel.

Built in florid neo-baroque, it dated from a period before the
Great War when the site was much frequented by Germans, since
it had figured, somewhat romanticised, in a passage of Hof-
mannsthal. The fashion was long past and the place had fallen into
disrepair. One corridor of the main building led to double doors
that were crudely boarded up, with warnings in four languages
that it was dangerous to go on, and the ruined side-wings were
given over to goats. Most tourists these days went to the Club
Méditerranée on the other side of the bay. But the hotel still
maintained a little bathing establishment on the beach (an attendant went down each morning and swept it with a rake) and there
was still, on a cliff-top above zig-zag terraces, a pergolated
belvedere filled with potted begonias, geraniums, and dwarf citrus—an oasis of cool green that the island itself, at this time of
year and this late in its history, no longer aspired to. So Alec, who
had a professional interest, thought of the ruins as being what
kept them here, and for Jason, who was five, it was the beach; but
Sylvia, who quite liked ruins and wasn't at all averse to lying half-
buried in sand while Jason paddled and Alec, at the entrance to
the cabin, tapped away at his typewriter, had settled at first sight
for the hotel.

It reminded her, a bit creepily, of pre-war holidays with her parents up on the Baltic—a world that had long ceased to exist except in pockets like this. Half-lost in its high wide corridors, among rococo doors and bevelled gilt-framed mirrors, she almost expected—the past was so vividly present—to meet herself, aged four, in one of the elaborate dresses little girls wore in those days. Wandering on past unreadable numbers, she would come at last to a door that was familiar and would look in and find her grandmother, who was standing with her back to a window, holding in her left hand, so that the afternoon sun broke through it, a jar of homemade cherry syrup, and in her right a spoon. "Grandma," she would say, "the others are all sleeping. I came to you."

Her grandmother had died peacefully in Warsaw, the year the Germans came. But she was disturbed, re-entering that lost world, to discover how much of it had survived in her buried memory, and how many details came back now with an acid sweetness, like a drop of cherry syrup. For the first time since she was a child she had dreams in a language she hadn't spoken for thirty years—not even with her parents—and was surprised that she could find the words. It surprised her too that Europe—that dark side of her childhood—was so familiar, and so much like home.

She kept that to herself. Alec, she knew, would resent or be hurt by it. She had, after all, spent all but those first years in another place altogether, where her parents were settled and secure as they never could have been in Poland, and it was in that place, not in Europe, that she had grown up, discovered herself, and married.

Her parents were once again rich, middle-class people, living in an open-plan house on the North Shore and giving al fresco parties at a poolside barbecue. Her father served the well-done steaks with an air of finding this, like so much else in his life, delightful but unexpected. He had not, as a boy in Lvov, had T-bone steaks in mind, nor even a dress factory in Marrickville. These were accidents of fate. He accepted them, but felt he was living the life of an imposter. It added a touch of humourous irony to everything he did. It was her mother who had gone over completely to the New World. She wore her hair tinted a pale mauve, made cheesecake with passion-fruit, and played golf. As for Sylvia, she was simply an odd sort of local. She had had no sense of a foreign past till she came back here and found how European she might be.

Her mother, if she had known the full extent of it, would have found her interest in the hotel "morbid," meaning Jewish. And it was perverse of her (Alec certainly thought so) to prefer it to the more convenient cabins. The meals were bad, the waiters clumsy and morose; with other jobs in the village or bits of poor land to tend. The plumbing, which looked impressive, all marble and heavy bronze that left a green stain on the porcelain, did not provide water. Alec had no feeling for these ruins of forty years ago. His period was that of the palace, somewhere between eleven and seven hundred B.C., when the site had been inhabited by an unknown people, a client state of Egypt, whose language he was working on; a dark, death-obsessed people who had simply disappeared from the pages of recorded history, leaving behind them a few common artefacts, the fragments of a language, and this one city or fortified palace at the edge of the sea.

Standing for the first time on the bare terrace, which was no longer at the edge of the sea, and regarding the maze of open cellars, Alec had been overwhelmed. His eyes, roving over the level stones, were already recording the presence of what was buried here—a whole way of life, richly eventful and shaped by clear beliefs and rituals, that rose grandly for him out of low brick walls and a few precious scratches that were the symbols for corn, salt, water, oil, and the names, or attributes, of gods.

What her eyes roamed over, detecting also what was buried, was Alec's face; reconstructing from what passed over features she thought she knew absolutely, in light and in darkness, a language of feeling that he, perhaps, had only just become aware of. She had never, she felt, come so close to what, outside their life together, most deeply touched and defined him. It was work that gave his life its high seriousness and sense of purpose, but he had never managed to make it real for her. When he talked of it he grew excited, but the talk was dull. Now, in the breathlessness of their climb into the hush of sunset, with the narrow plain below utterly flat and parched and the great blaze of the sea beyond, with the child dragging at her arm and the earth under their feet thick with pine-needles the colour of rusty blood, and the shells of insects that had taken their voice elsewhere—in the dense confusion of all this, she felt suddenly that she understood and might be able to share with him now the excitement of it, and had looked up and found the hotel, just the outline of it. Jason's restlessness had delayed for a moment her discovery of what it was.

They had been travelling all day and had come up here when they were already tired, because Alec, in his enthusiasm, could not wait. Jason had grown bored with shifting about from one foot to another and wanted to see how high they were.

"Don't go near the edge," she told the boy.

He turned away to a row of corn- or oil-jars, big enough each one for a man to crawl into, that were sunk to the rim in stone, but they proved, when he peered in, to be less interesting than he had hoped. No genii, no thieves. Only a coolness, as of air that had got trapped there and had never seeped away.

"It's cold," he had said, stirring the invisible contents with his arm.

But when Alec began to explain, in words simple enough for the child to understand, what the jars had been used for and how the palace might once have looked, his attention wandered, though he did not interrupt.

Sylvia too had stopped listening. She went back to her own discovery, the big silhouette of what would turn out later to be the hotel.

It was the child's tone of wonder that lingered in her mind: "It's cold." She remembered it again when they entered the grand but shabby vestibule of the hotel and she felt the same shock of chill as when, to humour the child, she had leaned down and dipped her arm into a jar.

"What is it?" Jason had asked.

"It's nothing."

He made a mouth, unconvinced, and had continued to squat there on his heels at the rim.

. . .

ALEC HAD grown up on a wheat farm west of Gulgong. Learning early what it is to face bad seasons when a whole crop can fail, or bushfires, or floods, he had developed a native toughness that would, Sylvia saw from his father, last right through into old age. Failure for Alec meant a failure of nerve. This uncompromising view made him hard on occasion, but was the source as well of his golden rightness. Somewhere at the centre of him was a space where honour, fairness, hard work, the belief in a man's responsibility at least for his own fate—and also, it seemed, the possibility of happiness—were given free range; and at the clear centre of all there was a rock, unmoulded as yet, that might one day be an altar. Alec's deficiencies were on the side of strength, and it delighted her that Jason reproduced his father's deep blue eyes and plain sense of having a place in the world. She herself was too rawboned and intense. People called her beautiful. If she was, it was in a way that had too much darkness in it, a mysterious rather than an open beauty. Through Jason she had turned what was leaden in herself to purest gold.

It was an added delight to discover in the child some openness to the flow of things that was also hers, and which allowed them, on occasion, to speak without speaking; as when he had said, up there on the terrace, "It's cold," at the very moment when a breath from the far-off pile that she didn't yet know was a hotel, had touched her with a premonitory chill.

They were close, she and the child. And in the last months before they came away the child had moved into a similar closeness with her father. They were often to be found, when they went to visit, at the edge of the patio swimming pool, the old man reading to the boy, translating for him from what Alec called his "weirdo books," while Jason, in bathing slip and sneakers, nodded, swung his plump little legs, asked questions, and the old man, with his glasses on the end of his nose and the book resting open a moment on his belly, considered and found analogies.

After thirty years in the garment trade her father had gone back to his former life and become a scholar.

Before the war he had taught philosophy. A radical free-thinker in those days, he had lately, after turning his factory over to a talented nephew, gone right back, past his passion for Wittgenstein and the other idols of his youth, to what the arrogance of that time had made him blind to—the rabbinical texts of his fathers. The dispute, for example, between Rabbi Isserles of Cracow and Rabbi Luria of Ostrov that had decided at Posen, in the presence of the exorcist Joel Baal-Shem, miracle-worker of Zamoshel, that demons have no right over moveable property and may not legally haunt the houses of men.

Her father's room in their ranch-style house at St. Ives was crowded with obscure volumes in Hebrew; and even at this distance from the Polish sixteenth century, and the lost communities of his homeland, the questions remained alive in his head and had come alive, in diminutive form, in the boy's. It was odd to see them out there in the hard sunlight of her mother's cactus garden, talking ghosts.

Her mother made faces. Mediaeval nonsense! Alec listened, in a scholarly sort of way, and was engaged at first, but found the whole business in the end both dotty and sinister, especially as it touched the child. He had never understood his father-in-law, and worried sometimes that Sylvia, who was very like him, might have qualities that would emerge in time and elude him. And now Jason! Was the old man serious, or was this just another of his playful jokes?

"No," Sylvia told him as they drove back in the dark, with Jason sleeping happily on the back seat, "it's none of the things you think it is. He's getting ready to die, that's all."

Alec restrained a gesture of impatience. It was just this sort of talk, this light and brutal way of dealing with things it might be better not to mention, that made him wonder at times if he really knew her.

"Well I hope he isn't scaring Jason, that's all."

"Oh fairy tales, ghost stories—that's not what frightens people."
"Isn't it?" said Alec. "Isn't it?"

2

THEY SOON got to know the hotel's routine and the routine of
the village, and between the two established their own. After a
breakfast of coffee with condensed milk and bread and honey
they made their way to the beach: Alec to work, and between
shifts at the typewriter to explore the coastline with a snorkel,
Sylvia and the child to laze in sand or water.

The breakfast was awful. Alec had tried to make the younger of
the two waiters, who served them in the morning, see that the child
at least needed fresh milk. For some reason there wasn't any, though
they learned from people at the beach that the Cabins got it.

"No," the younger waiter told them, "no milk." Because there
were no cows, and the goat's milk was for yogurt.

They had the same conversation every morning, and the waiter,
who was otherwise slack, had begun to serve up the tinned milk
with a flourish that in Alec's eye suggested insolence. As if to say:
There! You may be Americans (which they weren't), *and rich* (which
they weren't either) *but fresh milk cannot be had. Not on this island.*

The younger waiter, according to the manager, was a Communist. That explained everything. He shook his head and made a
clucking sound. But the older waiter, who served them at lunch, a
plump, grey-headed man, rather grubby, who was very polite and
very nice with the child, was also a Communist, so it explained
nothing. The older waiter also assured them there was no milk. He
did it regretfully, but the result was the same.

Between them these two waiters did all the work of the hotel.
Wandering about in the afternoon in the deserted corridors, when
she ought to have been taking a siesta, Sylvia had come upon the
younger one having a quiet smoke on a windowsill. He was barefoot, wearing a dirty singlet and rolled trousers. There was a pail
of water and a mop beside him. Dirty water was slopped all over

the floor. But what most struck her was the unnatural, fishlike whiteness of his flesh—shoulders, arms, neck—as he acknowledged her presence with a nod but without at all returning her smile.

Impossible, she had thought, to guess how old he might be. Twenty-eight or thirty he looked, but might be younger. There were deep furrows in his cheeks, and he had already lost some teeth.

He didn't seem at all disconcerted. She had, he made it clear, wandered into *his* territory. Blowing smoke over his cupped hand (why did they smoke that way?) and dangling his bare feet, he gave her one of those frank, openly sexual looks that cancel all boundaries but the original one; and then, to check a gesture that might have made him vulnerable (it did—she had immediately thought, how boyish!) he glared at her, with the look of a waiter, or peasant, for a foreign tourist. His look had in it all the contempt of a man who knows where he belongs, and whose hands are cracked with labour on his own land, for a woman who has come sightseeing because she belongs nowhere.

Except, she had wanted to protest, it isn't like that at all. It is true I have no real place (and she surprised herself by acknowledging it), but I know what it is to have lost one. That place is gone and all its people are ghosts. I am one of them—a four-year-old in a pink dress with ribbons. I am looking for my grandmother. Because all the others are sleeping . . .

She felt differently about the young waiter after that, but it made no odds. He was just as surly to them at breakfast, and just as nasty to the child.

THE BAY, of which their beach was only an arc, was also used by fishermen, who drew their boats up on a concrete ramp beside the village, but also by the guests from the Cabins and by a colony of hippies who camped in caves at the wilder end.

The hippies were unpopular with the village people. The manager of the hotel told Sylvia that they were dirty and diseased, but they looked healthy enough, and once, in the early afternoon, when most of the tourists had gone in to sleep behind closed shutters, she had seen one of them, a bearded blond youth with a baby on his hip, going up and down the beach collecting litter. They were Germans or Dutch or Scandinavians. They did things with wire, which they sold to the tourists, and traded with the fishermen for octopus or chunks of tuna.

All day the fishermen worked beside their boats on the ramp: mending nets and hanging them from slender poles to dry, or cleaning fish, or dragging octopus up and down on the quayside to remove the slime. They were old men mostly, with hard feet, all the toes stubbed and blackened, and round little eyes. Sometimes, when the child was bored with playing alone in the wet sand, he would wander up the beach and watch them at their work. The quick knives and the grey-blue guts tumbling into the shallows were a puzzle to him, for whom fish were either bright objects that his father showed him when they went out with the snorkel or frozen fingers. The octopus too. He had seen lights on the water at night and his father had explained how the fishermen were using lamps to attract the creatures, who would swarm to the light and could be jerked into the dinghy with a hook. Now he crinkled his nose to see one of the fishermen whip a live octopus out of the bottom of the boat and turning it quickly inside-out, bite into the raw, writhing thing so that its tentacles flopped. He looked at Sylvia and made a mouth. These were the same octopus that, dried in the sun, they would be eating at tomorrow's lunch.

BECAUSE THE BAY opened westward, and the afternoon sun was stunning, their beach routine was limited to the hours before noon.

Quite early, usually just before seven, the young waiter went down and raised the striped canvas awning in front of their beach cabin and raked a few square metres of sand.

Then at nine a sailor came on duty on the little heap of rocks above the beach where a flagpole was set, and all morning he would stand there in his coarse white trousers and boots, with his cap tilted forward and strapped under his chin, watching for sharks. It was always the same boy, a cadet from the Training College round the point. The child had struck up a kind of friendship with him and for nearly an hour sometimes he would "talk" to the sailor, squatting at his feet while the sailor laughed and did tricks with a bit of cord. Once, when Jason failed to return and couldn't hear her calling, Sylvia had scrambled up the rockface to fetch him, and the sailor, who had been resting on his heel for a bit, had immediately sprung to his feet looking scared.

He was a stocky boy of eighteen or nineteen, sunburned almost to blackness and with very white teeth. She had tried to reassure him that she had no intention of reporting his slackness; but once he had snapped back to attention and then stood easy, he looked right through her. Jason turned on the way down and waved, but the sailor stood very straight against the sky with his trousers flapping and his eyes fixed on the sea, which was milky and thick with sunlight, lifting and lapsing in a smooth unbroken swell, and with no sign of a fin.

After lunch they slept. It was hot outside but cool behind drawn shutters. Then about five thirty Alec would get up, climb the three kilometres to the palace, and sit alone there on the open terrace to watch the sunset. The facts he was sifting at the typewriter would resolve themselves then as luminous dust; or would spring up alive out of the deepening landscape in the cry of cicadas, whose generations beyond counting might go back here to beginnings. They were dug in under stones, or they clung with shrill tenacity to the bark of pines. It was another language. Immemorial. Indecipherable.

Sylvia did not accompany him on these afternoon excursions, they were Alec's alone. They belonged to some private need. Stretched out in the darkened room she would imagine him up there, sitting in his shirtsleeves in the gathering dusk, the gathering voices, exploring a melancholy he had only just begun to perceive in himself and of which he had still not grasped the depths. He came back, after the long dusty walk, with something about him that was raw and in need of healing. No longer a man of thirty-seven—clever, competent, to whom she had been married now for eleven years—but a stranger at the edge of youth, who had discovered, tremblingly, in a moment of solitude up there, the power of dark.

It was the place. Or now, and here, some aspect of himself that he had just caught sight of. Making love on the high bed, with the curtains beginning to stir against the shutters and the smell of sweat and pine-needles on him, she was drawn into some new dimension of his still mysterious being, and of her own. Something he had felt or touched up there, or which had touched him—his own ghost perhaps, an interior coolness—had brought him closer to her than ever before.

When it was quite dark at last, a deep blue dark, they walked down to one of the quayside restaurants.

There was no traffic on the promenade that ran along beside the water, and between seven and eight thirty the whole town passed up and down between one headland and the other: family groups, lines of girls with their arms linked, boisterous youths in couples or in loose threes and fours, sailors from the Naval College, the occasional policeman. Quite small children, neatly dressed, played about among rope coils at the water's edge or fell asleep over the scraps of meals. Lights swung in the breeze, casting queer shadows. There were snatches of music. Till nearly one o'clock the little port that was deserted by day quite hummed with activity.

When they came down on the first night, and found the crowds sweeping past under the lights, the child had given a whoop of excitement and cried: "Manifestazione!" It was, along with "gelato," his only word of Italian.

Almost every day while they were in Italy, there had been a demonstration of one sort or another: hospital workers one day, then students, bank clerks, bus-drivers, even high-school kids and their teachers. Always with placards, loud-hailers, red flags, and masses of grim-faced police. "Manifestazione," Jason had learned to shout the moment they rounded a corner and found even a modest gathering; though it wasn't always true. Sometimes it was just a street market, or an assembly of men in business suits arguing about football or deciding the price of unseen commodities— olives or sheep or wheat. The child was much taken by the flags and the chanting in a language that made no sense. It was all play-like and good-humoured.

But once, overtaken by a fast-moving crowd running through from one street to the next, she had felt herself flicked by the edge of a wave that further back, or just ahead, might have the power to break her grip on the child's hand, or to sweep her off her feet or toss them violently in the air. It was only a passing vision, but she had felt things stir in her that she had long forgotten, and was disproportionately scared.

Here, however, the crowd was just a village population taking a stroll along the quay or gathering at café tables to drink ouzo and nibble side plates of miniature snails; and later, when the breeze came, to watch outdoor movies in the square behind the church.

It was pleasant to sit out by the water, to have the child along, and to watch the crowd stroll back and forth—the same faces night after night. They ate lobster, choosing one of the big, bluish-grey creatures that crawled against the side of a tank, and slices of pink watermelon. If the child fell asleep Alec carried him home on his shoulder, all the way up the steps and along the zig-zag terraces under the moon.

3

ONE NIGHT, the fifth or sixth of their stay, instead of the usual movie there was a puppet-show.

Jason was delighted. They pushed their way in at the side of the crowd and Alec lifted the child on to his shoulders so that he had a good view over the heads of fishermen, sailors from the College, and the usual assembly of village youths and girls, who stood about licking ice-creams and spitting the shells of pumpkin-seeds.

The little wooden stage was gaudy; blue and gold. In front of it the youngest children squatted in rows, alternately round-eyed

and stilled or squealing with delight or terror as a figure in baggy
trousers, with a moustache and dagger, strutted up and down on
the narrow sill—blustering, bragging, roaring abuse and lunging
ineffectually at invisible tormentors, who came at him from every
side. The play was both sinister and comic, the moustachioed figure both hero and buffoon. It was all very lively. Big overhead
lights threw shadows on the blank wall of the church: pine
branches, all needles, and once, swelling abruptly out of nowhere,
a giant, as one of the village showoffs swayed aloft. For a moment
the children's eyes were diverted by his antics. They cheered and
laughed and, leaping up, tried to make their own shadows appear.

The marionette was not to be outdone. Improvising now, he
included the insolent spectator in his abuse. The children subsided. There was more laughter and some catcalling, and when
the foolish youth rose again he was hauled down, but was
replaced, almost at once by another, whose voice drowned the
puppet's violent squawking—then by a third. There was a regular
commotion.

The little stage-man, maddened beyond endurance, raged up
and down waving his dagger and the whole stage shook; over on
the wings there was the sound of argument, and a sudden scuffling.

They could see very little of this from where they were pressed
in hard against the wall, but the crowd between them and the far-
off disturbance began to be mobile. It surged. Suddenly things
were out of hand. The children in front, who were being crowded
forward around the stage, took panic and began to wail for their
parents. There were shouts, screams, the sound of hard blows. In
less than a minute the whole square was in confusion and the
church wall now was alive with big, ugly shadows that merged in
waves of darkness, out of which heads emerged, fists poked up,
then more heads. Sylvia found herself separated from Alec by a
dozen heaving bodies that appeared to be pulled in different
directions and by opposing passions. She called out, but it was like
shouting against the sea. Alec and Jason were nowhere to be seen.

Meanwhile the stage, with its gaudy trappings, had been struck
away and the little blustering figure was gone. In its place an old

man in a singlet appeared, black-haired and toothless, his scrawny
body clenched with fury and his mouth a hole. He was screaming
without change of breath in the same doll-like voice as the puppet, a high-pitched squawking that he varied at times with grunts
and roars. He was inhabited now not only by the puppet's voice
but by its tormentors' as well, a pack of violent spirits of opposing
factions like the crowd, and was the vehicle first of one, then of
another. His thin shoulders wrenched and jerked as if he too was
being worked by strings. Sylvia had one clear sight of him before
she was picked up and carried, on a great new surging of the
crowd, towards the back wall of one of the quayside restaurants,
then down what must have been a corridor and on to the quay. In
the very last moment before she was free, she saw before her a
man covered with blood. Then dizzy from lack of breath, and
from the speed with which all this had occurred, she found herself
at the water's edge. There was air. There was the safe little bay.
And there too were Alec and the boy.

They were badly shaken, but not after all harmed, and in just a
few minutes the crowd had dispersed and the quayside was
restored to its usual order. A few young men stood about in small
groups, arguing or shaking their heads or gesticulating towards
the square, but the affair was clearly over. Waiters appeared. They
smiled, offering empty tables. People settled and gave orders.
They too decided that it might be best, for the child's sake, if they
simply behaved as usual. They ordered and ate.

They saw the young sailor who watched for sharks. He and a
friend from the village were with a group of girls, and Jason was
delighted when the boy recognised them and gave a smart, mock-
formal salute. All the girls laughed.

It was then that Sylvia remembered the man she had seen with
blood on him. It was the older waiter from the hotel.

"I don't think so," Alec said firmly. "You just thought it was
because he's someone you know." He seemed anxious, in his cool,
down-to-earth way, not to involve them, even tangentially, in
what was a local affair. He frowned and shook his head: *not in front
of the boy.*

"No, I'm sure of it," she insisted. "Absolutely sure."

But next morning, at breakfast, there he was quite unharmed, waving them towards their usual table.

"I must have imagined it after all," Sylvia admitted to herself. And in the clear light of day, with the breakfast tables gleaming white and the eternal sea in the window frames, the events of the previous night did seem unreal.

There was talk about what had happened among the hotel people and some of the guests from the Cabins, but nothing was clear. It was part of a local feud about fishing rights, or it was polit-ical—the puppet-man was a known troublemaker from another village—or the whole thing had no point at all; it was one of those episodes that explode out of nowhere in the electric south, having no cause and therefore requiring no explanation, but gathering up into itself all sorts of hostilities—personal, political, some with their roots in nothing more than youthful high-spirits and the frustrations and closeness of village life at the end of a hot spell. Up on the terraces women were carding wool. Goats nibbled among the rocks, finding rubbery thistles in impossible places. The fishermen's nets, black, brown, umber, were stretched on poles in the sun; and the sea, as if suspended between the same slender uprights, rose smooth, dark, heavy, fading where it imper-ceptibly touched the sky into mother-of-pearl.

But today the hippies did not appear, and by afternoon the news was abroad that their caves had been raided. In the early hours, before it was light, they had been driven out of town and given a firm warning that they were not to return.

THE PORT that night was quiet. A wind had sprung up, and waves could be heard on the breakwater. The lights swayed over-head, casting uneasy shadows over the rough stones of the prome-nade and the faces of the few tourists who had chosen to eat. It wasn't cold, but the air was full of sharp little grits and the table-cloths had been damped to keep them from lifting. The locals knew when to come out and when not to. They were right.

The wind fell again overnight. Sylvia, waking briefly, heard it suddenly drop and the silence begin.

THE NEW DAY was sparklingly clear. There was just breeze enough, a gentle lapping of air, to make the waves gleam silver at the edge of the sand and to set the flag fluttering on its staff, high up on the cliff where the sailor, the same one, was watching for sharks. Jason went to talk to him after paying his usual visit to the fishermen.

Keeping her eye on the child as he made his round of the beach, Sylvia read a little, dozed off, and must for a moment have fallen asleep where Jason had half-buried her in the sand. She was startled into uneasy wakefulness by a hard, clear, cracking sound that she couldn't account for, and was still saying to herself, in the split-second of starting up, *Where am I? Where is Jason?*, when she caught, out of the heel of her eye, the white of his shorts where he was just making his way up the cliff face to his sailor; and in the same instant saw the sailor, above him, sag at the knees, clutching with both hands at the centre of himself, then hang for a long moment in mid-air and fall.

In a flash she was on her feet and stumbling to where the child, crouching on all fours, had come to a halt, and might have been preparing, since he couldn't have seen what had happened, to go on.

It was only afterwards, when she had caught him in her arms and they were huddled together under the ledge, that she recalled how her flight across the beach had been accompanied by a burst of machine-gun fire from the village. Now, from the direction of the Naval College, came an explosion that made the earth shake.

None of this, from the moment of her sitting up in the sand till the return of her senses to the full enormity of the thing, had lasted more than a minute by the clock, and she had difficulty at first in convincing herself that she was fully awake. Somewhere in the depths of herself she kept starting up in that flash of time before the sailor fell, remarking how hot it was, recording the flapping of a sheet of paper in Alec's abandoned typewriter—he must have gone snorkeling or into the village for a drink—and the emptiness of the dazzling sea. *Where am I? Where is Jason?* Then it would begin all over again. It was in going over it the second time, with the child already safe in her arms, that she began to tremble and had to cover her mouth not to cry out.

Suddenly two men dropped into the sand below them. They carried guns. Sylvia and the child, and two or three others who must have been in the water, were driven at gun-point towards the village. There was a lot of gesticulation, and some muttering that under the circumstances seemed hostile, but no actual violence.

They were pushed, silent and unprotesting, into the crowded square. Alec was already there. They moved quickly together, too shocked to do more than touch briefly and stand quietly side by side.

There were nearly a hundred people crushed in among the pine trees, about a third of them tourists. It was unnaturally quiet, save for the abrupt starting up of the cicadas with their deafening beat; then, as at a signal, their abrupt shutting off again. Men with guns were going through the crowd, choosing some and pushing them roughly away towards the quay; leaving others. Those who were left stared immediately ahead, seeing nothing.

One of the first to go was the young waiter from the hotel. As the crowd gave way a little to let him pass, he met Sylvia's eye, and she too looked quickly away; but would not forget his face with the deep vertical lines below the cheekbones and the steady gaze.

There was no trouble. At last about twenty men had been taken and a smaller number of women. The square was full of open spaces. Their group, and the other groups of tourists, looked terribly exposed. Among these dark strangers involved in whatever business they were about—women in coarse black dresses and shawls, men in dungarees—they stood barefoot in briefs and bikinis, showing too much flesh, as in some dream in which they had turned up for an important occasion without their clothes. It was this sense of being both there and not that made the thing for Sylvia so frighteningly unreal. They might have been invisible. She kept waiting to come awake, or waiting for someone else to come awake and release her from a dream that was not her own, which she had wandered into by mistake and in which she must play a watcher's part.

Now one of the gunmen was making an announcement. There was a pause. Then several of those who were left gave a faint cheer.

The foreigners, who had understood nothing of what the gunman said, huddled together in the centre of the square and saw only slowly that the episode was now over; they were free to go. They were of no concern to anyone here. They never had been. They were, in their odd nakedness, as incidental to what had taken place as the pine trees, the little painted ikon in its niche in the church wall, and all those other mute, unseeing objects before whom such scenes are played.

Alec took her arm and they went quickly down the alley to the quay. Groups of armed men were there, standing about in the sun. Most of them were young, and one, a schoolboy in shorts with a machine-gun in his hand, was being berated by a woman who must have been his mother. She launched a torrent of abuse at him, and then began slapping him about the head while he cringed and protested, hugging his machine-gun but making no attempt to protect himself or move away.

4

THERE HAD been a coup. One of the Germans informed them of it the moment they came into the lobby. He had heard it on his transistor. What they had seen was just the furthest ripple of it, way out at the edge. It had all, it seemed, been bloodless, or nearly so. The hotel manager, bland and smiling as ever, scouring his ear with an elongated fingernail, assured them there was nothing to worry about. A change of government, what was that? They would find everything—the beach, the village—just the same, only more orderly. It didn't concern them.

But one of the Swedes, who had something to do with the lega-
tion, had been advised from the capital to get out as soon as possible, and the news passed quickly to the rest. Later that night a
boat would call at a harbour further up the coast. The Club had
hired a bus and was taking its foreign guests to meet it, but could
not take the hotel people as well.

"What will we do?" Sylvia asked, sitting on the high bed in the
early afternoon, with the shutters drawn and the village, as far as
one could tell, sleeping quietly below. She was holding herself in.

"We must get that boat," Alec told her. They kept their voices
low so as not to alarm the child. "There won't be another one till
the end of the week."

She nodded. Alec would talk to the manager about a taxi.

She held on. She dared not think, or close her eyes even for a
moment, though she was very tired. If she did it would start
all over again. She would see the sailor standing white under the
flagpole; then he would cover his belly with his hands and begin to
fall. Carefully re-packing their cases, laying out shirts and sweaters
on the high bed, she never allowed herself to evaluate the day's
events by what she had seen. She clung instead to Alec's view, who
had seen nothing; and to the manager's, who insisted that except
for a change in the administration two hundred miles away things
were just as they had always been. The child, understanding that it
was serious, played one of his solemn games.

When she caught him looking at her once he turned away and
rolled his Dinky car over the worn carpet. "Hrummm, hrummm,"
he went. But quietly. He was being good.

Suddenly there was a burst of gunfire.

She rushed to the window, and pushing the child back thrust
her face up close to the slats; but only a corner of the village was
visible from here. The view was filled with the sea, which
remained utterly calm. When the second burst came, rather
longer than the first, she still couldn't tell whether it came from
the village or the Naval College or from the hills.

Each time, the rapid clatter was like an iron shutter coming
down. It would be so quick.

She turned away to the centre of the room, and almost immediately the door opened and Alec rushed in. He was flushed, and oddly, boyishly exhilarated. He had his typewriter under his arm.

"I'm all right," he said when he saw her face. "There's no firing in the village. It's back in the hills. I went to get my stuff."

There was something in him, some reckless pleasure in his own daring, that scared her. She looked at the blue Olivetti, the folder of notes, and felt for a moment like slapping him, as that woman on the quay had slapped her schoolboy son—she was so angry, so affronted by whatever it was he had been up to out there, which had nothing to do with his typewriter and papers and had put them all at risk.

"Don't be upset," he told her sheepishly. "It was nothing. There was no danger." But his own state of excitement denied it. The danger was in him.

THE TAXI, an old grey Mercedes, did not arrive till nearly eight. Loaded at last with their luggage it bumped its way into the village.

The scene there was of utter confusion. The bus from the Club, which should have left an hour before, was halted at the side of the road and was being searched. Suitcases were strewn about all over the pavements, some of them open and spilling their contents, others, it seemed, broken or slashed. One of the Club guests had been badly beaten. He was wandering up the middle of the road with blood on his face and a pair of bent spectacles dangling from his ear, plaintively complaining. A woman with grey hair was screaming and being pushed about by two other women and a man—other tourists.

"Oh my God," Alec said, but Sylvia said nothing. When a boy with a machine-gun appeared they got out quietly and stood at the side of the car, trying not to see what was going on further up the road, as if their situation was entirely different. Their suitcases were opened, their passports examined.

The two gunmen seemed undangerous. One of them laid his hand affectionately on the child's head. Sylvia tried not to scream.

At last they were told to get back into the car, given their passports, smiled at and sent on their way. The pretence of normality was terrifying. They turned away from the village and up the dusty track that Alec had walked each evening to the palace. Thistles poked up in the moonlight, all silver barbs. Dust smoked among sharp stones. Sylvia sank back into the depths of the car and closed her eyes. It was almost over. For the first time in hours she felt her body relax in a sigh.

It was perhaps that same sense of relaxation and relief, an assurance that they had passed the last obstacle, that made Alec reckless again.

"Stop a minute," he told the driver.

They had come to the top of the ridge. The palace, on its high terrace, lay sixty or seventy metres away across a shallow gully.

"What is it?" Sylvia shouted, springing suddenly awake. The car had turned, gone on a little, and stopped.

"No, nothing," he said. "I just wanted a last look."

"Alec—" she began as their headlamps flooded the valley. But before she could say more the lights cut, the driver backed, turned, swung sharply on to the road and they were roaring away at a terrible speed into moonless dark.

The few seconds of sudden illumination had been just enough to leave suspended back there—over the hastily covered bodies, with dust already stripping from them to reveal a cheek, a foot, the line of a rising knee—her long, unuttered cry.

She gasped and took the breath back into her. Jason, half-turned in the seat, was peering out of the back window. She dared not look at Alec.

The car took them fast round bend after bend of the high cliff road, bringing sickening views of the sea tumbling white a hundred feet below in a series of abrupt turns that took all the driver's attention and flung them about so violently in the back of the car that she and Jason had to cling to one another to stay upright. At last, still dizzy with flight, they sank down rapidly to sea level. The driver threw open the door of the car, tumbled out their luggage, and was gone before Alec had even produced the money to pay.

"Alec—" she began.

"No," he said, "not now. Later."

There was no harbour, just a narrow stretch of shingle and a concrete mole. The crowd they found themselves among was packed in so close under the cliff that there was barely room to move. A stiff breeze was blowing and the breakers sent spray over their heads, each wave, as it broke on the concrete slipway, accompanied by a great cry from the crowd, a salty breath. They were drenched, cold, miserable. More taxis arrived. Then the bus. At last, after what seemed hours, a light appeared far out in the blackness and the ship came in, so high out of the water that it bounced on the raging surface like a cork.

"We're almost there," Alec said, "we're almost there," repeating the phrase from time to time as if there were some sort of magic in it.

The ship stood so high out of the water that they had to go in through a tunnel in the stern that was meant for motor vehicles. They jammed into the cavernous darkness, driven from behind by the pressure of a hundred bodies with their individual weight of panic, pushed in hard against suitcases, wooden crates, hastily tied brown parcels, wire baskets filled with demented animals that squealed and stank. Coming suddenly from the cold outside into the closed space, whose sides resounded with the din of voices and strange animal cries, was like going deep into a nightmare from which Sylvia felt she would never drag herself alive. The huge chamber steamed. She couldn't breathe. And all through it she was in terror of losing her grip on the child's hand, while in another part of her mind she kept telling herself: I should release him. I should let him go. Why drag *him* into this?

At last it was over. They were huddled together in a narrow place on the open deck, packed in among others, still cold, and wetter than ever now as the ship plunged and shuddered and the fine spray flew over them, but safely away. The island sank in the weltering dark.

"I don't think he saw, do you?" Alec whispered. He glanced at her briefly, then away. "I mean, it was all so quick."

He didn't really want her to reply. He was stroking the boy's soft hair where he lay curled against her. The child was sleeping. He cupped the blond head with his hand, and asked her to confirm that darkness stopped there at the back of it, where flesh puckered between bony knuckles, and that the child was unharmed. It was himself he was protecting. She saw that. And when she did not deny his view, he leaned forward across the child's body and pressed his lips, very gently, to her cheek.

Their heads made the apex of an unsteady triangle where they leaned together, all three, and slept. Huddled in among neighbours, strangers with their troubled dreams, they slept, while the ship rolled on into the dark.

In Trust

THERE IS to begin with the paraphernalia of daily living: all
those objects, knives, combs, coins, cups, razors, that are too
familiar, too worn and stained with use, a doorknob, a baby's
rattle, or too swiftly in passage from hand to mouth or hand to
hand to arouse more than casual interest. They are disposable,
and are mostly disposed of without thought. Tram tickets, match-
boxes, wooden serviette rings with a poker design of poinsettias,
buttonhooks, beermats, longlife torch batteries, the lids of Doul-
ton soup tureens, are carted off at last to a tip and become rubble,
the sub-stratum of cities, or are pulped and go to earth; unless, by
some quirk of circumstance, one or two examples are stranded so
far up the beach in a distant decade that they become collectors'
items, and then so rare and evocative as to be the only survivors of
their age.

So it is in the life of objects. They pass out of the hands of their
first owners into a tortoiseshell cabinet, and then, whole or in fragments it scarcely matters, onto the shelves of museums. Isolated
there, in the oddness of their being no longer common or repeat-
able, detached from their history and from the grime of use, they
enter a new dimension. A quality of uniqueness develops in them
and they glow with it as with the breath of a purer world—meaning only that we see them clearly now in the light of this one. An
oil-lamp, a fragment of cloth so fragile that we feel the very grains
and precious dust of its texture (the threads barely holding in their
warp and woof), a perfume flask, a set of taws, a strigil, come wobbling towards us, the only angels perhaps we shall ever meet,
though they bear no message but their own presence: *we are here.*

It is in a changed aspect of time that we recognise them, as if the substance of it—a denseness that prevented us from looking forward or too far back—had cleared at last. We see these objects and ourselves as co-existent, in the very moment of their first stepping out into their own being and in every instant now of their long pilgrimage towards us, in which they have gathered the fingerprints of their most casual users and the ghostly but still powerful presence of the lives they served.

None of our kind come to us down that long corridor. Only the things they made and made use of, which still somehow keep contact with them. We look through the cracked bowl to the lips of children. Our hand on an axe-handle fits into an ancient groove and we feel the jarring of tree trunk on bone. Narrowly avoiding through all their days the accidents that might have toppled them from a shelf, the flames, the temper tantrums, the odd carelessness of a user's hand, they are still with us. We stare and are amazed. Were they once, we ask ourselves, as undistinguished as the buttons on our jacket or a stick of roll-on deodorant? Our own utensils and artefacts take on significance for a moment in the light of the future. Small coins glow in our pockets. Our world too seems vividly, unbearably present, yet mysteriously far off.

Each decade a new class of objects comes into being as living itself creates new categories of use. After the centuries of the Bowl (plain or decorated with rice-grains, or with figures, some of them gods, in hieratic poses, or dancing or making love) come the centuries of the Wheel, the age of Moving-across-the-Surface-of-the-Earth, from the ox-cart to the Silver Spur.

Later again, it is not only objects that survive and can be collected. Images too, the shadowy projection of objects, live on to haunt us with the immediacy of what was: figures alone or in groups, seated with a pug dog on their knees or stiffly upright in boating costume beside an oar; a pyramid of young men in flannel slacks and singlets holding the difficult pose for ever, blood swelling their necks as they strain upwards, set on physical perfection; three axemen beside a fence, leaning their rough heads together; the crowd round an air-balloon. Bearded, monocled, or in hoop skirts under parasols, and with all their flesh about them, they stare boldly out of a century of Smiles . . .

NOT LONG AGO, in the Museum of the Holocaust at Jerusalem, a middle-aged American, an insurance assessor, gave a sudden cry before one of the exhibits, threw out his arms, and while two maiden ladies from Hannibal, Missouri, looked on in helpless dismay, fell slowly to his knees—then, clutching his chest, even more slowly to the pavement at their feet. They tried to help him, but he did not get up again.

His tour companions had found him difficult, a loud, dull fellow. He had informed them that he made eighty-five thousand dollars a year, had a house at Fresno and a ranch near Santa Fe, was divorced from a woman called Emmeline who had cost him his balls in alimony, had a son who was on heroin, voted for Reagan, hated the Ruskies and that goddamned Ayatollah—the usual stuff. He wore a gold ring on one finger with a Hebrew letter (he was Jewish) and now, right in the middle of a nine-day tour of all the holy places, Christian, Jewish, and you-name-it, he was dead. He had, it seems, been confronted here with the only surviving record of his family, a group picture taken forty years before on the welcoming-ramp at Treblinka: his mother, father, two sisters, his six-year-old self, all with the white breath pouring out of their mouths in the January cold, heads turned in half-profile and slightly lifted towards the darkness just ahead, with beyond it (though this they could not have foreseen) a metre of roughened museum wall and the door into another country.

It was that vision of himself in the same dimension as the long dead that struck the man and struck him down: that rather than any recollection of the moment when the shot was taken. To see thus, from the safe distance of an American travel-group he had joined in Athens, Greece, that lost gathering to which he most truly belonged, and to see at last just where it was (despite the forty years' detour) that he was headed, had pushed him to the only step he could have taken—straight through the wall; and an error made nearly half a century ago, when an officer had breathed too lightly on a rubber stamp, was righted at last and a number restored to sequence. His cry was a homecoming.

His fellow-travellers on this later occasion, though shaken, went on to the rest of the experience: images, objects, carefully worked facts and descriptions. Only that one man went right to the centre, stepping through a wall that was in the end as insubstantial as breath, and on into flame.

GILLIAN VAUGHAN came back from her great-aunt Connie's with a present, a large and rather dog-eared envelope that she was clutching with fervour to her schoolgirl breast and which she refused at first to show.

Her mother was disconcerted, and not for the first time, by the child's intractable oddity. At just eleven Gillian was old-fashioned—that was the kind way of putting it, and stubbornly so; it was something she would not outgrow. It worried the mother, since her own nature was uncomplicated, easy (or so she thought), and she would have wished for the same qualities in her child. "Gillian darling," she protested now, but mildly, she was easily hurt, "what on earth?—I mean, what are we to *do* with them?"

"Nothing," the girl replied. "Look after them, that's all. I said I would and I will. You don't have to worry. I'll do it. They're Aunt Connie's most treasured possessions."

The envelope contained five x-ray photographs, and the curious child had chosen them.

Connie Hermiston, Great-aunt Connie, was eighty-seven. For the past year or more she had been passing on to her various nieces, and to those grand-nieces with whom she had contact, the family relics she was responsible for and which she wanted to leave now in younger hands.

She was not herself a collector, but she had, because of her extreme age, become the custodian over the years of other peoples' treasures—though treasures was too large a word for the jumble of bits and pieces she had stacked for safe-keeping in cupboards, drawers, and odd cartons and hat-boxes beside her wardrobe. Other peoples' sentiments or passions might be more accurate, as they attached themselves, mysteriously sometimes, to a kewpie doll on a black crook, from the Brisbane Exhibition of 1933, a fan made of peacock-feathers, several evening bags, pearl-handled cake-forks, a little lounge-suite made of iridescent china, medals, pushers-and-spoons, Coronation cups, christening dresses, handpainted birthday cards with celluloid lace edges. None of it had any real value, it was just family stuff; but each item had its pedigree, with the name attached (so far as Great-aunt Connie's memory could be trusted) of a Hermiston or a Cope or a Vaughan or a Glynn-Jones. Offered something out of this treasure house that should be hers, some piece of family history that she should be the one to carry forward, Gillian had chosen the x-rays. Only now, when she regarded them with her mother's eyes, did she see that her choice might be peculiar. She sighed, unhappy to discover that she had put herself, yet again, on the *odd* side of things.

"His name was Green," she said solemnly, as if the specific detail might make a difference. "John Winston Green." She meant the subject of the x-rays, which showed, in various degrees of ghostliness, in left and right profile but also frontally, the thorax and jaw of a young man.

Her mother's sister, Aunt Jude, who had been at the window, came up now, and leaning down she kissed the child on the top of the head, at the parting where her hair was drawn in pigtails.

Gillian looked up at her. Jude Hermiston smiled. She took the dusty package from her sister and examined it. "Let's look," she said, "shall we?"

She slipped the first x-ray out of the package, then one by one the rest.

She had seen them before. Years back, on visits to Aunt Connie's, she too had been allowed to take from their envelope the stiff, transparent sheets, and holding them to the light had seen him, this bit of him: John Winston Green, Aunt Connie's young man. Odd emotions stirred in her. They seemed her own, but were too deeply overlaid with what she had heard and caught breath of from Aunt Connie for her to be sure. Except that the emotions were powerful and real—a kind of astonished awe as before a common mystery.

The profile, its lovely line: where the base of the skull, so round you could feel it in the cup of your hand, swooped down to the neck, with the vertebrae, all ghostly grey, stacked delicately one above the other, almost pearly, and the Adam's apple a transparent bump. The left profile; then, minimally but perceptibly different, the right.

The Adam's apple: how touchingly present and youthful it was. You felt it in your own throat like a lump of apple, or like a difficult word. And the firm line upwards to the jaw. In the third and fourth image the head was turned sharply right—John Winston Green might have been giving the eyes-right salute to an unseen general; but the thorax appeared straight on and all the elements were changed; you saw the contained energy in the throat muscles, the strain of the tendons of the neck. The power and will of a whole being was there. You felt the squareness, the solidity of it all the way down to the footsoles, the stern discipline, held breath in the ribcage, the pushing upwards of the skull, the way gravity tugged, created weight (say eleven stone six) and held it to earth.

The neck seemed thick in the front views. The vertebrae in their pile like children's bricks were too squarely packed. But in profile you caught the delicacy of the thing, and it was this that touched and moved Jude now as it had moved her twenty years ago. The young man's Adam's apple rose in her throat. A word it was, that he had intended to speak but could not, because he had to hold his breath for the machine; a thought that had sparked in the skull, travelled at lightning speed down that luminous cord and got stuck in his throat. It was there, still visible.

John Winston Green, Aunt Connie's young man, had worked as a clerk in the Bank of Queensland. He was an oarsman as well, wrote poetry, and had died at Bullecourt in France, in 1917. The x-rays were Aunt Connie's last memento of him. All the rest, letters with poems in them, snapshots of occasions she still

remembered and could describe—picnics at Peel Island, tennis
parties, regattas—and all the small gifts he had sent her when he
was away on rowing trips in the south, and from Paris and Egypt,
had been consumed in a fire nearly thirty years ago. Since they
hadn't at first been worth keeping, the x-rays had been stored in a
garage and had alone survived. "They were the only thing he gave
me that lasted," Aunt Connie would say in her dry, no-nonsense
manner. "Isn't it odd? The most faithful representations of all they
were—in the end. Why shouldn't I love them best of all?" This,
Jude guessed, is what she must have told her grand-niece Gillian.
It is what she had told Jude.

There are natural lines of descent in a family. They are not
always the direct ones. It is proper that the objects people care for
should find their way down through them, from hand to hand and
from heart to heart. "She is my true mother," Jude Hermiston had
told herself once, "and this young man, of whom I have only this
brief, illuminating glimpse, is my true father. That lump in his
throat must be my name."

She restored the last of the x-rays to their package. She smiled,
and so did the child. And Harriet Vaughan, who was fond of her
sister, watched her daughter take the package and clasp it once
again, so solemnly, to her breast.

"What was the choice, darling?" she asked, though of course it
could not matter.

"Oh, spoons," the child told her lightly, "that belonged to
Grandma. Moya Cope got them. And a little case for jewels."

Harriet looked again at the ancient envelope the child had hold
of and was resigned: not to the entrance of these odd relics among
them, but to her daughter, this child who had come to her, she
thought, like a stranger, having no likeness she could discover
either to Eric or to herself, an utterly dear and separate being
whose very difficulty she loved.

"You don't mind, Mummy, do you? I mean—I know the spoons
were more *valuable*."

"Of course I don't," her mother told her, and leaned down to
kiss the child. "You funny bunny! Of course I don't."

A Traveller's Tale

1

THERE IS A POINT in the northern part of the state, or rather, a line that runs waveringly across it, where the vegetation changes within minutes. A cataclysmic second a million or more years back has pushed two land masses violently together, the one open savannah country with rocky outcrops and forests of blue-grey feathery gums, the other sub-tropical scrub. You arrive at the crest of a ridge and a whole new landscape swings into view. Hoop-pines and bunyas command the skyline. There are palm-trees, banana plantations. Leisurely broad rivers that seem always in flood go rolling seaward between stands of plumed and scented cane. It is as if you had dozed off at the wheel a moment and woken a whole day further on.

Poor white country. Little makeshift settlements, their tin roofs extinguished with paint or still rawly flashing, huddle round a weatherboard spire. Spindly windmills stir the air. There are water tanks in the yards, half-smothered under bougainvillea; sheds painted a rusty blood-colour, all their timbers awry but the old nails strongly holding, slide sideways at an alarming angle; and everywhere, scattered about on burnt-off slopes and in naked paddocks, the parts of Holdens, Chevvies, Vanguards, Pontiacs, and the engines of heavy transports, spring up like bits of indus-trial sculpture or the remains of highway accidents awaiting a poor man's resurrection. A tin lizzie only recently taken off the road suddenly explodes and takes wing as half a dozen chooks come squarking and flapping from the sprung interior.

Nothing is ever finished here, but nothing is done with either. Everything is in process of being dismantled, reconstructed, recycled, and turned by the spirit of improvisation into something else. A place of transformations.

At one point on the highway, surprisingly balanced above ground and about the same length as the Siamese Royal Barge, is the Big Banana, a representation of that fruit in garish yellow plaster. Two hundred miles further on and you come to the Big Pineapple, also in plaster, and with a gallery under the crown for viewing the surrounding hills. Between the two you are in another country. Men work in shorts in the fields and are of one colour with the earth, a fiery brick-red. Kids go barefoot, moving off the track on to the tufted bank with a studied slowness, as if they had heard somewhere that there is a fortune to be made by getting struck. Little girls in faded frocks hang over gates, dispiritedly waving, or in bare yards sit dangling their legs from an elongated inner-tube that has been hoisted aloft and found new life as a swing.

Every significant happening here belongs to the past and was of a geological nature. A line of extinct volcanoes whose fires were dashed out several millennia back, leaving a heap of dark, cone-shaped clinkers, are the most striking components of the scene. Cooling as they have in odd shapes, they have ceased to be terrible and are merely curious. Even their names in the Aboriginal language, which were often crude but did at least speak up for the mysteries, have dwindled on the local tongue to mere unpronounceables, old body-jokes whose point, if there was one, has been lost in the commonness of use.

It is one of my duties as an emissary of the Arts to bring news of our national culture to this slow back-water. My name is Adrian Trisk, livewire and leprechaun; or more properly, Projects Officer with the Council for the Arts.

The routine is always the same. Advertisements are placed in the "Canefarmers' Gazette" or the "Parish Recorder" and the Shire Hall hired for say Tuesday night at seven thirty, with supper provided and no charge. I show slides of contemporary Australian painting and sometimes a film, using the projector that is housed, along with the paraphernalia for Sunday Mass, in a hutch at the back of the hall; or I lecture on the life and works of an Australian poet. Nothing rigorous. Usually there are no more than a dozen in the audience; sometimes, in bad weather or when my appearance coincides with a meeting of the Country Women's Association, just two or three. Most difficult of all are places like Karingai where the population is "mixed"—that is, part Australian, part Italian, part Aboriginal, part Indian; and worst of all is Karingai itself, where even the Indian population is split into sects that worship at rival temples. I make certain, so far as these things can be arranged, that towns like Karingai appear on my itinerary no more than once every two or three years. Bridging the gap is all very well, but there is a limit to what a man can do with the discovery poems of Douglas Stewart and a slide evening with William Dobell.

The culture business, it's a box of knives! I could show wounds. I have been at it now for half a lifetime: twenty years as an expatriate with the British Council in Sarawak, Georgetown, Abadan; a stint at a West African University; two years as tutor to the brother-in-law of a sheikh—I'm not altogether without experience. But at fifty-six I have no firm foot on the ladder. There are always the young, pouring out of the universities with their heads full of schemes for converting the masses; little blond geniuses, all charm and killer-instinct, looking for cover while they finish a novel; girls with a flair for doling out rejection-slips and serving coffee to visiting celebrities; streamlined lesbians who know *just* how to re-organise everything so that it *works*. I have enemies everywhere, and they have not scrupled to poison the ear of authority with insinuations that I am not what I claim to be: that my post at that flyblown university, for example, was not on the teaching side but in catering. Life is a constant struggle.

I meet it with energy. Boundless energy. Nothing disarms people so completely, I have discovered, as breathless enthusiasm. Hopping about on one foot, crowing, chuckling, slapping one's thigh, pinching people's elbows in an excess of delight at finding them alive, well, and just where they might be expected to be;

peppering the speech with absurd formulations like "*Aren't* we all having a marvellous time? *Isn't* this just what the doctor ordered?," or such patent insincerities as "Hello there, all you lovely, lovely people!"; above all buttering the ear with flattery, flattery so excessive that only the most hardened egotist could take it seriously and lesser men curl up with embarrassment—these are powerful weapons in the right hand, and immediately establish the user as a harmless crank, too clownlike, too scatty, too effusive and highly strung to be a master of calculation.

Well, it's one of the strategies. In fact I am full of good will and want only to be left alone to make my way and to enjoy a moment of late sunshine at the top of the tree, but to achieve that I must protect myself, and protecting myself means playing the buffoon and avoiding places like Karingai where for reasons quite beyond my control (like the fact that the wretched Indians have rival temples) I will be left presenting my Brett Whiteley extravaganza to the wife of the Methodist minister, a retired timbergetter who is rewriting the works of Henry Lawson, and the hapless two-year incumbent of the one-teacher school.

2

I HAD FINISHED MY LECTURE and was waiting for the minister's wife, C. of E. on this occasion, to lead me to supper. The coffee-urn and the trestle table laden with sausage rolls, anzacs, rainbow cake, date-loaf, and pavlova were waiting at the end of the hall, presided over by two large-bosomed ladies who had spent the whole of my talk in setting it up, its impressive abundance determined less by the expected size of the audience than by their own sense of what was due to the Arts—the Arts, out here, meaning Cookery, of which the higher forms are cake-decoration and the ornamental bottling of carrots. The platform lights had been removed, the extension lead and projector, like some image of local veneration, had been restored to its hutch.

"If y' don't mind, Mr. Trist, I'd appreciate a few words. You might 'ear somethin' t' yer advantage."

It was the legal phrase that startled me—I was used to the little confusion about my name.

The speaker was a diminutive woman of sixty-five or seventy, very battered looking, whom I had taken when she first came in, she was so dark-eyed and brown, for one of the Indians; except that she wore a hat, a crumpled straw with two roses pinned to the brim, and a pair of white gloves that suggested Anglo-Saxon formality, the effort a woman makes who has to see her lawyer about the terms of a separation, or a doctor for what might prove, if luck is against her, to be a fatal illness—occasions she would want, later, to remember and be dressed for.

She had made no pretence, I noticed, of following my lecture, though it is one of my finest and had been delivered with all my customary verve. "Arthur Boyd and the Mystic Bride" was not, it seems, her cup of tea. Easing off her shoes with a series of gasps and sighs that was itself very nearly mystical, and which she in no way attempted to hide, she had slumped deeper and deeper into the canvas chair, blinking her eyes at one moment, as if what she saw on a vivid slide alarmed her, then once more sinking from view; and had difficulty, when it was over, in getting back into her shoes. An inconsiderate woman, who astonished me now by announcing: "It's t' do with that article you writ on Alicia Vale."

Now there is such a paper. It is one of several on a wide range of topics—West Nigerian gold-weights, Renaissance scissors, house interiors in Muscat and Oman. My publications at least are indisputable and can be produced as proof positive of their own existence. It's a little *coup* it gives me great satisfaction to produce. But that my Vale monograph, which isn't entirely unknown to followers of the Diva, should have found its way to Karingai! And into the hands of this odd, ungrammatical woman!

"You've read it?" I said foolishly.

She ignored the question. "I can't talk 'ere, it isn't the right place. But I reckon you'll be interested in some information I got." She worked her mouth a little, having lost control for the moment of her teeth, which she must also have assumed for the occasion.

She snapped, got them fixed again, and went on. "And *things*. I got some 'v 'er things. 'Ere's me address. I've writ it on this bitta paper. I'll expecher round ten."

She thrust a page of ruled notepaper into my hand, said "Thanks"—once to me and again to the minister's wife—and was off.

"Who was *that?*" I asked, and stood staring at the floral back.

Mrs. Logan allowed her lips to form a superior smile. "Oh that, poor soul, was our Mrs. Judge. She's quite a character. Lives out near the Indians."

My first thought, I should admit, was that it was a trap. My passion for the Diva, my obsession we might as well call it, with her life, her records, her relics, is pretty well-known at the Council, and I have enemies who would be happy to see me discomforted.

As a matter of simple caution I pushed the scrap of paper into my breast pocket as if it were of no importance, rubbed my hands together in a gesture of exaggerated delight at the prospect of sausage rolls and pavlova (overdoing it as usual to the point where it declared itself to be quite plainly an act), and waited for Mrs. Logan to move. She did not. She was observing me with amused but dangerous detachment.

She was a tall young woman whose husband had hopes of being a bishop. She was bearing their period in the wilderness with a good grace but was impatient. It showed. Her words snapped, her fingers flew at things, the tendons in her neck were strained. Her intelligence, finding no object out here, had begun to spin away from her, and since she leaned so much towards it, had set her off balance. She was poised but unstill, and seemed quite capable, I thought, of taking an interest in me, and in the unfortunate Mrs. Judge, out of boredom, or because no larger opportunity offered itself for revealing how superior she was to the follies and passions of men.

"You mean to go?" she asked.

I tried to laugh it off.

"Oh well, it depends, doesn't it? On how the morrow feels. I mean, you never know, do you? Perhaps it will be a Mrs. Judge day."

She seemed to find this very comical. I did a little jig as if I too recognised the absurdity of the thing; and experienced a wave of nausea at my own impiety. The bishop's wife, no doubt, had other notions of what was holy.

But I had saved myself, that's what mattered, and looked on the three sausage rolls I forced down, and the two slices of pavlova, as a proper expiation, and a proper snub to my hostess, who had assumed that in the matter of pavlovas at least there would be a certain complicity between us. In fact I loathe pavlova; but this is a question of taste, not Taste, and I took two slices very willingly to make amends. It was only when I got outside at last, and felt the dense sub-tropical night about me, the restless palm leaves fretting and rising, the low stars, the beating of wings and bell-notes in distended throats, the heavy scent of decay that is also the sweet smell of change—it was only then that I let myself off the leash and felt my heart quicken with a sense that even the dreaded Karingai might be the site of a turn in my fortunes, some unique and unlooked-for revelation. A magic name had been spoken and Mrs. Judge's address was burning above my breast.

But of course I would go!

3

I FOUND THE HOUSE easily enough. One of five unpainted weather-boards on high stumps, it stood apart from the rest of the town on a narrow ridge. The other houses belonged to Indians. Plump dark children, the youngest of them naked, splashed about in mud-puddles in the front yards; chickens rushed out squawking; a lean dog tied to a fence post stood on its four legs and yowled. Morning-glory, running wild in every direction, hauled fences down till they were almost horizontal, swathed the trunks of palms, was piled feet deep above water tanks and outhouse roofs. The big purple blossoms were starred with moisture. From beneath came the faint hum of insects and the smell almost overpoweringly sweet, of rotting vegetation.

Climbing the wooden steps, which had long since lost their rails, I paused at the lattice door and prepared to knock.

The woman was there immediately. She must have been waiting in the shadows beyond. Darker than I remembered, she had, in the clear light of day, a driven look, as if she had been hungry for twenty and maybe thirty years for something that had hollowed her out from within and which the black eyes had slowly sunk towards. She wore the same blue floral, but it was beltless now, and her feet on the dry verandah boards were misshapen and bare.

"Come on in," she said, peering over my shoulder to make sure there was no one with me; then stood and smiled. "I reckoned you wouldn' let me down." She turned into the hallway with its worn linoleum. "Come on out t' the kitchen an' I'll make a cuppa."

Indicating a chair at the scrubbed-wood table, she used her forearm to push back mess—jam-tins, scraps of half-eaten toast, several dirty mugs; then filled a kettle, scooped tea from a tin with Japanese ladies in kimonos on each of its faces, and sat. Behind her, on the wood stove, the kettle began to hiss.

"As I was sayin'," she began, as if our conversation of the previous evening had never been interrupted, "I got information t' give, seein' as yer interested in 'er."

"Alicia Vale?"

She laughed. "Well I don't mean the Queen a' Sheba."

She glanced round the smoke-grimed kitchen, cleared a further space between us, as if she were preparing an area amid the chaos where large facts could be established, and with a new light in her eyes, thrust her hand out and opened her fist.

Coiled in her palm was an enamel bracelet of exquisite red and gold, in the form of a serpent. Beside it, two tiny Fabergé eggs.

She was delighted with my look of astonishment and gave a harsh, high-pitched laugh.

"There! You didn't expect that, didja? I thought that'd surprise you." She set the three pieces down and turned away to haul the kettle off the stove. "You oughta know that piece if you're an expert. She wore that in *Lakmé*. New York, nineteen o-five."

It looked even more extraordinary among the breakfast litter of the table than it might have done in the museum where it belonged: one of those elaborate pieces that were created for her first by Lalique and later by Tiffany—lilies, serpents, salamanders, birds of paradise, all in the blue-green or red-gold of the period and intended to be worn off-stage or on, tributes to the fact that her own plumed splendour was continuous with that of the creatures she played, and that these ornaments of her fantasy-life in Babylon or India belonged equally to the world she moved in at Deauville and Monte Carlo, at Karlsbad, Baden-Baden, Capri. The thing writhed. It flashed its tail and threw off sparks. It was solid metal and had survived. I turned it and read the signature.

"Oh, it's genuine alright," she told me, pouring tea. She gave a wry chuckle. "I took one look at you and I reckoned you'd be the one. I knew it right off. This one, I told meself—he'll believe, if on'y the bracelet. And he does! Here, young feller, drink yer tea."

She sipped noisily and watched me over the rim of her cup.

"Y'see," she said, suddenly serious, "I trustcher. I gotta trust someone and you're it. I've decided t' come out a' hiding."

She let this sink in.

"I s'pose you know she was back 'ere in o-six."

"O-eight," I corrected, glad at last to prove, after so many surprises, my expertise. "There was a tour in o-three and another in o-eight—*Lucrezia, Lucia, Semiramide, Adriana Lecouvreur.*" I had it all off pat.

"Yair," she said. "Well she was 'ere in o-six as well, that's what I'm tellin' yer. O-six."

I was in no position to argue. Nobody in fact knows where Vale was in nineteen hundred and six; the whole year is a blank. In o-five she was in San Francisco, New York, Brussels, London, Paris, and St. Petersburg. In o-seven in South Africa, Vienna, Budapest, Warsaw, Berlin, and was back in London again to close the season. But in o-six nothing. The theory is that she had a minor breakdown and was hiding out in the south of France. More romantic commentators suggest a trip to China in the company of a Crown Prince, or a time in Persia with an Armenian munitions manufacturer who later, it is true, bought her a house in Hampstead and her first motor. But no one, so far as I know, has mentioned Australia.

"She spent the time," the woman informed me without empha-
sis, though her little black eyes were as lively as jumping beans—
she was enjoying her moment of triumph—"in a suite in the Hotel
Australia in Melbourne. And that's where us twins were born, me
and a brother. I am Alicia Vale's daughter!"

She opened up like a fist and presented herself, as she had previously presented the bracelet; all without warning, a glittering
jewel. As if to say: "There! If you believed in that you should
believe in me. We're all of a piece."

She sat back sucking her gums and grinning, delighted at having played her little scene with so much skill, and at having, for a
second time, so convincingly set me back.

"You can put that down now," she told me, indicating the
bracelet. "We're talking about me."

I HAVE SPENT nearly twenty years following the career of that
extraordinary woman, through newspaper articles, reviews, pro-
grammes, opera house account-books (my little paper is a run-up
to what I hope may be a full biography), and had, even before I
made my first venture upon the documentary records, been spell-
bound for another twenty by the legend of her and by the thin,
pure voice (unhappily a mere ghost of itself) that comes to us
from the primitive recording-machines of the period.

She was still singing after the war—after 1918, that is—but
only small things: a Schubert lullaby, "Home Sweet Home." Such
is the magic of her art that even these become, in her rendering of
them, occasions of the most poignant beauty; as if the simple
melody of "Home Sweet Home" were being plucked out of the air
by an angel banished for ever from the forests of Ceylon or the
Gardens of Babylon, bringing with it, out of that lost world, only a
radiant and disembodied breath. As an adolescent I would listen
to those recordings with locked eyes; imagining from photographs
the exotic realm out of which it was climbing, in which a common
farmgirl from the South Coast had been transformed by her own
genius, and elaborate machines for making ground-fog, clouds

and columns that can dissolve before the eyes on a view of endless horizons, into a creature of mythical power and beauty, a princess with the gift of immortality or abrupt extinction in her, a bird of paradise, an avenging angel—though she might also on occasion, and without one's sensing the least disjunction, appear in the pages of an international scandal-sheet, where her notorious language and ordinary, not to say vulgar affairs, like the exploits of the gods in their earthly passages, were transfigured and redeemed by the glory that came trailing after.

A coruscating meteor. Given that a meteor, all light and sparkle as it pours across the heavens, is at centre stone. Nothing so convinces us of her ethereal majesty as the fact that she was also a hard-headed businesswoman, who swore like a navvy (and got away with it), drank three bottles of Guinness at breakfast, and was surrounded wherever she went by a motley circus of book-makers, card-sharps, stand-over men, and a whole chorus-line of pale young fellows with shoulders, who made her every entrance a spectacle. Onstage she was, as often as not, a queen disguised as a gipsy. Offstage she was the gipsy itself, demanding that she be treated as a queen.

In her later years, when she lived on the harbour at Kirribilli, she became a kind of native Gorgon. I have a photograph, taken at her seventieth birthday-celebration at Anthony Hordern's, where she is caught, very grand and baleful, among a group of admirers— all elderly, all male, and all looking strangely fossilized, as if she had just that moment turned her hooded eyes upon them. Yet the occasion itself is as innocent as a children's party. The little cakes in their silver dishes are made up to look like snails, frogs, piglets; there are jelly-moulds, and a huge, heart-shaped cake with a knife in it and a ring of hard-flamed miniature candles.

She had survived and would live to eighty. Not for her the tragic destiny of Phar Lap or Les Darcy, done to death, their proud hearts broken, by foreigners. They're a tougher breed than the men, these colonial girls: the Alicias, the Melbas, the Marjories, the Joans. They conquer the world and come home to die in the suburbs, in their own swan's-down beds . . . But to be told now,

after nearly half a century, that the catalogue is incomplete; that
to the collection of Riccio grotesques and Kaendler Meissen, the
gold Rolls-Royce, the Louis Seize commodes by Dubois and
Riesener, the Daum vases, the Tiffany lamps and jewels, the costumes in which she filled out with her own marvellous presence
courtesans, princesses, village girls afflicted with somnambulism,
we must add an unacknowledged child—real, human—and especially, after so long *this* child, "our Mrs. Judge," a weatherbeaten,
slatternly but oddly impressive woman at a grubby kitchen table
in Karingai, who has appeared at last to claim her place in the glittering tale and to demand, with an authority that might be a
shadow of the Diva's own, that I should stand up now and be the
first to acknowledge her! Is this how the great tests present themselves to us? At ten thirty in the morning, in a country kitchen, in
a place like Karingai?

The woman set herself before me. She dared me to believe and
take up her cause.

I WAS SPARED at the last moment by a footstep on the verandah.
A man appeared, a big man in wellingtons. He had the soft-footed,
respectful air of a visitor, but one who knew the place and was at
home. The woman turned to face him. She made no attempt to
hide the bracelet, or the fact that there existed between us a state
of high drama.

"This," she said, and might have been speaking to herself, "is
my husband George." She got up, turned away to the dresser, and
brought another cup.

The man looked abashed but came forward, extending a large
hand. He was a man of seventy or more, wide-shouldered and
strong, with a head of wiry grey hair and long hairs, also grey,
sprouting from between the buttons of his flannel shirt. He seated
himself at the table, and when the kettle was ready she poured tea.

"You've told 'im then," the man said. He seemed embarrassed
to be addressing her in another man's presence.

"Yes, I told 'im. Not the whole of it, but."

He nodded, sipped, gave me another sidelong glance. He was oddly defensive for so large a man. As if he saw in me a kind of power before which his strength would be of no account. Faced with whatever it was, he flinched, and his largeness, now that it had been dismissed, was like a burden to him. He seemed unhappy with his own shoulders and arms, handling the china cup with difficulty. But when the woman put her hand on his for a moment, and their eyes met, they seemed beyond any harm that I or anyone else might do them, inviolably contained in their own concern for one another. His hairy Adam's apple worked up and down. He fisted his cup and drained it.

"Well," he said, "I'll be gettin' back."

He got to his feet, and when he turned to go she called after him. "Don't worry, George. It's oright, you know."

He was framed for a moment in the light from the doorway.

Sunlight was streaming down the hallway behind.

"If you say so, Mother."

He gave me a curt nod.

"I'll be back at five."

She listened while he crossed the verandah and went on down the seven steps, and when she faced me again she had a look of command that I would not have predicted in so small a woman. She glowed; she rose to the heights of what she must have seen as her true self; and was imposing enough to convince me then that she might be just what she claimed to be, the daughter of one of the greatest performers of the age.

"Now," she said, "I'll tell you the whole story, and you will believe."

4

I SHOULD POINT OUT that the facts of the Diva's life, as I know from twenty years of attempting to follow her course from a South Coast dairy farm through half the capitals of the world, are so meagre as to be almost non-existent. A secretive woman, deeply suspicious of even her closest friends and advisers, she seems to have protected the truth about herself by spreading conflicting accounts of her parentage, her marriage, even of the place and date of her birth. It isn't that she lied exactly, any more than Bernhardt did. Rather, she allowed others to make suggestions, the wilder the better, and then herself added the flourishes. As the years wore on and she moved further from the source, the flourishes increased and predominated, grew more extravagantly baroque. The common truth, if it had been laid bare, would have had to be rejected. It no longer fitted her style.

In the early days, when she was just a prodigious voice that had appeared, almost miraculously it seemed, out of a far and empty land, she had let journalists tell people whatever they wanted to hear; to dream up previous lives for her that were appropriate to Odabella or Semiramis, since her own outlandish country was to her present admirers every bit as fantastic as theirs. So her father was said to be a nephew of Napoleon, who had settled in New South Wales in the Fifties and married a local heiress. Later her parents were *saltimbanques* in a travelling circus, Hungarian Jews, and she had been born on the Dunolly goldfields on the day the continent yielded up its most spectacular nugget, the "Welcome Stranger." Later again, when she was firmly established, she confessed (which again may not be true) that she came from a poor farming family near Bega and offered romantic views of herself wandering about the paddocks and singing as she brought in the cows. (A marvellously evocative image this: dusk in the green pastures above the surf, a barefoot girl sleep-walking through the gathering dusk as the first notes of that angelic voice touch the colonial air; to be heard, like some as yet undiscovered spirit of the landscape, by a stranger who pauses a moment on the road and wonders if he is dreaming, then shakes his head and goes on—her first obscure admirer, quite unaware of the grace he has been afforded.)

Evocative but unprovable. The versions of her past that are promulgated tend to mirror her current status. It is only late in life, when she had abandoned her more extravagant roles and become a household favourite, that the farmgirl appears.

Did she really marry at nineteen the keeper of a small-town hardware store, and pass bags of nails, and nuts and bolts and screws over the counter? What happened to the man? Why didn't he come forward in the days of her ascendancy to claim his bride? Did she pay him off? Did she hire bullies to scare him off? She was capable of it. Did he never realise that the great Vale and his sullen bride were one? When she makes her first appearance in the early Nineties she is in the company of an ageing tenor from an Italian touring group; but he too disappears and is just a name.

And in a way, of course, none of this matters. It is part of the legend that she exploded into the consciousness of an adoring public as a fully developed Voice, clothed in the jewels, the satin folds of a savage empress; that she came into existence as what she always endeavoured, after that, to remain: a dramatic illusion with no more past in the actual flesh than the characters she played. As well ask what Norma or Lucrezia Borgia were doing between seven and thirteen as imagine the Diva's childhood. Living legends are not born, brought up, schooled in this place or that. They burst upon us. They are spontaneously, mysteriously, inevitably, *there*.

It was always like that. Between seasons she simply disappeared; and though the rumours were many there were no facts.

Was she the mistress, the morganatic wife even, of the Comte de Paris? Did she marry and then abandon the Armenian munitions manufacturer? Her relationship with the court at St. Petersburg was close enough for her to have had access to some of its most exclusive circles; but whether this was based on her quite unprecedented success in the theatre there or on some more personal tie cannot be confirmed. She destroyed the letters she received and herself wrote none—a few surviving notes are very nearly illiterate. Even her fortune cannot be traced. Terrified of being stranded without funds, she opened bank accounts in false names in some thirty or forty cities from Pittsburgh to Nanking, a good many of them still undiscovered and still accumulating interest, and when she died left no will.

Whether she herself believed the stories that circulated about her or was satisfied simply to be what she had become, the Earthly

Angel, the Incomparable, la Vale, we shall never know. But there
had been a childhood—parents and a home; there must even have
been an original and quite ordinary name. She herself can't have
forgotten. But they were her secret. What image she turned to
when the costumes, the jewels, the bold lines of an Amelia or an
Elisabetta were laid aside—that is the greatest of her mysteries.
Who was she when she looked into her glass at five in the morning? Who was she in her sleep? (Imagine it, the Diva's sleep!)
Inside the gestures of a dozen great characterizations, murderous
queens and princesses, vengeful lovers, wronged maidens, and
other monsters, was a lost and secret child that only she could
have recognised, and it was that child, grown into a sixty-year-old
stranger, who came home at last and looks out at us, terrifying but
also perhaps terrified by her own strangeness, in the photographs;
a woman who has survived the life she created and is left now to
resume the earlier, ordinary self she sailed away from and has
never entirely outgrown.

So Mrs. Judge's story, improbable as it might be, was not irreconcilable with the known facts. No story could be. Nor was it too
wild to be believed. I listened in a dream. When she had finished,
and we heard the man's step on the verandah, it was already dark.
She gave a great sigh and leaned back, exhausted by the telling or
the living of it—her own life, and seemed so touched for a
moment with the grandeur and remoteness of tragedy, that I felt
that if I so much as addressed her she might disintegrate like a
being from another world. Better to get up and leave as one leaves
a theatre, with the illusion still glowingly intact.

"You haven' lit the lamp," the man said, looming in the doorway, surprised to find us in the dark.

She started then, and made a move.

"No, I'll do it," he said. "You sit and finish your talk."

"We're finished," she said, staring trancelike before her. "We're
almost finished."

He moved about, pumping and lighting the lamp, and by the
time he was done, and had set it on the table, she was once again
the small, tired woman who had begun her story all those hours

ago. She looked at her gnarled hands, then upwards and met his gaze. She gave a soft smile.

"Don't worry, I'm oright. I'll see about gettin' yer tea in a minute. There's some corned beef."

She got up heavily and went to the meat safe.

I declined her invitation to stay. The moment of communion between us had passed. The man's presence, and the sound of him washing now in a tin basin at the back, snuffling noisily as he splashed, put a kind of restraint upon her. She no longer belonged entirely to herself. She saw me out to the verandah steps.

It was still light outside. Palm-tops and bananas stood in silhouette against the sky and high overhead was a fast-moving cloud, a flock of what I took to be birds. It was the flying foxes, making their way from the rainforests further north to their feeding place on the other side of town. Millions of them. Having unfolded themselves out of the darkness under the boughs of trees, they were flying, now that the light was almost gone, in a dense and flickering cloud that might have been the coming of the dark itself. The sky was black with them.

On the top step of the verandah, set out like an offering, was a covered saucer, with beside it a frangipani; on the second step another. She leaned down and took them up, one in each hand, the rival offerings.

"My Indians," she said smiling, and stood holding them up for me to see. More visible proof. There was a moment's pause while she let it sink in. "So then," she said, "what will it mean?"

I didn't know. What could it mean, sixty years after the event, thirty years after the main character was dead?—No, that was wrong. *She* was the main character.

"I don't know," I told her, a little alarmed by the possibilities, and not only for her. "We'll have to see."

She nodded.

"You know," she said, "I'm trusting you with me life. 'is as well." She jerked her head towards the lighted hallway.

I went on down the steps.

"I wouldn' dawdle if I was you," she called after me, suddenly practical. "From the looks a' that sky I'd say we was in for a storm. It'll be a thumper."

5

THE WOMAN'S LIFE. Incredible. But the details of it demand to be believed, and so, now that I have looked into her eyes, does she. She has a kind of grandeur, our Mrs. Judge, and for all her lack of education, an intelligence that immediately imposes itself. But she *is* uneducated, and much of what she has told me, if it is not her own experience, can only have come to her through the most painstaking research. She has at her fingertips dates, cast-lists, the names of even the most obscure of the Diva's colleagues and friends. The local chemist, who knows all the history of Karingai, assures me that she has spent the whole of her life here, or the whole of his life anyway, and he is a man of fifty. She and her husband keep to themselves. They are visited only by her Indian neighbours and one or two related Indians from towns close by. For years now the other whites have avoided them. The rumour is that she is herself part-Indian and the man part-Aboriginal. After listening to her story I have come to the conclusion that the fairy-tale childhood she describes can only be her own.

Two of her memories especially impress me.

One is the story of her flight from St. Petersburg to the Polish border in 1917, when she would have been ten.

She and her brother had been taken in their earliest infancy to Russia and were brought up there on the fringes of the court, the offspring, officially unrecognised, of a Grand Duke; so that as well as being the daughter of the Diva she is also, by her own account, a cousin of the Romanov children murdered at Ekaterinburg, and for that reason, she believes, still on the Bolshevik murder list. It was to escape their local agents that she took refuge, fifty years ago, at Karingai.

Of that earlier period she remembers almost nothing till the night of their flight over the snow: herself, her twin, and two ladies of high rank from the palace, all packed into a single sleigh.

Winter light, more glowingly blue than daylight, held the domes of the city in a dreamlike stasis as they made their way, closely covered against detection, over the Neva bridges and through the roaring streets; among carts, horses, peasants with swaying bundles, torches, confused cries, and faces. Then, with the sleigh hissing and sighing on the hard-packed snow, out at last into a countryside that might have been laid under a spell: the birches crusted a sugary white, all sound damped and distanced—the old Russia of her childhood laid for ever asleep in her head. Groups of stained wooden huts with alleys of ice-tipped mud between; tea fuming in cups, and strips of charred pork that grimed and burnt the fingers; forests, rivers of ice, a long swooning into an immensity of white where the days fell endlessly without sound and their passing left no track. Later, towards the west, lines of grey-coated, grey-faced soldiers, some with their feet in rags, many of them maimed and bandaged, who turned out of half-sleep to watch their sleigh recede into the distance, as they turned in their own dream to watch the grey lines dwindle behind. A whiteness at last without detail; which is amnesia, oblivion; a blankness in which the boy, the twin brother, strays and is lost in some town swarming with refugees, carried off in a contrary direction on the tide of Russians, Ruthenians, Letts, Poles, Jews that is pouring south, east, west out of the mouths of war.

The lost brother still haunts her dreams. Her male counterpart. That Other who would guarantee the truth of who she is.

She recalls their sleeping together in the same hammock, innocently fitted together, spoon-fashion, and sharing perhaps the same dream. Two blue moths are hovering over them, borne back and forth on the breeze. There is the scent of pennyroyal.

Sometimes over the years she has woken to that scent and to the slight motion sickness of the hammock, and has almost recalled what dream it was they were sharing that had later taken the shape of moths, and almost recaptured the feeling of completeness with which their bodies fitted together, their lovely congruence.

Catching sight of herself sometimes in a glass, she has had the

odd sense of being no longer one; has seen the mirror's depths
swim a moment and another figure come to its surface. She stands
face to face with herself then, but in some different time and
place; feeling her limbs harden, her chest grow flat, the hair
coarsen on her upper lip, as a deeper voice fumbles for words in
her throat, and in a language she no longer speaks. Her feeling
then is of painful incompleteness, of someone unrecognised and
lost now for nearly sixty years, who wears a semblance of her own
face and gropes through her for a memory of that forgotten
dream, their childhood; stopping dead perhaps on the platform of
some Polish border-town where he might be an inspector of
trains, and half recalling, as the distant names are called over the
station loud-speaker, the dazzle of a courtyard, and a monk's
bearded face leaning over them, a holy breath falling on their
brows as they sit wrapped for their journey; or further back still, a
garden with bowls of porridge cooling on wooden benches,
lemons cut in segments, a deep resonance as of bees in the honey-
coloured light of a hexagonal dome; his thought fluttering with
hers in a scent of pennyroyal, but no longer knowing, as she does,
what it refers to, and if he did know, or thought he knew, finding
no one now to believe him.

Her second recollection, which has perhaps crystallized the
first and given it coherence, is of a garden that descends via a tunnel and steps to a wide and dazzling harbour.

It is Sydney, 1920. She is thirteen. She has come to Australia,
and this she remembers perfectly, from India, having been spirited south out of Poland into Transylvania, and from there, with
the remains of their party, to Turkey; then south again on the caravan routes. Weeks of swaying across a landscape of blinding light,
with nothing to break the horizon but an occasional outcrop or
the bristling gun barrels of a band of brigands. Then, one cool
morning, India, valley on valley falling among threads of smoky
water, long sighs of relief after the desert-places, and a ridge of
mist-shrouded deodars. On narrow paths among the rhododen-
drons, pilgrims approach to the sound of bells.

What happened there is another story. After negotiations carried on between her own women and some local dignitary she was gathered into the rich, precocious life of a palace, betrothed, in a ceremony she recalls only as involving elephants and a great many fireworks, to a minor prince.

But destiny acted yet again to push her on. At barely twelve she bore a child, a son. He was snatched away at the very moment of his birth by a rival faction at court, and when she woke after a drugged sleep it was to find in his place a little rag doll. The doll too she has by her still. I knew that immediately, from the look in her eyes when she spoke of it, a little gesture of her head towards the door of the bedroom; but she did not produce it. It is, I know, the deepest of all her secrets. I imagine her sitting alone in the house, behind the lattice, in the evening cool, nursing it, crooning to it, speaking its name. After so long the lost child still comes to her in dreams that leave her whole body racked and torn. A small mouth tugs at her breast. She recalls a pain that for long hours fills the room, beats against the walls, then breaks and falls away, to become in the long years afterwards the same pain but no longer physical, a heart-wrenching emptiness. That child, if it survived, would be a man of sixty. They are almost contemporaries, she, her brother, and the child. He is, perhaps, living the life of a common peasant, quite unaware of his origins, working, hard-handed, hollow-thighed, in the mud of a paddy-field, always at the edge of starvation; another part of her, like the twin brother, that she has lost contact with but which moves in a separate and parallel existence in her mind.

Once again she was spirited away. And in Bombay, far to the south, no longer a wife or mother, was called one warm evening, lugging her rag doll, to a room in one of the great hotels on the waterfront, where a lady wearing a great many jewels shed tears, drew the child to her spiky breast, and claimed her as her own child recovered.

One sees how the scene might have gone. The Diva in fact had played it before. In *Lucrezia*. Finding in herself, to her own surprise and the delight of her admirers, the lineaments of a new and unexpected passion: beyond carnality and the lust for power or vengeance, the great emotion—maternal love. It was one of her triumphs.

She must herself have felt the oddness of it, that meeting in Bombay: of life's coming at last to imitate art—or had the fictive scene already had the real child in view? granting that there was a child; drawing on that as the source of its extraordinary power—of the emotion created to fill a role being required now, and in some ampler and more convincing form, to take on life itself. Clearly, in the Diva's case, it could not. When the great scene was played out and they came down to dusty daily existence, the child must have been just another traveller in the Vale circus, that rag-bag of managers, dressers, advisers, lovers, gambling cronies, and other hangers-on that moved with her from capital to capital for as long as she was on the road. The child might have been with her for a season or two (no need to specify on what basis) and then she was not.

So now, in the smoky light of a summer afternoon in Sydney, she is lying in a hammock slung between thick, flowering trees. A voice drifts through the open window of the house above. *Batti, batti,* it is singing while someone plays the piano, the unseen hands fluttering up and down the keyboard on effortless wings, and the voice also disembodied, of the air ungraspable. She is a child again. And found.

Lying alone here, half dozing in her white party dress, she gazes through flickering lids and an archway of stone to where the harbour, in a film of blue, gently rises and falls like the skin of some strange and beautiful animal that has come to sprawl at her feet, and whose breath she feels tugging the silk of her sleeves. The garden is full of scents: bruised gardenia, cypress, the ooze of gum. Insects are brooding over a damp place in the bushes where something is coming into existence, or has just left it. Clouds are building to a storm. Suddenly, up the long steps from the water, through the light of the archway, disguised now as a sailor and with his eyes burning in a wilderness of hair, his beard electrically alive, comes the monk Rasputin with a finger to his lips.

She knows him immediately. He reassures her of who she is and of where they have both come from. He too has escaped, lived through seven bullet-wounds in a frozen courtyard, after the murderers, terrified of his advance towards them—a mad dog dancing in the snow, that had already eaten poison and taken seven rounds of lead into his body—had turned on their heels and fled. Now he too is moving unrecognised through the world, waiting only to declare himself.

He has enemies and is pursued. He stays only long enough to warn her that she too has pursuers. When a voice calls from the house above he is startled, kisses the child's brow, raises his rough hand over her in a last blessing, and slips away in his sailor's garb down the long stairs to the water, where he pauses a moment and is framed against the stormy light, then descends to a waiting dinghy. Only the dark smell of his beard, which stirs her memory and is unmistakable, still remains with her. And it is this that she uses to evoke him, her one protector: his gnarled feet—the feet of a monk—retreating over the stone flags. And the water rhythmically lifting and falling, the breath of a drowsing beast . . .

Sixty years ago.

The voice calling from the terrace, having come to earth again, is her mother's. Alicia Vale.

6

I WAS WRITING UP the report of my Karingai lecture, comfortably at ease in dressing gown and slippers, with a bottle of whisky at my elbow.

These things write themselves. Comfortable clichés, small white lies to convince the holders of the country's purse-strings that big things are being achieved out there in the wilderness, that we missionaries of the Arts are making daily converts to the joys of the spirit and to higher truth. I'm a whizz at such stuff. Devoting myself for half an hour to the official lie was a way of not facing my own difficult decision: how far I was prepared (Oh Adrian, not another of your discoveries! Yes, yes, my dears, Uncle Adrian's at it again!) to risk my reputation and face a cruelly sceptical world in defence of Mrs. Judge's problematical birth.

The rain had come down as the woman predicted. Sheets of it! The earth turned to mud, bushes thrashed, trees swam in sub-aqueous gloom, the din on the roof of my motel cabin was deafening. So that I did not hear the tapping at first, and was startled when I glanced up out of the pool of lamplight to see framed in the dark of the window, and wordlessly signalling, like a man going down for the third time, the woman's husband, George. I hurried to the door to let him in but he refused to come further than the verandah. He stood there barefoot, his waterproof streaming.

"I jus' slipped out," he told me, "while she's sleeping. I wanted t' tell you a few things." He set his lamp down on the boards.

"But you must come in," I said. "Come in and have a drink."

He shook his head.

"No," he said very solemnly. "No I won't, if it's all the same." He looked past me into the lighted room with its twin chenille bedspreads, its TV set, the hinged desk-lamp. "I'm too muddy."

He was, but I guessed there was another and deeper reason. It represented too clearly, that room, the world I had come from, a world of slick surfaces and streamlining, of appliances, of power, that threatened him, as it threatened the woman too at the very moment of her reaching out for it.

"I'll stay out 'ere, if you don't mind."

So our conversation took place with the rain cascading from the guttering just a few feet away and in such a roaring that he could barely be heard.

He began to unbutton his cape. "I jus' wanted," he repeated, "t' tell you a few things." He paused, his thumb and forefinger dealing awkwardly with a stud.

"Like—like them people she thinks 'ave been makin' enquiries about 'er. Over the years like. Well, I made 'em up." He looked powerfully ashamed, standing barefoot with the streaming cape on his shoulders and his brow in a furrow. "I wanted t' tell you that right off like. T' get things straight." He met my eyes and did not look away. I turned up the collar of my gown, though it wasn't at all cold, and nodded; an inadequate representative, if that is what he needed, of the forces of truth. In other circumstances I might have got out of my embarrassment by doing a little dance. But he wasn't the man for that sort of thing, and at that moment I wasn't either.

"Y' see," he said, "I didn' want t' lose 'er. I didn' intend no harm. I wanted 'er t' think she needed me. I don't reckon it'll make all that much difference, will it? I mean, you'll still do what she wants."

"I don't know. I don't *know* what she wants."

"Oh, she wants people t' know at last. Who she *is*." He shook his head at some further view of his own that he did not articulate, though he wrestled with it. "I suppose it means she'll go back, eh? To them others."

Which others? Who could he mean? Who did he think was out there— out *where?*—that she could go back to? Didn't he realise that sixty years had slipped by, in which day by day a quite differ-ent story had been unfolding, in the papers and out of them, that involved millions and was still not finished and held us all in its powerful suspense?

He began to button the cape again, which was easier to deal with than silence; then said firmly: "I'm a truthful man for the most part, I reckon I can claim that. On'y—I didn't want t' lose 'er. She's a wonderful woman. You don't know! We've been happy together, even she'd say that. I tried t' make 'er happy and I've been happy meself. No regrets, no regrets at all! There hasn' been a cross word between us in all the years. That ought t' count for somethin'. When I first met 'er, y' know, she was just a girl—that light and small I was scared of even brushin' against 'er. I was a carter then, and she was workin' f' rich people, out at Vaucluse. We used t' talk after work, and one night she told me the whole thing. I never knew such a world existed. She wanted t' get away where they wouldn' be on to 'er, so we just kep' movin' till we holed up here." He looked again, with a furrowing of his brow, at his own view of the thing. "I better be gettin' back," he said, "before she wakes up an' starts worryin' where I am. She does worry, y' know. She was sleepin' when I left. Knocked out." There was another silence. Then he put his hand out, as he had earlier in the day, and we shook.

"You do believe 'er, don't you?" he said, holding my hand in his giant grasp. "It'd be best if you did, whatever it costs. She wants t' be known at last. But it's up to you. You just do whatever you reckon is the right thing. For all concerned."

He broke his grip, took up the hurricane-lamp, and with a curt little nod went down into the rain, leaning heavily into the wall of it, and I watched the light, and the play of it on his cape, till it flickered out among the trees. Holding my dressing gown about me, though it wasn't at all cold, I turned towards the empty room, its welcoming light and warmth, and was unwilling for a moment to go in. The sky roared, the big trees rocked and swayed, the water came sluicing down. The truth is that I have a great fear these days of being alone.

But this is Mrs. Judge's story, not mine—or it is the man's. He after all was the first of her believers, and has spent fifty years keeping faith with his convictions and translating them, even in minor dishonesty, into the dailyness of living. Of everything I had heard it was this that most touched me: the vision of what a man might, after all, make of his life in the way of ordinary but honourable commitment, and the plainness with which he might present himself and say, *This is what I have given my life to. This is what I am.* If I hadn't been convinced by the woman's claim, her passionate certainty that she was something other than what she seemed, I must have been by his steadier one that he was, even in her shadow, himself.

Compared with his part in all this my own is trivial. I am the messenger, the narrator; and if the narrator too needs to be convinced of the truth of what he is telling, it isn't the same as laying his life down and presenting that as the measure of his belief. The scepticism of my colleagues, a flicker of irony on the lips of even the most straight-faced listener—that is all I will have to bear. I see already how the improbable side of my nature (how does a man become improbable, even to himself?) will immediately declare itself as with a twitch of an imaginary cloak I clap my hands, flourish my fingers in the air, and present out of my own longing for the extraordinary (that is how they will put it) a small, dark, barefoot woman in floral, the daughter of Alicia Vale. "But she was perfect!" (They will be telling the story to others now, in a crowded bar, or over lobster shells at a business lunch, embellishing a little as all story-tellers do.) "She couldn't have been more appropriate if he'd invented her. But then he did, didn't he? He must have!"

Oh yes, she is appropriate all right, our Mrs. Judge. Too appropriate. She puts me to the test—not of belief but of the courage to come out at last from behind my clown's make-up, my simpering and sliding and dancing on the spot, to tell her story and give myself away.

The stories we tell betray us, they become our own. We go on living in them, we go on living outside them. The Bloody Sergeant comes on, announces that a battle has been won, bleeds a little, and after twenty rugged lines retires into oblivion. But what he has been called upon to tell has to be lived with and carried through a lifetime, out there in the dark. His own end comes later and is another story. Which another man must tell.

A Medium

WHEN I WAS ELEVEN I took violin lessons once a week from a Miss Katie McIntyre, always so called to distinguish her from Miss Pearl, her sister, who taught piano and accompanied us at exams.

Miss Katie had a big sunny studio in a building in the city, which was occupied below by dentists, paper suppliers, and cheap photographers. It was on the fourth floor, and was approached by an old-fashioned cage lift that swayed precariously as it rose (beyond the smell of chemical fluid and an occasional whiff of gas) to the purer atmosphere Miss Katie shared with the only other occupant of the higher reaches, Miss E. Sampson, Spiritualist.

I knew about Miss Sampson from gossip I had heard among my mother's friends; and sometimes, if I was early, I would find myself riding up with her, the two of us standing firm on our feet while the dark cage wobbled.

The daughter of a well-known doctor, an anaesthetist, she had gone to Clayfield College, been clever, popular, a good sport. But then her gift appeared—that is how my mother's friends put it, just declared itself out of the blue, without in any way changing her cleverness or good humour.

She tried at first to deny it: she went to the university and studied Greek. But it had its own end in view and would not be trifled with. It laid its hand on her, made its claim, and set my mother's friends to wondering; not about Emily Sampson, but about themselves. They began to avoid her, and then later, years later, to seek her out.

Her contact, it seemed, was an Indian, whose male voice croaked from the delicate throat above the fichu of coffee-dipped lace. But she sometimes spoke as well with the voices of the dead: little girls who had succumbed to diphtheria or blood poisoning or had been strangled in suburban parks, soldiers killed in one of the wars, drowned sailors, lost sons and brothers, husbands felled beside their dahlias at the bottom of the yard. Hugging my violin case, I pushed hard against the bars to make room for the presences she might have brought in with her.

She was by then a woman of forty-nine or fifty—small, straight, business-like, in a tailored suit and with her hair cut in a silver helmet. She sucked Bonnington's Irish Moss for her voice (I could smell them) and advertised in the *Courier Mail* under Services, along with Chiropractor and Colonic Irrigation. It was odd to see her name listed so boldly, E. Sampson, Spiritualist, in the foyer beside the lifts, among the dentists and their letters, the registered firms, Pty Ltd, and my own Miss McIntyre, LTCL, AMEB. Miss Sampson's profession, so nakedly asserted, appeared to speak for itself, with no qualification. She was herself the proof. It was this, I think, that put me in awe of her.

It seemed appropriate, in those days, that music should be separated from the more mundane business that was being carried on below—the whizzing of dentists' drills, the plugging of cavities with amalgam or gold, and the making of passport photos for people going overseas. But I thought of Miss Sampson, for all her sensible shoes, as a kind of quack, and was sorry that Miss Katie and the Arts should be associated with her, and with the troops of subdued, sad-eyed women (they were mostly women) who made the pilgrimage to her room and shared the last stages of the lift with us: women whose husbands might have been bank managers—wearing smart hats and gloves and tilting their chins a little in defiance of their having at last "come to it"; other women in dumpy florals, with freckled arms and too much talc, who worked in hospital kitchens or cleaned offices or took in washing, all decently gloved and hatted now, but looking scared of the company they were in and the heights to which the lift wobbled as they clung to the bars. The various groups hung apart, using their elbows in a ladylike way, but using them, and producing genteel formulas such as "Pardon" or "I'm so sorry" when the crush brought them close. Though touched already by a hush of shared anticipation, they had not yet accepted their commonality. There were distinctions to be observed, even here.

On such occasions the lift, loaded to capacity, made heavy work of it. And it wasn't, I thought, simply the weight of bodies (eight persons only, a notice warned) that made the old mechanism grind in its shaft, but the weight of all that sorrow, all that hopelessness and last hope, all that dignity in the privacy of grief, and silence broken only by an occasional, "Now don't you upset yourself, pet," or a whispered, "George would want it, I know he would." We ascended slowly.

I found it preferable on the whole to arrive early and ride up fast, and in silence, with Miss Sampson herself.

Sometimes, in the way of idle curiosity (if such a motive could be ascribed to her), she would let her eyes for a moment rest on *me*, and I wondered hotly what she might be seeing beyond a plump eleven-year-old with scarred knees clutching at Mozart. Like most boys of that age I had much to conceal.

But she appeared to be looking at me, not through me. She smiled, I responded, and clearing my throat to find a voice, would say in a well-brought-up, Little Lord Fauntleroy manner that I hoped might fool her and leave me alone with my secrets, "Good afternoon, Miss Sampson."

Her own voice was as unremarkable as an aunt's: "Good afternoon, dear."

All the more alarming then, as I sat waiting on one of the cane-bottomed chairs in the corridor, while Ben Steinberg, Miss McIntyre's star pupil, played the Max Bruch, to hear the same voice oddly transmuted. Resonating above the slight swishing and breathing of her congregation, all those women in gloves, hats, fur-pieces, packed in among ghostly pampas-grass, it had stepped down a tone—no, several—and came from another continent. I felt a shiver go up my spine. It was the Indian, speaking through her out of another existence.

Standing at an angle to the half-open door, I caught only a segment of the scene. In the glow of candlelight off bronze, at three thirty in the afternoon, when the city outside lay sweltering in the glare of a blue-black thundercloud, a being I could no longer think of as the woman in the lift, with her sensible shoes and her well-cut navy suit, was seated cross-legged among cushions, eyes closed, head rolled back with all the throat exposed as for a knife stroke.

A low humming filled the room. The faint luminescence of the pampas-grass was angelic, and I was reminded of something I had seen once from the window of a railway carriage as my train sat steaming on the line: three old men—tramps they might have been—in a luminous huddle behind the glass of a waiting-shed, their grey heads aureoled with fog and the closed space aglow with their breathing like a jar full of fireflies. The vision haunted me. It was entirely real—I mean the tramps were real enough, you might have smelled them if you'd got close—but the way I had seen them changed that reality, made me so impressionably aware that I could recall details I could not possibly have seen at that distance or with the naked eye: the greenish-grey of one old man's hair where it fell in locks over his shoulder, the grime of a hand bringing out all its wrinkles, the ring of dirt round a shirt collar. Looking through into Miss Sampson's room was like that. I saw too much. I felt light-headed and began to sweat.

A flutter of excitement passed over the scene. A new presence had entered the room. It took the form of a child's voice, treble and whining, and one of the women gave a cry that was immediately supported by a buzz of other voices. The treble one, stronger now, cut through them. Miss Sampson was swaying like a flower on its stalk . . .

Minutes later, behind the door of Miss Katie's sunny studio, having shown off my scales, my arpeggios, my three pieces, I stood with my back to the piano (facing the wall behind which so much emotion was contained) while Miss Katie played intervals and I named them, or struck chords and I named those. It wasn't difficult. It was simple mathematics and I had an ear, though the chords might also in other contexts, and in ways that were not explicable, move you to tears.

There is no story, no set of events that leads anywhere or proves anything—no middle, no end. Just a glimpse through a half-open door, voices seen not heard, vibrations sensed through a wall while the trained ear strains, not to hear what is passing in the next room, but to measure the chords—precise, fixed, nameable as diminished fifths or Neapolitan sixths, but also at moments approaching tears—that are being struck out on an iron-framed upright; and the voice that names them your own.

CHILD'S PLAY

Eustace

1

THE DOOR to the corridor was closed, but a soft light from out there flowed through the tilted fanlight, displaying, in a puzzle of shadow and highlights like a landscape on the moon, the bodies of the sleeping children, some crouched knee to chin in the centre of the bed, some spread-eagled face downwards with a foot-sole extended into the dark, others again laid out straight with their toes to the ceiling, the sheet rucked under their chin and their breath lightly coming and going. There were ten children in the dormitory, all girls. The room was full of their breathing and the faint scent of frangipani from the garden below.

All this, glimpsed from the washroom door, was like something the youth had never seen before.

Even after his eyes had grown accustomed to the half-darkness he found it difficult to interpret details. Was it a pillow one of the children was clasping to her, or another body? Was that a shadow or the dark strands of her hair? Was it an arm or a leg whose rounded flesh the light fell upon and made luminous? Piecing the ten bodies together as his gaze travelled from bed to bed, disentangling shadow from substance, smoothing out the creases in sheets and nightdresses to discover limbs, all this took long minutes in which he simply stood perfectly still and stared.

Then there were the sounds. Locating each of them—the murmurs, words, the long slow outpourings of breath—and tracking them to an individual child so that he had each of them, each of the ten, clearly in mind; separating out the ticking of a clock,

insect-noises from the park, and the dripping—was it?—of a tap
in the washroom behind him, or a shower, or a cistern, together
with his own breathing and the beating of his blood—it was a task
to be carried out methodically and with great patience, but at
some lower level than the part of him that simply observed.
Something was thinking for him; that is how he might have put it.
As when, with a speed and assurance that would have astonished
the casual observer, he would lay out, on a sheet of newspaper he
could barely read, all the working parts of a machine. Machines
were the most complicated things he knew: more complicated
than people—though of course he had only himself to judge by—
and more reliable as well. Machines he was utterly at home with.
Things fitted together part by part according to a settled order,
and all the parts were congruent, screw and nut to bolthole,
thread to thread. His long fingers could solve any problem of that
sort in minutes, no trouble at all. His intelligence was all in his fingertips, and in his eyes.

One of the children began to mutter words out of a dream and
the sounds caught his attention. He could make nothing of them.
But the idea of a dream breaking into the room like that, the idea
of its lying submerged under the silence (which wasn't really
silence at all) and breaking surface in those unintelligible syllables, disturbed him; it introduced an unmanageable element. He
took a small step forward.

It was a child in the second bed from the end. On the right. Who
now turned in her sleep, changing not only her own position but
all the highlights and shadows in the room, breaking his grasp of
it. The dream had started a ripple that involved all the other
sleepers as well. One by one they translated it, more or less
according to the depth of their sleep, into stirrings, murmurs,
little groans, till the whole room at the level of the beds was a
shifting surface of light and dark, of rising and falling contours.
He was almost sick with the unsteadiness of it. Everything was out
of hand.

He turned back into the dark of the washroom with its row of
hand-basins and its dripping cistern or shower, sat on the tiled

floor, and began to haul on his boots, which he had been holding in his right hand, first the one, then the other; carefully knotting the laces. While he was still engaged in this the crack of light on the wall opposite began to widen, a shadow filled it, and when he jerked his head around, one of the children was there, standing barefoot in her nightdress, through which he could see the darker outline of the body.

She stood and rubbed her eyes, frowning. She must have been nine or ten years old. She stared and frowned, but didn't seem at all alarmed.

"Hullo," he said huskily, because he couldn't think of anything else, and because the word, being the ordinary one, seemed immediately right. He gave a nervous smile.

She considered him a moment, then turned away as if he might be merely illusory and went to one of the washbasins.

He got shakily to his feet, suddenly too tall and thin, feeling out of his element in this big empty room with its checkerboard tiles, its row of handbasins and mirrors, its cubicles at the darker end where something dripped. He stood with his back to the door in case she panicked and tried to pass him. She was bent over a basin, drinking from the tap. Then she turned, wiping her mouth with the back of her hand, and considered him again, her brows drawn together in childish puzzlement. He lost his head. "Look, you won't tell anyone, will you?" he stammered.

She grew thoughtful but said nothing, and he began to move towards the window.

"It's a secret," he said.

She continued to watch. She seemed puzzled rather than afraid.

Fearful that if he took his eyes off her for even a second she might break or cry out, he felt his way to the sill, swung a leg over, eased himself down till only his fingertips clutched the cracked paintwork, and dropped. Once safely on the ground he moved swiftly into the shadow of a tree, but did not move away. Something made him stand there, still in the half-darkness, and look up. The garden trembled all about him on tiny waves of sound that might have been wings.

CHILD'S PLAY

The child had come to the sill, her nightdress billowing a little in the breeze. She stood there, quite calmly, looking down at him. Then she did a strange thing. She raised her right hand briefly and waved.

2

SHE TOLD no one.

Waking as usual in the narrow bed, with Miss Ivers in the doorway briskly clapping her hands and calling, "Now children, now girls!" and the room already filled with groans, giggles, little shrieks, as the nine others in their different ways took on the new day, sat dangling their feet over the edge of the bed a moment, unwilling to kick off, or wandered about half asleep till the first water struck them, exuberantly teased, slapped at sheets and punished pillows, or brushed their hair with long strokes, counting, or practised whatever rituals they had need of to make the crossing from the deep privacies of sleep to this lighter, brighter world that was embodied in Miss Ivers standing straight and slim in the doorway, the exclamation mark of her body making its own clear point: "This, girls, is how we should bear ourselves in the face of Monday morning," the clapping of her hands, and the "Now girls," providing the first little hook on which they would hang the many wandering minutes of their day—waking as usual into this utterly orderly disorderly world, she thought she must have dreamed him, the boy in the washroom, he seemed so alien to it all; she put him away with her other dreams as she swung out of bed and drew on her slippers.

But no. In the act of reaching down to ease her finger under the right heel, she saw again the laces drawn tight over his index finger, the freckles on the back of his hand, and knew he was real. Though surrounded still by the soft unreality of her sleep, so that he existed in the continuation of whatever she had been dreaming just before, he had been, none the less, utterly bulky and solid— bare-legged, gangling, freckled, with a smell, a mixture of sweat and car-grease, that did not belong to dreams. Dreams were odourless, she knew that at least. Moving with the others into the washroom she couldn't believe that they too would not catch some trace of his presence, feel some displacement he had made in the ordinariness of the room, with its mirrors above white basins, its shower and toilet cubicles. But the others were washing noisily. They caught no scent of him in their boisterous, not-quite-female world.

He had left no sign.

She told no one, and the day went on as if nothing had occurred. It was organised so tightly, and they moved through it at such a keen pace, that it was difficult to let any new thing in to find a place there: doing mental sums as fast as you could and then sitting up very straight when you had the answer, with your hands on your head and your elbows pushed back—straining, but not too obviously, to be called; vaulting the horse with your chin up and your eyes straight ahead as each of the others, one, two, three, four, went off before you, blonde, black or brown ponytails swishing; copying, but fast, before the blackboard was turned over, the chief products of Western Australia; all this kept your head filled with so many immediacies that there was no time for daydreaming, and no corner, with so much that was public and organised, in which anything unusual could lurk. Even when they wrote a composition and had to use their imagination the lines were strictly drawn. Miss Wilson wrote the opening paragraph on the blackboard. It was an old house on Dartmoor, in England, deep in fog, and they went on from there, filling the house with darkness and the sound of creaking doors, that might be ghosts but would more likely turn out to be tramps or stray dogs that left all mysteries explained in a last paragraph, which they were required to label *conclusion*.

Faced with the open invitation to confess a mystery, she might have let the boy in. But he didn't seem to fit. He was too tall, too ungainly, too much part, in his desert boots and T-shirt, of the sprawling sub-tropical town that began at the walls of their park, to enter the realms of the imagination as Miss Wilson defined it or to find himself on Dartmoor, in England. But she did think of him briefly. She allowed him to approach out of the fog and come up, in his floppy desert boots, to the door of that deserted cottage. Looking vaguely scared, he stood at the threshold, his whole body tense with what might now be required of him. Then she relented and let him off. She let him move away from his meeting with the perfectly conventional spirit she now introduced, who had once, in the olden days, been a witch whom the village people had drowned (though she wasn't really a witch at all, just a crazy old woman) in a greasy millpond, along with her cat called Lock.

There was an occasion during prep when she considered telling her best friend of the moment, Adele Morgan, who slept in another dormitory; was on the very point of it; but didn't. She had the odd sense that she would not be believed. There was no detail she could produce that would be at all convincing, and she was too matter of fact, had too clear a sense of the real and too high a regard for the truth, to invent one. She would wait till such a detail presented itself.

Besides, she had already anticipated the questions Adele would ask and they were not interesting. "Did he do anything? Weren't you scared?"

No, he did nothing at all. He was just there. And she hadn't been scared because there was nothing to be scared of. He was just an ordinary boy with red hair. Very tall when he stood up, and very shy. When she first saw him he had been sitting on the floor with one bare knee drawn up so that he could tie his shoelace (one was tied already, the other, drawn taut, was still, after the first simple knot, looped over his forefinger) and she had been reminded of how her younger brother, Jack, had learned to tie laces by practising it over and over, all one morning, on the veran-dah steps. The boy had had that same look of anxious concentra-tion. It was perhaps his coming to her thus out of her own past that made her believe at first that she was still asleep in her bed and dreaming. That is why she had turned away a moment to look at her cool face in the mirror, to see that her eyes were open, and to drink. When she turned back he had got to his feet and was staring.

A tall boy, carrot-haired and unexplained; but he didn't scare her any more than if she *had* dreamed him. At that odd hour, and in the lingering heaviness of sleep, he seemed like a continuation rather than an interruption of her dreams; as if she had first dreamed him and then found him there. What was there to explain?

Of course his presence wasn't related to her daytime life, to the world of corridors and stairs and stairwells and rooms where the blackboards were filled, even in darkness, with chalked up facts. But then neither were her dreams. These hours that were for sleep belonged to nowhere. They were outside the rules. No bells governed them, they were free. She had dreamed the strangest things, and had sometimes been very frightened indeed. Once she had dreamed of being on a picnic with her family when a ship rode up the beach that had no sail. The sailors, who were very ragged and foreign-looking, begged for some garment they could rig up to sail home and she had offered her dress, a bright yellow one. They had fixed it to the mast and sailed right out of view on the still moonlight, out of sight of her parents and her two brothers, while she, in one of those strange dreamworld experiences of being quite palpably in two places at once, stood both at the water's edge watching and at the rails of the ship, while the yellow dress (which had not been hers in fact but her cousin Millie's) stood out stiffly in the breeze.

Compared with that, an unexplained but entirely ordinary boy with red hair wasn't extraordinary at all. He had just gulped and said "Hullo." But when she stood at the windowsill and watched him, where he was half-hidden below the Chinese elm, he had looked, she thought, like a painting. She saw him in a field struck by the wind, all agitated gold. His long legs, bare, his arms long and hanging at his side, his face tilted towards her, had made him at that moment not "too tall" as she had first thought but like someone drawn out, drawn upwards with the strain of being where he was, or who he was, as in one of the swirly paintings in the school corridor. It was the heightened reality of him that attracted her. As if he belonged to a world with other rules of perspective, or to another order of beings, and had come to induct her into other possibilities than she had so far discovered at home or at school, to reveal to her how she might cross into the further reaches of herself. Until he came into her life she had not known how suffocated she felt here, where every moment of the day was *for* something and had to be filled; or how it frightened her that the whole of life might be like this, that those corridors where you must never run, and stairs you went down only on the left, and *quietly*, might lead to places where the rules that applied were different only in detail, not in kind, and were invisible to her only because no one had ever pointed them out (that was for later, as Miss Ivers said of so many things) or given them names.

So she kept his secret because it was her own, and knew he would come again. She did not even bother to wait for him, since she knew she had only to fall asleep and he would be there; and when he was there she would immediately be awake.

3

STANDING AGAIN, boots in hand, at the washroom door, he recognised in the scene some benevolence of nature that was reserved only for him. He had not expected it, but there it was. The world often surprised him like this. Behind him the raised window was a funnel for moonlight and the gathered noises of the garden, which he found comforting: soft wing-beats that might be an owl or a flying fox, the shifting of leaves, a stirring of furred creatures hunting. Beyond that, the wall he had come over; which formed in his mind a barrier he had passed between the world outside, that still made itself heard in the distant sound of a car (a Falcon, he guessed, changing gears as it turned uphill), the self they knew from the overalls his mother washed and the underthings she laid out for him, and this other self standing in socks and shorts at the threshold of a different world entirely, a strange still world of children sleeping in rows under bluish sheets, which belonged to the night, to this place only, and was female.

It was to him as if these children slept here always; as if this room were always closed and moonlit, even when it was light elsewhere, because this was the only way he had seen or could imagine it, or cared to. The room hovered above the nightsounds of the garden like a spaceship in a wood, with rows of encapsulated virgins. They slept. They awaited his arrival. The door at the end of the room led nowhere, and the light out there came not from a corridor but from space; nothing familiar lay beyond: no stairways to other parts of the building. This room was its own place, afloat on the children's breathing and on his own will. When he blinked it was not there. It had been waiting—for how long?—till he should at last appear. It was always half-dark and could never be otherwise. Never. Because if he let the light in he would have to let in along with it all those ordinary, exterior events and conditions that belonged to daylight and the sequence of days, which would put it for ever beyond him, whereas this way it was entirely his. No past led up to the room and no future away from it. It simply was. And it was here because he had found it here.

He listened to the children's breathing. That too, strange as it might be to him, was a comfort. Its regularity calmed him. Could he find her out, he wondered, by the note of her breath?

He had not seen, on that last occasion, which bed she had come from, but had decided—*he* had decided—that it was from the second bed on the right, in which last time, as he stood here, a body had spoken and stirred. All his re-enactments of that last time, achieved under the pressure of his need to come back here, if only in imagination, had begun with the turning of that body under the sheet, the first mysterious disturbance and coming alive of the still room as he had originally seen it. In his re-living of that moment he had made certain changes; he had allowed himself to see what he had, in fact, only heard. A child rose up out of the second-last bed on the right, met his gaze, swung her legs slowly over into the dark between the beds—he loved this moment, the contact of her bare foot with the cold pavement—and came down between the rows of sleeping forms, her nightdress transparent in the bluish light, holding out her hand to him.

He had been over it so often that he had quite erased that other version in which she surprised him from behind, caught him sitting cloddishly on the floor, struggling with the laces of his boots. In his new version of their meeting he woke her by the force of his own gaze upon her and she came quickly and willingly.

Now he fixed his gaze once more on the second-last bed on the right and waited for her to stir. And was again surprised.

From the first bed on his left came a small gasp; a child pushed herself into a sitting position and their eyes made contact in the dark. She drew down the sheet, swung her legs over. And he thought with a moment's passionate fury that he had been foiled, that the initiative had been stolen from him, and from *his* child, by an impostor. But she did hold out her hand to him, and when she came and stood before him he saw that it was the same child after all.

4

MARYLYN SHORE had come back to school in the new term with a hamster.

Pets were not allowed, but the hamster had lived for nearly two weeks in a wardrobe in the dormitory. It was Marylyn's, but in sharing the secret of its presence the others had come to think of it as theirs as well. They had fed it biscuits smuggled in from tea, and bits of lettuce and carrot, and were allowed briefly to stroke its fur. It became part of their dormitory life. Their sleep perhaps had a new quality because of their knowledge that it was there at the bottom of the wardrobe, and because, being nocturnal, they knew it was abroad, a tiny heartbeat in the darkness, while they slept. It moved in their sleep. It gave the night a different texture.

But the animal was discovered at last and transferred to the science lab, where Marylyn and the others were still able to feed it but where it passed out of their private world, and the glamourous light of a shared secret, and became just one more of the school's public properties.

Since Marylyn and the rest refused to tell the hamster's name (they had in fact called it Eustace), Miss Wilson, the headmistress, decided on Ruggles.

Because she was so pleased with herself for having found a neat and happy solution to the problem, Miss Wilson made rather a cult of Ruggles; she frequently referred to him in her pep-talks, and pretended, in a way the girls thought childish and affected, that he was a real personage and a full member of what she called "our raft," so that Ruggles became, in the end, as much one of Miss Wilson's attributes as the moth-eaten gown she wore, her Eiffel Tower brooch, her green-ink corrections, and the tiny bobble of flesh on her left eyelid.

Meanwhile, the creature's shadow, in his incarnation as Eustace, continued to occupy a place in the life of the dormitory, which had substance in a smell they might pick up from the bottom of the wardrobe, or a memory of how his small heart had beaten when they held him, very carefully, between the palms of their hands. Eustace became a code-word. Having left behind his essence, his secret name, the forbidden animal could be evoked out of the darkness of almost any occasion and went on dwelling among them in a form that was invisible to the eyes of authority and no longer needed feeding with anything but their childish complicity.

It was with the thought of Eustace clearly in mind that Jane decided to keep her visitor entirely to herself. She thought of him now under a code-name, like Eustace, and when he was about to tell his real name once she warned him quickly, "No, no, you'll spoil it. You mustn't tell your real name. Not to anyone, not even to me." She knew he would not remain undiscovered for ever, that sooner or later the others would certainly find out; but it seemed to her that if she kept her secret name for him, and if, for the others, he remained nameless, she would have something at least that was her own and that the boy would be safe.

The others did find out of course, it was inevitable. First Sheryl Payne, then Jill McArthur, then everybody. They sat up in their beds now, except for the sleepiest of them, whenever he came, and watched, and questioned, and tried to steal him away with all sorts of tricks—a different trick in each case, but she always recognised it, she knew them all so well—and with foolish, little-girl stories (how could he be interested in such things?) about their horses, their houses, the places they had been. She had never tried anything like that. It wasn't necessary. It was her bed he sat on; and the others, when gradually over the nights they got used to his presence and had gathered into the familiar atmosphere of the room his odd smell of car-grease—the others, when he had been made safe at last (she at least knew that he was *not* safe) came on tip-toe over the cool floor and sat cross-legged on the beds opposite. From there, gravely, in a little hum of female excitement, they watched. But did not enter the charmed circle. They came only to the edge of it, their faces lit by what they did not understand but felt the glow of just the same, while she and the boy, just the two of them, burned at the centre. There was nothing now, she felt, as she looked out at their scrubbed faces, still a little fuzzy with sleep, that would ever take her back and make her one of them. She had crossed some border in herself that was still, for them, far in the future. There was no way back.

5

THE OTHERS, watching, saw them as through glass, in a luminous bubble, they were so utterly absorbed in one another, had been drawn into such a distant dimension; and this both fascinated the children and freed them. Accepting the strangeness of the thing, and its attendant glamour, made them spectators and left them untouched.

What they might have been thinking, with a worldliness that was already an aspect of the women they would become, was "What does she see in him?" It was a mystery, but the question made it ordinary. What-does-she-see-in-him referred to the boy's patent unattractiveness, to his being too tall, too red-haired, too freckled, to his having bony knees and bitten-down fingernails that were lined with car-grease. These facts set him in a light so common (as the question itself set the whole situation in the light of "boyfriends" and "romance") that they quite forgot the unusualness of his being there at all in the more interesting mystery of his having chosen Jane and of Jane's having chosen him. His ugliness, since it wasn't their affair, seemed endearing. It was only later that they would see these characteristics that had made him safe as part of what also made him monstrous—his grease-stained hands, his being all arms and legs. But by then he would have passed out of the dormitory world, where everything was softened by the hour, the lingering glow of sleep out of which he had woken them, and their own hunger for fairy-tale, into the panicky blaring of police sirens and arc-lamps that made the school park with its millions of leaves into a dangerous jungle. Then some of these children, who had sat entranced by the spectacle of Jane and her visitor, and had even flirted a little with the unusualness of him, would fly into hysterics; he would rise up out of their sleep, with red hair on the back of his wrists, as a terror they could get around only by crying out aloud, till they found themselves safely awake again in their father's arms.

"This is Eustace," she had told them on that first occasion. And they stared. Was it a joke? Who would have suspected Jane, dumpy Jane, of having a sense of humour? Or did she mean some sort of transformation? They stared.

Jane concealed a smile at her own cunning. The secret significance of the word, which was already informed with both these possibilities (and was not her name for him) immediately cast its spell, not upon the boy, who remained unchangeable, but on her foolish schoolfellows, for whom he was immediately softened and silvered over and made familiar and small. He slipped into the circle of maidens like a changeling prince; puckering his brow a little, poor boy, and wondering where all this might lead.

She took his hand then, and he relaxed and felt safe. But he thought of the moment later as the point where he first lost control of things, where he was taken over and made an instrument of her more powerful will. What did it mean: Eustace?

But he was delighted at first by these others; by the glow they made in the room, by the increase ten times over of the specifically female atmosphere they created. They were a magnetic field of which he was the centre. Only gradually did it dawn upon him that this wasn't really so. Their attention wasn't a single force, but a set of forces that pulled him many ways. He couldn't keep track of himself. He felt torn apart, felt odd bits of him being passed around from one to the other of these children like sections of an enormous doll, an arm off here, there a leg. They didn't actually touch him, it was something stronger than touching. He felt parcelled out into so many places he no longer knew where his real centre was, if not in the one part of him they seemed unaware of, though he made no attempt to hide it. Their innocence, which had its own wilder aspects, its knot of chaos, had stolen the initiative from him. He became first resentful then cunningly resourceful. These others were a mistake. They wanted to make a pet of him, whereas what he wanted to make of himself was something quite different.

That was his real need here: that the situation should make of him something that he painfully longed for and had come here, all unwitting, to have revealed. He had no idea what it might be. He had simply followed some clue in himself and arrived. He hadn't even suspected, before now, that such a situation might exist, that high up here among the trees there was this room, magically sealed off from the rest of the world, where children slept and awaited his coming. He made no connection between these misty creatures in their nylon gowns and the crocodile of noisy schoolgirls in bottle-green tunics and straw hats that he sometimes passed down at the shops. Wandering about in the dark, blindly, hardly knowing what he was after, driven by his own restlessness, his dissatisfaction with himself and everything about him, simply lunging out into the air, down unfamiliar avenues and side streets, he had come to a wall that suggested climbing, since there must be something on the other side of it, then a garden, then an open window that could be entered, and there it was. It was as if he had climbed into a high place of his own head where he could breathe at last, and confronted it: a situation that had always been there and from which he was to force now the long withheld revelation.

But it had begun to go wrong. He had lost his grip of it.

He wondered sometimes how different things might have been if he had chosen another of the children: the child in the second bed on the right for example. They represented, these nine others, a set of possibilities he had not wakened, dreams or stories he had failed to enter, full vessels stored here unused because he had already chosen, or been chosen by—

So many possibilities confused him. They would have to be removed. He must go back to the beginning and take her with him. To a place where they could make things simple again, just the two of them. To their own place. To the tiled bathroom with its rows of mirrors above handbasins and that slow dripping from one of the cubicles.

6

THAT WAS the first step and she made no protest. She too seemed glad to get away. He half-closed the door behind them. It wasn't necessary to close it altogether, that might have alarmed her; and he wouldn't then be able to hear any disturbance from the dormitory. The half-closed door was enough. Here they could be alone, and here he felt the initiative was in his own hands again. He had separated her from whatever there was that she shared with the other children, and which their presence, however supernumerary, might represent. Here in the washroom, with its naked tiles and its own rituals, as of the ordinary public life set aside and the body laid bare, they could rediscover some of the magic that was theirs alone. He could bring his own body into focus here and rediscover what part it was to play in all this. He could see her not as one of a group of maidens, all washed and white in the alien power of their united but generalized sexuality, which if anything set her at a distance from him and disarmed him of his own power, but as herself—soft, real, touchable, as she had been previously only when he summoned up her image during the day, leading her off in his imagination, and being surprised in that dimension how far she was willing to go into his world, how deeply she herself led him on.

So the washroom was the first step.

They took it.

Returning later to the silence of the dormitory, to the hush in which the others almost breathlessly waited, he felt extraordinarily liberated and sure of himself. He would have liked to laugh right out, to throw the door open and shout into whatever lay beyond, or start a pillowfight and see the feathers fly, to do something loud and exuberant and alive with energy; he felt so filled with the joy of things and the power of his own voice and limbs. He would think of this later as perhaps the happiest he had ever been, when between him and the world there had been perfect concord.

If he had given way then to his boyish desire to whoop and break out everything might have been different. But he was thwarted; and not only by his fear of discovery, which in the recklessness of the moment he might have forgotten. The attention of the others, which was focussed entirely on her, had pushed him away to the edge of the scene.

"O Jane, Jane," their eyes were saying, "what have you been *doing*?"

She too saw it, and her hand touched his in an attempt to reassure him, but it was too late. He felt a surge of anger, and saw, in the blind fury of it, that he must take her further than the room next door. He must eliminate these others altogether.

So it was that he began to talk of a time when they would run away together. He sulked, he cajoled, he was insistent.

"Will you?" the others asked. Their eyes were hungry for it.

"Yes," she said firmly. It was as simple as that.

He dared not ask when. All he could do, as the nights mounted up and the pressure grew in him, was to force her closer, till the link between them was stronger than anything that might tie her to the others and their shared existence, till she stood so far beyond their understanding that she no longer had anything to say to them, and the circle in which they glowed when they sat together on her bed in the dormitory dazzled and even burned the gaze; till together they were so far beyond these others that their going would barely be noticed. He thought of their simply rising where they sat, in a kind of air-bubble, and climbing straight up out of sight.

They stood together at the sill, her hand in his, and looked down into the garden. It murmured and was heavy with the scent of night-flowers and the tink-tink of tree-frogs and crickets.

"Will you?" he said. "Tonight?"

He was, at that moment, the more innocent of the two. The next step, beyond the intimacies of the washroom, appeared to him only in terms that were vague and unimaginable, as some going beyond a point he had not yet glimpsed and therefore dared not press for. Once they were free of the building, down there among the leaves, with earth under his boots and the night all around them, the garden itself would provide the revelation of what it was to be, would speak directly to the blood in his hands. He felt the quickening rhythm of it deep within him.

He had never had a plan. His cunning, such as it was, dealt only with immediate events, and the shape of each occasion as he stepped into it was determined by the elements of the occasion itself and his response to them: a landscape of broken surfaces—light and shadow, cloth and limbs, the black-and-white checkerboard of a bathroom floor, the softness and warmth of her belly under the nightdress, the breathing of leaves under the moon.

"Will you then?" he repeated. "Tonight?"

She looked down into the pool of nightsounds and saw that to put it off any longer would change nothing, since she had already decided. Another day or two, or twenty. She would have to go beyond this point sooner or later. That had been clear from the start.

"Tonight then," she said, and heard the long sigh he gave, and felt his slow breath pass her. He was utterly happy. Utterly unaware of what lay before them.

For one last moment they sat together, hand in hand on the sill, and did not move.

7

LATER THERE was to be no reasonable explanation for it. The whole affair would remain, especially to Miss Wilson, for whom they had always been her very own little girls, and models of good behaviour, an impenetrable mystery.

She regarded them now with a kind of horror as they copied from the board and embarked on one of her flights of fancy, starting, as always, from the given paragraph: they had fallen, while out walking, into a cave full of brilliant jewels. Marylyn Shore chewed the end of her biro—"Don't, dear," she told the child automatically, "you don't know where it's been"; Gillian Bell sucked a pigtail, others gazed wide-eyed at the ceiling, or in the case of Bettina Falk, who was left-handed, turned at that odd angle to the desk; each of them already following her own idiosyncratic path, but all just children really, ordinary healthy little girls who would go on from this point (they all hoped) to normal lives. Watching them she felt it as some deficiency in herself that she could not connect them with the children who had sat there night after night with *him;* watching, keeping his secret, allowing Jane—

She felt a little jump of panic at letting Jane back here among the others, as if she might bring into the room, poor child, some of the terrible knowledge she must have acquired *out there.*

Miss Wilson put her hand over her mouth, not to cry out, it was too awful. It threatened to send the whole afternoon flying in splinters. She had to hang on.

But how could they have permitted it? She simply could not comprehend. Allowing Jane to go off like that, without a word of protest, without the least signal of alarm. And even worse perhaps, since it wasn't a single occasion but a matter of days—no, weeks—sitting night after night watching the boy, and even, since they were impenetrably united these children, inveterately secretive, touching him, allowing him to touch them . . .

At first they had refused to speak at all, they simply shook their heads and were dumb; even when, as gently as possible, they had been made to *understand;* when the awful facts were made clear to them—or as clear as was necessary: what had happened to Jane, and how close they themselves had been to ultimate harm. Even then they revealed no details, they refused to speak out. Had they failed to comprehend the horror of it? Or were they merely stubborn in the defence of their own complicity, or unfeeling, or—yes that, surely—protecting themselves from the full knowledge of what they knew. They had simply gone on, in a way that alarmed and affronted her, as if nothing had occurred at all.

They were writing now with their heads bent to the task, filling the first page with the fruits of their imagination. Later she would read what they had written and give it a mark. She comforted herself with the thought that if their imagination stopped at a certain point it was just as well. It would save them, as she could no longer save herself, from the enormity of the thing.

She glanced quickly at her watch. "Time, children," she said briskly. "You have two more minutes. Make sure you have a concluding paragraph, label it, and see that your name is printed clearly at the top of the page."

She stood at the window, with her arms clasped to her breast as if she were cold, though it was in fact too warm today. The garden below was approaching the full thickness of summer, every leaf separate and astir in the afternoon breeze, discovering darkness as an edge of shadow, the hungry little birds dipping and feeding on berries and squabbling disgracefully over the remains.

And in one way or another they had accepted it, the others. They allowed Jane, who had never been popular among them, and whose face soon grew dim in their minds, to walk out of their lives as she had walked out of the dormitory, and made as little as possible of her failure to come back.

The event itself remained for them a series of glowing but unreal moments when they had sat on a bed in the unlighted dormitory and watched Jane and the boy, two figures already touched by the strangeness of distance and the night; high dreamlike occasions between stretches of sleep, when they had, briefly, touched on something outside the rules of their daily existence, the rules that would govern their lives afterwards, and which they knew now was *there*, had always been there, and would never, even in their own case, and despite the rules, be entirely exorcised; though it did not have to be confronted—or not yet. They would recognise it again later, at a point further on, past the husbands and the children still to come. It was ten years off for one, at the bottom of twelve feet of water; twenty years for another, for others fifty, sixty even. It would reappear in a different and quite unpredictable form to each one of them: as a tree trunk suddenly illuminated on a country road, every scribble in its bark clearly readable; or a lump secretly nourished in one of the soft parts of the body; or a welling up, beyond the faces of children and grand-children, of a sea of blood. At that moment they might understand her at last, their lost schoolfellow, and in whatever part of them-selves they harboured a memory of all this, without precisely recalling it, see themselves getting up out of their solid childlike bodies to follow.

Meanwhile there was Miss Wilson's essay to finish—the mar-vellous cavern to be got out of.

They wrote on.

The Prowler

1

THERE IS more goes on in this suburb than meets the eye. But naturally.

Waiting at McAllister's newsagency yesterday for a magazine order I overheard a conversation between our popular newsagent and Doctor Cooper of Lancaster Road. "You know, McAllister," the doctor remarked, "you must be about the most regular man, time-wise, in this whole city. I hear your wagon turn into Arran Avenue in the morning and I say to myself, 'That's McAllister. It must be five thirty. Time to get back into my clothes and go home.'" McAllister was delighted. Three minutes later he was repeating the story to a new customer as an example of the complete reliability of his service.

There's no better place than a newsagent's for finding out what goes on in the world. And I don't mean by reading the papers.

2

OURS IS one of the older suburbs, no longer fashionable as it was forty or fifty years ago but still retaining a certain desirable elegance, and still, with its expansive gardens and tree-lined avenues, a place where a mode of life can be observed that has not yet surrendered to the patios, clothes-hoists, and drive-in supermarkets of the Estates. Houses here are of painted weatherboard in the colonial style: with gables, turrets, pepperpot domes, bull's-eye windows of emblazoned glass, verandahs, wrought-iron railings,

and venetians that hum in a storm. Bougainvillea and Cardinal
Creeper grow thick over outhouse roofs and the lattice-work that
keeps out the westering sun. Lawns planted with old-fashioned
natives like hoop-pine and bunya, along with the deodars and
Douglas firs of empire, make secluded spaces, some of them close
to parklike, where willy-wagtails feed and fat grasshoppers wob-
ble in flight above the cannas. It's a quiet area. Lawn sprinklers
weave elaborate loops and figures-of-eight; kids on bicycles hiss
over the gravel; a station wagon driven by a young housewife rolls
along under the bouhineas, delivering a kindergarten group or a
riot of small footballers. Deep in a garden somewhere, a splash,
then laughter as children lark about in a backyard pool. That's the
nearest you might come to a disturbance of the heavy stillness. At
night a tennis court, one wire wall thick with cestrum, suddenly
lights up in the sub-tropical dusk and there will be, for an hour or
two, the leisurely *thwack thwack* of a ball.

So that the assaults, when they broke out, seemed especially
shocking.

3

THE EARLIEST VICTIMS were disbelieved. They were written
off as hysterical. Two of them were unmarried, one was a young
mother of three with a history of mental illness, another a schoolgirl of sixteen. It was only after the sixth or seventh attack that one
of the newspapers got on to the story, and almost overnight, it
seemed, we had a prowler. From that point on, the assaults ceased
to be imaginary.

Scarcely a day has passed since then without a new report.
Once the prowler entered our lives, via the columns of the paper,
he was everywhere. He dominated the headlines and became the
obsessive subject of even the most casual conversations. He began,
little by little, to change the fabric of our lives. So local schoolgirls
no longer walk up from the bus-stop alone. They ring from town
and are met by anxious fathers in the Holden Kingswood. Wives,
returning home from a meeting, have learned to drive with the

doors locked and the windows up, waiting in the garage till someone appears on a lighted verandah to see them safely inside. What
did we do with ourselves before there was the prowler? What did
we talk about? He is as much part of our lives now as the milkman
or the newsagent. Every suburb has its prowler and we have ours.
It is, the newspapers tell us, the price we pay for modern living.
Prowlers come to us as part of that "way of life" that elsewhere in
the papers we are urged at all times to defend.

4

NOT ALL of the attacks follow the same pattern.

Sometimes the prowler does no more than watch a sleeping
woman from the windowsill or from the foot of the bed. When she
starts awake at last, suddenly aware of a real presence in her
dreams, he signals with his forefinger to his lips that she should
not cry out, shows the edge of a knife, and then just sits, holding
her thus—captive, mesmerized—till the light begins to grow in
the room and his face, a darkened blank against the sky, is in danger of becoming clear. Then, without a word, he rolls over the sill
and is gone.

Often, while the woman is washing up at the sink, he slips in
behind out of the darkening house; an arm goes round her waist, a
hand covers her mouth, she feels his breath, his fingers, but sees
nothing. On some of these occasions, startled by the sound of a
step on the verandah, or a train whistle, the attacker will break
and run, and the last she will hear of him is the banging of a wire-
screen door—which from that moment onwards will always mean
"assault." Sometimes the man is naked. More often he is not.
There are times when he has been sighted by a curious neighbour,
but only rarely are these sightings reported till after the event.
One wonders why. What, standing there at the bathroom window
or behind the slats of the venetians, did the observer make of a
naked figure stalking across the lawn? What area of a neighbour's
secret life did he think he had stumbled on, that might be
observed but not violated? There are lines, it seems, that we are

conditioned not to cross. Does the prowler know this, and feel certain that in nine cases out of ten, even if sighted, he will not be betrayed? His assurance comes perhaps from the very fact that he is a prowler: that is, one for whom the lines exist to be crossed.

<h1 style="text-align:center">5</h1>

UNDER PRESSURE of public opinion, and after a series of heavy editorials, the Police Department has decided to set up a special section to deal with the assaults. Called the Incident Squad, it is under the direction of Senior Detective William Pierce, who has two full-time assistants. One of them, following on a petition to the Department from local women's groups, is a woman.

Senior Inspector Pierce is a widower, aged thirty-nine, with two small boys.

<h1 style="text-align:center">6</h1>

IT MIGHT be anyone.

A fresh-faced kid running round an oval after dark stands panting for a bit with his hands on his hips, then dips his head like a big wading-bird to ease the muscles of his neck. After a brief burst of running on the spot, he resumes his training, alternating stretches of steady jogging with fifty-metre sprints, a lone figure on the darkening oval, a speck of white, moving fast, moving slower, moving fast again against a field of green. Minutes later he is dropping on all fours under a lighted window.

To watch.

At last, slipping out of his gym-shoes, unzipping his track-suit, easing the elastic of his shorts, he stands for a moment in the summer dark—still, poised as if before a barrier he must clear, preparing himself inwardly for the effort it will take, raising himself lightly on the balls of his feet. Then he moves.

Or a man rolls to one side of the bed where his wife is turned heavily away and sets his footsoles on the floor; pushes himself upright, slowly, lest the bed creak; stands, creeps to the hallway.

Having learned the cat-like quietness of his movements, and also perhaps his need for violence, in this very house and from the woman he leaves dreaming in the bed behind him. He pauses outside the room where his children sleep and listens a moment to their breathing. Then goes on.

It might be either of these.

Or a painter's apprentice already naked under his white overalls (who sets his lunch-tin down very carefully beside a garden tap) or a grease monkey naked under his blue ones.

Or a man in shorts and singlet, slap-footed in thongs, who has been walking a muzzled Greyhound. He ties it now to a tree, flicks his lighted butt into a camellia bush, and smiling, eases up a window. Already in his imagination he is halfway in. Behind him the dog stands tense, quivering, then as the garden sounds grow familiar settles to wait.

It might be any of these.

It might be anyone.

7

THE INCIDENT SQUAD had issued an identikit picture, assembled from the evidence of nearly seventy victims.

Each victim is presented with the outline of a face and a booklet containing page by page a variety of features; as for example, eyes close set or far apart, small pig-eyes, gimlet slits, round eyes frank and open, eyes that bulge a little, eyes that slant upwards at the corner, eyes that slant down, eyes with heavy lids, flat lids, no lids at all; eyebrows far apart or joined at the bridge of the nose, arched, pointed, straight, tilted up or down; eyebrows thick, thin, tufted etc.; and so on for the various shapes of nose, mouth, chin, ears, the various colours and kinds of hair. When each of these features has been considered, and the chosen eyes, eyebrows, nose, mouth, hair, affixed to the plastic outline, a face takes shape and the prowler begins slowly to emerge out of the victim's memory, out of the fog at the back of her head. Feature by feature he comes into focus; and so vividly in some cases that the victim has immediately gone into shock at conjuring up, once more, the image of her assailant.

So then: seventy men re-created out of the dark experience of seventy different women. These seventy images are then super-imposed one upon the other to discover what is common to them.

The results are puzzling.

Three separate types emerge, and have now been promulgated as possible likenesses of the prowler.

Three? Can the prowler then change his form? Is he perhaps an expert at disguising himself?

For the fact is that some of the features the women are most insistent upon—as for example black hair closely cropped and a zapata moustache—cannot be reconciled with others, long blond hair like a surfie's, thin pale beard, etc. The various images have been further sorted and amalgamated, and so we have the prowler's three faces, one young, one middle-aged, one old, rather like that mysterious portrait attributed to Titian in which the three heads of youth, maturity, and old age rise from a single trunk and look in three different directions—a whole lifespan, as it were, telescoped into the space of a single frame. In Titian's case the triple portrait has a pendant, a reflection, in which the three human heads are replaced by those of animals: lion, fox, and dog.

But to return to the identikit pictures. What seems strangest is that when the sharply detailed memories of these women have been laid one over the other to produce a composite picture, the face that emerges is both immediately recognizable (because typ-ical) and at the same time quite useless as a key to identification. The three faces are clichés. They look like everyone and no-one. Blondish baby-faced youth, lean, shy-looking, with the begin-nings of a moustache—student, bank clerk, apprentice plumber, railway porter. Clean-cut young married with short back and sides—an architect perhaps, or a schoolteacher or swimming-pool contractor, someone in advertising or the Town Clerk's office. Older man, distinguished-looking but with a hint of loose-ness about the mouth; might be a travelling salesman, a green-keeper, or a professional soldier recently cashiered or the owner of a small grocery business.

But these images will get us nowhere. Half the male population of the suburb, of the city even, might move without difficulty into these familiar outlines.

What does it mean?

Are there, quite simply, three prowlers of different ages? Or are the women's memories in some way inaccurate—or not so much inaccurate as so creative, so deeply stimulated, that they have added to their experience and remade it, so that what they reproduce is not what they saw at the moment of the attack (some of them can have seen very little) but what sprang into their minds as a visual equivalent of what their hands encountered in darkness, rough cloth, metal, the coarseness of hair, of what forced itself into their nostrils as an unforgettable but unidentifiable odour, and into their ears as a series of obscene monosyllables or grunts or beery endearments. These details do not interest the police; they can do nothing with them.

"His breath on my neck"—what use is that?

"His body was so hot—like an oven."

"There was a smell of mice."

"Salt. His hand tasted of salt."

The visual features of the identikit picture are attempts to render, in another language, what the women did not see but sensed, or heard, or smelled, and the translations are clichés, they derive from the common pool of their reading or from the movies. What the identikit pictures provide us with is not the composite picture of a prowler—some citizen engaged at this moment in delivering bread or sealing envelopes in an office or teaching his kids to box with a bag under the house—but a picture of the man these women fear most, or know best, or most long for, or have dreamed of once on some remote occasion and forgotten.

It is no coincidence that if we treat these pictures as caricatures, the man who most resembles the victim's assailant is often a member of her own family: a father, an uncle, a brother-in-law, a son.

8

A BURGLARY takes place. Nothing much is stolen. But a man, turning afterwards to the drawer where his handkerchiefs are kept, discovers that one of them has been used. He stares at the patch of quite ordinary wetness and feels panic. Not disgust but panic. As if his house could never be his own again; as if it stood roofless and could never again offer him refuge or protection because there is no such thing in the world; as if he himself stood naked. Whimpering with shame he tumbles the handkerchiefs out on to the floor and removes them with a stick.

What unnerves him is not the patch of wetness itself, but what it forces upon him—the fact of the burglar's ordinariness and at the same time his utter strangeness. He has before him the man's bodily juices, but no face, no name, and it comes home to him that he lives among strangers, more than half a million of them, who might at any moment break the unwritten contract and force their way into his bedroom, open his tallboy, put to use one of his initialled handkerchiefs.

Later he comes to think of his reaction as excessive and finds it difficult to isolate the precise cause of his panic. It seems irrational. But it is precisely this irrationality that continues to exert an influence on him. When he thinks of the incident he burns with shame.

So it is that many of the attacks—perhaps even the majority— go unreported.

9

EACH MORNING nearly a dozen women appear at the office of the Incidents Squad with information they will impart only to Senior Detective Pierce in person.

Senior Detective Pierce has become a popular figure in our little world. Smilingly reassuring when he appears on television, grim and determined when he is snapped at press conferences, he is a sort of prowler in reverse who has caught the imagination of the public in much the same way as the prowler himself. What did we do, we ask ourselves, before we had Senior Detective Pierce?

Even the genial detective's two small boys have entered the pantheon. They are called Sam and Harry, aged ten and seven.

They bear no clear resemblance to Senior Detective Pierce but are said to be the living picture of his dead wife, whose absence lends a touch of pathos to the policeman's rugged assurance and brings to an image that is otherwise all assertiveness and power an engaging ambiguity. It allows him to be a family man, very solid and reliable, but also turns him loose.

The two boys, tough-looking blonds, keep the mother's figure clearly in view (did she really look like that?) but in their cocky imitation maleness it is disturbingly redefined. When Senior Detective Pierce and his boys are photographed together at a swimming carnival or at one of our local rugby matches, this simultaneous absence and presence of the wife and mother constitutes a mystery that women respond to (and some men as well) without at all knowing what is in play. Around the rough edges of the two boys, all grazed elbows and knees, glows the aura of the missing wife, and the hard outline of Senior Detective Pierce, ex-lifesaver and League forward, is softened as he stoops to see that Sam's windcheater is buttoned, or with the corner of a handkerchief wet with spit, cleans ice-cream from Harry's shirtfront, by the lineaments of the tender, all solicitous mother.

"How are Samnharry?" women tend to enquire as a way of easing themselves into their story, slipping thus, as they might see it, into the role of family friend or next-door neighbour.

Then immediately, breathlessly, before the proud father can answer: "I have *seen the prowler!*"

10

THE INFORMATION provided by many of the victims has no basis in fact. That is quite clear. But it is not therefore false. They *have* seen the prowler, but in one of those dreams that nightly crowd the streets of our suburb with a life as intense, as busy, as any it knows by day. Here is just one of them.

The dreamer is a woman of forty, a pharmacist. She is walking at dusk along the grassy footpath of a street planted with poincianas, so thick (it is early summer) that they meet above the roadway, making a tunnel that the light of the street lamps barely penetrates. In the woman's dream the darkness in which she is walking is thickened by an unseasonable fog. It swirls so densely about her that she cannot see her feet. She wades in it. (This is dream weather. No such conditions occur in our damp subtropical city at the hour at which the woman is walking, though they are not infrequent, in another part of the year, in the hour before dawn—that is, at the time of her dream.) It is in a state of great weariness, as she drags her body through the warm fog, that she hears behind her, or in front, for she cannot tell which, a soft thudding, the footsteps as she quickly perceives of an approaching jogger.

She stops, flattens herself against the trunk of a tree; hoping that the runner, whoever he may be, will not see her.

The footsteps get closer.

She presses her body closer to the tree trunk, trying to pass through the rough bark into it, to become part of its life, and seems for a moment to have succeeded. She is not there. Only the roughness of the bark, its pressure round her thighs, gives her some sense of her own separate being as the runner (it is the blond boy in the tracksuit we have previously imagined) materializes out of the fog.

And at that moment a woman she recognises, with horror, as her perfect double steps right into his path. The runner has to pull up with a jerk to avoid colliding with her. They stand face to face. The youth steps to the left in order to pass her, and her reflection steps to the right. Again they are face to face. She tries to scream but cannot, her voice belongs to the double. She wakes with her face contorted in a silent shriek, and the boy's features are so clearly before her that she can describe them in detail: colour of eyes blue; a scar under the right eye high up on the cheekbone, which gives him a slight squint; hair heavy with sweat, hanging in bangs over his brow; a day's growth of stubble; a film of spittle that makes his teeth gleam, when recovering his breath at last, he opens his mouth to defend himself. She shakes her head. No! No! No defence! No defence possible!

It is the boy in the tracksuit, no doubt of it. She gives his picture to the life. For a whole week, each night of fog, he pads softly through her sleep and confronts her, always at the same point; comes so close she can smell his sweat, feel his breath on her face. He is too breathless to speak and she too terrified to cry out. They do their strange dance on the grass in utter silence.

After the seventh night of this silent intimidation she goes to the police. The boy enters their files. He contributes his features to one of the three identikit pictures, but is never sighted.

11

IT IS EASY of course to get things out of proportion, to forget that on a night when one, maybe two attacks take place, hundreds of innocent girls sit at their dressing table mirrors with the window open, rubbing coldcream into their face and neck, smoothing it gently upwards, then lower themselves into untroubled sleep; that schoolboys, tired after late football practise and an hour of television, roll gently over the touchline into absolute oblivion before they have even resolved the question, with fingers round their cock: "Will I tonight or won't I? Did I do it last night?"; that young lovers in cars angle-parked towards the drop on Bartley's Hill are softly rediscovering one another, moving into a lifetime together as they uncover the familiar unfamiliarity of one another's bodies in the hot darkness; as their parents, in a space of dark between the streetlights below, are also moving through one another (having graduated from here more than twenty years ago) like palpable ghosts, towards the mystery of sleep and the odd messages, important, uncatchable, that come to them in flashes before dawn.

The suburb sleeps. Most of its dreams are dull, bursting like bubbles in the light, and as clear as bubbles. Entirely guiltless. The sleepers drift, go under, climbing back into the shallows every hour in phase after phase, feeding on stillness; pulse slow, breath regular, renewing themselves with huge draughts of space in which there are no objects to catch the eye or engage the body's idling senses; free for a time of the body's demands as it goes its own way through the dark. Cats are abroad. Their eyes redden under a culvert. Flying-foxes row in to raid a patch of Moreton Bay figs at the edge of a golf course or a backyard mango tree; they hang there, upside down under the boughs, like the souls of a suburb of sleepers, ranked in the dark. Just before first light the newsagent, McAllister, from a car with one whole side cut away, tosses the morning papers rolled into a cylinder on to dew-damp lawns, and Dr. Cooper, hearing him turn into Arran Avenue, will know that it is time to get back into his clothes and go home. The papers lie there in the growing light. They carry the news. But the night's real occurrences will not be in them. One or two extraordinary moments, yes: a car-smash on Ipswich Road, a fight in a roadside café on Petrie Terrace, another assault. But not the familiar couplings, the exchanges, the busy life the suburb pursues in its sleep. This is anti-news, and from this point of view the papers are unreliable. Too much that happens here is of no interest to them. *A hundred and fifty thousand potential victims un-attacked in a single night.* What sort of news is that?

12

THE CIB has just announced that according to their experts the Nundah prowler and our prowler, who were thought to be one and the same, are indisputably different.

How, one wonders, do they know?

Nundah is the next suburb from here, the boundaries being the suburban railway line, a park, and the winding course of a creek that is quite visible in old photographs of the area but has long since been filled in to make an equally winding street; both sides of the street are planted with bouhinia, which all flower in the same exuberant pink and at the same season, but one side is Nundah and the other is not.

Does the Nundah prowler never cross the street? And if not why not?

I can understand that he might hesitate at the railway line, which does after all represent a real obstacle and where the character of the two suburbs is distinct, our side being older and better established, with big parklike gardens and, as the real-estate agents put it, a better class of resident. One can imagine that the Nundah prowler, used to small houses on sixteen-perch allotments, mostly treeless and unsewered, might feel intimidated before the big verandahed mansions on our side, might find the gardens, with their clumps of dark shrubbery and shade-trees, off-putting in some way, being unused to their odd pattern of moonlight and shadow or the sound of creatures rustling and breathing in the boughs. Insufficiently urbanized is what he might find them, and threatening to his sense of space. And the same would be true of the old-fashioned interiors. Too many rooms, too many corridors and stairways. Or it might be the unfamiliarity of the life that is lived here that makes him insecure. Or the kind of woman. One understands well enough that there may be social frontiers, and with them a whole set of sexual associations, that a prowler is unwilling to cross. At the railway line anyway.

But what about further down, where the boundary between the two suburbs is little more than a bureaucratic convenience? Does the Nundah prowler really stick to one side of the street, leaving the other to our prowler? Is some sort of territorial instinct in operation? Do prowlers lay down a scent that keeps off rivals, creating a magic fence around the borders of their fantasy world that a stranger recognises and is repelled by or finds himself unable to penetrate? And if this is so, how extraordinary that these private boundaries should follow exactly the line laid down on a map in the Surveyor's Office and recognised by most citizens only when their water rates arrive in a different post from their neighbour's opposite—should follow, that is, all the twists and turns of an underground creek filled in nearly sixty years ago and chosen then, quite arbitrarily (we can imagine the debate that was to determine so much in the lives of future prowlers and their victims) as a surburban dividing-line by a committee of respectable aldermen.

No doubt these considerations have occurred to the Incident Squad and been properly dealt with. But they have not published their reasons. When they do so, a great deal may be revealed that at the moment remains inexplicable, and valuable light shed on the secret life of suburbs—not to mention the anthropology of prowlers.

13

DESPITE THE WARNINGS that are published almost daily in our papers, and the growing number of assaults, women continue to make themselves vulnerable.

Driving slowly round the suburb in the gathering dusk I see window after window in the dark gardens ablaze with light, open to the cool summer breeze and all the scents, sub-tropical, overpowering, of the night: jasmine, honeysuckle, cestrum—that heavy night-walker.

The scenes that appear in these brightly lit squares constitute a series of frames between spaces of dark, a living peepshow. Here a girl in a half-slip is ironing, her thin shoulders moving to the music behind her, which as I drive on, bounces a moment and is gone. Another woman at a kitchen bench is decorating a birthday cake in the shape of an open book; my kids will be at the party where it is to be eaten, among party-hats, whistles, bowls of jelly and ice-cream (two dozen moulds of raspberry jelly are cooling on the laminex bench), and off-key renderings of "For He's a Jolly Good Fellow." Yet another woman stands in half-thought at a washing machine, holding an armful of overalls and waiting for the cycle to begin.

They are all unaware, these women, in their ease of movement or in their dreamy repose, that they are not only clearly visible as they hang aloft there in the dark, but have been endowed, in their detachment within the single frame, with a special quality of significance, so that the smallest of their gestures strikes the senses, is incised on the memory, is given, in all its ordinariness, an aura of the exotic that suggests a pose, as if what we were really watching were a set of professionals acting out a series of domestic scenes in such a way as to emphasize what is specifically erotic in them.

Even later, towards midnight, when the bluish-silver of the television screens has drained away down a pinhole and the suburb sleeps—all its citizens still present but communally engaged now in reassembling the facts of their daily life into the other language of dreams—even then, I notice, there are casements ajar, obliquely taking the moonlight, a curtain's drift and fall shows where a sash window has been raised a little to let in the breeze.

Not me is what is being proclaimed. *Others may fall victim, but not me.*

Some of these windows are open invitations. But which? That is the point. Obviously the prowler cannot judge or his attacks would not be reported. Do the reported attacks, then, represent only the tip of an iceberg, the prowler's *errors*, his misreading of what a window left unlatched or a woman moving half-clad across a stage-lit space might innocently suggest? Are there rooms where women wait night after night for the sound of a footfall, the creak of a board on the verandah, or a doorhandle being tried, only to suffer, night after night, the entry of nothing more than moonlight, thin, disembodied, that in the morning leaves no mark on the flesh?

The signs are not clear enough. What we need is a more specific means of communication. If only so that some women may discover the signals they should avoid.

14

I WONDER, since so much of the objective evidence has led nowhere, if the Incident Squad shouldn't try something quite

different; as a way, I mean, of releasing the crimes for a moment
from the world of fact into the world of fantasy where they properly belong. Since fantasy and its irrational associations are the
language the prowler speaks, mightn't we try thinking in that language as a way of anticipating his moves? At the very least the sort
of games I am proposing would loosen things up, get rid of pre-
conceptions that may be standing in the investigators' way, would
send them back to the evidence with a more open and intuitive
understanding of that pattern of analogies that lies often enough
under the confusions of mere event. Several "Letters to the Editor" have suggested the employment of a clairvoyant. But this is so
much simpler. And there is something liberating in the very idea
of a group of policemen and women, under the direction of
Senior Detective Pierce, abandoning their files for a morning to
play party-games.

So then, a questionnaire:

What colour does the prowler bring to your mind?

Apple green.

What fish?

A squid.

What great novel?

Elective Affinities.

What pop record?

Dark Side of the Moon.

What flower?

Datura.

What cloud formation?

Cumulus.

What animal?

Puma.

Could the prowler be a Gemini?

When they had learned to enter into the spirit of the thing, and
felt properly confident, the investigators would apply this method
of questioning to some of the victims. It would be interesting,
anyway, to see what might emerge.

15

THERE ARE those of us, I think, for whom the final identification of the prowler would be a terrible disappointment. He has become a kind of hero. Jokes that used to be told about a commercial traveller or the milkman invariably begin these days: "Have you heard the one about the prowler?" Not only is he endowed with a quite fabulous member and a back, as one of our great writers once put it, "to encounter a hundred in a night," he also, it seems, has a social sense (he is the Robin Hood of the boudoir) and a sense of humour. "I hope the prowler gets you!" a four-year-old hisses at his mother, who has denied him a second slice of chocolate cake in a department-store café. Bogey man, outlaw, sexual athlete, violator of middle-class security, hero of Husband's Lib—who could possibly want to see all this reduced to the inevitably smaller and commoner dimensions of the truth?

Besides, if the man were identified at last as the one and only prowler, his crimes too would be identified—the real ones—and the rest would be revealed as fantasy, crimes of the mind. Rumours would immediately fly about that he wasn't the real prowler at all but a scapegoat, and that the real prowler was still loose. Women would refuse to recognise him. "No. *My* attacker was quite different. Taller. More brutal looking. It's not him at all." The police would be accused of a cover-up of their own inefficiency. And sure enough, the attacks would immediately resume. If the prowler ceased to exist we would have to re-invent him. Perhaps he has already been re-invented several times over.

The police, of course, are well aware of the difficulty. They have to catch the prowler but also to put a stop to the assaults. The first is still a possibility, the second is not. "You can arrest a prowler, but how do you arrest an epidemic?"

This little joke is attributed to Senior Detective Pierce; who also, it seems, has a sense of humour.

16

AND WHAT are his thoughts, the prowler, when eavesdropping in the supermarket on the endless speculations about his identity, or consulting the headlines in McAllister's newsagency to discover where it was precisely, in the maze of suburban streets, that he made his appearance the night before, waiting—perhaps for the newspaper to confirm that he was there after all and to provide details he failed to collect in the confusion of the event itself—the woman's age, whether or not she was married, the number of her children—what does he think when, searching the pages for a full account (for public interest has waned, he has been relegated to page seven), he finds that assaults he never committed are now being attributed to him and others that he did commit have been distorted out of all recognition, either by the woman's account of his activities or the newspaper's reporting of them? Has he begun to realise that the real acts have long since been stolen from him, that events to which he brought his whole body and a lifetime of passionate fantasy have passed out of his hands into the public imagination and been stripped there of all the details that made them significant (for the attraction of the ritual lay in a secret order that made no sense to others), decked out instead with journalistic clichés and given a spurious shape that reflects only the moralism of our newspapers, their preference for the monstrous, and their dependence on the rhetoric of romantic novels, television serials, and softcore pornography? He has become a victim of the newspaper's hunger for events, but only for those events it has already created in its own dream-factory. How could he ever break through and make them report one of his crimes as he sees it, as it really is? Meanwhile he feels used, manipulated. In his passage across strange gardens, through strange rooms and the bodies of unnamed women, he is no longer pursuing his own will, or even his own fantasies, but acting out a scenario whose lines have already been determined by the newspaper and its readers and will be fully revealed to him, the actor, only in the dirty black-and-white of a few paragraphs of print.

Does he long now to be caught at last, our outlaw, and released from the burden of other men's compulsions, other men's dreams?

17

THE CIB has decided to take further measures. The Incident Squad, retitled the Special Assaults Section, is to be increased from three to seven and will have access to a computer.

Of course bureaucracy tends to increase quite independently of demand, but this new move does seem to be justified. The number of assaults has reached triple figures.

Budgetary considerations, the Minister announces, will allow for a second expansion at the end of the financial year, "should eventualities require it." And of course they will.

18

NOW THAT the number of victims has reached the magic figure of a century there are seven identikit pictures, and the strange thing is that they are no longer the clichés of three months ago; each of them has now developed a distinctive character. What we are faced with, it seems, is seven prowlers, all working in the same strictly defined area and using the same methods.

This surely is too much of a coincidence. The work of the prowler begins to look like the cooperative efforts of a gang; except of course that by their very nature these crimes are private and solitary. Or perhaps a club has been formed to act out the attacks as they have been described in the newspaper. A bizarre notion! Who would devise such an entertainment and why? Still, imitators there are, and more than one of them. Of this the police have no doubt.

And how does the prowler himself feel about this, the original prowler, I mean, the initiator, whose integrity consists in his commitment to his own crimes? How strange if his path should cross that of one of the others, if they should meet face to face over the body of a victim; or stranger still, if two of the false prowlers

should meet, each just sufficiently like the original to be recognizable but each seeing in the other enough that is different to make
clear how much of themselves they have allowed to creep in, to
what an extent they are no longer imitators of the prowler but significant variants. If two of the false prowlers were captured would
there be enough in common between them for the real prowler to
be identified? And supposing all seven to be taken, would it be
clear which of them was real? All seven, as the police know, would
lay claim to the first attack, might even create a prior one, in order
not to be deprived of the rest. (Perhaps one might guess that the
least insistent of them, assured of his authenticity, would be the
true original.) This is clear from the large number of men who
have already come forward and confessed to the crimes. Men of
all ages and occupations, from a fifteen-year-old schoolboy to a
retired shipbuilder of seventy-seven: widowers, pensioners,
young men newly married, metho-drinkers, known homosexu-
als—all desperate, it would seem, to have the prowler's acts define
them.

   Some of these men simply want to draw attention to themselves. Others have become obsessed with the assaults and long to
be their perpetrator, to appropriate to themselves the daring, the
fierce aura of sexuality they believe the prowler must be possessed
of, his deep sense of relief when, returning to his own house, he
stands naked before the mirror and says, "Yes, I am the prowler,"
or, concealing his violence behind a front of patient domesticity,
slips in quietly beside his wife.

   There are those among these men who genuinely believe they
are the prowler. Faced under the glare of the arc-lamps with
indisputable proof that they are not, they break down and sob,
they plead with Senior Detective Pierce to examine the evidence
again, to find something, some small detail, that will convict them;
they resist, they fight, they clutch at straws. Senior Detective
Pierce finds these men pathetic. Of all the males in the suburb,
they alone are above suspicion, since the one thing they lack
(what else does their behaviour mean?) is the courage to commit
the crime.

As for the others, the self-confessed prowlers who know they are lying, Senior Detective Pierce has begun to dread their arrival, more even than a new victim. Each of them has a bad conscience. Confessing to the prowler's crimes is a kind of diversion tactic. It is meant to save them from confessing to the real crime they have committed—or think they have committed. They are men who are laden with guilt, who hope that punishment and conviction for one crime, even if it is not their own, will be sufficient and will relieve them of dread. The real crime, in some cases, is trivial, the anxiety is not. And it is the weight of all this secret guilt that Senior Detective Pierce finds so oppressive, since he cannot absolve the men of it, and could not, even if he were to extend to them the one thing in his dispensation, the recognition that the prowler's crimes are theirs. Faced with the men's despair when he declares them innocent, their deep sense of grievance, their sullen hostility, Senior Detective Pierce, on one or two occasions, has come close to breaking down. He has been trained to deal with crime—specific incidents—not with deep, unspecified guilt.

Still, information about all these men is fed into the computer; they become part of Senior Detective Pierce's memory bank. Even if they did not commit the prowler's crimes they reflect them. Only when all the facts have been collated, and many things that are not facts as well, will some sort of pattern emerge.

But when will that be? And what pattern?

Senior Detective Pierce has come to believe, as the number of victims continues to rise and the identikit pictures top thirteen, that sooner or later the whole male and female population of the suburb will find its way into his files, every man a potential prowler, every female a victim. And what then?

19

IN THE MIDDLE of the last century in Rome, the old stone prison of the Mammertine on the Capitoline Hill, where St. Peter is said to have been jailed, was set up as an oratory. Here, among the usual votive offerings, silver hearts, limbs, eyes with little filagree bows and angels about them, symbols of a miraculous return to wholeness, hung offerings of another sort: knives, meat-cleavers, clubs still wet from the skulls they had broken, and damp hair sticking to them, cords that had been used in a strangling, a dirty pillow, a pair of blood-stained scissors. The whole place, one writer tells us, was haunted; as if all the city's murders had gathered there and hung about, palpably, in the dark. Blood and the odour of blood had seeped into the stones. The air was thick with unspoken confessions and pleas for absolution. Within the city, a temple had been dedicated to the city's secret crimes. The criminals had crept away, but the instruments they had used were left to speak for them in a language, at once concrete and abstract, that made the whole place a whispering hall for abominable declarations, where the guilty might come, under cover of dark, to relieve themselves of the tokens of their guilt . . .

20

SENIOR DETECTIVE PIERCE, who is surprisingly literate, has read of this place and begins to be haunted by it. He also has dreams in which he imagines himself to be a computer, softly whirring as the pieces tumble into place within him and the day's facts are fed in, some dark act committed in the streets of the sub-urb, a new face (victim or violator, it hardly matters which), a private fantasy brought to light at last and tucked away in the memory bank, which is his own head. His head is filled with the crimes, real and imaginary, of a whole suburb, it bursts with them, the violence calmly subdued in compulsive rituals or breaking out in savage bloodshed. He staggers up out of these dreams in a cold sweat, terrified of where he might have been and who might have seen him there.

Often when Senior Detective Pierce has these dreams he is awake.

What frightens him most is that he has begun to predict the crimes: the time, the place, the kind of woman. Has his accumulation of so much information, his entry into the pattern that lies under the facts, given him insight—unconscious as yet, but accurate into the real nature of the crimes, so that a part of what is still to occur becomes visible to him? Does he begin to have so godlike a knowledge of us all that every detail of what we will, even those things that have not yet entered our heads and become the focus of will, is already clear to him? Or is there some simpler and more sinister explanation?

Senior Detective Pierce has asked twice now to be relieved of his duties and sent back to the Vice Squad, but on both occasions his request was refused.

Why? he wonders.

Is it because they have their eye on me and want to keep me where I can be watched? Even these notes are a dead giveaway. I know too much. I have become a primary suspect.

Confess! Confess!

ALSO BY DAVID MALOUF

*"A richly imagistic writer, philosophical and literary in
the best sense."* —The Washington Post Book World

REMEMBERING BABYLON

In this rich and compelling novel, written in language of astonishing poise and resonance, one of Australia's greatest living writers gives an immensely powerful vision of human differences and eternal divisions. In the mid-1840s, a thirteen-year-old British cabin boy, Gemmy Fairley, is cast ashore in the far north of Australia and taken in by Aborigines. Sixteen years later, he moves back into the world of Europeans, among hopeful yet terrified settlers who are stalking out their small patch of home in an alien place. To them, Gemmy stands as a different kind of challenge: he is a force that at once fascinates and repels. His own identity in this new world is as unsettling to him as the knowledge he brings to them of the savage, the aboriginal.

Fiction/Literature/978-0-679-74951-6

HARLAND'S HALF ACRE

Frank Harland's mother dies from the prick of a rose thorn; his irresponsible father gives him up and then takes him back. Frank grows up to be a dreamer, who feels helpless except when he is putting lines on paper and whose attempts to rescue his remaining kinfolk bear tragic consequences. In exploring the enigma of Frank Harland, Malouf tells a story of abandonment and desperate love, of aboriginal landscapes and haunted car parks, of families that refuse to stay together and others that cling until they strangle. Beautifully written, humming with psychological nuance, this is a major work of fiction by a writer who makes us see the world with an almost hallucinatory vividness.

Fiction/Literature/978-0-679-77647-5

THE GREAT WORLD

Absorbed as it is by the twentieth-century history of Australian life, *The Great World* focuses on the unlikely friendship of two men who meet as POWs of the Japanese during World War II: Digger Keen, strong yet gentle, ruminative, unambitious, and Vic Curran, an orphan from a poor mining community, a tortured, self-made entrepreneur. For both men, war was supposed to be a testing ground of masculine and nationalist virtue. Instead, it becomes an ordeal that lays bare the painful reality that lies behind the nation's myth of itself.

Fiction/Literature/978-0-679-74836-6

AN IMAGINARY LIFE

In the first century A.D., Publius Ovidius Naso, the most urbane and irreverent poet of imperial Rome, was banished to a remote village on the edge of the Black Sea. From these sparse facts, one of our most distinguished novelists has fashioned an audacious and supremely moving work of fiction. Marooned on the edge of the known world, exiled from his native tongue, Ovid depends on the kindness of barbarians who impale their dead and converse with the spirit world. But then he becomes the guardian of a still more savage creature, a feral child who has grown up among deer. What ensues is a luminous encounter between civilization and nature, as enacted by a poet who once cataloged the treacheries of love and a boy who slowly learns how to give it.

Fiction/Literature/978-0-679-76793-0

ALSO AVAILABLE:

Child's Play, 978-0-375-70141-2
Conversations at Curlow Creek, 978-0-679-77905-6
Dream Stuff, 978-0-375-72449-7
Fly Away Peter, 978-0-679-77670-3

VINTAGE INTERNATIONAL
Available at your local bookstore, or visit
www.randomhouse.com